LIKE *a* F
OUT *of* WA

LIKE *a* FISH OUT *of* WATER

SECOND EDITION

EDWARD EVANS

edward_r_evans@yahoo.co.uk
www.edward-evans.com

Worthside Holdings Ltd
Worthside House
2 Belle Isle Road
Haworth
West Yorkshire BD22 8QQ

First published in Great Britain in 2015
Second Edition published 2018

Printed in Britain by Short Run Press
Typesetting and page layout by McColm Design

A catalogue record for this book is available
From the British Library

ISBN 978-0-9928642-8-6

Acknowledgements

I would like to express my gratitude to my wife, Lilian, whose tireless help has enabled me to complete the book, especially with regards to the more sensitive aspects of the story, and who, together with myself, corrected the errors of historical fact that had crept into my writing. I will always be grateful to her. I also wish to thank Jill Buchanan and Margaret Waterhouse for their generous input into all the various aspects of this story.

Part 1

Boyhood

Chapter 1

It's not that I didn't want to answer the phone; I was just simply too busy when Josh Rawlings, covering the mouthpiece, shouted over the office:

'Clive, there's a call for you; it sounds like some old dear wants to talk to you.'

I frowned, shaking my head and waving an arm, when Josh again shouted, 'She's insistent she wants to talk to you.'

'Oh Christ, give it to me then,' I responded ruefully, as Josh transferred the call.

I answered the phone. 'Clive White,' and immediately a soft well-educated voice came back at me.

'Mr White, I've read many of your articles over the years and I would like you to write my story.'

'Look, I'm sorry . . .' I paused for a moment. 'You didn't give me your name, but I really am far too–'

She interrupted me.

'Oh, I'm so sorry. My name is Alexandra Fraser and I know you are busy,' she said politely, 'but I do feel you are the only one who would have the compassion and understanding to do it.'

'I'm flattered but at the moment I'm really busy. I genuinely don't take on private work and I am not sure how this would fit into my Editor's plan.'

'Oh, but I think it would. You will, I promise, find it a very interesting story . . .' She paused. 'At least, will you come and talk to me so you can make your own judgement?' she continued, almost pleading.

I tried throwing up every excuse to avoid getting involved, but she had an answer for every one of them and I was beginning to run out of ideas. It was difficult in the end to say no. Anyway, what would half an hour be, despite my busy schedule? I arranged to see her the following Tuesday, latish on in the afternoon, fully intending to go home as soon as possible after. It was my wedding anniversary and would give me an excellent excuse to leave early.

I still don't know why I agreed: perhaps I was flattered she had said she had read many of the articles I had written for the Mail*; perhaps, deep down, I was intrigued. Whatever it was, I found myself driving through the gates of a beautiful old mid-Victorian house, reminiscent of those in northern towns which were formerly owned by wealthy industrialists. Sadly, so many of those handsome old houses have become dilapidated or have been divided into flats. This house, however, in its spacious grounds, was immaculately kept.*

I parked the car in front of the house and walked to the front door, looking as I did into the large bay windows on the ground floor. Everything looked clean and in its place. I wondered what on earth there could be here for me. I rang the bell, which was answered by a housekeeper, and I was invited in. I left my hat and coat on the stand at the side of a beautiful broad staircase where the landing was dominated by a large double portrait of a young couple; from its somewhat pared-back style I guessed it was painted some time in the 1940s.

I stood for a second or two admiring it, when I was interrupted by Alexandra Fraser, a tall well-groomed woman with steely-grey hair. She was, I later learned, eighty-nine years old, but she wore those long years rather well.

'It's a lovely picture, isn't it?' she said, interrupting my thoughts. 'It was painted from a photograph of my husband and me, on our holidays, just after the war.'

I turned to introduce myself, but she beat me to it.

'Thank you so much for coming, Mr White. I do appreciate it and I hope you will not think it a waste of your time.' Then, with a wave of her arm, she directed me into her sitting room.

It was a warm cosy room, in spite of its high ceiling, and was crammed full of photographs and memorabilia. I stood in silence for a second or two admiring the many sporting trophies. She invited me to look around, saying proudly, 'My husband was a wonderful rugby player!'

'And cricketer as well, it seems,' I added, though she chose to ignore my

comment and allowed me to continue to browse.

Over the fireplace was another large portrait and once again it was of a young couple, both of whom in military uniform. He was in the RAF and she was in the WAAF.

'It's another of us,' Mrs Fraser said. 'William – that's my husband – loved me in my uniform and I loved him in his, so we thought it would be good to have a picture of us both. He was a gallant officer and very brave . . . I was so, so proud of him,' she said, sighing with emotion.

We were disturbed by the housekeeper who entered and asked if we would like a cup of tea or coffee.

'Sybil makes a lovely cup of tea,' Mrs Fraser said affectionately.

'That will do nicely,' I replied, as I continued to look at the photographs and the abundant objets d'art scattered around the room. 'There is a lot of family history here,' I said, not really knowing what to say and waiting for her to come to the point as to the reason why I had been summoned. Then I suddenly saw a family photograph that included a Rolls-Royce.

'It's II PY!' I exclaimed, somewhat astonished.

'Yes,' she replied, 'that's one of the reasons why I wanted you to do the story.'

In the recent past I had written many articles for the Mail involving this car, and now I had discovered one of the first owners.

'It was the family car for many years,' she continued. 'We bought it from a titled family in 1934 or 35 and my father sold it just after the war ended. What was so sad, Mr White was that I only actually rode in it on one occasion, but the photograph was a good one of my father and I liked it for that reason and that reason only.'

It was then she began to show me around the room, fondly talking about each photograph as we came to it. 'This one is of my mother, Alice, and father, just as the First World War broke out and he went into the Army. This one is of my sisters, Lucy and Alice, who of course was named after my mother . . .

'. . . This one's my favourite. It's of me at my first dance with William, my husband,' she said proudly, for the second time, as if she wanted to make sure I had taken this in. 'He had it tinted, but it does not show the real colour of my dress, which was very red. Really daring for the day, but I will tell you about that later, if you wish to hear about it . . . This one's *of my wedding and those are of our children's weddings.'*

'Where's this one taken?' I asked.

'Oh, that's at Le Touquet in France. It was a favourite place of my mother and father and turned out to be my favourite place of all; we as a family spent many happy hours there. We had a beach hut, which was something special in those days you know. Le Touquet was my second home and I loved every minute there and I never wanted to come back to England . . .'

'This will be your father,' I remarked as I picked up a photograph of a dashing Army officer from the First World War.

'Yes, he joined up with all the others in 1914 and unlike many, he survived. He had joined the special tank corps where he was quickly promoted. Throughout the war he became well thought of as a leader and tactician and was frequently promoted. He won the Military Cross twice,' she said with evident pride. 'He always said he was lucky and that many others were more deserving, but at the end of the war he was already a brigadier. He was also a shrewd investor and managed to get out intact before the big crash of the late 1920s, which ensured all of us had a privileged time.'

'Is this your brother?' I asked as I looked at a picture of her parents holding a little boy's hand.

'No that's me,' she replied, 'and the reason I wanted to see you . . .'

The astonished silence with which I reacted to her remark was interrupted by Sybil, who brought in the tea, and I was invited to sit down. We waited for Sybil to leave before we recommenced our conversation.

'Sybil isn't a real housekeeper, of course. She has been a family friend for fifty years; she lives with me as my companion and looks after me. We are finding the house too big for us now and we've decided to "downsize" as they say today. My son will be taking over this house and we will be moving to a smaller one. I don't know for how much longer – my time, I'm afraid, is running short. That really, Mr White is the reason I have asked you to come and yes – I know what you are thinking – it is to do with that photograph.' She looked directly at me as if intent on capturing my interest. I must admit – she had succeeded.

'My tale,' she now went on, 'is one of love and security, followed by

pain . . . real pain . . . and hatred. Mixed in it are courage, determination, humiliation and even murder, but it will come back to love and true happiness. You see, Mr White, if you do agree to write down my story, I want it to be a lesson for others. The world has been full of hatred and violence for years – we've had two world wars – and still we are unkind to one another; I would have thought we should have learned something from it, but we haven't, have we, Mr White?'

I nodded, trying to disguise my impatience. What exactly was her story? She was certainly a mistress of suspense.

I caught a glint of merriment in her eye as laughingly she said, 'Well, let me begin at the beginning.'

'Yes, please, it's the best place,' I replied, smiling. And with her hands placed gently in her lap, she began:

I was born just before the end of the First World War in 1917. Europe was in turmoil. The Americans had joined the war and one could now see the end in sight. The Russians had assassinated the Tsar and my father and many others among his fellow officers thought it was possible that we would soon be in conflict with the new Russian leaders.

I was led to believe that, when I was born and my father had been told he had a boy, he couldn't stop smiling and told everyone he met great or small. I'm sure he would have told all in the German Army if he could! Instantly, I was the apple of his eye; he had always wanted a boy and, after having two daughters, he got what he wanted. I was christened Alexander George Chillington-Henry – the kind of double-barrelled name I have always despised.

I, apparently – at least everybody used to say so – was a pretty baby with big brown eyes and dark hair. My sisters – Alice was five years older than me, and Lucy, seven – both had independent streaks. Lucy was a wild one and would do anything she wanted to, and damn the consequences; Alice was very good-looking and never looked her age; she always envied Lucy's approach to life, although she herself was a free spirit, especially when my father was away; I thought of her like a pent-up genie in a bottle!

These two girls used to push me around in the pram, dressing me up as though I was their doll, and people would ask 'Is this your new sister?' or would comment: 'He should have been a girl; he's too pretty to be a boy!' My sisters made matters worse by encouraging me to play with them and of course being the baby, I was always being dressed up. What by today's standards would be considered normal behaviour was abhorrent to my father as he wanted a real boy and was determined to have the real thing. He was always furious with the girls when he caught them playing their 'silly games' with me.

'Leave the boy alone!' he would shout. 'Let him play with his own toys.' And quite frankly that is what I wanted to do. My father was in the Army and I wanted to be like him, to sit astride a tank and command a battalion of men. I would follow him around marching, especially when he was in uniform, and he would shout, 'Stand up straight, shoulders back and stomach in . . . Left foot forward and quick march! Left right, left right . . .'

He spent every bit of spare time he had with me, playing cricket or throwing a rugby ball to me. I much preferred cricket and apparently often had tantrums when he wanted to do something else; but gradually he gave in and spent hour after hour bowling to me. My mother told me I had my first cricket bat at the age of three and, by the time I was five, my father had difficulty in bowling me out, or at least that's what he used to tell me.

I used to love it when he came home: he would throw me up in the air and catch me as I fell and hug me tightly. It was a wonderful feeling to be secure in his arms and to know that he cared.

I know my mother felt the same, but it was in a different way. 'Don't be so rough with him,' she would say to my father. 'You know he's only a little boy.'

'Nonsense! He's a big boy. Aren't you, Alexander?' He didn't wait for the answer, but simply threw me into the air again, adding, 'He's my big boy and he's going to be a soldier like his father.'

It was a wonderful time for me. He would never allow me to slouch. 'Stand up straight, my boy. You'll never make a soldier standing like that.' I must admit it did me good in later life as I looked taller than the five feet five that I am which, even then, wasn't that tall for a boy.

My mother, of course, let my father have his way. She knew he was very proud of his son and that I was very proud of him. She was also a very sensitive person, a very good homemaker and she loved my father dearly, but in a strange sort of way she was always terrified of losing what she had. He never beat her or in any way touched her aggressively, but still she was scared of losing what she held most precious. She wouldn't dare to contradict or suggest anything unless my father had mentioned it first and she was absolutely forbidden to suggest anything that concerned my welfare without Father's blessing.

She was very kind and, if she had heard someone in the village was ill, she would be the first to go round and often I heard she had paid doctors' bills when others couldn't afford it. She would never talk about her acts of kindness, but the villagers would. When the financial crash of 1929 came, she was the first to race to help all those suffering and yet it was never given with any hope of receiving anything back. In these matters, when she was acting on behalf of others, she showed enormous strength.

It was lovely to belong to such a close family, but eventually my father began to worry about the influence my sisters might be having on me and decided I should go to boarding school. 'It will make him stand on his own two feet and make a man of him,' I heard him tell my mother.

I didn't know what it would mean, except I knew that she did not want me to go and neither did I, especially when I realised I would be staying there for long stretches of time and not coming home. My father and mother rowed bitterly over the decision.

'You will make lots of new friends and we will come to see you every weekend,' my father promised me. 'Won't we, Alice?' he added, turning to my mother. 'Yes, of course,' she replied, though from her tone of voice I could tell she didn't quite believe what she was agreeing to.

I at least had almost a year before the dreaded day arrived. My father had been promoted to General Staff and was able to spend more time at home with his boy. That last summer we spent at Le Touquet and I didn't really notice at the time, but Le Touquet was a very fashionable place. Everyone who was anyone went there. There were new gleaming-white hotels and the shops were every bit as good as those in Paris. Nearly every day my father played cricket on the beach with me and it was about this time when he decided that just being a good batsman wasn't the end of it all; I had to be a good fielder as well; so from then on, he put a stick in the sand and made me throw a ball at it until I learned to hit it every time. This felt like a kind of torture and I'm sure the others on the beach thought so too and felt sorry for me; but my father thought it was the right thing to do and that was good enough for me. I did eventually become a good fielder, particularly when throwing on the run, which was to prove useful later on.

Unfortunately, September arrived all too quickly and the fatal day had come for me to be taken to my new school. I was dressed in my new school clothes. There's a picture of me. Look, Mr White, on the table there. I suppose it was typical of many a public school of those days – the short trousers, the double-breasted belted jacket and a very silly cap – but that is how it was.

Everyone turned out to see me off. 'It'll make a man of you,' they all said, echoing my father's words. 'You're a big boy now.' But still it didn't seem real. And then it was Alice and Lucy's turn to say goodbye and it was the first time things became difficult. Both gave me huge hugs and kisses and began sobbing. I now realised something was happening which I didn't like and I too began crying.

'Go inside, Lucy,' my father almost shouted. 'You're upsetting the boy. You too, Alice!'

The girls did as they were told and I clung on to my mother's hand, which she squeezed in a way only mothers can do. She leaned over and quietly whispered, 'Don't worry, darling, you'll be all right,' which calmed my fears, at least for a short time.

My father had arranged for a little pony and trap to take us to the station, where we then caught the train to London and then out to Bankworth, my new school. I was becoming terrified; I could sense there was a tension between my parents as hardly a word was spoken. 'Don't worry, you'll be all right,' my mother kept on saying but it was slowly dawning on me that perhaps everything wouldn't be all right.

Bankworth looked like an old Victorian hospital – very dark and austere. It appeared to be three schools rolled into one: the first was a mixed junior school, which had only about twenty girls, but with eighty boys residing; then there was the Senior School which was divided into two – a school for girls up to eighteen years of age and about forty pupils in total, and a school for boys with about a hundred or more pupils. There was, I later learned, absolutely no connection between the two senior schools; each operated as if the other did not exist.

Mr White, can you imagine what it was like for a five-year-old boy to be left on the doorstep of the school, like the one I have described, with only a big brown leather suitcase, which was as big as me, and then having to say goodbye to all the life I had known. Even now I can remember the tears rolling down my poor mother's cheeks as she said:

'Don't worry, darling, Do it for your father. He loves you very much and he is doing this for you. He doesn't want you to leave really, but he believes it's best for you.'

Those words haunted me for years because I knew my father loved me dearly and yet he was, in some ways, wrong. It is the hardest thing, Mr White, to forgive the mistakes of those who you are closest to; those of strangers are easy to pardon. As my parents were driven away, I stood on the great stone steps of the school, craning my neck until the very last moment just to get a last glimpse of my old life. A new, less pleasant chapter had begun.

Chapter 2

'Come on now, young man,' Matron Horsefield said as she pulled at my hand and led me away from the front door.

She almost dragged me to the boys' dormitory where I was shown my bed and my cupboard and told to unpack my case and put my things into the cupboard.

'Now, young Alexander, from now on you will address me as Matron. Do you understand?'

'Yes,' I replied, while Matron bent over, waiting for the next word.

'Yes, what?' she asked but didn't wait for the answer, before repeating, 'Yes, M . . . a . . . t . . .'

I twigged at last and replied, 'Yes, Matron.'

She smiled. 'Good. Now let's get on with unpacking, shall we? . . . Have all your clothes got your name on?' she asked in a less tender way. 'Let's have a look, shall we?' She efficiently checked all the items in the case, leaving them on the bed for me to put into the cupboard. There was two of everything, all with name tapes sewn into them: 'Alexander George Chillington-Henry.'

Once Matron Horsefield had finished checking my clothes, she summoned the handyman, who took hold of my case; but to me, the suitcase represented my last link with home, a potent symbol of the possibility of return, and I tried to take it back again, but the handyman, of course, was much bigger than I and he soon vanished out of the door with it; to stow it away God knows where.

Matron then took me to the main hall where there seemed to

be a vast number of boys and girls playing. Only a few newcomers stood nervously to one side, waiting for something Eventually, a bell rang and all the old boys and girls went into the various four corners of the room, which, we quickly found out, were the 'house corners'. We, the newcomers, were simply left standing in the middle of the room, like a herd of lost sheep.

Just then a short, fat woman marched into the room, followed by a beautiful young assistant. The first lady was the headmistress, Mrs Waggott, whom everyone feared; the second was Miss Roberts, whom everyone adored, but the atmosphere soon worsened as the booming voice of Mrs Waggott echoed around the hall.

'Welcome back, children, and a very warm welcome to all the new boys and girls who have just joined us. For those who have not met me, my name is Mrs Waggott and I'm your headmistress. On my right is Miss Roberts, my assistant. Now our first job is to put the newcomers into the allocated houses and introduce them to the House Captain. That's right, isn't it, Richard,' she added, turning to a tall eleven-year-old with blond hair who stood nearby.

'Yes, Mrs Waggott,' he responded dutifully.

'Richard is our head boy for this year and Lilian is our head girl,' Mrs Waggot announced. 'Where are you, Lilian?'

Lilian stepped forward gingerly, a rather pretty-looking girl with red hair.

'Several of our newcomers haven't arrived yet, but we must get on with things . . .' She quickly went onto name the four junior houses, each named after, we were told, one of our 'great prime ministers': Peel, Asquith, Balfour and Russell. 'Now I'm going to call out each of your names,' she continued in that concise, correct way all headmistresses adopt when talking to their charges, 'and you will go to your new house.'

She called out our names in alphabetical order and soon enough I was despatched to Asquith House where I was welcomed by John Maynard, my House Captain. I was very lucky because even at the tender age of ten Maynard showed a great deal of sympathy towards his new house members. It was a custom of the school for the House Captain to allocate each newcomer to a 'friend', whose job was to ensure they got to know the ropes and got to know all the other members of our house. My friend was David Frost.

David was a very competitive lad who was responsible, with the house master or mistress, for picking the house sports teams. The houses were mixed, with an even amount of boys and girls allocated to each, and the house teams were mixed too, which was totally unheard of in the circles my family moved in. However, the girls did not play rugby – that was one step too far. Frost quickly introduced me to David Rice, another newcomer and the boy who was to be my 'bedfellow'. That, of course, simply meant that he was to sleep in the bed next to mine – nothing more sinister than that, I can assure you, Mr White. One must always be so careful with terminology nowadays, don't you agree?

The bell went again. This time it was the signal for tea and Maynard escorted us into the dining room and told us at which table we had to sit. We all sat down on long wooden benches at the long wooden tables with all the newcomers wondering what was going to happen. Soon enough one of our house members handed out the plates and cutlery, while another brought the mugs for the tea. When that was done, we had to queue up for our mug of tea, already sweetened, our two slices of bread and butter and a not very generous blob of jam. I had been spoiled and used to having tea with not just bread and butter but cakes, scones and other treats, too. I was shocked by the rudimentary nature of the food, though fortunately, like the other newcomers I suppose, I didn't feel hungry; I just wanted to go home.

After tea we were allowed to play for a while. David Rice and I went to play in the playground along with the others, just running around, playing tag or something simple like that, before it was time for bed. At six o'clock we, the five-year-olds, were taken to the washroom by our friends and shown how to wash ourselves and clean our teeth. Then we were shepherded to the dormitory to bed down for the night. The curtains had been drawn and it was pitch black, except for a very small light at the end of the dorm. We were all very scared and many of us started crying, pleading to go home and asking to see our mother. I couldn't believe it: how could my parents have abandoned me here? The bed was like iron and much smaller than mine at home and no one came to say goodnight or read me a story, which my parents had done ever since I could remember.

As I went to sleep, I heard the sound of sobbing coming from David in the bed nearest mine; he obviously felt as bad as me. Eventually, I must have got off to sleep because the next thing I remember was Matron shouting, 'Come on, boys! Time to get up!'

She made a point of going up to each new boy and asking them how they had slept.

'I didn't!' I said truculently, 'I hate it here,' then added, 'I want to go home to see my father.'

'Ooooh, we are in a bad mood, this morning,' Matron replied loudly, making sure everyone heard and causing them to laugh.

When she had finished her little chats, Matron went to stand at the end of the dorm and shouted, 'Good morning, boys!' to which we all had to respond, 'Good morning, Matron!' – a ritual that did not change in any way for the next five years.

Once up, our 'friends' took us first to the washroom, where we again washed and cleaned our teeth, and then to the toilet, where we were supposed to do our 'number ones' and 'number twos' and if we hadn't done our 'number twos' we had to tell Matron. Of course I hadn't and nor did I for the next three days, for which I earned a small dose of Senna pods, which within a few hours caused a revolution in the bowel department.

Breakfast consisted of a boiled egg with bread and butter and a mug of tea. I was interested to see how I was going to take the top off my egg, as my mother had always done this for me, so I watched everyone else. My first attempt was unsuccessful as the egg was very runny and the mess went everywhere. Matron, who noted everything of course, commented loudly, 'Poor Alexander can't do it! Come on, Robert, you show him how.' I was determined from that moment to get it right and avoid further humiliation.

Breakfast was followed by twenty minutes' playtime and then, at nine o'clock, by assembly in the school hall.

Again Mrs Waggott marched in, dutifully followed by Miss Roberts two paces behind and then by a whole string of masters and mistresses. She stepped onto the dais and in one movement turned and said, 'Good morning, School,' to which we all sang: 'Good morning, Mrs Waggott.'

We were then introduced to the staff and told which classes we were to go to. And so term and the inevitable routine started. It's surprising how resilient one is in circumstances you cannot do anything about and it was only a short time before we were all used to our routine and settled down. David Rice became my good and close friend and we spent many hours playing games together, running around; in fact for little lads we became quite fit. The only difference between us was that he was a brain box and I wasn't.

At first, it was the weekend visits from my parents that were the unsettling factor. I remember the first few visits. It was a joy to see them; they would bring me a few sweets – not chocolate, that wasn't allowed – but pear drops and the like, and occasionally a new tennis ball. But over time, even the visits became normal and the crying became less and less.

The first term, from September until December, was called the Christmas term. There was one hour of physical training or sport every day. This was my favourite and was spent doing all sorts of things, such as rugby and running. If the fields were too wet, we would play rounders and practise catching the ball. I was quite good at that. I wasn't too bad at rugby, either, but with five- and six-year-olds, the whole game appeared to be just one big rough scrum; everyone just piled on top of one another.

I remember it wasn't long into the term when a plague of nits hit the girls and one or two boys. This was very embarrassing as we were all told it was caused through having dirty hair, which as we know today simply isn't true. The boys suffered especially because they were moved into the girls' dormitory and had to stay there until the outbreak was over, which took about a month.

Those unfortunate boys hated every minute and were shunned because their hair, like the girls', was plastered with a foul-smelling cream, yellow in colour, which was enough to put anyone off. We would tease them unmercifully, often until they cried in despair. It's something children have in them at that age. They don't realise what they are doing; they don't realise that they are being hurtful and unkind. And I confess, I was one of those who joined in. However, in my case it was something that came back to haunt me and I was to suffer the torments of the grown-up version of teasing a million times more than I had dished out as a very little boy.

Of course, as it was coming up to Christmas and there was a Nativity play and of course the most angelic-looking among the boys and girls were chosen to play angels – David and I amongst them. At that age you don't mind dressing up and even the boys didn't balk at wearing long flowing robes and silvery wings, just like the girls.

The first term was over and we, as the newcomers, were all glad to be going home and no one more than me. It was a wonderful sight to see my father and mother arriving at the school's front door, ready to take me home with my big leather case, which seemed just that little bit smaller than when I had arrived. I can remember I didn't stop talking the entire journey and I seem to remember my parents dutifully answering yes and no in the right places. It did, however, give my mother some comfort that the school hadn't done me too much harm.

Alice and Lucy were at the house to see me arrive, along with a few friends of my parents, who all remarked, 'Hasn't he grown?'

There was an avalanche of inevitable questions. Do you like school? What have you done? Are you looking forward to going back? It was a ridiculous thing to ask me when I had only just arrived home. I wouldn't have told them the truth anyway because even at that age I knew it would disappoint my father if I said I hated the place.

Christmas was a happy time with all the family together, but as with all holidays it was soon over and once again, my father and mother dropped me off at the school with my big suitcase to begin the next term, which was known as the Easter Term.

Everything continued much as before except now, for the first time, I encountered problems with the junior sports master, Fred Arnett. For some reason he disliked me from the start and began to make things difficult for me at every opportunity.

We had child-size parallel bars where we were expected to do pull-ups and hold the position and for some unknown reason, I couldn't hold myself up for more than a second or so. 'Go and play with your knitting!' he would shout at me, much to the amusement of the other boys and girls, and he would make me sit at the back of the class. Then, when one of the girls also showed herself incapable, he would send her to sit with me, shouting something like, 'You two go off and play, there's good girls!' A peal of laugher would go through the class, echoing through the cavernous space of the gym hall.

Easter came and went and once again the three weeks' holiday were soon over. My father had taken me out as often as he could to play and time just flew by. 'Let's hope you get picked for the cricket team this term!' he shouted at me from the platform as my mother and I left Upper Hayfield Station.

The summer term was on us and for the first time I enjoyed school a little and the only reason was that I enjoyed cricket. At that time I could only indulge my passion in the playground, as we were only allowed to play rounders on the sports field. There, though, I proved my worth and I actually got into the house rounders team. I was frustrated, however, that they wouldn't trust me in the cricket team. I was considered not old enough and far too small.

I complained to my father that they wouldn't let me play cricket, but he would always respond: 'Don't worry, your time will come and when it does no one will be able to touch you.' It was to be another two years before they would pick me for anything. I would watch the others playing and longed to have a go.

The first year had finished and we broke up for the long summer holidays. My father was obliged to go away for several weeks, leaving my mother in charge with strict instructions not to mollycoddle me, but in fact she did nothing else. I always had the impression that she was worried about me; I actually thought that it was because she had not wanted me to go to boarding school and I often used to tell her not to worry. 'I can cope!' I said in as grown-up a fashion as I could muster.

The following year was almost a carbon copy of my first; lessons went on as usual and the sports activities were almost the same; I was only a somewhat bigger angel in the Nativity Play. The only real difference was the school had an outbreak of mumps in the Christmas Term. Even in the 1920s they realised that it was advantageous for boys to catch the disease at an early age, to avoid problems later on, and to this end I was encouraged to go into the sick bay and play draughts with some of the sufferers, but for some unknown reason, I didn't catch it.

This year was also the start of our elocution lessons: once a week for half an hour we would be taught to speak 'the King's English' and to purge any trace of a regional accent from our voices. Our models were to be the new BBC wireless announcers.

We also started learning French, which of course was one subject in which I did well because of our holidays at Le Touquet.

I suppose you could say each year was marked by some natural catastrophe. My next year, my third, was no exception;

the whole school, both senior and junior departments, had an outbreak of scarlet fever, which in those days was considered very serious. I caught it just before Bonfire Night in November 1924 and was rushed off to the Stone Gate Fever Hospital in an ambulance along with two other boys.

We arrived at Stone Gate, which I remember was like Bankworth, an old sinister-looking Victorian building, and were quickly hustled through the hospital and out into the grounds behind, where there was a row of long wooden buildings, reminiscent of an army barracks. which were known as the isolation wards. From each hut ran a covered path, just wide enough for a stretcher, but when it was raining, and two stretchers had to pass each other, one had to move out into the rain.

It appeared that our entire ward had been taken over by the boys from Bankworth with all age groups there and in all stages of recovery; the better you were the nearer to the exit door you were put; naturally we started at the far end. It was an unpleasant place for us juniors as we were all very vulnerable to bullying by the senior boys. We were not allowed visitors because of the infection, but were allowed to receive anything sent in and in consequence our parents sent many gifts, sweets and comics, which the senior boys swiftly confiscated especially as the latter was banned at school. However, they were returned a few days later all dog-eared and torn. The sweets were also shared out by the seniors, who allocated us very little, if anything at all. It got so bad at one stage that the nurses put our names on our bags of sweets and gave us a few each day to prevent them being stolen.

I was in quarantine for three weeks – I had, it turned out, only a very mild attack – and afterwards I was immediately returned to school; it was so good to be back with my own kind and to see my father and mother again, for the first time in ages. On the first weekend after my release my parents took me into the local town to shop for presents and to have tea in my favourite café. I loved that café which, after the austerity of the school was like paradise, with its dark tables and chairs set in an oak-beamed room with whitewashed walls, and its long half net curtain across the front window, just low enough for you to see in and watch the customers enjoying their freshly made scones and tea served in white bone china. My favourite treat was a giant disc of Lyons Swiss roll, which was quite a new delicacy then. I liked to unroll it and eat it bit by bit, like a snake disappearing down a hole – much to the annoyance of my mother!

Although I felt so much better after their visit, I wasn't allowed to do sports for another four weeks. Instead I knuckled down and honed my reading skills and learned my part for the Nativity Play: this year I was one of the Three Wise Men. I think I actually said three sentences and, when that was over, it was the end of term.

My father picked me up from school and we took our usual ride on the train, back to Upper Hayfield and home. It was a treasured sight made more so by the welcome that awaited me. My mother had arranged a party for all the family; even a few of my uncles and aunts were there.

'Why are we having a party, Mother?' I asked.

'It's because you have been so very ill and now you are better,' she replied.

My father apparently had been beside himself with worry and had actually taken time away from work until he knew I was on the mend. I had no idea scarlet fever was so dangerous.

It wasn't the kind of children's party one would have today; it was rather formal, more like a grown-up dinner party. I was put at the head of the table with my father and mother either side of me and unusually, my father stood up and gave thanks that I had recovered and was healthy and strong again. I won't bore you with details of the five-course meal that followed, but, needless to say, for a boy my age it was far too much.

I had a lovely Christmas and my most important recollection of that time was I had my first full-size cricket bat; signed by none other than W.G. Grace. During the previous summer, my father had been involved in some inspections with the Royal Gloucestershire Regiment and, while there, had been invited to attend a day watching Gloucestershire play Kent. He had been introduced to the great doctor and had asked for his autograph on my behalf, which he duly received, but he got an even bigger surprise when the Gloucestershire club also gave him a bat for me, with all their names written on the back, including that of W.G. Grace. My father had saved it to give me at Christmas.

At this point my hostess took a bat out of a stand close to where she was sitting.

'Look, Mr White, you can just see the signatures on the back, though they are very faded. It was too big for me initially, but I kept persevering and, silly as it may seem, I soon grew into it. I used it for years at school and then I thought it better to have another.'

'It must be worth something now,' I remarked.

'Oh I'm not interested in the money, Mr White. If the MCC want it, they can have it,' she replied. 'It's worth more to them . . . Now where was I?

'It was Christmas and you had had a grand dinner party,' I replied.

'Ah yes. You are listening, Mr White!'

My family will never forget the 28th December. It had snowed heavily during the night and I had woken in the morning feeling ill and running a temperature. My mother thought it was flu and sat me down covered by a blanket in front of the fire. I didn't feel any better by lunchtime, so she decided we should walk the short distance down to the local doctor, a Dr Palin, who ran an afternoon surgery. My mother told me the walk in the fresh air would do me some good, even though the snow was some twelve inches thick on the ground. The truth of the matter was, as my father had had to go away, my mother wouldn't have been able to get the car out and was, in any case, terrified of driving in the snow.

We therefore tramped the quarter of a mile to the surgery and by the time we got there, I was feeling terrible. We were greeted by Dr Palin.

'Mrs Chillington-Henry, how nice to see you! Come on in. Now I can see its young Alexander who has come to see me, isn't it?' he said in his usual cheerful manner,

'Yes, he's running a temperature and at the same time feels very cold,' my mother replied.

'Let me have a look at you, young man. It looks as though he has the start of flu. There is a lot about at the moment,' he said, as he took us into his room and sat us in front of his roaring fire. He gave me a thorough examination and then looked concerned. 'I think the boy has scarlet fever.'

'No, that's impossible, Doctor,' my mother replied. 'He's already had it. In fact, he was released from the fever hospital a couple of months back and I thought you can only catch the illness once.'

Dr Palin sat for a few moments thinking. 'Yes, that's right . . .' He paused as if unwilling discuss the matter. 'Look, Alexander, you stay here in front of the fire. I need to go and get some medicine. Perhaps your mother will be so kind as to come with me?' he added, addressing my mother, who now looked very concerned. 'Is that all right, young man?'

'Yes, sir,' I responded dolefully as my mother and the doctor left the room with me shivering in front of the fire.

I don't know why they left the room as I heard everything that was said in spite of their lowered voices.

'You say he has not long recovered from the disease?'

'Yes, as I said, last November. Is there anything wrong, Doctor?'

'I'm afraid I have bad news for you. I think he may have infantile paralysis.'

There was a deathly silence and I heard a dull thud as something fell onto the wooden floor. This was enough for me.

I ran into the next room to find my mother on the floor with the doctor bending over her.

'What have you done to my mother?' I shouted, forgetting all my own aches and pains as well as all my manners.

'Alexander, your mother is all right. She has just fainted. I think it must be the cold. Please go back into the room and sit by the fire, there's a good boy.'

But I wouldn't leave until I had seen my mother come round and begin to get back onto her feet and even then only when she herself told me to go and sit by the fire.

Infantile paralysis was a killer in those days and, perhaps even worse, some of its victims could be left in a state of full or partial paralysis, with one or several limbs completely useless. We call it polio these days and it is easily cured or prevented by modern drugs, but then it was feared.

'I'm sorry, Mrs Chillington-Henry, but you are going to have to be very careful and do exactly as I tell you . . . *to the letter!'* Dr Palin emphasised.

My mother simply nodded.

Dr Palin continued: 'Take him straight home to bed and confine him to his room. He must *not* come out of his room for any reason. No one must be allowed to come into the house; in fact it would be safer if no one came near it. Get George Williamson to leave the groceries at the gate and tell Fred to do the same. We cannot risk this disease being spread and I would suggest that Lucy and Alice are prevented from close contact with Alex. In fact, if after three days, they have not shown any symptoms, they should go and stay with their aunts.'

'I'll see to that,' my mother replied.

Fred Dunton was a lovely man and local farmer who delivered his milk by pony and cart and it was always a joy to spot him coming along the road, with his great silver churns sparkling in the early-morning sunshine, together with his three copper ladles: one, a quarter of a pint, one, a half and the other, a pint which he would use to ladle whatever milk you wanted into your own jug or jar and you would then take it to the pantry or the cellar, if you were lucky enough to have one, as they were colder. No fridges in those days, Mr White. Well, he wasn't going to let my mother walk any distance in the cold and still came to the door.

The next three days, the doctor told my mother, would be the most important. If I survived those, things might improve.

My mother was in a daze when we left the doctor's and struggled back to the house amidst yet another snowfall. I remember her taking me straight to my room, stoking up the fire and then going to tell our housekeeper and gardener and others about my plight. Mrs Fanshawe, the housekeeper, refused to leave; she wasn't going to see my mother on her own, to face all these problems by herself. This was the loyalty my mother had generated by helping all those in need. Even John Wilson, the gardener and odd-job man, whom my mother had had to order to go home, as he had four children of his own, came every day and filled all the coal scuttles and left them by the outside doors.

When I look back at it now, I find it so moving that these people – these friends! – placed themselves and their families at considerable risk to help our family.

By the following day I had fallen into a massive fever. I was delirious, falling in and out of consciousness, boiling hot one moment, freezing cold the next; there was nothing anyone could do except to keep me warm, to wipe my head with a hot damp flannel and to hope! I remember the doctor calling twice a day, advising my mother to keep up with the same routine and to try and get me to drink a lot of barley water. This was something we made ourselves in the 1920s and Mrs Fanshawe was a mistress of medicine manufacture. Armed with her prized Mrs Beeton's cookbook, she could make anything from shoe polish to barley water.

By the second day, things looked desperate; there was still no chance of an ambulance getting through as we had had further flurries of snow, which were making things that bit more difficult, and by now Dr Palin feared the worst.

My father had not been contacted as my mother did not want him worried, but now Dr Palin felt he should be informed in case the patient did not recover. John Wilson was charged with the job of going to the post office and sending a telegram to my father. It read: 'Alexander very ill. Stop. Essential you return home. Stop. Time is short. Stop.' It was signed: 'Your loving wife, Alice.'

My mother sat with me for hours, mopping my brow and encouraging me to drink, hardly stopping to eat or drink herself. Mrs Fanshawe was an angel, making sure my mother did at least take a nap from time to time and taking over the bedside duties. By the third day, however, my poor mother was at the point of exhaustion and the housekeeper sent her off to bed.

It was whilst my mother was in bed that my father arrived home, together with Dr Palin and a specialist doctor from London, whom my father knew from the Army. He was none other than Sir Harry Crabtree, who you may remember was an important pioneer in the treatment of polio.

'Where's Alice?' my father asked Mrs Fanshawe, as the three men entered the house.

'I'm sorry, sir, but she's not had much sleep for these past days. I was afraid she would become ill and I sent her to bed. I'll tell her you're here,' the housekeeper replied.

'No, let her rest. The doctors and I will just go and have a look at the boy. I will see my wife later.'

Mrs Fanshawe led the entourage into my room, which was like an oven.

As soon as he entered the room, Sir Harry almost shouted: 'For God's sake, open the windows and let some fresh air in! The boy will suffocate to death!'

Mrs Fanshawe jumped to it, almost as though she was a private under orders. I can still remember that breath of fresh air as it drifted over my bed.

'Come on, young man, let me have a look at you,' Sir Harry said as he gently pulled the bed clothes off and began to examine me. He gave me a thorough examination and then he whispered, 'My, you have got a fever! But I think we may be over the worst.'

He then turned to my father and, careful not to humiliate Dr Palin, he commented: 'Your doctor was wise to consider infantile paralysis because the fever is so extraordinary. However, I'm sure we can rule that out. I'm convinced he has another dose of scarlet fever. Look, Doctor,' he said, inviting Dr Palin to check his diagnosis, 'see how the rashes are forming. It's a straightforward case. Don't you think?'

Dr Palin agreed. It would have been a brave man to go against such an eminent character.

Sir Harry turned to my father: 'Tell Alice that all is well and he should start to recover within the next two or three days. She can stop worrying. You, too, William! You won't be losing our fine future English cricketer that soon!'

He turned to Mrs Fanshawe. 'I want you to destroy *all* his bedding when the fever has subsided and tell Mrs Chillington-Henry that the room must be cleaned thoroughly before it is used again. It is very important to prevent the disease spreading.

'William,' he said, returning to my father, 'he will be very weak when the fever goes and I don't think he will be fit for anything for at least six months. He will need to convalesce for many weeks. But he will get back to normal, I promise.'

My mother had been woken up by the commotion and had walked in to hear the last few words spoken by Sir Harry. My father turned, as he heard her sigh of relief.

'It's scarlet fever and he's getting better!' my father said, almost having to wipe tears of joy from his eyes. My mother cried unashamedly as she and my father embraced.

'I seem to have brought you some good news,' Sir Harry said as he turned to leave the room.

'Come on, Mrs Fanshawe, let's all have a cup of tea,' my father said, his relief apparent to everyone.

Well, I did recover, but it was several weeks before I had the strength to do anything physical; in fact, I missed the entire spring term at Bankworth, although my mother had the sense to obtain a private tutor.

That must have been the cue for Sybil to enter; she hadn't waited to be asked and now carried in a tray of tea with home-made scones and jam.

'Sybil, dear,' Mrs Fraser said, 'I've just been talking about your mother and how she looked after me when I was ill. Yes, Mr White, Sybil was Mrs Fanshawe's daughter and since those days we've been good friends. I hope you don't mind me mentioning it, Sybil.' Sybil nodded her approval.

'Her husband was killed during the war. He was in the Navy and won the Distinguished Service Order. He was a brave man. She has two lovely children and four grandchildren. They all regularly come to stay with us. We'll miss that I think when we move to our little house. Won't we, Sybil?'

She nodded. 'I will miss the house; it is a wonderful place to live and has so many lovely memories,' Sybil said quietly as if she was already thinking back to those days.

As we had our tea, Mrs Fraser continued:

You know, Mr White, my father didn't want to take any chances with my health and felt a warmer climate would be beneficial to me and in consequence he packed me off, with my mother and a tutor, to Nice. We stayed there all winter; I was bored out of my mind. I wasn't allowed to do any physical exercise, except walk along the Promenade des Anglais, which was about two miles in length and which I had to do at least once every day and often twice. I was allowed to go into the sea but it was too cold.

However, in Nice, the winter was soon over and as my strength returned, my mother took us all to what became my second home in Le Touquet. My father had purchased a house there as an investment and sometimes we would even fly there across the Channel. When I think, Mr White, how at that time aviation was still in its infancy, I wonder how on earth I was persuaded to go on one of those early passenger aircraft. We were all much braver in those days! However, it was only a short flight to Le Touquet and a short ride from the aerodrome to our French home, so my father was able to spend more time with us. He hadn't been able to visit us in Nice and I had missed him.

On his first visit during my convalescence, my father told me he had been reading in the newspaper about a new young cricketing phenomenon in Australia, Don Bradman. Apparently, he had represented his town or village at the age of ten, scoring a century on his debut. He had honed his batting skills by playing a form of tennis, using a cut-down broom as the bat and hitting a golf ball against a wall. At this point, my father produced a cut-down walking stick, to which he had fitted a rubber handle and told me to start doing the same.

It proved an impossible task. I don't know, Mr White, if you realise the speed at which a golf ball can travel when it rebounds off a wall, but I can assure you it is very quick indeed. And add to that a bat only an inch or so wide, and you can appreciate the difficulty it gave me. I loved being with my father, but this was torture; however, for him I persevered and managed to practise about an hour a day. By the time I returned to school for the summer term, which was the second week in April, I could regularly hit the ball two or three times in succession; but the most important thing for me was that my father was proud of me.

I returned to school for the start of the summer term to an enthusiastic reception from my friends, who, it seemed, had missed me. Even Matron with her stern manner commented: 'It's good to see you, Henry. Are you better?"

'Yes, Matron,' I replied with a smile.

It was good to be back, even if it was business as usual. However, for the first time in my scholastic career I started getting good marks. My private tutor had naturally taught me on a one- to-one basis and my spoken French, of course, was really excellent.

The problem now, oddly enough, was with sport. Mr Arnett, the sports master I mentioned earlier, was now the master in charge of cricket and, if anything, his dislike of me seemed to have intensified since my illness. There were twenty-one pupils in our class and for the first match Arnett picked the two teams, with him playing in one of them. Our side was to bat first and he picked the batting order for both sides; I was to go in at number seven.

Of course he loved to show off and he put himself on to bowl. Remember, he was playing against eight-year-olds! I think we had scored a miserable 10 when it was my turn to bat.

'You should be playing netball with the girls,' he shouted even before he had bowled me a ball.

He started his run-up to bowl at me, but in fairness, it was nothing over the top: just three paces and very slow right arm over.

I sent it for four, to the cheers of my team.

'Catch it!' I heard him shout peevishly to some unfortunate, fielding down the leg side. The boy didn't have a chance and anyway it was pretty much along the ground.

It was a glorious day. I reached my fifty so quickly, to the further cheers of our team, that Arnett made me declare to give the others a chance to bat.

Arnett made us suffer when he went into bat, where of course he had an easy time of it. He too scored fifty, but didn't retire to give his teammates a chance. He wanted to win . . . and of course he made sure of it.

It was the first time boys began to judge him as unfair, and it soon got around what had happened. Even the headmistress made a point of congratulating me in assembly the following morning.

I had a wonderful season and scored a lot of runs, but during each good innings, Arnett would make me retire. I was out only twice, though sadly one of those was the Annual Junior Founder's Day Match when I was picked to represent the school against the parents. For me it was an exciting day: the first time my father and mother had been able to see me play in a proper match. The parents were always gentle with us, as we were still only little lads, although, I often thought this was just an excuse they made, just in case they were beaten.

Arnett put me in to bat at number three. The openers actually did rather well and had put on 30 for the first wicket. I went in to bat and the bowler began to dolly a few up to give me a chance, which I took full advantage of. I had quickly scored 33 when the new bowler dollied another ball down the leg side. I just hit it high into the air and was caught.

My father was furious. 'You should have looked where the fielders were before you took the strike,' he said angrily as we walked back to the pavilion.

I must admit I was a bit shocked and upset, as, even though I had scored only 33, I thought I had done well. To give him his due, my father soon relented and said, 'Well done!' as he gave me a hug. He couldn't help adding, though: 'Let this be a lesson and look next time!'

The juniors were easily beaten, but it was a lovely day for all of us.

My remaining years at Bankworth Juniors followed the same pattern as all of them, except for the obvious: we were all becoming more grown up and more competitive and developing our own characteristics. My last year at the Bankworth Juniors, however, was my best and in spite of the indifference shown to me by Mr Arnett, I was made the House Captain.

I was determined to make Asquith House the best, not only in sport, but also on the academic side. Stars were awarded to individuals for good work in whatever field and at the end of the year they were all tallied up and, of course, the house with the highest number of stars won a trophy. David and I worked as a team, encouraging everyone in Asquith to do their best, so much so by, the middle of the summer term we had an unassailable lead.

At the Junior Prize-Giving Mrs Waggott called both David and I up to receive the trophy and as she handed it over, she commented: 'Seldom in my life, as a teacher, have I seen two children show so many leadership qualities at such a young age! Well done, boys!' I felt myself blush with pride and embarrassment.

This wasn't my only achievement that year. I actually captained the Junior School cricket team and made the local newspapers on several occasions. Arnett still tried his best to belittle me, but he had no option when it came to cricket; I was without doubt the best prospect with the bat the school had ever had.

It may seem as if I'm boasting, Mr White, but whatever I might say, this was all down to my father and the time he had spent with me over the years!

The cricket season started with our first match against St Jude's, another public school in the area, against whom we always played a home and away. I had won the toss and elected to bat; our openers had scored 15 when one was out and I went onto the field. I remember there was an air of expectancy as I had scored a lot of runs in the form and house matches.

I faced the first ball and to my horror I was bowled out for a duck. Arnett greeted me coming off the field and for the first and only time in my entire stay at Bankworth he made some constructive criticism: 'Bad luck, lad, but you were overconfident. Remember in future to take your time and look at the ball for the first over or so and only hit the loose ones.'

'Yes, sir,' I replied sadly. I felt as though I had let everyone down. We lost the first match easily and I remember overhearing Arnett commenting the following Saturday that perhaps the responsibility was too much for me.

Our next match was against All Saints and this time I didn't let anyone down. I scored 86 not out and I even took a wicket bowling. I continued in this vein all season, scoring nearly 800 runs in total and with us not losing another match. We then had the return match with St Jude's, who teased us about the previous match, particularly when we lost our first wicket for only ten runs.

I was about to go in when I heard Arnett shouting, 'Take your time, lad!' and it made me think of my father's criticism several years before.

'Right, sir,' I replied and walked slowly to the crease.

I didn't face the first few balls, though they didn't look that difficult, but when I did face them, it was my day. I scored 122 not out, out of a total of 167 for seven and they were all out for 35. Revenge was sweet!

The annual match against the senior school first years and the Founders Day Match against the parents were the ones I remember most. I scored 127 and 132 not out and it was the first time the juniors had won both matches for many years and I had scored three successive hundreds. Needless to say when I collected the batting prize, the headmistress once again painted a glowing picture of my achievements.

My final prize, and my only academic one, was for French, which in fairness was easy as I lived there for many weeks each year, so I had a distinct advantage over the others. Nonetheless, Mrs Waggot was proud of my achievements and announced: 'And for the third year in succession Alexander receives the prize for French.' You can imagine what my father and mother were feeling like, especially when some of the other parents came up to congratulate me.

My father and mother came to pick me up at the end of term and at the end of my days in the Junior School. I can still remember my tears when I had first arrived and how much I had hated being left by my parents and now I was crying because I was leaving!

'Thank you very much, Mrs Waggott, I've had a wonderful time,' I said to the headmistress, a little shyly.

'It's been a pleasure, Alexander. And I for one will miss you, though you won't be very far away!'

She turned to my father. 'I know your son will do splendidly in the seniors, Mr Chillington-Henry, and not just at cricket!'

My father waved his hand deprecatingly as I went to put my case, which now didn't seem very big at after all, into the back of the car. We drove out of the drive and I waved to Mrs Waggott through the back window until I could see her no more and then settled back into my seat.

'You're quiet,' my father said as we drove home.

'I'm thinking about the last two weeks. They were possibly the best of my life,' I replied.

'They certainly were!' my father replied. 'We're both very proud of you, aren't we, Alice? You are a credit to the family.'

Those words made me so happy. I just closed my eyes and let the memories drift over me. The next thing I knew we were arriving home.

'Come on, Alexander darling, we're home!' I heard my mother say amidst my dreams of the cricket field.

Chapter 3

Mrs Fraser was interrupted by Sybil who came to ask if we would like another cup of tea, 'or perhaps something a little stronger?' I was about to accept when I looked at my watch: it was seven o'clock.

'God!' I almost yelled, getting to my feet. 'It's my wedding anniversary and I promised to take my wife out. I've booked the table for seven thirty and I'm late already.'

'I'm so sorry, Mr White. It's my fault,' Mrs Fraser said apologetically. 'Is there anything I can do?'

'Thank you, but no thank you. I will have to rush,' I replied.

'What is the restaurant called and I'll give them a ring for you. It will save you time.'

'That would be kind; it's The Three Feathers at Medwith.'

'Oh I know it very well. Jamie Montrose is a friend of mine. I'll say you are running late and will be there for eight. Is that acceptable?'

My wife wasn't as irritated as I feared she might be, especially when I told her about the curious tale I heard and especially its extraordinary narrator. And so it was in a buoyant mood that she and I arrived at the Three Feathers shortly before the allotted time.

At reception, our conversation with the pretty young receptionist was interrupted by a dapper man in his late eighties.

'Mr and Mrs White? How nice to see you. I'm Jamie Montrose, the proprietor. 'I hope you will excuse the liberty but I have a gift for you . . . no two!'

A pair of enormous bunches of flowers appeared out of nowhere, one from Mrs Fraser and the other from the restaurant. This epiphany of blooms caused a bit of a stir as most diners turned to see which of the royalty it was that would have provoked so ostentatious a display.

After a delicious meal Mr Montrose joined us at our table. His very first question was: 'So how do you know Alexandra?'

'I don't yet,' I replied honestly. 'I'm writing a story of her life and we've only just started.' My admission startled me; it wasn't until that moment that I had thought I would accept the commission, but somehow it seemed to have been decided without me.

'It's a fascinating tale,' Jamie Montrose began. 'We have known her for more than sixty years; she is a remarkable woman, very talented and a very human person. Her husband was one of my best friends. We played rugby together.'

I couldn't resist asking, 'What do you find interesting about her?'

The question clearly unsettled him. His tone became reserved though polite. 'You must find that out for yourself, Mr White, but I can promise you, you will not be disappointed. I hope you enjoyed your meal and perhaps we will see you again one day soon.' He got up and we shook hands, but there was a new embarrassment, perhaps even mistrust in his whole demeanour.

The following day I phoned to thank Alexandra and to arrange another appointment, but to no avail; Sybil who had answered the phone promised she would get Mrs Fraser to call as soon as possible. A couple of days passed and still no call, so I rang again, with the same result. Sybil promised once again that she would let Mrs Fraser know that I had rung and get her to ring back as soon as possible; she also assured me that she had let her know I had called previously.

Three days later I was tearing my hair out, wondering what the hell to do next when Josh Rawlings shouted across the office, 'I've got that woman on the phone again. What shall I tell her?'

'Who is it?' I asked impatiently, as I was already on the phone.

I heard Rawlings ask the question and then shout over, 'An Alexandra Fraser.'

'I'll be with you in just a minute,' I shouted, and politely told the person to whom I was on the phone that I would ring him back as I had an urgent call waiting.

'Put her through,' I called over anxiously.

Rawlings covered the mouthpiece up and whispered loudly so that the office could hear, 'She must be something. I've never seen Clive so anxious to speak to someone!'

'Good morning, Mrs Fraser,' I quickly said as the phone clicked over.

'Good morning, Mr White . . . and let that be a lesson to you,' she added,'

'What lesson?' I asked.

'I wanted to see what reaction I would get from keeping you waiting and ignoring your calls and I got just what I wanted.'

'And what's that?' I asked somewhat stupidly.

'Now I know you do want to write my story and I'm sure you won't make another late afternoon appointment.'

From the tone and manner of her voice I could feel her smiling at me. There was a second or two of silence, which I'm sure she engineered just to make me feel worse.

It was things like that which made her character all the more fascinating. She knew exactly how to control the situation, unnerving even a hardened reporter like me.

I broke the silence by thanking her for the wonderful flowers she had given Jill and me. 'Now I mustn't waste your time,' I continued, turning to my real subject. 'When can I come and see you?'

'Now there you go again, Mr White. You should say what you mean. It's your time we are wasting and you are the busy one. You've forgotten I have all the time in the world, as long as I'm alive.'

That brought me down to earth with a jolt. I had been behaving as though I was talking to some young woman whom I was trying to impress, instead of an eighty-nine year-old lady.

'Would tomorrow morning be OK?' I asked. 'About nine o'clock?'

'Oh, Mr White, when are you going to learn? A lady does not start work until ten thirty.'

'Ten thirty it is then. I'll look forward to it.'

'So will I, Mr White, so will I. Goodbye.'

I put the phone down and for a moment or two I simply stared into space, only to be brought back to earth with a bang, when my colleagues in the office wolf whistled, with shouts of: 'He's in love!' 'He's got it bad!' 'I've never seen Clive like this before . . .'

'She's eighty-nine for God's sake!' I shouted at them.

Perhaps I had fallen in love with her, I thought to myself, but it was her character, her humour and her joie de vivre. I couldn't wait until tomorrow, but with a story like this, I felt I had better clear it editorially.

George Stevenson was an old hand in the editorial stakes; he had held several senior positions with several newspapers and had previously been the Editor of the Morning Echo, *which had one of the biggest circulations of all, but he had been head hunted and offered a huge rise in salary to come to the* Mail *and put it back into order as it had been losing circulation, and he had succeeded in his efforts. He was a tough cookie and I knew that I wouldn't be able to do this one without his agreement. I had even been contemplating doing it in my own time and thus avoid the difficulties, but I thought perhaps I had little enough spare time with my family as it was.*

I walked into George's office full of trepidation only to be greeted with a broad smile and a laugh. 'I hear you've got another woman, Clive. You be careful, a man of your age, too!'

'Yes I have and she's eighty-bloody-nine and still as sharp as a needle,' I retorted. 'It's her I've come about. She wants me to write her story and I don't know why . . . I just can't put my finger on it . . . but I want to do it.'

'Who is it?'

'A woman called Alexandra Fraser. She lives with her housekeeper in Upper Hayfield on Thames.'

'I've heard of her. She's lived a somewhat privileged life. Father was a General, I believe. Why does she want you to write this story?'

I explained she had read the II PY articles we had published a few years ago and that her family had previously owned the car. But there was something extraordinary about her story, I told him, though I held fire on exactly what this might be.

'How much is she asking?'

'Nothing so far.'

'She will,' George added cynically. 'She obviously needs the money to maintain her lifestyle.'

'Maybe, but there's no indication of that yet.'

'OK, do it! But keep me informed. If you think it's going nowhere, drop it quickly.'

I was relieved, but I suppose I knew deep down George would go with my instinct.

I arrived once more at the house and drove up the small drive. This time Mrs Fraser herself greeted me. She was gardening at the front of the house, or perhaps I should say picking the odd few flowers, as she had a part-time gardener for the real work.

'Mr White, how nice to see you again, but then I knew I would,' she said with a smile and a little friendly push of my shoulder.

'Good morning, Mrs Fraser, and it is a lovely morning. It seems a pity to have to work.'

'This isn't work for me, Mr White; it's a pleasure and I know you will enjoy it too. Anyway I think I know you well enough to call me Alexandra. A privilege I have given to few people in my life, as I like to keep my distance. How long have we got today?'

'Well, actually I'm yours until the story is finished or to be honest until I feel we can go no further,' I replied. I don't know why but I couldn't bring myself to call her Alexandra at the time, in spite of her permission to do so. There was just something about her that familiarity wouldn't allow.

'Mr White . . .' she began.

'Please call me Clive,' I asked, but she never did, except on this first occasion.

'Good, Clive it is then. Let me take you round the garden, it will give you a feeling of life in the twenties and thirties.'

We walked to the side of the house where she opened a wrought-iron gate, perfectly painted black, without a mark of rust anywhere.

'My husband, William, would never allow things to get dirty or marked and would insist things were cleaned or repainted the moment something showed. My grandfather planted this yew hedge, my father put the gate in it and my husband shaped it. I now try to keep it as they did.'

The gate fitted snugly into an arch cleverly shaped into the hedge, and which led out into a huge two or three-acre garden, still fully maintained in a style that was pure Gertrude Jekyll. There were cascading flower beds that were straight out of an Impressionist painting, exquisitely shaped lawns for croquet, elegant summerhouses and gazebos; walkways of scented roses and an ornamental pond full of fat, glistening goldfish. At the far end of the garden was a small pavilion that faced out onto a small cricket pitch. We stopped for a minute or so where she just gazed before sighing.

'This is where my father and I played cricket. I had such a wonderful time. He did love me dearly and I him!'

I could detect a tear being pushed aside as she turned and led us back to the house.

'I can appreciate why you will find it difficult to leave this house,' I commented.

'It's the memories that I shall miss,' she said quietly as we entered the house through the back door.

As we passed through the spacious kitchen Sybil asked if I would like a cup of tea with a toasted tea cake, to which I readily assented. Mrs Fraser continued through to the drawing room which we had sat in previously.

'This really beats working for a living,' I quipped as I settled into a cosy armchair and took out my notebook.

She smiled. 'Now, Mr White, do you want me to continue where I left off or do you wish to approach things from a different direction?'

'I would like to play it by ear, so please continue as you will. You were at the point of having to start at the Senior School . . .'

The summer holidays were over. I had had my eleventh birthday and now had to start a new year at Bankworth, but this time I was a senior boy. My father was so proud of me; he had a look of satisfaction on his face every time he looked at me, as if to say, 'That's my boy!'

I was driven to the station by my father, accompanied by the family, minus Lucy of course, as she was now well and truly married and was expecting a child of her own. I'm not sure to this day whether it was planned or not. Alice came along, but she too was always busy now and I wondered if it would be the last time that she would see me off.

I was put on the train, the heavy door slamming behind me. I lifted the window to kiss my mother and Alice goodbye and then I remember the guard waving his green flag, the shrill noise of his whistle warning people the train was starting and the whoosh of steam as the train began to move; slowly at first then quicker and quicker, as I leaned out of the window waving madly as my mother shouted, 'Be careful, you'll fall out!' Alice ran along for a little way until the train began to pull away from her and I could see my father giving his last dignified wave, but still with that look on his face that said, 'That's my boy!'

I was on my own for the first time, armed only with my leather case, which seemed to grow smaller every time I used it. I must admit I was afraid and yet in some way proud of the fact that I was trusted to be on my own. I sat down on the seat in a second-class compartment, with my case beside me and despite my best efforts, it was far too heavy to lift onto the rack. There were far more items needed for the Senior School, from running shorts to a pair of 'Sunday best' shoes, as well as more personal items such as a pot of home-made raspberry jam which my mother had made from the raspberries we had picked together during the holidays.

I was alone in the carriage until we reached London, giving me time to dream about the now vanished holidays – a long hot summer spent at Le Touquet, special times playing cricket with my father, the picnics in the country, the parties in the garden, swimming and learning to do the crawl. I thought about my mother; how she would give me gentle hugs and kisses on the side of my face and almost jump away when she heard or saw my father approaching. She used to pull me close to her as though she needed to protect me. My father hated it and would shout, 'Alice, for God's sake, leave the boy alone!'

The train arrived at London St Pancras and I now faced the prospect of making my way by taxi to Waterloo. I don't mind admitting it, I was scared. My father had given me money for the taxi, which he told me would be on the rank outside the station, so with my two-ton case I struggled along the platform, handed my ticket to the collector, who clipped it and returned it to me.

Without my asking, he added, pointing, 'Taxis are over there, son!'

'Thank you, sir,' I said politely, wondering how on earth he knew what I wanted.

I was struggling along once more when a kindly porter took the case off me.

'Where do you want to go to, son? The taxis?'

'Oh, thank you,' I replied with some relief.

He deposited me at the taxi rank and I waited my turn, which duly came. The driver alighted, nodded at me, then took the case and strapped it to the open side luggage stand and off we set, arriving well in time for me to catch the train to Bankworth.

To my great surprise and pleasure I saw my great friend David Rice and he too was looking lost, so at least we could be lost together. I'm sure my smile was as big as his when he first saw me and to have a companion at this time was a real bonus. We sat in the train talking about the holidays and reminiscing about old times at the Junior School, when some other, older lads in our school uniform came into our compartment. One of them looked across at us.

'New boys then, are you?' this lad asked.

'Yes,' we said nervously.

'What are your names?' he asked firmly, showing off to his friends.

'Rice,' David replied.

'And yours?' he demanded from me.

'Henry.'

'I want your last name, stupid.'

'That is my last name. My Christian name is . . .'

He shut me up. 'I don't want to know your other names. We are known only by our surnames at Bankworth. Well, no doubt I'll be seeing you there,' he continued, before turning away to talk to his friends and totally ignoring us from then on.

Neither David nor I had the courage to ask him his name; we simply looked at each other with raised eyebrows and continued our conversation in whispers to avoid disturbing them.

The train arrived at Bankworth Station and even before it stopped, many of the carriage doors were opened, revealing dozens of Bankworth pupils of all ages and sexes alighting and then racing out of the station to the awaiting buses. Of course, the newcomers didn't realise what the routine was and walked slowly to the bus stop, only to find we had missed the bus and would have to wait for the next one, which was a good half an hour.

We were joined at the bus stop by one or two others whom we'd known from the Junior School and at least we felt safety in numbers. We were all worrying about the senior boys and what it was going to be like when the next bus arrived and we all piled in. The journey was familiar enough, except the bus turned right instead of left for the Junior School. When we arrived at the gates, we were ordered out and told all newcomers were to carry their cases to the school front door and wait in the entrance hall. We then went through a similar experience to that at the Junior School.

This time we were individually taken into a master's office where we were given our house name and our school number. Curiously, I was assigned the number 1, which had now become vacant, and I felt a surge of anxiety as I thought of the attention this might draw to me. How I would have preferred the anonymity of David's number, 23! Next we were to go to our House Captain's room, where he would send someone to take us up to our dormitory and show us where to unpack our things, after which we were to return to see the House Captain, in his room. There was no question of having a 'friend' at this school: you were dumped in at the deep end and had to make the most of it.

I waited outside his room where, on the door was displayed a big sign with large black letters: 'Welcoming Committee'. This was far from the truth.

I seemed to wait a very long time before I decided to take

matters into my own hands. I entered the room and was immediately ordered out by several of those inside, who seemed to think I wouldn't be able to hear unless their instruction was yelled at the top of their voices. I was told to knock and wait for permission to enter.

I went out shaking like a leaf, closing the door behind me and this time I knocked and waited . . . and waited and waited. The Welcoming Committee were really proving their authority. I had almost given up when a huge yell emitted from the room.

'Get in here now!'

I was petrified as I nervously walked in.

I was so relieved to see David was a member of my house, but he was the unfortunate one who was being interviewed when I entered. They had obviously given him a hard time. He passed me on the way to the door, looking pale and rolling his eyes to heaven as he left. Before me was a long table at which six of the senior house members sat in judgement.

'Stand up straight and look straight ahead,' one of them barked.

'Name?' the House Captain yelled.

'Henry,' I replied swiftly.

'Surname, idiot!'

I was about to respond when I recognised the big lad on the train; he leaned over to the House Captain and said, 'That is his surname, Peter.'

'What's your Christian name then?' the House Captain said loudly as if not to be outdone.

'Alexander.'

'Ah, so you're the little runt who's good with a cricket bat I hear.'

'I don't know,' I said, trying to be modest and at the same time too scared to open my mouth.

'Of course you know. How many did you score at the last Junior Founder's Day Match?'

I hesitated.

'Come on, answer me, boy,' the House Captain ordered again.

'One hundred and thirty,' I replied nervously.

'It's a new record, isn't it?'

'Yes, I believe so.'

'Well, you'll be very useful to this house. What else can you do? Can you swim?'

'Yes.'

'Any good?'

'Yes.'

'From now on you will address me as "House Captain". Do you understand?'

'Yes, House Captain.'

'Harry, he's all yours,' the House Captain said to one of the other senior boys. Harry was the House Sports Captain and responsible for picking all the teams for all the sports activities. Now he took over the questioning.

'What else do you do?' he asked to which I replied, running and tennis. Harry, who was clearly impressed, then announced he was taking me for his fag.

'Come with me,' Harry ordered.

'Be careful, Harry, he's a pretty boy,' the House Captain said, causing great amusement amongst the others.

Harry gave the V sign.

In those days Mr White, the fagging system still operated in the school. I don't think it was a bad thing as long as they didn't bully; you have a batman in the Army, after all, so I suppose it was the same. The rule was you had to pay your fag threepence a week in cash and not in kind.

Harry instructed me to follow him and I was led to the prefects' room and then on to his bedroom, followed by a trip to his locker and various other places, on each occasion detailing all the duties I had to perform – making beds, cleaning shoes, tidying his locker and insuring his clothes were put out for the wash.

Inside I was furious, especially as I had been called a pretty boy.

'Well, that's it, Henry. Not much really. I'm sure you'll do fine,' Harry said condescendingly. 'My name is Harry Whelan, by the way. I'm sure we will get on, providing you do things properly and if you do, I'll let you call me Harry.'

Whelan was a new prefect and an equally new house official. He had been a good all-round sportsman and had therefore been made House Sports Captain. In the end, I suppose I was grateful to have been chosen as a fag, as the bosses tended to protect the individual chosen, as anything bad reflected on them. I was equally fortunate as Harry had two years in the job, but I'll come to that later.

After I had been shown the ropes, I raced to rejoin my friends.

'Hard luck, Alex!' David said sympathetically, as I apprised him of my misfortune.

We spent the rest of our first day walking round the school, getting to know the place. It was enormous, full of corridors and staircases, with numerous places where one could hide. The communal washroom was massive in itself, more like an assembly hall, and was the focus and matrix, as I soon discovered, of every plot, plan and prank.

There was row after row of wash basins, just like in the juniors, but now they all had mirrors in front of them so that you could shave properly. It was a sacred school rule that no one could show even the slightest hint of whiskers, and God help you if you disobeyed. The toilets, as you would imagine, were Victorian, with very old urinals, bearing the date 1855. The doors and sides of each unit were only about six feet high, so you were lucky if you could finish what you were doing without someone throwing something over or jumping up to see what you were up to.

There were over one hundred and fifty pupils, so naturally all washing activity had to be done in relays. The youngsters, the first- and second-year seniors, would get washed for bed at 7 p.m., the next two years at 8 p.m. and so on with a similar situation in the morning, except the youngsters had to be washed and changed and out of the way by 6.15 a.m.! All kinds of shenanigans were hatched and carried out in the washrooms, but the worst torment was the flicking of wet towels and I was grateful when the practice ended up being formally banned when a youngster sustained a serious eye injury.

During that first day in seniors we were suddenly called by a bell sounding and, like all good sheep that had lost their way, we followed everyone else. It was a similar format to the Junior School, except the Senior School was blessed with an electric bell which sounded all over the school. The bell sounded for Assembly and the beginning of lessons, and for breakfast, lunch and supper. This was the teatime bell.

We followed the line which led into the dining room, where all the boys were now racing to their allotted spaces. We new boys didn't as yet know the ropes, so we made our way to where we thought we should be. David and I were lucky; I caught the eye of Harry Whelan and he indicated that we should sit at the end of his table, which of course we did.

Each house official was also a prefect and they sat at the head of the table lording it over the rest and even Harry, bless him, was no exception – he loved it. It was the head of table's duty to allocate the various duties to each person: who collected the bread, who collected the butter, who laid the tables with the cutlery, who set out the plates, cups and saucers and so on. For once I wasn't involved in it, as I had already been allocated the duties of a fag. I sat next to David at the table so at least we had each other's company, as it appeared the people in higher forms did not talk to those in the lower echelons. In other words, you did not speak to them unless they spoke to you.

There was always one teacher present at meal times, something deemed necessary, because there were often fights in the dining room, which resulted in a Friday punishment and no one was allowed to leave their table until every boy had finished eating, which for those who perhaps didn't like what they were eating and were very slow, was a great embarrassment. You soon learned that if you didn't like anything, the handkerchief was your salvation. You really suffered if you kept the table late.

That night when we went to the dorm, I found that David was sleeping a long way away from me. I didn't know who my neighbour, or bedfellow, was, but I knew he must be an older pupil because he wasn't yet there. I snuggled down into the bed, hoping I could get to sleep before he arrived, just in case he was a bit of a bully, but I had no such luck. He arrived about nine o'clock, so I knew he must be a fourth or fifth year.

He saw me peeping at him. 'Hello, I'm James.' He must have seen the relief on my face as he continued: 'Don't worry, I won't bite you! What's your name?'

'Henry.'

'Henry what?'

'Henry is my surname, really!'

'No, I want to know your Christian name. If we are going to be bedfellows for the next couple of years, we might as well know each other's names, don't you think?'

'Yes, that would be good. My name's Alexander.'

'Right . . . Alexander. I'll call you Alex. You get to sleep now and I'll see you in the morning. Good night.'

'Good night, James,' I answered. I was so happy that I had made a friend of one of the seniors; I actually slept like a log.

Six thirty came far too quickly as the bell rang for the first years to get out of bed and get washed. We were all rushing about too much, to spend time talking to one another, but I managed to give the thumbs-up to David before racing to get dressed. I finished dressing and went down to the recreation area to wait for David. I met several others who had been to Junior School and it was like some grand reunion, reminiscing and planning for the future at the 'big school'. David soon joined us and we chatted until the bell went for breakfast. Breakfast was porridge, buttered toast and tea. Each table lined up in order, each boy armed with a plate and cup, to receive his helpings. The tricky bit came when you had to help yourself to the milk and sugar as there was hardly room enough to put your cup down, let alone your plate. After a few days, I developed a knack for it worthy of a juggler.

Breakfast over, I had to quickly go to Harry's room where I began cleaning his shoes and by the time I had finished, both his and mine shone. Harry was appreciative and even gave me a pat on the back.

'Not bad, Henry, Not bad at all!'

We were interrupted by House Captain.

'Good morning, pretty boy. I need to speak to Harry. Would you mind?' He waved me out of the room.

'Of course,' I replied, and immediately knew I had made a mistake.

'Yes what?'

'Yes, House Captain.'

I quickly left the room, inwardly seething that he was still calling me 'pretty boy'. He didn't care when, where and whom he said it in front of, and I knew that the nickname would catch on, especially in the House Captain's company.

The bell rang for assembly and we all had to stand on parade in number order and then file along the corridor to the main hall, where we were to sit in the same seat until the day we left the school. Needless to say, as Number 1 I was nervous, but as James, my bedfellow, was Number 2 he was able to steer me in the right direction and I led the way. We filed into the hall where I sat on the front row at the far side of the central gangway, while all the others followed suit according to the number. As soon as we were all there, the Head Boy announced: 'Silence in the hall and stand!' The whole school stood up and waited.

The Headmaster, James Peters, now entered the hall, in full cap and gown, walking from the back to the front without looking in any other direction than straight ahead. Directly behind him was the Revd William Pitt, the Padre, and behind him all the other teachers in order of importance. The deputy was Mr Rhodes, a weakly, snivelling little individual who got his pleasures from exacting corporal punishment. If he were crossed, you would suffer, and what was worse, you could actually tell he was enjoying it. I despised him for it, but I must say he was kind to me later on. Last in the procession was the Matron, Miss Patricia Rumbalow, a dour Scottish woman with an accent to match that was often difficult to understand. She was as hard as nails and wouldn't tolerate anyone who tried sickness as a means of avoiding school activities.

And so the daily ritual of Assembly began – the Headmaster with his big booming voice threatening hell and high water for any boy who dared infringe the school's myriad rules, and the Padre, with his low, gentle voice, intoning the daily prayers. There were endless announcements and stern reminders of duties and obligations; the homilies and sermons.

Prayers over, the Head ordered us to our classrooms. There were twenty of us in my class and only eight of us had been to the Junior School, so we tended to stick together as we had history in common. We were all in different houses: only three from Dryden, seven from Keats, and five each from Wordsworth and Tennyson. There was intense rivalry between the houses, with no love being lost when any competition was commenced. Dryden was at a disadvantage with only three members but the camaraderie was good.

Monday to Saturday noon was almost entirely regimentalised. The routine lessons and the homework in an evening were a chore, and each and every one of us longed for the bell to sound and we could go out into the playground to play any game you could think of, even football, which wasn't officially recognised.

'Gentlemen do not play soccer,' the Headmaster would preach. 'That is for hooligans.'

Only Saturday afternoon offered a brief respite from the routine – that is, if you were clever enough to elude the tasks imposed by the seniors. Sundays, of course, were different, again as everyone had to go to church for both the morning and evening services. We all walked to the church in number order, which meant I led the way as I was number 1. I was directed into the third pew from the front, leaving the front two rows empty, and the rest of the school followed on behind, taking their places in order. However, the right-hand side of the church was reserved for the girls. There was obviously some clandestine liaisons going on, as there was much chatter and knowing looks exchanged across the central aisle. The Padre rang a hand bell, which signified that the service was about to begin, and the Headmaster and Headmistress led the rest of the teachers to their places in the two front pews of the church.

This was the day, of course, when Revd William Pitt came into his own and once the congregation was settled, he solemnly came down the aisle, following the cross, which was always carried by the youngest member of the choir, while behind him came the rest of the choir, whose members consisted of both teachers and pupils. William Pitt had been a padre to the Forces in the 1914–18 war and he peppered his sermons with tales of bravery, humour and sadness from that time. Strangely, his Sunday sermon was the one thing I looked forward to, as he genuinely made me think about others in difficult situations and gave me a little more strength to do what I had to do.

The rest of the Sunday, until the evening service that is, was your own, but you were still dressed in your Sunday best so any idea of rough and tumbles with friends was out of the question. Matron would exact fearsome punishments if you got your clothes dirty . . .

We were interrupted by Sybil asking if we would like a sandwich for lunch. Would I still prefer tea or would I like something stronger? I looked at my watch. It was 1.30 p.m. I couldn't believe my eyes. I had become totally immersed in Mrs Fraser's story and fascinated by the way in which she was telling it.

'Now, Mr White, What's it to be?' Alexandra asked.

We spent half an hour chatting generally before she adopted a somewhat businesslike approach to bring the 'lunch break' to its conclusion.

'I'm sure you would like to move on, but first I thought you would like to

see the school photos at the time.' She went to open a drawer and pulled out several rolls of long pictures with all the pupils from all three schools on them.

'That's me next to David!'

She then lovingly pointed out her close friends – James, her bedfellow, Harry, the House Sports Captain, and so on.

'They were happy times in that first year. I'll point out the others when we get to them . . . I was talking about Sundays, wasn't I?'

It was a boring afternoon, really; even our free time was strictly monitored, especially for us younger ones. Forms 1 and 2 were lined up and taken for a walk over to the nearby fields, and the entire girls' school followed suit. But the older boys, Forms 3 and above, could actually go out on their own . . . Well, that's not strictly true; they could go out in pairs or more, and were not allowed to return in any other way. So for two years every Sunday most of us were walking to the fields and back in a long line. It was a two-hour round trip; but if you became a runner, you could go on a training run on the Sunday, again in pairs, but with less restriction and with no supervision. Forms 1 and 2, however, could only run around the school sports field. But at least that was unsupervised, so it was the direction I took. It was infinitely better than the long chattering line of junior boys just walking round with a teacher.

Following the afternoon exercise, we would shower off and hoped we would be finished before some idiot came along and turned off the hot tap! By the time you had cleaned up and got back into your Sunday best it was just in time for a quick supper in the dining hall and then straight back to church again.

We had been at Senior School for about a month, and were beginning to get used to the routine, when during Assembly we were asked if anyone would like to take part in a production of *The Mikado*, which was to be performed as part of our Christmas season. There was no obvious sign of enthusiasm and the Headmaster called on the House Captains to find 'volunteers'. In the end, of course, the House Captains simply delegated the task to those boys they did not particularly like. My House Captain did not like me and volunteered my services.

'But I have to work for Harry, House Captain,' I protested.

'I've spoken with Harry and he has agreed,' he retorted and, turning to his hangers-on who were lounging in his room, he added, 'We want to make sure we've at least one of our pretty boys in the play, don't we?'

Naturally I didn't respond, so he yelled, 'Don't we?'

'Yes,' I replied in a whisper.

'Speak up!' he bawled.

'Yes, House Captain,' I responded.

'Now leave us, pretty boy, and report to Mr Pounder tomorrow. Don't let me down, pretty boy.'

I left his room devastated. Why did he have to be so cruel, I thought to myself and why did Harry agree to it without talking to me first? It turned out that Harry hadn't agreed. He was having a little trouble with the House Captain and I was the means of getting back at him.

I reported to Mr Pounder after lessons the following day, as ordered, introducing myself as 'Henry, sir, and that *is* my surname.'

Mr Pounder, the English Literature teacher, was tall, thin and bespectacled, with long wisps of hair that barely covered his large bald pate. He was widely held to be a 'queer', as the terminology then had it, but for all that, wasn't unpopular among the boys.

'Well, young Henry, I have just the part for you,' Mr Pounder said, smiling. 'I think you will be just the job, don't you, Mrs Rogers?'

Mrs Rogers, his assistant in the production, was one of the master's wives. She was very pretty, but very vague.

'What's that?' she asked.

'One of the maids,' Pounder replied.

'Oh no!' I exclaimed. 'Please, sir. I don't want to do that. Isn't there another role?' I said, almost begging.

'It will be fun, boy. You'll enjoy every moment. Anyway someone's got to play the role,' he said insistently.

That was the end of the matter. I was now one of the damn maids and the only consolation was that within the next thirty minutes I had met the other two maids and they shared my frame of mind. At least there was security in numbers. Fortunately, it was a small part and in no way difficult to learn. You know the line: 'Three little maids from school are we.' It has stuck with me all my life. For any young lad, the thought of dressing up as a female was worse than death itself, so you can imagine the tortures we suffered as we tried the costumes on and attempted to act as butch as we could!

Fortunately, my being good at sport helped to dissipate any untoward aspersions with regard to my masculinity. I had in any case quickly recognised, even at the Junior School, that those boys who had sporting success were 'looked up to' and treated better than their less sporty peers, even if it was subconscious. I was determined to do well at sport and spent as much time as I could honing my skills on those activities which would give me recognition. Oddly, perhaps, during that first term I applied myself in particular to table tennis, at which I spent as much time as I could and playing with as many boys that would give me a game.

One of our house masters, Peter Wilkes, was a keen sportsman and in his spare time, coached those boys in his house whom he deemed worthy of his attention. It was the case with me and table tennis. There were four of us from Dryden House whom he used to give coaching to for an hour a week in two half-hour sessions on Tuesdays and Fridays. This was fantastic as we had the tables for that length of time and of course it was something to look forward to and without doubt, it made our house a strong junior side. I didn't win anything that year, but I did come second in the junior knockout and I was part of the under-thirteen team which won the house cup.

It was soon half-term and boys who lived locally could spend three days at home. My father upset me a little by telling me to remain at school on this occasion as it would be too unsettling for me to go home. I was really disappointed as I was dying to see him. However, he decided to come and see me instead. I had been picked for the Dryden House under-thirteen team to play rugby and we were playing against Keats. As I've told you, I didn't really like rugby, but nonetheless I was there to do my best, especially as my father and mother were coming to see me.

I remember the day well. It hadn't stopped raining for a week and the field was absolutely waterlogged, so you can imagine the mud bath and what we all looked like at the end of the game, which I remember ended in an honourable draw. Under the circumstances that was a fair reflection of the situation. None of us could hold onto the ball – it was far too slippery – and I certainly couldn't run on the wing for the same reason. However, my father had watched the game and was so proud that I had played for the house team.

My parents took me into Bankworth and we spent the rest of the day enjoying each other's company. I told them about being Harry Whelan's fag.

'It'll do you good, son,' my father commented. 'Do a good job, that's the most important thing.'

Then I told them about *The Mikado*.

'Oh! Wonderful! Wonderful!' Father exclaimed. 'Which part do you play?'

I could hardly get the words out of my mouth.

'I'm one of the three little maids from school,' I replied.

My mother smiled, detecting my discomfort, but my father patted me on the shoulder and proudly said, 'Good sport, son, good sport. You'll get teased a bit, but you do your best. Well done!'

I could hardly believe it. My father was always behind me

whatever I did. He made me feel wonderful and it did make me try my best.

My mother tried to give me a little cuddle, but one look from my father and she became distant.

'You'll be all right,' she whispered when she thought my father wasn't watching.

It was about this time that I noticed my nipples were getting bigger. I found myself becoming a little embarrassed, in fact a little scared because I knew it would be a source of ridicule, especially what with me dressing up for *The Mikado* as one of the maids. I became very self-conscious and every day I would look in the mirror, when I thought no one was looking, to see if they had become any bigger. But of course, when you look every day, you do not notice any changes.

The other great discovery of that first term in Senior School was smoking. Not that I indulged myself but it was clearly a rite of passage for the first formers. It was very fashionable in those days to smoke, and, although it was banned at school, nearly everybody tried it. Every lunch time, several juniors would go to the outside toilets and light up a Woodbine, a Senior Service or a Player's and pretend to smoke them. By pretend, I mean suck in and blow out immediately, without inhaling. Then you would hold the cigarette between your two fingers, nonchalantly in the air, as long as you could, hoping you wouldn't have to repeat the operation. Mr Wilkes, like every master, knew it was going on and tried to discourage his pupils from doing it. Perhaps because he was a sportsman, but also he was an enlightened man for those days, instinctively knowing that it was bad for you even without the scientific evidence to back it up. Gathering a group of culprits around him, he would inhale the smoke from a cigarette and then blow it straight back into a white handkerchief, showing a big brown stain of nicotine. 'That's what's going into your lungs, lads,' he would say.

Mrs Fraser paused as she got up to pull a large photo album off the bookshelf.

'We were coming to the end of the first term and it was now time for our production of The Mikado. *These are some of the pictures taken by the local newspaper. You may be interested to see them.' She opened the album and passed it over. 'Can you find me, Mr White?'*

I knew The Mikado *well as I'm a Gilbert and Sullivan fan, so I knew what the three little maids would look like and I really did not know what Mrs Fraser wanted me to say. However, there was one picture that showed just one of the little maids. 'Is that one you?'*

'Yes!' she replied.

'You were a beautiful child!' I said to her, unable to conceal my astonishment.

'Yes, you see, Mr White, that was the trouble. And you can imagine what the other boys thought and said to me. I was a boy and that picture made me look like a pretty girl. It also made the front page of the local newspaper, with the Headmaster bragging that the make-up artist, Mrs Rogers, deserved a round of applause for doing such a great job. My House Captain made the usual comments and some others even started blowing me kisses in a mocking way, of course.

'My father and mother came to see us and my father told me how proud he was that I had been such a good sport, I could put up with all the jibes and insinuations. I knew better. All my mother could say was, "Well, my dear, you certainly looked very pretty." She gave me a sly, gentle little cuddle and once again hoped my father hadn't seen.'

Chapter 4

That Christmas holiday there was a wonderful surprise waiting for me. My father could see how I was developing as a cricketer and wanted to ensure I had every opportunity to hone my skills. He had therefore embarked on a new project of constructing a full-size cricket pitch in the garden, which he wanted ready for the summer season. In the New Year, the workmen arrived and set to, with my father supervising every little thing; he wanted it perfect in every detail and wouldn't accept any excuse that might hold the project up, even though we had deep snow.

I loved it, Mr White, my own 22-yard strip and I could bat and bowl every day to my heart's content and even when my father was away. I could get the gardener to bowl for a while or some of the lads from the village.

The Easter term started in the usual way. Harry Whelan our House Sports Captain called a meeting of the house to discuss our present sporting situation. There were always new boys at the beginning of every term, all of them anxious to enter or do something that would ingratiate themselves with the captains of this and that, and I suppose I was no less eager to show willing and listed all the sports I was prepared to participate in that term. I even enrolled for the boxing team as I felt I would get less teased if I took part in a tough sport.

Harry smiled. 'Yes, Henry, we know what you can do!'

I didn't know whether or not to be flattered; instead I felt embarrassed as though I had been stamped on for bragging and being a bighead. It turned out that Harry meant it in a flattering way, but at the time I simply held my head down and shut up for the rest of the meeting.

David volunteered for chess, which I will say at this point he soon excelled in and won his house colours tie within eight weeks of the term starting. I was as jealous as could be, but in fairness I was really pleased for him. He wore his tie every day and was the first of our group to win colours.

On the second Saturday of the new term, all those boys, including me, who had said they could swim were taken to the baths and were all put through their paces. Some of our boys had exaggerated their abilities and could only just swim. I fortunately had been taught by my father and was able to do well; David also had a go but was really more of an academic than a sportsman. I don't think I'll ever forget that day, though. We were all changing after the swimming trials. David suddenly looked at me and remarked, 'Alex, are you growing tits?' Until that moment, I had suppressed any anxieties about my swelling breasts, but now this was the first time anyone other than myself had noticed them. And, of course, it had to be David.

'No I'm not!' I snapped back quietly.

'Sorry!' he whispered and left matters there.

I did have a successful time in the pool and helped the house to come runners up in the competition and I did win one or two of the heats.

Adolescence is always a difficult time and the body does all sorts of strange things and I was becoming very confused and resented the fact I was somewhat different. I consoled myself however with the thought that many of the boys had something different about them which drew comment or even ridicule. Many wore spectacles, for example, and were teased by being called 'four eyes'; one boy's eyes were so bad his spectacles were bottle-thick; we even had a lad with a harelip, and so on. And so I could easily have buried my worries had not certain incidents from time to time forced me to face up to my growing differences.

Among the most important aspects of the school's rituals were the random inspections carried out by the Headmaster, to ensure the cleanliness not only of the fabric of the buildings but also of all the students. It was on one of these occasions that he found traces of mice and went absolutely mad. On the following day, during Assembly, he announced that we must all sharpen up.

'I have even noted that beds have not been made properly and boys have been sent out of meals to wash their hands! This also is not good enough,' he bawled.

'Now, prefects,' he continued, 'I'm charging you with this responsibility: you will see that every boy is clean and well shaven and that his hair tidy. Woe betide any boy brought to me who is not!'

For all the junior boys this was a recipe for disaster, as it gave the prefects carte blanche to bully, which they did with relish. At wash time that evening, we were lined up naked and inspected.

One of the prefects came along with a cane, lifting our penises up one by one, on the pretext of checking to see if we had the crabs. He was followed by another prefect who checked our hands and faces to see if we were clean. When he came to me, he remarked that I had shaved well and a so-called friend of mine threw in: 'He doesn't even shave yet!' much to the amusement of all those present.

Following this remark I vowed to shave and a few days later, I was there with shaving soap all over my face and with a safety razor. I gradually removed the foam to reveal exactly what had been there before: a smooth skin and a clean face. I went through this charade many times, just for peace and quiet, knowing full well it wasn't necessary. Unfortunately, my facial hair never grew and after a couple of years I didn't even bother to pretend.

We had been back at school for about four weeks when the draw for the boxing took place and I was against an old minor adversary. I wasn't what you would call a stylish boxer; I just had unabated aggression and that is how I fought. I just went in with fists flailing, banging away at the boy's face. I remember that first fight: it went the full three rounds, which I won, but I was so worn out I could hardly stand. I had three more fights before the final which was to be held at the end of term, I was lucky as I won them all and then had to prepare for the final, which my father would be watching.

On the night of the final, I went to my corner and proudly heard the announcer shout my name. I held my hand so high; I knew my father must have seen it. Round one I went out absolutely blazing, fists going like mad, but my opponent caught me with a cracker on the nose. The referee stopped the fight to look at it, as it was bleeding heavily. He wiped my nose.

'I'm all right, sir,' I said, determined to carry on. 'It often bleeds.'

'Carry on boxing,' the referee said and I started to pummel his face again.

The second round was a repeat of the first.

'Stop boxing!' The referee again looked at my nose. By this time there was blood everywhere.

'Really, I'm all right, sir,' I insisted.

'Carry on boxing.'

The third and last round was the worst. Two cracks on my nose and I had to defend or the fight would be stopped. Needless to say I lost. But my father thought I had won – in the higher sense of the word – and that was good enough for me.

I had spent far too much time training for the various sports with the result my academic studies had begun to suffer; so much so I was warned by the teachers I would have to stay down if they didn't improve and the moment the cross-country race was over, I came sixth incidentally, I heeded his warning and, with David's help, I really did knuckle down and caught up. This is what real friends will do for you. He was marvellous.

The summer term was the one I had really been looking forward to, as I knew I would do well with the bat. In fact, during the Easter holidays, I couldn't wait to leave home, especially as I was going to be taking my precious W.G. Grace and Gloucestershire County Cricket Club autographed bat along with me!

Back at school, Harry Whelan once again called a house sports meeting. Almost at once he shot me a smile.

'And we all know Henry is interested in playing cricket. Is that right, Henry?'

'Yes it is,' I said confidently.

'I also want some volunteers for the athletic team and once again we all know that Henry here is going to volunteer. Don't we, Henry?'

I nodded and could not stop myself from blushing. Harry's ribbing was always a strange mixture of affection and deprecation.

The following week all the potential house cricket players met together for net practice. There were about thirty of us, all anxious to be picked for the house team. Although I did well in the nets, Harry felt I had had it easy so far and warned me there were some very fine bowlers in the other houses. I suppose he was trying to make sure I kept my feet on the ground, not get too cocky, which could be disastrous as I had already learned.

Nonetheless, I had a good season playing cricket for the house and I was awarded my house colours. I also enjoyed a fair one playing for the school's junior team, but my moment of glory came with the last two matches of the season. The penultimate one was the Founder's Day Match when the juniors of the Senior School played the seniors of the Junior School plus two teachers to make it more even. Mrs Waggott, my old headmistress was there and pleased to see me.

'I hope you're going to give my boys a chance, Alexander,' she said with a smile.

I laughed. 'No not a chance, Mrs Waggott. We are going to win!'

She laughed, too. 'Well, best of luck, Alexander.' She knew

my competitive instinct wouldn't allow me to give anyone a chance.

I went in number three, a position which seemed to be becoming my normal one and which seemed to be the most advantageous too and as with the previous year's match, nothing could go wrong. I rattled up a quick 101 before losing concentration and was bowled next ball. The team scored 204 all out and the juniors were all out for 77.

'Next year, Alexander, I want you to play for us. I'll make you a teacher for the day,' Mrs Waggot quipped, as she presented the cup to our Captain, Paul Meadows.

The final match was on Prize Day when the parents played the Senior School juniors. Once again I had a good day with my bat, scoring 110 not out and winning the junior batting prize for the first time. I had actually broken the record for the number of runs scored by a junior in any season by a long way and was awarded my house colours for cricket.

What was more, and certainly more remarkable: I managed to scrape through my exams, again thanks mainly to David, who was always there to show me the rudiments of any of the subjects.

All in all, I had had a good first year at Senior School and returned home feeling almost heroic. My father, I knew, would only be interested in my sporting feats, whereas my mother would concentrate her interest on my academic achievements, which were rather lacklustre by comparison.

By the time the train pulled in at the Upper Hayfield Station, I was so excited I couldn't open the door. A gentleman who had travelled down with me kindly opened it for me.

'Good luck!' he shouted as I jumped off the train.

I didn't have time to say thank you for I could already see my father on the platform, in his full military uniform. I dropped my case and ran along the platform as fast as I could. He opened his arms and I jumped into them, wrapping my legs round him as I did so. I squeezed his neck tightly as he hugged me and he even deigned to give me a big kiss on the cheek. I could see my mother smiling at us proudly as the hug lasted for what seemed like minutes.

He put me down and I stood in front of him, sticking out my chest so that he would notice my tie. I coughed as if to attract attention, and out of the corner of my eye I saw my mother signal to my father with a slight movement of her eyes and a nod of the head towards my tie. He twigged and shouted proudly:

'He's won his house colours!' He gave me another hug and an even bigger kiss than before. Not the sort of thing one does, you know, in a military family. But he did it and it was wonderful.

'Oh, I'm sorry, Mother,' I said as I went to her and gave her a big hug too.

'Don't worry, but you know, darling, I'm proud of you too,' she said, squeezing me.

'Come on, my boy, let's get you home.' My father took my hand and we collected the case and made our way to our new car waiting outside the station. It was I think one of the new MG Sportsman saloons. In fairness, it wasn't new, it was three years old, but you couldn't get cars then for love or money. There was a long waiting list, so we accepted this rather than wait. It was a wonderful car and do you know, my father took us up to sixty miles per hour, and only stopped there because my mother started to panic. But it was very sporty and I felt good sitting beside my father in the front.

I mentioned to you earlier, Mr White that my father was a shrewd investor. Well, he was always one to listen to advice from all quarters, weigh it all up and then make his own judgements. He had made excellent investments in the Stock Exchange which had been booming for many months and in early 1929 decided it would be sensible to invest in other things and not just the Stock Exchange, which day after day was achieving record highs. One or two of his friends had been telling him that the bubble wouldn't burst for a few years yet, while others were already warning of catastrophe. These days can't go on forever, he was often told by his soothsayer friends.

But he was, in any case, a man of caution and perhaps this was down to his Army training: you never throw everything into the attack especially when there are two opinions and so he invested a sizeable amount of his money in a London house. The property was very glamorous – it was a terraced house in a beautiful square – but my mother thought it very extravagant as we already had a beautiful house in Le Touquet. However, father had been promoted yet again and in the end, convinced her that we could afford the upkeep of all the properties. For me, as yet, London had no attraction and I just loved Le Touquet and my home, Glengarry.

The summer was beautiful. We spent most of the time at Le Touquet and scarcely moved from the beach and our lovely beach hut. My father could spend only a few days here and there with us due to Army business, so really I spent most of the time with my mother. We became very close when we were alone together, but so distant when my father was on the scene. It was strange, but I had the feeling she was worried about me. I put it down to my being away at school and perhaps it was because she was spending more and more time alone. She would call me her beautiful child, never boy or girl, just her beautiful child. The moment my father was with us she would become reserved and remote, as if she had literally faded into the background. I'm sure this was the reason she never actually discussed my problems with me: the sheer fear of losing what she had, built a wall between us when it came to these matters.

Times are different now, Mr White; you can get help from all quarters; but then freaks were locked up, hidden away, even in the best of circles, or perhaps especially in the 'best of circles'. The Royal family, for example, kept certain members from the public gaze, so what chance did I have? Do you understand what I mean? Whatever my mother would have thought at the time, she wouldn't be able to say anything for fear of losing her security. Women had no protection in those days, so I can understand her keeping quiet.

The summer holidays were soon over. September always

seemed to come round too quickly, making it time for me to return to Bankworth. It was 1929 and I was now twelve, nearly a teenager. It was the Christmas Term and my seasonal departure from home had become almost mundane. My mother and father still came to the station to see me off, but Alice, my sister, of whom I was very fond, was now almost engaged to an RAF officer and was hardly at home.

I was no longer a junior in the Senior School; I considered myself to be an experienced senior and now had a form below mine . . . Mr White, Clive, sorry! Do you realise what power that gave me? To be actually off the bottom rung and no longer everyone's dogsbody was tremendous. I was, however, still Harry's fag and still had his duties to do, but now I didn't mind so much.

I arrived at Bankworth Station and ran for the bus as did all the other older pupils, leaving the newcomers to work out for themselves what they had to do. The moment the bus arrived, I raced up to the dorm, unpacked my case and raced down again to find my friends. I was, I would point out, wearing my house colours tie, just to let everyone know how good I was. I soon found out, however, you are only as good as your present success and that all my heroics of last year had long been forgotten. You couldn't rest on your laurels.

That term simply flew by. What I suppose was most remarkable about that term was my deepening friendship with Harry. I continued to fag, of course, but there seemed to be growing camaraderie between us, a mutual recognition as equals. I kept in contact with him after leaving school and even saw him several times over the years, but unfortunately he died about six or seven years ago. I'll always remember one of the last things he said to me: 'You were always too beautiful to be a boy.'

The Christmas production at the end of term was *Peter Pan*. Mr Pounder came to me and asked if I would take a part. After my father's praise the previous year, I foolishly agreed to do it and I was once again offered . . . no, that isn't strictly correct . . .

I was given a female part. He wanted me to play Wendy – an enormous part for a youngster of my age and a bit of a challenge.

'Can't I play a boy, sir?' I once again pleaded.

'Don't be silly, Henry. You know how good you were in *The Mikado* last year and I think you will be even better this year.'

I tried to use my charm. 'But, sir, so were the other two!'

'You're better looking. And that's what's needed for this part.'

'But it's a girl, sir! It's not fair.'

Here the discussion was ended and I knew that, if I refused, someone somewhere would make me do it. I was mad and miserable at the same time. I had to break the news once again to my friends and I got a fair amount of teasing.

We had had a reasonable start to the year and now it was approaching half-term. My father had decided to let me go home for the three days as he was very busy at work and couldn't find the time to come and visit me. For me that was always tremendous, especially as I would see a new family pet which my father had bought to keep my mother company when he had to stay in London. It was a black and white Border Collie named Rafter; he was the fluffiest puppy I had ever seen and the most playful. It wasn't a pedigree breed in those days but we didn't care – he was lovely. I was always sorry to leave him.

October arrived and on the 29th we all got up as normal and started the day with the usual assembly in the main hall, but we could all sense that something was amiss, that there was panic in the air. One or two of the teachers were missing; several others were anxious to hurry matters on. There was only Mr Wilkes and one or two others who seemed relaxed. At lunch time we were all in the dining room when the meal was interrupted by the Headmaster.

'We are giving you the rest of the day off and there will be no prep. All prefects will report to my office immediately and the rest of you will remain here until they return,' he ordered sternly.

We all knew something dreadful had happened but none of us knew what and all waited for the prefects to return with any news. Harry Whelan was given the task of telling the school what had happened.

'Right, quiet everybody. There has been a disaster on the New York Stock Exchange and many Americans have lost a great deal of money. Unfortunately, this panic has spread to the London Stock Exchange and many people are losing their savings over here, too . . .' He paused momentarily to let things sink in and then went on to explain a few things about what became known as the Wall Street Crash. Quite frankly, almost all of the younger boys, me included, didn't understand what it all meant, but some of the older boys seemed perturbed. They probably knew their own futures were in jeopardy.

The prefects were virtually put in charge of the school for over a week – in fact, until we broke up for half-term at the end of that week. The Monday and Tuesday before half-term saw the Stock Exchange fall almost 25 per cent in the two days and continued to plummet for the rest of the week. There was absolute panic everywhere and factories began closing down; shops were shutting and people were thrown out of work, with no means of supporting their families. There was a lot of political discontent and in consequence the Government cancelled all leave and put the troops on alert, which meant my father couldn't, after all, come home to see me at the half-term holiday.

I arrived at St Pancras on my way home and found it was strangely quiet; in fact there was an eerie atmosphere. There were few rushing down the platforms to get to the taxis first, no one wanting a porter to save the few coppers it may have cost and then there were dozens of taxis waiting for the odd passenger to hail one of them.

During that short holiday, my mother was able to dote on me unhindered. She even came into the bathroom to help dry me off after a bath, but as she looked at me, the hot water still glistening on my skin, I became nervous and angry. 'Mother, I'm a big boy now. You mustn't come in!'

She let her gaze linger a few seconds on me, with that worried look on her face, which was becoming more and more common. In her anxiety I saw my own, but mirrored and magnified. My peers had begun to look and notice the differences and I tormented myself with questions. Would my nipples continue to grow and swell? Did I have some terrible incurable disease? I can talk about all this now, Mr White, but back then I couldn't talk to anyone – simply out of fear of ridicule.

On returning to school we found that a handful of boys had left from our intake and we had even lost two of our teachers. Matters seemed to be getting worse and everybody was feeling unsettled, though superficially the school's routines remained the same.

One day, Mr Pounder called all the *Peter Pan* cast into a meeting, explaining that, owing to the dire economic world situation, we had a duty to cheer everyone up with a good performance. He then gave us all our parts to learn and told us to have the first scene ready for the following week. Pounder's stiff upper lip attitude was shared by many adults of that time. The general attitude was: We have to make the best of things.

Even the Headmaster started to take an interest in the production and would call round in the evenings to see what progress was being made and would make a point of talking to me. 'Good sport, lad, well done,' he would say as if I was doing my patriotic duty by playing a girl. I was flattered by the attention until, that is, I got my costumes for the show including a long blonde wig with an Alice band and then I hated everything.

Mr Pounder noticed my change of attitude. 'You didn't think you were going to play Wendy in your school clothes, did you?'

'No, sir,' I replied miserably.

'Well, don't be so damn stupid and do your best! The school needs you at this time.'

I was going to do my best anyway, but doing my best was going to cause me a great deal of personal grief.

The day of the dress rehearsal came and, as I climbed into my night gown for the opening scene, I knew that all the school would be present. However, I put a brave face on it and the play went really well. It was ruined for me at the end, though, when we were taking our bows at the final curtain. For a joke, some of the prefects came onto the stage with a bunch of flowers for me; it caused uproar and even the teachers were laughing. I just had to stand there and take it. I laughed with them but in reality my stomach was churning. Things didn't get any better when the girls' school came to watch on the Saturday afternoon. Even before the play began, I overheard one of their teachers asking if I was male or female. To make things clear, this time I took my wig off at the final curtain, but was told not to do it again as it spoiled the scene.

My parents came to the evening performance and once again my father thought what a good sport I had been, but suggested I volunteered for a more masculine part next time. I didn't like to tell him I had been given no option.

My mother simply said, 'You looked beautiful, dear,' and stroked my wig.

'Don't do that, Mother,' I pleaded. 'Others may be looking!'

'Quite right, son, quite right,' my father added.

The local press were once again in attendance and I got a good write-up and of course the inevitable photo on the front page. 'Wendy Steals the Show' was the headline for the article and it even gave the impression that it was one of the girls who had taken the part. I didn't care as it took the spotlight off me.

The end of the Christmas term brought a new wave of anxiety and uncertainty. None of us knew what our family position would be or how our parents had fared in the financial turmoil. Which of us this time would fail to return to school? Which of the teachers would simply vanish?

St Pancras Station was once again quieter than normal. Outside that stately pile, people were begging, carrying banners and slogans: 'No Food, No Money, No Hope!' It was a very, very sad state of affairs.

I caught the train and arrived at Upper Hayfield to be greeted by my mother in a very distressed condition. Several of our friends in the village had lost their money in the Crash and were selling up. There were many farm workers who were losing their jobs because even the farmers had been sucked into the investment bubble and they too had lost their money and were having to sell their farms to pay their debts. My mother felt a kind of curious sense of responsibility for the state of affairs and began to help out as many people as she could.

Christmas came and, although my father was at home with us, my mother's time was spent in helping neighbours. On Christmas Day and again on Boxing Day all the unemployed people of the village and their families were given a Christmas dinner. She had also purchased sacks of potatoes and vegetables and distributed them as they left, and every week after that, until they managed to get a job, she did the same.

When I look back on those troubled times, I am pleased to say there was no bitterness or jealousy from anyone. Those who suffered appeared to accept things in the spirit they were given, that of kindness and Christian charity. They did not envy or sneer at her because she remained unaffected financially; they appreciated her acts of kindness for what they were and did not feel debased or humiliated by being its recipients. Several years after, when the crisis was over, our neighbours continued to treat my mother with such reverence; they would have done anything for her.

It was now time to go back to school and this time I was by myself door to door, as my mother hadn't wanted to use the car because it seemed too ostentatious when we had so much poverty around us. I took the bus to the station and there was the normal railway journey to Bankworth. Unfortunately, I was sitting in a compartment with a group of boys who were determined to make my life a misery by calling me Wendy. I tried to shrug it off and pretended to laugh, but all the time I wanted to run away. I was so glad when we arrived at Bankworth and was once more among my friends, especially David.

Chapter 5

This term I was determined to prove my sporting prowess more than ever. Once again the boxing ring was my arena.

I had success in the first fight with my usual aggressive attitude, but I had considerable pains in my chest every time I was punched. I won the next fight, too, but this time I explained to Mr Wilkes the problems I was having. He advised me to see the Matron, but unsurprisingly she was unsympathetic and didn't even bother to examine me.

'I'm not afraid, Matron,' I protested. 'I came second last year and I've already won two fights this year.'

'Well, maybe it's the next one you're frightened of. Go on with you and don't be so silly!' As she shooed me out of the surgery, she patted me on the bottom.

The next fight was to be, I'm afraid, my last and I lost badly because I was too busy trying to stop myself from being hit. It was such a terrible performance that Mr Wilkes asked if I had seen Matron and if so had she suggested any reason for my pains. When I told him what she had said, he was disgusted and went to see her; after which I was told to report to Matron again, but if anything she showed even less sympathy.

If I couldn't cope with it, she told me, I should stop boxing. This time she examined me and I know she noticed my enlarged nipples but was too embarrassed to do anything or even talk about it. Mr Wilkes, nonetheless, gave me tremendous support, telling me to put these little problems behind me and concentrate on something else, like table tennis. While I did very well, I didn't seem to have the enthusiasm I had had in previous years. I had become obsessed with looking at my body: what had been enlarged nipples had now become walnuts, which were impossible to conceal all the time. I noted too that my testicles hadn't developed in the way the other boys' had. More and more, my physical anomalies were drawing attention, both curiosity and laughter. I couldn't understand what was happening to me.

One morning I woke up to find there was blood on my sheets. I immediately went to the surgery and told Matron what had happened. She took one look at me and announced, 'Well, boy, you are full of complaints these days, aren't you? All you have are some nasty haemorrhoids. Eat more slowly and do not strain when you are trying to do a number two and you will be all right. Try not to complain so much; it will make you feel better,' she added in her normal supercilious way.

'Thank you, Matron,' I replied and promptly left, relieved it wasn't anything serious.

Here again, Mr White, the times have changed; no one then would talk about problems like this; it just wasn't done and you accepted what the doctors or nurses told you and you were certainly not to question them.

My one great joy that term, I suppose, was cross-country running. I still had problems with Arnett, who worked in both junior and senior schools, but at least I had other things which I could do without his input. I was virtually excluded from his lessons, as he still sent me off to run round the fields. This had a positive result, as I had become a reasonably good distance runner. Arnett always had his favourites and always wanted them to do well and I remember on one occasion him telling everybody that Peter Jacks was going to win the cross-country race. He hadn't even contemplated that I could be considered a contender and had totally underestimated the potential of someone who ran several miles twice a week during his PE lessons.

I volunteered to compete for my house but, as there were also several other boys who wanted that honour as well, we all had to take part in a run-off, which Mr Wilkes arranged for the following Saturday afternoon. There were thirteen of us who set off on the cross-country course, which was three and a half miles long. The first eight back were to be in the team, so there was everything to play for. There was no official timing for the race, but our house master, Mr Wilkes, did put the stopwatch on to see what sort of time we would do it in. He was also the adjudicator and, to make sure no one cheated, he insisted we had marshals around the course.

The gun fired and we were off. I set off at an incredible pace and only later settled down to a more sensible one. It was an unusual strategy for me as I normally kept a sound steady pace throughout. I remember looking round after the half-mile marker and saw there were at least 150 yards between me, the front runner, and the boy in second place. I kept up my rhythm and won easily and was back in the changing room well before anyone else got back.

The Junior Cross-Country team was duly posted on the house notice board and the inevitable rumours spread about how easily I had won; so much so that Arnett was asked by one of the boys what my chances were against Jacks.

'Gloria doesn't stand a chance against him!' Arnett was one of those people who had to be nasty at every opportunity, not just about me, but with anyone whom he felt was different or whom he didn't take to.

Mr Wilkes called me to his study and when I arrived he was with Harry Whelan; they had been discussing the tactics for the race.

'Alex, you ran a fantastic race the other day. Do you know how well you did?' Harry asked.

'What do you mean?'

'Your time, you idiot!'

'Henry, you were three minutes inside the course record!' Mr Wilkes said almost nonchalantly.

I was flabbergasted. 'I only did enough to get selected. I had no idea–'

Mr Wilkes interrupted me. 'Now don't be conceited, boy!'

'No, sir, I'm not. I promise I didn't mean it to sound like that.'

'I'm sure you didn't, Henry . . .' He paused. 'We want you to be the Junior House Cross-Country Captain.'

'Oh that's wonderful. Wait till I tell my father!' I was ecstatic.

'Right, Henry, thank you for coming. Please don't tell any one your time; we don't want to warn the opposition, do we? I'll be announcing tomorrow that you are to be the Captain and we'll see where we go from here.'

'Best of luck, Alex,' Mr Wilkes said as I left, for once using my Christian name.

I went out of that room feeling ten feet tall and was thrilled that I had a chance of winning. I continued my little runs around the sports field, and even pretended I was struggling when I knew Arnett was watching.

Race day came and we all made our way to the starting area. The juniors were to go off first, followed some thirty minutes later by the seniors, who were to run seven miles. The four house teams lined up with the captains in front and their seven representatives behind them. Our house master wished us all the best and took our photographs as the gun fired to set us off. As before, I raced away as fast as I could, once again taking all my rivals by surprise, though this time I noted that Jacks wasn't so far behind.

At the mile mark he made his great effort and I could hear his heavy footsteps on the long stretch of tarmac we had to run along before returning to the fields. He was coming close to me. Then he was at my shoulder. I put everything into it and ran flat out as we ran shoulder to shoulder for at least four hundred yards.

The last thing I heard was a huge groan from Jacks as he dropped back. He was exhausted and I didn't seem to have much more left myself, but I continued, regained my rhythm and finished the course. I won, beating the old record by just over three minutes and it was almost five minutes before any other competitor finished.

I was able to race again, but every time I ran or was involved in strenuous activities I found my physical differences beginning to make a difference to my performances, particularly in athletics.

'Mr White, there is a big difference, no matter what people may think.'

I nodded as yet another tray of tea and cakes were brought in by Sybil.

'Still interested, Mr White?' Mrs Fraser asked as she poured the tea.

'Of course I am,' I replied. 'There's a lot of water gone under this bridge and I can't wait until it reaches the sea.'

'A regular philosopher, aren't we, Mr White?' Mrs Fraser asked but without waiting for an answer, continued with her story:

After the cross-country race, I was awarded my second set of house colours and felt rather pleased with myself, but I was still a little in awe of David as he won house colours again, this time not only for chess but for badminton, too.

I was beginning to worry about my place in the various teams as I knew, apart from Harry, they didn't want me and my only consolation was I knew they couldn't leave me out because they needed me for both cricket and swimming. I also knew deep down they would do anything to exclude me, particularly as several boys had begun commenting on my appearance.

I had been entered in the various swimming heats just as I had been the previous year, in spite of the fact that I had not really wanted to take part. The physical changes I was undergoing, which had been in remission for many months, were now beginning to develop by the week, and by the time the swimming started I had quite a shapely figure for a thirteen-year-old, so much so that after the first round in the competition, the entire school knew about the 'developments', shall we say, and when I took part in the next round, half the school turned up to watch.

I stood straight up on the blocks, with everyone cheering and whistling at what they were seeing. Half of them had never seen a naked pair of breasts before, even if my own were small . . . but to see them on a boy! They were naturally curious, but matters were made worse for me as the master in charge insisted I wore my running singlet, which as soon as it became wet was almost see-through and caused even more delight.

All the same, I did well. It was following the swimming that I had further problems, as once again I found that I had bled in bed and once again had to go to see Matron. Even before she examined me, she scolded me for not having done what she had advised, but at least she did make an appointment for me to see the doctor. He agreed with her and confirmed that I had a very bad bleeding pile and that I should be confined to the sickroom until it was better. I was excused all sports and rigorous activities.

Apart from Mr Wilkes, the only person who showed any kindness to me was one of the housekeepers, Mrs Dorothy Singleton, who worked in the sewing room opposite my bed.

'Good morning, Mrs Singleton,' I said, as she came over to see me.

'Good morning, young man,' she said, as she inspected my bed. 'What on earth has happened to you then?' she asked. 'It's Alex, isn't it?'

'Yes, Mrs Singleton,' I replied.

'Call me Dot,' she said. 'You've been having this trouble for some time, haven't you, dear?'

'Yes, not quite as bad as this, but it seems to be getting worse. I have tried everything Matron has suggested but it doesn't work,' I replied and then explained what Matron and doctor had said. Even back then I felt that Dot didn't believe their diagnosis. She even went on to tell me that she had heard some of the boys teasing me about having periods.

'How often does this happen?' she asked 'Is it regular?'

'I don't know,' I replied. 'What do you mean?'

'Well, do you get it happening once a month, twice, three

times?' Mrs Singleton asked, showing great concern.

'I don't know exactly, but I think it happens every four or five weeks. I haven't really taken any notice,' I replied.

I know now she felt desperately sorry for me and genuinely wanted to help. She knew exactly what the real problem was and took me into the sewing room where she tried to offer me some advice, all the while desperate not to hurt my feelings.

'Look, Alex, I know you may be embarrassed at what I'm going to say, but I think it will be the answer to the bloody sheets.' She went over to a cupboard and took out a box. 'I think this might be of some help . . .' She handed me a sanitary towel and, seeing my shocked look, added, 'I know it's for ladies, but if you wear it at night in bed, it will soak up any blood and you won't have messy sheets. The others won't find out –you can put them on under the bedclothes.'

'That's very kind of you, Dot. I will try it because it really is getting worse,' I replied gratefully.

'What about during the day, dear? Do you have any difficulties then?'

'Yes. Sometimes I have to wash my pants out two or three times a day.'

'Look Alexander, you can use these during the day as well. I'll get you a special belt for you to wear. It holds the towel underneath and from then on you won't have many problems. It is for girls, but if you don't let anyone see it, no one will know, will they? Anyway, it will be better than the mess you seem to be in, won't it?'

'Anything will be better than what I have to put up with at the moment,' I replied.

'One thing, Alexander, I'm very sorry but the school cannot afford to give you these things. Can you pay me for them?'

'Of course I can. I'll get you the money tomorrow,' I replied with some relief. I was grateful to anyone who tried to help me. I went to the school bank the next day and drew out two shillings to give to the housekeeper. But what a performance!

'Why do you want it? Why do you want it now? What's it to

be used for?' It took all my persuasive powers to get the master to grant me my own money. In the end I told them that the housekeeper was going to buy me a set of new underpants as I had torn my others. This was accepted, but the master added that the expenditure would be noted in a letter to my father.

I gave Dot the money the following day. She had already bought the towels for me and promised to buy more as and when I needed them. She did this for me until the day I left school.

The end of term arrived and for the first time I was grateful it had come as I was being teased almost every hour of the day. No, Mr White, 'teased' is not the right word; I was ridiculed every moment of my waking day. I was glad to get away, if only for the three weeks' holiday.

Once again my father wasn't at home. He was still unable to get leave, as the Government was still worried there would be an uprising. My mother seemed relieved, however, to have me to herself.

I told her what was happening to me and how my body was developing and what was being said by everyone at school and even how I was having to wear a sanitary towel for my 'piles'. Anyway I'm sure she knew I wasn't troubled with haemorrhoids but she couldn't bring herself to admit what the real problem was. She got into a terrible state and was desperate to hide everything from my father. It was as though my situation was unimportant as long as my father was kept happy.

The last three months at school had given me an interesting figure, which quite frankly, Mr White, many a young lady then and today would be jealous of, but if you could imagine the mental torment I was in, not knowing what I really was – whether I was a girl or a boy and desperately trying to remain the latter; it was terrible. Every time my mind was not occupied, it would drift back to my body. I would do anything to avoid being seen naked or even to talk about my problems, which I suppose made matters worse for me. Even my mother didn't want to think about it.

I'll always remember when she stamped her authority on the situation.

'Alex, my dear, I want you to promise me that you will not talk to your father about this. I want it to be our little secret. You promise?'

'Yes, of course I promise,' I said to her, trying desperately to stop myself from crying.

With her words the sudden realisation dawned on me that I was on my own.

You know, Mr White, some women will put up with anything rather than lose what they have got, particularly where a man is concerned. Look at the cases of domestic violence we hear about today, when so many women who have been badly beaten up by their husbands will refuse to give evidence against them. Why not? 'Because I love him,' is often the reply and still she goes on living with him.

I think in some way my mother was one of that type. She was prepared to let me suffer in order to protect her safe little world.

While at home I resigned myself to believing I was a boy who was simply a freak – that was it until I had to return to school. Then I didn't know which was worse, being at school where I was ridiculed all the time or being at home where I was rejected by the people I loved the most.

At least it was now the summer term when I could do something of note.

Harry called his usual meeting to find out where the cricket talent was and this time he didn't make fun of me. He had become a true friend and wouldn't do anything to make my position worse.

I naturally played cricket for the house with much success and was initially selected for the school second eleven, but after three matches during which I had scored 57 not out, 104 and 84 not out, they could no longer keep me out of the first team and then as I did so well in the first eleven, I kept my place and finished up top of both first- and second-team averages.

My great moment was when I was awarded my school colours, which were presented in the main hall in front of the school, and for that brief moment they forgot my personal disfigurement and applauded, especially when the Headmaster told them I was the youngest ever cricketer to be awarded his school colours. I was being reported in the local press as a child cricketing prodigy and on several occasions throughout the season the press would come and watch, which made the Headmaster proud as it reflected well on the school. It did, however, put pressure on me, but every time I had a problem, Mr Wilkes was there with his advice and coaching.

Sports day went very well, but by now I could feel my physique becoming a disadvantage, in that I couldn't easily compete with my peers on equal terms, but also I had to suffer the indignity of the shouting and the whistling whenever I did anything. Furthermore, I couldn't bear the thought of my parents being embarrassed by my predicament and was glad that neither of them could make the sports day. I suppose I knew anyway that my mother would avoid the day at any cost.

I did, however, have reasonable success, winning several races, but it wasn't without cost as once again as I drew more attention to myself. Everyone knew by now I didn't have to shave; everyone knew my voice hadn't changed; everyone knew I was growing breasts; everyone guessed I was having periods and everyone was guessing that I was really a girl.

The result of this was that a prefect called Hazard, who had been aggrieved that I had been selected for the first eleven at his expense, decided with several others to exact revenge on me.

I was asleep in bed when suddenly I was woken up by Hazard and the two Barratt brothers insisting I went with them. I told them I was too tired, at which point they tipped me out of bed and pulled me to my feet.

'Come on Gloria, get yourself down to my room before I kick your lovely little arse from here to breakfast time!' Hazard threatened.

By now James, my bedfellow, was awake, too. 'Leave him

alone, Hazard! He's done nothing to you.'

'Bugger off!' one of the Barratts sneered. 'She's coming with us.'

I tried to get my dressing gown on but I was simply dragged and pulled through the dormitory by these three rather large teenagers. The noise of my pleading woke most of the boys as we passed their beds and some sat up to see what the problem was.

'Lie down! Unless, that is, you want some of the same!' Les Barratt shouted. Of course, everyone duly did, and who could blame them as the Barratts had always been bullies, prone to throwing their weight around and they were formidable when together.

I was pulled into Hazard's room and ordered to strip.

'Come on, let's see these beautiful tits you've got,' Barratt One whispered loudly.

I just stood there, not moving, not saying a word and trying to be brave. 'I've told you,' Hazard said forcefully, 'take them off or we will!' He looked at the others for their approval and naturally the Barratt brothers nodded their agreement.

I still stood there in defiant silence, ready for anything and then suddenly they made their move. It all happened so quickly: they tried and succeeded in tearing my clothes off, but not before I had fought like a wild thing. I used everything in my armoury: fists, feet, head, nails and teeth, and my opponents certainly go what they deserved.

The moment I was naked they stopped and just stared at me, like sex-starved perverts, not knowing what to do next. I was marked from head to toe with scratches and blotches, but I was still game to fight on. Hazard made the first move and slowly advanced towards me. I clenched my fists and waited.

'Come on then, you bastard!' I shouted at the top of my voice, hoping someone would hear and come to help me, though knowing that the Barratts' reputation was enough to put most brave souls off. 'See if you can fight me on your own, if you dare!' I taunted.

He started on me and for a second or two and I gave as good as I got, but the Barratts wouldn't let Hazard fight alone. They hauled me onto the bed and held me firmly down, leaving Hazard to strut around menacingly. He started commenting about my breasts and then came over to stroke them slowly and even tried to kiss them. I began shouting for help, screaming, writhing and wriggling . . .

Thank God Harry Whelan raced in.

'You dirty bastards!' he shouted and charged over, punching Hazard full on the nose. 'You two get out now! I'll deal with you later.'

The Barratts had started to leave when one of them muttered, 'Do you fancy her then?'

Harry turned sharply. 'What did you say?'

'Nothing, Harry,' they replied in unison.

'You lying cretins!' he shouted and struck one of them on the side of the face. 'If any of you touch him again, I'll beat you to a pulp. Do you understand?' Harry snarled. They made no answer. 'Do you?'

'Yes.'

Harry borrowed Hazard's dressing gown and wrapped it round me.

'That's mine,' Hazard pointed out.

'Fuck off, you animal,' Harry replied and took me back to my bed, which some kind soul had remade for me.

The following morning, in Assembly, the Headmaster instituted a big investigation into the uproar of the previous night. As no one would own up as to who had been responsible, the whole school was punished. All had to stand to attention in the main hall for the whole of the following day's free time.

I should have twitted on them but I knew what would happen if I did. I was even asked by Mr Wilkes how I had got the marks on my face and body, and he knew I was lying when I told them I had had a fight. Hazard had the ignominy of also having to lie about the marks on his face, too.

I was very worried that this sort of behaviour was going to be the forerunner of what was to come, especially as my guardian angel, Harry, would soon be leaving. I did earn a bit of respect for not twitting on the three of them, but it was short-lived.

There were now just two weeks to the end of term, and the big event, of course, was Founder's Day. We had the usual number of Old Boys and Girls who had returned to see how the school was getting along. Some of the very successful men came back in their fancy cars with their beautiful women in their beautiful clothes and lovely hats. They would occasionally venture onto the grounds where a few of us would be playing cricket and they would offer a shilling to anyone who could get them out; they often were and would nonchalantly spin the shilling through the air towards the successful bowler, as if to say 'It's just coppers. I can afford it.' The average wage then was about £1.00 per week so in reality it was a lot of money to throw away. But it added to the fun of the day and it gave dozens of us the opportunity to earn a little extra pocket money.

The highlight of the day was the cricket match between an Old Boys' XI and the school first team, though it had been several years since the school had been successful and beaten them.

The Old Boys had a formidable side which included two men who were playing County cricket, albeit not always for the first teams. I had been selected much against the Captain's wishes, as he preferred to play older members in his team. Had it been his decision I'm sure I would have batted number eleven, but fortunately Mr Wilkes had drawn up the batting list. The team selection had been posted on the school notice boards and had caused a stir as I was still a junior. It also created a little bit of jealously from the more senior members, who felt that they should be playing instead. But there it was: I was in and I had to justify my selection.

I had written to my father and mother and told them I was to play, and you can imagine my joy when I saw them there, together with Alice and her new boyfriend. It seems her relationship with the RAF officer was short-lived.

We had a beautiful ground, surrounded by mature trees, and with a very green pitch. When the weather was fine, as it was on that day, it was a joy to see. Of course, it had its slight slope, which Mr Wilkes had taught me to overcome, and which encouraged square cuts to the right-handed batsman as the ball would rattle to the boundary down the slope, but it was a joy to be playing there. The match started at two o'clock prompt. We had lost the toss and the Old Boys had elected to bat. Our Captain, Paul Webster, had put me on the boundary out of the way.

I suppose I looked a bit out of place as I was the only one in short trousers and looked very young. Harry Whelan was the wicketkeeper, so at least I had a friend on the field and at least he kept acknowledging me and keeping me in the game – often signalling for me to walk in as the bowler began his run-up.

It was a mistake to put me deep on the boundary because although I was accurate, I hadn't got the best of throwing arms especially on the long boundary and, after all, I was still very young and with the Old Boys rattling up the runs at a fair pace, it was a difficult job for me. The Captain would clap his hands and yell, 'Come on, Henry, chase it!' or 'Come on, Henry, throw it!' as if I was the sole cause for all the run scoring that was happening. By tea the Old Boys had declared 211 for seven and now it was our turn.

I couldn't eat my tea; the tension was getting to me. I simply had a drink of squash and went to sit with my parents and Alice. While I was there with them, some of the Old Boys came to congratulate me: 'Well done, young man!' and such like, which made me feel much better, but I was quiet and my father could see how nervous I was and began to give me words of encouragement.

'Come on, I know you can do it! And remember you have been selected because they know you can do it as well, so don't worry!'

Already we could see the boys coming out of the tea tent, so I made my way over to join them. I had nothing in common with them, except the cricket, as I was so young; it was like being a fish out of water.

'Come on, young Henry,' Paul Webster commanded. 'Get padded up. We've got a team photo and we don't want your little legs showing, do we?'

Harry came over and said, 'Don't take any notice. You've earned your place. Come and sit next to me.'

I was so relieved. I quickly went in and put my pads on, took hold of my bat and walked out to the team, who were preparing for the photograph. I sat next to Harry on the front row, as proud as punch. The photo call was over and we walked back to the pavilion to await our fate. Webster and Harry were the openers and I was number three. Webster was a dramatic batsman and very loud; it was as though he wanted everyone to know he was the captain and that he was there. He faced the first ball and returned it with a straight bat back to the bowler; the next delivery he hit for a run.

'Come on, Harry, one run!' Of course, Harry had already started running before the call came, but Webster had to impress.

Harry hit the first ball he received for four, very luckily off the edge, but they all counted. The next over Webster hit a beautiful off-drive for two runs, which brought applause from the crowd.

'Come on, Harry, two runs,' came the inevitable cry.

The next ball he received was a snorter and was hit full on the pad. All the Old Boys appealed and he was given out LBW for three.

It was now my turn. I stepped onto the field and passed Webster coming out. He was furious. 'It wasn't out! I hit it,' he said, shaking his bat.

I didn't know what to say; I just walked out to the square. The applause was tremendous and people actually stood up and clapped this little lad in shorts walking out to bat and even the Old Boys' team gave me a warm reception.

Harry walked over to me and said one of the loveliest things anybody had ever said: 'Now don't you worry; you've been selected because you've earned it. And just remember, I have always wanted to bat with you today, so come on, let's show them.'

'Thanks, Harry,' I replied.

His words gave me so much confidence. I knew I could do well. I took the leg stump guard, the way Mr Wilkes had told me to do. The butterflies in my stomach were terrible as the bowler ran down the pitch and released the ball, which was fast down the leg side and which I glanced for four. I had broken my duck to the delight of the crowd.

The next hour was pure delight. Harry and I scored freely, until he was bowled out for 51 when the score was 87 for two. He came over to me on the way out. 'I knew you would do it: you've made my day. Don't get out! The rest aren't as good.'

Winstanley came in next followed by others, but I was in full flow: my fifty came up in a few overs or so and my hundred, about an hour later. I finished up with 132 not out and the match was won. The applause was sensational and the press, who always attended these functions, made a meal of it. The reporter from the local newspaper, the Bankworth Echo, even sent for a photographer to take my picture.

I was carried on the shoulders of my teammates to the winners' ceremony and given an honour I didn't expect. The Captain, Webster, invited me to go with him and take part in the presentation ceremony. We walked over to the dais where he was presented with the cup and to my astonishment, he immediately handed it to me and held my hand in the air. He then clapped with the rest. I couldn't stop crying: tears of joy are always more difficult to stop.

My family were so proud of me, so much so my father wouldn't let me out of his sight. I know he was basking in the reflected glory of what I achieved and why not? It was him who had given me the talent; those hours and hours he had spent bowling the ball to me. It was really his success; I was just the tool that carried it out.

After Founder's Day, of course, came Prize Day. David, my friend won three prizes: for English, English Literature and History, and, as he walked up to pick up his prizes, none of us realised it would be one of the last occasions we would see him. His father had been one of the victims of the Wall Street Crash and could no longer afford to pay his fees. His father had already paid a full year in advance so at least David got to complete the year. But in any event he was here now and we were cheering like mad at his success.

I confess that I didn't win any academic awards that year; my prizes were just for sport. I had been fortunate in my year, winning a whole string of events. The first announcement was made: 'For the winner of the Junior 220 yards – Chillington-Henry . . .' I had also won the 440 yards, the 880 yards and the Junior Cross-Country, which got a special mention from the Headmaster.

'It seems unbelievable that the winner actually knocked three minutes off the previous record and that winner was Chillington-Henry . . .' And when the Headmaster presented the prize to me for the Junior Cross-Country, he added, much to the amusement of the audience, 'This is getting very boring!' Next he presented the prizes for cricket and finally came to mine. 'And now we come to the batting prizes. The junior batting prize was won by Chillington-Henry, but as he has won the senior prize, too, we are awarding it instead to Michael Spiller.' This was a decision that received a huge applause.

'. . . Now we come to the junior Victor Ludorum for all-round performance, which goes to Chillington-Henry. But before I ask him to receive his trophy, I would like to say I have never seen a batting performance like the one he gave last week. I'm sure that one day he will play for his country.

'Finally, I would like to add to that the splendid performance he gave as Wendy in our theatre production of *Peter Pan*. I'm surprised that a girl beat all the boys!'

This brought tremendous laughter, cheers and wolf whistles in the hall as I walked up to receive my trophies, with the proudest father in all the world looking on. The cricket team lined up to applaud as I came down the steps.

After the presentations I said goodbye to Harry, which was one of the saddest moments of my life. He hugged me and thanked me for all I had done for him and asked me not to lose contact and then said the strangest thing: 'Goodbye Alex and chin up!' It was as if he knew what the future would bring.

That term ended one of the best periods of my life. We all parted in such a wonderful spirit especially as we all knew we were no longer to be considered juniors and when we returned, it would be in long trousers. I really did feel ten feet tall. However, I couldn't wait to show my father my best trophy, which was of course my school colours tie.

That night, when I got back home, I didn't sleep a wink; I was so excited about everything and I was not even a bit tired the following day. We were all having breakfast together when my mother made an announcement.

'Alexander, I've got a surprise for you. We are going shopping.' For a moment my heart sank; I hated shopping. Surely it was for girls?

'Don't you want to know what for?' my mother continued.

'Yes of course!' I replied, trying to sound enthusiastic.

'I'm going to buy you a pair of long trousers!'

Suddenly my life was complete. What more would any young man want, other than a pair of long trousers? Once again I was so excited I raced over to her and she went through the ordeal of hugs and kisses, thoroughly enjoying the reception I gave her but still trying to maintain some decorum.

'Now come on, don't be silly! Sit down and finish your breakfast,' she said. 'It's only a pair of trousers.'

Only a pair of trousers, I thought to myself. Doesn't she realise what that means? My life will change forever. I was in a daydream.

'Come on, Alex, let's go to the town and get it over with. I know you don't like shopping.'

'I do now,' I said, smiling.

I couldn't believe my eyes when my mother got into the driving seat of the car.

'Mother, you're driving!' I said as I climbed into the front seat next to her.

'Yes, darling, there's been a lot of talk about bringing in a compulsory driving test for all new drivers so I thought I would get a licence before they did!'

'I'm impressed!' I said, as she reversed out of the garage and swung the car round in front of the house and on into town.

A few minutes later we were walking into the shop, Wilberforce Bespoke Tailoring, to be greeted by the proprietor, Mr Wilberforce himself.

'Ah, good morning Mrs Chillington-Henry and I suppose this is the young gentleman who has come for his trousers. Well, they are almost ready; it's just the length; but we will need to try them on, so that we can finish them. It should only take an hour or so.'

I was mesmerised as I watched as Mr Wilberforce bring in the trousers, as though he were carrying some wonderful dish of food. I watched him place them on the table and gently unfurl the legs, then pick them up and gently brush them with his hand. They were light grey and long and I remember I just stood there, admiring this creation that was going to change my life forever. He handed them to me and asked me to try them on.

Naturally, they were too long, but I didn't want to take them off; I felt so important and grown up.

'What do you think, Mother?'

'They look lovely, Alex.'

Mr Wilberforce finished the final measurements, marking all the lines with a piece of chalk and I reluctantly returned to wearing my shorts.

'I'll have them ready in half an hour. I can see the young man is anxious to have them,' he added, as we left the shop.

We returned after forty-five minutes. I was burning with impatience, as the last fifteen minutes were absolute mental torture. My mother wouldn't hurry in the grocer's, indulging in inconsequential chit-chat with the shopkeeper and then at the butcher's, it seemed he dawdled over cutting the meat on purpose. Didn't they realise what trouble they were causing me? In the greengrocer's I was even a little sharp with the errand boy, earning a mild rebuke from my mother.

'I haven't brought you up to be rude,' she said quietly.

'I'm sorry, Mother. I just can't wait!'

I pushed open the door of Wilberforce's and went in, only to be admonished once again by my mother.

'Alex!' she protested loudly, waiting for me to open the door for her. 'You're a gentleman now. That's so unlike you.'

'I'm sorry, Mother; it won't happen again,' I said, opening the door and standing back to let her through. 'It's just the excitement.'

'I know, dear, but you must never forget: ladies first.'

Now came the good bit. I tried the trousers on and they fitted perfectly and from then on I wouldn't take them off.

'Come on now, don't be silly,' my mother insisted. 'You can put them on tonight and show your father.' That night we were having a dinner party to celebrate one of my father's promotions and, by way of marking my road to manhood, I was to be present, too.

'Oh go on, Mother, let me! Don't be mean!' I added, almost going into a tantrum.

She gave in.

'All right, all right!' she agreed, just for the sake of peace I imagine. 'However, don't get them dirty before your father has seen you in them . . .' She paused and turned to Mr Wilberforce. 'I think you had better make another pair, Mr Wilberforce.'

'Please put these in the bin, Mr Wilberforce,' I added, proffering my shorts and smiling.

'No, we'll take them home . . . just in case,' my mother interrupted.

As we left the shop I felt I had gone into the shop a junior and come out a senior. I walked along with my mother, linking my arm in hers: I was now a man with responsibilities. There hardly seemed any time for me to show off my new trousers before the guests started to arrive. The trouble was I didn't want to take them off, not even to wash, and even though I was careful, I got them splashed with water.

I can't go down like this, I thought. I'll wait until they dry, then no one will notice.

It wasn't to be. I was disturbed by my mother shouting: 'Alex, come on down now. Our guests are here and they all want to meet you.'

I felt like a prince walking down the stairs to meet the guests, standing at the foot of them and making sure at the same time they could see my long trousers and school colours. All my pretences of being grown up soon disappeared, however, when I saw my sister, Alice waiting for me; I hadn't seen her for ages. I quickly went up to her outstretched arms, which held me tight as she hugged and kissed me.

Lucy arrived with her husband and I felt rather sad, as there appeared to be an undercurrent of bitterness between her and my father, and especially between her husband and my father. I found out later that Lucy had been obliged to get married. That sort of thing was all a bit of a disgrace back then, although the family had cleverly hushed it up by sending her away to relatives in the country until the baby was born. My father had still not forgiven them for what they had done, but Lucy seemed to have grown up a lot since I had last seen her and had become very attractive; she really got some attention from the other men present, much to the annoyance of her husband.

My father called us into the dining room and we all sat round the table, all twenty-eight of us! My father sat in the middle, with my mother on his left and me on his right. You cannot imagine how I felt: it was the pinnacle of my life so far. My mother had sought help from the village and for that evening we had a cook and two waitresses, with my mother organising all things in military fashion.

Without doubt it was a successful evening but the crowning glory was yet to come. The meal was over and the gentlemen had started to smoke and drink their port or brandies, when my father stood up and tapped his spoon against his glass.

'My friends and family, I want to make a toast to my son. First, for the phenomenal score he made at the Bankworth Founder's Day Match – 132 not out . . .' At this point he was beaming all over his face as he looked at me, and I beamed back. '. . . And secondly, for the way he had played throughout the season to win his school colours.' He pointed to my tie. 'I'm sure that one day a member of this family will be playing cricket for England . . .'

I could hear one or two of the guests agreeing with him. Then there was silence and they all stood up.

'To Alex and good luck!' they cried.

'Speech, speech, speech!' they all started chanting and banging the table.

My father leaned over. 'Alexander, you are going to have to respond. It is a custom whenever someone is toasted that they make a speech. A short one, mind you!'

At least Bankworth had given me the confidence to stand up and speak, but now I was lost for words. I was so happy that once again, the tears started to roll down my cheeks.

'I did it for my father,' I said, the tears almost choking the words.

There was silence as no other word would come out. Then someone shouted: 'Well done, Alex!' and they all started clapping and cheering. It was the culmination of a wonderful year but it was something that would never happen again.

Chapter 6

I arrived at school and received a lovely reception from my friends. We were all in our long trousers and our new jackets; I was wearing a tight pullover under my clothes to lessen the feminine appearance of my body and I always wore my blazer open, which was more comfortable for me, although not quite de rigueur. However, my first real blow was the realisation that David was not coming back to school and I was devastated as he had been my only real friend.

Mr White, I suppose in life you can count on one hand how many people you can really rely on when the chips are down. David would have been one of them. We had been inseparable for seven years and, I don't mind admitting it, I did shed a tear. What's more I was no longer a fag so I had lost Harry as well. I felt really alone. I knew the others would be friends but not real mates, if you know what I mean.

The Christmas term started in the usual way, with the new Sports Captain, Philip Wilson, calling a meeting of the house to see who would do what. I could no longer box so all I had was table tennis, with the result I began to spend a little more time on my studies. We soon were back in the normal routine. James, my bedfellow was tolerant of me, but kept his distance for fear of being linked with me. You know what boys are; peer pressure can be an awful thing.

We were now in Form 3. The bell had just gone to start classes, when one of the boys told me the House Captain wanted to see me immediately. I ran up to his room and of course he wasn't there. I walked quickly back to my classroom and for the first time I realised no one wanted to sit next to me. In fact, as I entered the room I was wolf whistled. It was obvious that, prior to going into the classroom, the boys had already decided to get me to sit right at the front of the class on my own. I therefore had to walk to my seat in front of my classmates who were all whistling or cat-calling. I even saw the teacher trying not to smile and even he didn't stop the row until it got out of hand. I tried hard not to cry without a great deal of success, much to the amusement of the others. What was worse, I had to sit there for the entire term.

'Oh, she's crying, sir!' one of the boys commented.

'Come on settle down,' Mr Fisher shouted over the laughter. 'Leave him alone.'

'She's a "her", not a "him",' one of the boys said, to more laughter.

Fisher at last got angry. He could see my distress and realised matters were getting out of hand. He swiftly restored discipline to the class but I now felt like a freak. I knew I was on my own and couldn't rely on anyone, so I kept my head down as much as I could. My father's words rang in my ears: 'Don't worry about the teasing, always do your best!'

As ever Fred Arnett, the sports teacher, was my nemesis. It was obvious to everyone that he saw me as something of a freak and he also knew the other boys were constantly making fun of me so now he joined in.

We had all lined up at the bars ready to pull ourselves up and several times he called me out to do it first. But I could only manage one pull-up and hung there desperately while the others catcalled.

'Come down, Gloria darling. Sit over there and I'll get you some knitting,' he said in an affectedly effeminate voice, much to the amusement of the class.

I left the gym in spite of his orders and did five laps round the track instead. During the next sports lesson he gave me a ball of wool and two needles.

My unhappiness spilled into other areas, too. I refused point-blank to take part in the theatre production, much to the annoyance of Mr Pounder.

'I've done it two years running and I don't want to take part in it this year,' I said firmly.

The production was A Christmas Carol by Charles Dickens. Pounder had the gall to say, 'Well, there isn't much of a female part in it this year.'

This rather insensitive comment played on my mind so much over the days that I eventually went and spoke to him about it. Amazingly, he apologised and said he was just disappointed that I hadn't volunteered as I always did so well for him. I promised that I would take part in next year's production. This was a promise I would live to regret.

I managed to get through the term without too much difficulty; in other words by keeping out of the limelight. I almost believed people had begun not to notice me, but then the swimming competition came round and I knew that I was in for trouble. My breasts were continuing to grow and my nipples had begun to swell and turn pink. The House Sports Captain insisted I take part, as the House was so short of talent.

When I entered the swimming pool, everyone took it as a bit of a laugh. However, after I won my heats and had the chance of points for the house, the teasing became less aggressive, though I did have to endure the inevitable adolescent comments: 'It's not fair, sir, she's got extra buoyancy!' You can imagine the sort of things that were said. In the end I got to the finals, which were always held at the town baths. However, the Headmaster called me into his office.

'Henry young man, I've got a bit of a problem . . .' I could sense that he was very, very uncomfortable with what he was trying to say. 'You have been successful in the swimming competition and you are to be congratulated. However, as I said, I have got a bit of a problem . . .'

'Yes, sir?' I said, almost asking him to continue.

'The problem is . . . your body. When you are in the pool . . .'

He paused with embarrassment, '. . . it is unsettling the other boys and I feel it may be necessary to cover your body more.'

'What do you suggest, sir? I already wear my running vest,' I commented.

'I think it would be more appropriate if you wore a costume similar to that . . . that worn by ladies,' the Head continued.

'But, sir, I can't! Things are difficult enough. I'm not a girl and it's not fair.'

'Then, young Henry, I'm afraid you cannot compete.'

I protested long and hard but the Head wouldn't relent, so I took my case to Mr Wilkes, who thought it was wholly inappropriate that the Head should have spoken like that and he would go and see him. He did and convinced him that my present garb would be sufficient, though the Head insisted he would review the situation next year.

So I did attend the finals and won three races, although the whole experience was very painful.

It was my last year in the Junior Cross-Country and once again I won it easily, but once again, my success aggravated Mr Arnett because for the second year running I had beaten his boy and he wasn't going to let me forget it. At every opportunity he would make a fool of me and would praise anyone else who made a fool of me and most of all, Hazard who was still a junior prefect. He had already been warned off by Harry Whelan, but now Harry had gone and I was undefended.

On one occasion, Hazard saw me run back from cross-country training and jump into the communal bath. I always tried to do this early to avoid difficulties, but this time he was passing the door just as I got in. He came in. 'Well, Gloria, we are a pretty little thing, aren't we?'

I ignored him, hoping in vain he would go away, but he just leaned over the side of the bath and leered. He looked like an pervert and couldn't take his eyes off me. I was covered in mud and wanted to wash it off, but every time I rubbed myself over he became more and more aroused.

I did the best I could and jumped out of the bath and ran to get my towel, but he ran after me and caught me. He snatched the towel from me, leaving me naked and facing him.

'Come on, give me just one little kiss!'

'Don't be so bloody stupid!' I replied angrily, but I was in no position to fend him off. I was soaking wet, the floor was like ice, very slippery to those with bare feet, and, of course, I was naked.

Hazard grabbed hold of me as I tried to get away, then pulled me towards him and started to kiss the back of my neck. I was struggling and slipping all over the place, so he picked me up. Thankfully, we heard someone coming and he just dropped me onto the floor. The pain for a moment was excruciating as I landed on my backside, but what did that matter when I was released from his clutches.

'See you later!' he said sinisterly.

That evening I knew something was afoot as I saw the Barratt brothers with Hazard looking at me; it was obvious that they were discussing me and planning something. I deliberately made myself scarce and made sure they didn't see me.

After supper I went round to the laundry to collect some towels, as that month I was a house orderly, responsible for ensuring clean ones were available. The duties for this lasted only a month and then it passed to another boy, but it enabled me to stay out of harm's way for half an hour or so. I entered the washroom and was met by Norman, the boiler man. We chatted for a while and he invited me to have a cup of tea and a round of toast, which I accepted gratefully; it was another way of keeping out of Hazard's way.

We went into the boiler house and sat down chatting. He opened the furnace and placed a piece of bread onto a toasting fork and asked me to hold the fork while he made the tea. I made four pieces of toast and then spread the butter, which ran into the hot bread. That, together with the sweet Sergeant Major's tea, was an absolute treat. He invited me to sit next to him on his little sofa while we ate it all. He had a really cosy little den.

To the right of the boiler with its furnace, Norman had a three -seater settee and two armchairs, a table and two chairs and a cupboard, where he kept his milk and food; add to that a sink and a toilet in the far corner and it was home from home and for me – safety from Hazard.

'Are you Alex Henry?' Norman asked.

'Yes. Why?'

'Oh I've heard a lot about you. You're very good at cricket, I hear.'

'Not bad,' I replied.

After I had drunk the tea and finished the toast, I was a little worried about the time and made my excuses.

'I have to go now. Thank you for the tea and toast. See you soon, Norman.'

'Bye,' he replied. 'If you want to come round tomorrow, about the same time, you can have some more toast,' Norman said. 'I like to have the company.'

I was thankful as it was another place I could hide.

That night I washed early, went to bed and tried to get to sleep, but it was a complete waste of time. Hazard came along to my bed, shouting, 'Gloria!'

I ignored him so he shouted again. 'Gloria, I'm talking to you.'

I still chose to ignore him, so he tipped me out of bed as he continued to abuse me. 'It has been brought to my attention that you have made a mess in the bathroom and I'm going to make sure that you clear it up. Get down there now!'

I put my dressing gown on and walked to the washroom, which was a large room, partitioned into twelve sections; each section had its own bath and wash basin and an area to put your clothes while bathing. I walked into the room and Hazard followed, immediately shutting the door behind him. I knew I had problems when I saw the Barratt brothers, his little henchmen, already in the washroom, waiting for me.

I turned round to find Hazard bearing down on me. I pleaded with him to leave me alone, but it fell on deaf ears. They were animals, sheer bloody animals. I clenched my fists and prepared for the worst. I only managed to punch one of the brothers once before they grabbed me and threw me fully clothed into a bath of cold water. I screamed for help, but Hazard pushed me under the water. I came up spluttering and in no fit state to retaliate, a situation they took full advantage of.

'Oh, you're wet,' Hazard said. 'Let me get these damp clothes off you.'

I remember I was shivering with cold and fear as they took off my clothes and gave me a towel to wipe myself. They leered as they watched me dry myself. One of the Barratts started to play with himself and asked if I wanted a bit of 'it'. I would have loved to have thought of something smart to do or say, but I was too cold and too frightened.

Only then did they let me go. I had to walk all through the dorms past the beds, with all those brave little boys pretending to be asleep and not to have heard anything. I had only my towel to cover me and a bundle of wet clothes. I had no other nightclothes and had to turn my bed over and remake it before I could get in. Needless to say I didn't get any sleep that night.

Mr White, when I look back, I realise that Hazard was besotted with me; he couldn't leave me alone and, because he couldn't be seen to fancy me, he took it out of me by being unkind. There were times when he was on his own, I could tell he just wanted to admire me; I could see it in his eyes, a kind of love. Then there were the other times when he behaved like an pervert, but only and always when he had an audience.

Hazard and his henchmen were becoming very powerful in the school hierarchy and like most bullies they had a considerable following. They were ruling the roost and because of this, anyone and everyone, was prepared to join in with whatever torments they dreamed up for me. But it was the incessant comments that really began to get me down: they told me how I looked, how I was allegedly behaving and how each and every one of them would like to screw me.

I can tell you, Mr White, it was a very miserable existence, though when I look back I can see how it made me a stronger more determined person. But what if I had been a different kind of a person . . . what then?

There were many forays to my bed during that term, when Hazard along with others would tip me out of bed, strip me, either in his room or the washroom. Things were becoming more serious and I threatened to report them on several occasions. But all this elicited was a scornful, 'Who would believe you? Everyone knows you behave like a tart and who would be expelled first: a boy in a boy's school or a girl in a boy's school.' I was powerless really. My overriding concern was that I couldn't dare risk trouble, as my father would never forgive me. It was the only thing that kept me going, my fear of losing my father's affection.

There were now eight boys involved in this 'ring' and for them I was fair game at all times. They made sure they were the only ones allowed to touch me up – not with my blessing I would hasten to add – but at anytime, anywhere, and no one else was allowed to do anything.

Rumours were rife that I was 'whoring it around', which made more and more boys despise me and ostracise me. No matter what I said, no one would ever believe me, except David that was, but he was no longer there. When I look back, his loyalty must have already been stretched to the limit, with the stick he got for standing by me, although he never complained or turned against me, not even under peer pressure.

I was always covered in bruises and scratches as a result of my trying to defend myself and I was forever having to explain to the masters that I had hurt myself falling. Some of the ring leaders actually enjoyed seeing me struggle and fight; they began to get more and more aroused and began trying different scenarios.

Several would masturbate and ejaculate all over me and they didn't care where; but always they would be holding me down while they took it in turn to have their fun. If I screamed, they simply stuffed my mouth with a towel; if I struggled they became more violent and all of them in turn would lie on top of me, fondling me, then ejaculating between my legs. I had almost got to the stage when they called me I would have just gone because that way it was easier. When the end of term came, I had never been so relieved in my life.

But even at home I felt dejected. I just needed someone to talk to, not about my problems, just someone to talk to. That first day back, I found my mother sitting in the garden taking tea with a few friends. I walked across the lawn.

'Oh hello, Alex,' she said, then, turning to her friends, she carried on, 'He's home from school for a few weeks, aren't you, dear?'

'Yes, Mother,' I replied. I desperately wanted to talk to her.

'Do you want to join us?' she asked. 'I don't suppose you do, do you?'

'I'll see you later then,' I replied. 'Good afternoon,' I said, turning to the ladies and went off to my room to unpack.

My mother was organising some charitable works for the unemployed but had forgotten that charity should begin at home.

During the second week of the holiday Alice came over to see me and at last I had someone to talk to. We spent hours together and I told her everything, to such an extent that we spent most of the time in tears and in each other's arms.

'Alex, we've got to do something. You shouldn't be in a boys' school. Couldn't you transfer to the other side?' she asked.

But it always came back to my father. 'He wouldn't like it, Alice.' I made her promise not to say anything, a promise she kept, albeit reluctantly.

Alice and my mother came to see me off on the train back to school and as it started moving, Alice ran alongside, our hands touched for a second or two as she shouted, 'Chin up, darling!' Harry Whelan's words came flooding back as the train left the station and once again I was on my own, left to my thoughts and worries, trying not to shed a tear.

The summer term was the only one where I could more than hold my own. I was able to concentrate on cricket and athletics, which at least helped to take my mind off matters, but not off the immediate problem, which was that my features were becoming more feminine by the week. In an attempt to ward off staring eyes and lascivious jibes, I bound a scarf tightly around my chest in an attempt to flatten my forming breasts. I cannot tell you how difficult they were to conceal and how painful it became.

However, it didn't take long for the eight perverts, as I'll call them, to start back on their old routine and, as before and I had to fight long and hard to fend them off. The most difficult problem, however, was that four of the gang were regular members of the cricket team.

I was naturally picked for the First XI and scored a 50 in the first match. I was feeling pretty pleased with myself and for a moment let myself relax. It was Stephan Davies' turn to look after the bath towels and, as he was involved in some other activity, asked if I could do his duties for him; it was just for the rest of that day and at the back of my mind I probably thought it would get me out of the way. I went into the towel room and once again bumped into Norman, who after a chat, offered me tea and toast in the boiler house. He had never been difficult before so I accepted.

We sat on the couch chatting for a short while, but this time I felt a little uncomfortable as he began patting my knee, albeit in a manly fashion, but the second time he did it, he left it there and I had to casually move away. The boiler house door creaked open as only heavy steel doors do and in walked Hazard with several others of his cronies.

'Hello there, Norman,' Hazard said, as he made his way towards me.

'Good evening, Mr Hazard . . . gentlemen,' Norman replied as he got up from the settee to allow Hazard and a boy named Joseph Smith to sit either side of me. One of the Barratts slammed the door and instantly the entire place became soundproof. It had all obviously been planned and it seemed even Norman had been in on it.

'Don't worry, little girl! We're not going to hurt you. We just want to see you naked,' Hazard said in a quiet, odd voice.

I made a move to get up, but Hazard quickly pulled me back onto the settee.

'Come on, Gloria, take your shirt off and let's see!' Hazard continued, more aggressively.

'Please, Hazard, let me go. Don't do this to me!' I begged. But my fear only seemed to goad them more.

'Come on, take it off or we'll rip it off!' Smith shouted excitedly.

I saw Norman pick up his pruning knife, and pass it to Morton, who then came round to the front of the settee, opened the blade and began to rub it down the front of my clothes. I began screaming for help, but it was useless as the noise of the boilers took the sound away. My struggling and screaming seemed to arouse and encourage them further and all of them approached and surrounded me.

Suddenly, Hazard and Smith grabbed hold of me by the arms, whilst Barratt made sure I didn't make a further sound by tying a towel round my mouth. The knife was razor sharp as Morton began very slowly but surely to cut my shirt open. I began to struggle and fight furiously.

Norman, who by now was shaking and sweating with excitement, threw two large wide leather belts over to Barratt. These were used to tie the bunker open when the coal was delivered.

'Tie them to her ankles and then hold the belts. She won't be able to move!' Norman shouted.

I hadn't a chance. Within a few minutes I was totally incapable of stopping them. Morton continued to cut my clothes off, but Smith would have none of it. 'Give it to me! Let me do it!' he shouted as if in a frenzy.

Morton handed him the knife and Smith, who by now had undone his trousers, finished cutting my shirt off. He began kissing me as he did it, licking my face; he was by now past caring what the others thought. He began to rub his penis all over my face as I lay prostrate across the arm of the settee. Then, as if in one frenzied motion, he cut the rest of my shirt and vest off and ejaculated over my breast. I could see his eyes; he was like a mad thing.

His depravity seemed to encourage the others, as they too began to pull the shreds of my clothes from me, only stopping from time to time to admire their handiwork. Then each in turn did a variety of different things to me, all whooping for joy as they ejaculated over different parts of my body, mainly my breasts and head. Smith was by now totally naked himself and began writhing all over my body, rubbing the semen into both of us until he too added more to the slime.

Then Norman, the dirty pig, began to show them how to bugger me and explained that it was just as good as the real thing.

Smith began shouting, 'Come on, come on, come on, let me do it!' He was almost jumping around as they turned me over and spread-eagled me across the arm of the settee. The Barratt brothers held my arms. Morton and Peter Wales held my feet with the belts, almost on the ground, while Norman greased a candle with Vaseline and shoved it into my bottom, 'We don't want to hurt ourselves, do we?' he sneered, as he smeared more grease into my bottom with his fingers. The others laughed unnaturally.

Smith was at it again. 'Let me do it!' he cried, almost begging Norman to give him the Vaseline. He began to smear it around my bottom, gently at first and then more roughly as he pushed his fingers deeper inside. The pain was excruciating.

I couldn't move a muscle. I tried to wriggle and scream to no avail. I heard that pig Norman explaining it needed to be bigger as he pushed something hard inside of me. I turned my head and could just see Norman pulling the handle of a trowel out of me. He had a frightening wild look in his eyes as he watched how the others were becoming worked up. I was terrified. I could now feel the blood trickling down my legs and I thought they were going to kill me.

Then the first of those beasts started on me. It was Smith. He was determined to be first; he leaned over and began pushing himself inside me. He took his time, each time pushing harder, and then screaming with delight as he ejaculated again.

The others were uncontrollable in their haste to be next. Wales couldn't wait as he ejaculated over Morton who by then was on top of me. Then it was Shepherd's turn and he just dribbled it around my mouth to the delight of the others and I couldn't even wipe it away.

The next was Hazard. 'Come on, my little lovely, you've got the best now!'

He too pushed himself inside, but even through the pain and the haze, I detected he was unhappy. He didn't want to share me; I was his, but I could only feel hatred and disgust as each in turn followed suit and took me. Then, finally, it was Norman's turn. He grabbed me like a vice as he thrust himself inside me, snorting like a pig as he pushed in and out.

The others had become strangely silent from the moment they had finished and had even let go of the belts. I tried to free myself, but Norman wasn't finished.

'Hold the fuckin' bitch. I'm not done yet!'

They tightened their grip until he had finished, pushing harder and harder until at last he came.

I swear he sounded like some wild boar rutting and now the boys were looking at him for what he was, a filthy fifty-year-old rapist, who had led these boys into eternal hell . . . not that they needed much leading, but as an adult he should have . . .'

***

Mrs Fraser stopped for several minutes, feeling the pain again, no doubt for the umpteenth time. I could see a tear roll down her cheek as the pain became too much. She pushed the tear to one side and continued:

The boys, no, those beasts, now realised what they had done and were terrified; they couldn't put the clock back and they knew they had got to live with the consequences. They saw me lying there, almost unconscious. I was naked, all my clothes were torn and I couldn't walk. The boys started to panic; they had to do something quickly; to concoct a story just in case I got them into trouble. Norman was a different kettle of fish – a hardened paedophile – as he would be called today.

'She could go missing,' Norman suggested.

'We could put her in the furnace,' Smith enthused. 'No one would ever know. They would think she had run away!' Norman thought this was a good idea.

They didn't even consider that I was still alive. Norman simply opened the furnace door and motioned the others to pick me up, but somehow I found the energy to sit up and scream.

'Please don't kill me! I won't say anything! *Please!*

'Shut the bitch up,' Norman yelled, throwing a towel to Morton, who shoved it in my mouth and tied the towel round my face again.

Norman and Smith were jointly trying to get the job done.

'Open the furnace wider, quick!' Smith shouted to Norman, who immediately opened it further, but even then it was only just wide enough to push a body through.

Norman grabbed hold of my legs and told the others to lift me up and carry me over to the furnace. I could see the evil look on Smith's face as he took my waist and encouraged the others to pick me up. It was as if he wanted simply to wipe the whole event away by destroying every last bit of me.

They took me over to the boiler where I felt the extreme heat on my feet as Norman tried to feed my body in. He momentarily let my legs go as the heat was too much for him and I opened them wide, pushing them against the front of the furnace, burning myself in the process. They couldn't push me in and had no chance to do so unless they tied me up again.

'Kill her!' Smith yelled in a frenzy of madness. 'Kill her!' he yelled again.

But the rest were beginning to sober up. I exchanged glances with Hazard and he could see the sadness and fear in my eyes.

He pushed his way over to me. 'Don't be so bloody stupid, you bastard! No one is going to kill her. We are going to get her out of here.'

With that he picked me up and carried me from the boiler house and into the towel room. He washed me down and gently bathed my burned feet, while the others looked on in total silence.

I had no clothes of any description to put on. To get rid of the evidence, Norman had already put them all into the furnace. I was bleeding profusely and my feet were too sore from the heat to stand up.

'Help me lift her up. You can see she can't walk,' Hazard ordered Shepherd. Then he and the others lifted me up and carried me to the washroom, where Hazard ran a hot bath. I was invited to get in. I had no life or strength to refuse. I lay in the bath almost lifeless and began hoping that I could drift away and never come round. But they were worried and kept coming in to see how I was. The water was red with blood as they lifted me out and gave me a hot shower to clean me off.

'Get her to bed!' Hazard ordered and between them they carried me to the dorm, hoping they wouldn't be seen, but there was one kindly soul who had seen some of what had happened and had told Mr Wilkes, who came rushing up to see me. He immediately contacted the Headmaster, who also came to my bedside.

'What has happened?' he asked.

'I've been raped,' I replied simply.

'Don't be silly, boy. How could you be raped?' he asked angrily.

I knew I was fighting a losing battle but I was determined to get that animal, Norman and simply told the Head it was him and that he had torn all my clothes and burned them in the boiler.

'Why were you there?' the Head asked suspiciously. I could see Mr Wilkes bristling at this line of questioning.

'Collecting towels, sir,' were the only words I managed to utter.

'I'll telephone the police,' Mr Wilkes said to the Head.

'No. No. *No*!' the Headmaster shouted. 'I'll not have the police brought into this school. I'll deal with it!'

He didn't want any scandal and the police were not informed. Norman, however, was dismissed on the spot. Mr Wilkes later told me he was given the choice to leave then with no references, or the police would be brought in, and he knew what the consequences of that would be. He left immediately and I do know he became an alcoholic, as he couldn't get a job anywhere.

He lost his family and friends and died in poverty. Poetic justice, wouldn't you agree, Mr White? As for the others . . . well, I'll tell you about that later.

Mr Wilkes took me up to his house to make sure I was all right. I confided in him almost everything that had happened and the names of all those who had been responsible and what they had done to me. He told me to take a bath and he would have a look at what damage had been done and then I could have my supper with him and his wife. I took the bath and relaxed as never before. There were no prying eyes, no nasty comments, just a hot bath and a slow, relaxing soak. I came out of the bathroom, just wrapped in a towel, to be greeted by Mrs Wilkes.

'Poor lovely Alex,' she said in her gentle sympathetic way, handing me a dressing gown. 'It's not fair, all this unkindness, is it?'

I didn't answer, but I knew I was in safe hands so an answer was unimportant.

Mr Wilkes took me into his bedroom with his wife present, and looked at what those animals had done and said that he was going to do something about it. I begged and pleaded with him not to and that, if he did, my father would never forgive me. I remember assuring him that in some way I would get my own back.

'They don't deserve to be in this school; in fact, they deserve to be in prison! And Guest should never come out again,' Peter Wilkes said angrily, almost spitting the words out. 'I'm not going to let it go, but I'll hold off for a few weeks.'

'Thank you, sir,' I said softly.

I spent a lot of time with Mr and Mrs Wilkes, who, you could say, nursed me back to health again and gave me the old-fashioned affection I needed as well as what we would now call counselling. It helped me enormously to face my problems, as all along I didn't want to upset my father. I somehow felt he would believe the words of eight boys rather than mine but, whatever, I didn't want to lose what bit of him I had left.

One of my worst moments at school happened shortly after this incident, when I was sent for by the Headmaster and was surprised to see my father in his office in full military uniform, towering above the Head as he sat at his desk. I walked in and we were invited to sit down.

'Hello, Father,' I said happily, as I hadn't seen him for some time.

'What's all this about then?' he asked impatiently.

The Head began, but was totally out of his depth, especially with a man like my father. 'Well, Mr Chillington-Henry . . .'

'Well, what? Get on with it, man,' my father almost yelled.

'Well, we would like you . . . to . . . to remove your son from this school . . .' The Head stuttered out the words.

'Nonsense! What for?'

'Well . . . you must surely have noticed he has developed breasts. They're . . . it's a huge distraction for the other boys. In fact, we've had to dismiss one of the staff because of the advances he had been making to your son . . .'

'That's a lie!' I said loudly.

'Shut up, boy!' my father snapped. 'Go on,' he ordered the Head.

'Well, other boys are known to have been . . . interested in him and it's very disconcerting both for him and them. I would say that we have, at all times, told these individuals to behave themselves and they have. Haven't they, Alex?'

I had my father with me and I was brave. 'No not really, sir. In fact . . .'

'Shut up, Alexander. Don't speak to the Headmaster like that.'

Immediately my father stood up and leaned over the Headmaster's desk, almost touching his face and shouted:

'It's clear that no fault lies with my son, Headmaster. I'm not going to take my son out of this school and as far as I'm concerned, it's you who have created this problem and it's you who are going to cure it. Furthermore, if any harm comes to my son, I'll hold you personally responsible and, I can assure you, I make a terrible enemy. You will never work again and I'll make it my duty to ruin you and anyone connected with you. Do I make myself clear, Headmaster?'

The Head was trembling under the onslaught and didn't answer.

'Do I?' my father shouted.

'Yes, sir,' the Headmaster replied, as if he were a private in the Army.

'I don't think we've anything more to say to each other. You make sure you have everything back to normal before he comes home at the end of term. Do you understand?' he concluded, almost yelling the last words.

'Yes, sir!'

'We'll bid you good day, then,' my father added as he turned and left the office. 'Come with me, Alexander.'

I followed him out of the office, leaving the Headmaster sweating profusely. I'm sure he had never been spoken to like that before and it was obvious he was terrified of the consequences of upsetting my father, who by now was a very high-ranking military man.

We passed Arnett walking down the corridor and my father acknowledged him. 'Arnett!' he said sternly.

'Sir!' Arnett replied, acknowledging my father, as we continued on our way.

'Father, how do you know Mr Arnett?' I asked curiously.

'I had difficulties with him when I was in command of the Tank Corps during the war. Why?'

'Oh nothing, Father. He's not very pleasant to me, that's all.'

'Alex, what is all this about really?' my father asked when we were on our own.

And then I just came out with it matter-of-factly, surprising myself as much as my father. 'I've grown breasts and I'm even having periods.'

My father's reaction was intense. 'Don't be so bloody filthy!' he shouted at me. 'I do not want to hear any more of this rubbish. I expect you to win the batting prize again this term. You make the best of it, do you hear?'

'Yes, Father,' I replied as I watched him climb into what was now his chauffeur-driven car and simply leave me standing there alone. He didn't even turn and wave goodbye.

The following day, the Headmaster called me into his office once more. This time my house master, Mr Wilkes, was also present. The Head made it clear that if I had any further trouble, I was to contact either him direct or Mr Wilkes.

'I mean it, young man, any sign of trouble you come to me.'

The Headmaster was trying to appear sincere and in control.

'Thank you, Headmaster. I will,' I replied.

I left his office accompanied by Peter Wilkes, who took me to have a chat with his wife.

'Alex,' Mrs Wilkes said gently, over tea and cakes, 'Peter and I have given your situation a lot of thought and feel that it would be better for you if you came and had your baths here. It will be safer. In fact, if you ever feel vulnerable, you must come to us. I want you to promise you will . . .' She paused for a second or two, allowing her offer sink in. 'Come on, promise,' Mrs Wilkes insisted.

'I do promise and I want to thank you awfully. I really don't know when or how I'll be able to repay your kindness,' I said, becoming somewhat tearful.

'You don't have to. It's a pleasure,' Mrs Wilkes said, stretching out her arms to give me a hug.

The boys, meanwhile, thought they had got away with it, especially as Norman was the only one who had been punished. So as soon as things were more or less back to normal, they once more began all their little tricks. Like all beasts when their wounds are healed, their confidence grows again, little by little.

They were all brave enough when in a pack and yet none of them could look at me when they were on their own, with the exception of Hazard and, as I said before, I genuinely believe it was because he was besotted, in some strange sexual way, with me. Occasionally, I would see him staring at me but the moment he saw me looking, he would turn sharply away.

It was Joseph Smith who haunted me. He was the one who I felt would really have burned me alive and the one who seemed to have gained the most sexual gratification from it all. Yet when I look back, he was the one who seemed to feel the most guilt. He could never look at me. Even when I used to stare at him as he passed, he would simply bow his head and hurry away from me. There were times when I knew he wanted to speak to me but could never rustle up the courage. In fact, the incident seemed to destroy him as he was never as cocky and clever as he was before. In fact, he became somewhat of a loner.

I tried to keep out of everybody's way because it didn't take long for the rumours to spread round the school and nearly everyone I knew thought I had brought it on myself as I was too free and easy. One or two even thought Norman had been unfairly treated, but no one ever got to know the truth of the matter.

Mr White, I know I'll probably repeat myself a few times on this point, but I made a vow that, one day, I would get my own back on all these individuals and that any revenge I could exact wouldn't be bad enough.

It wasn't long before the four boys in the First XI tried to get me out of the team and made a complaint direct to the Headmaster, with Morton as their spokesman. I heard all about it later from Mr Wilkes.

'Sir,' Morton apparently said, 'it's embarrassing having a girl playing in the team, regardless of how well she plays. It causes the school to be ridiculed and we get a fair bit of stick from our opponents and we feel it affects our performance. We think it only fair too, that she should have her own changing room as it again causes embarrassment to other members of the team.'

The Headmaster picked up his phone and called the staffroom. 'Ask Mr Wilkes to come to my office, please. We've got a bit of a rebellion in the cricket team.'

They waited in silence until Mr Wilkes arrived and with a quick knock on the door, he entered the Headmaster's study.

'Ah, Mr Wilkes. Young Morton here and his friends want me to make a few changes to the cricket team. Apparently, the team no longer want our star batsman in the side. He has become an embarrassment.'

'Headmaster, I wonder if I might have two minutes with Morton on his own. I'd rather we kept it in the family. Oh, by the way, Morton, who are these others you're talking about? It wouldn't be it Hazard, Shepherd and–' Mr Wilkes didn't have to continue.

'Yes . . . sir,' Morton interrupted.

Wilkes turned to the Headmaster. 'I'll deal with it now, Headmaster.' The Head duly left his office to Mr Wilkes.

'Now, Morton, I'm not going to waste my time talking to you, save to say, you and the others have a choice. Lay off Henry, or I'll go the police.'

Morton went white. 'But, sir, wh–'

'Shut up and listen, Morton. We all know you were one of the people who raped that poor child and we've all the proof we need. In fact, Norman made a statement to say you were the ringleader.'

'That's not true!' Morton shouted, panicking. 'It was Smith!'

'I don't care who the hell it was, but I'll tell you this, if it wasn't for Henry, you would be in prison right now and for a very long time. Now what is it you have to say about the cricket team?'

'Nothing, sir.'

'The thing is, Morton, one, you are nowhere near as good as Henry and, two, you will have to live with your crime for the rest of your life and mark my words, you will have to pay for it eventually. Now get out before you lose your place in the team and the school!'

'Sir!' And with that, Morton promptly left.

For all that, they still tried to make things difficult for me and often did things to embarrass me, hiding my clothes and so on. On one occasion, they managed to steal all my clothes with the exception of my cricket sweater, hoping I would have to walk back to the school like that. Fortunately, the umpire's coat came to the rescue.

It wasn't an entirely wasted year, though. My studies had gone rather well and in particular I had shown a vast improvement in Maths and, although I was no longer able to compete in athletics on equal terms, I won the three prizes for swimming and the cross-country, but they were the last. The worries I had experienced with the bullying did spoil my performance on the cricket field but I still managed the batting prize. Ironically, we had a very successful season and only lost one match, thanks to an all-round team effort, including Hazard's bowling.

The final ignominy of that year took place on the last day but one of the final term. The prefects always had a leaving party and this generally included all those in the cricket First XI, and the rugby XV. It usually meant that it was for the fifth and sixth forms, but occasionally, and it was very occasionally, a younger boy would have been good enough to have been selected.

However, although I had been a First Team member for two years, I was considered too young and was never invited. This year I had been invited, but I genuinely felt it would not be in my interests to go and made my excuses. In the end, I didn't have any choice in the matter as I was pretty much ordered to go to the prefect's private rooms to join in the leaving celebrations. I was told that John Walton would also be there as he was the only other non-fifth or sixth former to be invited (he had been selected for the team as wicket keeper), so I thought that I would have at least one ally.

I arrived at the room to be greeted by the Head Boy.

'Well done, Miss Henry! You have done us proud again,' he said, already slurring his words. 'Have a drink!'

I helped myself to orange squash and sat down, wondering why I had been invited as no one talked to me and I was just left on my own in the corner, giving polite smiles when anyone looked in my direction. I made several attempts to leave, but was ordered back, but by now those eight perverts had joined the group and they were already worse for wear. Then Walton, the only other youngster, was excused and left the party. I thought I would be able to go with him, but they wouldn't let me. Everyone was by now very tipsy and once again I began to fear for my well-being.

I sat and considered what options I had and I decided attack was the best form of defence. I calmly went over to Joseph Smith and quietly asked him whether he was going to try and kill me again and how was he going to do it this time *Poison*? To my utter astonishment, he didn't say a word and simply left the party.

Hazard, who had been staring at me for at least half an hour, only averting his eyes when I returned his glances, suddenly got up and announced in a semi-drunken way, that we were all going to have a dance. A strange idea for a boy's school, if you take my meaning, Mr White, but by now my whole life had become surreal.

Morton was put in charge of the wind-up gramophone and the music started. Hazard immediately asked me to dance and I quietly refused.

'Look, little Miss, I only want a dance. If you make things difficult, I'll make the next hour or so very hard indeed. The choice is yours,' he whispered nastily.

I got up to dance with him, feeling sick as he put his arm around me. I saw him nod to Morton, who changed the music to a slow waltz. Hazard tried to dance, cheek to cheek, which must have been a very odd sight as the other boys began to chant:

'Oooh! Look. Hazard fancies her!'

Their jibes made him act even more strangely. He seemed not to want to let go and when the music stopped, he made a grand show of kissing my hand and bowing. 'Thank you, madam,' he said. He walked me back to my seat, where I turned to him and, with as much dignity as I could muster, said:

'Thank you for not letting those animals kill me. I owe you my life.'

Hazard went deathly pale and was unable to reply.

Fortunately, I was taken off to dance with another prefect and left Hazard simply sitting and staring into space, becoming more and more drunk.

Things took a turn for the worse, however, when someone suggested I should do a striptease. Naturally, I refused, so the boys decided to strip me instead. There were twenty or more of them and I didn't even bother to struggle. They stood me on the table in the middle of the prefects' room and all just leered. I was thankful that this was as bad as it got, but was surprised that some of them had allowed it to happen at all.

The Head Boy called a truce and said I had been a good sport and allowed me to go. All the same, I felt sullied by the whole business, especially when the rumours went round the dorms that I had actually done a striptease and had had intercourse with several of the prefects. Not one of them denied it.

The summer term ended the unhappiest period of my life. I couldn't have imagined that people could be so cruel and no one, apart from Mr and Mrs Wilkes, treated me as a boy anymore. I even heard the teachers referring to me as 'her' or 'she'.

How relieved I was to be back on that train home.

Chapter 7

Mr White, I know you will find it difficult to believe, but home was becoming the better of two evils. Of course, my mother didn't want my father to know what was really going on and in any case he would have refused to listen, so for me the summer holidays were never the same again. I knew what my mother was like and I even pitied her, but my father, who was out in Belgium and France on military business, was a bitter disappointment to me. I always hoped he would try to understand, see things from my point of view. After all, I couldn't help what was happening to me.

We spent most of the time in Le Touquet with my mother and Alice, who was now married but whose husband was abroad with his unit. In some ways I was relieved my father was away because you know, Mr White, whenever a child is in trouble they always turn to their mother and I was no exception, but as I received no help from that direction, I turned to my lovely sister, Alice.

My mother and I hardly spoke to each other during the first two weeks. I spent many hours by myself on the beach, away from everything, just daydreaming about former days when I had enjoyed life and that special Founder's Day Match when I batted with Harry. But I could never quite get away from the problems with my body and the dreadful things that had happened to me.

What was I to do? Whom could I go to for help? Would it get any worse? What would happen when I went back to school? I couldn't stand another year like the last, especially when my father had visited and threatened the Headmaster to keep me in school. I knew in my heart I hadn't got a chance.

You cannot hide anything from your close family and mine was no exception. Alice naturally asked me what was happening to me and I broke down and once again confided everything to her: all my problems, everything – the good and the bad.

'You know, darling, I think we should do something. Just look at you. How could anyone think you were anything other than a girl? We will have to do something and never mind Father. I'll take you to a doctor.'

'No!' I almost wailed. 'I couldn't do that. Please, Alice, I couldn't cope with that,' I added, tears streaming down my face.

Alice said no more and simply put her arms around me, and we stayed like that for several minutes.

From then on Alice became my close confidante, my friend and counsellor; without her I know I would have never pulled through. For some reason – and I really don't know why – from that moment on she wanted me to make the change, burn my boats and become a woman, which in reality, of course, I was. I think it was the fact that she thought my life would be easier that way. I believe Alice did attempt to discuss my difficulties with my mother, who simply ignored her, and that made Alice furious. She knew that my parents' refusal to see the truth left me in limbo.

I remember lying on the beach with Alice just chatting when she suddenly announced: 'You know Alex, you have got to face it: you really are a girl with a tail, not a boy with breasts. I think it very cruel to keep you in this situation. You should be one of us . . . Come on, let's have some fun!' she added.

'What do you mean?' I asked.

'I want you to try it for size.'

'What, for God's sake?' I asked.

'Darling!' she exclaimed. 'You're becoming a woman of course,' Alice replied with that wicked smile on her face when everyone could tell she was up to mischief.

'Alice, I couldn't. Please don't put me through this,' I said, almost pleading.

'Darling, no one knows us here. Try being a girl for a while. Do it for me. We could have some fun. Please just try it. You're very pretty!'

Mr White, I loved my sister dearly, but when I look back I can see that, unintentionally, she brought a lot of confusion in my life. She was so persuasive and I did everything to please her, even dressing up. But as soon as she had gone, I was consigned to limbo again, totally bemused about who and what I was.

No matter what I said, Alice had an answer for everything and I reluctantly agreed to do as she asked. We went down to the beach and sat outside our beach hut and I looked at her; she had everything and I must confess I was a little envious. Maybe I was biased, but she still looked young and attractive and was wearing a very pretty swimming costume with a hat to match. I, on the other hand, was wearing a pair of swimming shorts and my running vest.

Much to Alice's amusement, we were chatted up several times. She even deliberately enticed lads to come over to us. All I wanted to do was to tell them to go away, to tell them that I was really a boy.

'Come on,' Alice pleaded. 'I'll treat you to an ice-cream. I'll race you there!'

She started running and I jumped up and raced after her. It was all done for effect as she had noticed two English boys looking at us; they were obviously trying to decide whether or not they had the courage to come and talk to us.

We arrived at the ice-cream seller who had one of those bicycles with a big tub on the front; you could only have vanilla in a cornet or wafer, not the selection you can have today. We waited in the queue and, sure enough, just as Alice had calculated, the two boys came over to talk to us. Needless to say, she did all the talking.

'My name's Alice and this . . .' she said, standing gently on my toe, '. . . is my little sister, Alex.'

I was dumbfounded. Alice kept looking at me, frowning, trying to stop me from saying anything that would spoil things.

Alice asked the ice-cream seller for two cornets.

'Let me get these for you?' one of the boys asked.

'Oh thank you! That would be nice. Would you like to join us?' Alice asked.

'Alice! What on earth are you playing at?' I whispered to her.

'Just play along. We'll have some fun and God knows you need some!'

We walked back to the bathing hut and sat down on the rugs. Alice moved over to allow Phil to sit down next to her and I had to sit next to David, who seemed intrigued by me.

It was David who opened the conversation. 'Why have you cut your hair so short?'

Alice chipped in: 'You're very rude. It's the latest thing. It's all the rage in Paris.'

'Oh I'm sorry, I didn't mean to be rude. I was just thinking how nice it was,' David replied.

The conversation continued in a similar vein as we ate our ice-creams. Alice answered their questions in her usual extravagant way and I tried to speak as little as possible, hoping that soon it would all be over. Finally, Philip got up and asked Alice if she would like to go for a walk with him. She could see I was petrified of being left on my own with David and suggested we threw ball to each other instead. It was at that moment that Philip spotted the cricket equipment in the hut.

'Who's the cricketer then?' he asked jokingly.

I was just about to answer that it was me when Alice interrupted:

'Our brothers. They're back in England.'

Phil took hold of the bat and proudly announced: 'I like cricket. Come on, we'll teach you how to play.'

'Girls versus the boys and you've got to give us a chance,' Alice demanded. 'The losers can pay for the next round of ice-cream.

That's fair, isn't it?' She gave me a sly wink.

'Well, no, I wouldn't want you to pay at all,' David said, smiling.

'Fair's fair,' I said, suddenly enjoying the situation.

There were some other adolescents, boys and girls, on the beach who were laughing and smiling at our antics and, at Alice's invitation, they joined us. 'It's girls versus boys and the losers buy the ice-creams!' she said with gusto.

Alice was elected captain and she demanded that the girls bat first.

We went to sit on the sand to decide who should go in first And, of course, Alice thought I should.

'Don't let them think you've played before! Hold the bat wrong or something,' she whispered.

I went up to the wicket.

'Come on, Alex!' I heard Alice shout.

I faced the first ball, holding the bat all wrong, and John, one of the other boys, ran up and proceeded to show me the correct way.

'Like this?' I asked.

'Yes, that's it!'

'Now not too fast,' I shouted, which encouraged the bowler to bowl underarm. It was easy to hit for 6. I swung round, pretending to have been lucky.

'Like that?' I asked.

'Yes, like that,' John replied, bemused.

I went on to smash every ball any of them could throw at me, even when they got annoyed and started to bowl fast. After about ten minutes, I handed the bat to the other girls.

'Where did your sister learn to play like that?' Phil asked Alice.

'She didn't! It's the first time today, but she's a fantastic tennis player,' Alice replied, grinning.

It was our turn to bowl and David took delight in showing me how to bowl properly, first putting his arm around my waist, to hold me tight and then holding my right arm straight and accidentally touching my breasts. Afterwards, he didn't stop apologising.

I pretended to get the hang of it, especially as I knew what would happen if I didn't.

John was first in to bat.

'Are you ready?' I asked.

'Yes!'

I bowled and down went his wickets first ball.

'I'm sorry. Were you really ready?' I asked.

'Yes of course,' he replied, baffled.

'Are you sure?' I asked again, 'because if you weren't, we can start again?'

'Yes!' he almost snarled. He threw the bat down onto the sand. Now Phil came in to bat. He hit the first, second, third and fourth for successive runs, but then I sent him a quicker one which bowled him.

'Sorry,' I said politely. 'Am I doing it right?'

'You know you are, you little tinker!' he said, gritting his teeth and trying not to laugh.

I asked the others if they wanted to bowl, but they didn't, so I continued and the boys were all out within a few balls.

'Well, it looks like you have to buy us the ice-creams then!' Alice said, clearly delighted.

We all went off to be treated yet again.

'Come on, you terrible twins, where did she learn to play like that?' David asked.

'Shall I tell them, Alex?'

I looked at her, wondering what the hell she was going to say next.

'She plays for the English junior ladies' team and is their top batsman.' Alice said proudly. 'Now, how about that walk?' she asked the boys, who had stopped in their tracks.

'Well, I hope we can at least do that right,' Phil said.

Alice handed Phil and David our ice-creams while we put the mats back into the beach hut and locked it ready for the walk.

'Alice! What on earth are you doing? What am I supposed to do?'

'Oh, just hold his hand!' she said impatiently 'He'll be satisfied with that.'

'And if he isn't?' I whispered in sheer panic.

'He better be, or he'll answer to your big sister! Now, come on, let's have some more fun.'

We went back to the group, picked up our melting ice-creams and the eight of us began to walk along Paris-Plage with the sun beating down. Eventually, David plucked up courage to ask if he could hold my hand, which, although deep down I was totally embarrassed, I allowed him to do so. I thought how polite he was in the way he had asked but then he spoiled it by once again apologising for touching me where he shouldn't have.

'Forget it! Don't worry about it. I'm not,' I replied a little haughtily.

We all walked slowly along the beach hand in hand, Alice and Phil sauntering close to me.

Alice gave me a sly dig in the ribs, followed by one of her naughty winks. 'I think my sister likes you, David.'

'You bloody . . .' I whispered, to which Alice once again gave me one of those naughty but nice smiles. She was a mischievous creature but I was fond of her. Anyway, it seemed to make David feel good for a while.

We finished our walk and Alice told them we had to go home to dinner.

'Can we see you later?' David asked, but Alice was in command now. Her age and experience was taking over.

'We would love to . . .' My heart sank. '. . . But I'm sorry, we've to go out with our mother tonight. Maybe another time?'

I could see David's face light up. It was a holiday romance in his eyes and it was all because my sister wanted to have a good time. I felt mean and wanted to tell him everything but there was no point as the boys would be returning home long before we were and it would be terrible to ruin their holiday by admitting I was a boy and that David fancied a boy.

'Will you be on the beach tomorrow?' David asked.

'Yes, after luncheon,' I replied unthinkingly.

Both David and Phil were clearly delighted they were going to see us again. As Alice and I walked home, we were unable to stop laughing as we talked about the afternoon and how we had conned them into buying the second ice-creams.

'It's the first time I've seen you laugh for ages,' Alice said, as she grabbed my hand. 'You ought to get out more!'

'Alice, it's easy when I'm with you. But you know I don't feel like a boy or a girl. I'm in the middle somewhere. I think like a boy and react like a boy, and yet I'm a . . .' I couldn't bring myself to say it.

'Alex, darling, you're not a boy and you are going to have to learn how to be a girl. Otherwise you'll be in permanent misery. Come with me tomorrow and we'll have another lovely day.'

The following day we went back to the beach and, of course, our admirers were already there waiting. Alice invited them to join us and we sat on the mats just talking until Phil asked us if we would like to go for a swim. I was wearing the same clothes as the day before. Alice, of course, was wearing another creation. I refused, telling them I had forgotten my bathing costume, but Alice, bless her, had thought of that.

'Don't worry, Alex, you can borrow one of mine. I've brought two with me,' she said as though this was the most natural thing in the world to do. 'Come on, little sister, we'll go in and change,' she said, giving me no chance to argue.

I felt absolutely embarrassed by the whole business, but didn't have the courage to make a fuss. We went into the beach hut to change and, to boost my confidence Alice gave me one of her favourite costumes and helped me get into it.

'Alex, darling, you look wonderful!' she said, as she coaxed me out of the hut. 'Ta-da!' she cried as she walked down the steps onto the sand, holding her arms out wide. I followed behind, hoping no one would notice me, but David's eyes were popping out.

'You look lovely, Alex,' David said, just standing staring at me. I didn't know what to say. I didn't know whether to be flattered or embarrassed. I couldn't really believe that a boy was actually being nice to me.

'Say thank you then Alex,' Alice said as she locked the door and put the key round her wrist.

We all ran down to the sea. It was beautiful day; the sea looked lovely and inviting with hardly a ripple to be seen. I couldn't help but dive under the waves – I hadn't swum since last summer – and did the front crawl, then swam about a hundred yards out, much to the amazement of the others, even Alice.

'Where did you learn to swim like that?' she asked me when I returned.

'Father taught me and so did school,' I replied.

'Is there any end to her talents?' Phil asked Alice.

'She surprises me sometimes,' Alice replied, smiling at me.

We played around in the water for a couple of hours and then dried off in the sun, each getting a little sunburned, but it had been another pleasant afternoon.

David had a bad case of puppy love and followed me round like a lost soul. I think he would have done anything to please me. Then came another nightmare moment when he asked me if I would like to go to the pictures with him that evening.

'Yes, of course she would!' Alice replied before I could gather my wits.

I looked at her, furrowing my brow, hoping that she would shut up.

'Do you speak French then?' I asked.

'No, but the film is a musical and I don't think it will matter that much,' David replied excitedly. 'Do you? Speak French, I mean.'

Again Alice answered for me. 'Yes, she does and very well.'

'Will you meet me at six thirty then?' David asked.

'She'll be there. I'll make sure she is. But remember, David, she's only fifteen and has to be in before ten o'clock.'

'Of course. I'll see you at the cinema then, half past six?' David said, with a smile from ear to ear.

'Yes that will be lovely,' I replied reluctantly.

I watched David walk away as though he were on air.

I was absolutely furious with Alice for putting me in this position and was still remonstrating with her as we walked through the gate of our house, when suddenly Alice almost screamed. She had only just realised I hadn't changed out of the bathing costume. We dared not let my mother see me like that. Alice went in first and made sure my mother was occupied, and then I crept in and went straight to my sister's bedroom.

'Alice, this is not fair,' I told her when she joined me. 'I can't go through with this. I need you there,' I pleaded.

'I can't. Phil's taking me out.'

'Alice, you can't! You're married, remember,' I exclaimed.

'Don't worry, I'm only flirting a little. Of course, I'll be there. Do you honestly think I would let my little sister do this alone? I wouldn't go out alone myself. Anyway, Alex, it will do you good to go. He's harmless and very polite and very, very shy. See if you like it and enjoy everything while you can.'

She lent me a dress and helped me to get ready. Then, to my horror, she called out, 'Mother, come and see Alex!'

'No, please, Alice, don't tell mother! Please!' I begged, but it was too late . . .

My mother walked into the room. I thought she was going to die of shock; it hadn't been that long since she bought me a pair of long trousers. She stood in the doorway and went white, unable to say a word.

'Mother!' Alice said defiantly. 'Let me introduce you to your daughter, Alex. This is what your son really is. Doesn't she look pretty? When are you going to realise that what you're doing is wrong? You have to speak to Father? It's unkind to treat Alex like this . . .'

Mother was almost shaking with confusion. She didn't know what to say and then the words just stumbled out.

'Take that off, Alex, and don't be so silly!'

'She can't, Mother. She's got a date tonight. He's a lovely boy and Alex is going out and I'm going with him,' Alice shouted angrily. Even poor Alice couldn't get the gender correct and often referred to me as him or her.

'Don't be silly! What if someone sees you? Please, Alex, for my sake, take those clothes off.' My mother was close to tears.

I was about to give in when Alice took over again. 'Mother, if you don't let him go, I'll speak to Father and tell him everything . . . I mean it!'

My mother was also in a strange new world; she was very uncomfortable with everything and stormed out of the bedroom without making another comment. Alice put her arms around me.

'Darling, you can't keep on living your life like this. As a boy, everybody is rejecting you, and what has Father done to help you? Nothing except make you into something he wanted you to be . . . a fine cricketer. You grasped at the chance when you were little, but you're not that little boy anymore and you have got to do what's best for you. Not Father! No one knows us here. We can have some fun and I'll be with you all the time and I'll see no harm comes to you. Your big sister will protect you!' She smiled and squeezed my shoulders.

'Come on now, darling,' she continued, as she gave me one of her scarves.

A little later I was waiting at the cinema with Alice in the background. I began to wonder if David had stood me up. But no, I could see him coming along the footpath, grinning all over his face, with Phil close behind, veering off to join Alice and leaving me to face David by myself.

'Hello. Thank you for coming,' he said, trying to break the ice between us.

Few people in the last few years had been so kind to me, so at least I should be kind to the one who had, I was thinking to myself.

'It was nice of you to ask,' I replied warily as he took hold of my hand and led me inside, followed by the dutiful Alice and Phil.

David didn't see too much of the film, as he spent most of the time mooning over me. I suppose it was very flattering and I even let him put his arm around my shoulders, which made Alice smile.

'Alex, we leave tomorrow,' David said, as we walked slowly back to our house, 'Can I write to you?'

'Yes, of course, if you like,' I replied, not really knowing what to say.

David put his arm round my waist and pulled me gently closer to him. I tried to discourage him, but thought what the hell; he's leaving in the morning. We arrived home and stood by the front gate to say our goodbyes. Alice went in to get a piece of paper to write my address on and came straight back. 'Well, aren't you going to kiss her goodnight then?' she asked David.

'Alice!' I shouted in disgust.

'Go on, don't be silly!' she said to me.

'May I?' David asked.

'You might as well,' I said, trying to "play it cool" as they say today.

David took me in his arms and kissed me full on the lips. I was shocked and pulled back a little, but then he kissed me again and I responded. I actually found it quite nice. Alice and Phil left us alone for a few minutes before Alice intervened in loco parentis.

'Come on, David, I've told you she's only fifteen and will have to go in.'

We had our last kiss and said goodbye to each other. David was clearly very upset, but *c'est la vie*, Mr White. It was lovely while it lasted and he really was a nice boy. He even wrote me a letter before we left for England. It was a mushy, sentimental sort of one and it made Alice laugh, but I felt quite sorry for him.

That summer Alice and I spent many more happy hours on the beach, and I always wore her costumes. We drew a lot of attention and, do you know, Mr White, I think I was almost happy. It was as if I was living in a make-believe world, a Neverland far from the real world of my school. I was Wendy all over again.

On the way back to England my mother hardly spoke a word to either Alice or me and I thanked God that there wasn't very much of the holidays left and that I would soon be back on the train to Bankworth. Indeed, September soon came around.

Alice went back to her home in London and I was taken to the station by my mother, still hardly speaking to me. My father was still away and I suspected he was staying away deliberately. Quite frankly, I always thought it was one of the reasons we had spent the whole holidays at Le Touquet, just in case he needed to return to Glengarry. I was sure my mother didn't want him to see what was happening to his wonderful son.

At the station I got into the compartment of the train and put the carriage door window down. My mother moved closer and, as the whistle went and the train began to move, she reached out to touch me.

'Don't worry, darling. I'll be thinking of you!' It was a total surprise.

Alone in the compartment, I wept bitterly.

Chapter 8

It was the usual routine back at school. I still had to sit on my own in class and now even at the dining room table. I think I must have been the first fourth former to be treated badly by everyone, even the first-year juniors; it was humiliating. There wasn't anything for me to do except study, and I spent many of my spare hours with Mrs Wilkes in her home. She even gave me cookery lessons and I often prepared their meals and helped her with the housework in an effort to thank them for their kindness. It was awful to be pitied, but I found that whatever pity there may have been was followed by a genuine fondness for me.

Quite early on in the term, Mr Pounder came to see me and reminded me of my promise that I would play in that year's Christmas production, He confessed that this year he had selected a play with a part which would "utilise your feminine attributes", as he put it.

'What's the play?' I asked.

'It's Shakespeare,' Mr Pounder replied.

'Come on, which one?' I asked, fearing the worst. 'Viola? Rosalind? Imogen?'

'The Taming of the Shrew. I want you to play Kate, of course. I know you'll be very good in it.'

'You must be kidding me. Don't you think I've got enough troubles? When do you want to know?' I asked.

'As soon as possible,' Mr Pounder replied.

I telephoned Alice, who was staying with my mother as her husband was once more in the Middle East, and told her what

Pounder had had the cheek to ask.

'Well, what should I do?' I asked.

'You know me,' she replied. 'You know what I think: do it. Don't hesitate and have some fun. Don't care what they say or think; just do it, darling!'

Alice always gave me so much confidence when we were together or when we spoke to one another but, as soon as I was away from her, it was back to normal. I went to Thelma Wilkes and told her what Alice had said. Thelma was more measured.

'Do you enjoy acting? Can you put up with the teasing? Have you got time to do it?'

'I've got nothing else to do. I can't compete in the sporting activities anymore and, yes, I do enjoy acting once I'm immersed in it. As for the teasing I don't know. I don't think it could get any worse.'

At this moment, Mr Wilkes arrived. He had already heard about Mr Pounder's intentions and that the Head was all for it too; I would add sparkle to the show, apparently.

'It's a big part. Alex. It could help take your mind off other things.'

Mr Wilkes' comment made my mind up for me and the following day I spoke to Mr Pounder and agreed to do it and began in earnest to learn the part. Imagine my horror, then, when Hazard came to see me and told me he was playing Petruchio, Kate's suitor. I felt absolutely sick and couldn't get to sleep the whole night. The following morning I immediately went to see Mr Pounder and found out it was another one of Hazard's sick jokes.

'I can assure you I wouldn't have that young man in my troupe, especially where you are concerned, my dear,' Pounder reassured me. 'Sorry, Alex,' he added, realising his mistake.

'Thank you, sir,' I replied, sounding really relieved.

Alice came to see me at half-term and took me out to my favourite little teashop. We had our usual heart-to-heart where she told me she was still cross with Father and apparently he and Mother had made friends again and that things were back to normal on that front. I hadn't even realised things were so bad between my parents and I felt rather guilty.

Immediately after half-term, Mr Pounder took me into London to visit a theatrical costumier's where I was to be kitted out professionally. I had four different outfits to wear, all very daring and all based on real Elizabethan dresses. The costumier was a right little Mary Ellen and adored sorting things out for me. It was so funny when he tried to work out how I could be from Bankworth Boys' School with a bosom like mine.

'She's from the girls' side,' Mr Pounder said, just to shut him up.

There were naturally a lot of rehearsals and the last few were in full dress because we needed to get used to all those ruffs and the like. My décolletage caused something of a sensation with the boys, so much so the audience grew day by day. This caused some of the other teachers to investigate why there was such a sudden interest in Shakespeare.

Mr Wilkes walked into one of these rehearsals and was disgusted quite frankly; in fact he was so angry that he took me there and then to the Head's study, with Mr Pounder tagging along, for him to decide whether I was decent or not.

The Headmaster looked me up and down and then sent me to the ante room which was attached to his study.

'Shut the door, Henry,' the Head said as I left the room.

I shut the door and sat in a beautiful leather armchair and waited to be called back. I'm sure they didn't realise I could hear every word they said.

'That is my very point, Headmaster,' Mr Wilkes said firmly. 'You addressed him as Henry. If he was a girl, you would have said Alex. This child has already had a very difficult time at this school without us making it even harder and allowing him to be made a fool of. It's unforgivable. I have told you before, Headmaster, I think it's immoral and unfair for him to remain with us. He should transfer to the girls' school . . .'

Mr Wilkes paused to let all sink in before continuing: 'Alex will do anything to help the school and anything to avoid confrontation with his father.'

The Headmaster acknowledged that point.

'I'm sure,' Mr Wilkes went on, 'that's the reason he had agreed to do it in the first place. But what Mr Pounder here is doing is sheer exploitation. It's like some damn freak show and it's not fair on him!'

'I chose her, Mr Wilkes, because she's very good . . .' Pounder protested.

'That's just it, Pounder,' Mr Wilkes said, raising his voice.

'What is?' the Head and Pounder said in unison.

'You've just referred to Alex as her and she! You can't have it both ways. If we think she's a girl, she should be sent to the other school! What chance has the poor child got here?'

'Look, Mr Wilkes, I asked Alex, and she . . . sorry, he said he would do it. It's too late to make any changes now, especially to those dresses. They are specially hired for the job. Even if we had a boy taking the part, the bosom would have to be padded,' Pounder added.

'There we go again!' Wilkes interjected angrily. 'Even if we had a boy! This is a boys' school for God's sake.'

The Headmaster called matters to a halt and said that I should decide what happened for myself. He called me in but before he could begin I told him I had heard everything.

'Well then, young Henry, you've heard it all and now I'm going to ask you to decide. I'll give you until tomorrow evening to make up your mind.'

'Headmaster, that's not fair,' Mr Wilkes remonstrated.

The Head had made his mind up and put me in a terrible position: Heads I win, tails you lose. The decision was made worse as it soon became apparent that the other boys had somehow become aware of the decision I had to make and began putting pressure on me to carry on with the play. I knew what Alice would say and even Mr Wilkes had to agree that really I had no choice. I duly went ahead and the rehearsal audiences grew larger and larger.

Soon after Mr Wilkes' argument with the Headmaster, I

noticed that the attitude of the staff began to change. They all began to call me Alex and not Henry and they began to say more supportive things. It was the first step to improving my lot.

I confess, Mr White, the play was a roaring success and I was its star. In fact, I had never seen anything like the applause we received at the end of the show. Even the staff cheered. The Headmaster made his usual comments about how good we were, but the most amazing comment came from David Wright, who was now the Head Boy.

He stood up and said loudly: 'Alex, you were fantastic. Well done!' The entire audience erupted into cheers again. I thanked them and said I couldn't have done it without Jeremy – he played Petruchio – and we held each other's hand and bowed, which caused some of the boys to whistle.

What had started as a joke by the prefects two years previously was continued as the youngest and smallest boy in the school brought me a bunch of flowers from the prefects and even Hazard smiled as I acknowledged them. The Head had one criticism. My bows apparently showed too much cleavage and this was unsettling the boys.

'Perhaps you had better curtsey, Alex,' he suggested.

The play was so good we were asked to perform it at the Civic Hall to allow members of other schools to see it. It was, you see, one of the Shakespeare plays that had to be read for the English Literature Matriculation Examination.

I had been so disappointed that Alice hadn't been able to make it to the school performances, but she made a special effort to come to the Civic Hall and to my delight, she brought my other sister, Lucy. Once again the play got rave reviews and I was even introduced to the Mayor and Mayoress. The Headmaster was so proud that the school had achieved such good publicity that he announced that there was an open invitation to the Mayor and Mayoress and Bankworth Council to next year's production. 'So put it in your diaries,' he added spiritedly.

'What will it be next time?' the Mayor asked.

'We've not decided yet, but I can promise you it will be every bit as good as this, Mr Mayor.'

'Well, Headmaster, if it's half as good as this one, it will be fantastic,' the Mayor said, and then asked the press photographer to take a picture of him alongside Jeremy and me. Not once, Mr White, did anyone mention that I was a Bankworth boy. No one ever questioned it and I just went along with it for everyone's sake.

Lucy came backstage after the performance to see me.

'You were wonderful, Alexander,' she said, looking me up and down. We hadn't seen each other for over two years, possibly three, and clearly no one had filled her in. I know it was the same for her as she asked 'How did you make your bosom look so . . . realistic?'

'I'll explain later. It's a trick of the trade,' Alice said, not giving me the chance to speak.

'No come on, tell me. I shan't say anything.'

We were interrupted by Mr Pounder and the Headmaster coming into the dressing room. Oh, by the way, Mr White, as we were in the Civic Hall, I had my own dressing room. Jeremy, Petruchio, had the star's dressing room because he was a prefect, but I had the number two room, which made me feel wonderful.

The two men once again congratulated me. The Headmaster turned to Alice and Lucy.

'And who are these young ladies?' he asked.

'They are my sisters, sir. This is Alice and this is Lucy.'

'Oh, how do you do? It's a pleasure to meet you,' he said, shaking their hands. 'Hasn't she done well? I think it's her best performance yet.'

I was dumbstruck. In fact, if there had been a big hole somewhere, I would have jumped in.

Mr Pounder compounded the fracture. 'For her age, she's incredible. Well done, Alex, well done!' And then they both left, oblivious to the ruins they left behind.

I could see Lucy eyeing me more closely.

'Come on, you two. What's all this–'

Alice interrupted and, with no thought for anything, simply said, 'Look, Lucy, Alex is a girl . . .' And pointing to my bosom, she added, 'Those, darling, are real!'

'No!' Lucy collapsed into a nearby chair. Eventually, she managed to say, 'How embarrassing! What on earth are we going to tell people?' Appearances were everything for Lucy, I'm afraid.

'Don't you start, we've had enough of that from Father without you becoming another bloody stupid person,' Alice retorted, defending me to the hilt.

I began to change out of the costume, Lucy looking on as though I was a freak. Quite frankly I was hurt. Alice saw it and tore into her.

'If you knew what our sister has been through since she was eleven you wouldn't look like that.'

Alice then gave Lucy a potted history of my short life including the rape. I hardly heard a word. I sat in front of the mirror with my head in my hands, sobbing. I don't remember much else until Lucy came and put her arms around me and kissed the top of my head.

'You poor darling, I had no idea what you've been going through. I'm so sorry,' Lucy said, kissing my head again.

'Well, Lucy darling, let me introduce you to our new sister, Alexandra,' Alice announced, trying to cheer me up.

There was a knock at the door as Mr Pounder once again marched in. 'What on earth is the matter with you?' he asked when he saw my tear-smudged make-up.

'She's just so happy that everything went so well,' Alice replied. Lucy nodded in agreement.

The Christmas holiday was a strange affair. Only Alice really wanted me to stay with her. Then Lucy invited me for three days as her husband was away. I know she didn't want me to meet him in my state and anyway, I suspected she only wanted to hear the juicy side of the story. I spent a little time at home, but my mother left me to look after myself; it was a case of never the twain shall meet. My father, of course, stayed right away.

I returned to school with only a simple, 'Goodbye, I'll see you soon,' from my mother.

The spring term was like no other I had faced. I was bored stiff. All I had was my studies. I wasn't allowed to swim. I couldn't compete in the Senior Cross-Country. It was considered too much for a young lady and yet I knew deep down I would have given them a run for their money. I wasn't allowed to do PE with the boys anymore as Arnett had complained that it put the others off, especially in the gym. It was his way of getting rid of me for good: there was no one now to compete against his favourites. I just simply ran round the fields on my own, keeping fit and occasionally playing with my father's training bat against the wall in the playground.

Towards the middle of the term, Hazard gave one of the other prefects a beating because he had teased him about liking me. Hazard had to prove he didn't and once again he began to torment and to bully me. The routine of tipping me out of my bed began and I was dragged down the dorms and taken to his room, which was now out of sight. Once again my body was covered in blotches and bruises from the onslaughts and once again, Mr Wilkes asked me where I had got them and knew I wouldn't tell him; but we all knew that, if I was honest and told him, my life would be less worth living than it already was.

Hazard took every opportunity to prove he was 'anti-Alex'. One day, when he was competing in the Senior Cross-Country race, I happened to be passing by when the house team were having their communal steaming-hot bath in the washroom.

'Come here, Gloria,' he shouted through the open door. I took no notice and walked on. Hazard, with several of the others, jumped out of the bath stark naked and ran after me. I ran like fury as they chased after me. It took only one shout to others boys in the area and I was caught and handed over to the naked Hazard and his merry men. I was carried into the washroom and thrown fully clothed into the bath, immediately followed by the ten or so other boys who had left the bath to chase me. They sat round the edge of the bath as they passed me round like a parcel, pushing me under water as they did so.

Eventually, I was allowed to get out of the bath with everybody's hands groping everywhere and allowed to change. Into what? That was my next problem; I hadn't got a clean or dry set of clothes. I had two alternatives: one was to go to Mr Wilkes and ask if I could go there and have some tea with them and dry my clothes at his place, or go with the rest of the boys in my dressing gown and have tea in the dining room. I did just that and walked into the dining room with just my dressing gown on, watched in absolute silence by everyone.

I seemed to be gaining more and more courage from adversity and simply walked to the table and sat down. George Wilberforce, the new French teacher, was the master on duty asked. 'Alex, what has happened to your clothes?'

'It would appear I have got them all wet, sir,' I replied in the still deathly silence.

'Well, you can't sit around like that,' he continued.

'Tell her to take them off then, sir,' one of the boys shouted, which caused uproar in the dining hall and soon everyone was chanting: 'Off, off, off, off!'

It took some time for Wilberforce to restore order, but a few clips round the ear brought us quickly back to reality.

'What am I supposed to do then, sir?' I asked when the din had died down.

Wilberforce was stumped.

'Just hurry up and finish your tea and go to the dorm. I'll see what we can do to get you some dry clothes . . . and you lot . . .' he continued, ' . . . I want to know what happened to Alex's clothes. If I don't know by the end of the evening there will be trouble. Do I make myself clear?' There were a few feeble "Yesses".

'Well do I?' Wilberforce repeated more sternly, to which the whole dining room erupted with a loud, 'Yes, sir!'

It wasn't my fault and yet I knew I would be blamed for what had happened. Hazard and his cronies owned up but were punished lightly as they told the Head I had been walking on the side of the bath fully clothed and had fallen in by accident when one of the lads had grabbed my leg. No one could remember which one it was, so they all took the blame. The Headmaster didn't believe them one jot, but had to accept what was said: ten against one, of course. The five prefects among them lost privileges for a week and the others were grounded for two weeks. It was becoming more obvious to everyone that I wasn't really wanted in the boys' school and perhaps, deep down, I no longer wanted to be there.

Cricket, of course, Mr White, should have been my great consolation that term. But even that proved less than a pleasure. I didn't perform as well and Hazard, who was a good bowler and very popular with the rest of the team, contrived to make my life a misery even out on the field. I didn't make a score over forty for most of the season, but it was still enough to keep me in the team. It was half-term and I didn't want to go home and face the possibility of meeting my father, which in itself tore me apart, and I was sure my mother couldn't face any further strain on their relationship, so instead, I elected to face a worse torment.

It was Saturday 14th June 1931. We had played our arch rivals, Richton, away and won, largely thanks to Hazard's bowling. I had scored a measly 32, having been bowled by a very straight ball, I had simply lost concentration and, to make matters worse, when we went out to field, I dropped an easy catch off Hazard, who was bowling as if he were on fire.

'You stupid woman!' he yelled at me, much to my and everyone's embarrassment, and then to my eternal shame, he sent me out to the boundary.

'You can daydream out there all you like. At least you won't do any harm!'

I walked to the boundary with my head bowed. Our Captain, John Banks, admonished Hazard, but the damage had been done. Mr Wilkes, who was our umpire, also made a comment to Hazard at the end of the over. Nonetheless, he was the man of the match, taking seven wickets for 54 runs.

'It could have been eight!' he snarled at me as we walked off the pitch victorious.

'Don't worry!' John Banks said quietly. 'You did well.'

That was scant consolation, as now I had to face more torment from Hazard in the changing room.

'What's she doing now?' he asked rhetorically. 'Trying to cover her tits up, no doubt.' He grabbed hold of my chest, which he began forcefully massaging. 'If I had a pair of these,' he said, 'I would be playing with them all day. Do you play with them all day, Gloria?'

'Hazard, shut your bloody mouth and leave him alone!' John Banks shouted. 'We've had enough of your behaviour.'

Mr Wilkes had heard the commotion and reiterated what Banks had said and matters calmed down. Even so, some of the lads had sided with Hazard and had joined in the banter. We all got on the team charabanc, minus Mr Wilkes and the Captain, who had both gone to look after another boy, one of our supporters, who had been taken ill. He had given strict instructions that the prefects were to ensure everything and everybody returned to school. Hazard and his cronies were the most senior prefects so I'm sure you can imagine what the result was. He immediately started to throw his weight around and directed his efforts towards me. The poor unfortunate sitting next to me was physically lifted from his seat and jettisoned to another and Hazard sat next to me.

'Gloria wants me to sit next to her. Don't you, Gloria?' he whispered, rubbing his hand around my cheek and chin in a mock show of tenderness.

I didn't answer. 'Don't you, Gloria?' he repeated more loudly, but again I didn't answer.

The Barratt brothers now also got involved. One stood

behind my seat and the other in the gangway. I could see they were ready for action.

'Don't you, Gloria?' Hazard shouted.

'Yes, yes, yes, *yes*!' I yelled. 'Now leave me alone. Please leave me alone.'

The driver pulled in and stopped the coach; I think it was to tell us to calm things down, but Hazard would have none of it. He stood up on his seat and sarcastically announced: 'She wants to be left alone and I thought she wanted me!'

'Come on, let's see your tits,' he continued shouting. 'Come on, Gloria. Show us your tits. We want to see them. Don't we, boys?'

Several of the boys began chanting, 'Show them! Show them! Show them!'

'Come on, Gloria, don't be mean. Let's see them,' Hazard yelled, whipping up more and more support.

'Oh for God's sake, leave me alone,' I cried, but my plea fell on deaf ears. I was pulled into the gangway and they began. It seemed as if everyone was trying to get involved, in spite of the gangway being small, but I fought and struggled with every bit of strength I had and used everything I could, fists, legs and feet, teeth and even my fingernails.

'Oooh, she's scratched me,' came the inevitable jibe.

I was screaming for them to stop, but even the coach driver carried on as though nothing was happening; perhaps he was too terrified or perhaps even he wanted to see what it was all about. They tore my shirt from my body, then my vest and the scarf I used to hold in my breasts, but still they hadn't finished. My underpants and socks were also pulled off with such force, I screamed in pain.

Finally I was naked and by now the driver had pulled in.

Hazard shouted in triumph: 'Look, she hasn't got any balls.'

But no one answered.

There was complete silence; they had achieved their goal. I was naked on the floor and had nothing to cover myself with. Most just stared – they had never seen a naked woman before in their lives and this was the nearest thing to it. I struggled to my feet sobbing. I wanted to shout and scream but nothing would come out. I saw a piece of my clothing in front by the driver and walked towards it, the boys parted, allowing me to pass. Even the driver was open-mouthed as he took in my feminine curves. I picked up my shirt and put it on; every button had been ripped off. One of the boys at the back picked up another piece of clothing and held it out to me, and once again I slowly walked between them, covering as much of my chest and body as I could, like some coy young woman who had been seen by the opposite sex for the very first time.

Other pieces of clothing were picked up and handed back to me, all in complete silence. For once I had the impression that some had realised they had gone too far. I got dressed and sat down, but Hazard wasn't satisfied; he felt he was losing the initiative and started again.

'Move over, Gloria. Let me sit next to you. After all, you know you like me.' Only his creeps laughed this time but now there was something forced about their chuckles.

The driver restarted the coach and pulled out onto the road. After a few minutes, Hazard asked the driver to stop at the next pub as it had an off-licence. Hazard, who was eighteen and looked even older, left the coach, returning with a crate of beer and, I think, bottles of whisky. He and his cronies then proceeded to conceal them in among their cricket gear, tipping the coach driver a few coins to keep his mouth shut.

Back at school, I wanted nothing more than to have a bath and go to bed. I wanted to bury myself in some hole and hide myself until the end of term. In earlier years, my sporting abilities had won me respect of sorts, but now even that was away from me. I had become a mere object of curiosity, a spectacle subject to a hundred inquisitive little eyes that wanted a quick look at some freaky thing that might or might not be a female.

It was around eight o'clock that I finally got into bed, but sleep was out of the question. The stress and mental fatigue, I suppose, were too much. I couldn't get to sleep and kept tossing and turning and hoping everything would go away and let me return to happier times.

James came to bed about half past nine and in his way I knew he was trying to comfort me when he said: 'Well played today, Alex! Good knock. Night.'

'Night, James,' I replied, knowing full well he would have heard everything – all the rumours, all the lies, all the gossip – and that even he wouldn't want to talk to me or acknowledge me too much, for fear of being 'tainted'. I turned over and tried to relax.

It was about eleven o'clock when Hazard came to my bed.

'Come on, Gloria, get out of bed.'

I pretended I was asleep and ignored him.

'Gloria, I'm talking to you. Get out of bed. Now!' he shouted. I still ignored him and with that, he grabbed hold of the bed and tipped it over, throwing me onto the floor.

James tried to intervene. 'Come on, Hazard, leave him alone!'

'She's not your girlfriend. She's mine, so mind your own bloody business.'

'Come on, don't you think you've done enough today already?' James persisted.

'Were you listening?' Hazard said as he turned over James' bed, too. James leapt up and held up his hands as if to fight, but Hazard didn't wait for further comment. He grabbed me by my hair and pulled me through the dormitories to his room. For the boys, it was another peepshow, as they watched the spectacle of this crazed boy hauling me past them all, pleading and screaming.

'Lie down!' Hazard yelled at the first and second years. 'If I see any of you with your head up, you'll suffer the same fate. Understand?'

Of course no one answered; they were all too scared to show their faces.

'Please, Hazard, please let me go,' was all I could say as I was pulled the final few yards to his room. He dragged me in, almost throwing me the last few yards. The moment we were in, the door was locked and the light switched on, to reveal the Barratt brothers, Les and Dennis and Ian Williamson; they were all fully dressed and had been drinking. The room stank of alcohol and body odour and so did their breath as they taunted me.

'Strip off!' Les Barratt ordered.

I ignored him.

'You heard him, Gloria,' Hazard said.

'Please leave me alone. I've never done anything to you,' I pleaded.

'You have! You dropped a bloody catch,' he replied.

'Please, I didn't do it on purpose.'

'Gloria, you have two choices: either you strip yourself or we strip you off and that way will not be pleasant.'

'If I do it, can I go then?' I begged.

'Yes,' Hazard replied. 'Is that all right with you boys?'

They all nodded, so I began to strip off. I undid my pyjama jacket, button by button, finally leaving the jacket partially open. Hazard and Les Barratt were clearly aroused. They were just staring at me as I trembled in fear. Suddenly, Williamson pulled my pyjama cord and my trousers fell down to my feet. A murmur of desire went through the room. Williamson gently slipped my pyjamas off me and once again I was standing naked.

I bent down to pick my trousers up and put them on again.

'What are you doing?' Hazard asked nastily.

'You said I could go if I stripped off.'

'That was then. This is now,' Les Barratt breathed in my ear, giving it a little kiss as he did so.

He put his face near mine. 'Do you want another?'

He started to smile but my spit aimed directly at his face hit him in his eye. He jumped back in disgust, wiped his face on my clothes and slapped me hard across the face, knocking me to the floor. I tried to crawl to the door only to be stopped by Williamson, who jumped on my back like some jockey. They all began stripping off and were ready to take whatever they could get. I managed to grab my trousers and tried again to pull them up but couldn't. Hazard lifted me up so my trousers fell to the floor. I was fighting like an injured dog, knowing that losing would mean the end. Hazard couldn't manage with my onslaught and was forced to get Williamson's help.

'Hold the little bitch still,' Hazard called to Williamson.

They passed me to those Barratt bastards, who began, gently at first, to massage me and then lifted me on the bed and began to feel me all over, more roughly now.

Panic set it and I screamed. 'Don't do this to me!'

But they took no notice and carried on as though I was the victor's spoils, enjoying it all the more I struggled. I continued to scream until Hazard covered my mouth with a pillow to stop me.

I struggled to free my mouth from the pillow and wriggled violently to stop their hands from groping me, to no avail.

Williamson had taken over from Hazard and covered my mouth; the Barratt brothers had got hold of my arms and legs; and Hazard was on top of me. I'm talking about four very fit eighteen-year-olds against one very sensitive fifteen-year-old child.

'Do you remember this, Gloria?' Hazard asked. 'Do we need the grease today?'

He didn't wait for an answer. 'Turn her over and don't let her scream,' he ordered the others.

I saw his eyes. He was once again like a wild animal after the female, the dog after the bitch, and he must have seen my eyes fill with terror the moment before they turned me over.

My face was pushed into the pillow. Williamson held down my head and shoulders, while those two bastard brothers opened my legs wide apart, and Hazard leaned across my body to prevent me wriggling. The moment my legs were fully open Hazard forced himself into me once again. There wasn't a thing I could do. I couldn't even scream in pain. He spent at least five minutes assaulting me, watched by the others as they eagerly awaited their turn. By the time the third one was on me I couldn't resist anymore; I was too hurt and exhausted and once again, I was bleeding profusely. When those three animals finished their turn, they made way for Williamson but he declined. I was thankful for that but it wouldn't have made any difference. They had had their way with me for the second time and now they sat on the bed exhausted.

Thank you, Gloria,' Hazard said sincerely and then added, 'I think you should get dressed now and go back to your bed.'

They threw my pyjamas at me, but I couldn't move. 'Get up!' Hazard ordered, but I couldn't.

Williamson was beginning to panic a little and said hurriedly, 'Come on, sit up, Alex, I'll help you get your jacket on.'

'Get her to the bathroom!' Hazard ordered, now beginning to panic too.

Williamson ran ahead to the prefects' bathroom to draw a hot bath and I was carried along and almost thrown into it.

'You should be getting used to that by now,' Barratt remarked.

I could have killed him there and then. Hazard could see I was angry.

'I think she's cross, I'd watch out if I were you!'

I got out of the bath and collapsed to the floor. Williamson dried me and helped me put the jacket on. I stood up, revealing a massive pool of blood beneath me.

'Christ!' Williamson exclaimed. 'Look at this!'

'Give her a few towels. They'll just think she's had a period,' Barratt said, laughing.

Williamson was stony-faced. 'It's not bloody funny. This will take some explaining,' Williamson said, trying to get the others to see some sense.

Williamson wrapped me in a few towels and Hazard told me to go my bed. I was wet through and it took me nearly ten minutes to reach my bed, a journey which would normally take just one. A few boys were sitting up in bed, watching me as I passed, sliding my feet across the polished wooden floors as it was my only means of movement. One or two of them uttered words of comfort and sympathy to me.

'Hard luck, Henry. Don't worry, they're leaving soon,' one whispered.

James, my bedfellow, and one or two others got out of bed to come and help me into bed. It seemed like the first real kindness anyone had shown for several months.

As they lifted me up onto the bed, James saw what had been done to me.

'Oh God, the bastards, look what they have done!' he exclaimed to the others.

One of the other lads broke into the sewing room and stole a couple of sheets and James wrapped them round me.

Everyone went back to bed and eventually I fell asleep, vowing revenge on the whole pack of them.

I missed another weekend of cricket and once again I had Mr Wilkes asking what on earth the matter was. I confessed that it had happened all over again but this time I wouldn't give him the names of those involved. He knew very well, however, who they were.

My first act of revenge came quite by accident. I was back on the cricket field, playing in the house match. I was facing a spinner from the opposition and had noticed that Peter Wales was fielding at square leg, which, as you will know, Mr White, is just behind where the batsman is standing, about twenty feet away from the bat. The bowler had made a few good balls, giving me a little difficulty in hitting them; in fact I had popped two of them up and they could have easily been caught. The bowler consulted with his captain and Peter Wales was brought in and was only about four or five feet from the bat. The next ball was similar and I popped this one up too, but Wales missed it.

I don't know whether it was my imagination or not, but I saw that grin on his face, the one he had when he raped me and I was angry. The next ball was a bit wider and I cracked it with all my might, He didn't stand a chance: the ball hit him full on the nose, slitting his cheek almost from nose to ear. He was out cold and had to be taken to hospital. The match was abandoned, to be replayed on another day, and when it was replayed, he was still absent.

Wales returned to school some four or five weeks later in a terrible mess; there was no reconstructive surgery in those days as we have today, so he was left with a terrible scar on a squashed face. I couldn't say sorry – he'd never said that to me – in fact, I said something terrible.

He came up to me with his hand out. 'I hope there will be no bad blood between us, Alex?'

I ignored his hand and walked away. 'Your face is as ugly as my arse. I hope it's as painful.'

But my first real chance of revenge came when Hazard and his cronies had once again been drinking and were being very loud. The whole school knew what was going to happen to me. It was the same procedure, except that this time Hazard and Les Barratt didn't even ask me to get out of bed. I volunteered to go along.

When we arrived at Hazard's room the others hadn't yet arrived.

'Come on, Gloria, get them off.'

I began to remove my clothes and I could tell they were both excited, so I played along a little and then I had an idea. I tried to be a little sexy, pretending to do a striptease. They were well and truly into it, and I persuaded them both to strip off. I would give them something else, I told them, something that they would never forget. You have never seen anyone take their clothes off as quickly as those two did. They were desperate for the experience.

'Come here!' I said as sexily as I possibly could. 'Come on . . . closer,' I whispered. I began to stroke their penises gently. 'Lie down!' I commanded.

They were like lambs to the slaughter.

The one thing that all that cricket practice had given me was very strong wrists and hands that had a grip of iron and it wasn't long before I had Hazard's testicles in my right hand and Les Barratt's in my left. I began crushing them with all my might.

Both were screaming with pain and both were incapable of movement. I dug my nails deep into Hazard's testicles and stood on his stomach and pulled. The blood came pouring out of him and I could see one of his testicles almost out of its bag. His screams must have been heard by the whole school, but no one came.

Barratt started pleading with me, saying how sorry he was and that he would do anything and, of course, Mr White, I let him go . . . after he suffered the same fate.

They were in a terrible mess and were unable to get up and unable to stop the bleeding.

I ran down to the other Barratt's room, knowing he would be along to Hazard's shortly. I knocked on the door.

'Come in!'

I couldn't believe my luck: he was in bed. I pretended to be terrified.

'Hazard has ordered me to come and give you a thrill,' I said, showing him a hint of bosom. 'Can I get in?' I asked him.

'Yeah!' he answered excitedly and pulled the sheets back to allow me to jump in. It was all too simple with him, as he was already enlarged. I simply grabbed his scrotum, squeezed as hard as I possibly could and twisted it around as I jumped out of his bed. The blood spurted everywhere and I knew they, all three would need surgery.

I walked back to the dorm, passing by Hazard's room on the way and I remember popping my head round the door and shouting, 'Perverts!'

I walked along the dorm. Everyone was wide awake and smiling. 'Well done, Henry!' 'Good for you, Alex!'

I made a slight detour and went to the bathroom and took a bath, totally against the rules at this time of night, but at this moment I felt good with the world and I wanted to wash the smell of them off me. I eventually returned to my bed and listened as the ambulance men took the three unfortunates away to hospital. I confess, Mr White, it was sweet. I enjoyed shouting 'perverts' again as they passed. The ambulance men would think they were homosexual, which as you know was still illegal in those days, and they would be frowned on. I knew they wouldn't dare say how it had really happened as they knew I would have had no hesitation in revealing all. The upshot of it all was that they were suspended from school and never returned and my life became just that bit better.

I reported Williamson for his small part in the second affair and he was caned in front of us all and suspended until the next term. He was eternally grateful I didn't let the Head have quite all the details.

The following day I went to see Mr Wilkes, who simply asked, 'Were they at it again, Alex?'

'Yes. I knew they would be. They were drunk and for the first time I took advantage of them.'

'Well done, Alex, but be careful!'

The next four weeks until the end of term were a delight. I was much happier and it showed. I played in five matches, scoring 400 runs, including 160 not out in the Founders Day Match, which is still the school record. And I still retained the batting prize.

I was happy the year was out and prayed that, now Hazard and his cronies had gone, I would have a better life.

I returned home with my honour intact; I was dying to show my father my batting prize, though I suspected somehow he wouldn't be around. I arrived at our station to be greeted by Alice and I wanted to tell her what I had done, but she wasn't herself and seemed very anxious.

'Hello, darling,' she said as I walked up to her.

'Hello, Alice. What on earth is the matter?' I asked.

'I'm afraid Father and Mother have been arguing bitterly about you.'

'What about?' I asked

'About what to do about you, of course,' Alice replied.

I couldn't believe it. I had experienced all that trouble at school and now I feared I was going to get it at home, too.

Alice and I took the bus to our village and walked slowly back to the house. I didn't want to go in, but Alice linked my arm and we walked in together.

My mother came to greet me.

'Hello, Alex, dear. How are you?' I saw that she looked tired and haggard.

'I'm fine, Mother. Where's Father?' I asked stupidly, eager to show him my new cricket trophy.

'He's busy in the study right now,' she replied. 'I shouldn't disturb him at the moment. He's not in the best of moods and I think he wants to be left alone.'

I was devastated and my mother really didn't know what to say. I could see that she was nearly in tears and didn't want to talk, but it was Alice who broke the painful silence:

'Come on, Alex; let's get your things upstairs.'

Mr White, I know this is going to sound strange, but I actually felt as though I was walking to my own funeral. Everything was happening in slow motion; it all seemed unreal and I thought I was having some kind of bad dream that wouldn't stop.

Somehow, Alice got me upstairs and I sat down on the bedroom chair, completely numb. The world began turning in the opposite direction and I didn't know which way to go. Alice brought me a drink and suggested we went out for some fresh air. I remember agreeing, but I don't remember doing it. We walked back down the stairs and I saw my mother walking into the study to talk to Father, slamming the door behind her. It didn't shut properly and was left ajar.

Alice wanted me to go straight into the garden, but I stood on the bottom step of the stairs as I heard my mother's raised voice.

'You can't be like this! You can't ignore him. He's your child, whatever he is!'

'What am I supposed to do? Dress him in ladies' clothes after all these years telling my friends what a wonderful sportsman he is and how well he is doing, winning this and that. He's a damned embarrassment!'

'But he's still done these things and they are still things we can be proud of . . .' my mother replied in obvious distress, her voice shaking with emotion.

'I'm going to stay in London until he goes back to school,' my father roared.

'Please don't do this,' my mother begged. 'Please don't do . . . !' Her voice broke as she began crying loudly.

'I don't want to live under the same roof as that . . . that boy, that child . . . Whatever he is . . . he's a bloody freak!' he shouted.

Alice was touching me as my father stormed out of the study. Later she told me that I had just stood there, my mouth wide open, trying to scream, but nothing would come out. My father stopped and looked at me and just for a few seconds, I saw deep regret in his eyes.

That was the last time I saw Father for many years.

I was ill for about three weeks in all and every day Alice would sit on my bed and reminisce about all the good times we had shared together, especially our holiday in Le Touquet. Gradually, under the influence of her unremitting cheerfulness, I began to pull myself together. Eventually, Alice decided that it would be a good idea if we were to spend the rest of the summer at Le Touquet and get some sun on us. I was getting very pale and thin, she chided and then news came that my school would be closed for an extra three weeks as they were fitting new boilers. For Alice and me this was like manna from heaven: seven whole weeks in Le Touquet! Alice was even more excited than me. My mother decided she would come for just the first week.

'Wait till I get you there and wait till Mother's gone!' Alice whispered, laughingly.

That first week in Le Touquet, my mother tried to convince me that my father hadn't meant what he had said. It was only said because he had lost his little boy. To Alice, this was like a red rag to a bull.

'Oh so he does recognise he has lost his son. Why then does

he leave him in a boys' school? Why, Mother? Why? How can he be so insensitive?'

My mother couldn't answer but on the day she left to return to England, she promised she would speak to my father about transferring me. Deep down, I didn't want her to as I thought that somehow there was still a chance that I would be normal again, that my father would come round, that he would become what he had always been – my best friend.

As soon as my mother stepped onto the ferry, Alice and I began our heart-to-hearts. I once again confessed everything to her, all the terrible things that had happened to me since our last holiday, not leaving a thing out. She was desperately sorry for me; every time I mentioned something terrible, she would squeeze me tight.

Our conversations took me out of myself. She made me come to terms with my situation and move on.

My greatest worry was my real sexual position in life. What was I? In my head, and by upbringing, I was a boy, but in reality I was a girl, and at that point in life when you are mixed up in any event, life was a nightmare.

'Darling, I know what I believe, and I'll never refer to you as him. From now on you are going to be my little sister. You can't go back and from now on I'm going to call you Alexandra.

Anyway, darling, whatever you do, you can't get rid of those lovely tits, can you?'

'Alice!' I shouted. I was utterly shocked at what she had just said. I had never heard anyone in the family use disgusting words before.

'Oh tits, tits, tits, tits!' she said and we just sat laughing.

Alice took me into Le Touquet window-shopping and to buy a few groceries. She saw a new bathing costume in the window of this very fashionable boutique. We walked in, with Alice looking as vampish as ever and with me wearing my normal masculine trousers and a sailor's top.

I was waiting for Alice to come out of the changing room, when suddenly I heard the young shop assistant say,

'Monsieur!' I turned round to see her holding a chair for me, inviting me to sit down. In the changing room, Alice's ears pricked up and in her perfect French she admonished the young assistant.

'Mais c'est ma petite soeur!' she said almost angrily.

'Je suis désolée, mademoiselle!' the assistant replied, clearly flustered and bemused.

Alice came out of the changing room.

'You look lovely, Alice, really lovely!' I said to her.

'Yes, I agree, but I think you should have one just the same, but in a different colour. She gave her orders to the assistant.

'Alexandra, come on, try this on,' Alice said, handing me the costume.

'Alice! What are you doing?'

'Never mind, try it on; do as you are told. Go on, put it on,' Alice ordered.

I reluctantly went into the cubicle and tried the costume on, stepping out to let Alice see.

'You look sensational, darling!' Alice exclaimed as I made my entrance.

'Oui, absolumment ravissante!' the assistant said, obviously trying to make amends for her error.

'I'll take them both,' Alice said as I went back into change. But she hadn't finished with that and insisted I had a skirt and shirt as well. 'They'll be good for everyday casual wear, shopping and the like,' Alice remarked.

I could do anything as long as I had Alice with me, but it was what would happen when she wasn't there that worried me.

It was the height of the season at Le Touquet and the August sun brought everyone out onto the beach. We made the most of it. It was a repeat of last year with the exception that it was Alice who got most of the attention. Several young men fell for her, but of course got nowhere. We went everywhere together; she looked after her little 'sister' almost as a mother should and by the time it was necessary to go back to school, I was almost back to normal, whatever that meant. I don't mean that I had overcome the trauma of my existence, but I had come to terms with it and I had begun to rationalise things. Alice had almost convinced me that I was her sister and I even thought my life would be easier and better if I was. The problem was I always had my father in the back of my mind and I didn't want to hurt him.

Chapter 9

Back at Bankworth, I made the usual dash to get the bus straight away on arrival. I felt almost optimistic: at least Hazard and his cronies would be no longer at the school to torment me. I went to my dorm and unpacked my case. James was now a first-year prefect and no longer slept in the dorm, so I waited eagerly to find out who my new bedfellow was.

However, it soon became clear that I was still considered a leper. No one wanted to sleep next to me and for several days, I had no bedfellow. Then, when a late-arriving first-year finally had to been given the next-door bed, he showed obvious reluctance and this in spite of the fact he didn't even know me.

I had no alternative but to concentrate on my studies. I had been reasonably successful with Maths and obviously French and I decided to concentrate on those subjects for my matriculation. Mr Fisher, of whom I wasn't that fond, persuaded me to take German more seriously and add it to my repertoire, quite wisely as it turned out. He had fought the Germans in the Great War and he anticipated more trouble in the future. All the same, he loved nothing better than to quote from the great German poets, Goethe and Schiller, Heine and Rilke.

Quite soon into term, Mr Pounder came to see me, to remind me that the Headmaster had invited the Mayor and other important guests to our next Christmas play. This year he intended to build the play around me. I was naturally flattered but just as naturally worried, too.

'Alex we all know what you have been through and I must admit I have thought long and hard before asking you to play this part. But I know that, if you do it, you will be good . . . no, superb!'

Even at that age I knew a sales pitch when I heard one. 'You want me to play another female part, don't you?'

'Yes. It's to play Alice in *Alice Through the Looking Glass*. It's especially important this year as we are having His Majesty's Inspector of Schools visiting us at the time of the production and we would like the very best for him. Will you do it? If not for me, then for the school,' Mr Pounder asked.

This year I was determined to decide for myself, by myself and now I didn't care what others thought of me.

'I'll do it, sir!'

'Really?'

'Yes, sir.'

Later in the week I was summoned by the Headmaster as he and Mr Wilkes had matters of great importance to discuss with me. I duly arrived to be greeted by both men with smiles all over their faces.

'Henry,' the Head said, beginning in his normal formal way. 'First of all, I would like to thank you for being courageous enough to take the part in this year's play. You have been told how important it is to the school.'

'Yes, sir. I'm very happy to do it,' I replied.

The Headmaster continued: 'We know you have had to face terrible problems at school and we've done our best to punish the culprits. That business–'

'It was rape, sir,' I interrupted. Out of the corner of my eye I saw Mr Wilkes put his finger to his lips.

'Well, whatever, young man. Anyway, we've decided to give you your own room, like the prefects have, but at the end of one of the girls' dormitories . . .'

For a moment I was shocked: they wanted to put me with the girls. I stood absolutely flabbergasted and silent, until Mr Wilkes broke the silence.

'Alex, I feel it will be better for you . . . and safer. You will still have your lessons in the boys' school; still have your activities with the boys . . . Unless you want to do some with the girls?'

'No fear, sir. I'll take my chances with the boys.'

Mr Wilkes continued: 'You will still eat in the boys' dining room, unless, that is, you want to eat with the girls, but you will sleep in your new room. This is the only condition you will have to keep to. The rest is almost voluntary. Oh no, there is another condition that is compulsory. You will play cricket for the First XI.' He smiled.

I was in tears. 'Thank you, oh, thank you very much,' I said, sobbing my heart out. 'You don't know how much this means to me.'

'We do, Alex. We do know how much it means to you; it means a lot to me, too. We should thank the Headmaster for all his efforts.'

'The room will be ready next week,' added the Headmaster and I'll introduce you to Miss Sidebotham, the Headmistress, and she will explain what she expects from you.'

'Thank you, sir,' I replied and turned to leave.

'Before you go, young Henry,' the Head said. I stopped in my tracks. 'Were there any other boys who are still in school that were involved in the incident with Mr Guest the boiler man?'

'There's an old saying, sir: what comes around goes around and I prefer to leave it at that.'

I left the Head's office absolutely delighted with everything. Even Mr Wilkes, who followed me out, couldn't believe the turn of events. I went with him to his house and had tea with him and his wife. Mrs Wilkes was wonderful.

'I'm so pleased for you, Alex. You deserve it for what you have already done for the school and for what the school has done to you!' she said. 'I would give some consideration to transferring full time to the girls. It doesn't take a genius to see what you are, Alex.'

'Leave him be, dear. We've achieved a lot today already,' Mr Wilkes added.

'Why has the Head done this?' I asked.

'To be honest I don't know, but rumour has it, he's terrified of your father. I doubt that deep down he's undergone much of a conversion. He's a bigoted old sod.'

'Now then, dear,' Mrs Wilkes interrupted. 'We don't want to run the Headmaster down, do we?'

'No, dear, you're right,' he replied.

Later that week, the school odd-job men moved all my stuff and I moved in straight after. It was simple and plain and I had my first night's sleep without worry for two years. Eventually, I got my room how I wanted it and for the next few years I called it my 'little flat'.

I had my interview with Miss Sidebotham and was absolutely amazed at her common sense. It was obvious she had been fully briefed on my condition and the only rule she placed on me was that no boys were allowed in my room; to my utter astonishment, she had no objection to how many girls I had in, as long as there were no real juniors.

It wasn't long before the more inquisitive of the girls started to venture into my room. It was rather nice as there was no animosity. They just accepted me as one of them. The problem was I didn't want to be accepted by them.

Mrs Sidebotham also invited me to take part in any activities I wanted to and I did join in some of the sports, but refused many, as I couldn't bring myself to compete against girls.

I wrote to Alice and told her what had happened and her reply was so lovely I could feel myself filling up as I read it. She was delighted for me, but suggested I went over to the girls' full time; to burn my boats, as she put it. All the same, she did understand why I preferred to lead a kind of double or in-between life.

In the early days, I decided to have breakfast with the girls, as it was really more convenient, but then joined Form 5 with the boys for my lessons. I'll never forget the first day I went into the girls' dining room for breakfast, still dressed as a boy, but displaying the female attributes. There was total silence and every pair of eyes just followed my every step.

'Good morning, girls,' Miss Probert, the duty mistress said. 'This is Alex and she will be joining us for breakfast and will perhaps take part in other things; but she will be attending classes in the boys' school. I'm sure you will make her welcome. Won't you?'

'Yes, Miss!' was the dutiful response.

I sat down at the table to be waited on by various girls; it was far more civilised than with the boys, but of course you would expect that. I had to get used to the idea as eventually it was my turn to do the waiting on table. I loved every minute of it; I loved being part of a regime that made me feel secure and wanted.

There was never any sympathy required; they just accepted me as one of them, with the result that I made some very good friends from the girls' side, some of whom have lasted until today.

My room became a social hub and many of the girls just used it as a drop-in, for a chat, or for help with prep. It was lovely to have so many friends without any hints of animosity or bullying and it felt as good as my last year in the Junior School. After breakfast I returned to the boys' side and it was like stepping into a different world.

But, Mr White, the strangest thing happened: where in the past I was ignored and ostracised, with no one wanting to sit next to me, I was now treated differently. I put it down to the fact that, because I was effectively in the girls' school, they now looked on me as actually being a girl and no longer a freak. The boys themselves had no fear of girls and accepted it was normal to talk to girls, so there was no longer a problem with anyone sitting next to me. Furthermore, the girls were out of bounds and they put me out of bounds, so I was no longer touched.

Anyway, as a result of the change I started to enjoy school once more and, although I was naturally still worried about my body, I no longer strapped my breasts down. I did however wear my clothes in such a way as not to emphasise what I had, particularly when I was with the boys. (On the other side, though, I didn't bother.) It wasn't satisfactory but it made the best of a bad job.

My studies really improved and by the end of the term I felt that I was doing well, but the most important job I had to complete was playing Alice. I really put my heart and soul into this part and actually looked forward to the performances.

The rehearsals from the very beginning were heavily patronised and even more so when we started wearing the costumes. Mr Pounder was constantly turning away prying eyes and commenting they had only come to see the star, or that they were members of my fan club. It was very flattering and satisfying, especially now that there was no disgrace in looking at me. Finally, the day of the dress rehearsal arrived, which, as in previous years, was for the boys of the school.

Mr White, the changed attitudes of the boys was obvious as soon as I walked onstage in my costume. You can imagine, from all the drawings and pictures, what Alice looked like. Well, that's exactly how I looked. The audience of pubescent boys was totally silent, looking at me in amazement. Mrs Wilkes had helped me on with the costume and before I had finished, she said, 'Alex, you are lovely! In fact, tonight you look positively stunning. You're going to set a few hearts a flutter.'

It was an unbelievable dress rehearsal and at the end of the performance, when I came on to take my final bow, everyone stood up and I was cheered. I felt as though my rehabilitation was complete. The prefects did the same again and bought me a bunch of flowers, but again this time I knew it was done in the right spirit.

The Headmaster came onto the stage and thanked the cast, the production team and then gave a special thanks to me.

'I do not believe we could have had a better-looking Alice if we had gone to the West End and hired one!' This caused further cheers.

I curtseyed, which caused more cheers and whistles from the boys, as my cleavage could be seen clearly when I bent down.

'Not too low!' the Headmaster whispered.

'No sir. Right sir,' I replied, quietly hoping no one else heard.

The first performance for the His Majesty's school inspectors was equally spectacular and again went off without a hitch. And at the end, when we were taking our final bows, a boy came up onstage and gave me a bunch of flowers. The Headmaster had thought it was an important little touch. We had formidable write-ups in the press and, needless to say, both the Headmistress and Headmaster played the mutual cooperation card. I was in the programme as Alex, so no one was the wiser.

Alice, my sister, came the following night and all the little extras were left in, including the bunch of flowers, the little special bows and the thanks to everyone. When I curtseyed she stood up and shouted, 'Well done, Alex!' and the audience followed suit. It was a wonderful night and it was lovely to see Alice after the show. I started to take my wig off, but she stopped me. 'Darling, leave it on, you look beautiful.' Mrs Wilkes overheard and agreed. 'Yes, she does, doesn't she?'

I introduced Alice to Mrs Wilkes.

'This is my big sister, Alice.'

'I can see the likeness,' she remarked.

Alice got up to her usual mischievous tricks when a reporter from the previous night returned with a photographer to take our pictures. Alice somehow got the man to one side and the following little headline appeared: 'Bankworth Girl Steals the Show', and then a little story. Neither the Headmaster nor Miss Sidebotham denied the story, so that's how it was left.

Mrs Wilkes invited Alice and me for a cup of tea at her house, which we gladly accepted, but Alice wouldn't allow me to take the outfit off; she wanted to see me looking as happy for a little longer. Mrs Wilkes told Alice all about the changes to my situation and how lovely it was to see me smile once again. We talked for ages, so long in fact as it was now too late for Alice to catch her train home. The invitation by Mrs Wilkes to stay overnight was accepted which reminded me of the happiest days of my early childhood, to see Alice around so early in the morning.

The final performance was for the girls' side and the Junior School, which was the first time the latter had been invited, and this too was a success with this audience also giving me a huge round of applause, when I took my final bow.

Do you know, Mr White? I couldn't believe I had so many admirers at school. Several boys actually watched every performance and some even wanted to chat with me behind the scenes.

'They fell in love with the dream, but they woke up with reality.'

I think Rita Heyworth's quotation went something like that when she played Gilda in one of her films. Some were very keen and it's funny when I look back; but I remember Mr Pounder commenting about one boy, 'I think he's fallen in love with you,' and then laughing. I also remember him coming to me after the performances were all over and saying, 'Alex, you were excellent and I think you are very brave. But I'll tell you something, young man. You have won the hearts and minds of the boys and all, and I mean all, members of the staff. It was obvious to everyone that you put your heart and soul into this part and for that I'm eternally grateful.' I was so happy. I felt as though I had been released from captivity and allowed to resume my life from where it left off in my first year at Senior school.

When I returned home for Christmas armed with all the photographs, I felt good in myself for the first time in a long time. I didn't even mind that my father had decided he wouldn't spend Christmas with his family. I spent a week with Alice and the remainder of the time at Glengarry with my mother, and for the first time for a very long time I was actually looking forward to going back to school for the spring term, even though I could not compete in any sporting activities.

The cross-country was out as was the swimming, and, although I did have the opportunity to swim with the girls, I couldn't bring myself to do it, especially as the Headmistress insisted that if I did take part I had to wear a bathing costume.

I was too bashful, Mr White, without my Alice around and, to be honest – without blowing my own trumpet too much, Mr White – I would have found it too easy, as my times were so much better than any of those the girls achieved. I was given the chance of going to watch them swim, which many of the boys would have given their eyeteeth to do, and it was pleasant, but they were perhaps not as competitive as we were. I did, however, have a few games of tennis and table tennis with them and was on a par with their abilities, so at least I got a good game.

Year 5 had been good and ended very well with me passing my matriculation in seven subjects and being allowed to stay on and take my advanced subjects to get into university. I suppose my one disappointment that year was that I was told I couldn't be a prefect the following year, as it was considered inappropriate.

The cricket season was amazing and even here there were a few changes; there was no pretence about what I was and I consequently became more relaxed, with the result that I had a fantastic season. It did, however, annoy some of the opposition when they thought a girl had hit a fifty or a century off their bowlers, but as the Captain said on more than one occasion.

'You wouldn't want us to field an inferior side, just to give you a chance, would you?'

I received prizes for Mathematics, French and German and, of course, the batting prize yet again, and once again the Headmaster congratulated me on the performance in the Christmas play.

The whole summer was spent in Le Touquet, away from it all; unfortunately most of the time I spent on my own. Alice had her husband home and naturally wanted to spend time with him. My mother was better off without me, so it was a question of simply improving my French. Mrs Wilkes' domestic science lessons had served me well as I was able to look after myself to a reasonable standard.

I did, however, return to school for the Christmas term in the lower sixth looking very well indeed and again, as in the previous Christmas terms, I was asked to take part in the Christmas play, which I did. However, the Headmaster thought it was better if I wasn't the major attraction and just had an ordinary role. I attempted Dame Edith's Lady Bracknell *avant la lettre* in Oscar Wilde's *The Importance of Being Ernest,* which was fun.

I must be honest, Mr White, I did miss the adoration of the audience, but, as Mr Wilkes told me, it was becoming more and more difficult for the school to conceal the truth and could be difficult for both me and the school if the story became commonplace; the press would have a field day.

Until the cricket season started I just became a swot and spent much of my time studying in the school library. I was becoming exceptional at Mathematics and was without doubt being recognised as a possible Oxford candidate. In fact, throughout the two final school years, I was being groomed to try for Oxford, which was quite exciting for me. The possibility of playing first-class cricket with the University was for me the most fantastic opportunity I could have wished for. I therefore put my mind to it and tried to obtain a place. I was made Vice Captain of the school cricket team and just enjoyed life.

The summer holidays were lovely that year as I had Alice again and converted back to being her little sister. Her husband had been sent abroad, as had my father. The Germans were beginning to worry us and Winston Churchill was warning everyone that we should be preparing for another war and was being called a warmonger for doing so. Mosley's Blackshirts were beginning to create difficulties and the Jews in Germany were having a terrible time and had just suffered what we now know as Kristallnacht, when much of their possessions were burned in the streets and their shops and homes were raided and looted; it all pointed to further trouble. Senior officers were sent on missions to ensure we had full support from our friends and allies.

But for now Le Touquet was fabulous and we had the most fantastic time. We both managed to gain many admirers and were taken everywhere, always together. As far as I was concerned, I had developed an inner strength and was able, to a much greater degree, to look after myself, but I still preferred Alice around. She tried to teach me a few feminine ways, as I tended to walk like a man, with big, ungainly steps, and in many ways, although I looked very feminine, I sometimes didn't behave so.

My last year at Bankworth began. I was determined to get into Oxford and worked very hard for my Advanced Matriculations. My little flat was almost like a little classroom in itself, filled with all the books I could get my hands on. I had made a special friend of one of the girls, Jennifer Bleasdale, who was from Haworth and who also wanted to get into Oxford, with the result we spent many hours together. A friendship grew from small acorns and to this day we still correspond. She's eighty-eight years old and, like me, a great-grandmother.

My year in the upper sixth was almost a carbon copy of the lower sixth, with just a few exceptions. I was allowed to appear in a 'starring role' in the Christmas production, playing Juliet in *Romeo and Juliet*. It was another rip-roaring success and, because it was another Shakespeare play, there were four performances for local schools, again at the Civic Hall, as well as the four in Bankworth itself, which gave a total of eight.

We had to work really hard on this play, which to me was enjoyable as I had little else to do. It didn't seem to matter now, whether I showed bosom or not, as it was just taken for granted I was from the girls' school and even Miss Sidebotham had some input on what I was to wear and whether it was suitable or not.

I honestly believe that, had I been transferred two years earlier, I wouldn't have had the option to study with the boys.

Despite no longer being on the boys' side, I was made School cricket Captain and again with no worries I was able to play as never before. I overheard Mr Wilkes talking about me and said my batting was joy to watch. The school had an extremely successful season and was drawing much attention from the press and many stories were abounding on how well I was doing. However, taking Mr Wilkes' advice I didn't in any way allow the press to talk to me, referring them all the time to the Headmaster and Mr Wilkes.

The Founders' Day Match had arrived and it was the first time I had been involved in this annual match as Captain of the school team. To my utter astonishment, however, Hazard had been selected to play for the Old Boys XI. Oddly, he had been rehabilitated by the Headmaster, despite the scandal that had caused his departure and despite his appalling treatment of me. Mr Wilkes protested strongly against this insensitivity, but to no effect. Furthermore, Hazard still had a reputation of being a very fast and dangerous bowler, which caused some of our boys to be a little scared. So all in all, it looked set to be a very difficult match, in many different ways.

From the very moment he arrived, it seemed, Hazard could not stop himself making comments such as 'How is Gloria these days?' or asking other members of the team, 'Is she still having periods?'

I managed to shut him up by asking in front of the others, 'Are you still a eunuch and were they able to sew them back on?'

'You can fight it out on the pitch and not in the dressing room,' Mr Wilkes said, trying to ensure my antipathy didn't ruin my chances.

The match started promptly at two o'clock. I had won the toss and elected to field and the Old Boys had made a respectable 140 for the loss of four wickets when Hazard came into bat.

He was at the non-strikers end for the rest of the over and began preparing to face the bowler at the other end. I called John Petty, the bowler, over and apologised for taking him off, but told him I was going to bowl at Hazard.

I called the wicketkeeper and the slips over for a conference, which can often be unnerving to the new batsman; I was determined to unsettle him.

'We can get Hazard out easily, if you do what I say,' I said and then gave my instructions. 'If the ball hits the pads, I want you all to appeal as loud as you can. If the ball just misses the bat, appeal as loud as you can. It will definitely unsettle him. Got it?' I said as I caught the ball thrown to me. 'Right arm over, Mr Wilkes,' I added, pacing out my run-up.

Hazard was ready and I began to run down the wicket and just as I got to the crease, I stopped.

'Sorry!' I shouted and walked back to my mark. I ran down again and, putting everything into it, I bowled fast and low. The ball rattled the pads; I jumped up in the air and joined the roar of 'Owzat?' as we all appealed.

'Not out,' replied Mr Wilkes.

The next ball whistled passed the bat like a rocket and once again we all roared, 'Owzat?' and again I jumped in the air making my appeal.

'Not out!' Mr Wilkes replied. It was easy to see Hazard was getting rattled.

The next two balls were identical and once again we all roared with the same result, but this time Hazard protested to the umpire. Mr Wilkes admonished me so that Hazard could hear, but when he turned away from Hazard, he winked and smiled at me. He knew what I was doing. It was pure gamesmanship. The next ball was pure delight; it ripped out his off stump like some magical wind. Hazard stood there, astonished and angry, his petulance showing as he banged his bat down on the floor.

My teammates ran over to congratulate me, showing their delight; it was pure poetry. I started walking back to bowl my last ball when I heard Mr Wilkes say, 'Well done Alex!'

To make matters worse for Hazard, I took myself off the bowling and brought Petty back on. The old boys declared at tea for 235 for seven and now it was our turn to go out to bat.

Hazard was fired up. 'If you think you can get away with that, you've got another think coming!' he sneered as he passed our dressing room on the way out to field. I could sense the apprehension in the team and suggested that I go out as an opener.

I was nearing the crease to take my guard when we all heard Hazard remark, 'Come on, Gloria, you're playing with the men now.'

John Huffer, the Old Boys umpire, told him not to be so silly and called on me to take my guard. Mr Wilkes quietly demonstrated by waving his hand to me to calm down and take no notice.

As Hazard ran down to the crease, you could see the venom in his face and feel it in his manner. He let go of the ball; I went down the pitch and knocked it right out of the ground. There was a massive cheer from the crowd. Hazard was devastated and the whole Old Boys team were very embarrassed. It took three or four minutes to find the ball and, when it was returned, Hazard looked at me as though I was dirt and that it was just luck. He ran down for the second ball and it was a carbon copy of the first except I hit the ball that far they never found it. I could see Mr Wilkes laughing to himself and one or two others. I scored 28 off the over, which is still the school record. The next over was a maiden and I had to face Hazard again. This over was mild; I scored only 14 but Hazard had been punished with 42 runs off his two overs. He never bowled again and spent the rest of the match on the boundary out of harm's way. But his last ignominy was when I reached my fifty, after just five overs. I retired to give the others a bat. We won the match with two wickets to spare and, as I received the cup, the Captain of the Old Boys commented:

'At least Alex is leaving and we won't have to face his

formidable bat. Maybe he will play for us?' Hazard left early and I never saw him after the match; he was obviously too embarrassed.

It was a similar story when we played our last match on Prize Day; it was my last one at Bankworth as a pupil. It was a lovely day and I elected to bat first. I scored 150 not out and retired, giving the others the opportunity to bat. Our team scored a record 301 all out; the visitors, parents and friends that is, were all out for 123.

It was a fitting end to my years at Bankworth which culminated in my winning the batting prize for the sixth year running. We all assembled in the prize-giving tent for the ceremony and the Headmaster began to present all the prizes. Suddenly, he broke off from his litany to announce: 'For the next prize I'm not going to announce the winner; I'm breaking with precedence and I'm going to ask Mr Wilkes his house master to introduce him.'

There were a few polite ripples of applause as Mr Wilkes rose to his feet and stood in front of us all, not speaking for several seconds. There was a deathly silence in the tent, only punctuated by the occasional clearing of a throat.

He began: 'This is one of the saddest days in my career as a teacher. Why? Because we are losing one of the most courageous young people I have ever had the pleasure to be associated with. Many of you present will not have seen this young man in his heyday; you're too young and your parents wouldn't have been told about him because you, the pupils, will not have heard.

'He came to this school as a junior and before long he developed into a boy of courage and determination. He caught scarlet fever twice and was very ill but still returned a very fine cricketer. I think there's a moral in there somewhere. If you want to be a good cricketer you have to catch scarlet fever.' There were ripples of laughter around the audience.

'Mrs Waggott, the Junior School Headmistress still remembers how he led his house into winning the school cup by the biggest margin ever achieved and how he scored 132 runs at the age of ten, which enabled the school to win the Junior Founder's Day Match for the first time for many years. She too was sorry he left the Junior School and she too says he was one of the most popular students she had ever had, not only with the boys and girls, but with the staff.

'However, I want to talk about his achievements at the Senior School and how well he did in his first year and the standard he set in 1930. He was a semi-finalist in the boxing. He won the Junior Cross-Country, breaking the record by three minutes – a record that still stands today; He won the 220, 440 and 880 yards, as well as the mile, on Sports Day. He won two cups for swimming in the 50 and 100 yards. He then scored over a thousand runs during the cricket season.

'He holds every batting record at the school and I'll never forget that Founder's Day Match when he was twelve years of age. He walked out to bat in his short trousers, a little boy compared with the others; the score was eight for one wicket. I could tell he was nervous, but the first ball was easy which he hit for four and after that he had a field day. This little lad went on to score 130 and win the match for us. We carried him shoulder high off the field and the Captain allowed him to receive the winners' cup on behalf of the team. He had won his school colours and several house colours by the time he was twelve.

'I'm not going to mention the 50 runs he scored last week on Founder's Day in only five overs, or the 150 he scored earlier today, because you all know about those. But that is how he has performed at everything he has been given the opportunity to do – always his best.

'I know he won't mind me finishing the story, as fate was to change his world. He developed bodily changes and became ridiculed, despised and ignored by many who had cheered him the years before. He could no longer enter the boxing ring and it became too embarrassing for him and the school to allow him to swim.

'He could no longer compete in the cross-country or on Sports Day for fear of the comments that would be shouted at him. The only thing he had left was his wonderful gift with the bat and he even had to fight to be allowed to continue with that.

'He suffered unbelievable pain from the ridicule he received because we all know boys can be very cruel. He was tormented because he looked more feminine than otherwise and yet he had the courage to give three tremendous performances in the female leads in *Peter Pan, The Taming of the Shrew* and *Alice Through the Looking Glass,* knowing he would be ridiculed for doing it; but he did it for the school, so well in fact that the school production had wonderful write-ups in the local papers.' By now tears were rolling down Mr Wilkes' face.

'He became ostracised and no one would sit next to him in class, but this didn't dampen his courage or his tenacity; he had nothing else left in the sporting world, a place where he had excelled almost unrivalled; but then he buckled down to succeed in some other field and this effort has also been rewarded by his winning a scholarship to Oxford to study Mathematics and Modern Languages.

'I know of no other person who has displayed so much courage and determination and who deserves this prize more than Alexander George Chillington-Henry.'

Harry Whelan, who, I'm proud to say, was there, led the applause by standing up; followed by my heavily pregnant sister, Alice. Then everyone stood up and clapped and cheered for almost five minutes and I too like Mr Wilkes had tears rolling down my face. The audience sat down as I accepted my prize, almost sobbing.

'Thank you very much for this wonderful bat! I shall treasure it for the rest of my life. I would like to say a special thank you to Mr Wilkes for those kind words and for the fact that he and his wife have helped me enormously through the last few years. I did the best I could for my house and my school but most of all for my father.'

I walked down from the platform and I could see Alice at the front. She had broken down in tears; I went to console her.

'Darling, what have we done to you?' she asked rhetorically.

'It's been so unfair. I'm so pleased for you now. You do deserve everything!'

'Hello, Alex.'

'There's a voice from the past,' I said as Harry came over to talk to me.

'Did you have it rough after I left?' he asked.

'No not really. It's old Wilky; a bit prone to exaggeration you know. Oh Harry, it's lovely to see you. I really missed you when you left,' I said, now sobbing almost uncontrollably. 'You were a good friend, Harry . . .' I paused to introduce Alice. 'Harry, this is my lovely sister, Alice and she's another good friend,' I said, making Alice tearful again.

Harry and I chatted for a couple of hours before he had to catch the train. Alice too had to leave, as her husband was arriving home the following day and she wanted to be prepared, but not before we had a laugh about our holidays in Le Touquet.

'Do you remember David?' she asked.

'Of course, he gave me my first kiss,' I whispered.

'He was in love with you!' Alice said.

'Yes I know, poor chap, but he was nice. If he could see me now, he would be in for a surprise.'

'Shocked I think is the word, Alex . . .' She paused for a moment. 'You should never have gone back. You were happy, regardless of what you may say. You looked happy for those few weeks.'

'And miss all this?' I asked.

'Darling, it would have been worth it,' Alice replied.

We said our tearful goodbyes and I returned to my room to clear up several years of memories ready for the end of term. My special goodbye to Mr and Mrs Wilkes tore me to shreds. They had taken the place of my mother and father; they had been my confidants, my board of advisors, my shoulders to cry on, and I genuinely did not want to leave them. They both hugged and kissed me as we said our goodbyes.

'If ever we have a son, I would like him to be just like you, Alex,' Mr Wilkes said. But Mrs Wilkes added in a whisper, 'Or a daughter!' as she kissed me again on the cheek. We both smiled.

It was a sad day as I walked away from the school, looking back many times to wave to the Wilkes' and other members of staff who had been so kind to me over those last few years. I got on the bus for the last time with two large boxes as well as my big leather suitcase which now quite frankly seemed absolutely tiny. On the bus I took my last look round and gave my last wave with tears rolling down my face.

Everyone was so kind to me and felt the distress I was in. Even the youngsters said, 'Cheer up, Alex!' and one even said, 'We shall miss you!' which made matters even worse for me. It was a far cry from what had happened a few years earlier with the Hazards and Barratts of this world. Some of the boys even helped me carry my cases to the station and helped me onto the train. Why did I have to go through that pain? Why was it not always like this I thought as I sat in a compartment with boys of all ages wanting to talk to me?

St Pancras was the end of the line. I said my last tearful goodbyes to my school companions and shouted for a porter.

'Where to, miss?' he asked, as I wasn't wearing my jacket.

'The taxis,' I replied.

'Are you sad to be leavin' then, miss?' the somewhat observant porter asked.

'Yes I am. I've had a wonderful last year and I shall miss my friends,' I replied.

He took my luggage to the taxi and with a quick 'Good luck, miss!' was away. I began loading my stuff into the taxi.

The driver too made the same mistake as he asked, 'Where to, miss? and then proceeded to interrogate me about my love life.

'Have you got a boyfriend yet?'

'No!' I replied.

'What, a pretty girl like you! You don't want to be left on the shelf , do you?'

'I've only just left school; I'm only eighteen,' I replied, wondering how I had got myself into this conversation.

'Me and me wife were married when she was eighteen,' he continued.

At Waterloo I was glad to get away from him. I called another porter, who took my luggage to the platform to await the train to Upper Hayfield.

I was cross that the taxi driver made the comments he did, but while waiting on the platform for my train, it made me think about the problems I faced in the future. Who and what was I to be? I desperately wanted to be friends with my father and believed that the only way I would achieve that would be to remain a boy. Certainly that would have to be the case, if I was to carry on playing cricket. But then, as a boy, I risked being seen as a freak . . . It was a dilemma I could not yet resolve.

I took the train home, crying all the way. There was no one there to welcome me and I simply caught the bus to my stop. The only welcome came from the driver, who said, 'Home for good, Alex?' He didn't wait for an answer before continuing: 'I've been reading about your batting in the paper. They say you're good enough to play for England. Well done!'

At least he didn't say, 'Miss', I thought to myself, as I thanked him for his good wishes.

I walked up the drive, opened the front door and walked in. There was silence.

'I'm home!' I shouted to be greeted by Rafter the Border collie. He at least seemed genuinely pleased to see me.

'Mother, I'm home!' I shouted again.

Then I heard a baby cry in the lounge and walked in.

'Darling, welcome home!'

It was Alice together with baby Isobel, her daughter, and surrounded by Lucy and my mother. For the first time for years

I was actually being welcomed home by my family and I broke down yet again and sobbed my heart out as I hugged each of them in turn.

Even so, I saw my mother shudder as Alice handed Isobel to me and said, 'Come on, Issy. Go to your Aunt Alexandra.'

Part 2

The Student

Chapter 10

My father was still unwilling to see me and told my mother to tell me that he had provided a self-contained flat at the house in Chelsea for me and if I moved into that, he would finally come home.

My mother tried to convince me it would be good for me and that I would enjoy life in the big city, particularly as I was going to Oxford where I would meet many new sophisticated friends and the flat in the city would be an advantage. I didn't even put up an argument; I just accepted it was my lot and within a week I had packed all my things and, with the help of my mother, had moved in. I was still allowed to go to Le Touquet and, after a week on my own in London, I went to France to get some sun.

Both Alice, with Isobel, and Lucy, with Edward, her five-year-old and youngest child (having now had three by two different fathers, something totally unknown in those days), came to stay with me for a month and once again, Alice persuaded me to address my feminine side. This time Lucy joined in, too. They didn't realise what utter torment they gave me; it was as though they were pushing me to make up my mind; something I could do when they were there, but something that was impossible when they were not. The two of them paid for a nanny to look after the children during the day and we had a fantastic time. I was actually persuaded to go out with several boys on my own, which was quite interesting, but damn confusing for me! Alice, of course, thought it would do me good.

It was here I made my biggest mistake. In my head, I knew I should have taken the advice that Alice kept offering, but in my heart, I still wanted to please my father and 'win back his affection', if I can put it like that, and the only way I thought that was possible was by playing cricket and being his boy. So the moment my sisters left I reverted to type and returned to London for the last week to get myself ready for Oxford.

On my return I had a letter from my Bankworth friend Jennifer Bleasdale, who informed she was going to be at St Hilda's College the following Monday and asked if we could meet. Now I recognised I had created my own problems, as I had elected to go to one of the other colleges which were male dominated, while St Hilda's was an all-female college. However, I managed to get in touch with her and arranged to meet on the following Tuesday.

I made my way to Oxford and the start of a new life, arriving at my assigned hall of residence where I booked in and was allocated a room. I immediately made my way there and began to unpack to get my house in order. It was a lovely little room, a little bit bigger, perhaps, than I had been given at Bankworth, with its own wash basin, but no toilet. This was communal as were the bathing facilities, and I had to share with some fifteen people, all male with the exception of me. I had made a rod for my own back, it seemed, but I decided to tough it out, be all grown up and pretend I was male. I put the fact that I had grown breasts to the back of my mind.

I realise now, Mr White, I had set myself an impossible task and on reflection I too should have gone to St Hilda's, but then there was the small problem of my birth certificate.

All freshers had to meet in the main hall where we had to say what activities we would be interested in and of course I went straight to the cricket 'stall'. I put my name down to be considered for selection as a member of the college team, adding that I would also like to play for the university.

'There are a lot of extremely good players waiting to be

considered for that, young sir,' the head of the college team replied.

I also enrolled in the amateur dramatic society, but again I realised I didn't stand much of a chance, as I was too feminine to be a man and they had many 'real' girls who could take the feminine leads. It wasn't like being at school, where I was a big fish in a small pond; here I was a little fish in a large pond.

The first day passed without too much difficulty. I managed to make some acquaintances with whom at least I could talk and then took myself off to the city, where I bought myself the obligatory bicycle. The next day I went over to St Hilda's and met Jennifer and we both felt the same: it was wonderful to see one another and at least we each had a friend. I parked the bike up and wandered around Oxford with her, getting to know the place. There were some lovely little cafés and restaurants to take tea or have luncheon and we enjoyed most of those pleasures. We made a pact that we would meet every Monday and Friday whatever we had on; it would maintain our friendship.

You know, Mr White, we kept that promise until I left, that is, at the end of the year, but I'll come to that.

I wasn't very happy as I could hear people talking about me and some of the students came right out with it. 'Alex, are you a lesbian?' 'What are you?' they would ask. Both male and female students wouldn't be seen in my company and I was so grateful that Jennifer stood by me and I had at least two days a week to look forward to. It was becoming as bad as Bankworth, only worse. The first semi–violent act that took place was when a group of freshers took all my clothes when I was in the bath and I was made to walk back down the corridor back to my room in front of many gawping men and women. It's a terrible thing when you see people of whatever age and class being unkind to another and there is nothing the 'odd one out' can do except grin and bear it.

***

'It's terrible, Mr White, truly terrible – man's inhumanity to man,' Mrs Fraser commented, sighing sadly. 'Even though this was on a very minor scale, it still hurts. These people knew nothing about me and yet they could bring themselves to be cruel.'

I had to agree with her. We had lived through some terrible times in the twentieth century.

'I think the secret is', I said, 'how the individual himself reacts to this situation: if he allows himself to be influenced by others, or if he is prepared to stand up and be counted and not let these sorts of things happen to the other more unfortunate.'

'Ah yes, Mr White, but there are so few who are brave enough to fight for the rights of the persecuted,' Mrs Fraser added. 'They themselves are a heroic minority!' She sighed once more before taking up her story again.

I was very much a loner; not that I wanted to be – I loved having people around or even being around people. I suppose I was one of those who were vulnerable to being used by others, simply because I longed for friendship, particularly during the first few months at Oxford when I was trying to find my feet. No one really wanted me for company and I found myself in a similar situation to that which I had been in at Bankworth. So I tried to work hard at the subjects I was taking, in particular towards my Mathematics degree. It was only after I had been in college a few weeks that they recognised I had a special ability in the subject, with the result they asked me if I would like to take on a little extra work solving mathematical problems, which naturally I accepted.

However, I was also studying Modern Languages. I was already almost fluent in French and was pretty good at German. No, I am being modest, Mr White, I *was* fluent in French. However, to improve my ability in German, I began exchanging conversation with a German student, Eberhard Leist, and we spent several hours a week in each other's company, excluding Mondays and Fridays, which, of course, were reserved for Jennifer. Eberhard took me out to the pub for the odd drink or two and my German quickly improved. It was my friendship with Eberhard that was to lead to one of the most bizarre events of my life.

I remember the day as clearly as anything. It was Armistice Day, 11th November, and I was invited to a dinner party given by a Helen De Witt, a woman who purported to be Dutch but whom I suspected was really German. Eberhard was one of the guests and we went along as a pair. I say a pair very loosely, because I believe he already knew what sex I really was. I must admit I thought at the time it was peculiar no one ever mentioned or questioned me on the subject, but perhaps they were just too polite.

We arrived at Pentland Villa, Helen De Witt's house, which was early Victorian or even late Georgian. It had several large rooms with high ceilings; the dining room was large enough for thirty or more to dine, as well as having three settees, several matching armchairs and a grand piano. It was so tastefully done, you wouldn't have believed it was just one room. Mrs De Witt introduced me to the other guests (like most Germans she could not quite manage the English *v* or *w*): 'Velcome to Pentland Filla. I vant to introduce you all to our new guest, Alex Henry.' The other guests turned to me and smiled. Soon after, Mrs De Witt took me to one side.

'Ve often have dances here. It is big enough.'

I remember sighing with delight at the thought, something Mrs De Witt duly noted.

'Alex . . . May I call you Alex?'

'Yes of course,' I replied.

'The next party ve have, vhich von't be long avay, you must come too. I promise you vill enjoy it, but there may be several other students there and you vill not be allowed to talk in English,' Mrs De Witt continued.

It was strange. She never asked me to call her by her Christian name, so it was always Mrs De Witt. Seeing the delight I took in looking at her furnishings, she began to show me round the room, with its Adam fireplace, its Chippendale furniture, and its wonderful paintings and sculptures; even the piano was a masterpiece in its own right. It was, Mr White, a sight to behold; I was truly impressed.

A little later, the staff brought in trays of canapés and a choice of drinks – champagne (it was actually Sekt, the German equivalent of champagne), rosé and Riesling – and the conversation quickly warmed. Mrs De Witt brought over a somewhat thickset gentleman, who wore unfortunate bottle-glass spectacles that made him look a bit sinister, but like the others he was really a charming man.

'What a beautiful English accent!' I said after he had introduced himself as Norbert Lisek. He was a German professor of English and was on a visit to Britain, trying to improve cultural relations between the two countries.

'We must try and speak the language properly, if we are guests in foreign country,' he commented after my compliment.

'That's very true! That's why I want to learn your language properly.' The champagne was beginning to loosen my tongue.

'Well, we must make sure you do. Let me say this, Alex, if you ever need help getting through your degree, let me know.' He gave me his card and for one of the few times in my life I felt the thrill of being flattered. Norbert seemed to be showing a genuine interest in me and I spent much of the first part of the evening with him just chatting. He was asking about my interests, which of course meant talking about cricket and France.

'You've spent some time in France then?'

'Yes we have . . .' I answered. 'I mean my father has a house in Le Touquet. I love it there. In fact, I think it is the only place where I am truly happy.'

'Yes one does tend to love a place when you can communicate with the natives, so to speak,' he added. His use of the word 'native' struck a sour note. I adored the French and would never refer to them as 'natives' however it was meant.

He could see he had touched a nerve and changed the subject quickly. 'Where do you live?'

'At the moment I live in college, but my father has given me a little flat in Chelsea. Well, it's not so little; it has two bedrooms and is very comfortable.'

'You are very lucky. I wish I had had a father who gave a present like that!' Norbert continued. 'What does your father do then?'

'Oh, he's a bigwig in the Army, a major general I believe,' I said proudly. 'But it wasn't really a present; it was purely and simply to give me somewhere to stay if I was ever in London and couldn't get home.' I wasn't going to tell a bunch of people I hardly knew that I was estranged from my father and that he simply wanted to get rid of me.

However, by the time we sat down for dinner my tongue had been loosened enough to have given my fellow guests a potted history of my life, although I steered clear of the 'difficult' bits. I was enjoying myself for the first time in ages and liked the attention.

It was a lovely meal, with plenty of wine, and I must confess I did have too much, though not quite enough to lose total control of myself.

Mr Lizek was sitting on my right, and a large plump woman named Petra Hunsfeld, from the German Embassy in London, was on my left and I had the strangest feeling that my dining companions had been specially chosen for me. Mrs De Witt, of course, was at the head of the table, but formed part of our little group.

'For those of you who vere late arriving and who haven't met our special guest this evening, Ladies and gentlemen – Alex Henry,' she said, pointing me out. 'He's at the university and studying German, and I'm pleased to say, ve are going to help him!' Everyone turned to me and clapped politely and I nodded my thanks in return.

'It's very kind of you, Mrs De Witt. I do appreciate it,' I replied, a little astonished at being singled out in this way.

Mrs De Witt continued: 'Ve are in exulted company. Alex is the son of a major general in the Army and, as anyone from

Germany knows, that is a werry impressive position indeed.'

Everyone nodded in agreement and then returned to their conversations.

'Vat are you hoping to do vhen you leave Oxford?' Mrs De Witt asked.

'I suppose I would like to go into research, mathematical research I mean. One of the professors has already suggested that I try aeronautics as I have already been given some special calculations to do.'

'Ach, but how interesting!' said the plump Embassy woman with a smile. I saw her glance at Eberhard.

At the end of the meal our hostess proposed a toast to our King and Queen and then to the German Chancellor, Adolf Hitler. Everyone, including me, raised their glasses. At that time, Hitler did not seem as threatening as he would appear only a few short years after, but even then I regretted raising my glass to him, especially as there was a growing feeling against fascism in the University. When the evening broke up and we all went our separate ways, I tried hard to forget that toast.

'Thank you, Mrs De Witt. It has been a wonderful evening. I hope to see you soon,' I said graciously as I was leaving.

'You vill, my dear, you vill. Next Wednesday you are invited to our little conversation class. I hope you vill come?'

'I most certainly will. Thank you!'

After the dinner, Eberhard and I went for a drink. He was fired up with all things Germanic and seized the opportunity to tell me about all the good things that were happening in Germany and how the Führer was improving the economy and the whole mood of the nation. Germany, he told me proudly, was going to be great again and take her place alongside Britain.

'Would you like to read a copy of his book?' Eberhard suddenly asked. 'It's called *Mein Kampf* –"My Struggle". It is good reading!'

I collected the book during one of Mrs De Witt's conversation classes and she seemed pleased, particularly as I took the German version, and when I handed it back the following week she asked, 'Vell, Vot do you think?'

She was clearly very keen on the book and so as not to upset my hostess, I told her that I had enjoyed it and that it had some very interesting radical ideas. It was naïve, I know, Mr White, but I didn't want to upset the apple cart as at least I had somewhere to go.

'It could work if done properly with the consent of the people,' I added.

'My fery thoughts, too, young man,' she said, smiling as though she had made a conquest.

During the following two weeks, I went to Mrs De Witt's several times and even accepted another invitation to dinner. I received the invitation at the college. It was in German and requested that gentlemen should wear a tie. At the bottom of the card was the injunction: '*Nur Deutsch darf gesprochen worden*!' (German only will be spoken).

Inexplicably, Eberhard seemed to have vanished, so on the day of the dinner I had to go on my own. I turned up with a bunch of flowers for Mrs De Witt, who once again made me feel most welcome. This evening was different: it was a buffet dance, with all the guests allocated to a table. At the end of the room, in front of the French windows, was a small band.

Once again I found myself next to Norbert Lizek and Petra from the Embassy and also on our table was a very petite attractive blonde woman named Christina Wakulat, who was about my age, together with a German husband and wife couple, Artur and Magda Schultz. The food, of course, was perfect and the Sekt flowed abundantly.

After dinner, Christina, who looked absolutely splendid in a beautiful straight dress, asked me if I would like to dance. Now, Mr White, imagine the situation! There I was being chatted up by a young girl, being invited to have a dance and, because of the way things had gone at school, I only knew how to follow! I don't think I have ever fallen over so many times in my life!

I'm sure the Sekt didn't help either. God knows how Christina put up with it but she took it in good spirit, laughing all the time. At least we got back to our table in one piece!

We sat and chatted about this and that and as the evening progressed she told me that it was her second time at Mrs De Witt's and that she too worked for the Embassy. Mrs De Witt was helping her to learn English. Our conversation was suddenly interrupted as the band began to play a waltz and Christina almost begged me to dance again. 'This time I know you will be much better!' she cried as she took my hand.

She was right. We slowly danced round the floor and each time she got closer and by the end of the dance we were cheek to cheek and our bodies were close. We parted momentarily for the band leader to announce another slow waltz and then we were close again.

It's difficult for any young man to hide his feelings when faced with a woman close to him and the reaction from her lower quarters, as she constantly pressed against my breasts, was only natural. I almost cried out in surprise as I felt Christina's erection through her shimmering dress. I quickly recovered myself.

'Whoops, that's different! Now how on earth did you get one of those?' I asked quietly.

'Please, keep close to me!' he, as I have to now call him, begged. 'Let's go into the garden and I'll tell you all about it.'

We sidled out of the French windows and onto the terrace. Our departure drew a few looks and smiles from the other guests.

'Well, that was a surprise, Christina!'

'Look, Alex, please don't say anything, they think I'm homosexual and I'm not, so please don't say anything,'

'I can't call you Christina. What's you real name?'

'No, Alex, you must! It must be Christina at all times. Please!'

'All right, Christina. What's all this about?' I asked, somewhat anxious as to my own delicate position, sexually speaking, as well as what Mrs De Witt might think if she discovered my complicity with 'Christina's' deception.

'We must be careful!' he replied as we sat down on a garden seat at the end of the terrace. He looked around before beginning and asked if I would hold his hand for appearance's sake and then began a most bizarre story.

'Christina' told me he had lost his parents during the Great War and was placed in a home until he was fifteen and was then released into the world with nothing. Soon after his release, he became so desperate that he broke into the orphanage and stole some money. He knew they would inform the police, so to help his escape he disguised himself as a girl. After several days of wandering he was taken in by an old couple and given food and a bed.

They asked him what his name was and just off the top of his head, all he could think of was the name of a nurse at the orphanage who had been kind to him and so he called himself Christina Wakulat. He stayed with the couple, working for them to earn his keep, but living as a girl all the time. Eventually, he ran away to Berlin where he fell in with a theatre troupe. They soon found out that he was really a boy, but used his talent for female impersonation in their shows. Times were changing in Germany and he had to be so careful, as homosexuals were *verboten* (forbidden). He wasn't homosexual, of course, and he made sure everybody knew he wasn't!

At this point he suddenly stopped telling his story and whispered, 'Kiss me. Please kiss me. Now!'

I didn't know what to do, but I leaned towards him like some person under hypnosis. He pulled me closer and kissed me; a kiss which lasted several seconds. I pulled away, suddenly aware that someone was watching us.

Christina took my hand and invited me to follow him for a short walk round the garden.

'You aren't all you seem either, Alex,' Christina began.

'No, I'm just unfortunate,' I replied, finding my voice at last. 'I'm a boy with breasts and a figure of fun to a lot of people and I think you are making fun of me!'

'No, don't say that, Alex! I won't make fun of you. I need you to help me!'

'How can I do that?' I asked, becoming more confused by the minute.

'I want to get away from these people, to lead a normal life, but I can't. I'm trapped by circumstances. I don't have anyone outside Germany, or inside for that matter who would be prepared to help me. They're all becoming too frightened.'

'What do you want me to do?' I asked.

'Mrs De Witt, as she calls herself, wanted me to find out if you were a homosexual. They wanted me to try and gain your friendship and eventually persuade you to stay the weekend here. We would be caught in bed together and then they would blackmail you into helping them.'

'That's ridiculous! What on earth could they want from me?'

'Your father is virtually a general and they want information.'

'Good God! This is unbelievable. This is the last thing I need!' I almost shouted and pushed him away. 'I have to go, Christina. Sorry, I can't help you.'

'No, please don't! They'll kill me! You have to help me, Alex.'

His words stopped me in my tracks. I looked at him and suddenly I saw myself begging for my life in the boiler house, Hazard looking down at me. I saw in Christina's eyes the desperation that I had felt then.

I nodded and arm in arm we slowly walked back towards the house, where we were greeted by Mrs De Witt.

I was a consummate actor, though inside I was totally confused and in turmoil. 'Oh, what a beautiful place you have here, Mrs De Witt. It has such a romantic atmosphere, doesn't it, Christina?' I said, squeezing her hand, which was returned with the sweetest look you could imagine from one boy to another.

Mrs De Witt glanced at us in turn.

'It is romantic to be young vherever one is!'

I did my best to blush like a schoolboy and let go of Christina's hand.

'I do hope you'll invite me again, Mrs De Witt,' I said, the smoothness just oozing out of me.

'Of course ve vill Alex, you have become quite part of the family, hasn't he, darling,' she said turning to a gentleman who was now standing next to her and whom I think Mrs De Witt didn't really want to introduce to me.

I leaned over and kissed her on the cheek.

'Thank you so much. You are very kind,' I whispered. And then turning to the gentleman, I added, 'I'm sorry, we've not been introduced.'

Mrs De Witt's companion seemed momentarily taken aback but, quickly recovering, introduced himself as Franz Helman. I shook hands with him.

I glanced at my watch. 'Well, I have to get back to my room for the curfew, Mrs De Witt. Will you excuse me?'

Finally, I turned to Christina. 'Would you do me the honour of seeing me out, Christina?'

At the door we had a hurried whispered conversation, but we were soon interrupted by Herr Helman who was leaving too, whereupon he clicked his heels and bowed solemnly to us as he passed.

I walked back to the college, worrying and wondering what on earth was going on at that place and whether I should go back at all. Very quickly, of course, I came to the conclusion that the whole lot were a nest of spies and that they had been grooming me all along. I felt both angry and bitter – I had not been accepted at all; I was being used. And by the end of a long and sleepless night, I had made up my mind to go to the police.

I was now so paranoid that I took the bus and went to the police station at Banbury. Absurdly, I suppose, I thought it was safer to go there rather than to a police station in Oxford, just in case they had been infiltrated.

You can imagine, Mr White, how ridiculous I felt when I found myself at the front desk, telling a fatherly-looking sergeant I had a matter of national security to discuss.

'Now then, son, what is so important that you can't tell me?'

the tall bearded desk sergeant replied.

'I'm sorry, sir, I can't tell you. I've travelled a long way today in order to make sure I wasn't being followed. I have to speak to the senior officer. You can ring my father at the War Ministry. He will vouch for my integrity,' I replied somewhat sternly.

'No need to adopt that tone of voice with me, young man,' he replied.

'Please get me the senior officer quickly,' I implored.

The Sergeant reluctantly went away and within a few minutes he returned with Superintendent James Baker, a tall willowy looking man with an aquiline nose.

'Now then, son, what's all this about then?'

'Can we go somewhere quiet, please, sir?'

'Of course, come with me,' he replied, directing me past the counter towards his office.

The moment we entered and the door was shut behind me I excitedly told him, who I was, where I was educated and which college I was at in Oxford. 'You can ring my father or Mr Wilkes at Bankworth and they will vouch for me. I'm not one to exaggerate . . .' I paused for a moment.

'Go on then, tell me what it's all about?' Superintendent Baker said, trying to get me to come to the point.

I then went into full detail about everything and everyone, before finally asking, 'So what shall I do?'

He had listened intently to all I had said and then quietly and calmly asked, 'Where can you be contacted if you are needed?'

I gave him the phone number of my college.

Leave it with me,' the superintendent said as I left. 'Someone will call you if they think it necessary.' He could see I was excited and anxious at the same time. 'Thank you for your trouble.'

Mr White, if the police acted as quickly today as they did on that day, we would possibly have little or no crime, but in this instance I was amazed. Before I got back to the college, there was already a plain clothes policeman waiting for me. I was quietly whisked away and taken to London, the porter being told I had had some bad news and I would probably be away for a day or two.

The car, a black Wolseley, drove along the Embankment and turned left into a building, I think at the back of the Strand, and we seemed to go below ground. I was taken out of the car and led past several windowless offices, before finally arriving at a large room, similar to a boardroom, with a large table and several chairs. The furnishings were sparse, but what was there served their purpose. Already waiting in the room were several men and one woman. They were obviously something to do with the police.

'Good afternoon, Alex, please sit down,' the senior of the group said as we walked in. 'I know you will want to know why we've brought you here. You mustn't be alarmed but I would like to ask you a few simple questions before I give you an explanation. Is that clear?'

'Yes certainly,' I replied.

Suddenly one of the other officers began talking to me in German and I was momentarily terrified. I thought I had been tricked and was now in German hands.

I protested vigorously. 'Why is he speaking in German? Tell him to speak to me in English. I won't answer any of his questions otherwise!'

'That's the spirit, young Mr Henry!' the senior officer said in English.

The questioning seemed to last for hours and oddly not once was I asked about Mrs De Witt. I was beginning to feel absolutely tired and hungry.

'I'm sorry,' I interrupted. 'I'll have to have something to eat I'm starving.'

The senior officer quickly ordered some tea and ham sandwiches, but there was no question of actually stopping to eat; everything was done on the hoof so to speak.

Finally all the officers left the room, leaving me alone. A few minutes later the senior officer returned.

'I'm sorry about that, Alex. I hope you don't mind us calling you Alex?'

'No, not at all.'

'We needed to know you could be trusted. Even the sons of important people can be corrupted.'

'I came here of my own free will, sir. I have nothing to hide,' I said indignantly.

'Yes, I believe you did Alex, but this is a very serious matter. You have stumbled into what we believe is a spy ring, one which we've had our eye on for some time. So now I want you to tell us everything from start to finish.'

So I went through everything, all that had happened, when, where and why. I told them that I thought they were planning to compromise me with Christina and how he or she had said she wanted a way out. By the end of all the questions I was shattered and falling asleep, but I wasn't allowed to go back to college until they had finished with me. Instead, I was shown to a room complete with bed and the normal facilities which they had laid on for me and I was invited to stay the night. It was sumptuous compared to my college room and the moment my head touched the pillow, I was asleep.

The following morning I was taken down to breakfast in a small canteen. Four of my interrogators were already there and they invited me to join them at their table; all the time there were little searching questions.

Immediately after breakfast, I was returned to the boardroom and the hard questioning continued. After a lunch, I had an embarrassing hour with the woman interrogator who asked me about more 'personal' matters. 'I'm a man,' I insisted, 'a man who has unfortunately grown breasts. It's not the first time this has happened and it won't be the last!'

I was physically and mentally worn out by the time the interrogation finished, when once again I was left alone until the senior officer came back into the room.

'Alex, I want you to do something for me. I want you to make friends with these people and go along with everything, and do everything they expect you to do and find out everything you can. I can't force you to do this, but if you do, I must warn you that they could be very dangerous people. It's up to you!'

I just wanted to get out of that place, to return to normality, so I reluctantly agreed. I didn't mind helping my country, in fact I thought it was an honour, but I didn't like being used once again by both sides because I was unusual. Once again, I was a bit like a fish out of water.

'I'll give you a bit of advice, Alex,' the officer said, having thanked me. 'It's a classic trick to be asked for help by someone who says they want a way out. It's a quick and easy way to gain your trust.' They were warning me, of course, about Christina.

'Now I want you to go to your flat in Chelsea,' the officer continued: 'Spend the rest of today and all tomorrow there and then return to Oxford the day after. Your father is spending three days away from the office at his home in Upper Hayfield and the story you both will have is that he felt poorly and was at home. I want you to telephone Christina and explain the problem and invite him down for the day and see what happens. Play it by ear!'

I wondered if this was this my opportunity to once again become friends with my father? A foolish thought as it turned out.

'Now we'll be arranging contacts for you in Oxford. There'll be a new porter when you go back to your college. The present one will be given compassionate leave . . . I'm sure he will appreciate the extra funds in his wage packet . . . Well, thank you again, Alex, and for now, goodbye . . . and good luck!'

I took a taxi to Chelsea and telephoned Christina as requested. He was unable to come without permission, but would see what he could do. I had a feeling things would be all right for him and within a couple of hours he was knocking on my door.

He kissed me on the doorstep and then entered. His English wasn't too good, so our conversation was mainly in German.

'I'm sorry about that,' he said as soon as he was inside, 'but they may be watching.'

'Who, for goodness' sake?' I asked, almost in irritation.

'Mrs De Witt and her friends,' Christina replied. 'Alex, they're dangerous!'

I left matters at that and began to chat about trivial things – English food, how lovely London was in spring . . . I studiously avoided mentioning Mrs De Witt. I didn't trust myself yet not to give the game away.

'Shall we go to the pictures?' I asked as we had all the evening free.

'Yes, good idea,' Christina replied. 'But, Alex, we will have to hold hands and act as though there is something between us.'

'That's all right. There may be, given the chance!' I replied, keeping my options open in case he was setting me up. I was becoming as devious as them.

We left the flat like two young lovers. Christina looked fabulous, even though I knew everything was false; I had even seen the special padding in her bra, but it didn't matter. It was a night out at someone else's expense and for my piece of mind. However, I was relieved when I found out that the security service was actually watching the flat round the clock, just in case the Germans tried to bug it, which fortunately they didn't.

We held hands as we walked to the cinema just off the Kings Road and watched some B movie; stopping off afterwards at the fish and chip shop, and walking home, eating them out of newspaper (something I always loved). Christina put his arm round my waist and I his and we walked the last few yards to the house like that. I honestly felt so uncomfortable about the whole thing. For some odd reason I couldn't bear to be seen with a girl's arm around me – it didn't feel natural – and yet it wasn't a girl, it was a boy! Still I felt uncomfortable. However, I decided it was all for King and Country and went along with it to see how things developed.

Back at the flat I teased Christina about her fake breasts. The padding device was very advanced for the day, Mr White, but even so they had to be helped with cotton wool and handkerchiefs. Then very naughtily, I showed him what he should have. We fell about laughing. It was good being open like that and then he spoiled it by saying, 'I've told them I think you are a lesbian.'

'Well, I'm not! Goodnight!' I shouted angrily.

'Sorry, Alex,' he said as I slammed my bedroom door, leaving him to sleep on the couch.

We returned to Oxford the next day, both going our different ways and both a little irritated with the other. It wasn't long, however, possibly a couple of days afterwards, that I received a call from him inviting me to go to a soirée at Mrs De Witt's the following weekend.

'I'd be delighted,' I replied, thinking of my duty to my country, and duly reported to the temporary new 'porter'. He gave me a phone number to remember, and I still do remember it. Oxford 4941. It was a safe line which I could use to pass on information.

Of course, I no longer looked on my visits to Mrs De Witt's villa in the same way. In fact, I now began to feel hatred for her and her friends and it took all my acting powers to continue being civil to them. On the other hand, I was pleased to see Christina, although of course I had to be wary even with him. He greeted me with a big kiss as I walked in, obviously for the benefit of the others.

Mrs De Witt was, she said, overjoyed to see me again. She kissed me affectionately. 'You're almost one of the family now, Alex,' she said with her beautiful smile.

She's a better bloody actress than me, I remember thinking as I was led upstairs and shown my room. Yes, Mr White, I was staying the weekend and I had taken my suitcase with me. It was a stupid thing to do, but I had grappled with my conscience and thought, 'Cry God for Harry, England and St George!' or whatever the saying was.

Mrs De Witt took me into the room and I stopped in the doorway. It took my breath away. It was a beautiful room and so luxurious in every way – its double bed, its furnishings, the glimpse of a gleaming bathroom through an open door; it genuinely took my breath away.

'Is this for me?' I asked, totally astonished.

'Do you like it?' Mrs De Witt asked.

'Like it! 'I exclaimed. 'I love it. Can I keep it?' I replied jokingly.

'Well, Alex, it's certainly yours for the veekend and remember, ve are not like your college, ve do allow guests in the bedrooms, male or female!' she replied with a knowing smile.

I bet you do, I thought, as I too put on a knowing smile and added, 'You really are too kind, Mrs De Witt.'

That day Christina and I spent several hours wandering in the garden talking German and sometime later, during the afternoon, we were joined by Norbert Lisek and Petra from the Embassy.

'How nice to see you again, Alex,' Norbert said as he walked over to meet us.

'Good afternoon, Mr Chillington-Henry,' Petra said, in her usual starchy manner.

'Good afternoon,' I replied.

'I'm pleased you have made the effort to continue with your German,' Norbert went on, 'and even more so that you still come to see us.'

'Why shouldn't I? It's a lovely place, after all, and you have all been so friendly. I almost feel as though I am one of you!'

At that point I caught Norbert signalling to Christina with just a twitch of an eyebrow. Christina took the hint.

'Alex, I have to go for a minute. I have forgotten to do something,' she said. Back in a tick!' she added in English with a smile.

I was very wary, but I thought it was broad daylight; nothing could happen here. But as I looked round I saw we were in a walled garden where no one could see in or out.

'Come now, Alex,' Norbert began, 'I want to know your real

opinion of what you have seen or heard while you have been here. Simply from the educational point of view, that is.'

'What do you mean?'

Norbert continued: 'You are an educated young man and we want to know if you think that we are getting things right. Are our little sessions up to the right standard?'

'Very much so. I have been really impressed. Yes, very much so.'

'And what about that book you were lent . . . *Mein Kampf*?' He leaned over and whispered. 'It's a load of rubbish, don't you think? Its message is far too extreme.'

I quickly saw the trap he was laying for me. 'Look, Norbert. Forgive me, but you and Mrs De Witt have been wonderfully hospitable, and I don't think it's really right that I should criticise your culture and beliefs. Whatever your Chancellor's ideas, I think he has to be respected as your head of state. To be honest, though, I don't agree with you about Mein Kampf. It has lots of interesting ideas, though many may need refining . . . But I don't want to fall out with you, Norbert. Let's not discuss politics any further.'

Norbert could not stop himself from smiling at Petra. 'Alex,I'm sorry, I didn't mean to offend . . .'

'Listen, Norbert, you have your view and I have mine, but I'm a little surprised that you can criticise your leader while working for him. I wouldn't do that. In fact,' I said, smiling, 'I think I'm more loyal to him than you are!'

'You may well be,' Norbert said with a sigh.

We then spent an hour or so talking, steering clear of politics, yes, but all the time I could sense Norbert was still probing, with dear Petra just nodding in the right places. In the end I was convinced he was satisfied I was no danger. Quite the contrary: I could be of use, even at my age.

I returned to the house alone and took the opportunity to nose around. Just off the main hall was a closed door. I had been shown most of the house, but this room I had been purposefully steered clear of. I knocked on the door and walked in. I saw a group of people gathered around a desk: Mrs De Witt, Lisek, Petra and another tall, sinister-looking man. Mrs De Witt turned at the interruption, her face filled with rage.

'Get out! Get out! Here it is private! You must never come in here. Do you understand?' she shouted. The rest of the party were clearly shocked at this outburst.

'I'm sorry! Please forgive me, Mrs De Witt. I was looking for Christina.'

Mrs De Witt quickly calmed down, but by now the others were looking at her with some disgust.

'No, it is me who is sorry, Alex. My friends and I were having a little argument and I am a little stressed. Where is Christina? She ought to be with you.'

'I'm not sure, but she can't be very far. Please excuse me, Mrs De Witt.'

I turned and left, shutting the door as I went; however through the door I heard raised voices in German; it was obvious they were all admonishing Mrs De Witt for her stupidity.

I waited a short distance away and tried to listen in, but I heard someone coming to the door. I quickly went to another doorway just down the hall and hid there, hoping I wouldn't be seen. The door opened and the sinister-looking man popped his head out and looked both ways to see if I was still about. I stood absolutely still, unable to move out of fear as he closed the door again. I was still petrified when two or three seconds later, he repeated the exercise and once again looked both ways. I heard him return to the group; the raised voices continued and I could hear everything perfectly. They were discussing me and my loyalty to the cause!

Lisek was taking the helm. 'Look, Günter,' he began, obviously addressing the sinister visitor, 'I have questioned Alex for well over two hours. I really think he is sympathetic to Herr Hitler's ideas and I'm sure will commit to us. Unless Mrs De Witt here has frightened him off with her little outburst.'

Günter sounded irritated. 'Well, I'm not sure we can trust him so easily. I would prefer to carry on with our stratagem – to compromise him and then blackmail him. It's simpler. That way we will be able to get more information out of him about his father and the Ministry–'

'But if he comes round to our way of thinking, we won't need to stoop to all that kind of thing,' Lisek interrupted.

'The last thing we need is another blind convert to the cause. No we need to frighten him! That way, he will work all the better for us. Petra, go and get Christina . . .'

I hurried to the front entrance and pretended to have just come in as Petra came out of the room.

'Have you seen Christina?' I asked. 'I've been waiting ages.'

'She's wanted by Mrs De Witt. I'll tell her you're waiting for her,' she replied.

'I'll be in the garden,' I said, as she went off in search of Christina.

I sat in the sun and thought about the whole situation. It was obvious that this little fascist cabal was going to exploit my differences just as everyone else had, but this time I had grown up a little and was a little braver and I almost knew what to expect.

I waited a couple of hours before Christina came to meet me in the garden, followed immediately by a servant, bringing out tea. As we sipped the hot liquid, Christina seemed very sheepish and hardly spoke a word, which concerned me.

'Have I upset you?' I asked finally.

He had hardly replied, 'No' when Mrs De Witt arrived and tried to mend fences. The conversation was very stilted, but I did ask if I had got Christina into trouble by going into that room.

'Not at all Alex, she's very tired. We've been working her too hard this last couple of hours, haven't we, Christina?' The last three words came out almost through gritted teeth.

'Yes, that's right, Alex, they have. But I'm free now. I'll take you for a walk when we've finished our tea,' Christina added.

Soon afterwards, Christina and I went upstairs. I took her into my room and we sat on the bed. He put his hand on my knee and we sat there for a few minutes in silence. Then, without warning, he gently rocked me over onto my back, leaned over and kissed me on my cheek.

'There's no one watching at the moment, he whispered, 'but there will be tonight. They plan to take pictures, to compromise you!'

'I won't let them!' I said angrily, 'and I'm leaving. Now!'

'You can't, Alex. Please! I know what they will do to me. They will kill me, make me disappear. I know it. You are the only one who can get me out of this. Please.'

It was those four words again: they will kill me. I couldn't put him through what I had been through. I had to help him, but I felt I had to discuss the matter with my contact first.

'Christina, can we leave here for half an hour. I want to go back to the college for a bit.'

'Of course, they'll have no problem with that. Though I should warn you, you'll be followed.'

'But you'll be with me!'

'And you think they trust me? They are security mad at the moment,' he added.

We left the house holding hands and casually strolled back towards the college. As we passed through town, Christina discreetly pointed out our chaperone reflected in the glass of a shop window. We stopped at a little café and popped in for a quick cup of tea. The man was waiting across the road for us to come out.

'I would like to get rid of him, if possible,' I said anxiously, 'and I've an idea. A few doors away, the shops back onto an alley and there are back exits. Let's do it!'

We left the café and continued to saunter along. I pointed to a mannequin in a window, displaying a braided Chanel suit. We wandered inside and after a few minutes wandered out the back and then raced along like a couple of kids up to mischief.

I left Christina outside the college gate and made my way to the porter's lodge. My man, thank God, was there. I quickly told him everything.

'Go to your room. Someone will be with you within half an hour,' the porter said, almost shoving me out of his little room. I did as I was told and sure enough, almost thirty minutes later there was a knock on the door. It was the senior officer.

'Alex, good to see you,' he said, shutting the door firmly behind him. 'Now quickly, tell me what's happened.'

Again I told him everything. 'I just don't want my father to be hurt if some nasty report gets into the papers! He'd be devastated and he'd say it was all my fault . . . for being a . . . freak! What should I do?'

'It's up to you, Alex, but my advice is to go through with it. In the end, I don't think they would actually do what they threatened to do. It would risk exposing them as well as you . . . And someone will be close by, I promise. It's whether you can bear to . . . to get along with Christina. If you do it, you'll be able to play along and we may get more information about them.'

I looked at him and blushed. He, too, was very embarrassed by the whole business.

'Now tell me about this room you burst in on,' he said, hurriedly changing the subject.

'It was an office. There were lots of bookshelves.'

'Did you see anything odd or unusual?'

I tried to visualise the room again. 'Yes, actually there was. Some of the bookshelves seemed to stand further back than the other, as if they were part of a door. I didn't think much of it at the time. Mrs De Witt's outburst really shocked me. Do you think there was another secret room?'

'Perhaps . . . Now I want you go back and do your best. It's up to you,' the officer said, getting up to leave. 'And, like I said, don't trust Christina. She may sound plausible, but very likely she's in the whole thing. You know where we are should you need us.'

He held out his hand. 'I must go, best of luck Alex . . . and thank you!' And with that he was gone.

I quickly returned to Christina and we sauntered back to Pentland Villas. In the High Street we once again spotted our tail in the doorway of a bookshop. He was looking very annoyed. We walked in through the main door and made our way to my room, where once again we lay on the bed. I felt sorry for Christina's predicament as I knew what they really thought of him and that 'win or lose' he was really not much use to them. I vowed I would try my best to save him, as long as I believed he was not truly one of them as the senior officer suspected.

For all his difficulties, he was still a man, Mr White. He rolled over on top of me and kissed me on my cheek.

He was a man, Mr White, through and through, and I was a woman. There would not have been anything wrong with what we were doing, had it not been for that little piece of paper called my birth certificate. I was becoming more confused than ever, about what I was or what I should be. Perhaps what was hampering me was only the mental control that my father still had over me. I had always been his boy. How could I stop being that boy now?

Christina began to kiss me more firmly, but I kept moving away which upset him.

'Don't you want to do this?' Christina asked with desperation in his voice.

'I'm not sure,' I replied somewhat sheepishly.

'Then kiss me . . . I won't bite!'

I let myself go, convincing myself it wasn't a proper kiss, so it didn't count. It was for King and Country. We kissed full on the lips and he held me so tight, it almost took my breath away. I couldn't believe I was beginning to enjoy sleeping with the enemy.

As he stripped his clothes off, it became only too obvious that he was a man. I let him take off my shirt, whereupon he began to caress and kiss my breasts, but that's as far as I went except to distract him. I played with his manhood until he ejaculated over me and the bed. He lay back beside me, panting.

I could not help laughing, which caused him to get cross, but when I think about it, it is just as funny – the stuff films are made of. There I was with a beautiful top half and nothing below and there was Christina with nothing up top and something different below and we were both involved with some kind of Nazi spy ring.

It was almost time for dinner, which was to be another grand affair and after duly sprucing up, we went downstairs to the lounge, where the guests were already assembled and listening to the pianist specially hired for the evening. Christina and I went to sit on a sofa, where we were offered a glass of Sekt by one of the maids.

'This is so much better than champagne, don't you think, Alex?' Norbert said as he came to join us, sitting between us.

'Have you two been having a good time?' he asked.

'Lovely!' I replied in English. I looked at Christina fondly. I even gripped his hand and squeezed it a little. I think I had grown to like him a little; and he certainly seemed fond of me. He, after all, had been the one who hadn't wanted to blackmail me.

At dinner I sat next to Christina and on my other side was a German I hadn't met before, a Manfred Willemer, who was tall and blond and vaguely schoolboyish even in middle age.

'Call me Manfred,' he said, introducing himself to me.

Hello, Manfred,' I replied. 'You know Christina?' I added.

'Yes of course. I understand you two have hit it off . . . are abit of an item, as the Americans say. Don't you know?'

The one thing in my life that I dislike is a foreigner trying to use the colloquialisms. It never sounds right and didn't on this occasion. But I really disliked him for another reason – he had clearly been given the job of finding out more about me. He was a slick professional.

It wasn't long before I realised, Mr White, that my drink had been spiked. I became tipsy very quickly and very woozy and eventually, I knew I would have to leave the table.

'I think I have had too much to drink, Mrs De Witt. I'm so sorry. I think I will have to go to bed. My voice sounded strange, drowsy and disconnected.

'That's all right, Alex, ve have all been like that at one stage or another in our lives, haven't ve?' Mrs De Witt replied graciously.

'Christina, could you help Alex upstairs and make sure he is all right.'

What followed was like a dream. Christina took me to my room and lay me down on the bed. 'I'm sorry Alex,' he whispered in my ear as he pretended to struggle with my jacket. Then suddenly the room appeared to be full of men and women and I was being stripped off. I can remember struggling a bit but quickly giving in. Words drifted in and out of my head. 'I knew he was a woman!' There were the blinding flashes from photographs being taken as I was splayed out on the bed, my face and breasts prominent, and then more, as others – both men and women – did various indecent things to me. I don't know how long it all lasted, but I know they put Christina in the bed next to me and, when I came round the following morning, I found myself naked with his arms round me. He was fast asleep, or unconscious, I don't know which.

Oh God what have they done, I thought as the horror hit me of what the pictures may show. They know all my secrets. I would . . . I would hate my father to see them.

Christina woke up, looked across at me.

'I feel absolutely terrible that I did this to you last night,' he whispered as he stroked my head. He told me again and again how sorry he was and how fond of me he was. I was worried he was beginning to convince me!

We eventually got up. I was still naked and still not a hundred per cent, but I managed to get dressed and go downstairs to take a quick walk in the fresh air to help clear my head. I was soon joined by Christina and once again we sat on a bench and talked. It was the only place that was safe to talk.

'So where are these photos now?' I asked him.

'In the room above your bedroom. I know where they develop the film, too. We may be able to sneak a look,' he replied. 'We Germans have developed some very small cameras and some highly sophisticated technical surveillance equipment,' he said somewhat proudly.

He must have seen me shudder at his use of the words, "We Germans".

'Sorry, Alex, I didn't mean it to sound like that . . . Look, it's possible they'll have another go this evening; they may not have got the right shots.'

'Not again!' I sighed. 'Look, Christina, they really know what you are. I almost heard them say so and you're right, they're only tolerating you because you're helping them trap me. I can get you out of all this if you want?'

He was very wary, but I decided to go on. 'Trust me. I'm going to tell them I'm in love with you and I want to stay with you and see what happens. Trust me, please! It might get you out of here.'

We went into breakfast where I noticed the other guests could not help giving us knowing looks. The strong tea brought me back to earth and gave me the confidence to walk down the corridor and knock on the forbidden door. I heard scurrying about and conversations, but no answer. I knocked again, this time hard.

'It's me, Mrs De Witt . . . Alex. May I come in?'

A second or two later she replied, 'Yes, of course, Alex. Come in.'

I opened the door and walked in, to be faced by Günter and Petra as well as Mrs De Witt.

'Now vot can I do for you?' she asked.

I was a good actress, Mr White, and after this performance I should have gone on the stage. I know I would have succeeded.

'Mrs De Witt, I'm so sorry about – '

She didn't give me a chance to finish before she asked, 'Vot about, Alex?'

'I seemed to have had far too much to drink and I made a fool of myself,' I replied, trying to appear coy and embarrassed.

'No you didn't. Ve all go through this stage. Don't vorry about it!' she continued.

'But it was the other matter, I really meant. I . . . I slept with Christina!'

'That doesn't matter either,' she said, again interrupting me.

'It does . . .' I paused for a second for effect. 'You know as well as I do that Christina is a man and I think you realise my own predicament . . .' I paused again. 'My problem is that I think I have fallen in love with him and I want to be with him and I don't want you to sack him because he slept with me . . . I just want to be with him . . .' I paused again. 'Please don't sack him,' I said, almost sobbing. 'I don't think he loves me, but I know I want to be with him!'

They were visibly taken aback by my performance and without doubt it could have altered their thinking about me and put Christina in a safer position.

'Don't you vorry yourself,' Mrs De Witt said as she put her arm round me as though she was comforting her daughter. 'Ve von't tell Christina off and ve do understand.'

She took me to the door and smiled.

She's as good as me, I thought, as she released me into the hall. A proper Sarah bloody Bernhardt!

I stayed outside the door and was sure they had taken the bait hook, line and sinker. I even heard them laughing about it – my naïvety, my innocence. I quickly went to find Christina and told him what had happened. He was to pretend he wasn't in love with me and that he had told me that the relationship wouldn't be going anywhere. A few minutes later, Mrs De Witt called him into the office.

It was a hour or so before they released him again and he had been well and truly briefed. He was told to keep me dangling, to play a little hard to get, be a bit ruthless with me and a bit cruel, to test what my reactions would be and to find out if I really cared as much as I had implied. He had abandoned his women's clothes and he looked really quite attractive in his male attire – a simple roll-neck and slacks – though a little bit thin perhaps.

That evening – it was now Sunday – they persuaded me to stay the night again; they would take me back to college on the Monday morning. Quite honestly I didn't want to. Regardless of this little adventure, as I saw it at the time, I didn't want to miss my studies and wanted to see Jennifer. However, I stayed and I acted up the part of a love-smitten youth. Over dinner, I gazed at him calf-eyed and even tried to serve him the best morsels of food. A little way through the meal Chris, as I shall now call him, suddenly snapped at me, just loud enough for the others to hear: 'Stop fussing, will you, Alex!'

'Don't be like that,' I said. I pretended to be hurt and made my excuses.

'Please excuse me. I have college in the morning and I have to go to bed. Goodnight everybody and thank you for a wonderful weekend, Mrs De Witt.'

I left the dining room and gave a final wistful look back at Chris. He simply affected indifference.

He joined me about an hour later, when I was in the bath. He sat on the edge of the bath and told me what had been said after I had left. Mrs De Witt was obviously pleased by the turn of events and had even tried to defend me.

'She's such a nice girl and a lonely one. I don't know vhy she pretends to be a man, because she's quite pretty and it's obvious just from her appearance and ven she speaks, she cannot be anything else. I don't vant her upset! Ve need her.'

We laughed at the success of our ruse; at how they thought they were taking us in when in fact we were taking them in. Things got lively when Chris climbed into the bath. We spent another night in each other's arms. By now I was absolutely convinced of Chris's sincerity. I began to feel nothing but warmth towards him.

The following morning, we had breakfast and I said my good-byes to Chris and even managed a tear or two, for De Witt's benefit.

'You really like him don't you?' she said as she drove me to college.

'Yes. Yes I do,' I replied, 'but he doesn't want me, only what he can get out of me,' I added like some lovesick girl who has just realised she was being taken advantage of.

'I don't think he's like that, Alex,' she said. 'In fact, he told us last night he actually cares for you too.'

'He did?' I asked excitedly.

'Yes, he did.'

From then on I behaved like an excited schoolgirl. She dropped me off at the gates. I kissed her on the cheek and almost skipped through the college gates. On the way in I stopped at the porter's lodge. I waved back to Mrs De Witt.

'See you Vensday, Alex!' she shouted.

'Yes,' I replied with a beaming smile all over my face.

There was a new porter on duty, but he identified himself the moment he saw me. I quickly apprised him of the situation and was told to meet the senior man here at one o'clock.

'If anybody asks you, he's a senior technical liaison officer with the AVRO aeronautical establishment. He'll be discussing the possibility of you working with them.'

You would have thought it would have been impossible for me to concentrate on my studies, with all the excitement and activities going on, but I could actually divorce the two. I attended the lectures as though nothing else was on my mind. It was strange, but it was a skill that was to prove very useful later in my life.

Lunchtime soon arrived and I was met by the senior officer, whom I knew as 'George', though I doubt that was his real name.

'I'll take you to lunch,' he said, smiling and took me to the local chip shop where we bought good old-fashioned fish and chips, wrapped in paper. We ate them sitting on a park bench where I told him everything that had happened, leaving as little as possible out. I drew a discreet veil over my intimacy with Chris, alluding to it only in the most general way.

'You're a brave young man. Well done!'

"I don't know about the man bit . . .' I began to say but was abruptly cut short.

'We won't go into that . . . Now, Alex, I want you to tell them you have been offered some research work at AVRO. It's top secret and only a few members of the firm know about it, but here's a letter which explains what they want you to do and I want you to show it to the young man. He's bound to pass the good news on to them. Go and see Christina as soon as you can and be as thrilled as possible, implying you may have to move. You know what to say,' he went on, becoming somewhat embarrassed. 'Let's see how the hare runs. As soon as we've got evidence, we will pounce. Remember you mustn't tell a soul, not even your father.'

'I won't. Thanks for the fish and chips,' I said as he left and I returned for my afternoon lectures.

Straight after supper, I did as I was told and cycled over to Pentland Villa and asked to see Chris. I couldn't believe it. He was dressed as a woman again, and this upset me. I thought he was playing games with me.

'I just like being like this,' he explained as I looked him up and down quizzically.

He took me out into the garden, 'Why are you doing this to me, Chris? I like you as a man, not as a woman. You know that I really love you and I thought you loved me. At least you told me so . . .'

As you can see, Mr White, I was no longer quite in command of myself; the divisions between play-acting and reality had become blurred.

'Oh come on, Alex,' Chris protested. 'You know how fond I am of you. Is that what you wanted to see me about?'

'I don't think I want to tell you now. You have spoiled things for me,' I replied like a petulant, spoiled child.

'Come on!' he said, putting his arm round me, trying to comfort me and kissing me on the cheek like a dutiful lover. 'Come on, tell me!'

I took out the envelope with the letter. 'Give me a kiss and I'll show you.'

He kissed me full on the lips and I pretended to, or perhaps really did, melt into his arms and then showed him the letter.

'Gosh! That's not bad at your age,' he commented. 'Why you?' he asked.

'You cheeky devil! Why not?' I replied. 'I'm very good at maths and way ahead of the others in my college. They want me to help with some research. It's secret, I think,' I said, whispering the last few words. 'Trouble is, if I accept it, I won't be able to see you so much and if you didn't want me to take it I won't. I would prefer to be with you. You know that, don't you?' I asked, trying to squeeze out a tear.

'I do now,' he replied, holding me. I saw him look up quickly as if he had seen something, but I couldn't turn round to see.

'You seem uncomfortable with me today,' I said. 'Please can I come and see you later? I need to see you. I want to know what to do,' I asked, pleading.

'I can't tonight. I have to work. I'll see you tomorrow,' he said, almost pushing me out along the long gravel drive.

'What time?' I turned and asked when we had reached the gate.

'When you like,' he replied and went back along the drive.

I cycled back to college just in time to meet Jennifer in the evening. I was dying to tell her about everything, but I had promised to keep mum and that was that. We had a lovely night out, but I did feel as though we were being watched, but by which side I didn't know.

The following evening, after lectures, I again made my way to Pentland Villa.

Mrs De Witt met me at the door. 'Your young man is not here at ze moment, but come in. You and I can have a chat. He tells me you have had some good news . . .'

'I don't think it is,' I replied. 'It means I may have to go away. I don't know yet if it's all the time or a few days a week. He obviously told you I have been offered a job in research at AVRO. It's one of our very biggest firms,' I said proudly. 'If Chris doesn't want me to go, then I won't. I don't want anything else except him.'

'Vell, you do have it bad, don't you?' Mrs De Witt said, leading me into the forbidden room.

'Do you know,' she continued, 'he has asked me if he voud be allowed to marry you.'

'No!' I almost screamed. 'Really?' I asked.

'Yes, really,' she replied. 'He has a real opportunity at our Embassy for promotion and I think a girl like you would be a great asset to him. Vould you be prepared to help him?'

I had never heard such a load of rubbish in my life. How on earth Mrs De Witt had dreamed up this next little charade I'll never know; it seemed so idiotic. I knew that Chris had no real designs on me anyway. I had no illusions about myself, but I couldn't believe that Mrs De Witt, with all her so-called intelligence, would think I could fall for it. I actually felt embarrassed at the lengths they were going to in order to entrap me.

'Of course I would!' I answered, trying to appear sane, 'but would he really be allowed to marry me? If it's true, I'm the happiest person alive!'

I walked over to her smiling and kissed her hard on the cheek. 'You have done so much for me, Mrs de Witt. How can I ever repay you! . . . When will he be back?'

'I think I heard him come in a minute or two ago. I'll go and see.'

She walked out of the office and left me on my own. I knew it was a test and just smiled and beamed with excitement and even waltzed and spun round. When I heard her come back, I raced to a chair and sat down.

'You know vere your room is, of course. You know it is *your* room now, dear Alex. Vell, if you go up there, I think you may be in for a surprise,' Mrs De Witt said.

I walked upstairs and opened the door. Chris stood waiting, now in his male clothes. I knew we were still being watched as Chris was always nervous when he knew the cameras were on him.

'Alex!' he said softly, 'I know we've only known each other a few weeks now, but as far as I'm concerned it's long enough. 'Will you marry me?' I grabbed hold of him and squeezed him for the camera and replied, 'Yes, yes, yes!' and I kissed him passionately.

With my fingers crossed of course, Mr White. At that very moment I realised, despite all our intimacy, I was fond of him. His life had mirrored mine but I was very far indeed from being in love with him.

I don't think in all my life that an enemy could be so bloody stupid, idiotic or naïve as to think anyone would fall for what happened next. And when I look back, I feel almost offended to think they thought I would.

Chris handed me a little engagement ring and made a great show of putting it on my finger. But there was one detail they hadn't thought about: it didn't fit.

'Never mind, we'll get it altered later. I don't want to spoil the moment,' I said coyly.

Chris seemed to think that the ring gave him carte blanche to do as he pleased and within minutes my new fiancé began to take my clothes off in front of the camera and once more we began a session, Mr White, for England and King George.

They persuaded me to stay the night again, which I did. I must admit the bed was very comfortable compared to my narrow little bed at the college. During dinner, Chris made advances to another woman at the table, which was undoubtedly stage managed to make me jealous, but I played along and pretended to be a little cross with him. I surprised myself as this made me realise my acting ability was second to none.

Chris actually came up to me and said, 'Don't worry, *Liebchen*, it's you I want. You know, Alex, I believe you really do love me, don't you?'

Mr White, it was a statement and not a question, and now I knew I had him thinking I really was in love with him.

I answered him as sincerely as I could. 'Yes, yes, of course I do. I can't help it but I know I'm now lost without you. Pretending to be in love with you has made me actually fall in love with you. Is that strange?'

Mr White, excuse the modern expressions, but for me, everything had at last clicked into place. Let's be honest, what man in his right mind would propose to a person like me, purporting to be a man, dressed like a man . . . It was too ridiculous to contemplate. I was truly sorry; but now I was convinced Chris was in on it too, that it was all a scheme to entrap students and others into helping or spying for the enemy. Chris was the good guy who would confide in you and gain your confidence, while the others were the potential bad guys. At least in my mind, I now knew where I was and I can only believe they thought I was some lonely pathetic little soul whom they could manipulate like a puppet on a string . . .

That night Mrs De Witt made our engagement public in the drawing room.

'*Meine Damen und Herren*, I have some vonderful news to give you: Alex and Chris, who haven't known each other for more than a few weeks, are to be married . . .'

There was a round of applause and then someone proposed a toast: 'To Alex and Chris!'

I smiled and having thanked everyone, made my excuses and disappeared to my room. I needed time to think. Ten minutes later, I went back downstairs to the sound of raised voices. It was Chris and Günter. I stood at the bottom of the stairs for a few seconds, trying to listen to what was going on. I couldn't hear what was being said, but then Günter's voice seemed to boom throughout the entire house.

'Go and get her! Bring her to me now!'

Chris came out and saw me standing by the stairs. 'Günter wants you. Please come with me.' This was spoken more like an order to an inferior rather than a lover to lover. We walked into the drawing room and were soon joined by Mrs De Witt.

'Now, young lady,' Günter said in English. 'I have got to be straight with you. Chris has been recalled to Germany and he'll be leaving in a day or two.'

'Can I go with him?' I immediately asked, feigning dismay.

'Not at this point in time,' he continued.

'What if we were married?' I almost pleaded.

'But that couldn't happen for several weeks. But I know he will wait for you to go over there, won't you, Chris?'

'Of course, I will,' Chris said, as he came over to kiss me on the cheek.

Suddenly, Günter spoke excitedly: 'I have an idea. If you wanted be useful to him and to Germany, we might be able to get you over there quicker!'

'Really?' I asked, as Chris squeezed my hand a little and smiled what I now knew to be one of his fake little smiles.

'I think I can manage it if you are prepared to help the Fatherland. It may, of course, mean taking German nationality. Would you be prepared to do that? To give up your country?'

'To be with him?' I paused and looked at him. 'Yes, yes I would!'

Chris grabbed hold of my face and, squeezing it, kissed me full on the lips.

Günter continued: 'Let me ask you . . . and you must think very carefully before you answer. If I can get you to Germany quickly to be with him, or better still, if I could stop him being transferred and get his promotion here, would you do something very delicate for us?'

'I wouldn't commit murder,' I said, laughing. 'But I love him and that's enough for me.'

'Alex, you told Mrs De Witt you were going to AVRO next week.'

'This week!' I replied.

'Oh good,' Günter said. 'Well, would you be prepared to take some photographs for us when you visit? It really would help you and Chris, as well as doing a small favour for the Fatherland.'

'Oh no, that would not be right,' I answered. 'I would not want to betray my country,' I continued, trying to make it sound I wasn't a soft touch.

For the next hour or so what had begun as a no-no became a maybe and then, 'I'm sure I can! . . . Just a few photographs . . . that's nothing . . . But when will I know what Chris is doing? I can't bear the suspense.'

'I promise I'll sort it out for you,' Günter said reassuringly.

'I haven't got a camera, though.'

'Don't worry, Alex. I'll give you one tonight and when you get there, just take what you can and I'll look at them after. If you can take a photograph of the inside of the factory, that would be good, but anything will do.

'Now I'm sure you two want to be on your own. You have a lot to discuss. I'll see you later. Chris, I just want a quick word, please, before you go . . .' he added as we were leaving.

He shut the door behind me and I stayed as nearby as I dared. I heard Günter congratulating Chris on his conquest.

I saw the handle on the door move slightly, so I made my way quickly to the dining room. As the two Germans came out, Günter made the point of saying as loudly as he could: 'Now you go and look after that fiancée of yours. She's a wonderful girl!'

Chris came out and raced upstairs, thinking I had gone up there, so I had a few minutes to think about my next move. I still had to pretend I was in love and still had to sleep with him; but that was losing its flavour, I don't mind telling you.

Chris eventually found me in the lounge drinking a glass of Sekt. He helped himself to one and we took them out to the garden, sitting as far away from the house as we could. It's exactly what a clever operator would do particularly when trying to gain the confidence of others, I was thinking as we gazed across the twilit lawns.

'You know, Alex, you don't have to pretend to me,' Chris suddenly remarked.

I had decided to play it my way and presumed he was doing it the same. 'What about?' I asked.

'You loving me.'

'Are you blind? Do you really think I would do this if there wasn't a chance of having you? Of course I love you and I do want to be with you. I would cheerfully give up my country to be with you,' I replied.

He took my hand and walked me back into the house and on the way up to my room, we were intercepted by Günter.

'May I come into your room? I've got something to show you.'

We all trooped into the room and he gave me the smallest camera I had ever seen. It was a Leika and was about the size of a box of Morning Glory matches.

Günter gave a quick demonstration. 'You only have to click it and turn the film on like this. As you can see, it's very easy. It can take twenty pictures in all . . . I'm sure you'll put it to good use,' he finally said as he bade us goodnight.

I got into bed beside Chris. He was especially gentle; I think I had actually fooled him into believing what I had said. Anyway, he cuddled up, telling me to be very careful, that what I was doing was espionage and very dangerous.

Mrs De Witt took me back to college in the morning and I clocked in as usual, stopping at the porter's lodge. It was the original officer again.

'I need to speak to George! Urgently! Tell him, the bait's hooked.'

Once again we met at lunchtime and ate fish and chips in the park where I gave him the Leika to look at.

George was really pleased with my efforts and arranged for me to go to AVRO on Thursday to look round the place. 'Of course, we'll be the ones taking the photographs,' he remarked, smiling. 'All the same, it's probably best you actually go there, just in case they're watching you.'

AVRO proved a fascinating place and whatever was reported in the papers, we really were preparing for war. Aircraft production was being stepped up and the new engines were being tested.

At the end of the visit, George handed the camera back to me. 'The films have been taken in such a way to look as though you are an amateur. Play dumb about the things you have photographed and you'll be all right.'

We returned to Oxford late in the evening and it was too late to visit Pentland Villa. However, Günter had left a phone message with the porter asking for me to contact him as soon as possible. He was clearly very anxious about the whole affair.

The following evening I went to the villa and handed the camera over to Günter, who rushed off to get them developed. Chris had obviously been told to keep me entertained as he was very attentive – a job at which he succeeded as he managed to keep me there at least two hours. Finally, Günter returned and asked us both to go into the forbidden room.

'I have some good news for you,' Günter began. 'The photographs are wonderful! Your fiancée has done her job very well, Chris and it should stand you in good stead.' He announced this with such an artificial smile on his face it could have cracked a mirror. Then almost without taking a breath he was straight back to business. 'Are you going again, Alex?'

'Yes, as a matter of fact I am. I think the technical officer wants to see me next Tuesday. They're arranging for me to have security clearance. Obviously, they've got some extremely sensitive projects. You'd think we were still at war, wouldn't you?' I added, in effect having a quiet dig at them.

'Well, I'd like you to take some more photographs,' Günter continued, oblivious to the irony of my comment.

'What about us?' I asked, holding Chris's hand tightly.

He just looked at me, smiling blandly, as if to say, 'Well, that's enough for now.'

We left the office and went into the lounge and to my surprise I saw Eberhard.

'Hello,' I enthused. 'How nice to see you! I've missed you. Where have you been?' I asked.

'It's nice to see you too. I had to transfer to another college. My lodgings made it too awkward to remain there. I was sorry to go,' Eberhard replied.

'Who's your friend,' I asked, looking at a very spotty, shy individual sitting next to him.

'Hello,' the spotty lad said as he stood up to shake my hand. 'I'm Peter Spillsbury. I'm at Cambridge studying German and Applied Physics.'

'Oh, how interesting! I'm studying Maths and Languages here, though it looks as though I'm going to be put on a big research project soon.' I could not help boasting a little.

Peter was a classic case for the people at Pentland Villa. He was obviously a loner and highly intelligent, destined, no doubt, for some very sensitive research. Mrs De Witt and her cronies certainly had a nose for it.

I sat in the lounge for a good half an hour by myself, trying to out think their next move. I was beginning to think of the whole thing in terms of a game of chess and didn't really pay much attention to the possible seriousness of the consequences.

I returned to AVRO on the following Tuesday and once again George took the photographs and handed the camera back, only this time he had one juicy picture, which was guaranteed to wet their appetite.

However, I delivered the pictures virtually a week later than I had promised the Pentland people, thinking I would make them sweat a bit and they did. They had left many messages for me, but I had simply told them I had to finish some work urgently and would be there possibly on the Tuesday. I eventually went to the villa on Wednesday. I walked into the house and went straight to the forbidden room and knocked on the door.

'Mrs De Witt, it's Alex. I want to speak to Günter.'

The lady of the house came scurrying to the door.

'Alex, he vill be back in half an hour. Go and make yourself at home upstairs.'

She had obviously forgotten what was afoot upstairs, for when I opened the bedroom door there was Chris as Christina with another man. I heard the sound of a camera clicking and whirring. I did not need to feign shock. Chris looked up but seemed unfazed, as he smiled across at me. I quickly shut the door and went downstairs in a bit of a daze.

I waited in the lounge and by the time Günter had arrived to see me, I had recovered my senses. I remember being very angry mainly because of the time I wasted.

'I've just seen Chris on the bed with another man. They're taking pictures. He obviously doesn't think much of me, otherwise he wouldn't do it!'

'Grow up, girl! It's only work.' It left me to guess exactly what kind of work Chris was engaged in. Pentland Villa obviously did some kind of sideline in pornography. Was there no end to the depths to which these people could sink?

'Have you got that film for me?' Günter suddenly asked.

'That's all you're interested in, isn't it. Not me!' I said, now with my full dramatic hat on. 'As long as I can be of use, you'll just string me along, is that it?' I asked.

'Give me the camera, young lady, and then I'll listen to you.'

'No I won't!' I replied like a spoiled child.

'Give me the camera *now*!' He was becoming more aggressive and there was a gleam of menace in his eye. Perhaps I had overstepped the line.

I really was scared, so I pushed the camera across to him, shaking a little as I did.

'Now go into the library and stay there until I call you.'

'Yes, Günter,' I said timidly and went to the library and sat and waited. I tried to cry for effect, but in reality a deep rage was boiling inside me. I waited, seething, for well over an hour when Mrs De Witt called me into the office. Günter was already there and so was Chris as Christina. They were all smiling sweetly as if nothing untoward had happened.

'The pictures are fantastic, young lady. I don't think it will be too long before we'll have an answer whether Chris can stay or not,' Günter said calmly.

Somehow or other I managed to play my part. I began to sob. 'I don't think I want this anymore. Every time I come here I don't know whether I'll see a male or female. I don't think he really wants me.'

'I do! But I have to work and this is part of what I do,' Chris said soothingly, as he hurried across to me and hugged and kissed me.

'You . . . you still want to marry me then?' I asked, looking up at him with red eyes.

Günter was clearly getting impatient with this sentimental scene and interrupted to ask when I was going back to AVRO.

'Oh, every week now!' I said innocently.

'Well, that is wonderful. You can help us a lot here, my dear,' Günter said.

'No I don't think I can. I think you are stringing me along. You're making Chris work and I don't think he will be able to marry me. It's all one-sided,' I replied, getting upset again.

'That's not true, my dear. When he gets promoted there will be no need to earn the extra money he gets now and he will be able to spend more time with you, won't you, Chris?'

'Of course I will,' Chris replied, squeezing my hand.

What a comedy we were playing, Mr White! No one was sincere.

'So when are you going next?' Günter asked, returning to his theme.

'I've already told you, every week, but I've made my mind up: I'm not doing it anymore. That's all you're interested in, not me . . .' And then, much to their consternation, I flounced out.

'Go and get her now!' I heard Günter shout. But I was taking a quick run between wickets and was out of the grounds like a flash. The ball, to my sporting metaphors, was in their court. What would they do next?

I returned to the college and reported to the porter and soon found myself meeting George down by the Isis. Understandably, I think in retrospect, he thought I had overplayed my role a little, and I was a little shamefaced. Perhaps I was enjoying all this role playing a little too much.

George now gave me strict instructions. I was to become friendly with the Germans again, let them know I was working on some calculations for a new jet engine and that I had a copy of the plans in my room. 'We want to see,' George explained, 'how far they will go in their espionage. We'll give you some fake plans and calculations to plant there. You'll do all your real work on site.'

Naturally, I was all for it.

'The next thing is,' he went on, 'I want you to draw up a plan of Pentland Villa. I know it's a lot to ask of you, but I have every confidence in you. You may over-egg things a little sometimes, but you're doing remarkably well for a newcomer to this business.'

It was a tall order for any young woman, let alone one with my problems, but I was resolved to do it to the best of my ability. And on top of that, I had my own agenda: to get back the incriminating photographs they had taken of me several weeks before. I duly made friends with the Pentland people again and casually told Chris about the engine I was working on.

Only a day later, Mrs De Witt called at the porter's lodge during afternoon lectures and asked if she could wait for me in my room. The porter, of course, was on the ball and politely refused. He would let me know she had called. I telephoned her the following day.

'Alex!' she cried. 'How nice to hear from you! Vot have ve done that ve don't see you so often now?'

'Nothing, Mrs De Witt. I'm just so busy.'

'Alex, please come to dinner tonight and let me make it up to you. About seven then, yes?' she said, as she put the phone down, before I could refuse her offer.

They made me more than welcome; it would have turned any cream sour. Even Günter was pleasant. Chris was actually in a dinner jacket, thinking he looked wonderful, when he looked quite the opposite. He was really too thin and it made the jacket look too big. I now found him faintly disgusting.

It was a pleasant dinner, of course – wonderful food and wine, and plenty of other guests. Some, I think, were in the same boat as me and were friendly enough. I tried to be as pleasant as possible myself, though in reality I was busy making my calculations. The conversation inevitability came round to what everybody was doing for Christmas.

'Where are you going, Alex?' Mrs De Witt asked.

'My parents are going away, I think. My father has some military business in France or Belgium, and he has arranged to take my mother. So I'll be here on my own . . .' I paused as I wiped a little tear from my cheek.

It was, after all, pantomime season, Mr White.

'Alex, I want you to stay with us where you belong,' Mrs De Witt remarked.

'No, Mrs de Witt, I couldn't!'

'I'll hear no more about it. You are staying here with Chris.'
'You are too kind. You really are,' I said, throwing Chris a radiant smile.

They persuaded me to stay overnight and of course Mrs De Witt put great store in telling everyone: 'Alex knows where her room is.' I felt myself blushing. God, what must these people think of me?

I had made friends with them again and now for my punishment I had to sleep with Chris.

The following day I cycled back to college and, as it was the last day of the term, I spent that time with Jennifer until she went home. I phoned Alice and found myself spilling the beans about the whole business. Perhaps I was more nervous than I thought. Anyway, Alice took the whole thing in her stride; for her it was just a bit of fun. She would send up a very pretty dress so that I could wear it on Christmas Eve which is the most important part of Christmas for the Germans. I remained in college until the 23rd and then went to stay with the Germans.

On Christmas Eve, I stayed in my room until the very last moment, having paid a great deal of attention to my appearance. It was as if I was about to go on stage for a first night, in a new role. I was so late that Mrs De Witt came upstairs to ask if everything was all right.

'I'm coming now, Mrs De Witt, I'm sorry to keep you waiting.'

'That's all right, dear,' she said as she went back down the stairs. I followed a few seconds later.

I walked into the dining room in Alice's dress to shocked silence; even Chris couldn't speak. I must have looked good because the flattery was amazing. I had a lovely evening and this time I was able to dance, following, not leading, as I had always done at Bankworth. Everyone made a fuss of me and Chris seemed almost desperate to get me into bed. I took this opportunity to reverse roles and to take control. I took a bottle of Sekt to the bedroom and made sure he drank far too much.

'Look, Chris, I want to help out with your work. You know the picture stuff. I confess it excites me!' I told him. 'So can I take part in the next session?' I asked excitedly.

'Yes, of course,' he said in an inebriated way.

'So where do they keep the camera and films then?' I asked.

He put his finger to his lips and said, 'Ssssshhhh!'

'Come on!' I said as I started to undo his trousers. 'Let's make a film now!' I begged as I pulled his trousers to the ground. 'Show me where to switch it on, or I'm not playing anymore!'

He tried to grab hold of me, but I pushed him away.

'Come on, or you go to your room!' I commanded.

You see, Mr White, I was learning what power I had over sex-starved males.

He told me to follow him and he took me to the room above mine, where there were three cameras set into the floor, capturing the action from three different positions. It was amazing. I couldn't see them in my room and yet from here you could see everything in my room completely. On the walls were shelves piled with archive boxes and discarded reels of film.

'Now where were those compromising photographs they had taken of me?' I said to myself as I searched around. I needed to get them back, because through all of this, Mr White, I was still concerned about my father and what he would go through if such images became public.

I pretended to switch the cameras on and took Chris back to my room, where, thank God, he quickly fell into a drunken stupor.

On Christmas Day, I dressed as a man and tried to make myself useful, mentally noting where everything was. I stopped for a few minutes to chat to Günter, who was being very pleasant to me.

'How has college been this session?' he asked.

'It's been really good, though very busy. As well as my studies, I'm working on a new jet engine for AVRO. It's revolutionary and very hush hush, but I'm enjoying working on it very much.'

I knew that he must know all about this already – after all, Mrs De Witt had tried to gain access to my room – but there was no harm in enticing him a little more.

'Where do you do this work?' Günter asked, unable to stifle his curiosity. 'At AVRO?'

'Oh no, I do it in my room. I have all the papers there and when I have finished them, I take them back to AVRO. It's really good,' I said, as if I were an excited child, anxious to tell the world about a new toy.

'You haven't brought them with you, have you? It would spoil Christmas if you had to start working while you were here.'

'Oh no, they're in my room back at college,' I replied, sensing he had taken the bait.

'In the New Year I'll want you to take some more photographs. Will that be possible?' he asked.

'Günter, you may not realise this, but I love Chris and, well, if I have to do certain things to keep him, then I have to do them. Not nice, but that's the way it goes,' I added somewhat firmly.

Günter looked pleased, as if I were a real convert to the group. I had certainly convinced him of my loyalty. He kissed me on my head and left the lounge.

On the 27th December, Günter invited me into the forbidden room to have another chat with him. He poured himself a glass of cognac and invited me to have one. The conversation quickly took a slightly surprising turn as he began to tell me how much he had enjoyed taking those photographs of me. I was a very beautiful young woman, he told me.

'Please, I'm engaged to Chris and I want to marry him,' I said, protesting mildly.

'He doesn't want you really and he's not a real man. You were beautiful in those photographs.'

'Günter, please, don't upset me!' Then like a flash of lightning it dawned on me. He might take me to the darkroom. 'Can I see those pictures if they are that good?'

'Not now.'

'Please, please, Günter,' I begged, almost simpering.

That was enough. He took me to a room in the basement. To my astonishment, I saw they were lined with hard files. They had been doing this for years! He took down one of the files, took out the photographs and spread them over a table. He invited me to sit down and placed himself next to me. I glanced at the pictures spread out before me, trying not to look too closely. Günter, however, seemed to become excited. I put my hand on his inner thigh and stroked him, at first gently then harder and harder. From that moment he was putty in my hands.

'Kiss me!' he demanded.

'I can't! I'm engaged to Chris.'

'Kiss me!' He didn't give me a chance to answer and pulled me across his knee and kissed me.

I kissed him back hard on the lips for several seconds and then pulled away.

'We can't do this – it's not fair!'

All the same he kissed me again.

We left the photographic room, unfortunately seen by Chris, who, like any man when he sees a woman who is supposed to be his, with someone else, becomes intensely jealous.

I stayed at the house until 6th January and during that time, I was being treated like one of them and was able move around the house un-chaperoned. I was able to sketch a fairly detailed plan of the house and got a good idea of the extent of their operations. On New Year's Eve, we entertained an industrialist who had something to do with the Arsenal in London and was an expert in the development of munitions. He was a married man but also a homosexual, and that night, I know, he was given the usual treatment. I would have to warn George about this one.

Almost every night now, Günter invited me into the darkroom, asking me to wear Alice's dress, but all he wanted me to do was to sit on his lap and caress his inner thigh.

He would always lock the door and on one occasion, Chris tried to get in. 'Go away!' Günter replied to the knocking on the door.

'Alex, I know you're in there. Please come out,' he pleaded, sounding somewhat pathetic, as though he was being two timed.

'We're busy,' Günter shouted.

Chris kicked the door hard and you could hear him swearing all down the corridor as he walked away.

Unfortunately, Mrs De Witt could feel the tension rising in the house and reported the matter to a higher authority in London, which resulted in another, more ruthless individual being sent in to sort out the place.

Major Hartman looked the epitome of a Gestapo officer; he even had the hallmark – a long leather coat. His Embassy car drew up and he stormed into the building, with everyone scurrying out of the way. He didn't knock on the door of the forbidden room but just marched in.

He shouted at all of us in German: 'What the hell is going on here. You are all endangering our operations and we cannot put up with this stupidity any longer and who is this?' he bawled, pointing at me.

Günter sent me out of the room, though I stayed close enough to listen. 'What stupidity?' he asked.

Major Hartman told him that Mrs De Witt had implied that they were fighting over me and the place was no longer secure.

The one thing Günter was able to do was to think on his feet and this time was no exception.

'Alex is a very good informant,' he explained coolly. 'She is totally infatuated with Stelzig.' This, I now found out, was Chris's real surname. 'She will do anything to be near him, but she is not the most attractive female. In fact, she wears men's clothes and behaves like a man and, of course, Stelzig doesn't want to get involved. I am trying to be nice to her to keep her on our side. We need her, she's a potential gold mine. Her father is a general and she's involved with engine research at AVRO. She's already given us some excellent photographs.'

Outside the door, I sniggered. To which photographs was he referring?

'You have already lost one man because of her. Prinz was arrested and taken by the police. Why was that?' Hartman asked.

'He was a fool! We got hold of some of the papers the girl's been working on. We checked it all out with Glazzard at the university and it's all correct. We think there may be more, though we couldn't find them.'

This was news to me; I could hardly believe they had fallen for this ruse. Well done, George, I thought, but who was this Glazzard at the university? I wanted to listen more, but a maid came along the corridor, carrying a coffee tray to the dining room and I followed her in. I was soon joined by Chris who sat down next to me and took my hand. For once, his emotion felt real and I even felt a little sorry for him. It wasn't long before he was called into the forbidden room and given a strong telling off. Then it was my turn.

I walked in. I was wearing men's clothing and must have looked distinctly odd.

'Is this the thing that this whole affair's about?' he almost roared at Günter.

'Yes it is and that is why I tried things my way,' Günter replied, careful not to look in my direction.

'I understand you are helping us, young lady . . . man . . . whatever you are,' Hartman said sharply.

'Yes,' I replied.

'Why?' he asked like a professional interrogator. 'What possible benefit could you gain from us?'

I forced myself to play it cool, imagined myself back on that stage at Bankworth. 'You may or may not believe this,' I said lucidly, 'but I have effectively been on my own for years and here for the first time I have found a family of people of whom I'm very fond and a man I would like to marry.'

'Then why do you go around like that?' he asked as he came over to me and tugged at my jacket. 'You're not a homosexual.'

'It's my upbringing,' I said.

He looked at me bemused.

'You're talking rubbish. I can see through you even if the others can't.'

I forced a tear across my cheek.

'You can stop that! It doesn't wash with me,' Hartman snapped. 'And he doesn't want you either.' He pointed to Chris.

'That's not true!' I yelled. 'He does love me. I know he does.'

'Well, my dear, that remains to be seen.' He paused and handed me the photographs. Once again I tried not to look too closely.

These ones were different from those Günter had shown me. They were obscene, disgusting. I was visibly shocked.

'Now, my dear, I'm not going to beat around the bush, as you English say. You will now go back to your college and you are going to bring back all those papers you have been working on. Then you are coming to see me. If you refuse, then

I will give copies to the principal of your college. Your poor father will no doubt be very interested to see what his son gets up to at college.' The Major had clearly done his homework.

I was dismissed and for the first time, Mr White, I was genuinely scared.

The following day, Major Hartman left and it was as though a weight had been lifted off the staff. Günter was back in charge. He tore into Mrs De Witt for telling tales and then into Chris for causing all the trouble in the first place. That evening he was back with me in the photographic room, kissing me all over.

'Where do I stand with all this, Günter?' I asked as soon as he was somewhat aroused.

'Don't worry, Alex, you'll get the papers from your college and everything will be all right. Hartman is just trying to throw his weight around.'

As we went back upstairs, Günter asked me to wear Alice's dress, which I duly did; but Chris saw us once again and went absolutely mad with him. As soon as he could, he grabbed me by the hand and pulled me into my room.

'I thought you were supposed to be in love with me!' he said angrily.

'Don't be silly, you know I am. It's me who's trying to save you from going away. Do you think I would do this for anyone else?'

'Well, it seems like it. You're spending a lot of time with Günter. It's got to stop . . . and there is something else . . .' His anger was making him indiscreet. 'They were never going to send me away anyway. I'm too useful to them. Günter just said it to make you work for us.'

I pretended to be shocked and insisted I wanted to be alone for a while. As I lay on my bed, I heard all pandemonium breaking out below. Chris and Günter were having a blazing row, to which Mrs De Witt was contributing. I had really stirred things up. I think they would have destroyed themselves eventually, even without the Security Services doing it for them.

From time to time there were silences, but then the war would commence again. It was during one of the quiet periods that Mrs De Witt came to see me again. 'Look vot you've done. They are fighting over you!' she shouted at me. 'Vot are you? Some sort of devil?'

'Not you too!' I said. 'I couldn't bear it if you turned against me too, Mrs De Witt. You're like a mother!'

But Mrs De Witt was obdurate. 'I'm not stupid, Alex. You are not all you are cracked up to be, young lady. I think ve vill regret meeting you. I can't quite put my finger on it, but ven I do . . .' She paused.

We were disturbed by what sounded like falling furniture and Mrs De Witt ran downstairs. This was my moment for exit stage right, Mr White. I put my coat on, packed all my things, and simply went downstairs. As I pushed open the front door, Mrs De Witt tried to stop me with kind words.

'Alex, please don't go. It's all been a terrible misunderstanding. Please vait. I'll get Günter.'

'No, please don't bother! No one wants me here anymore.'

'Vait, vait!' she pleaded. 'I'm getting him.'

I pretended to wait but as soon as she was out of sight, I left the building as quickly as I could. The moment I was out of the drive, I ran in the opposite direction to which they might have thought and made my way into town.

Soon I found myself being slowly followed by two men in a car and I was beginning to panic. I ran faster but they were still there. I dared not go down a side road as it was too dark; even the main road was bad enough. I ran faster and faster but the weight of my case was too much for me. I saw a little fish and chip shop open across the road. I'll be safe there, I thought, but I had to cross the road. I took a chance and ran. They stopped and watched as I went in.

To my dismay I had forgotten I was still dressed as a woman and now would have to act the part. I pushed my way through the queue to the counter.

'Please, help me,' I begged. 'I'm being followed by two men

in a car. Have you got a telephone? I need to phone the police.'

'What two men, love?' the owner asked from behind the counter. I turned round to show him and the people in the queue, but they had gone.

'Please can you help? I'm not pretending. They were there,' I replied.

'I'm sure they were, but they're not now, love, so you don't 'ave to worry. Anyway we don't 'ave a phone 'ere, but if you go to The White Hart, the pub a couple of hundred yards up the road, they've got one,' the chippy said.

I looked both ways before leaving the shop and ran out, towards The White Hart. I was petrified. It was difficult to keep the pace up but I tried. I had run about half the distance when I had to cross a side road and to my horror, they were there. For a split second, I couldn't do anything but stand and stare at them and then the adrenaline kicked in and I set off once again.

I had almost reached The White Hart when their car screeched to a halt, the door opened and I and my luggage were hauled in. I screamed at the top of my voice to no avail. No one saw me being pulled in and I thought I was going to be killed.

'Get down, Alex! They're looking for you. Get down!' the man shouted as the car sped off.

'Who are you?' I asked.

'We work for George and it's our job to look after you,' one of the men replied.

I was so relieved, Mr White, I just burst into tears and within minutes I had fallen asleep. The next thing I remember was being woken up by George, gently shaking me by the shoulder. He led me out of the car and into a police station. I was given tea and then he sat down to talk to me. I handed him the plan I had sketched and told him everything I had discovered. I told him where all the pictures were and where they kept all the equipment; what the names of their most recent victims and as much about their future plans as I knew. Now I was being cold-blooded. I hid nothing.

George's gentle manner soothed me. He told me they would

raid the place that night as they had enough reasons to.

'And those pictures . . .' I began to ask.

'. . . Will be destroyed and thank you for what you have done. You need not worry.' He ended by saying I looked lovely.

He was as good as his promise. That night armed officers surrounded the house and arrested everyone inside. Günter, it transpired, had killed Chris and was busy concealing the body with Mrs De Witt when the raid took place. A few months later, Günter was hanged for murder at Winson Green. Mrs De Witt and the others were sentenced to many years in prison. All the photographs and films of me, thank God, were destroyed.

You know, Mr White, in many ways I hated doing what I did, the lying and cheating, the whole sordid business, but for a short time I was made to feel wanted, even if it was for the wrong reasons. I was able to hide away from what were the normal realities of life. At Pentland Villa I was what I should have been in the beginning – female – and now I had to return to my normal life again, vulnerable and vilified. On the other hand, I had become harder, more able to stand up for myself.

Chapter 11

I was glad, Mr White, nonetheless to return to my normal student life and the following term, which thank heavens, was completely uneventful, I even achieved some good results from my work. Sadly, however, apart from Alice, no one wanted to spend the Easter break with me. I longed for the following term and the cricket season to start, as I could at least then hope to restore some of my battered pride. You see, Mr White, I had readopted my male persona. It felt like a haven – a protective shield.

At the beginning of the summer term, I was on fire with enthusiasm. I was reluctantly invited to the nets for a practice session and from the attitude of all the men present it was clear they thought it was a laugh with me there. The Captain, a third-year student, told me in this supercilious way to pad up, which I did. I was then invited to go into the nets for the practice session.

I was put in the third net with the 'no-hopers' and very quickly showed them what for as I carved the second-rate bowlers everywhere, so much so the bowlers from the other nets came to have a go at me. I wasn't out the entire time and knocked everyone everywhere. The stuffed-shirt of a captain came over to me and contritely asked if I would be good enough to attend the following day. He would give me a real test, which I naturally agreed to do.

It was a Friday, my day with Jennifer, and I wasn't going to let her down so I invited her to come and watch. Once again, I had a fantastic net practice and was picked for the 'Probables' against the 'Possibles' the following day, Saturday. Jennifer asked if she could come along and watch that too, which was wonderful for me.

The match was being played on one of the university grounds down by the river and began at two p.m. The Probables were batting and I put my foot in it when I asked our Captain if I could go in number three. I was virtually told I would go in when I was told to and that the club had some excellent batsman who had already proved themselves; he put me in at number six to give me a lesson in modesty. Someone up there was on my side as we had just 40 runs for four wickets when I went in. I knew if I was to get into the university side, I would have to perform better than anyone else. I walked to the crease, passing the outgoing batsman on the way in; he looked as miserable as sin and didn't even acknowledge me. Mr Wilkes' words came flooding back to me: 'Take your time, study where the fielders are and take your guard.' I did just that. I scored 129 not out, so we were all out for 201. We lost the match, but I had done enough to get selected for the college team.

When I walked off the field, Jennifer was so excited she ran out to meet me and gave me a kiss on the cheek. It was a lovely gesture but it drew attention to our relationship, which was construed in the worst possible light.

The following Saturday we were playing Balliol College and I was selected to play. This time the Captain dropped his 'I'm in charge' stand and asked me where I would like to bat. I chose number three as it had become my own. Jennifer again accompanied me to the match and was asked if she could help prepare the teas for the players, which she did and enjoyed doing it. All the same, she was quizzed unmercifully about our relationship but all she would say was that we had been friends for a long time and that we had been at Bankworth together.

The match started with Balliol batting first. We had an excellent start with three wickets down for 30 runs, but the middle order really piled on the runs. They declared at 270 for seven wickets. After tea we went into bat, feeling a little daunted. We had another batsman in form, a Fred Dinage and when I went out to bat he had already scored 50.

'Leave it to me!' he said. 'I'll call you when I want you to run.'

'Rightio,' I replied and began my innings; but I wasn't in favour of letting him decide what I was to do.

I faced the first ball which I clipped for two runs.

'One run!' Dinage said, full of superiority.

'No, two!' I shouted as I scampered down the wicket.

Fred only just made it in and at the end of the over he came up to me and said, 'If I tell you to run, you run. If I say no, I mean *no*. Do you understand?'

'Yes, of course,' I replied, but I had never played cricket like this before. It went against all my instincts. And when it was my turn to face the bowling I did just what Mr Wilkes had said and only hit the loose ball, and at the end of the over I really tried to hit a long one so he had to run and I could face the bowling again. He only scored a further six runs when I passed his total and a further twelve when I reached my hundred. I scored 150 runs and he scored 89 as we passed their total and were 273 for one wicket.

'You were lucky out there!' Dinage said as we walked back to the pavilion. 'You could have been out many times. You were really lucky!'

'Thanks, Fred. I'll remember that next time,' I said out loud.

'Supercilious bastard!' I whispered under my breath.

Once again Jennifer was over the moon at my success and once again her exuberance drew comment. This wouldn't happen in this day and age – we are far more enlightened – but it was considered almost shocking for two girls to be 'going out' together. To be honest, though, that wasn't my real concern; it was the fact that I was considered to be a woman, despite the fact that I dressed in men's clothes. Anyway, the whole thing caused an almighty fuss and the upshot was I was hauled up in front of the college committee.

'For God's sake, we've been friends since school. I was at the boys' side, she was at the girls, so don't be so bloody stupid,' I replied angrily.

The situation was too difficult for the committee to deal with, so fortunately matters were left at that – at least for the time being.

I had considerable success for a newcomer and it was raising many eyebrows – not only from those who admired ability, but also from those who were jealous and those who simply wanted to get rid of me just because I was different. There was a lot of speculation and talking behind my back and they would even make lewd comments when they knew I was in hearing distance. It was beginning to cause difficulties; difficulties which my enemies knew would give the college an excuse to get rid of me. The usual reason for rustication – being sent down – apart from failure in academic work was gross misconduct, which included being homosexual or lesbian and associating with prostitutes.

Well, some of them seemed to believe I fell into all those categories, if you were to go by the comments they made.

That evening after my hearing in front of the committee I had a good time in the nets, not only with the bat but also with the ball, and was feeling pretty satisfied with my performance. In fact, it seemed that all of us were happy with the practice that evening, so much so that several of the team wanted me to go out with them for a drink afterwards. I must be honest I didn't really want to go and initially I refused. They made sure, however, that I changed my mind.

'We'll drop you off,' David Cranbrook said as we all piled into the two cars we had brought to the grounds.

'Thanks, that will be great,' I replied. However, he began to take an unusual route. 'I thought you were going to drop me off, David.'

'Oh God, I'm sorry, Alex,' he replied. 'It was me talking; it made me completely forget. I'm so sorry. Look, come with us. We're just going to have one quick drink, and then we're coming back. Will that be all right? I'll go back if you want to; it's a little out of our way, but never mind.'

You see, Mr White, it was the classic 'make someone feel awful' trick, and I fell for it. I'm sure we've all done that in our time.

I was sitting on the back seat of the car, a little Ford 10; not a bad little car for a student, though of course there were still a lot of 'rich kids' at Oxbridge. Fortunately, I caught Peter Widdowson giving one of the others a quick wink when I finally gave in, so I could sense that something was amiss.

'Sorry, Alex,' David said as we all got out of the cars. 'We won't be long.'

'That's all right,' I replied, by now totally wary of the situation.

We walked quite a long way from the car and found ourselves in the seediest part of Oxford you could imagine and, although it was still quite light, the area seemed dark.

'They sell good beer here,' one of the team commented, as he put his arm round me as if to give me confidence. He led me down the steps and we entered into the club. The moment we entered I realised the club was for 'degenerates', for prostitutes, homosexuals and the like. In the middle of the room was a dance floor and at the end of the room a tiny stage, where a three-piece band was in full swing.

'What would you like to drink, Alex?' Peter asked as we all stood at the bar.

'I'll just have orange, thanks. I've got to keep fit,' I replied.

'You should have something stronger,' he insisted.

I was adamant and kept to my orange. The barman, however, didn't; I saw him add gin or something similar to the drink.

Students in such a place were a rarity and few of the clientele came over to us, good-time girls and someone, I instantly suspected, had been specially ordered for me: a big attractive-looking girl in men's clothes. I was being set up. She wouldn't leave me alone and eventually she, with the aid of the others, dragged me onto the dance floor, where she made a spectacle of herself and me. She was holding me tight, fondling me and making various suggestions, which I did not enjoy in any way.

As soon as I could, I left the room and went to the gentlemen's toilet to have a few minutes on my own. It was obvious what they were trying to do. Hadn't I seen it all before? They wanted me to fall foul of the college rules about lewd behaviour with prostitutes and the like. I had to keep my reputation intact so I decided to carry out a little plan. My experiences at Pentland Villa had made me devious.

I went back into the bar and pretended to be enjoying the woman's attentions. After a while, I asked if she would like to go somewhere more private. I called Peter over.

'Peter, would you take my kit home and put it in my locker?' I asked.

'Yes, of course, Alex. Be careful,' he said with a wink. 'She might be a bit more than you can handle.'

'Shall we go then?' I said to my companion.

'Yes, come back to my place, darling.'

'Let's sneak out the back door. I don't want everyone knowing my business.'

In the rather squalid doorway at the back she made to kiss me, but I pushed her away.

'Wait here a moment, will you. I've forgotten to mention something to the Captain.'

I went back inside the club, quickly and quietly made my way out of the front door, and raced as fast as I could back to the college. At the porter's lodge I made sure he noticed me and also asked him the time, so that he would remember. I was safely in bed at half past ten.

The following morning I was called to the Principal's office and was advised that I had been seen in disrespectable company, and that I had spent the night with a woman of very uncertain character.

'Where on earth did you hear that rubbish?' I asked.

'Please address me properly, Mr Chillington-Henry. I have a

good witness who says that you were seen leaving a club with this woman.'

'What time, sir, was this incident supposed to have taken place?' I asked snootily.

The Principal nervously shuffled his papers, as if to be looking for them, before replying:

'Approximately ten o'clock. I might add the gentleman who reported this incident is a well-respected young man.'

'This paragon of virtue isn't by any chance Peter Widdowson, is it, Principal?'

'I'm not at liberty to say.'

'I think I have every right to ask, sir,' I snapped, becoming very brave. 'Even in a court of law I can see and question my accusers and yet you deprive me of this right.'

'Very well, young man, it was Widdowson, but his testimony is also confirmed by others,' he replied as though he had played the trump card.

'Principal, this is a disgusting attempt to get me ejected from the college. I know the rules as well as anyone else. I'm fairly new to Oxford and don't know my way around. I do not have many friends so when I was invited to have a drink with members of the cricket team I reluctantly went. They took me to this seedy place where they tried to get me drunk and at the same time fix me up with that ghastly woman. I was so disgusted I left the place. No, I ran away from the place and was at the college at seventeen minutes past ten. This can be confirmed by the porter, who saw me as I came in.'

A smile came over the Principal's face. 'Why on earth didn't you say, Henry, it was just high spirits. The boys were just having fun.'

'I hardly think it was fun when they reported the incident to you. Do you, Principal?' I replied fiercely.

'It was high spirits. We'll say no more about it,' the Principal said as I left, sighing with relief that he had found a way out of the mess.

Cranbrook couldn't look me in the face when we took the

field the following afternoon. We were playing Merton and the university selectors were there to watch the match. We had elected to bat and were 21 when the first wicket went down and I walked on to face my first ball.

I was met by Fred Dinage, who had the gall to repeat his usual Instructions, 'I'll call you when I want to run. These bowlers are a bit tough, so leave it to me.'

I was so annoyed I simply said, 'Don't be so bloody daft!' I walked to the crease.

Fred had scored ten when I began to face the bowling. The first ball I faced was a full toss down the leg side, which I hit for six and the second ball I hit for four, so in two balls I had equalled his score. I scored my first century when he had reached 23 and my second century when he had scored 41. Soon after he was bowled and in walked Cranbrook. He looked so embarrassed and was unable to concentrate. The first ball almost bowled him and before he had the chance to face the next one, which bowled him for a duck, I was on 230. The Captain declared and as we walked off the pitch I turned to Cranbrook and said nastily, 'I know you don't want me in your team, but how on earth did you get your place?'

I meted out much the same to Fred Dinage. 'I was lucky again this time, Fred. I could have been out on many occasions, but I'm surprised you only got 47. The bowling was atrocious, wasn't it?'

This wasn't my usual style and it only gained me enemies, but I was becoming more and more fed up with the way I was being treated. I was getting braver, too.

My performance got me selected for the university first-class side and I was almost immediately picked to play at the county ground at Worcester. The season was to be the zenith of my cricketing career. At Worcester I went out to bat and from the moment I was on the square everything went well. I had scored 119 when I was bowled middle stump by a spinner of all things. We were all out for 277 and they were 353 for five declared when rain washed the rest of the match out. All the same, my batting had created a bit of a storm and several of the newspapers even tipped me for the England side. I was selected again to play against Kent at Canterbury and had scored 115 when I broke my finger. Owing to my injury, I missed the next match but was selected to play against Surrey at The Oval and here I scored my highest first-class century: 166 not out.

It was too much for the press. I was hailed as the English answer to Bradman and it was even suggested I be picked immediately. However, one or two newspapers starting dropping strange insinuations about me and suggested that I was not eligible to play. One or two reporters started snooping round the college looking for a story.

After the match at The Oval my teammates invited me out to celebrate my 166, and foolishly I agreed to go. We all set off to a certain gentleman's club in Mayfair, where Willoughby St John- Peters, one of the players, was a member. He phoned ahead to reserve a private room. As soon as we arrived the head waiter, Fellows, took us to a beautiful Georgian room with a long table running down the middle. It was set out for twelve of us but there were eleven of us in all, seven members of the team and four other friends.

I might be the hero of the match but from this point on I was pretty much ignored. By the time we had eaten our meal, most of the company had become very rowdy and almost drunk. Even I felt a little worse for wear, so I knew my drink had been spiked again. Still I had my wits about me, so I thought I would be able to cope. The meal finished, Willoughby stood up to propose a toast.

'Gentlemen, I want to propose a toast to Alex here, for the superb innings against Surrey . . . George, just shut that door and lock it. We don't want anybody walking in, do we?' he shouted raucously. George locked the door and threw the key to Willoughby.

'As I was saying, well done, Alex, and here's to many more.'

They all stood up to repeat the toast.

'Thank you, gentlemen,' I replied.

'Gentlemen. Now for tonight's entertainment!' Willoughby concluded.

He clapped his hands and two very busty women came into the room dressed in French maids' outfits. They were carrying several more bottles of claret and began refilling our glasses. I declined the offer of a glass, but the others continued enthusiastically.

Now the maids, as I'll call them, began to caress the students sitting around the table, one of the girls paying particular attention to Willoughby, placing herself astride his lap, undoing his trousers and then having intercourse with him. The second maid attended to another of the players. A third maid now entered and I saw Willoughby as he signalled for her to pay attention to me. She took the hint and slowly wiggled across the room and stood at the back of me; she ran her fingers through my hair and began to slowly caress my face.

As you can imagine, Mr White, I was made decidedly uncomfortable by this action. No, I was terrified. The first two maids were now nude and were going from guest to guest undoing ties, unbuttoning shirts and so on. It was turning into an orgy.

The third maid continued to stroke my hair and began running her hands down my arms. I stood up to leave, but was pulled back down by the two students on either side of me. They took hold of my arms and at the same time began to rip my shirt open.

I had my running vest on, but one of my teammates picked up a knife and cut through it. It fell away and I was exposed. I was shouting desperately for them to stop, but they were all too drunk to take any notice. I was in a position where I couldn't fight back as my arms were almost forced to the back of my chair. Everything stopped for a second or two as they admired their handiwork and exposed my bare chest. They were clearly wondering what to do next, when at a signal from Willoughby, the maid began to kiss, lick and caress my breasts. My teammates began to chant 'Alex is a lesbian' over and over. Suddenly, I was back at school. The nightmare was beginning all over again, only now the boys had become men.

I heard Willoughby yell, 'Get her on the table and hold her down.'

Like automatons, they pushed me onto the table, scattering all the cutlery and crockery onto the floor. I saw the third maid strip off in a teasing fashion, inciting the men to ever greater outrages.

I struggled violently as I tried to get up, but my legs and hands were pulled apart across the table and held very firmly. I was prostrate, half naked. The maid slid on top of me and started caressing my body, her tongue licking every exposed part. She could see the disgust in my face but still she tried to kiss me full on the lips. I spat at her and my spittle hit her full in the face. She jumped back in horror and two of the men momentarily let go of me. I struggled to sit up, but almost at once the maid began to attack me.

I rolled over and fell off the table as the woman hit me repeatedly. The idiots loved it, the spectacle of two bare-chested females fighting. They were in frenzy, cheering the woman on, encouraging her to continue her attack. She was getting the better of me, but I somehow managed to roll under the table and get to my feet before she had chance to follow. As she got up, I punched her full on the face and she fell backwards dazed.

I was immediately grabbed by two of the men and held firmly.

'Let me go, you bastards!' I screamed.

'You can't leave yet, Alex,' Willoughby cried out, 'the fun's only just beginning. Come on, join in the fun.'

'No, I just want to go. Please let me go!'

'Sorry, Alex, you can't go yet. Anyway I've got the keys in my pocket. If you want to go, you will have to work for it. You have a lovely pair of tits and if you're nice to me, like the other girls are, I'll let you go.'

'All right,' I replied, playing for time.

Willoughby nodded to the two men holding me and they let me go. I slowly walked towards Willoughby.

'Lie down on the table!' he ordered his voice full of menace. I did as I was told and at once I was held down by a dozen pair of hands.

'Give her to me!' Willoughby shouted.

They pushed me along the table contemptuously, as if I was nothing more than a platter of meat. Then Willoughby pulled me upwards and on top of him. His penis was exposed and vulnerable.

It was now that I saw my advantage. After all, I was sober; they were all drunk. Quick as a flash I grabbed a knife from the table and held it against his manhood.

Everyone froze in shock. Willoughby began to whimper as his penis rapidly deflated.

'Get those bloody keys from his pocket,' I shouted to one of the maids. The maid did as she was told, placing the keys on the table.

'Come on, Alex, it was only a bit of fun!' Cranbrook said. They were all beginning to sober up quickly now.

'You call this bloody fun?' I said witheringly as I held the knife more closely against Willoughby's penis, allowing it to press into his skin. 'Don't think I'm not man enough to do it!'

One of my teammates made a sudden move towards me but then stopped in his tracks.

'Tell them to bloody keep away or you'll be a eunuch,' I screamed.

'Get away! Don't come near!' Willoughby yelled.

'That's right. Now one of you put those clothes over my shoulder, and one of you unlock the door and give me the key. Then go and stand with the others by the fireplace and don't move a muscle. You!' I said to another lad, 'Take Willoughby's trousers and throw them out of the window.'

As soon as this was done, I barked out my next orders. 'Now, everybody, get down onto the floor and lie on your backs!'

They did as they were told and then before dropping the knife, I crushed Willoughby's testicles as hard as I could and immediately picked up the rest of my clothes, ran out of the door, locking it behind me again. The maître d' didn't seem at all surprised to see a near-naked woman come out of the room. He assumed, I suppose, I was just one of the hired prostitutes and he let me change in one of the toilets.

It didn't take long for the rumours of the event to spread around the college and I was hauled in front of the university selectors. Willoughby's father was an influential figure and the professors seemed determined to find any excuse to be rid of me.

They told me they had evidence that I was having a lesbian affair with Jennifer and that if I agreed to leave without a fuss, she would be spared any accusations and allowed to stay. They were never less than polite, but the upshot was that I was given no choice except to agree.

I immediately went to the pavilion at The Parks to collect my kit. I was enraged, but tears of humiliation were rolling down my cheeks. My former teammates had clearly got wind of what had happened and arrived at the pavilion just as I was leaving. They all lined up on either side of the door and slow-handclapped me off the grounds. It was a devastating moment – one of the cruellest things that had ever happened to me.

There was a silver lining to the whole affair, however. As I was packing my things, my Mathematics tutor came into my room. I had been his brightest star and he was angry about what had happened. It was an injustice and he told me he had taken the liberty, however, of phoning the Dean of University College London and had told him about my ability and also something of my difficulties. The Dean had agreed to see me himself in the first week in July with the view of offering me a place.

I knew I would never get the chance to play first-class cricket again, but at least I might be able to pursue my academic career.

***

'Good morning, Alex,' the Dean said, smiling, as I walked into his office some weeks later, dressed smartly in a suit and tie. 'Sit down and make yourself at home!'

What a change from the stuffed shirts at Oxford, I thought as

I sat in what was a very comfortable armchair in the corner of his cosy room. He pulled another up to sit opposite me and explained what the tutor had said before adding:

'I met another friend of yours the other day,' he said almost at once.

I looked at him curiously.

'He also said you were a very good student and didn't deserve the treatment you were getting and he also asked me if I could help you. You seem to have lots of enemies, Alex, but some very good friends, too.'

'Peter Wilkes!' I said smiling. 'My guardian angel!' I continued almost in tears.

'Yes, Peter Wilkes, and he told me some of the things you have suffered at school and I want to help you.'

'You're very kind. Thank you!' I replied.

'Well, I contacted your professor at Oxford and he kindly sent me some of your work from last year. It's excellent stuff and I think we can allow you to pass straight into the second year here, if that suits you, of course!'

'Of course it does!' I said, almost ready to hug him. I got up to go.

'One more thing, Alex. I've arranged for you to play for the university. You're to report to the Cricket Captain on Wednesday night at the sports ground. He's been told of your physical condition and there won't, I promise, be any fuss. Or he'll have me to contend with.' Incidentally, I was put in the 1st eleven straight away and had a fantastic season.

The icing on the cake came when Jennifer came down to London to spend a week with me. We had such a wonderful time. I invited her to Le Touquet, but about a week before we were due to set off, she wrote to me telling me she had fallen in love with a man from Ilkley in Yorkshire and had to call her holiday off. I was terribly disappointed, but such is life and I didn't let it worry me, especially as she insisted that she didn't want to lose touch. Don't laugh, Mr White, but I was a bridesmaid at her wedding.

Part 3

London

Chapter 12

I went to France on my own and spent a couple of weeks by myself thinking about my problems, trying to decide how I should proceed. Man or woman? I was trying to rationalise what my options were, to use a modern expression. I was always happier as a girl; all my real friends were girls and when I made myself up, I wasn't a bad-looking girl. All my adult friends wanted me to make the change and when I really thought about it, there wasn't much that was male left – just an aptitude for cricket. Finally, there was the fact that my father didn't want to know anyway, so why should I bother to please him anymore? I determined to return to London as a girl.

Back at University College, however, I lost my nerve and dressed once more as a man. I fell in love with London and the university, though I was still very much on my own, mainly because of my silly garb. It was totally ridiculous because, as I was later told, everyone knew the truth anyway. You know, Mr White, even at that time, London could be a very lonely place when you were on your own, despite the two or three million people living there. However, the university staff were very supportive of me and by the end of the Christmas term I had settled down and was well on my way to obtaining my degree. I exceeded all expectations and it was generally considered that I would gain my Bachelor's degree at the end of the year, one year ahead of normal.

It was a particularly cold winter, January especially, and what with the threat of war and Mr Churchill's dire warnings, it seemed much colder. It was an odd situation: everyone knew in their hearts we were soon going to be involved in another war, but they tried to turn a blind eye to it all and hoped it would go away.

During the spring term, the Dean asked me to work on various official mathematical projects, which I was advised would help me to get my Masters if I intended to stay on at university. The temptation was too much; I agreed to the job and was also accepted as a student to take my Masters the following year. I was living in a kind of academic bubble and my usual problems seemed far less important. That was, until the month of March.

It was a cold March day and I remember it as though it was yesterday. I was sitting in Lyons Corner House on the Strand at a table where I always tried to sit, where I could be alone and yet I could still see what was going on. It was a form of escapism as we would say today. Anyway, I was busy minding my own business when a group of lads, probably in their twenties, barged into the café. One of them knocked my books onto the floor and spilt my tea all over the table and over my notes. I gasped and immediately bent down to pick up my books. He too went down, apologising profusely as he did so and our eyes met as we momentarily stopped and stared at each other. My heart stood still for that moment as I stared into his eyes. I wanted it to go on forever and I knew from that moment I was in love and wanted to live with him for the rest of my life.

Do you believe in love at first sight, Mr White? Well, I do.

The spell was broken as he picked up my books and placed them where I had just wiped the table down with my serviette.

'I'm so sorry! It was careless of me. It's just we've been selected to play for Surrey and it's the excitement!' he spluttered as if he had to tell someone or anyone of his good news. I was so pleased it was me. He sat at the table for a few moments until one of his friends shouted across:

'William! Come on!'

I had just sat there, staring into his eyes, swooning at every word he said. He must have thought I was mad, but I just couldn't get any words out. He got up smiled and walked over to rejoin his friends. I tried to smile back, but I was suddenly filled with panic.

I pretended to get on with my work, but all the time I was sneaking a look at him. He was a big handsome man, with a powerful neck and shoulders. He must play forward, I thought as I saw him glancing at me too. I turned away quickly; I couldn't believe it: I was behaving like some silly little girl rather than a twenty-year-old freaky male. I looked up again and caught his eye. He smiled and I managed to smile back. It was too much. My heart was racing. How could I even try and look at my books when this was happening to me! We caught each other's glances several times before I heard one of them say, 'Who's the pretty boy then?'

'Oh I don't know, but know I've seen him somewhere before. I think it was at Oxford,' he replied.

I was sick in my stomach and even more so when another of the group said, 'Be careful, Billy Boy, that kind of thing can get you into trouble.'

He didn't look up again and I just wanted to cry. I kept glancing up in hope, but it wasn't to be. I tried to hold back my tears, but the odd one still trickled down my cheek. I wanted to get up and leave, but I couldn't; I had to wait until they left before I could pluck up the courage. I didn't want to let him see me upset, so I kept my head down and pretended to read the book. I must have been twenty minutes on that one page when I heard the group prepare to leave. I glanced up to see William bringing up the rear as the men passed me. He smiled and said loudly, so that the others could hear, 'I'm so sorry about your tea. Can I get you another before I go?'

'No, thank you. There's no harm done,' I replied with a sigh.

'That's good.' Then suddenly he whispered quickly, 'I'll see you back here at six o'clock. Don't be late!' He then just raced off to be with the others.

Can you believe it, Mr White because I couldn't! Here was a

man whom I had never seen before and whom I knew from that very moment I had fallen in love with, and what is more, he wanted to see me again. I sat there a few minutes in total disbelief and wondering if he would be warned off by his friends and how on earth he had seen me at Oxford. I was feeling wonderful.

I went back to my work at the college and sat at my desk, unable to think straight. However, it didn't take long for reality to sink in. I began to think there was an ulterior motive. What did he want with me? Was he homosexual? And in any case, how could I contemplate any relationship given my dubious situation? I was all mixed up. Every time I looked into space, I saw him. Every time I closed my eyes I saw him and every time I tried to work I saw him. In fact that afternoon, I was useless to everyone. It even drew comments from my colleagues. One of them even remarked, 'I think Alex is in love!' And another sang a few bars of 'Love's Old Sweet Song', which was very popular at the time.

'Don't be silly! I'm not interested in women,' I responded, which drew forth smiles from all present. I said it quite naturally, without irony. To some extent I still saw myself as a shy young boy.

I then began to convince myself it was all some huge joke and he wouldn't turn up and, if he did, so would the other rugby players and I would once again be the butt of other people's humour, and that, I couldn't bear. Several times, I decided I wouldn't go and put myself through the agony and then I would argue to the contrary. What was there to lose? Perhaps he was also lonely and wanted this freak for company.

In the end the 'go' vote won and I set off to the Lyons Corner House straight after work, packing up my things as quickly as I could, much to the amusement of all present, armed with their knowing smiles.

I arrived at the café at 5.15 p.m. and to make sure I looked nonchalant, I took one of my books out and buried my head in it. Then it wouldn't look too bad if he didn't turn up.

It was ten to six and I remember I was on my third cup of tea and desperate to go to the loo. But I dare not go in case I missed him. Nine minutes to six and he still hadn't shown. Eight, seven, six, five and there he was walking through the door. I couldn't pretend to be casual. I simply beamed from one side of my face to the other. He walked up to the table and held his hand out to mine. I took hold of it, and he shook it.

'Good to see you again. Would you like another cup of tea?' he asked, trying to be casual and talking loudly. I suspect it was to let the other customers in the café know that this was a platonic relationship between two males. The way I felt and the way I acted, I couldn't imagine anyone believing that charade.

'I'd love one please,' I replied. 'By the way,' he said quietly, 'my name is William. What's yours?'

'Alex,' I replied.

We sat drinking our tea, hardly saying a word. In fact, I could sense his difficulty, but I couldn't seem to do anything to help him.

He broke the ice: 'What are you doing at the moment?'

'I'm at London University studying Mathematics and Modern Languages, French and German.'

'You'll soon be needing those. It looks like there is going to be a war.'

'Oh I hope not. My father fought in the last one and was one of the lucky ones to come out alive.'

We continued to make polite conversation and all the time I felt him staring at me. I kept averting my eyes, but still felt his eyes pierce through me. It wasn't a nasty feeling; it seemed tender. He began to reach over to take my hands and suddenly stopped as he realised there were others in the café . He stopped and just looked into my eyes. Mr White, I know this will sound conceited, but I knew he had fallen for me.

'Come on. Let's get out of here,' he said. 'I need some fresh air.'

I stood up and remarked, 'I'll have to go to the toilet before we leave.' But to my horror, he said, 'So do I. I'll join you. Keep an eye on this stuff for us, will you?' he called out to the waitress behind the counter.

I marched to the gents with him a few paces behind. I pushed the door open and held it for him and then went over to the cubicle.

I never used the urinal and by force of habit I walked into a cubicle and sat down, while he went up to the urinal. I took a few minutes as I felt I had to stay a little longer, just for appearance's sake. When I returned to the table, he had already paid for the tea and was waiting to leave. I couldn't help noticing the two women behind the servery, one nudging the other as we passed. I'm glad William didn't see it or he might have forgotten the whole thing. I was used to looks like that, but he wouldn't have been able to cope with it, especially with the law as it was.

We left the Corner House and made our way to the Thames Embankment, strolling past Parliament, over Westminster Bridge and along to Chelsea Bridge and back to Parliament. It was a lovely walk and it was a fine evening. However, there was a sense of strain, for although we naturally gravitated towards one another, we steadfastly forced ourselves to keep a permanent gap of at least one foot between us at all times.

We chatted about our lives and he told me how much he loved playing rugby. He was very impressed that I knew so much about the game, though I didn't dare tell him that I used to play. He sat me down on a bench facing the Thames and began to open up, looking directly in to my eyes.

'Look, Alex, I don't know how to say this, but I know I have to, for my own piece of mind. When I look at you, I know you are not a boy and yet it seems you are trying to behave like one. You're ungainly in your clothes, you're trying to hide things and what is maddening to me is . . .' He paused for a few seconds. '. . . I want to be with you. From the moment I saw you this morning, when I looked into your eyes, I knew that was that and I didn't want anyone else.

'What's worse, my friends that were with me this morning could see what impression you had made on me and have given me some terrible stick. I'm not an invert or anything, not an Oscar Wilde type, and yet with you I'm lost. I want to hold your hand and I can't. I want to kiss you and let everyone know how I feel about you and I can't. I have known you for ten hours and I cannot let you go. Why are you like this?'

He put his hand down on the bench and drew it away as I placed my hand on it.

'Please don't! This is tearing me apart and I cannot understand why. I've had many casual relationships, but I have never found myself in a position like this before.'

I felt exactly the same way, but I was truly scared to tell him my secrets. However, I knew deep down that if I didn't, I would never see him again and possibly if I did tell him I would lose him anyway. I was totally unprepared for this situation; I had no control of these emotions, but win or lose I had to tell him.

'I have a flat not far away; it's in my father's house, but he doesn't live there. Would you come and have dinner with me tomorrow night? I'll tell you everything. I warn you, it's not very simple.'

'Yes. Yes, thanks. That's sounds nice.'

'I'll have to be going. It's getting late,' I said, trying to end what could turn out to be a disaster.

'I'll take you home. Then at least I'll know where to go.'

I tried to put him off, but whatever I said he had an answer for; for the first and only time I began to feel nervous in his company. William was six feet four and I was five-feet-five-ish and all I could think of was Hazard and the others at school and the times I had been raped and buggered by those bastards. I didn't have much option really. He stood up and immediately hailed a taxi. Within seconds we were on the way to Chelsea. We stopped outside my flat and William seemed reluctant to get out. Perhaps it was the look of disgust on the driver's face which he had noticed or perhaps it was the fact that I had asked him in for a cup of coffee.

As I got out of the taxi, William paid the driver and I heard him say, 'She's in a play in the West End. It starts tomorrow. I could see the change on the driver's face as he took the money.

Mr White, you can see the difficulty for him; he had already started to make excuses for being in my company. We were on a disaster course.

We walked up the steps to the front door. I fumbled with the keys, as my nerves were getting the better of me, but eventually opened the door and shut it again immediately he was inside.

Mr White! I had him trapped between the door and myself. I don't know what came over me, but I put my arms around his neck and pulled myself up, with my feet almost off the ground. I felt a little resistance at first and then he melted. I could feel the tension in his muscles change as he now held me in that position and we kissed. He wouldn't put me down and held me so firmly I thought my breath was being taken away from me, but it wasn't. The world had stopped at that moment and I didn't want it to start again.

Mr White, in spite of all my previous liaisons, it was my first real kiss and if it had all ended then, I would have been fulfilled. He pulled me once again close to him, pressing himself against my chest, only this time I could sense the relief at what he had confirmed. He squeezed me tightly, not wanting to let go, pushing his head close to mine as he whispered, 'I love you.' I was powerless. I couldn't believe what I was hearing. I went limp in his arms, but still he wouldn't put me down. Eventually, he did and I almost passed out. It's one of those wonderful experiences one never forgets.

I made the coffee in a complete daze. I know he was talking to me but I don't remember what about and then all too quickly it was time to go.

'You will come tomorrow, won't you?' I asked, almost begging.

'Of course I will! You just try and stop me.'

There were no big kisses, just his big hands grabbing my face and pulling it towards his, as he bent down and kissed me goodnight. 'Seven o'clock tomorrow then. Bye!' he shouted as he went down the steps two at a time. I watched him from the window until he went out of sight, still in a daze that this could be happening.

I returned to the flat and simply sat in the chair listening to the radio, still not really taking anything in, but now wondering what I was going to say tomorrow and how I was going to say it. I was absolutely tormented. He believed that I was a woman dressing up as a man, and I felt I wasn't either. I decided to play it with a straight bat: the truth, the whole truth and nothing but the truth, and if he still wanted me then, he would know everything and I would have nothing to hide.

I was deep in thought when I was brought back to reality by an announcement on the radio that Herr Hitler had annexed Austria into the German Reich. This was followed by discussions on how it was likely to affect the rest of Europe and one of the contributors was Winston Churchill. He was convinced that Europe would soon be once again at war. I was too mixed up to take much notice of what was being said, but the following night when William arrived, much of our early conversation was about this and how he agreed with what Churchill was saying and how we should prepare ourselves for the worst.

I cooked a lovely meal. Although I say it myself, I had become a reasonable cook, having had to look after myself for so long and having Thelma's tuition in the kitchen. I didn't have to skimp on the money side as my father still gave me a good allowance so I could afford to splash out on good ingredients. I had even bought a bottle of wine, some candles and flowers for each of the rooms.

We enjoyed the meal, but I dreaded what was coming. I knew he would want to know all about me. We sat on the settee in front of the fire, which crackled cosily. I had switched on the standard lamp and turned off the main light to create a more romantic setting. I was lying across him with my head and shoulders across his lap as I started my gruesome tale.

I began at the beginning and gave him my complete history, ending by telling him: 'I have the same menstrual cycle as any woman.' I think I had suddenly realised that if I wanted to keep him I had to convince him I was what he thought I was.

'Why don't you wear woman's clothes, for God's sake!' he asked in a sharp tone which took me back a little. 'It can't be that difficult, can it? You are a very pretty young woman and the sooner you realise it the better!'

'William, how can you say that? I don't know any different. I have been brought up for the last twenty years as a boy and to react as a boy. It's only the moment I met you yesterday that everything has been turned upside down. I'm totally confused, but I know that I have fallen for you.'

He squeezed my arm a little to reassure me.

'I'm scared,' I continued, 'I've always worn boys' or men's clothing and I cannot face the humiliation of changing. I have never had to buy ladies' things. I have never been told what to buy, how to buy them, what to wear, how to wear them and even how to put them on. How do you expect me to start and, William, think about it: all my fellow students and colleagues at university treat me as a man, so do my neighbours and the few friends that I have got.

'It has been a terrible experience for me – the comments, the looks, the nudges, the insinuations. I've got to the stage where I could accept all that and ignore them by putting my head down in a book. I suppose deep down I was also doing it for my father, but I know I'm wasting my time on that score. It's really too late with him. I know if I change, I'm going to have to face it all over again, this time from the opposite angle. Perhaps I need courage or perhaps I need encouragement; whatever it may be I'll have to have . . .' I stopped there. I thought I had said too much already and I didn't want to put any more pressure on him. We lay in total silence, the flickering fire casting its phantasmic shadows onto the ceiling: there was a tree, there was a cloud, there was a witch . . . Oh God, I felt so good and secure as he softly caressed my head, my arms and my chest. We both lay thinking our different thoughts, but I knew from this moment that this was the life I wanted.

Mr White, that evening was the turning point of my life!

We spent the rest of the evening talking about our futures and of our hopes and dreams as all young couples do. I was behaving like a girl, so much so that William suddenly said, 'From today I'm going to call you Alexandra.'

'That's what my sister, Alice calls me,' I said.

'Well, it sounds as if she at least has common sense then, doesn't it?'

During the next few months we spent many an evening together, but it was always at my flat and I could tell William was becoming a little impatient with me and even started to give me ultimatums. He wanted to take me out, but convention wouldn't allow it. He wanted to introduce me to his friends, but it would be too difficult to do so. As long as I dithered, we were trapped; he was too scared to be seen in public with me as a man. I was too scared to make the change.

I couldn't even go to watch him play rugby, which was terribly disappointing as he was now a regular for Surrey and a permanent fixture for the Wasps. Their club had won several trophies and he wanted me to attend the victory celebrations, but I couldn't.

I remember one afternoon we risked a little trip into the city and afterwards when we returned to the flat, I knew there was something on his mind as he had been unusually quiet throughout our little excursion. I finished preparing tea and sat on the settee next to him.

'Come on, what's on your mind?' I asked.

William then launched into one of his tirades. 'We've had a lovely day, I've walked a dutiful two feet away from you the whole time and quite frankly, it's getting on my nerves! You can't live the life your father wants for you; you must live your own life. You must take what happiness you can get and I promise that, as long as I live, I'll love you and look after you and I don't care if we can't have children. I just want to be with you.'

He finished what he had to say and we sat in total silence, just gazing at one another until I leaned over and rested my head on his lap. He put his hand over my head and gently stroked me. We stayed in that position for at least an hour. I was in heaven. Yet still I was too frightened to make a decision and I thought if we stayed like that I wouldn't have to. He went through several weeks of being miserable in my company, but he always ended by telling me he loved me and that all he wanted was for me to be normal.

Alice's words all over again and I knew deep down he was right. If only Alice was here to help me I knew I could do it. Every time she was with me I said yes and then couldn't do it as soon as she was away from me, and now with William it was the same. What was even worse, when I was awarded my BSc in Mathematics and a BA in Modern Languages, no one came to see me receive them. William desperately wanted to, but we were both too scared. Although the day was tinged with sadness, the university formally offered me a research place for the following two years to do a Masters, which I accepted straight away.

We were having a wonderful time together. I was truly happy and for the first time, I enjoyed being teased by my colleagues; I didn't want it to end, but I could feel William was losing his patience with me. I knew eventually he would grow tired of seeing his ultimatums passed over, especially as war was looking more and more certain as the days went on. In mid-October, William dropped the biggest bombshell: he was joining the RAF.

There was no argument, no discussion; he simply made the decision and told me he was joining the next day. I was devastated and quite selfishly didn't want him to go. He told me that, with him out of the way for a few weeks, it might help me to make up my mind.

We had a lovely week before he had to go up to the Officer Training Centre at Cranwell and I missed him painfully as soon as he was gone. He made many wonderful new friends and from the photographs he sent me of the mess parties, showing several pretty young girls in the background, I began to feel very vulnerable.

The summer brought some relief for me as I was picked for the University side; but it wasn't as glamorous as Oxford or Cambridge, as ours was not included in the County fixture list, but it did give me great pleasure to play against two Oxford colleges which we thrashed and I scored over one hundred and over two hundred in respective matches. But the best match of all came when I was selected for the Combined Universities team against the Australians and actually played against Don Bradman, who scored 210 not out in just over half a day. They declared 524 for three and in reply we were 172 for five when rain washed out the rest of play.
I scored 52; in fairness, it wasn't their strongest side, but it was the Australians and they never liked to lose. It was the last time I was shunned by anyone. The Oxford boys who had been selected and who were aware of my circumstances gave me a wide berth, but that didn't matter, I was the university's top scorer so far and that made me feel good.

By November, William had spent several weeks at Cranwell and he decided to spend the whole weekend with me. We had a fantastic time, but I began to feel that the sexual side of our relationship would be the cause of its failure and thought I would have to do something about it. At this point in time I had one friend that I could rely on and that was my old teacher, Mr Wilkes. We had corresponded regularly since I had left school and I had spoken on the phone to Mrs Wilkes on several occasions, but now I thought I would call and see them.

I had received many invitations to go and stay with him and his wife for a weekend, but what with my commitments to university I never seemed to have the time. However, this time I took full advantage. William had gone back to Cranwell to finish his training and I was left alone as usual, so I thought I would take the opportunity to try and sort myself out.

I tended to look on Mr Wilkes as a father figure and as Mrs

Wilkes had always mothered me a little, treating me almost as a daughter, it was almost my real family and quite frankly, I had no one else. My father wouldn't talk to me; my mother, who was so fiercely loyal to my father, was avoiding me and apart from William and Jennifer I had no other close friends.

I left Chelsea and arrived at Bankworth late on Friday evening. It had been a terrible day in London – there were problems with the trains and the rest of the transport system was at a standstill as a result. By the time I arrived at the Wilkes' house, I was shattered. Of course it had to be mid-term at the school and unfortunately, he was on duty in the evening, so it was left for Mrs Wilkes to entertain me.

'Come on in, Alex! It's lovely to see you. Peter is on duty, so it will be tomorrow before we see him.'

'It's nice to see you and a friendly face,' I said as I entered.

'I'm sure you would like a cup of tea.'

'Pretty desperate. Actually I've had a pig of a journey,' I replied.

I sat down in front of the fire and unwound for a few minutes, just enjoying the peace and quiet.

'This is very good of you, Mrs Wilkes, I do appreciate it,' I said, thanking her for having me.

'Nonsense, Alex, and it's Thelma. Please call me Thelma.'

'Thank you . . . Thelma,' I replied.

I don't know how the conversation started, as we had already been chatting for almost an hour when she asked: 'How are you getting on these days? How is the real Alex getting on?'

I remained silent for a few moments and then for some inexplicable reason, I suddenly started to tell her everything that had gone on. I can't explain it, but I told her that I had fallen in love.

She began to talk to me as my mother would. She said she had known my true nature from the outset but had hardly dared broach the subject back then. Suddenly, she seemed to open up a fresh perspective on my life.

'Alex . . .' She paused for a moment to get her thoughts

together. 'Both Peter and I have thought for a long time that you were a girl and we also thought that it was disgraceful that you were left with the boys for so long. We suggested to the Head that you be transferred to the girls' side, but he refused point-blank. He feared your case would become known and somehow tarnish the school's reputation. It was a terrible thing to do.

'Do you know it was your father who got you transferred to the girls? He came back to see the Headmaster and insisted on it.'

'Mind you, I think your sister Alice and Peter had something to do with putting your father in the picture . . .'

I was absolutely astonished that my father had *any* influence *or* input in my transfer to the girls' side, but now realised he must have had some insight into my problems.

'So what should I do now?' I finally said.

Thelma thought for a while and then calmly replied: 'I can't have children, Alex. I have been to see so many specialists and all of whom told me to do this and that, but all to no avail. They all accepted their fees and as long as I paid, they were happy to see me. I tried everything and then one day someone recommended Mr Geraint Evans, a gynaecologist in Harley Street. He gave me a thorough examination and after two weeks, he gave it to me straight. There was no chance I could have children as there was part of my womb missing, no matter what I did. His abruptness startled me, but at least it was the truth and after a time I could live with that and did not have to live with false hope.

'Now, Alex, I suggest that you see him and see what he makes of your situation. Then you can take it from there. It may be that you are luckier than me and you can have a baby.'

'Thelma, I'm not looking in that direction at all; I just want to see what can be done for me.'

I was even a little bit shocked by Thelma's last remark. The thought of having a child has never entered my brain. I was thinking only of my relationship with William and whether or not he could improve how things looked down below.

Quite frankly, Mr White, they were a bit of a muddle. The whole scenario opened up a lot of different avenues for me, which I had never considered before.

'Could you phone Mr Evans for me and make an appointment?' I asked, excitedly and yet desperate at the same time.

'Of course,' she replied. 'But he's expensive.'

'My father will pay,' I replied. 'At least he owes me that.'

'Do you see your father now then?' she asked.

'No. He doesn't want me,' I replied, trying hard not to cry.

She could see my distress and immediately changed the subject. What's this man in your life like then?'

I immediately opened the floodgates and began to tell her all about William. I was so excited; it was the first time I had ever been able to confide in anyone about anything, let alone my love life.

The tears soon disappeared and I must have had a lovely smile on my face as Thelma remarked, 'He must be someone very special, as I have never seen you look so happy.'

'Oh he is!' I replied. 'But he won't commit until I sort myself out.'

'Then do it, girl,' she replied, coming over and giving me a big hug.

It was music to my ears and once again, I felt things were on the up. I finished my tea as she returned armed with Geraint Evans' telephone number and she told me that I should telephone him, as it really would be better if I did. I promised myself I would ring on the following Monday.

I had a wonderful weekend with the Wilkes'. They took me round the local town where I had spent so many happy hours with my parents at weekends or half-terms and even to my favourite tearooms. On the Saturday evening, things became a little more serious as Peter, as I was now invited to call him, began to talk about my stay at Bankworth. I once again thanked him for the lovely words he said about me at Prize-Giving Day and for what he had done for me since, only to be told he regretted he hadn't done more. It was when he asked how things were with my father that he saw the pain I had to go through when I told him what the situation was. Peter himself became emotional and said, 'If you ever need me, or a shoulder to cry on, I'm here and I'll always be here for you, and I'm sure Thelma will be to.' She nodded her approval.

I had lunch with them and caught the midday train back to London. I left knowing I had two real friends on my side. I didn't sleep very well that night, as I was too excited at the thought of what Geraint Evans would say to me and of course very worried for fear in case his prognosis was that it would be simpler to improve the masculine side of me. In the end, I convinced myself I was, after all, only making an appointment and that was that. I telephoned Mr Evans the following day and made an arrangement for nine days later, explaining briefly what the problem was.

It was a terrible nine days. I hadn't heard from William, which was unusual, and I was deeply anxious about what the specialist would find. I arrived at 18a Harley Street at eleven sharp, the time of my appointment, and was greeted by Mr Evans' nurse receptionist.

'Good morning, my name's Alex Chillington-Henry and I have an appointment for an examination with Dr Evans at eleven,' I said as boldly as I could.

She looked at me agog. 'You do realise that Mr Evans is a gynaecologist and is a Mister not a Doctor,' she said in a somewhat supercilious manner.

She was interrupted, however, by Mr Evans. 'Nurse never judge a book by its cover. Come with me, Alex, will you?'

I followed him into his consulting room, where he questioned me for a good hour on my problems before he started to examine me closely. I was told to strip off and to wear a dressing gown and to lie on his couch, all the time asking questions. He seemed very interested in my case.

'Are you homosexual?' he asked, as he was examining my lower half.

'No, I'm not!' I snapped.

'I'm sorry,' he replied. 'But you have an enlarged–'

I stopped him in mid-sentence. 'I was raped and buggered by the prefects at my school on a very regular basis and no one helped me. Everyone turned a blind eye. Even my father wouldn't have anything to do with me when I developed . . . this way. I was thought of some sort of a freak so I was fair game, especially to my fellow cricket teammates, it seems.'

'Wait a minute!' Mr Evans suddenly said. 'Didn't I see you score a fifty against the Aussies the other day?'

'Yes!' I replied.

'You're a cricketer, young man?'

Then for a few minutes or so we talked cricket. I think he was trying to make me relax a little.

'Let's continue,' he said gently. 'Please lie on your back.'

At last he asked me stand up and button myself up.

'I'm afraid we might have bad news, but I'll need some x-rays. Would you to be able to attend St Thomas' tomorrow morning? We can talk some more then.'

'I'd like to know what you think now, Mr Evans. I can't bear not knowing the truth.'

He hesitated. 'We'll, I don't think we can do much. I think your cricketing days are over.'

'What's the problem?' I demanded.

'Well, young man, without a very major operation to remove the womb etc., which I wouldn't recommend, as it's very dangerous, I think you will always be classed as female. And we certainly wouldn't be able to reduce your breasts. So you are stuck with it.'

I felt a flush of joy. 'But, Mr Evans that is exactly what I wanted to hear! I have a boyfriend and I just wanted to know if I could have a normal relationship with him and get rid of this,' I said, pointing to the bit of gristle that was my penis.

'I don't think that will be too difficult, but I'll need to look at the X-rays. But how about the cricket? Won't you miss it?'

I almost laughed. 'Yes, Mr Evans! I think I would!'

'Well, I'll see you tomorrow morning then, young . . .' The doctor's voice faded away.

The following day I arrived at St Thomas' at the appointed time and was immediately taken to X-ray where Mr Evans was waiting for me. The X-rays were soon done and I was whisked up to his office in the hospital.

After a few minutes of studying the X-rays, he turned and began to advise me what he recommended.

'Look, young man . . .' he began.

'Look I'm sorry, sir,' I interrupted, 'but it's probably best you stop calling me that. It will be easier for both of us.'

'I'll call you Alex then . . . I told you yesterday you had all the female internal attributes. You also have a vagina, albeit small, but we can do something about that. The problem is that your penis is only an external means of going to the toilet. It has no other function. You do not have testicles. How on earth this wasn't discovered at birth, I cannot understand. I'll have to put it down to inexperience. You should have been registered as a female.'

'Are you sure?' I asked.

'Young man, I don't make mistakes,' Mr Evans replied haughtily. Alex, I mean.'

'Sorry!' I responded.

'I would need to tidy all that up, but it will be a shame to lose a good player.'

'They won't let me play anyway. They think I'm a freak.'

'I don't like that expression and you're not a freak. You only have a slight abnormality in the urinary tract, which can be altered and you will be right as rain.'

'Mr Evans, about other matters . . .' I began but found myself unable to continue.

'Everything else,' he said, guessing my meaning, 'when I'm finished, will be normal. I'll notify you when I can perform the operation. It may be several months, I'm afraid.'

I left the hospital on a high and I thought I was the luckiest person in the world.

Chapter 13

I had to wait two more weeks before William came home on leave, during which time, unfortunately, he had to spend half of the time with his parents. During the other half, he spent almost the entire time trying to persuade me to throw away all my male attire to buy a complete new wardrobe. He wanted me in short to burn my boats as a male. This would mean he wouldn't have the difficulty explaining to his parents what I was and we could spend more time together. He was over the moon, however, when I told him I had seen Geraint Evans and what he intended to do and it gave him a little more confidence that I was serious about moving in his direction.

I did however feel he was a little more distant this time, probably because he had such a wonderful time at Cranwell, having passed his training course with top marks and, of course, he told me they had had a big celebration dinner to which, he delighted in telling me, he had taken a local girl. You can imagine how I felt, particularly as it was Christmas the following week.

This period was one of terrible personal strain for me, as William now had a new career: he was an officer in the RAF and was being transferred to Flying School in Lincolnshire as he was now going to be a bomber pilot. I wasn't really helping myself as I was still suffering from a deep-seated inertia and feared that his changed life would lead to a change in his feelings for me. Pilots, even in those days, were the glamour boys of the Forces and were always in demand by the ladies.

I had him for three days at Christmas and we spent two of

them with Peter and Thelma Wilkes. They treated me like their daughter and were delighted when I told them about Mr Evans. We had a lovely Christmas, except William was too shy to show any affection to someone still in trousers, particularly in front of other people even though they were my new adoptive parents.

In the New Year of 1939, William joined his unit at the RAF Flying School and within a few weeks he had won his wings. As I said, William had achieved top marks in his group and was becoming well thought of, so much so, he was offered a training post abroad. He was initially sent to Lincoln under bomber command and began to learn all the new techniques which he was to pass on when he started his new post.

Two weeks later, in March, Hitler invaded Czechoslovakia and war became inevitable. The government of Chamberlain, despite his peaceful rhetoric, was making some efforts to protect the defence of the country. We were developing new fighters and new bombers and recruiting more men into the Forces and it became William's job to help train these future pilots so that we weren't totally defenceless when the war started.

I didn't see him as often as I would have liked during the summer, but I did have many letters, all of which I have kept, but in them there was always the feeling that he was holding back his real feelings and a hint of what he wanted me to do. While he was away, I became immersed in my work at the university and inevitability, as it was the summer, in my cricket. I had the most fantastic season I had ever had. It was a glorious summer and I scored over two thousand runs with an average of 88.

You see, Mr White, I'm still proud of my cricketing achievements. I was picked again for the Combined Universities to play against the West Indies, but this time, I didn't do very well, I was out for 35 and 40. We were well and truly beaten in two days, but I'm showing off now! We scored 125 and 176 all out in respective innings, with them having scored 440 for five declared. Cricketers have long memories. Mr White. Don't look at me like that. I said I was showing off!

It was a bad year, Mr White. Chamberlain was making his futile efforts for peace with Hitler and of course most people, except Chamberlain himself perhaps, knew he was wasting his time. Anyway, within a few days, as we all know, Hitler marched into Poland and we had to declare war once again on Germany.

I couldn't believe it when William told me he had been posted to Canada for six months to train bomber pilots there. I suppose in one sense I was being selfish, thinking he was out of danger from a possible war, but on the other hand, I wasn't going to see him and in my condition I was worried he would find someone else. He wrote to me every two or three weeks and it was wonderful to receive his letters and I know he missed me as much as I missed him. Naturally, he wasn't able to tell me what he was doing, and even the little things he thought possible were often obliterated by the censor.

The fifth letter from the Canada is the one I prize the most. Look, Mr White, I always have it close at hand. It was the first time he wrote he was in love with me and wanted to be with me for the rest of his life. I felt so happy. I wanted to tell everyone, but then it struck me what we were contemplating was suicide as long as I remained, in the eyes of the world, that is – a man.

I spent the next three weeks worrying about what would happen to us as a couple. Where would we live? Would he be thrown out of the RAF? Could we get jobs if people found out? A hundred and one problems came to mind and led me to think I was being unfair to him. I would be the reason his life would be ruined and did I want that? I had almost decided to give him up for his own good, when his sixth letter arrived and again it was so full of love and hopes for our shared future that my thinking changed all over again. You see, Mr White, I was like a pendulum, swinging back and forth between despair and optimism, just as my gender swung between male and female.

I had in the meantime tried to do my bit for the war effort. I had approached the RAF, the Navy and the Army, but all with the same results. Once they had seen me stripped off, I had no chance and was summarily dismissed with the usual comments: 'Darling, we want to win the bloody war, not distract the entire bloody Army.' I even heard one of the recruiting sergeants commenting that there was a bloody lesbian in there, trying to join up! Another made the lewd comment, 'that she only wants to join up to get fucked as many times as she can.' It was dispiriting stuff and I feared what some members of the public would say when they saw me – an apparently fit young man, not in a uniform.

My university undertook a lot of research for the Ministry of Defence during the war and we were all covered by the Official Secrets Act, so I comforted myself that I was at least helping the war effort and doing my bit in that respect. One evening, I was returning home to my flat in Chelsea in a fog when I saw in the murky distance a dark figure sitting on the steps at the entrance. I stopped dead in my tracks, wondering who on earth it could be and what was wrong. I began walking very slowly, but the nearer I got the faster my pace became until I was running. It was William and as he saw me approach he stood up and then stepped onto the pavement as I got nearer. I couldn't help myself. I ran right up to him and jumped, wrapping my legs around his waist and kissed him a thousand times.

He dropped the parcel he was carrying and tried to untangle me from him, which he found somewhat difficult.

'Not here! Let's go inside, I want to talk.'

He freed himself from my arms and then held on to them tightly. My feet dropped to the ground as I let go and for a moment I was in shock, a thousand and one things began running through my mind. Was he trying to say it's over? Had he found someone else? He saw the distress in my eyes and immediately calmed my fears.

'Don't worry! I'll tell you all about it inside.'

Relief returned and I grabbed his arm and walked up the steps to the front door. I was so excited I couldn't find the key quick enough as I fumbled in my jacket pocket, but eventually we walked through the door and into my flat. We were like two lovers who had just learned the meaning of the word as we hugged and kissed each other for what seemed like hours. It was so good to have him home in my arms.

'How long have you got?' I asked excitedly.

'Forty-eight hours.'

'Oh, is that all? It's not fair. Why can't you stay longer?'

'I just managed to hitch a lift on a flight of B56 Bombers. There were five which the Yanks delivered to Archbury and I have to go back with the pilots or I'll be in trouble, and what's worse, it's going to be another six months before I get back.'

'Six months!' I exclaimed 'What am I going to do without you?' I added despairingly.

'Well, hopefully after that I'll back for good. It looks like I'll be stationed again somewhere in Lincolnshire. Anyway, enough of that, I have to talk to you. I've been rehearsing this all over the Atlantic and I've got to get it off my chest.'

'Would you like a drink?' I asked, holding onto his hand for dear life as I pulled him into the kitchen.

'Let's just have a cup of tea. We need to talk,' he said, repeating himself, as if to emphasise the urgency of what he was so anxious to say.

We sat at the kitchen table and it was the first time I saw William really embarrassed and not knowing where to start.

He began with a cough. 'Darling, you know I love you very much. I don't know why, but I can't put you down.' He stopped as if to find words which didn't want to come out and then began again. 'I can't leave you alone and I want to spend all my time with you. Oh God! Look I don't know how to say this . . .' He paused again for a minute or two, drinking his tea and using that as the excuse not to continue. Then suddenly he just blurted out what he wanted to say:

'Look! You are a young woman and deep down you know

you are a young woman. You behave like one, at least you do when you are with me. Why don't you bloody well dress like one?

'I want to show people how much I love you. Do you think there is anything worse for me than walking out with you, with a permanent one-foot gap between us? I want to walk down the street holding your hand, without the worry of being seen, or having to tell the waiter you're my younger brother . . . It's driving me mad and I can't go on like this much more. Darling, you have to make up your mind! Soon . . . Now!'

He stopped speaking and we looked at each other across the kitchen table. He stretched out his hand and took mine into it and gently squeezed it as if to say, 'Come on, it's your turn.'

The tears began rolling down my cheeks. Here I had a man in front of me who was offering to love me and give me something I had not felt for many years and yet, still, I was too scared to change. I was totally mixed up.

When I was with him I could take on the world; when I wasn't, I drifted back into my shell where I felt secure. My tears stopped all my efforts to speak. I could only hold on and hope he would understand.

'I'm not going to let you wriggle out of this one!' he said firmly, 'as much as I love to see that little, beautiful, sad face. We are going to do something. Right?' His question being a rhetorical order.

I suppose it was what I needed; someone to make the decisions for me and that is what William had started to do.

'You can wear something simple to begin with. What about a skirt and jumper?'

I still couldn't answer and felt myself blushing.

'Well then, that's what we'll start with. You'll need underwear, shoes and stockings and we will start tomorrow and go out and buy them. Do you understand?' Again it was more of a command than a question.

'I'm not one of your subordinates!' I replied indignantly, still sobbing.

'Do you understand?' he repeated.

'Yeees!' I replied, not realising what I had let myself in for. In my heart I knew I had come to a crisis, the moment when I had either to make a complete break with the past or forever remain as I had been.

'Come on! Be brave, we're going to start today and we are never turning back! Never!' He squeezed my hand firmly and I brushed away the tears with my other. 'Come on, I'm going to buy you a meal tonight and we'll say farewell to my brother. Do we agree?'

I put my hand over my eyes and forehead. He squeezed my hand tighter. 'Do we agree?'

'Y . . . y . . . es! . . . I agree . . .' I replied, stammering the answer.

'Right, where do you want to go for dinner? It's the last time as Alexander. Tomorrow it will be Alexandra. Do we agree?'

I think it was in that split second that I finally made my mind up, to try and live in a different world. I know I couldn't have done it without William, but I was dreading the transition.

'Yes, to the second question and you choose for the first,' I replied, cheering up a little.

We went to a little restaurant close to the West End, down one of the side streets. I think it was called the Pig and Whistle. It was a lovely little place with very secluded tables in half-lit corners and what was more the food was good. We walked in and the head waiter greeted us with some disdain. William, however, started how he meant to go on, by announcing, 'Please excuse my fiancée's attire. She's just finished performing in a play and hasn't had time to change.'

'That's all right, sir,' the waiter replied, with a strong Cockney accent. 'We get all sorts in 'ere.'

We both laughed.

It was the first time William had shown the courage to almost tell the truth and it made me feel good. We sat down at a table in the most secluded spot and simply gazed at one another. At last I mustered up the courage to speak the question that was in my heart.

'Do you mean what you just said?'

'What's that, darling?'

'Introducing me as your fiancée?'

'Of course I do! But I can't marry a man now, can I?' he whispered. He paused as the waiter came for the order.

'I'm sorry, sir, but you're a trifle late and there are a number of items not available. There was a gas explosion at Covent Garden the other night and they're not back to normal yet and we can't get all the veg we need.'

'Oh don't worry,' William replied. 'There'll be a war soon and we'll have to get used to that kind of thing. Just serve us what you can. I'm sure we will enjoy it.'

'What play are you in then?' the waiter asked.

I was flummoxed but William had the answer at his fingertips. '*As You Like It.* She's playing Rosalind. Modern dress, of course. It opens next week at the Whitehall Theatre. It's been the dress rehearsal today.'

'No more lies. From tomorrow,' he added in a whisper as soon as the waiter had gone.

'Now, I'm going to make a bargain with you. I'm proposing we get engaged. So I'll only get engaged when I have in front of me my girl . . . the girl I love . . . How are we going to get your new things?' he asked, changing tack.

'I can't go into ladies outfitters dressed like this, can I?'

'You could. You could say you've been robbed and lost everything, or I could go and buy you the jumper and skirt and a pair of shoes and stockings and then you could go in.'

'You don't know my size,' I quickly retorted, like a petulant child.

'No, but we can measure tonight. Can't we?' he replied with a naughty smile.

We had a lovely evening, talking about everything and every- body, but always coming back to the same decision, that this was the last time I would dress as a man.

We paid the bill, left the restaurant and took a taxi back to my flat in Chelsea. It was the last time I walked up the steps dressed that way and it was the last time William made the excuse that I was an actress in a play.

I woke up late the following morning to find William wasn't in bed, but the momentary worried feeling soon disappeared when I saw the note he left me, saying he would be back in about an hour. He was always so thoughtful and to make sure I didn't worry he even put the time he had left on the note. I decided to stay in bed and wait; it was much warmer anyway.

I must have fallen asleep again as the next thing I remember was the sound of William making a cup of tea, which he brought up to me together with a few boxes, which obviously contained ladies clothing.

'You don't know my size,' I yelled almost automatically. It was part of my defence mechanism and an effort to put off the fatal moment. The moment of my transformation.

'We'll see.'

He sat on the bed and we drank the tea together and all the time William was looking stupid with a supercilious grin on his face. I knew he had been up to something, but then I didn't know what.

'I'll just take these downstairs,' he said, picking up the cups and saucers and placing them on the tray, still with that stupid look on his face. 'You get ready and I'll cook you breakfast,' he added as he left the room and returned to the kitchen.

I'll never forget this day, Mr White. Never!

I went to my wardrobe to collect my clothes. The scream must have been heard all over London.

'William, what have you done with my clothes!'

'I think they are in those boxes. Shall I come and help you look?' I heard him chuckling to himself.

'No you won't!' I said, running to lock the door and just succeeding before he got there.

We talked through the door. I say 'talked', but it was simply me pleading, half crying and half laughing. 'William please, please give me back my clothes!'

'Darling, they're there. You just have to try them on.'

I was terrified. This wasn't Wendy in *Peter Pan*. This wasn't a holiday prank, like in Le Touquet. This was real life and I spent the next half an hour pleading to no avail. William wouldn't give in until I tried on the clothes.

'I'll try them on if you tell me where my other clothes are,' I said like a spoiled child.

He agreed and I let him in.

'Where are they then?' I asked.

'I've given them to the Salvation Army.'

'*No*!' I screamed. 'You couldn't have.'

'Come on. Try them on, there's a good girl,' he continued, treating me like some naughty schoolgirl. He took them out of the boxes and gave them to me one by one. He could see I was embarrassed and whispered, 'Don't worry, darling, I love you.'

I felt an absolute idiot. Mr White. Try and imagine that for twenty years you have been brought up as a man; you have played like a man, behaved like a man, dressed like a man. I even had the mentality of a man and now, with my hormones all jumbled up, I had fallen in love . . . with a man. And now, in one fell swoop, I was to become a woman.

He had bought some lovely silk stockings and I put these on first. Like most men his attention to detail was lacking as he had forgotten to buy something to hold them up with. Then I tried a pair of satin knickers, a below-the-knee A-line skirt, and finally, a blue sweater. But, best of all, something I didn't appreciate at the time, was a tawny-coloured coat with a big collar. It was very fashionable.

I put them on slowly and William was mesmerised. I had never realised before that someone could captivate another with their sexuality. You have heard of a striptease; well, this was a dress-tease. William was captivated and when I had finished, he wolf whistled and shouted: 'Now, will you marry me?'

'I'm not going to answer that. Who would want to marry

someone so cruel?' I said, pretending to be angry. My newfound femininity was beginning to show.

'Come here.' He walked over with his arms outstretched.

'One more step and I'll deck you,' I replied, smiling with my fists clenched, like some boxer in drag. Only I knew I didn't look like a boxer.

William stepped back. 'Oh, it's a fight you want, is it?'

He charged at me, knocking me onto the bed and kissed me. Darling, you look beautiful, especially with your short hair.' He put his arms on my shoulders and held me down and just looked at me.

'Come on, get up!' William demanded, acting as if he was already my lord and master. 'We've a lot to do and talk about and we've only got twenty-four hours left.'

This pulled me up by my bootlaces. 'Couldn't they give you any longer? Couldn't you report sick?' I knew they were stupid things to say; the war wasn't going to stop for me, even if this was the first time I had been in love.

'Come on, let's have breakfast.' He took my hand and led me to the kitchen and as I moved, one of my new stockings fell down and William bent down to pull it up for me. 'Can't have my fiancée looking shabby, can we?'

Seeing him do this gave me goose pimples. To think that someone like William wanted to love me, wanted to be my friend, wanted to look after me . . .

We had our first breakfast as a true couple and it was delicious, even if it was just three rounds of buttered toast and a pot of tea.

After breakfast he helped me make the final adjustments to my dress. He enjoyed tying my stockings up and kissing my shoes before putting them on me. He enjoyed holding my coat as I gently slipped my arms into the sleeves, giving him a sly kiss as I did it. Fortunately, he had been sensible with the footwear, whether by design or luck I don't know, and I could just about walk in them.

Dressed in his RAF officer's uniform, he opened the front

door. Then he turned to me with his arm crooked, so that I could link my arm through his, and we walked down the front steps onto the pavement.

'Head up, shoulders back, let's go!' he ordered.

'You sound like my father,' I said, memories of my father in uniform flooding back.

'Come on. You've no need to slouch. You've got a good figure and you are very beautiful. Be proud of yourself.'

I did feel proud of being with William. He looked lovely in his uniform, but I was very self-conscious and I remember every time we approached someone, I would slouch, shoulders forward, to conceal my shape. William quietly reprimanded me. 'Shoulders back, stand up straight!' I did as I was told, but it was an effort.

We looked around Chelsea for a ladies' lingerie shop and soon found a quaint little shop on the Kings Road, very modern for the time. William completely took the wind out of my sails by walking straight up to the manageress and telling her a pack of lies.

'My fiancée has had an accident and has broken the thing that holds her stockings up. Have you such a thing?'

I rolled my eyes up to heaven in total embarrassment; I just wanted to run out of the shop. The proprietor saw my horror and smiled. I didn't know what to say or do; the only words that came out of my mouth were, 'He's a bit of a bully, you know!'

She smiled again.

'Of course we do. I'll show you,' she replied, pulling out a drawer and presenting me with a selection. William paid. I certainly wasn't used to this. I had ample funds as my father always made sure I had more than sufficient.

'My dear,' the proprietor said as she began wrapping the goods, 'have you seen these new petticoats? They have just arrived . . .'

She didn't give me time to answer and immediately opened two other boxes, displaying the contents on the counter top.

'They're very nice,' William said.

'You shouldn't be looking, sir.'

We all smiled. It was like manna from heaven to have advice like this.

'What size are you?'

I was stumped for a second or two.

'You look a medium to me,' she said, fortunately not giving me much time to answer.

I eventually chose three with William's help. It was then that my worst nightmare happened. Like a true saleswoman she then decided to sell me a bra to match the petticoats.

'They are very pretty,' I said to her, trying to conquer my shyness.

She continued with her sales pitch, but then I realised I had to do something which took extraordinary courage.

'Could I have a word?' I asked, whispering in her ear.

'Yes dear. Come with me,' she replied.

'You wait there, bully,' I called out to William.

William asked the proprietor if he could use the phone as she took me into her backroom where I had my first 'girly chat'.

'I'm not wearing a brassiere at the moment. I never have. I haven't felt the need to, and I'm a little embarrassed to talk about it, especially in front of my fiancé.'

'Well, you should wear one, dear. Hasn't your mother told you what can happen in later life? I really think you should start. Look, take my advice. Just try one and see how you go. It's more dignified and you won't be young forever. Come on, what size are you?'

I looked at her bemused. 'I don't know!'

'Well, let's have a look.' She took her tape measure from her pocket and began to measure my chest. 'Lift your jumper, please. Don't be embarrassed.'

She could see me blushing. 'I can promise you, you will regret not wearing some support with your chest, particularly as you get older.'

She went and fetched the correct size and I, somewhat

clumsily, put it on and she fastened it.

'May I try the petticoat with it?' I asked, gaining more confidence, as she had been so nice.

'Of course you may. Go into the changing room and I'll bring it to you.'

It took some time for me to dress myself, especially to undo the knots that William had tied in the string. I plucked up the courage to look in the mirror and gasped. There was a lovely young woman I had never seen before. I called the proprietor in to see.

'Well, that looks very nice,' she commented. 'How is the brassiere?'

'Strange, but comfortable,' I replied. 'I'll take your advice. I'll wear one. May I keep it on and the petticoat?'

'Of course you can. Shall I wrap the rest up?'

I went back out into the shop and secretly gave William the two pieces of string and whispered, 'A souvenir!'

Mr White, in that cup over there you will find two pieces of string. William took them with him on all the operations during the war. They were his good-luck charm.

I had finished buying my new lingerie or I should say William had finished buying me my new lingerie when the proprietor suggested I might like to have look at the new dress shop along the Kings Road and perhaps buy a hat to go with the outfits.

'I don't want to press you, but ladies always wear hats,' she said, and Bessie Casson the milliner, just down the road, has just had a wonderful delivery of hats which will just suit you with your short hair.'

William looked at me and I shrugged my shoulders. I had never even thought of wearing a hat.

'You know, dear,' the manageress said, 'you have a beautiful face and figure. A hat would set everything off. Anyway, dear, think about it. Manners maketh man, or so they say, but a hat maketh the woman.'

'We'll certainly think about it,' I said to her, as she handed the parcels to William to carry.

We left arm in arm and walked to a café near the Underground at Sloane Square, for a cup of tea and a chat. I don't know whether I was shaking with excitement or relief that the ordeal was over. I used that shop right through the war; I never went anywhere else until the day it was hit by a doodlebug. You know a V2 bomb. The proprietor was killed outright along with several others, right at the end of the war. It was terrible. I felt quite proud of myself and eventually told William what I had done.

'Come on, you,' William said. 'You need at least one or two dresses and then we should take a look at those hats.'

'Yes, a hat would be perfectly lovely. You heard what she said, "A hat maketh the woman."' I flounced around in my new outfit, pretending to be all feminine, and then spoiled the act by stumbling in my new shoes.

Having bought two simple dresses, we entered the milliner's full of the joys of spring. 'I want to buy a couple of hats for my fiancée. You came recommended. So here we are,' William declared joyfully.

We spent another wonderful hour as I tried on dozens of hats before coming round to the two I preferred, or rather the two which William said suited me most of all. And do you know, Mr White, the simple act of trying on a lady's hat, looking in the mirror face on, actually made me feel more feminine. I also discovered that William liked a woman to be glamorous which meant I would have to work hard to make myself that way!

I kept one of the hats on as we left and, I confess, I looked stunning. Well, he said so and he hadn't finished yet. He took me on to Harrods in Knightsbridge and we bought several more frocks and three pairs of shoes and then lunch. I had a wonderful time and, for the first time in years, I felt important.

After lunch he announced he had a surprise for me. On leaving Harrods he hailed a cab and as we climbed in he whispered something to the driver.

' Close your eyes,' William said to me, 'and don't open them until I tell you. Promise?'

'I promise!'

I didn't open them until he told me to and when I did we were outside Gemstones, a little jeweller's in Hatton Garden. Inside we were greeted by the proprietor, a Jewish fellow named Isaac Fischer, who already seemed to know William.

Isaac left the front-of-shop and returned with a little box and in it was this . . . Look, Mr White, isn't it perfect? Three flawless diamonds! Not a bad gift for a woman six hours old!

He put it on my finger and Isaac blessed us as we left.

'I have another surprise for you. I'm taking you to meet my parents. He had phoned while we were in the lingerie shop and made all the arrangements with his father.

'No, I couldn't! No, please, it's been a big day for me today. I don't think I'm ready to face them.'

'You are and you will!' he ordered, brooking no contradiction. 'I've only got a few hours left. I've just got engaged to a very pretty woman and I want my folks to meet her. That's an end to it.'

'Do they know about me?' I asked.

'Of course they do.'

'Everything?'

'Yes, of course.' The shock on my face told the story. 'Yes everything. That you are a pretty clever girl who's working at the university . . .'

I was relieved but frightened. I think it's bad enough meeting prospective in-laws in normal circumstances, but in my situation it was terrifying.

Half an hour later we were knocking on the door of a handsome large double-fronted Edwardian House in Hampstead. I felt myself trembling at William's side.

'Dad, Mother, this is Alexandra, my fiancée,' William said as soon as we were inside.

'How do you do, sir,' I said as I shook his father's hand, almost sounding as though I was still a boy at Bankworth. I turned to his mother. 'Hello, it's so nice to meet you at last,' which I thought sounded better.

They were a prosperous-looking couple, still attractive in their fifties. He was the managing director of the Gas Light & Coke Company, an important company at that time.

'Congratulations!' his mother said, smiling with the double pleasure at seeing her son so unexpectedly and with such a lovely surprise. 'And when did this happen?'

'An hour ago!' William replied, 'and you are the first to know. There's no time to hang around now.'

I could tell they were happy and Mrs Fraser even more so when she learned we hadn't even told my parents yet.

William's father was having a very difficult time at work because the company was busy preparing for the inevitable Blitzkrieg, the mass bombing raids that Hitler had carried out everywhere else. Mr Fraser, the father that is, had the strain of being out night after night, organising the work, so I'm sure he wasn't at his best.

I sat down on what was clearly a new leather settee, with William sitting a discreet distance away, opposite me. I suddenly noticed William raising his eyebrows at me, and I suddenly realised I was sitting with my legs sprawled open. I quickly drew them together and sat in what I thought might be a more ladylike pose.

'I'll go and ask Cook about some tea and then we'll talk,' Mrs Fraser announced, before suddenly asking: 'But where is it? Let me see it. Let me see the ring!'

In ungainly fashion, I got up and held out my hand to show her the ring.

'Oh Wilf, it's beautiful. Look,' she said, directing me over to William's father sitting in a chair across the room. 'You are a lucky young girl,' she added, with William interjecting that he was the lucky one.

I felt like a spare part when William began to tell his father how he was and how things were. Mrs Fraser smiled at me and suddenly asked if I would like to look at her garden while the men talked about business and while we waited for the tea.

She took me out into the garden and, for a few minutes I was called upon to admire flowers and plants I had never heard of in my life. It was a very odd situation. I felt that I would much rather be back with the men.

When we returned, the maid had laid out tea and Mrs Fraser began to pour. 'Milk and sugar, Alexandra?'

'Yes, please.'

'William has told us you work for the Ministry of Defence. As a secretary?'

'No, Mother! I told you she's one of the boffins, you know. She's a mathematician,' William interrupted.

Mrs Fraser's eyes nearly popped out of her head.

'Yes, of course. It's just that I didn't take it in. She's so . . . glamorous. You expect a clever woman like that to look . . .'

'Dowdy?' William suggested.

'Different, I was going to say.'

'She also fluent in French and German.' William was obviously trying to make sure his parents were impressed.

'Then what's she want with you, eh?' Mr Fraser asked, laughing.

'I don't know, I'm just lucky, I suppose,' he replied and then got up and sat next to me.

'What does your father do?' Mr Fraser asked.

'He's a major general, but I haven't seen him for ages. His work takes him away a lot of the time,' I added, trying to cover up my embarrassment. I tried to steer the questions to safer matters.

'Who was the cricketer?' I asked, looking at some team photographs on a nearby table.

'Oh that was me when I was younger,' Wilf replied.

'He was very good,' Mrs Fraser added.

'Alexandra plays cricket too, Dad,' William added, rather stupidly I thought.

For the first time Mr Fraser looked at me a little oddly.

'Cricket's not for women,' he said sternly.

'Oh, I don't know. She played for Oxford University and scored a hundred against Worcester and I think 166 against

Surrey before they stopped her playing . . .'

'Is that true, Alexandra?' he asked in total surprise.

'Yes it is, Father,' William said, answering for me.

It was almost seven o'clock when William suddenly announced we would have to go as he had to leave very early in the morning to return to Canada.

'Oh! You can't!' Wilf suddenly announced. 'I've arranged a surprise party for you both. Alexandra, you'll be able to meet some of his friends.'

William gave me a look as if to say sorry and then, turning to his father, he said, 'Thanks but I mustn't be too late.'

'I can't wear these clothes if we are going out. I've been in them all day,' I interrupted.

'I can lend you something, Alexandra, if you like,' Mrs Fraser replied.

'Thank you . . .' I began, only to be interrupted by William insisting that I wore the dress we had bought in Harrods earlier. 'H.E.L.P!' I mouthed, hoping that his parents wouldn't see me.

'You can change in William's room upstairs,' his mother said as William rushed to my aid by taking the parcels up to his room.

'Don't be long, William! I'm sure she can manage on her own.

Women like to!'

'I'll just open the parcels for her,' William replied.

Half an hour later, I came downstairs, having sent William down a few minutes earlier to make things look more seemly. As I entered the lounge, William raised his eyebrows in pleasure.

We were then taken to a local hall, which I think was a Masonic Lodge, where to my surprise they had arranged a private dinner party for us, where we were the guests of honour and although it was a lovely affair, I longed to be alone with William for the last few hours of his leave.

Immediately after dinner, a wind-up gramophone was brought out and they began to play the old 12-inch records. I remember there was Jack Payne, Roy Fox, even some early Glen Miller and several others, and of course William and I were forced into starting everything off, to the shouts and cheers of everyone present. It was the first time I had danced with William and it was wonderful, even if he did have two left feet. I held him firmly and made him follow me, although I was the one going backwards and as there were more men than women, you can imagine the moment we walked off the floor, someone else was there to ask me to be their partner. I don't think I missed one dance.

I was the centre of attention, the belle of the ball. And I loved it.

'Where did you learn to dance like that?' William asked me, a little annoyed, I think, at the admiration I was attracting from the other young men.

'At Bankworth!' I replied, as I sat down beside Mrs Fraser, breathless from my exertions.

It was an idiotic thing to say so loudly.

'But isn't Bankworth just for boys?' Mrs Fraser asked curiously.

'It's for girls and boys.'

'Oh, I didn't realise.' Still she looked a little confused.

Suddenly, William's father banged his hand on a table and proposed a toast. There was silence as he spoke.

'We can all see what a charming girl Alexandra is and I can see that you all like her, but what's more important is that I and his mother can see how much our son loves her and I sincerely believe it's reciprocal. Therefore, I would like to propose a toast to the happiness and good health of William and Alexandra . . .'

Everyone raised their glasses. 'To William and Alexandra. Good health and happiness!'

It was now getting late and William thought it better we take our leave, when suddenly one of the young men came up us. William introduced him as one of the rugby team. He looked at me very curiously.

'I say, were you the boy in the Lyons Corner House that day

William spilled your drink?'

'Yes,' I replied, 'but please don't say anything. I was supposed to be under cover. I didn't make a very good job of it, did I?' I put my finger to my lips and said, 'Please don't say anything. I'll get into trouble.'

'I won't, but I knew I had seen you before. I knew you were too good-looking to be a boy. William's a lucky man. I wish I had seen you first.'

Back at the flat I walked up the steps a different person. For the first time I wondered what the neighbours would think.

'Darling, where did you put my clothes?' I asked the moment we were inside.

'I told you: I gave everything to the Salvation Army!'

'What!' I screamed. 'I thought you were teasing. What am I going to do? I've got to go to college, to work. I can't just turn up as a woman one day, after being a man a few days before. Imagine what will happen!'

William realised he had put me in a bit of a spot and there was no way out. He was leaving in less than six hours and I was stranded.

'Come into bed and let's talk about it.'

I set the alarm for five o'clock and we got into bed. He put his arms around me and whispered, 'I love you and thank you for a wonderful day. You don't need to worry. You looked lovely!'

Within seconds he was asleep, leaving me to worry about the following day.

It seemed only moments later when the alarm went off. It was still dark and it felt as if reality was rushing back at me. William was leaving and I had to make my mind up what to do. I got up and dressed quickly, then went to the kitchen prepared some toast which I took to William with a cup of tea. He was already awake and like me, didn't feel like talking; it was too distressing.

'You know, darling,' he said eventually, 'you had many admirers last night and it's the first time I have felt insecure.'

'Why should you? Who put this on my finger?' I said,

showing him my lovely ring. 'It was a fantastic evening, wasn't it? I've never enjoyed myself so much before.'

'Or had so much attention!' William said sarcastically.

'Well, that's your fault! You chose my clothes for me . . .'

'I've got impeccable taste, darling. I chose you for a start.'

'What did your parents think of me?' I suddenly asked.

'Dad thought you were a cracker and fell for you straight away. Mother . . . well, she was just amazed how clever you were, though she was a little suspicious of your motives. She thought you wanted to snap me up quick as I was a good catch. I told a lie and said you were very well off already and that I was the lucky one.'

'What a terrible thing to think. But she's right: I did want to snap you up.'

'Darling, I've got to be going soon. What are we going to do about your job?'

'You're not going to believe it, but I'm going to come clean and tell them I have only been pretending to be a boy and, now that I have fallen in love, I'm not going to pretend anymore.'

'You can't! You'll be ridiculed.'

'Darling, I've had ten years of ridicule. Another few days won't make any difference. If they don't want me, I'll have to do something else.'

'You're an incredible woman. No wonder I've fallen for you. You must write to me and let me know what happens.'

It was time to go. He grabbed hold of me and pulled me towards him and gave me a long lingering kiss before common sense took over and he had to depart. We walked out arm in arm and on down to the end of the road. William hailed a taxi. He turned to kiss me, but I said, 'I'm coming with you!'

'You can't!'

'Just to the train. Please?' I begged.

'Just to the station then.'

He turned to the driver. 'Euston, please.'

We set off, my head on his shoulder the whole way. I just didn't want any of this to end. We arrived at the station and confirmed which platform his train was leaving from and went for a quick cup of tea. Two of the American pilots who had delivered the bombers were also in the café.

'Well, if it isn't our Limey officer. How are you, Bill?' one asked in a strong American drawl. The other was giving me the once-over.

'Aren't you going to introduce us?' the second airman asked.

'Yes, I'm sorry. This is Miss Alexandra Henry, my young lady.'

'Hi Alexandra,' he said, 'I'm Dave from Texas and the less good-looking one is Wilbur from Michigan. Your boyfriend here has hitched a lift with us.'

'I know. Thank you,' I replied. 'I really am grateful. It's been wonderful to see him.'

Their train was announced and I felt the tears flooding to my eyes. The Yanks saw my distress and left us in peace. I bought a platform ticket and we walked slowly to his carriage, my arm around his waist and my head on his shoulder.

It reminded me of that awful day when my father refused to come and see me off. I began to cry uncontrollably. We arrived at the carriage door and stopped and for several minutes just stood hugging and kissing each other as if it was for the last time. Then the damn guard blew his whistle and William jumped into the carriage, slammed the door, dropping the window in the process. I put my hand out and he grabbed it and held on, not wanting to let go for a second.

The train began to move and I with it. I ran as long as I could and then William let go. I waved until the train was out of sight with the tears still running down my face. I couldn't believe the happiest moments of my life were over. I stood sobbing for a few minutes when a lovely porter came up to me and put his arm round me. 'Don't worry, love. He'll soon be back.'

'Yes, but in six months,' I sobbed.

'Yes, but it will soon go. Can I get you a cup of tea?'

'Yes, please,' I replied, wiping the remains of my tears off my cheek.

We walked into the café and the porter shouted: 'Give this

girl a cup o' tea. She's just said goodbye to her bloke. He's a flier and she's upset.'

The entire café turned to look at me and there were lots of friendly words. As I sat drinking my tea, people kept coming over and saying what a wonderful thing 'my fella' was doing for his country and how proud I must be. I thanked the lady for the tea and asked her to thank the porter for his kindness and got up to go.

'Good luck, dearie,' she shouted as I left. I turned and thanked her.

My next job was more difficult. I decided to go and see the Dean. He had always been so kind and would give me advice, so I went into one of the station booths and telephoned him. No time like the present.

'Come now, Alex. I'm free for the next hour.'

My heart sank as I thought of my ordeal. My God, would he even recognise me in my current garb. I took a taxi to the university and walked up the steps to the main door. The man on the door didn't recognise me, though the look on his face told me that he thought he had seen me before.

I walked into the Dean's office and waited at the counter for his receptionist to come. The butterflies were terrible and I was beginning to feel sick.

'Hello, Alex. He won't keep you a moment,' she said. 'He's just on the phone.'

I was absolutely dumbfounded and she burst out laughing. I turned to leave and began to walk away when she called me:

'Alex, don't go! We've known for a long time you're a woman and couldn't understand . . .' She was stopped in mid-sentence as Giles Prendergast called me in.

'Good morning, Alex, Take a seat. What are we going to talk about, I wonder?' he asked, with a huge grin on his face.

'This, I suppose,' I said, standing up to show off my attire.

'Alex, I heard what Penelope began to say to you and it's true. We've known you were a woman from the moment you left Oxford. We genuinely thought that you were just running away from all that and didn't want to spoil things for you. When you came here you looked beaten and we all felt sorry for you. But may I say, today you look different.'

'I hope I do, Dean! I'm wearing a dress.'

'You know what I mean, young man. Oops! Sorry, young woman. It will be lovely to see you out of those silly clothes. What's your real name?'

'Alexandra,' I replied, the butterflies fast disappearing. 'Can I keep my job?'

'Of course you can! You know your work is well thought of . . . Oh by the way, you had a good night last night, didn't you?'

I was taken aback and looked at him quizzically.

'Well, let's just say news travels fast. I think congratulations are in order. Anyway, let's have no more of this double life. Let us keep Alexandra and get rid of Alexander. Take the rest of the day off and enjoy yourself and come in tomorrow looking as happy as you do now.'

I walked out of the office but was stopped by Penelope.

'He told me all about it the moment he came in this morning. He told me you've got engaged. Can I see the ring?' she asked.

I showed my hand to her, the three stones sparkling in the light. 'Gosh, you lucky thing. He must be worth a few quid. What does he do?'

'He's a pilot. He's just gone away for six months so you can imagine how I'm feeling.'

'Well, I'm just glad those silly clothes have gone and what a change! You're going to give some of the girls a run for their money. Even your short hair is very attractive. You may start a fashion. Good luck, Alex!'

I took a taxi and went straight home. I had never felt happier in my life. I had a spring in my step and I felt wonderful. I almost skipped up the stairs to the flat I was so happy. All the same, once in the flat I instantly felt lonely. I spent the rest of the day moping around, wanting to get on with my new life. Things had started so well that I just wanted it to continue.

I was brought down to earth with a bang when I was

listening to the six o'clock news. Hitler had invaded Poland and Mr Chamberlain had given him an ultimatum to get out or we would declare war on Germany. We knew Hitler wouldn't, so effectively we were once again at war. It was a strange feeling because for those first few weeks nothing happened. We didn't attack Germany and they didn't attack us. It seemed surprising at the time as we had troops deployed in Europe.

I spent another Christmas with my friends, Thelma and Peter Wilkes. They made me so welcome; one could have believed they were my parents. My real ones hadn't really had much to do with me lately. My mother did at least send me a Christmas card and so did my sisters, but there was never a word from my father and that really hurt me.

The Wilkes' gave me a wonderful time, but the strangest thing happened. We had finished lunch and decided to take a short walk. Peter thought I would like to see the area where the new tennis courts were to be constructed, which was just at the edge of the playing fields. It was a cold day which was to be expected for the day after Christmas, so we all wrapped up warm as we made our way to the spot. It was also a clever way of letting me see the cricket pitch, which we had to pass on the way and where I'd had so many triumphs as a boy. The memories came flooding back as it had been the only place I was allowed to be myself.

We had a look at the tennis court area, which I must say was impressive and then set off back to their home. Suddenly, low and behold we saw the Headmaster walking towards us.

'Good afternoon, Wilkes . . . Mrs Wilkes,' he said, touching his hat.

'Good afternoon, Headmaster,' they replied in unison.

'And good afternoon to you, Alexander . . . How are you?'

'I'm fine, thank you.' And he went on his way again. The three of us were astonished. He hadn't noticed my appearance and we were still looking at each other in amazement when suddenly he turned and exclaimed: 'Alexander! What are you doing dressed like that?'

'I think you know that, Headmaster. I have been a girl all my life and should never have been at your school at all,' I replied with a slight hint of sarcasm in my voice.

'Well, I must go and it was nice to see you, Alexander. You do look well.'

'It's Alexandra and thanks. It was nice to see you, too.'

'Yes, goodbye.' He doffed his hat and acknowledged Peter by saying 'Wilkes' and then walked away smartly.

When he was out of earshot we burst out laughing: how on earth could he have walked past and looked at me without noticing my clothes. It made for good conversation afterwards.

The holiday passed all too quickly and I was soon back in my London routine and was progressing well with my Masters. One night in mid-January I returned home to find a letter from Geraint Evans, 'Consultant Physician, Harley Street London'. Evans, you'll remember, was a specialist surgeon dealing with gynaecological problems. I didn't have to read it; I knew what it was about. He wanted to see me as soon as possible. Could I please make an appointment? As the following day was my day off, I decided to try to see him then. I ran round the corner to the phone box and my luck was in: he could see me late on in the afternoon, about four o'clock.

I arrived at Harley Street slightly early and in a very nervous state, so much so the receptionist offered me a cup of tea to calm my nerves, which I gladly accepted. This time she was quite amenable. Mr Evans came out, shook my hand and led me into his consulting room.

'Well, young woman . . .' he said with a smile. 'See, I can tell this time . . . I can attend to your little problem next Monday and you will be in hospital for approximately two weeks. You'll have to take things easy for another month and I'll need to see you at least once a week during that time. Do you understand?'

I nodded.

'Good,' he added. 'My receptionist will give you all the details, appointment times and what you should bring with you. Wonderful! I'm looking forward to this. It's a new experience for me. Pity about the cricket.' We both smiled.

I was worried and excited all at once and I began to prepare for the big day. I didn't dare write to William and let him know what was happening. He was doing a dangerous job and I felt this would distract him. I wrote a quick note to Peter and Thelma and advised the university that I was going into hospital and would be away for several weeks. They were very supportive. However, after a great deal of soul-searching, I decided not to tell my family.

The day came and once again I arrived at St Thomas'. There was a bed waiting for me. I had all my pre-meds the following day and was taken down. All I can remember is hearing Mr Evans saying, 'Good morning, Alex. Pity about the cricket, but at least I saw a good knock. See you soon.' And I was away, out for the count.

It took a few days to recover from the anaesthetic and each visit from Mr Evans confirmed I was recovering and at each visit he insisted on talking cricket.

'He's got away with it so far!' Evans announced to the ward and was then pulled up by Sister who pointed out he had got the gender wrong.

'Sorry, ladies. *She*'s got away with it so far. She scored a fifty against the Australians. You know, it would be a pity not to see her play again! . . . Sorry, young man, I keep making this mistake, but I only think of cricketers as men.'

All this sporty talk drew some odd stares from the other women in the ward and they didn't know quite how to relate to them. That didn't matter because, to be honest, I didn't quite know how to relate to them. The big surprise of the week was a visit from the Wilkes'. It was an enjoyable hour or so, especially as they had been granted special permission from the Matron herself to allow them to stay longer. It seems I was Mr Evans' favourite patient.

My colleagues from the university also came to see me, so the fourteen days soon went and I was able to leave. I was a little sore still but I was told that would soon pass. As yet I had not dared to feel or look at my new genitalia. I returned to the flat to find a pile of letters and cards from everyone I knew, including several from William, who somehow or other had found out about the operation. His final letter was short and sweet: 'See you on Saturday, darling!' William, it seemed, had been granted seven days' compassionate leave and he was going to spend the entire time with me.

'Saturday? That's tomorrow,' I yelled to myself. I wanted to make everything nice for him, but you know Mr White, operations undertaken yesteryear were very different to those undertaken today; you really did need time to recover. I was too exhausted to move a muscle.

That night I slept like a baby. The following morning I was up early and only just in time, for there was a loud banging on the door. It was a deliveryman from the florist's in Chelsea.

'Very special delivery, madam,' he said as he handed me a huge bunch of red roses, their heady fragrance already filling the air around.

'There's a card inside,' he added as I breathed in the aroma.

'Don't close the door, miss. I have another one in the van,' he said, opening the back doors to reveal none other than William.

'William, William!' I yelled at the top of my voice and regardless of the care I was supposed to take, I jumped the rest of the way down the steps and into his arms. We were locked like that for some time, oblivious to the fact that the deliveryman was still holding onto the roses that I had almost thrown at him in my haste to get at my William.

'Hum, hum!' He coughed to attract our attention.

'Thanks!' William said as he handed the driver a very generous ten-shilling tip.

The driver was over the moon as he handed the flowers back to William and we made our way inside. Once again, I shut the door, trapping him and once again we stood and kissed.

'Come on, tell me all about it,' he said, as he pulled me into the kitchen and sat me at the breakfast table. 'You look a bit pale, darling. Are you all right?'

'Yes, getting better every day.'

He was cross that I had not told him I was going into hospital, but he was all ears. I told him everything that had been done and everything that Mr Evans had said, including the comments that he feared England had lost a great batsman.

'Batswoman!' William interjected.

I told him there was every possibility I could have children, which took his breath away. I could tell he was looking at me in a new light.

It was over all too quickly, but we did manage another visit to see his parents and have a drink with a few of his friends; plus a little shopping trip for me and a visit to the Services Club, where I was taken purely and simply to be shown off. It was very flattering for me and satisfying for William. We had a lovely meal, but all the talk was about what was going to happen with the war, which hadn't really affected us much yet.

On the final morning, we went to Euston again. It was a repeat performance of the last, but this time I found it even more difficult to be parted from him. At least I thought he was safe, away from the conflict. William returned to Canada to finish his posting, having been promoted to Flight Lieutenant and almost given a promise of promotion to Squadron Leader when he returned to England.

I'm afraid I went back to work, in spite of Mr Evans' advice not to, as I was bored silly at home. I saw Mr Evans on a regular weekly basis and I'm pleased to say I was signed off with everything functioning normally after the allotted time.

Part 4

War

Chapter 14

It was the beginning of March 1940 and I was called into the Dean's office where many of my colleagues were already waiting. As I walked in they all clapped. I was standing a little dumbfounded when the Dean thanked me for all my good work and told me I had been awarded a Master's degree in Mathematics.

There it is, Mr White, framed on the wall. The certificate made in my new, now real name, Alexandra Georgina Henry. They had changed all the records in order to make everything official. I couldn't believe how kind they all were. I burst into floods of tears, but not before I had kissed the Dean on the cheek.

The following day I received a telegram from William saying that he would be arriving at Euston Station that day on the five o'clock from Edinburgh. It was all happening. I raced over, not bothering to change, and found that the train had been delayed for an hour so I decided to go into the buffet lounge and wait. To my utter disappointment, William's mother and father were already there waiting too. Without the protection of William, I was given the third degree about my operation, the true nature of which they had no idea.

To change the subject, I showed them a letter from the university saying I had been awarded my Masters.

I'm not sure the idea of a bluestocking daughter-in-law pleased Mrs Fraser very much and there was a somewhat disconcerting sharpness in her voice when she said: 'We are a clever young lady, aren't we?'

After that she immediately began to ask me more questions about my family, which I side-stepped as well as I could, until I was then rescued by the announcer. I began to wonder whether she had some suspicions about me.

I excused myself excitedly. 'I've got to go!' I ran out to Platform 14. I had already bought my platform ticket and ran through the gate to meet the oncoming train. The carriage doors were already opening long before the train had stopped, but I couldn't see William. I looked in all directions, jumping on the spot to see over the crowds who were alighting from the train. Then through the clouds of steam I saw him, a handsome RAF officer, walking towards me. I simply ran towards him. He dropped his kit bag on the floor and stood with his arms open.

I must have broken the long jump world record as I leapt into his arms. He was home and I loved him. He stood there for several seconds, holding me off the ground and only let go when he saw his father tactfully pulling his mother back, so as not to spoil our moment.

William only had a seven-day pass before he had to report to his new base near Lincoln. He had indeed been promoted to Squadron Leader and would be taking over his first command. He was genuinely pleased to see his mother and father and hugged them warmly, which made me feel a little envious as I no longer had the same relationship with mine. We walked down the platform with his father carting the kit bag. On either side of William, arm in arm, were his two favourite women.

Mr and Mrs Fraser had driven to the station in their car and they now offered to take me home. They knew, of course, that William would be staying with me for at least some of the time but they never once alluded to the fact – out of embarrassment or tact, I don't know. Mrs Fraser, probably, disapproved.

'It's a beautiful part of London, isn't it?' she remarked as we all got out of the car outside the flat. 'Is it yours?' she asked.

'Oh no! It's my father's house and I just have a little flat at the top,' I replied as I opened the door. 'Please come in. You can leave your coats here if you wish, or take them with you upstairs,' I said, pointing the way.

The flat wasn't small really. It had two bedrooms, a bathroom, a kitchen, lounge and dining room – quite impressive for a young person on their own. Of course, Mrs Fraser was impressed. I made them tea and biscuits.

'Go on! Tell him your good news then,' Mrs Fraser said, knowing full well it would spoil things for me. 'She's a clever one, this one. She's just got a degree!'

'My Master's degree,' I corrected her.

'That's fantastic news,' William said, hugging me and somewhat embarrassed at what his mother had done, especially as he could see I was disappointed.

Fortunately, they stayed only a few minutes before leaving. To my surprise however, William made to go with them, giving me a quick peck on the cheek. I began to wonder if I was somewhat of an embarrassment to him, particularly when with his parents. I was devastated but couldn't say anything because of his parents.

They left and I spent the whole night worried and depressed.

He did arrive the next morning very early, full of apologies, explaining that his mother was worried about his father's health and had wanted to ask his advice. He saw that my eyes were red from crying and guessed the cause.

'Oh, darling, I'll be spending the rest of my life with you. Surely you could spare a little of me for my parents. Anyway, I have a little present for you, a peace offering.'

'There's no need for that. I just wanted the first night with you, but it's over now. We'll start afresh . . . OK, let me have a look at this present then,' I asked, getting a little excited.

He went to fetch a couple of boxes he had left at the bottom of the stairs and inside them were the most beautiful red dress, a gorgeous pair of shoes, and ten pairs of the latest nylons. He wanted me to try them on, there and then; in fact he insisted I tried them on with his help. We went into the bedroom and I tantalisingly stripped off; he pulled me close to him and held me tightly in his arms and we fell on the bed. He began to kiss me gently and caress every inch of me.

It was exhilarating as his hands followed the contours of my body. It was as though I was in a dream . . . the passion was so soft and gentle . . . the kisses seemed to just whisk over my skin, sending tantalising shivers down my back and then the passion turned as we made love for the very first time.

I turned over and felt complete. He gently pulled me close to him and once again held me tight as if I was too precious to let go. Not a word was spoken and we fell asleep. It was late morning before I woke up. William was gently caressing my hair.

'Are you all right, darling,' he asked tenderly.

'Mmm, yes I am,' I replied, sighing with satisfaction. 'Oh I am and I love you.' I sighed again. 'Don't ask me to get up. I haven't the energy,' I continued, but William did, and raced to the kitchen full of the joys of spring to make me a cup of tea. I lay in bed daydreaming about what had happened, and sighing again and again as I bathed in the memory.

William and I spent as much time as we could together those next few days and we did have a wonderful time. I have to say, Mr White, your first time with someone you really love can never be eclipsed.

At least Lincoln was nearer than Canada, but even so he had great difficulty getting leave and it was a month before he could get a twenty-four-hour pass. Mr Hitler had invaded Norway and Denmark, the latter capitulating quickly, leaving Norway to fight on for another two months even with our support. The war was gathering pace and there was little time for leisure for our fighting men.

William's squadron made many sorties during that time. We, I mean the British people, felt some relief that at last we had a true leader at the helm of government as Winston replaced Neville Chamberlain as Prime Minister, but on that very same day Germany invaded Holland and Belgium.

The RAF – William included of course –was called upon to

defend our Expeditionary Force. Our troops were trapped at Dunkirk and were gradually being wiped out and it was the RAF's job to protect them and help them escape. I was worried out of my mind about William but at the same time I felt that I wasn't doing my bit when he and so many others were taking all the risks.

In June, Italy also declared war on us, by which time the Germans had overrun France in a very short time. We suddenly felt isolated and vulnerable, for all Churchill's brilliant oratory, and we knew it wouldn't be long before the Germans attacked us.

Late in summer of 1940 the Germans started bombing us in earnest, with devastating consequences, and by the end of the summer it was dreadful. We were, however, making great gains in the air as our fighter pilots were taking the fight to the Germans and winning, but we knew it was just a prelude to the Germans invading the country.

At around this time I started making enquiries about whether or not I could join up but my research was considered too important to allow me to go. I think it was the one male cell still left in my body that made me feel like this, but it wasn't to be.

That was until a certain air raid at the end of November.

London was now having, almost nightly, its fair share of bombing raids and to my horror, one evening the university was hit several times. I'll never forget the devastation when several of us turned up for work. Our college was almost obliterated. The shell of the building remained but the interior was still burning and the Auxiliary Fire Service was still trying to put out the fire. It was a terrible mess and we knew that our all our research had been lost. We were all congregating when the Dean joined us and invited us to a meeting in another college. We duly arrived only to be told that for the moment it would be better if we returned home. We would be contacted shortly.

After a few days moping around, I went to see the Dean and

asked if I could be released as I had decided to try and join the WAAFs – the Woman's Auxiliary Air Force, Mr White. I'm sure you will have heard of that illustrious organisation. I remember sitting at the desk with the recruiting officer as she went through my details.

'Name?'

'Alexandra Henry,' I replied and there followed all the usual questions. Address? Date of birth? Present occupation? Mathematician on research project. Qualifications? MSc and BSc in Mathematics. BA in Modern Languages. Fluent in French. Good German. Can you drive? Yes. The questions seemed to go on for Ever. Then I was ordered to move on.

'Wait over there,' the officer ordered and I went and sat outside what turned out to be the Medical Examiner's office. Name. Address. Date of birth. The same basic questions asked time and time again.

I had to lie, of course, about my medical history. What choice did I have? The medical officer, a male of course, asked me to strip off down to my knickers, which I duly did and I was given a full clean bill of health, but it was a disconcerting process. I dressed myself and was told to wait outside until I was sent for. A few minutes later, I was told I had been accepted and given a date and time at which I was to report to Blackwall Hill, which was the training centre nearest to London.

I spent the next few days at home tidying the place up and writing letters to William, though I didn't tell him I was joining the WAAFs. The only people I told really were Peter and Thelma who, replying to my letter, told me how depressed Peter had become as he had tried to join the Forces himself, but had been turned down because he was too old. They said he could probably be accepted in the Admin section, but he wasn't happy about that as he wanted to fight.

I arrived at Blackwall Hill at the appointed time and was ushered into a wooden Nissen hut where we were lined up to be given our uniform and allocated billets. Within a few minutes, I had collected mine and was taken along with nine others to our billet. I took the one furthest from the main door and Marjorie Davies, who became my best friend, was next to me. Opposite were Phyllis Drew and Ann Whelan and the four of us became inseparable.

Mr White, you can imagine it was a great ordeal for me. I was still not comfortable with 'girly' talk and I had never had to undress in front of a woman before and I was truly nervous.

The Section Leader came to the door and shouted, 'Come on, ladies, you have half an hour to get dressed and stand by your beds. Understand?' she shouted.

'Yes, Section Leader,' I answered, much to the derision of the rest.

'Ooh, she fancies the Section Leader!' one of them shouted, which immediately got a loud rebuke from the Section Leader, who was a large masculine-looking woman and was certainly not one to be crossed. We all started to strip off, though I did so rather more slowly, eager as I was to see how it was done.

I stripped down to my petticoat and knickers, which for this establishment I discovered were very glamorous and brought whistles from several of the women. I copied Marjorie, who from that day I called Madge, in the order in which she did things, including the liberty bodice which I hated and the Lyle stockings which were just as bad and then of course the uniform. The hat was the only thing that fitted perfectly and with everything else we had to make do and modify. Although I say it myself, Mr White, I looked quite good.

We waited by our bunks until the Section Leader came back with another regular volunteer, who showed us just once how to make the bunks up.

'From now on, ladies, your bunks will have to be made properly. Do you understand?' she bawled. 'Right, listen up,' she continued: 'I'm Section Leader Williams and you address me as Section Leader. Do you understand?'

'Yes, Section Leader,' we all answered quietly.

'Louder!' she bawled again.

'Yes, Section Leader,' we all yelled.

'Get outside onto the parade ground and wait for the other billets to join you. Understand?'

'Yes, Section Leader.'

We all waited in a group on the parade ground chatting in our little groups when she came out and yelled: 'Shut up, get into equal lines and stand to attention.'

There was a bit of confusion and of course the Corporal ridiculed the worst offenders. My little group was spared, thank God. We all stood to attention as the male Commanding Officer came out accompanied by the Senior Female Officer and addressed the new recruits before him. He told us that we were joining the war effort and after training would be going into various different sections doing different jobs. We would be interviewed when the training was nearly completed to see which section we would be going into.

It was a short training scheme. The first three weeks were to get us fit, which I already was; in fact, I was by far the fittest. My biggest downfall as far as the others were concerned was that I spoke too nicely. Anyway, it attracted a fair amount of ridicule, though it was nothing to what I had suffered in the past, and this time I had three good friends who were always on my side, no matter what.

Christmas 1940 was dreadful for the country. France had surrendered in June and now the Nazis had Atlantic ports from which the U-boats could operate. In consequence, our shipping was being sunk willy-nilly. Rationing had become the norm and, even if you had the coupons, you couldn't always get your share of food, particularly in London. We were all confined to barracks over the festive season, but I must admit we had a wonderful time at the numerous parties we were invited to.

Apart from the three days over Christmas and one day at New Year, we had no male contact until the fourth week of training when we were invited to go to a ranks' dance at a base nearby. Unfortunately or fortunately, whichever way you wanted to look at it, we were not allowed to wear civvies. I remember it very well and, I must be honest, I was really looking forward to it. The excitement started as soon as we began to get ready. All the girls were thrilled to be going out and everyone was giggling. I couldn't get excited in that way; I suppose it was the remains of the boy's education that was still in me. I sat on the bed waiting for Madge to finish making up, watching her closely, when she turned towards me.

'Don't you wear the stuff?' she asked, lifting her lipstick up to show me.

I didn't know what to say. At last I said, 'My parents never allowed me to wear any make-up so I never have.'

'Well, they're not here now, are they?' She didn't wait for an answer and called Ann and Phyllis over to give her a hand to make me up.

'Sit there and keep still!' she ordered.

Ten minutes later they had finished. She gave me her compact mirror to have a look at myself. I was amazed. Again, Mr White, I thought I looked at least presentable. The four of us flounced down the hut and hurried to catch one of the lorries which had been laid on to take us to the dance. I don't mind saying it, I was now excited. There were about twenty of us in this lorry-load and we set off, singing all the popular songs of the day and many of the war songs, too – 'Tipperary' and the like. We were soon there. The four of us stuck together as we walked into the dance hall, which, of course, was blessed with a bar.

I was amazed. There was a real band and the music sounded good. That, together with the ambiance, immediately began to make you feel good. It was made even better as several RAF types immediately came up to us and asked us to dance. My companions refused as politely as they could; they wanted to look at the lie of the land and judge what was available, but I grabbed hold of my partner firmly and took him dancing around the floor, causing a few eyes to open and stare. Soon the dance was over and after thanking him, I went back to the girls. Within seconds, another lad came up and asked me if I would have a dance, but I refused as I told him I was going to get a drink.

'What would you like?' he asked.

'No, don't worry, I'll get it,' I replied.

'You fool! Let him get it,' Madge whispered in my ear. 'It's the price for a dance.' It was just like Alice – the cost to hold hands was an ice-cream.

'Come on, let me get you a drink,' he asked again.

'Yes, all right then, thanks. I'll just have an orange,' I replied politely.

'An orange for the lady,' he told the bar staff. 'That's if she is a lady,' he added coarsely in an undertone to the barman, thinking I hadn't seen and heard.

I drank a little of it and then was invited on the floor by the baboon, whose name I discovered was Fred Bellinger. It was the Charleston, which I was good at. I'm afraid I made an exhibition of myself, as many of the dancers almost stopped to watch us. I didn't care; no one knew me and I was enjoying myself.

When I returned to the girls, followed by my partner, Madge once again whispered to me: 'Be careful! He's after you.'

For the next hour, I was enjoying myself, even though Fred wouldn't leave me alone. I kept being taken by other partners in the 'excuse me' dances, but after a few bars from the orchestra, he would chip in again. He began to lace my drinks with gin, but at last both Phyllis and Madge witnessed him doing the dirty deed and warned me.

I decided to sit out the next few dances and sat at the table with Ann. Again Fred asked me to dance, but I politely refused, but he then became aggressive.

'You're not having all those drinks off me and not dancing. Get on yer bloody feet now!'

I refused again and he went away, so I took the opportunity to go out for some fresh air as I was getting a little worse for wear.

'Tell Madge I'm just going out for a tick,' I shouted across to Ann.

It was a stupid thing to do, as of course, I was followed out by Fred, and I was just taking a few deep breaths when I found myself being pulled round the corner, pushed up against the wall and mauled all over.

'I spent all this money on you tonight and you're not getting away with this. You owe me a favour, darling,' Fred snarled.

'I didn't ask you to,' I replied haughtily. 'And I didn't ask you to spike my drinks.'

This put his back up. 'Yer stuck-up cow,' he said as he began to push against me.

He was a big man and with any other woman he might have got his way. He had already begun to lift up my skirt with one hand and undo his trousers with the other when I jabbed my knee right into his groin. Then, as he doubled up in pain, a well aimed kick put him sent grovelling on the floor.

'Touch me again and it will be your stupid head,' I shouted, much to the amusement of Ann and Phyllis who had run out to see if I was all right.

Unfortunately, that wasn't the end of the matter. We continued dancing and, in fact, had a very pleasant evening. The story of my little revenge soon went round and I became a bit of a celebrity with the girls in my hut. It was nice to be so popular and in demand; I had experienced so many lousy times and now I felt I deserved some good times and I was determined to have them.

We had the last dance with our respective partners and kissed them all goodnight. All this flirting made me feel a bit of turncoat, but, as Madge tried to convince me, William was probably doing the same so it was only fair. We made our way to the collection point, the four of us walking in line abreast, singing some of the tunes we had danced to. Suddenly, we were confronted by several men from the RAF, including, of course, Fred.

'What's the stuck-up little cow going to do now?' he yelled.

'Leave it out, we're going home,' Phyllis replied.

'Not with that little cow, you're not. She's mine,' he snarled.

'Leave her alone! It was your own fault. Get the MPs,' Madge shouted as Ann tried to leave, but her path was cut off by two of the men.

I felt terrible that I had got the others into this mess. I suggested that they went and leave me there, but the three of them wouldn't hear of it. We tried to walk on but gradually they herded us towards the Nissen huts. We resisted as long as we could, but at last they succeeded. In the darkness between the huts it was deathly quiet and I could feel we were all terrified.

'You stay out of this, my lovely ladies. This first one is for me,' Fred said as he came over and plucked me out of the group.

The other men held back my friends as Fred pushed me up against the metal skin of the hut. Madge started to scream, but was soon silenced by a slap. They struggled to free themselves as they saw Fred start undoing my clothing, his hand tight across my mouth. I remember biting his hand and getting a swift response from the back of it. He lifted my skirt and then began to pull my knickers down, all the time using his huge bulk to prevent me from moving. I could see the girls' fear and anxiety for me as they tried to struggle free. He had almost torn my knickers off when he decided to undo his own trousers and pull out his penis.

His trousers slid to the floor and he began trying to insert himself into my body. At this point my old defence mechanism kicked in, and I grabbed his testicles and squeezed with such force that he screamed like a severely injured animal. I didn't let go; it was Hazard all over again and this hazard, too, wasn't going to get away with it. His friends let go of the girls and came running towards me.

'Get back or I'll pull the bastard's cock off,' I yelled, squeezing even harder, with Bellinger screaming louder and louder. I gritted my teeth and growled like some tigress attacking its prey as I dug my nails into his flesh and pulled, as more and more blood ran down his legs.

'Get back!' he screamed at his mates. 'Get back! Let go! *Please*!' he continued to scream.

At this moment some MPs arrived. One of our lot had seen what was happening as we were leaving and had the sense to get help.

'What's all this about?' the Sergeant asked me as I was still holding Fred's testicles in my hand and I wasn't letting go until I was satisfied.

My friends quickly told them what had happened. The Sergeant, however, only seemed to find the whole thing amusing, laughing at Fred's predicament. He was a well-known bully, it turned out and the Sergeant was glad to see him get his comeuppance.

'All right now, Private, you can let go now. We'll take it from here.'

We left but not before I gave one last almighty twist, causing Fred to scream like some injured fox after it had been run to ground.

'Wait till my fiancé gets hold of you. He'll kill you!' I whispered.

I pulled up my knickers and tidied myself up.

'There's no need for further action, Sergeant. I don't think he'll be troubling the girls for some time.'

I walked over towards the other six men, still full of anger. They were so intent on looking at the unfortunate Bellinger that they didn't notice that I was aiming a punch at the one who had slapped Madge. It hit him full on the nose and actually knocked him to the floor.

'Oh, I'm sorry, I thought he was going to hit me.' I said, addressing the MP. We left the place looking like a war zone. That was girl power, Mr White, and it taught me to stand up and fight for my rights in the future.

'We'll get you for this!' I shouted at the remaining men.

Within a few seconds, shock had taken over and I began to cry and shake uncontrollably.

I couldn't believe what had happened and I couldn't believe that I had had the courage to stand up for myself and I couldn't believe that I had three friends who didn't leave me when I was in trouble and who were prepared to stand up for me. That was a real first for me. They comforted me as we caught the last lorry back to our camp and they began to talk about the night in an effort to stop me becoming too distressed about the attack. It helped, especially when they started bragging to the others in the lorry about what I had done. We arrived back at camp but all I wanted to do was get in my bunk and forget the whole incident.

The following morning after breakfast we were on the parade ground doing our routine marching when we were called to attention.

'Volunteers Henry, Davies, Drew and Whelan, dismiss and report to the CO immediately and hurry.'

'Yes, Section Leader!' we all replied and ran to the CO's office. We waited outside until I plucked up the courage to knock and walk in, where I was greeted by his clerk.

'I'm Volunteer Henry. I understand the CO wants to see me and Davies, Drew and Whelan.'

'Wait there, please,' she replied.

I waited for a few seconds until she returned and asked me to go in.

'You are?' the CO asked as I walked into his office. He had two other officers with him: Squadron Leader Jenkins and Wing Officer Berridge from the WAAFs.

'Volunteer Henry, sir.'

'Henry, I understand you had a bit of trouble last night?'

'No, sir. It wasn't anything I couldn't handle.'

'That's not the point, Henry. We've a very seriously injured man. Did you lead him on?'

'How dare you insinuate that, sir,' I said, almost shouting.

'And, Henry, how dare you talk to me like that!' the CO snapped back angrily.

'I'm sorry, sir, but he made two attempts to rape me. First when he pulled me behind the Nissan huts and secondly in front of the other girls.

'Why did you go outside with him then?'

'I didn't, sir.' I told him what had happened.

I could see the Squadron Leader trying not to laugh as the CO began to ask further questions about the incident. I finished up by saying that I didn't want the matter to go any further and that I had told the Military Police the same.

'Private Bellinger may have a different view,' the CO observed drily.

I felt fury boiling up inside me. 'Isn't rape a capital offence during wartime, sir? I'm sure Bellinger and his associates should ask themselves that question, sir.'

They were all taken aback by those remarks and matters were quickly drawn to a close. Strangely enough, I hadn't a clue whether I was right or wrong, but it did the trick as I heard no more about it, especially after the others vouched for my story, which, incidentally, Mr White, gave me a lot of street cred as we say today.

Things quickly quietened down. There were other more pressing matters, I suppose. The next week was a good one; we had all done well and were now being asked which sections we would like to train for and if there was any preference where we would like to be stationed. Although they couldn't promise anything, they would endeavour to station us where we wanted.

I chose to do administration or driving on any of the airfields around London. For obvious reasons I wanted to be near home; Madge also chose driving while Ann and Phyllis wanted to be involved with maintenance. The latter were immediately sent off for further training while Madge and I were left to finish the last week without them. We were simply the best of friends and on our last evening before our transfer to RAF Pangbourne, which was a fighter station, we went to our last dance.

There was no trouble and we once again had a whale of a time, dancing every dance and both having dozens of marriage proposals and proposals of other sorts as well. I couldn't believe things could be this good. We were given seven days' leave before transferring to Pangbourne and I was determined to make the most of it. I invited Madge to come and stay with me in Chelsea to have what she called a 'girls' London weekend and of course she jumped at the idea with open arms.

We left the training camp after saying cheerio to the Section Leader who genuinely seemed sorry we were leaving and made our way with our travel passes to Chelsea. Madge was impressed with where I lived and even more so when we went inside. However, I was thrown into confusion. Waiting for me was a letter from William, inviting me to a party at the officers' mess on the Saturday. It was now Wednesday and I had promised Madge that she could stay with me for the week. I decided to phone William at the camp, explaining my problem and asking if Madge could come too. There was no need to worry, he said, the more women the merrier and of course she would be welcome. She was delighted and when I returned to the flat, you would have thought I had handed her the Crown Jewels.

The next problem was that Madge didn't have any 'party' clothes with her and we had to buy some. Now this was a new experience for me as I was helping another woman to choose an outfit. Was I to make sure she didn't outdo me in the fashion stakes, or was I to tell her the truth if I didn't like something? Well, Mr White, I hadn't developed my feminine side enough to even give it a thought; I wanted her to look good and I wanted both of us to have a good time.

We certainly didn't have a good night that night. However, as the sky was absolutely clear we knew there would be more bombing raids, but, like everyone else, we didn't know how bad it would be. The blackout was in force, but by just peeping out with all the interior lights switched off, it seemed like half of London was burning.

The raids seemed to go on for hours, before the all-clear sounded and the last of our guns fell silent, as the last of the German bombers with their droning engines went out of hearing distance. We took a pasting that night and in the morning when we ventured out, we were thankful even to be alive.

We left London by train, for Lincoln early on the Saturday morning, arriving at the base around lunchtime. We had decided to travel in uniform as it did have advantages. Men would give up their seats for us and buy us drinks in the station buffets; it was though we had been put on a pedestal; it was rather nice.

I didn't know what sort of party it was so we carried our clothes in a little case, which would also come in handy if we were allowed to stay. We managed to catch the local bus to the base and walked smartly up to the office at the main gate.

'I have an appointment with Squadron Leader Fraser,' I said in a military sort of way, precise and to the point.

I heard the guard telephone William and report. I could even hear William's replies. 'I have two WAAFs at the gate, sir. One of them says she has an appointment with you. They're not half bad-looking, sir.'

'Two WAAFs, you say?'

'Yes, sir.'

'What's her name, the one who has an appointment with me?'

'What's yer name, miss?' the guard asked.

'Private Henry.'

The guard repeated the name to William, who then asked, 'Ask her her Christian name?'

'What's your Christian name?'

'Alexandra,' I replied and once again he repeated it to William.

'I'll be there myself in two minutes,' William said. I could hear the astonishment in his voice.

'Yes, sir,' the guard said.

Soon I heard William coming along, chatting to one or two of his officers and then I saw him. I wanted to run out and grab him, but I was in the Forces now so I stood perfectly still alongside Madge, as if we were on parade. We were both trying not to giggle. The three officers walked in, with William leading the way. He was dumbfounded to see his little girl in uniform.

Madge and I stood to attention and saluted. 'Private Henry reporting for duty, sir,' I said, grinning despite myself.

'Gentleman,' he said, turning to the other officers. 'This is my fiancée, Alexandra Henry and this is her friend . . .'

'Marjorie,' I said, interrupting him in mid-sentence. Then, turning to her, I said, 'Marjorie, this is my fiancé , Squadron Leader Fraser.'

The formalities over, William deigned to kiss me, even in front of the others. Everyone shook hands. I could see that Flight Lieutenant Tom Collingham had immediately taken a fancy to Madge.

We were treated to lunch in the officers' mess and everything seemed rather casual as the squadron was on stand-down for seven days whilst they were waiting for essential parts to arrive. William wouldn't talk about the operations they had carried out and wouldn't let any of the others either, partly due to security – as there were signs everywhere, 'Careless talk costs lives' and 'Someone may be listening' and so on – but mostly he didn't want us to worry. We were, however, given a tour of the station, Madge with Tom and me with my William. Afterwards, William suggested to trip to the village pub.

His car was a four-seater open-topped Bentley, borrowed from one of his officers, so we drove to the pub in style. We were followed by other officers in their cars. The men were in high spirits and William encouraged them. 'After all, he told me later, 'you never know when it may be their last time for a bit of fun.'

That was the point, Mr White; these men went out on missions every night, knowing that it might be their last, and few, and I mean few, ever gave a thought for themselves; that's how it was.

Some of them got a bit tipsy and a little silly with us, but in general, it was all taken in good fun. We returned to the base and prepared for the evening and I was allowed to change in the Squadron Leader's quarters. In fact, William insisted on helping me get dressed, even though he was just sitting on the bed watching my every move. Once again, I gave him a 'dress tease': standing naked before him, caressing the sides of my body and wiggling gently as I slipped on the girdle before running my nice new nylons through my fingers and sliding them onto my legs. I ran my stockinged toe across his knee as I clipped my suspender onto it and then leaned over to repeat the movement with the other. It was too much for William. He took hold of my arm and pulled me onto the bed. I had never realised the power a woman can have over a man until after he had made love to me again.

'They will all know what we've been doing,' I commented with a hint of embarrassment in my voice.

'Darling, it doesn't matter. I'm the CO, remember.'

I quickly washed and redid my make-up, something William had never seen me wear before. I put on the beautiful red dress he had brought back from Canada and when I had finished, I knew from the look on his face that I looked good.

It wasn't just the 'Wow!' he gave me; it was the fact that he couldn't leave me alone; he became extremely tactile, but it was lovely.

'I'll have to wear this more often,' I observed.

'You certainly will, darling,' he said, almost growling with excitement.

The evening was a buffet party in the officers' mess, with a dance to follow. The music was provided by a quartet, one of whom was a young woman who both sang and played the clarinet. The party had been going for about twenty minutes before we arrived and I remember we walked down the corridor, arm in arm, to make our grand entrance into the mess.

William opened the door and one officer shouted: 'CO present!'

The band stopped as all present slow-handclapped William into the mess accompanied by several flashes from the official photographer. This apparently was the tradition. William acknowledged all present and gave the order to carry on, and the merriment began again unabated.

William introduced me to all the officers and their wives and sweethearts. Walking round the room, I noticed a cricket bat propped up in the corner. I stopped and couldn't resist picking it up, feeling its weight and pretending to make a stroke. It was just habit, I suppose.

'Your lady friend seems to know how to use one of those,' one of the younger officers commented admiringly to William.

'She does indeed! She played for the Combined Universities against the West Indies and scored 52 against Bradman's Australians, as well as scoring 166 against Surrey at the Oval,' William said proudly with me becoming embarrassed.

'Do they have women's teams, then?' the officer replied, somewhat taken aback.'

'No, but she's so damned good, they let her play on the men's team!'

The dancing started with William and me taking the first dance. The young singer began with Astaire's 'Let's Change Partners and Dance', the idea being that every time the music stopped we had to swap partners. It was a lovely way to get to know people, but not if you wanted to stay with just the one. I could see Tom Collingham was smitten with Madge and was reluctant to change, but c'est la vie.

This was followed by an excuse-me quickstep, which encouraged a young officer to ask his CO's permission to dance with me. William politely agreed, though I could see he was not over pleased. The young man could dance very well and we looked very good together, so much so that some people actually stopped to watch us. All the same, I was relieved when the music stopped so that I could go back to William. Poor chap, he was half proud and half jealous and I wanted to reassure him I was all his.

That night we had little time to talk, so the following day he arranged for us to go to a little tearoom in the village. He ordered tea and scones and we sat in the corner, holding hands across the table.

'Why didn't you tell me you had enlisted? It was a bit of a

shock, I can tell you. A nice one, I will say, because you do look lovely in your uniform.'

'Well, the university had been bombed and I was left at home waiting for them to contact me and I was, well, bored. But, darling, seriously, I wanted to do my bit. I feel so much closer to you wearing the same colours. It sounds silly but it's true!' I paused for a minute and just looked at him. 'I passed out of training with Madge and we are going to Pangbourne in a couple of days' time.'

'Smashing girl, Madge,' William added.

'Hey, don't you get any ideas. You're mine!' I said, smiling, as he squeezed my hand.

'I know, but I do have one idea, darling. I want to get married as soon as we can. Don't let's have a long engagement. I can't risk the most beautiful woman at the dance falling into the hands of someone else, can I now?'

He could see my hesitation.

'You do still want to marry me then?'

'You know I do. I love you. Do you think I would be wearing this, if I didn't?' I replied as I held up my ring finger.

'I want to decide on a date now.'

'Darling, we can't! We've got to sort out one or two little problems first.'

'What problems?'

'Well, for one, my birth certificate . . . And then . . . well, I have to tell my parents . . . It's so complicated, darling. I think it would be up to my father to have my certificate changed . . . and I'm not sure he'll want to help me . . .' I was becoming emotional. I wanted desperately to marry William but I could see so many obstacles the more we spoke about it.

William looked desperate.

'Please, don't worry, darling,' I said, trying to put a brave face on it. 'We'll sort it out . . . Look, I'm going to have to go now. Madge and I have a train to catch. Let's decide where and when the next time we see each other.'

'That's what I feared,' William responded.

'Darling, don't say that. I would live with you anywhere and I wouldn't even need a ring to have to do it! But if you really want to marry me then . . . well, we're going to have to face up . . .' I stopped in mid-sentence, though it was more to stop the tears starting than anything else.

Outside, I put my arm around his neck and pulled his head towards me and kissed him.

'I love you!' he whispered.

'I love you, too, darling.'

On the train to London, Madge and I sat down facing each other, without a word spoken, daydreaming about last night's dance. Madge was full of her new romance, Tom Collingham. Suddenly she leaned over and gave me a kiss.

'He's wonderful! Thank you for taking me. I had such a lovely time. You're now officially my best friend, Alexandra,' she added, giving me another squeeze.

'It was lovely wasn't it, but it's so sad to be going back again.'

We made our back to Chelsea, collected our stuff and then caught the train to Pangbourne, exhausted from all the excitement.

Madge gave me a funny little smile. 'You never told me he was a Squadron Leader or that you were at university or that you played cricket. You're a secretive one, aren't you?'

'I was, but not now. I've lived a very private life and it's thanks to you that I'm now beginning to enjoy myself.'

'Well, I don't care what your past is. I only know I have got a new best friend.' She giggled.

'Have you been drinking?' I asked. 'Because it sounds like it.'

'I've only had one or two to celebrate,' Madge replied.

'Celebrate what?' I asked.

'Tom asked me to marry him, and I said yes.'

'What!' I exclaimed excitedly. 'But you've only just met him.'

'Yes, I know but isn't it wonderful? We've got a lot to be thankful for in this war. You can do just what you like! And that's just what I want to do.'

Chapter 15

We arrived at Pangbourne around lunchtime, logged in and were ordered to report to the Commanding Officer Squadron Leader Wesley at 2.30 p.m. in the afternoon. We were taken to the NAAFI beforehand and had lunch, which was laid on for us. It was a far cry from William's station, but there was a war on and Pangbourne was more in the firing line than Lincoln, so I suppose we had to be thankful for small mercies. We were on a merry-go-round as far as men were concerned; from the moment we walked in until we left, we were chatted up.

At two thirty sharp we reported to the CO and waited outside his office, saluting all the senior officers who passed. Madge was first in and allocated her duties. Initially, she was told to join the pool of drivers but that she would also be used in the radio communication centre. She came out delighted with her lot and then I was called into the office.

I saluted the CO and the Squadron Officer, which was the equivalent rank for the WAAFs, and was invited to sit down. We had a general chat about where I saw myself, why I wanted to be in the WAAFs and what I wanted to do. I gave them an outline and told them that my fiancé was in the RAF Bomber Command and that I didn't want to be left twiddling my thumbs when there was a war on.

He was reading my details on my entry form. 'I see you have a BSc in Mathematics and a BA in French and German.'

'Yes, sir,' I replied. 'But I was awarded an MSc for Mathematics a few weeks ago.'

The Squadron Officer was suitably impressed. 'You passed your training well, Henry.'

'Thank you, ma'am.'

'We feel you are wasted in this situation and that you should immediately attend an officer training scheme. We are several short on this base and we know you could fill one of the positions well enough.'

I've often joked that they must have been desperate to want me, but within two days I had been transferred to the officer training centre – much to Madge's chagrin as we had been billeted together and she would be on her own. However, it wasn't long before she too was put on the course and was made an Assistant Section Officer. I thought it was a combination of my education and my stay at Bankworth that gave me an edge. I realise now that it was probably because I was brought up as a man that gave me the edge over other women.

I found the training scheme easy and astonishingly enough on my return to Pangbourne, I was once again interviewed and then they immediately promoted me to Section Officer, which was the equivalent to a Flying Officer in the RAF.

'We need officers like you in the Service,' the Squadron Officer said as she held her hand out to shake mine.

'Well done, Henry! You deserve it,' the CO said and he too shook my hand. 'I've given you a twenty-four-hour pass so you can go and celebrate.'

I couldn't wait to tell William and when I did he was over the moon for me. We wanted to celebrate together, but he was on ops over Holland that evening so it was impossible.

Two days later, I was taken and introduced to my new section, which was at the moment rudderless. I was to be responsible for the control and ordering of essential parts for the Spitfires in the Squadron. The section was frankly in a mess and was causing many of the planes to be grounded for much longer than they should have been. The operation needed a thorough overhaul and I set about my task with enthusiasm. Madge had also passed her training and was made Officer in charge of Transport, at a rank below me. There was never an ounce of jealousy between us and we continued to be very close.

A month or so later, we were invited to a party in the officers' mess. Our special guest that evening was to be Group Captain Tony Wetherton, whom I realised, was just the man whose advice I needed to turn things around in my section. I wasn't above using my charms to get what I wanted and, of course, I donned my beautiful red dress.

We didn't have to wait long for the Group Captain and his entourage and immediately he was surrounded by a crowd. It was amazing how many friends he suddenly seemed to have and how many people who wanted to buy him a drink. How on earth would I get near him, I wondered. I suppose I was lucky the CO brought him over to our table to introduce three of his female officers and he delighted us all by sitting down with us and even ordering a round of drinks. Several other male officers joined the table and we began to have a good time. I don't know how but the subject got round to cricket and the Group Captain started to explain the rudiments of the game to us uninitiated females.

'Do you play any sport?' he asked, directing his attention to me.

'I love cricket,' I replied somewhat passionately.

The other officers looked at me disdainfully as I if I were trying to ingratiate myself with the Group Captain.

'Oh, do you now!' the Group Captain commented ironically.

'How lovely! What do you do: bat or bowl?'

'I can bowl but I suppose you would say I was a batsman,' I replied modestly. 'Batswoman, I mean, sir.'

One of the other officers tried to belittle me. 'What's your highest score then?'

'One hundred and sixty-six not out, against Surrey,' I said flatly.

You should have seen the open mouths around that table, Mr White.

'So which ladies' team did you play for?' the Group Captain asked curiously.

'I didn't, sir.'

There were noises of disbelief.

'And how was that then?' another disbelieving soul remarked. 'How could you play against men?'

'It was easy to play against the men, but if you mean how did I get picked, well . . .' I paused for a second or two. 'I loved cricket so much, the only way I could get a game was to pretend to be a man!' I said, laughing as the others joined in.

'How on earth could you fool anyone that you were anything but a glamorous young woman?' the Group Captain asked, clearly determined to get to the bottom of all this.

'I couldn't. That's why in the end I was thrown off the team. I don't think I'll ever be allowed to play again; but they did let me play for the Combined Universities against the Australians in 38 and the West Indies in 39!'

'Shame!' the Group Captain said. He looked at me closely and with obvious interest. 'Let me buy you a drink, Section Officer.'

'Thank you. That would be very nice,' I replied.

A few minutes later he asked me to dance and as we moved across the dance floor, he questioned me further. Here, I thought, was my chance.

'What are you doing now?' he asked.

I told him I was in Procurement and how difficult it was because of the bureaucracy and that at best we were only ever able to get 60 per cent of the aircraft into the air at any one time. I explained that the CO was having a tough time because of it and it was something he had no control over.

'It really upsets me,' I went on, 'because he really tries hard to motivate people and he's fighting a losing battle.' I may even have fluttered my eyelids a little as I said this, Mr White.

'Look, come and see me tomorrow and I'll see what I can do.'

We rejoined our colleagues at the table and almost immediately the CO asked me to dance. What a dancer he was!

We did everything from the quickstep to the waltz, and the Charleston to the latest craze, the jitterbug. I knew I had made a conquest with the Group Captain as every time the CO and I danced past him, he made a point of smiling at me. The CO and I returned to the table for a well-earned rest and we were soon rejoined by the Group Captain. The CO left us alone for a few minutes, when out of the blue, the Group Captain whispered in my ear:

'Look, would you like to have dinner with me tomorrow evening?'

'I would love to, sir,' I replied, though not without a pang of guilt.

'Don't call me sir when we are at a social occasion. It's Tony. Yours is Alex, isn't it?'

'Alexandra, sir.' I paused. 'Sorry, Tony,' I said, smiling.

'Excellent, I'll pick you up around seven then. No, you're coming to see me, aren't you? We'll go straight from there. I'll square it with the CO to make sure you are off duty.'

'I'm already off duty, so don't worry.'

'Excellent. Excellent!' he said. 'Now I have to leave. No rest for the wicked.'

Business over, I set about letting my hair down and having a good time, but I noticed how my chat with the Group Captain had not been too well received by some of the other girls and it showed when I had to walk home on my own.

I was up very early the following day and the moment the staff arrived, I was on their backs.

'I want a complete list of all parts for aircraft we are waiting for, then a list for all transport and finally, for everything else. And I want it for 1200 hours without fail and I want it accurate. Right?'

'Yes, ma'am,' they replied, though I could hear them muttering under their breath.

I exploded. 'There's a bloody war on, you know. I need it this morning.'

I got the list on time and thanked everyone for their efforts.

In the interests of team spirit, I explained what I was going to try to do and from their change of attitude it was clear I was forgiven. I went to see my Squadron Officer and explained where I was going and what I was going to do and she nearly had a fit.

'You can't do that, Section Officer! There are proper channels to go through.'

'But, ma'am, everyone has tried to go through proper channels and look where it has got us. Nowhere. And the CO has got everyone on his back because of it.'

'I have to tell you, you will be disciplined if you break the rules.'

'What can they do to me? I can always go back to do research on bomb blasts at the university, ma'am.' I was sailing close to the wind and I knew it.

'On your head be it,' she said.

'Thank you, ma'am.'

I left Pangbourne and arrived at Group Headquarters at three o'clock but it was at least four o'clock before Tony was able to see me. There had been a bit of a flap on and my visit was somewhat down the list of priorities. He opened his office door.

'Come in, Alexandra. It's good to see you.'

'Thank you, sir,' I said as he shut the door.

'Now what can I do for you?'

I went through the whole story again, almost verbatim, and he absolutely agreed with all my suggestions. He promised to do everything he could to help me.

'Now,' he finally said, 'let's call an end to the business part of our meeting. From now on it's Tony again. Agreed?'

'Agreed. Will I be all right like this? I didn't think to bring a change of clothes.'

'No, you'll be fine. Anyway, you look lovely in your uniform.'

He called for his chauffeur and we were driven all the way to London where he had booked a table at the United Services Club. I nearly died. I often went there with William and I was dreading I might see someone I knew. The driver dropped us off at the door and we were escorted to our table. Tony was, like William, a real gentleman, and pulled back the chair for me. He gave me the menu but I let him chose for me. Madge always said it made them feel important and that was the way to get them to do what you wanted.

'Where are you from originally?' he asked.

'Oh it's a lovely little village not too far away – Upper Hayfield on Thames. Do you know it?'

'No, I'm a northerner myself.'

'I have a little flat in Chelsea. It will be a bit cold but we can go back for a coffee, if you like?' I wondered whether I was risking things too far and I was relieved when he said:

'We won't have time, I'm afraid. We're expecting trouble over the next few days so I need to be back early in the morning. Perhaps next time?'

'That would be lovely!'

The meal was excellent, the company was good and we had a very pleasant evening; in fact, as usual it went all too quickly. We left the club and drove back to Pangbourne, stopping just before we arrived at the gate. He leaned over and kissed me.

'Thank you for a wonderful evening! And I'll make sure you get those spares.'

Tony got out and came round to open my door.

'I'll ring you if I may, but I don't know when it will be. Good night, Alexandra, and thank you again.'

I said, 'Good night,' and he took me in his arms and kissed me again. This time I responded.

Mr White I felt terrible afterwards. When I got back to my room, I cried myself to sleep. I felt such a traitor.

The next few days, in fact the next three weeks, were somewhat uneventful. The raids on London had been curtailed because of the bad weather or perhaps the Germans were losing their nerve when facing our boys. On the third week, we took delivery of our spares; almost everything I had asked for we received, with the result, I was sent for by both the CO and the

Squadron Officer and congratulated on my splendid work. Unfortunately, my success also drew accusations. 'You have to sleep with the boss if you want anything,' I even heard one of my subordinates say. I was labelled as the Group Captain's mistress, and perhaps I deserved it.

A week later the CO called me into his office.

'I have some terrible news for you.'

Before I had heard anything, I almost collapsed onto the floor. I thought it was about William.

'Group Captain Tony Wetherton has been shot down over the Channel and is believed killed in action. I'm very sorry. I believe you were close to him.'

I didn't know what to say. On the one hand, I was absolutely relieved it wasn't William and on the other, I felt deeply saddened. He was a lovely man and in no way deserved his fate. I think he had fallen in love with me and I had only toyed with him. I felt terrible.

I wanted desperately to see William. I phoned and told him I had a forty-eight-hour pass and asked him to come to the flat. It was a lovely surprise when he arrived with a big bunch of roses and torture when he tried to kiss me over the top of them. He had booked us some theatre seats to see Noël Coward's *Private Lives*, which we thoroughly enjoyed, though strangely enough when I've seen it since, I don't find it at all amusing. I suppose it was just a relief from the war; we would laugh at anything.

From the Haymarket, we walked to the Lyons Corner House where we had first met, sitting down in the same seats and ordering tea and toast. I would love to think the waitress remembered us, but perhaps it was the romance of the evening or she was just plain nice. I put my cards on the table explaining what I had done to get the spares and that the Group Captain had asked me out to dinner.

He stopped me abruptly. 'Just shut up and listen. I don't want to know. I know that you love me and would never do anything to hurt me, so there's no need for explanations.'

He was that sort of man, Mr White. On the way back to the flat we walked so close together you couldn't have put a sheet of paper between us. We felt like two old-fashioned lovers strolling down a country lane. It was a lovely evening, but, as with all forty-eight-hour passes, the time went too quickly. Neither of us could risk being late in case some flap was on, so it was a quick breakfast, a walk round the shops, tea and a sandwich in a little tea room and then the train back to our respective bases.

A week later, I was called in to see the Squadron Officer. I thought it was still in connection with the way I procured the stores and equipment and that I was perhaps going to receive yet another 'telling off'.

However, I marched into the office and saluted. 'Ma'am,' I said, acknowledging her rank.

'Section Officer Henry, I have some good news for you. First, though, I would like to congratulate you on the splendid job you've been doing these past few months. It's been noted by many. You may be a little unorthodox, but we know you get the job done, and in recognition of your work as of today you have been promoted to Flight Officer. Congratulations!' She put out her hand to shake mine and then handed me the insignia for my new rank.

'Thank you, ma'am,' I replied, almost beaming like a schoolgirl.

I turned to leave, but the Squadron Officer called me back.

'I haven't finished with you yet.'

'Sorry, ma'am,' I replied.

'Well, as I say, you've done such a good job that it's possible in the near future we'll be transferring you to another section . . . And before you ask, I'm not as yet at liberty to say . . . That's all. Thank you, Flight Officer,' she said, giving me one of her rare smiles.

I left her office on cloud nine, Mr White. I phoned William but unfortunately, I couldn't speak to him. I assumed he must be operational. I wanted to save it and to tell him first, but I couldn't keep a secret; I had to tell Madge.

Mr White! Talk about real friendship. Madge was more excited than me. We got two off-station passes for the evening and she took me out to dinner at a lovely little restaurant near the base. We were treated to drinks by some of the men, who joined us at the table as we ate our meal.

I phoned William the following morning around 7 a.m. as I knew he would be back safely by that time and in my excitement blurted out all that had happened.

'We've got to celebrate this!' he said. 'Can you and Madge get a four-day pass over Easter? Tom has suggested we have a few days together in Devon. He would drive us there.'

'That would be marvellous. I'll ask Madge. I'm sure it will be no problem for me – I'm the blue-eyed boy at the moment.'

'Girl!' William corrected, laughing.

The conversation ended abruptly as William was called away and I set about making the arrangements. Madge was over the moon. Imagine it! An Easter break in Devon; we couldn't wait. I wanted to go there and then.

The following day I was walking across the field towards the offices past the machine-gun emplacement when the air-raid siren sounded. I ran as fast as I could towards the shelter, some one hundred yards away, but I wasn't quick enough. Several Messerschmitts were already circling, preparing to attack the aerodrome. I was straight in the firing line. Our machine gun opened fire, causing the first fighter to veer away and giving me chance to make cover. I managed to get into the shelter just in time as we all heard the familiar screaming sound of the Stuka fighter bombers diving in to attack. It was a terrifying experience and was the first time that many of us had been caught up in the fighting and the war proper.

You could hear the machine gun open up again and again, as plane after plane attacked the base. There was pandemonium. We soon learned that several buildings had been hit, as well as several aircraft, but all those that had not been hit were now taking off or were already in the air. We heard the scream of another Stuka and then the stomach-churning whistle as it released the bomb. There was an almighty explosion and the whole area shuddered. Then for a few seconds, it was strangely silent until the fighters started coming in again.

I suddenly noticed that the machine gun had stopped firing. I looked out to see that the two gunners had been hit. I didn't think about anything else; I simply ran out of the shelter across the one hundred yards to the post and found the two men were badly injured from the bomb blast. I lifted the first up over my shoulder and started to hurry back. I saw one of the Messerschmitts turning and it began to attack me as I went across to the shelter. I instinctively threw myself and my burden onto the ground as the bullets were whistling around me but I wasn't hit. I picked the gunner up again and flung him over my shoulder as I saw another coming in for the kill. I managed to get into the shelter as I heard the bullets zinging into the sandbags that sheltered the entrance. I placed him on the floor and immediately ran back to help the other one.

I ran across the field and could hear the fighters coming in again. I fell to the ground, but the firing had stopped; there were no bullets aimed at me. I picked myself up and ran again to the emplacement. This time, however, I had to dive into the machine gun pit as the bullets sprayed the area like hail. The man was also badly injured and bleeding profusely. It was obvious that without medical attention, he would quickly die.

I picked the injured man up, put him over my shoulder and once again made my way back across the field to the shelter, only this time I was almost without strength and couldn't dive when the fighters attacked. I knew I wouldn't be able to get him back up again, as I was too exhausted. However, I managed to get back, almost unscathed, and laid him down, collapsing for a second or two; but as the attack was continuing my adrenaline and determination kicked in and once more I ran out to the machine gun, only this time I was somewhat protected as our spitfires were now engaging in dogfights with the enemy. It enabled me to run back to the machine gun almost unhindered.

I spun the gun round and, with a quick look and a few bursts of fire, I found out how to use it. Several more Stukas were now diving in. Mr White, the noise was unbelievable. I thought they were all going to fall on me. You looked up and you saw this aircraft coming straight down at you, screaming like a devil. You couldn't believe how fast it was travelling and you couldn't believe it was going to be able to pull out in time. It released its bomb and no one knew where exactly it was going to fall until it went off. If you were still alive after that, you were lucky.

Then the whole process would begin again as the next one came in and then the next and the next and so on; all the time they were being protected by their fighters. I aimed the gun at the first fighter and fired as he came at me, strafing the area with his gunfire. I wasn't hit, thank God, and faced the next one. Maybe it was the mathematician in me, but I thought if I could see the flight line of the next one, I could fire in front of him and he would run into the bullets. I know it sounds stupid, but that's exactly what I did. I refused to take cover and just kept firing. I followed him round with the gun, firing continuously, not noticing there was another behind. The second one sprayed my position with bullets and then winged away, but to my astonishment the first plane began to stutter, then smoke, then plummeted towards the ground at the far end of the aerodrome. The plane skidded along the ground, followed a few minutes later by a massive explosion as it blew up in a ball of fire, sending the flames and the thick black smoke high into the sky. It was only then that I wondered whether or not I had been hit. Surely I had; the bullets had fallen on me like rain; but apart from a few cuts and bruises I was entirely unharmed.

I suppose it only lasted about fifteen minutes, when the all-clear siren sounded and people started to come out of the shelter. The damage was extensive: we had lost seven aircraft on the ground and one in the air, although the pilot had baled out safely. Several buildings had been hit, with two completely destroyed. They had lost two fighters and three Stukas were also shot down.

I was working on autopilot as I watched the airmen bring a German pilot, who had managed to get out of his plane before the explosion, into the main building for questioning. He was obviously a senior-ranking officer by the amount of insignia he carried on his uniform, but at the time I didn't see what his rank was. He wasn't injured, but he was in a state of shock. As they passed close by, I spoke to him in German and asked if he was all right. He told me he was and stopped for a second to speak to me, but was pushed aggressively by one of the airman.

'Leave him be!' I ordered. 'You wouldn't want this to happen to one our pilots, would you? No, you bloody wouldn't.'

'*Danke*!' the German officer said in wonderment.

He carried on speaking to me in German and told me he had seen me on the ground and had stopped shooting because he wasn't at war with women. I told him, with a smile, that he was a fool. After all, I had taken advantage of his chivalry. He was quickly led away. I did see him again some months later, but I'll come to that.

I was totally exhausted and went to my room to lie down and was woken up three and a half hours later when the FCO asked for a report. I hadn't had the chance to change out of my uniform, which was filthy and covered with blood, and I hadn't a clue where my hat had gone. I walked slowly, half in a daze and the other half in shock, to the CO's office. I was just about to pass through the NAAFI when I was greeted by one of the junior officers who had never been particularly friendly towards me.

'Ma'am,' she said, as she stopped me in my tracks. 'Thank you for what you did for Pete Richards. It was very brave of you. Thank you!'

'Who's Pete Richards?' I asked, bewildered.

'He's my fiancé and I'll never be able to thank you enough!'

she answered, almost in tears and then came up to me and kissed me on the cheek.

'Anybody would have done it. I was just close by.'

'No. No they wouldn't! What you did . . . well . . .' She couldn't continue because of her tears.

I put my arm around her. 'Is he going to be all right?'

'Yes, thanks to you,' she replied and walked away quickly to hide her tears.

I couldn't believe the next few moments as I passed the NAAFI. I was clapped by everyone present and I too had to walk off quickly to hide my tears.

I arrived at the CO's office and the Squadron Officer shepherded me inside. I was greeted by the CO and the new Group Captain, Toby Beardsmore. The CO introduced me and I suddenly felt absolutely filthy.

'Please accept my apologies for the state I'm in, sir. I haven't had time to change.'

'It's us that should be apologising to you for waking you up!' the Group Captain observed. 'You must have been pretty worn out after your exploit. We are all very proud of your actions. You are a credit to your uniform and to your unit!' He held his hand out to shake mine as did the other two present. 'We would like you to join us for dinner in the mess tonight. I would be honoured if you said yes.'

'Thank you, that would be lovely,' I replied. 'But I'm sorry, I haven't got another uniform.'

'Come in civvies. We will make an exception this one time,' he added with a grin. See you at six thirty then?'

'Yes, sir. Thank you!' I turned and left the room.

I searched round for a billet which still had hot running water and ran myself a bath. It was that deep I could almost have swum in it. It was lovely. I just lay there and relaxed.

'Alexandra! 'I heard Madge shouting.

'I'm in here. Just a minute, I'll open the door,' I shouted back to her. I quickly got out of the bath and let her in and then jumped back in.

She came in. 'Are you all right?'

'It's all over the camp what you did. I couldn't believe it. It's fantastic.'

'Yes, I'm fine. I must have had a brainstorm or something and now I'm bushed.'

Madge leaned over the bath and gave me a hug and then sat on the side as we chatted about our four days in Devon.

'Wait till I tell them what you did. You're a little hero, you are.'

'Heroine,' I said, correcting her for my own amusement.

'Well, whatever you are, I'm proud of you.'

'Thanks, Madge. I've been invited to dinner with the new Group Captain, the CO and the Squadron Officer tonight in the mess. They've excused my uniform as I have ruined mine. What shall I wear?'

'That red dress of course. You'll knock 'em dead.'

'Good idea!' I got out of the bath and Madge helped me get dressed.

Back in my room I changed quickly and Madge, with her usual skill, put the greasepaint on me and made me look like some film star. I arrived at the door of the mess at six thirty prompt, knocked on the door and was invited in to three cheers from everyone present and a chorus of, 'She's a jolly good fellow'. To my delight Madge was there, too. They made a lot of fuss of me, to the point that I even became a little tired of it and I began politely asking people to forget it. The CO cracked open one of his rare bottles of wine at the end of the meal and with each having about a mouthful, they drank to my health.

The following day I was once again called into the CO's office to be told that the Prime Minister was going to visit the base to inspect the damage and that he, the CO, would like me around when he arrived.

'When is he coming, sir?' I asked.

'This afternoon . . . and we want to make sure we are all getting on with the job, pulling our weight so to speak. I'm sure you will do your best, Flight Officer, with all in your team.'

'I will, sir. Thank you sir,' I replied, saluted and returned to my post.

Everyone was excited that Mr Churchill was visiting as we all wanted to see him, so much so that when he arrived just before lunch, nearly everyone was outside waiting to cheer him wherever he went. I found him such an inspiration and you know, Mr White, Churchill had done it all. Whatever people thought of him or his politics, he had been a warrior. He had fought for his country; he had been captured and escaped and shown he was capable of considerable acts of bravery. What more do you need in a leader, Mr White?

The Prime Minister inspected the damage together with the Chief of Air Staff and talked at length to the CO and his staff, and several of the lower ranks before finally asking to see me. He had heard the story of what I shall call my 'bravery' from several quarters and was very curious to meet the 'heroine of the day'.

Once again, I walked into the CO's office and I found myself face to face with Mr Churchill, my idol, who, before I had time to salute, held out his hand to me and said, 'Well done, young lady. You are an inspiration to the nation.' He spoke to me for several minutes, though I've no idea what he said; I was so nervous and star-struck!

It does make you feel proud, Mr White, when someone you and others look up to, says that you have done well and praises you for little things. It makes you want to do better.

We had started to make some headway in the war. The Italians had lost three battleships in our raid on Taranto and we were having more success in the Atlantic with our convoy system. More of our goods were getting through, and then of course we had an enormous boost to our morale when we sunk the Bismarck, one of Hitler's pocket battleships and the pride of his fleet. Our spirits were slowly but surely lifting.

At last, Easter came and our trip to Devon. Madge and I went to my flat in Chelsea to meet William and Tom. However, we had our first disappointment when Tom found out that petrol had been stolen out of his car and for the moment he couldn't get any more, not even with help from his CO. We would have to go to Devon by train, instead. The second disappointment was they were late and we had already lost four hours of our precious four-day pass. However, they eventually arrived and kept the taxi waiting while we collected our stuff and piled it into it, before making our way to the station.

It was all a bit of a mad dash and we had only minutes to go, before the train left. We were lucky in one sense as we had a compartment to ourselves and could relax a little from the moment we set off. We were all in uniform, so it was relatively easy to reserve a table for lunch in the buffet car. The food wasn't too bad, especially with one or two beers to go with it. It loosened our tongues and conversation never stopped. Madge, of course, had to tell them about my act of bravery, which I genuinely didn't want to talk about, but it made no difference to William.

He simply remarked: 'I could expect nothing else from this beautiful little creature.'

Tom said I should have been given a medal.

It seemed we were cursed on this trip. The train was almost at Temple Meads Station, where we were to change for Torquay, when it was halted, owing to an air raid on the city. The train was stuck in the tunnel at Chipping Sodbury for two whole hours and it became suffocatingly hot. There was considerable damage to the line and we were slowly routed via other lines to the station.

Unfortunately, we had missed our Torquay connection.

Tom telephoned the hotel in Torquay, saying we would be arriving tomorrow and explained the circumstances and then set about trying to obtain accommodation for the night, which proved even more difficult until a friendly taxi driver took us to the Red Hill district, where his wife did bed and breakfast. It was adequate but that's all you could say about the place. However, we went for a meal to the Llandoger Trow, an old inn near the port, which, considering the circumstances, was wonderful. Both the starter and main courses were fish, washed down with old-fashioned porter. The most important thing was the atmosphere in the restaurant. It was electric and defiant; the owners were not going to allow Mr Hitler to put them out of business and they infected their customers with the same determination, which made us all have a good time with a devil-may-care attitude and a spirit of friendship.

We returned to our bed and breakfast very tired and glad to get to bed. We had to share the bathroom, the toilet and two of us had to sleep in a three-foot-six bed, which, as you will be aware, Mr White, is only just bigger than a single. We had both booked in as Mr and Mrs and felt a bit naughty and decadent, but I don't suppose the proprietor would have cared. It was the times: everything was being turned upside down and even our old-fashioned values were fast disappearing.

Breakfast the following morning couldn't be served unless we handed over food coupons, which, as serving personnel, wasn't something we carried about. The alternative was to pay an extra pound and she would forget the coupons. Well, it was a jolly good breakfast and certainly William knew the eggs were fresh as he was woken up in the early hours by the cockerel in the garden making a hell of a din. The morning, however, was taken up trying to get on a train to Torquay. Despite the station still in chaos, we were able to catch one; but then it didn't arrive in Torquay until four o'clock, which now only left us thirty-six hours to enjoy ourselves.

They were pleasant hours, I can tell you, Mr White. Torquay and its surrounding villages seemed far away from the troubles, even if they were on alert in case there was ever a landing. We left the other two to their own devices and strolled gently along the front. William seemed to be worried and didn't want to let go of me. I could tell he was unhappy.

We sat quietly for several minutes in one of the shelters on the promenade before I asked him to tell me what was troubling him.

'I didn't want to worry you,' he replied.

'A trouble shared, darling.'

'I lost twenty-four men and four aircraft last week.' He paused, before continuing with tears in his eyes: 'Three of them were my friends. You remember James, James Butler. You sat next to him . . .' I nodded. 'Then there was Willow. We called him that after your visit as he was always talking about cricket . . . and we lost John, too.

'We didn't stand a chance. They were waiting for us and we didn't even reach the target. Twenty-four men dead and several injured. It was a disaster and now I'm worrying about what would happen to you if I didn't come back.'

I snuggled my head onto his shoulder. 'Don't be silly, darling; nothing is going to happen to you. Only the good die young and you have been a very naughty boy.' I was trying to make him smile and not succeeding.

'We keep losing men and I'm constantly worrying it's going to be my turn next.'

'Rubbish! You're mine and I'm not going to let anything happen to you. So snap out of it and let's enjoy every moment while we can. Come on, I want to play on the penny slot machines.' I made him get up and shook the mood out of him.

We finished the holiday on a high, the four of us vowing 'to come back when it was all over'.

We caught the train back to Temple Meads and took the slow train back to London. There was a fifteen-minute stop at Reading where we managed to get something to eat and drink and then continued on our way to the city. It was a pleasant enough journey as we had the second-class compartment to ourselves.

The last bit of bad luck hit us as we approached London. There was yet another air raid and the train was stuck outside the station and this time there was no cover. We all had to wait, knowing the train could be seen and perhaps strafed or bombed or both. It was a nerve-wracking wait, but eventually we were taken slowly into the station as the all-clear sounded.

We were all very tired when the train pulled into Victoria

some two hours late, owing to the air raid, which made things very difficult as our passes were quickly running out. William found a phone box that was working and managed to tell his deputy he was stuck and that he wasn't to leave his post before he got back. Poor Madge and I, underlings that we were, just had to get back as quickly as we could.

Matters were again taken out of our hands however, when once more the air-raid siren sounded and everyone ran into the Underground to take cover. We ended up spending half the night down there, with what seemed like hundreds of people and for many, it was obviously the norm, as they were equipped with groundsheets and sleeping blankets, and even little primus stoves to make tea. The stench of so many bodies, after an hour or so, was terrible and I for one was glad when the warden spotted us and invited us into his little office, where we had a cup of tea with him.

As soon as the all-clear was sounded, we made our way back into the dark London night and hurriedly kissed our partners goodbye. We took a taxi to the edge of the city and started walking the forty miles or so to Pangbourne as there was no other means of getting there. We thumbed anything and everything that passed. In fairness, it wasn't hard to get a lift in those days; anyone in uniform could expect to get one quickly and we were no exception. After two different drops, we arrived back at base at two o'clock in the morning, some six hours late. We reported in at the guardhouse, made our report and went straight to our room. The following morning we explained what had happened to the adjutant and nothing more was said.

The next few days passed as normal. Our squadron was scrambled several times and we had a lot of organising to do, to ensure spares and materials were secured and I was given extra duties to oversee that the repairs from the bomb damage were organised and carried out. I was appalled at the amount of money that was being thrown at some of the works in the name of speed. We were not asked to get competitive quotes;

we were simply asked to get the job done. Some of the contractors were clearly profiteering. It was disgraceful when men and women were losing their lives for them.

Restoration work was well underway when I was called in to see the Wing Commander. Once again, he was accompanied by my Squadron Officer and the Squadron Leader. I walked into the office and saluted.

'Flight Officer Henry,' the Group Captain said.

'Sir,' I acknowledged.

'No, I shall cut out the formality . . . Alexandra. We have recommended you be awarded the George Cross for your act of bravery and this has been accepted. You have been invited to Buckingham Palace to accept the award from the King. Well done! You deserve it and we are very, very proud of you.'

I almost burst into tears, which seemed to have become a habit with me over the weeks. I seemed a bit shaky on my feet and was invited to sit down and have some tea.

I was told what was expected of me during the ceremony in London.

'Would you like your parents to go with you or any other person?' the Group Captain asked.

'Not really, sir, except my fiancé, Squadron Leader Fraser at Lincoln, sir.'

'I'll speak to him. The presentation will take place on the 30th of July at 2 p.m. I'll take you there and we will meet your fiancé wherever it suits.'

'Yes, sir. Thank you, sir.'

News soon got round about the award and everyone without exception was pleased for me. I received a phone call from William and he was so pleased, I was over the moon. William then broke the news to me that he had been awarded the DFC for his part in that disastrous raid when he lost his friends and he too had a presentation on the same day. He decided to ask for a forty-eight-hour pass so he could take us out for a meal in the evening. I would do the same.

The Group Captain had other ideas, however, and had

already booked a table at the Services Club.

I rang my mother to tell her my news and asked her if she would like to be there, though I knew she wouldn't come. We had hardly been in touch since the beginning of the war and she had only learned about my joining up from Alice, I think.

'Darling, I'm so proud of you,' she said, sounding very upset, 'but I don't think I dare. Your father wouldn't approve. I'll tell him, but you know what he's like. I miss you, Alex. I wish things could get back to what they were. I must go, darling. I'll be thinking of you on the day.'

'Thank you, Mother. Please try and see me soon. I miss you too . . .' I rang off, wondering whether to invite Alice, but I knew that she was too wrapped in her ever-expanding family.

Panic started to set in. I didn't even know how to curtsey; I tried practising in front of a mirror when I was on my own, but I could never get it right. You would think that all the practice I got as a youngster in the plays at school would have been sufficient, but this was different. Madge came to my rescue and we went through half a dozen rehearsals. Finally, the big day arrived. We set off at nine in the morning, with me wearing a nice new uniform. It was just like going out to bat: once you were there at the crease, the butterflies disappeared. We arrived at the Air Ministry just before midday and were taken into a grand hall where I was introduced to all the top brass. I was invited to have a drink, but refused. 'I'm sorry, I'm just a bit nervous.'

To my astonishment at that moment William walked into the hall. I stopped what I was doing and immediately went over to him and to his utter embarrassment, I kissed him.

'Sorry about that,' he said to the Air Vice Marshall. He was blushing up to the roots of his hair.

'Don't worry, Squadron Leader. It isn't so very often we are in such courageous company. I understand you are also picking up your gong today.'

'Yes, sir,' William answered as the Air Vice Marshall went off to greet some other officers.

From that second on, I was ready for anything. Suddenly, one of the officers banged on the table and announced that the Air Vice Marshall wished to say a few words.

'We are here today,' he began, 'to pay tribute to a very brave and courageous young officer. Raise your glasses, please, to Flight Officer Alexandra Henry.'

Everyone raised their glass and called out my name. I felt so proud, Mr White.

William and I were taken to Buckingham Palace and waited with the other honourees in the long hall for the presentations to begin. I was going out for the second innings and the butterflies had returned.

My award was the highest of the day and I was called first. 'Flight Officer Alexandra Henry is awarded the George Cross' and then they described what I had done. I walked up to the King and Queen who were standing on the steps. The tears were rolling down my cheeks as I stopped and turned towards him and curtseyed. It was perfect and then my medal was handed to the King, who in turn pinned it onto my chest and then shook my hand. Queen Elizabeth came down the steps to talk to me and made me feel terrible when she told me my curtsey had been very lovely but that awards were accepted by a salute. I burst out laughing, much to the amusement of the King and Queen; I made them laugh even more when I told him how long I had been practising.

I saluted them both and returned to the side area where William was waiting for me. This time he gave me a kiss and wasn't a bit shy as he looked at the medal. William was called a few minutes later to receive his DFC (the Distinguished Flying Cross) for gallantry. His had drawn much of the fire from his colleagues to enable them to escape the onslaught by the German fighters and regroup.

A little later, William and I were about to leave when I saw a tall Army officer taking a photograph of me. I turned and smiled, then hurriedly turned away again. It was my father. 'William, it's my father!' I shouted. I turned round but he was gone.

I knew then that he still loved me, even if it was in a strange sort of way. I would have loved to have seen him and told him about William and how well I had done at university and how well I had done at cricket, but it wasn't to be. Anyway, it was obvious that he now knew I was living as a woman, and, as William pointed out, now was perhaps a good time for me to broach the matter of the birth certificate with him.

We arrived at the Services Club with me still wearing my medal. I was like a little child; I was so pleased I didn't want to take it off. The door was opened for us and William stood back as someone announced: 'George Cross entering,' and everyone stood up. I was truly honoured as there were so many brave souls in that place, including my William. The Group Captain was already there, along with all his other guests, and as I sat down, he led a toast in my honour. I began to relax without the pressures of the day. It was a lovely meal and a good time was had by all. I took my medal off and placed it in its box, replacing it with plain blue ribbon above my pocket on my uniform.

William was an old sentimentalist and after the last handshakes and farewells, he took me to our Lyons Corner House for a cup of tea. All I now wanted to do was sleep, so we took a bus and a slow walk to Chelsea and home, with hardly a word spoken. We were shattered and the moment we arrived home we went straight to bed.

'Why didn't you ask your father and mother along today?' I asked as my head hit the pillow.

'I didn't want to spoil your day,' he replied. 'I know what a bore Mother can be!'

The next thing I knew was William bringing me a cup of tea in bed, together with the *Daily Mail Daily Mirror, Daily Express* and *The Times,* all of which carried a report on the courage of Alexandra Henry and a little about William and why he was awarded his medal. He then handed me a parcel wrapped up in newspaper. I thought it was a present and began to tear off the paper in my excitement. I couldn't believe it: it was my old jacket, the one I used to wear when I pretended to be a boy.

'You pig!' I shouted. 'Where was it all this time?'

'Why, do you want to go back?'

'What? And lose you? Not a chance. I don't even want to be reminded of all that anymore. Throw it away, darling. And all the other stuff?' he asked, laughing.

'Ooh you pig!' I shouted, launching my pillow at him and just missing the tray of tea.

He flung himself onto the bed to prevent the other pillow following the first, put his hands on my shoulders and pushed me back onto the bed and kissed me. It was becoming a habit, making love after a play fight and then he spoiled the moment.

'Well, it's the first time I've made love to someone who's won the George Cross. Victoria Cross, yes. But the GC . . . Hmm . . . let me think . . .' He paused. 'No, I haven't. Not the George Cross!'

The other pillow went thundering into his face.

We spent the day at his parents' home. While his father knew the value of my award, his mother didn't and both William and I heard her say to Wilf, 'But Bill has won the DFC.'

William was going to explain, but quite frankly I didn't want to talk about it. The excitement had worn off.

Do you know, Mr White, for really only the second time in my Life, I felt I had made it. The first time was at Junior School and now here, I was accepted by everybody for what I was. I was no longer the freak, no longer the outcast, no longer the fish out of water. The pond had grown and I had grown with it; not that I was any bigger, but I had more confidence in my own abilities and because of my dreadful childhood, I was now able to hold my own in a man's world.

Sybil entered with the inevitable tray of tea and scones. 'You'll be giving me a weight problem, if I keep eating these,' I said, bringing a smile to her face, especially when I added, 'And no, I won't refuse. I can't. They're too delicious!'

We chatted for a few minutes about this and that when Mrs Fraser suddenly announced: 'I would like a day or two to think about the rest, Mr White. I hope you don't mind. Alice and I and Sybil will be going to Le Touquet for a few days. We need a break from all our hard work,' she added, laughing.

I was disappointed and couldn't help showing it, but I wasn't the piper playing the tune.

'No, of course I don't mind. Just give me a ring when you're ready and I hope the next meeting will be as enjoyable as the others have been.'

We finished the tea and I was shown to the door and, with a final goodbye, Mrs Fraser commented: 'I do hope you will let me see what you have written so far.'

'Of course I will!' I replied as I got into the car and drove away.

Chapter 16

It was several weeks before I received another phone call from Mrs Fraser; both George Stevenson and I had almost given up. In fact, he had been pestering me to go and see her as he had thought my article, long as it was, was worth pursuing. In fact he was, like me, keen to know what happened after the first instalment, but wouldn't admit it. I was contemplating telephoning her to arrange an appointment, if only to keep George off my back, when my phone rang.

'Bet you thought I was dead, Mr White,' were the first words I heard as I picked it up.

'Mrs Fraser! What a surprise!' I yelled, causing my colleagues to stop working and look at me, now with a silly grin on my face.

'How did the holiday go?' I asked.

'Wonderful. Le Touquet is still a wonderful place and the villages around are beautiful too. I spent several days just milling round the area: Calais, Boulogne, and all the villages – Cap Gris Nez, Desvres, Wimereux, Hardelot – the war museums. It brought back many memories and of course the weather was lovely and Alice and I pulled a couple of old pensioners and persuaded them to play cricket. Winners pay for the ice-creams!'

I wouldn't have put it past Alice to have pulled a couple of blokes after what Mrs Fraser had told me about her, but having never met her one can only imagine. When would you like me to come and see you?' I asked.

'Any time you like,' she replied. 'We're here for the next few weeks.'

The following week I turned up at Glengarry to be once again greeted by Sybil at the door. 'Mrs Fraser is in the garden with her sister, Alice. Would you like to go through? She is expecting you,' she asked in her gracious manner, which always set the scene for the place so well.

'Yes thank you, through the gate there?' I asked, pointing to the little gate in the hedge, which was still looking as fresh as the day I first arrived.

'Yes through there. You'll see them.'

'Thank you.' And with that I left the front door and walked the few yards through the gate and into the garden. There they were, the two sisters, sitting at one of the tables enjoying what was obviously one of Sybil's cups of tea and the inevitable scone or cake.

'I knew you would be on time, Mr White. The tea has just been made. Now come here. I want you to meet my best friend and my sister, Alice,' Mrs Fraser said, beginning the conversation. 'Mr White, this is Alice.'

'I've heard a lot about you, Mrs . . .' I paused as I didn't know her surname.

'Oh, just call me Alice,' she responded.

I must admit I felt very uncomfortable as I could hardly bring myself to call Mrs Fraser, Alexandra, in spite of her invitation and yet with Alice it seemed easier.

'I've heard a lot about you,' Alice went on, 'and let me tell you, Mr White, if we were two or three years younger, you would be fighting us off,' she added with a twinkle in her eye.

I was forty years younger than both of them, but they still had a charm of sorts. I knew it was going to be an interesting time.

We sat in the garden as Alice remembered the amount of torturous cricket practice Alexandra had been put through by their father. 'He would bowl at him for hours. There you are, I've said it again, "him", but he was a him even then, weren't you, darling? Father would stand at the wickets, with his big thick gloves on and he would make Alexandra throw the ball at him from all angles. She could hit a stump nine times out of ten from any angle and from at least twenty or thirty yards away. I can hear him cheering encouragement now. Mr White, it was torture to watch.'

'Shall we sit out here while the weather is like this?' Mrs Fraser asked.

'Yes why not?' I replied. 'It's certainly very pleasant.'

'Can you remember where we had got to?' she asked.

'Of course,' I replied as I flipped open my notebook.

'Cheat,' Alice quipped.

'You had received your George Cross from the King following which you went to see William's parents and –' Mrs Fraser interrupted me.

Oh yes, I remember his mother didn't know the difference in the value of the awards and was determined to let everyone know about William's DFC and quite naturally, of course. However, the celebrations didn't last; there was a war on, so the next day it was business as usual and we had to return to our units to continue the war. You remember I was at Pangbourne. When I arrived, I was saluted by everyone on the base, which to someone like me was somewhat disconcerting, but it soon became the norm.

William, meanwhile, was immediately promoted to Wing Commander and ironically Tom was promoted to Squadron Leader, so they were still working together.

December 7th saw the greatest change in our fortunes as the Japanese attacked the United States fleet in Pearl Harbor, resulting in the Americans declaring war on Germany. The Yanks were now shoulder to shoulder with us and our spirits were lifted, although all the Axis Powers – Germany, Italy and Japan, to name a few, were still making huge gains. Christmas was spent at William's new command near Ipswich. He was moving up in the ranks and had many social engagements and many female admirers, which I think was designed to keep me on my toes and it did, but I had the advantage because at all RAF bases there were always far more men than women.

I returned to Pangbourne immediately after Christmas and shortly after New Year I was called in to see the CO and told that, in view of my qualifications, they wanted to interview me to see whether my languages were good enough and whether I would be suitable to be used in some other way. A little later, he depressed me by saying I was being seconded to assist in German translation. I could have thought of nothing worse than sitting in an office looking at documents and translating them into German or vice versa, when I could be active on one of our bases, helping to win the war. However, I was ordered to go, though the CO told me he was sorry to lose me and that I had done a good job. Madge was promoted into my job, and I was naturally delighted for her, though I knew I was going to miss her.

William phoned me early in January 1942 and invited Madge and I to a party to celebrate his and Tom's promotion. We were to stay over the weekend so I would have to get at least a forty-eight-hour pass. I must be honest, Mr White, the George Cross opened many doors for me and prevented many normal requests from being turned down. So getting a weekend pass to see my Group Captain fiancé wasn't the most difficult thing, in spite of the war. William wanted me to 'knock 'em dead', so I had to buy some new clothes, in particular a couple of new dresses. I hadn't had much to spend my money on in recent months so now it was to be one big spend-up. Then I had my first disappointment: the Friday night was to be a mess party with all officers and wives and he wanted me to wear my uniform for that. He was so proud of me he wanted me to show off the ribbon I wore for my GC. I would have preferred to wear a dress. However, I had the Saturday night to go down that route.

Madge and I set off to Little Whitton in Lincolnshire, the base camp of Wing Commander William Fraser DSO, arriving there around three o'clock in the afternoon. Once again we were stopped at the gates and asked for our identity. Within a minute an American Jeep arrived to take us to the Nissen hut which was the nerve centre of William's operations. I opened the door of his office and we walked in to be greeted by Williams's duty officer.

'Ma'am,' he said, saluting me. 'Can I help you?'

I returned the salute. 'We've an appointment with Wing Commander Fraser.'

'Oh, please go on through.'

We walked into the next office, but again there was no one there and by now I was losing my patience.

'Flight Sergeant,' I shouted, 'where is the Wing Commander?'

Then suddenly William appeared from behind the open door. I couldn't help myself. I just went up and kissed him. I couldn't have cared less who was there. Every time I was away from him made things more difficult for me and I just had to feel him next to me, to be held and to know that he needed me.

'Sorry, Madge,' William said, temporarily ignoring her in his excitement of him seeing me. 'How are you?'

William arranged for transport to take her to Tom.

'Take the Section Officer to Squadron Leader Collingham and return here as soon as you can. Thank you!' he said to his driver.

William shut the door, turned the key and we kissed. Long slow kisses that were never supposed to end. Warm, tender touches that made you tingle from head to toe. At last his orderly knocked politely on the door and told us the transport had arrived. There is always someone, Mr White, who has to spoil your pleasure, even if they don't mean to.

The driver took us into Lincoln and we spent a couple of hours drinking tea, eating scones and simply chatting about the future. William was determined to marry me this year and so inevitably the difficulties regarding my birth certificate came to the fore again. To my surprise, William confessed he had been trying to contact my father by phone, but had not had much success, but he wasn't going to stop trying.

'I want to marry you the moment he agrees to do something. Will you marry me?' William asked for the umpteenth time.

'Darling, I would marry you tomorrow, but we have to change that piece of paper.'

I had a feeling my father would do something for me, as I always remember the sorrow in his eyes at what he had said that day when I was fourteen. Now I felt he owed this to me and somehow he would repay his debt.

We returned to the camp. I was so excited and absolutely determined to have a good time, but I had only about forty-five minutes to get ready. At least we were in uniform and I didn't have to be too decorative, but I still wanted to 'knock 'em dead'. We, that is Madge and I, were given a double room separate to the main servicemen's block, as there was a strict policy of non fraternisation between the sexes, which was a real pity, because I was ready to devour William; but it was better than nothing and I would sooner see him than not.

I put on some snazzy Chelsea underwear, changed into my dress uniform with my one and only medal ribbon sitting proudly on my chest, painted my nails, or talons as some would call them. It was considered very daring, and, with lipstick to match, I felt good. I would say at this point it was entirely Madge's influence; on my own I was still a little insecure and wouldn't often dare, but I was getting braver.

I marched across the parade area and into the Wing Commander's Office and reported for duty. 'Flight Officer Henry reporting for duty, *sir*!' I shouted as William and two other officers came out to greet me.

'Come here. Give us a kiss and never mind these two!' William said, grabbing hold of me and kissing me full on the lips, smudging my lipstick. Of course he was left with an enormous smudge of bright-red lips across his mouth; Max Factor would have been proud.

He looked at himself in the mirror and turned towards his colleagues. 'I don't think this would be acceptable on the parade ground, gentlemen, do you?'

They all laughed.

I redid my war paint, without the help of Madge, and marched with my William to the mess hall where there was a banner saying, 'Welcome to our new CO!' We walked into the hall and were greeted by William's aide-de-camp and were immediately asked what drinks we would like. He scurried away like a little rabbit and I thought he was creeping around us a little, but William told me it was just his way and he was invaluable.

The main bomber unit was on stand-down as they had

carried out three solid weeks of sorties over Holland and Belgium and were having a well-earned rest, hence we had most of the officers and their wives and girlfriends present. One thing I had always admired William for was his ability to remember who each person was and a little bit about them and so we began to tour all the people present, with William introducing me to each and asking how they all were. We had been there about half an hour, when William went up to a group of young officers.

'These are Flying Officers Ridgeway, Brabbham, Seddon and Shepherd. They are our replacements and have only been here two or three weeks and are not yet full-bloodied,' William said, introducing them to me. I nearly died on the spot. For in front of me was Peter Shepherd, one of my eight rapists. I could tell from his eyes he knew me but just couldn't place where he had seen me before. That was until William introduced me: 'Gentlemen, this is Flight Officer Alexandra Henry, my fiancée.'

The moment the name of Henry was mentioned the penny dropped and poor Peter went pale.

'You look as though you've seen a ghost, Peter,' I casually remarked.

'You know each other then?' William asked.

'Oh yes, we're old friends. We used to play cricket together when we were little children. But Peter didn't like playing with the girls. He would always go off with the boys,' I remarked as Peter's ashen face turned beetroot.

'Do you play cricket then, Flying Officer?' William asked.

'Yes, sir.'

'Any good?'

'Not bad,' Shepherd replied.

'Could you score a 50 against Bradman's Australians?'

'I don't think I'm in that class, sir,' he replied.

'She is!' he said proudly. 'She scored 52 and then went onto score 166 not out against Surrey. Impressive?'

'Sir!' they all replied as we moved on to the next group of people.

'Darling, you seemed uncomfortable in his company. Is there a problem?' William asked.

'No, not a problem, just an opportunity to catch up on very old times,' I replied and William, good as he was, left it at that.

Tom and Madge arrived shortly afterwards and it was good to see him after such a long time.

'Congratulations on your promotion, Tom,' I said as he was just about to say the same thing to me about my medal, but then the band struck up with a drum roll and William's number one Squadron Leader, Will Meadows, jumped onto the stage to make an announcement.

'Officers, gentleman and ladies . . .' He paused until everyone stopped talking. '. . . This evening is a very special one.'

'It's belated in the sense that we've been somewhat busy of late, paying our early-morning calls to Germany and delivering our new 2000-pounder, to ensure that Adolf remembers we won't be long away . . .' There were huge cheers and whistling as he continued: 'We've not been able to properly welcome our new CO because he was thrown in at the deep end and has been too busy. It looks like he's been busy on the home front, too, so we would like to congratulate him and his beautiful fiancée on their engagement . . .' There were more whoops of approval and we took a bow. '. . . I haven't finished yet,' he said, gesturing with his hands for everyone to settle down. 'His fiancée is a very special guest. I'm sure you will have noticed her medal ribbon on her tunic. She only has one, not like some of us with several, but hers is special. She's the holder of the George Cross, which, as I'm sure you know, ranks with the Victoria Cross. Gentlemen and ladies, I want you to raise you glasses to a very brave woman . . . Alexandra Henry!'

I caught the eye of Peter Shepherd as he raised his glass and I could see he was shocked at what he had heard. Very few had then seen a George Cross ribbon, as it was a new award and not many people had won it. William was called up to say a few words, which were as eloquent as ever and was then invited to start the dancing. We waltzed around the floor like two professionals to the cheers of the assembled guests and then the others joined in.

William had his duties to do and left me with Tom, Madge and Will Meadows, who invited me to dance, just moments before Peter Shepherd was about to ask and was stopped in his tracks. We were having a wonderful time and I was really amused by Shepherd's misfortune, He tried several times but couldn't get near me, as I seemed to be in demand. William couldn't leave his duties and I was virtually a woman on her own. I knew Peter was absolutely desperate to talk to me so I took the ball to him. It was a ladies' excuse-me and I took the opportunity to go over to him and ask him to dance.

'Peter, may I have this dance, please?' I said politely.

'Yes certainly,' he replied, raising his eyebrows to heaven as if to say, 'Lads, look at what I've got after me – the boss's wife!'

You could almost tell from his attitude what he was thinking. We set off round the floor; he wasn't a bad dancer, but just him touching me made my skin crawl. I began to regret my rashness. I don't know how I could even let him touch me. The music changed to a slow smoochy tune and we were almost creeping round the floor. He dropped his hand down my back and I put it back up.

It made him realise I wasn't going to be as easy as before.

'There's no hard feelings between us are there, Alex?'

'Good Lord no, Peter. Why on earth would you think that?' I replied, trying to be sincere.

'Oh, no reason. You've done so well for yourself and you seem so happy with the Wing Commander, it would be awful if he found out about your past and everything became messy. You wouldn't want that, would you?'

'Oh no, I wouldn't!' I replied, trying to sound worried. I could once again see in his eyes what an evil *bastard* he was. 'You wouldn't tell anyone, would you?' I pretended to plead.

'Of course not, Alex; it'll be our little secret.'

'Yes, let it be,' I said, feigning relief.

'What happened to you after I left?' he asked.

'I was transferred to the girls' school where I saw my time out. I took a degree in Maths and Modern Languages and then took a Master's degree, also in Mathematics. I met William and we fell in love. I then played cricket for the universities against the Counties and the Australians and broke a few records. I joined the WAAFS and rescued two men under heavy aircraft fire and then shot down a German aircraft, for which I won the George Cross, and I've been promoted at work and I think I'm soon going to make Squadron Officer. Oh, and I've met the King and Queen and Winston Churchill and my father was made a Major General,' I said, smiling. 'So I suppose I've been fairly busy . . . So what have you done, Peter?' I asked.

Round one to me, I thought. Peter was totally taken aback. I could see it in his eyes, he was jealous and didn't answer; in fact, he changed the subject and asked:

'When are you getting married?'

'I don't really know. When William has time, I suppose,' I replied.

The music stopped and I thanked him for the dance and was walking away. He grabbed my arm and asked whether he could have the next one. I looked at his hand on my arm, as if to say, what the hell are you doing?, and he immediately let go, saying, 'I'm sorry, Alex.'

I smiled and again turned to walk away and remarked, 'Please don't call me Alex. It's Alexandra.' This embarrassed him, as others had seen and heard what I had done. He was visibly annoyed and started drinking heavily. I began to think I had an opportunity to get my own back.

He kept looking at me in the same way as before, but I didn't want to spoil William's evening with a so-called friend of mine making a fool of himself in front of everyone, so I asked him to dance once again. He was only just sober enough to appear normal, but I could feel he was becoming under the weather. I took him back to our table and introduced him to our friends.

'This is Peter. He's a friend of mine from my schooldays.' We sat down for a while and he seemed to sober up, but when he went to the toilet, he swayed a little.

I went over and interrupted William in his discussions and told him I was taking Peter Shepherd out for some fresh air. I whispered in his ear, 'Trust me!' He nodded his approval.

When Peter returned to the table, I told him I was taking him for a walk, to get a breath of fresh air. I couldn't look any of them in the face as I knew what I was going to do.

'Come on, Peter, let's go for a walk. You need . . .' I paused for a moment, thinking what to say. 'You need a breath of fresh air,' I said, grabbing his arm and directing him out of the room, followed by dozens of pairs of eyes.

We casually walked out of the hall and out into the fresh air. Outside lighting was at a minimum as a precaution against air raids, so when one left the main paths it was very dark, although your eyes would soon get used to it.

'Do you know, Henry, you're not a bad-looking woman,' he said in a domineering sort of way. 'It would be a pity if you lost everything because it all seems easy for you now. What would the dear CO think if he thought you were a man?'

'But I'm not! I never have been and that is why I was transferred to the girls' school,' I replied. 'Anyway you're not going to say anything to anyone, are you?' I asked, pretending to be scared of what he might say but hoping to make him feel he had some power over me.

'No I won't. Come here!' he ordered. He had the attitude that he was still in control, just like he was in the boiler house. 'We always knew what you were and you were a pretty little thing. That's why we all wanted you.'

I took him round the back of the Nissen huts and lifted my skirt. His hand slipped down and touched the silky feeling of my knickers. He began stroking the silk and helped by the alcohol he began to undo his trousers. I encouraged him by stroking his inner thigh. 'Drop your trousers and undo my skirt, quick!' I begged. He stepped out of his trousers and his pants, still swaying. I picked his pants up and began to caress his testicles. He began to sigh.

'Come on,' I said. 'Where's the big brave boy who raped a fourteen-year-old?'

He sobered up like lightning. I squeezed his testicles just to let him know he couldn't escape.

'Before I go, little Peter, I want you to know that my fiancé knows everything about me from beginning to end and the fact that I was raped by nine perverts. I have nothing to hide. It began to hurt him as the pressure intensified.

'Now, Peter, do you remember considering putting me in the boiler? Well, do you?'

'It wasn't me. It was Norman Guest. I didn't want any part of it,' he replied almost shouting, but frightened that we might be seen.

'Do you remember telling me that no one would believe my word against all those prefects? Well, do you? Because I do!' I paused to let what I had said sink in and tried to look at him with tender eyes, just to make him feel worse. 'Now who's the one that is nearly naked and who has just tried to rape his Commanding Officer's fiancée? Who will believe you now, Peter? Rape is a capital offence in wartime, isn't it? Who would believe a junior officer against a senior officer who has just been awarded the GC for bravery?'

I squeezed hard and he opened his mouth to yell.

'I'd be quiet if I were you. We don't want to bring them running to see what's happening, do we? Now open wide.' He ignored me and started to plead. 'Peter,' I said, 'open wide! Now there's a good boy, open wide.' I squeezed harder and he opened his mouth. I rammed his pants into his mouth as far as I could, making sure I squeezed just enough to prevent him from biting my fingers.

'Peter,' I said as I looked at his terror-filled face, 'do you remember the towel tied round my mouth to stop me from screaming? Well, how does it feel? Oh! You can't answer, can you?'

He began to struggle so I applied real pressure; he fell to his knees, but it was a controlled fall as I refused to let go; I was squeezing as I followed him down, gripping like a vice and forcing him to roll onto his back.

'Do you remember how you looked at me and called me a whore and how you told people I charged others for my services but that you had it free? Do you remember? Well, I do. Now, Peter, this is for old times' sake . . .' And with two hands, I cracked his testicles like two little nuts. His screams were muffled by the underpants.

I left him there without trousers, the blood trickling down his leg. I turned to him and quietly said 'Peter, I don't think there will be any hard feelings between us for a very long time, do you?'

I felt really satisfied as I walked into the ladies' toilet to wash the smell of that rapist from me. I was joined by Madge.

'Where the hell have you been?' she asked. 'Everybody's been looking for you.'

Madge and I walked back into the hall and thankfully, I didn't look a bit flustered.

'Hello, darling, you've been a long time and where's the Flying Officer?' William asked.

'Oh him! He began misbehaving himself, so I sent him on his way,' I said with a wry smile.

'Sure you are all right?' William asked.

'Darling, I feel wonderful,' I replied.

'Good, let's dance.'

The rest of the evening was fantastic. However, towards eleven o'clock William was called out. One of his officers had been beaten up and had to be taken to hospital. It had happened, apparently, a few minutes after he had said goodnight to the CO's fiancée. Four men set upon him and then he didn't remember what happened after that.

'Good Lord! That must be that Peter Shepherd. I would have thought he would have given a good account of himself. He was always brave, especially in a group!'

I spent the night with William, regardless of the rules, and it just felt so good feeling him next to me.

'Was Shepherd one of those boys?' William asked as I was almost asleep.

'Yes, darling. He was, but it's over now.'

'I thought as much. When I saw the look in his face when you first met him, I knew he was worried. I don't want him here anymore. I'll have him transferred.'

'There's no need, darling. He won't worry me anymore.'

'But he will me. I'll think of some way of moving him with good grace. We need pilots and he happens to be one of them.' We fell asleep, with me looking forward to wearing my new dress and feeling better in myself every day.

Chapter 17

Early the following morning I quickly got dressed and returned to my bedroom, having to cross the parade ground to get to it. I was so happy I marched across, pretending I was on duty and hoping that I wouldn't be seen. But of course the best-laid plans of mice and men... I had to run into the Guard of Honour who were raising the flag and blowing reveille. I marched past them and saluted, all of us having big smiles on our faces.

'Good morning!' I said, almost laughing.

'Good morning, ma'am.'

I arrived at my billet to find Madge still asleep. I crept in and began to wash and get myself ready.

'Where have you been, you lucky devil? Don't answer! I'm jealous,' she said, waking up and stretching as though she had had a rough night. 'That's the advantage of being the CO's girlfriend,' Madge said, laughing.

The men had to stay on duty during the day as there were plans being made to cooperate with the Americans on a significant number of bombing operations. It was just planning and discussions at this stage, but all senior officers were expected to attend. Tom lent us his car, and Madge drove us all into Lincoln in uniform and we had a whale of a time, being chatted up in the cafés and tea rooms. I remembered Alice in Le Touquet leading the boys on to get an ice-cream and I told myself I was going to do the same to get a cup of tea.

Mr White, I promise you it was only for devilment . . .

It was unusual as this stage of the war for many women to have decorations and I kept getting asked what it was for and

I would always say: 'I've kept the tidiest office for six months running' and I would always get the reply: 'Oh I thought it was something like that.'

Madge always went along with me. However, this afternoon we entered the little tea rooms and I must admit we did look an attractive pair in our officers' uniforms. We sat down at a table only to be joined by four others who brought two chairs with them and we sat as a table for six.

'What're your names then?' one of them asked.

'I'm Alexandra and this is Madge,' I replied, trying to be pleasant.

'Ooh Alexandra!' one of the others commented in a posh voice.

I knew then it was time for us to leave, but Madge said, 'Come on, lads, there's no need for that. All we want to do is have a cup of tea and go.'

'I'll get you a cup of tea, darlin',' he replied and shouted to the waitress to come over and take the order.

'Is everything all right, ladies,' the waitress asked, sensing something was wrong.

Madge answered, 'Yes, fine at the moment,' and gave our order for two cups of tea.

'What's the medal for?' the third imbecile asked, trying to touch the ribbon with his finger and at the same time 'accidentally' brushing my breast. 'Come on, what's it for?'

'I've kept the tidiest office for the last six months,' I replied, causing hoots of laughter and the questioner to lean over again to try and touch me. I just caught his ear.

'Darling,' I said, 'if you don't behave yourself, I'll pull it off. Now sit down. There's a good little boy,' I said as I saw the other make a move and immediately warned him 'Don't. I mean it. I'll pull it off.'

We were saved by the bell as the waitress brought the tea. She had called the police and the beat bobby now entered the place.

'What's all this about then?' he asked.

'Oh it's nothing, Officer. These young boys are just being a bit silly. It's just high spirits,' I replied.

'We were just laughing when she told us what she had been awarded the medal for. She's kept the office tidy for six months!' he said, starting to laugh again.

'What unit are you from?' the policeman asked the lads.

'Little Witton,' they replied.

'My fiancé is the Commanding Officer there, Officer,' I said to the policeman, which caused the young men to go pale.

'Do you know the colours of the medal ribbons?' the policeman asked.

'Yes,' one of them replied.

'Well, clearly you don't. This is the George Cross and just because it's worn by a woman, it's still one of the highest awards for bravery we have and maybe one day you may have the honour of cleaning her boots.'

'Do you want their names, ma'am?'

'No, as I said it was just high spirits,' I replied.

'Sorry, ma'am,' they said as the policeman took them outside and sent them on their way.

We thanked the waitress for calling the officer and enjoyed a good cup of tea and a fresh scone. We laughed about how they had looked when I said William was the CO.

We spent the rest of the day shopping before racing back in time for the dinner in the officers' mess. William was open mouthed as I entered, which made me tease him.

'Darling,' I whispered in his ear, 'your mouth's open.' He promptly shut it.

'You look sensational,' he replied.

It was a lovely evening, Mr White. But then all my evenings with William were like that. I may have loved being the centre of attention, but everything I did was really for him, as if we were alone together in that crowded room.

The following morning Madge said goodbye to Tom and I to William, but not before I went to his office and saw a photograph of myself wearing that lovely red dress, albeit in black and white. I felt so proud.

I'll never forget the 17th February 1942. It was one of the most important days of my life. I was summoned to the Commanding Officer's Office for discussions on a new recruitment programme. I thought it strange I had never been involved with recruitment but duly turned up. I was directed right into the CO's office and invited to sit down.

'Good afternoon. Flight Officer. Would you mind waiting there for a moment. I just have to go and collect something.'

'Not at all, sir,' I replied.

I sat daydreaming for a minute or two when the door opened and a voice said: 'Flight Officer Henry. Date of Birth: 15th October 1917. Name: Alexandra Georgina Chillington-Henry. Sex: Female.'

'*William*!' I shouted, turning round to see him holding this piece of paper. 'Oh, William, I don't believe it!' I said, beginning to cry. In fact, I cried and cried. My father had at last done something special for me; I just wanted to go home and kiss him.

'You've been granted a twenty-four-hour pass. We can go and celebrate and I've already booked a table at the United Services Club in London and we've got no time to waste . . .'

I raced to my quarters, changed into my best uniform, collected everything I would need and ran back to the CO's office. William's driver was outside waiting as we both hurried in.

'Good afternoon, ma'am,' the driver said, as I sat down.

'Come on, call me Alexandra. You've known me long enough,' I said, excited to know that was my real name at last.

'Yes . . . ma'am.'

William was absolutely mortified that I had invited a subordinate to call me by my Christian name, but at least he knew it was the excitement of the moment and at least the driver had the sense to ignore me. We called at Chelsea to enable me to change and then raced over to the club.

We entered the dining room to the announcement: 'George

Cross entering', with everybody standing up and everybody looking at William. The waiter pulled my chair out and I sat down at our little table for two. We were at last on our own. William had sent the driver away until ten o'clock the following day and for me it was bliss.

'Good evening. My name is William. What's yours?'

'My name is Alexandra.'

'Do you come here often?'

'Oh yes, but only when a very handsome young man invites me.'

'Well, I know you will find this strange, but I have suddenly fallen in love with this girl called Alexandra Georgina Chillington- Henry and I'm going to ask her to marry me. Do you think she would say yes if I asked?' William said.

'Who?' I asked.

'This young woman. I told you – her name is Alexandra Georgina Chillington-Henry.'

I stood up and walked round to his seat, sat myself down on his lap, much to his embarrassment and said, 'Yes, I think Alexandra Georgina Chillington-Henry would marry you if she was asked,' I replied.

'When do you think Alexandra Georgina Chillington-Henry would marry me?'

'Tomorrow,' I answered.

I returned to my seat only after he had given me a whopping kiss, much to the amusement of all those present. I couldn't choose anything on the menu as I was so excited; I had to leave everything up to William to order.

'Excuse me, Madam, do you think Miss Alexandra Georgina Chillington-Henry would enjoy chicken?'

'Darling, it's the first time you've referred to me as Miss. That calls for a celebration kiss,' and once again, much to the embarrassment of William, I went round and sat on his lap and wouldn't move until I had a celebration kiss.

'William,' I said a little later on, as we ate our first course, 'how did you get my father to do this for us? He never wanted to see me again and he never wanted to be near . . .' I stopped as I could feel myself getting upset.

He took my hand across the table and gently squeezed it while he described what had happened.

'I telephoned your father several times at the War Office until he finally accepted my call. He insisted I didn't call again and I agreed not to as long as he met me to discuss this one matter. After a great deal of soul-searching on his part I suppose, and persuasion from me, he agreed to see me at your home in Upper Hayfield. What a lovely little village it is. You don't realise these places exist until you drop in on them.'

'Never mind that, get on with it,' I demanded, wanting him to get to the point of his story.

'Well, I arrived at the house. Prompt at two, knowing that as a professional soldier he would require that. Tom Collingham had very kindly dropped me off and waited for me in the village.'

'Get on with it. Get to the point!' I asked anxiously.

'Well, after introducing myself, he asked me into the lounge where I met your mother, who was waiting for us.

' "Come on, young man, tell us what this is all about," he asked.

' "It's about your daughter, Alex, sir," ' I replied and I could see him wince as I said that word.

'I went on to tell him how you had suffered and all the terrible things that happened to you at school, even down to the rape, which caused your mother to cry. I then went on to explain what you had achieved at Oxford and how they wouldn't let you continue playing cricket, as you were too much of an embarrassment to the university. I could see your father's blood boiling as he became inwardly angry. I continued and told them of all your achievements and how you won your George Cross and how you met the King and Queen.'

' "I was there," he interrupted, "I saw it all." He was becoming very emotional but was trying hard not to show it.'

'I knew I had seen him there. I knew it!' I said delightedly.

'I hope you don't mind, darling; I told him about how you went to see the gynaecologist and his belief that you should never have been registered as a boy. I even showed him a letter from Mr Evans. Forgive me, darling.

'By the time he read the letter, he was physically drained. He passed it on to your mother and she couldn't finish it. She was too distraught.

' "What do you want me to do, young man?" ' your father asked.

' "I want to marry your daughter, sir, but I need the birth certificate changed. She is known to everyone as Alexandra and I would like her to be registered as that," ' I replied.

' "I don't know how, but I'll do it," he said sadly.

' "Can I bring her home. She desperately wants to see you and I know she loves you both very much. She often talks about how you used to teach her to play cricket." I saw your father's chest stick out. He was proud of your ability.

' "I know . . ." He couldn't continue the sentence as he had difficulty in saying it; I know it was the word "she", but then he repeated himself: "I know she is." '

' "I would have loved her to play for England," ' I said proudly.

' "So would I!" he added. "So would I!" '

That did it for me; I burst into tears, not of misery, but of joy.

'Don't tell me anymore. I can't bear it and it will spoil this beautiful day.'

'Needless to say, darling, within a week he had achieved the impossible. He went to Somerset House and told them he had made a foolish mistake with your birth certificate. It was the Great War and he'd been in such rush that he hadn't been thinking straight. Now he wanted to correct it. Who would dare argue with him? He said he had been very confused and thought he had been told he had a boy, especially as the name was Alexander George. It was easy in that sense to change it to Alexandra Georgina and that is now your real name.'

'What was that again?' I asked.

'Alexandra Georgina,' he repeated.

'I'm sorry, I didn't catch that.'

'Ah, shut up, or I'll come round there and smack you.'

'What was that name again?' I asked, taunting him and with that William gave me a playful tap across the table.

'Your father telephoned me at my office,' William continued, 'and arranged to meet me in London. That was yesterday. I asked again if I could bring you to see him, but, darling, I think it was too much for him to talk about. He was very sad. I don't know what to do on that score, but I won't give up. However long it takes.'

William ordered two glasses of beer to toast ourselves ' and we went on to agree the date of our wedding – the 6th September 1942. From then on all we wanted to do was to go back to Chelsea and relax.

We paid our bill and prepared to leave, the head waiter announcing, 'George Cross leaving!' and all the diners stood up.

William whispered in my ear to acknowledge the tribute, which I did to the astonishment of all those present.

The club allowed me to use the telephone to phone Alice. She was ecstatic and as thrilled as I was, especially when I told her Father had changed my name to Alexandra Georgina.

'I knew he would in the end,' she shouted excitedly down the phone.

After I phoned Alice, Mr White, I phoned my adoptive parents Peter and Thelma Wilkes and told them to reserve Saturday 6th September. At the same time I asked Peter to give me away, unless my father changed his mind.

We left the club and as I wanted to go to Westminster and walk arm in arm back to Chelsea because, if you remember, Mr White, the last time we had done that we needed to watch out for the law. This time there were no worries. William was a very romantic fellow and loved it when I remembered all these little events in our romantic history. It was pure joy.

The following morning, however, I was distraught at the

thought of our parting. I lost control of myself, behaving like some silly woman, as I probably would have thought several years previously; but now I just didn't want him to go. I was so worried he might never come back that I cried and cried and cried. The knock on the door put a stop to things as his driver had called to collect him.

'Come on now, darling, be brave. Don't let him see you have been crying. It wouldn't do!'

The parting wasn't how I wanted it to be; I wanted it to be slow with long lingering kisses, when in fact the opposite happened.

The driver announced, 'Sorry, sir. There's a flap on and they have asked me to collect you straightaway. We've to be at Command HQ by two o'clock, sir. We must leave now.'

'Right, Corporal,' William replied and turning to me said, 'Darling, I have to leave immediately.' It was a quick kiss and an 'I love you, darling' and he was away.

I cleaned up the flat, making sure everything was safe and caught the train back to Pangbourne, arriving in plenty of time. So much so Madge asked, 'Is everything all right?'

'He had to go back early. There was a flap on,' I replied somewhat sadly.

Britain and the Allies were having a torrid time against the Axis forces and had lost a great deal of territory all over the world; I think it was perhaps our low point in the war. I did my bit, everything the CO told me to, and dreamed of September. From July onward I spent as much time as possible organising our wedding.

It was to be at Upper Hayfield church at twelve o'clock. Mr Wilkes was going to give me away if my father wouldn't, and Alice, my lovely sister, was to be the matron of honour. Lucy's little girl was to be my only bridesmaid. Tragically, Lucy and her husband had parted so she would come unaccompanied. Tom was to be William's best man and all his family were arranging to come down too.

William gave an open invitation to all his senior officers and many did indeed make the trip. The biggest joy was that my mother accepted her invitation immediately and promised she would try to get my father to come too. He didn't, Mr White. Perhaps it would be better to say, he couldn't.

The banns were posted in William's parish and Upper Hayfield three weeks before and I had to explain to the vicar privately that there had been a mistake in registering me at birth and I showed him my amended birth certificate. He very kindly altered the parish records accordingly. My mother arranged for the local milkman to drive me to the church in that famous Rolls-Royce and now I counted the days away.

The big day arrived but, in spite of William being the Commanding Officer, he could only get a seventy-two-hour pass. His outfit was on twenty-four-hour alert and he couldn't be spared.

I had bought my dress from a little shop in Chelsea. I know I looked all right as both Alice and Madge came with me to buy it and neither of them would have said it was good when it wasn't. Would you, Alice?

The hour arrived and I walked down the aisle on the arm of my dear friend Peter Wilkes, the expected ten minutes late, full of apprehension, but my worries fast disappeared when I saw William standing there, waiting at the altar, with an enormous grin on his face. He gave me an adorable wink and whispered, 'You look lovely!' but his voice echoed throughout the church and was heard by everyone.

I couldn't resist a little joke when the vicar asked, 'Alexandra Georgina, do you take . . .' I leaned over and quietly whispered to William, 'What's that name again?' He smiled; in fact, he tried desperately hard not to laugh.

The service was soon over and we slowly walked out of the church to face an archway of RAF Officers with their ceremonial swords. It was wonderful and the photographs still send shivers down my spine when I look at them. The reception afterwards was held in the village hall and in spite of the war, it was a grand affair. Many of the villagers had repaid my mother's kindness after the financial crash and had given some of their ration coupons to help with the food.

When the formalities were over, the party, which had been organised by some of the villagers, began. What was so lovely was that everyone from the village was invited and most came. Dr Palin had announced that only death certificates were an acceptable excuse for not coming. The pub was closed for the day, as my mother had commandeered the publican and all his beer. My mother surprised us by telling us that her wedding gift was the flat in Chelsea, which was ours as long as we wished. All in all, I was floating on air.

Like everything, even that day came to an end, but there was one last surprise, which William had been party to: my mother had offered us Glengarry for the night. William had bought me some beautiful nightwear and had laid it out on the bedspread.

As we lay in each other's arms at the end of that wonderful day, we vowed to have our 'real' honeymoon in Le Touquet as soon as the war had finished. But to be honest, Mr White, that was my honeymoon – the sweetest night of my life.

Part 5

France

Chapter 18

We and our Allies were still having a rough time all over the place, particularly in the Atlantic where the Germans had sunk millions of tons of our merchant shipping. In North Africa we had been pushed back deep into the desert and in the Far East and the Pacific, the Japanese had conquered almost everything. Our backs were against the wall. Christmas 1942 was a very bleak affair, although everyone tried to keep cheerful.

In reality, the tide was already turning. In the early part of 1943 the Germans lost many men at Stalingrad. We had begun to gain ground in various sectors, particularly Italy, and even our destroyers were beginning to take control of the Atlantic. The RAF was in control of the skies around Britain, though this didn't stop the Luftwaffe from trying to penetrate our defences. Many German pilots were shot down and the few lucky enough to bale out were taken prisoner.

One day in February I was summoned by the CO to meet him in his office at ten o'clock sharp and told that there were several people who wanted to meet me.

'I think it's something to do with some publicity they want to do to help the war effort,' the CO said.

Ten o'clock sharp I was at his office and only his secretary was there. 'Go on in, ma'am,' she said, opening the door for me. I expected to see the CO but there were only two people there.

'*Guten Tag,* Frau Fraser,' the officer said.

'*Guten Tag,*' I replied, uncertain of what was going on. I asked in English and he answered in German: it was an interview to see what the quality of my German was; later we would all speak in French to see how good that was. Neither of the two men identified themselves so it was all very disconcerting. We conversed for about half an hour, then, somewhat absurdly, we all suddenly began to speak French. My German, I confess, was a bit rusty, but here I was in my element. The conversation finished and I was told to go back to my normal duties.

A fortnight later, I was ordered to report to the Air Ministry to attend another interview, as they wished to test further my spoken French and German. I was told it was unlikely I would be returning to Pangbourne, whatever the results were, which deep down was very distressing as I had been there for some time. What was worse, I only had three days' notice before I had to report to the Air Ministry in London where I would be given my new orders. Should matters be successful I had one big advantage: I could live at home, but of course I was missing out on the company I knew.

I had made wonderful friends at Pangbourne, especially Madge and even the CO knew we were almost inseparable. Before my departure he gave us both a twelve-hour pass and told us to enjoy ourselves, which we did, visiting all our usual haunts, the cafés and the pubs, as well as all the sections on the base to thank them for their support. It was hard saying goodbye to Madge: with tears in my eyes, I thanked her for bringing me back into the world. It was down to her, in part, that I now felt I could cope with anything.

The following day I was ordered to report to the Air Ministry, but before doing so I was asked to call at the CO's office to pick up my travel papers. On arriving, his adjutant asked me to see him on the parade ground as he was waiting there. Mr White, almost the entire company was assembled to salute me and wish me the best of luck. Can you imagine how humbling and yet uplifting that was? I was cheered off the station by everyone and then driven to the railway station in the CO's car. I had a lump in my throat the entire journey.

I arrived at the Air Ministry and was immediately taken to

meet my new temporary boss, Wing Commander Charles Drake. He was affectionately known as Winco. I walked into his office and saluted.

'It's I that should be saluting you, Flight Officer,' he said. 'Now is it Alex or Alexandra?' he asked.

'I prefer Alexandra, sir.'

'Then Alexandra it will be.'

'When we are alone we'll use our Christian names, don't you think? Mine's Charles, by the way.' He reached out to shake my hand. 'So Alexandra. Why have you come to me?' the Wing Commander asked.

'Orders, sir,' I replied.

'Charles, please,' he said, gently reminding me. 'I can't tell you how much all that formal stuff bores me.'

'Sorry, Charles.'

'Do you know what we do?' Charles asked.

'I haven't a clue. I was told it was something to do with translation.'

'Well not quite,' he began. 'We interview captured prisoners, deserters or anyone connected with the Luftwaffe. We may be required by any of the other services to assist them in matters of the same kind. I'm told you have a degree in German and you're fluent.

'I'm fluent in French, Charles. My German is a bit rusty, I'm afraid.'

'I think you're being a bit hard on yourself, Alexandra. A bit of practice and we'll soon have you up to scratch. Come on, I'll treat you to lunch and I'll let you buy me a drink. We will talk over the formalities as we walk.'

He took me to none other than the Services Club and the usual announcement was made as I entered, so that everyone rose to their feet and stared at Winco. He looked a little disconcerted at the attention.

'My God, is it like this everywhere you go?'

The waiter came and Wing Commander ordered a gin and tonic for himself and a half of bitter for me. I really fancied cod and chips and he, too, had a fish dish; despite all the water round Britain, fish was still a bit of a luxury.

Winco began to explain what his unit did:

'It's quite a small team really. There's me, you and just two others. You will be given the rank of Squadron Officer, as from 8 a.m. tomorrow morning. Basically we're required to visit areas where Luftwaffe officers have been captured. At the moment we've a flap on and we will be leaving for Presteigne in Radnorshire, where I'll hasten to add, we've almost a riot situation, as there are problems in the POW camp there. We're going to assist in sorting it out, in case we can glean something that will be useful to us.

'We'll be staying for two, possibly three, days, so you will need your normal changes of clothing. The rule is, you have to keep a suitcase ready in the office, as we often have to leave at a moment's notice. Where's your suitcase now?'

'It's at my flat in Chelsea. It's all packed and it's only a case of picking it up.' I paused before asking, 'Charles, why have you chosen me?'

'It can be a difficult job and you have shown character,' he said, pointing to my ribbon. 'You're the first woman to have been given the job, but initially you are only on six months' secondment.'

'What's your background, Charles?' I asked.

'Me? I'm just a boffin. I was given this rank and uniform, as it was fitting for the job I'm overseeing. I have never been in an aeroplane or worked in the RAF. But I'm good at the job, I can assure you.'

We had another drink with our meal and then left for Chelsea.

'Would you like a quick cup of tea?' I asked.

'I'd love one,' he replied and decided to keep the taxi waiting, so I took it upon myself to invite the driver in so that he could have one also. But, as with all drivers in those days, he refused to leave his cab.

'Never do that again,' Winco said sternly. 'One, they will

know what you have got inside. Two, he knows you work at the Air Ministry and you may have secrets at home and, three, he will know you are going away and the house will be empty.'

I felt well and truly told off. 'One cup of tea, made with dried milk and no sugar coming up,' I said humbly.

'Follow my lead,' he commented as we prepared to leave a few minutes later.

We entered the cab. 'Sorry, we were a long time, cabbie. Kings Cross, please.'

We settled down in the cab and looked out at the busy city streets. Charles spoke again.

'What time does your husband get home then?' he asked.

I twigged straight away.

'He's in mostly before three o'clock, but his hours are so unusual he sometimes doesn't get in until four.'

'Mm, interesting.'

We arrived at King's Cross and caught the LMS to Wolverhampton, travelling first class, and then changing for Shrewsbury and finally to Presteigne. It was a long day and we were shattered by the time our car arrived to take us to the camp, which by the way was well into the hills of Radnorshire. Rooms were provided for us, but as they were not expecting a woman, things were a little difficult. I slept till ten in the morning and woke only when I was asked what I would like for breakfast. I was surprised at the choice, considering there was a war on and we were all rationed.

Charles came into the canteen for his breakfast and briefed me. The camp was only for the Luftwaffe, German airmen, and trouble had been brewing for some time, as the prisoners were complaining about food and conditions and other matters. Charles decided that he would take the lead in questioning and I would act as second string. Our section took command of the questioning, he told me, but we were subordinate in matters of camp security.

Following breakfast we were taken to the interrogation room to await the first officer. I was open-mouthed, as he walked in accompanied by two guards and he was as surprised to see me. *'Mein Gott*!' he exclaimed and put his hand out to shake mine, which I took much to the guards' consternation.

'Ma'am, no physical contact with the officer, please!' one of the guards reprimanded me.

'Why not?' I asked. 'I know this officer . . . In fact, I shot him down.'

The guards looked at me, astonished.

'You talk to him,' the Wing Commander told me.

'I'm Squadron Officer Fraser and I've come to try and sort out the difficulties and this is my Commanding Officer, Wing Commander Charles Drake, and you are?

'I'm Heidrich von Helmstedt. I'm the senior-ranking officer in the camp,' he replied with an educated East Prussian accent.

'Tell me what the problems are,' I asked.

He went into detail about how poor the quality of food was and how there was insufficient to go round and that many were going hungry. There were no Red Cross parcels and the mail wasn't getting through.

I felt a sudden surge of irritation against this aristocratic German.

'You're grumbling about the quality and quantity of food! How dare you? Don't you realise that thanks to the Luftwaffe half our country is starving. Our children have no fresh milk, no fruit, no vegetables, little bread, no meat, no chicken and you have the nerve to complain about your food. Don't you realise we can't get our ships through because your U-boats keep sinking them?

'Don't you realise that so many of our factories have been bombed by your Air Force that we can't make bread and you have the nerve to complain about quantity and quality. Let me make it clear, if the British public knew what you are getting to eat, there would be a riot.'

Von Helmstedt was conciliatory; he was even a little shocked at my forthrightness. I suggested we and the camp Commander meet with the camp's twelve Luftwaffe officers to see what could be done. Winco concurred. Dialogue was best, he pointed out.

Afterwards, when Charles and I discussed the whole crisis, he said he felt the camp had mismanaged a storm in a teacup and quite frankly the affair didn't warrant any outside help. He said that I had responded well, but advised me to be a little more temperate in my language. 'Play it cool, Alexandra.'

That evening I telephoned William to tell him about my new work and that I had been promoted to Squadron Officer. I actually think he was more pleased than I was; even more so when I told him I was now staying at home and he would be able to see me more often. I knew it was difficult as things were very busy at the moment, with nightly raids on Germany and the Low Countries, but at least we were making strides to cripple Germany's manufacturing capacity. William had led a massive attack on industrial plants at Essen and once again had put himself in mortal danger to save others and won a bar to his DFC and earned another trip to London, which he invited me to. It was another grand affair and another chance for him to meet the King. We had our usual celebration dinner at the Services Club among friends and colleagues, but once again, we only had twenty-four hours together and he was back on duty.

The next few months, for me, were boring; we just interviewed pilots and airmen who had been shot down and baled out; it was very routine stuff. In fact, we were assisting the other services as things were so quiet. I longed for something to do to keep myself occupied, if only to stop me worrying about poor William flying all the time. Furthermore, I didn't want to put too much pressure on him by always telephoning him and complaining that I didn't see him.

We did have one break from our usual routine when we were called to assist in the interrogation of a U-boat crew who had been captured as a result of destroyer action in the Atlantic. It was interesting to note that the crew revealed how terrified they were when they heard our sonar tracking devices. They also let on about the chaos in the German Navy, where both organisation and strategy left much to be desired. U-boats were being sent in all directions and often they hadn't a clue what they were supposed to be doing.

I had been with Charles' section for just a short while and was transferred from secondment to being made a permanent member of the team, with thankfully a glowing report about my work and ability. As a result of this, when Charles was asked if he could help the Americans with certain matters, I was immediately asked if I would go with him to Dorset to take part in some operation and at the same time meet the other members of the section. The two I hadn't met before were Flying Officer Donald Bright, (known as Duckie for obvious reasons) a former dentist who spoke French, German, Russian, Spanish and Italian, all fluently, and Flying Officer Sam Reason. You would have thought he was German. I have never known anyone so perfect, without a whisper of an error in his grammar or his Berliner dialect. On several occasions when he had interviewed German prisoners, he had been called a traitor as they thought he was a German working for the British.

We arrived in Dorset late on a cold March evening and with Winco driving, we pulled up at the gates of the very large mansion which was being used by the Americans as one of their headquarters. We were waved directly on as soon as the guard saw us and as Winco began to drive on, I was so incensed, I shouted, 'Stop the car!'

Charles was absolutely flabbergasted as he saw me get out and storm back to the guard.

'Are you bloody stupid?' I shouted at the guard. 'We could be bloody Germans! You're supposed to protect this area, not give it up to the enemy. Now check the bloody passes and tell your command post we're coming through.'

'Yesss, ma'am,' the shocked private replied.

'There's my ID,' I shouted as I pushed it towards him at the same time as Winco was reversing back. The others also took their IDs out and handed them to the guard, who in turn dutifully checked them.

'I'm going to report this to the most senior officer I can because it's bloody ridiculous,' I said loudly.

'Well done, Squadron Officer!' Charles said as he drove to the front of the building.

We got out of the car to be greeted by Captain Gerry Weinsberger, who was the aide-de-camp for the newly appointed General John Grisman, who in turn was responsible for the project we were going to hear about.

The Captain took us into the building where we were invited to wait in a beautiful entrance hall; the kind where, Mr White, you could imagine all the guests being met as they arrived for a weekend hunting party. The General himself came down the magnificent staircase to greet us.

'Good morning, Charles! Good of you to come.' We all acknowledged him as he continued: 'Before we go upstairs I want to take you into the dining room,' he said with a smile.

The dining hall, such as it was, was enormous and had been divided up into a large open-plan office at one end while, at the other, there was a very large-scale model of the northern coast of France. It started from the Belgium border through Dunkirk, Calais, Boulogne and Le Touquet in the north, to Dieppe, Le Havre and Cherbourg in the south and almost fifty miles inland. The dining room was restricted access and this time we did have to confirm our identity before we entered.

'Charles, I heard about your little show at the gate. Well done!' he remarked. 'I cannot stand sloppy security.'

'It was Squadron Officer Fraser, not me,' Winco commented.

'Good for you, Squadron Officer!' the General added.

We were then taken to his office where he explained the purpose of our meeting and what he required us to do. In the short term, we were to be part of a group which would be preparing the ground for an invasion landing, as the first phase of ridding Western Europe of Nazi occupation.

'The project is secret and your section has already been investigated as to its security liability and we're satisfied that your work will help us greatly. The model you saw downstairs is an accurate copy of what's on the ground and all we have to do is fill in the blanks.

We've got to know where all the German fortifications are before we attempt to land in France.

'We're receiving many pieces of information from our own men, who are making regular sorties into France and receiving written information from the Resistance organisations. However, we don't have sufficient personnel with the appropriate security clearance to translate this information and that's where you come in.

'Well, young lady, do you think you can cope?' the General asked, turning to me.

I was just thinking, oh my God, not another patronising bastard when Winco spoke up for me.

'General, the Squadron Officer here has already been awarded the George Cross for Gallantry. She is an expert in both French and German and has an MSc in Mathematics. I don't think this little job will be too difficult for her, *sir*!' he said, showing a little anger and snapping out the word 'sir'.

'Your point is taken, Wing Commander,' the General replied, somewhat embarrassed. 'Do any of you know this area of France?' he asked, still feeling uncomfortable.

'Yes, sir, I do,' I replied. 'I have lived in Le Touquet several months a year for the last twenty years or so. So I know it very well.'

The General seemed even more uncomfortable.

'Now', the General continued, recovering a little. 'We're picking up four leaders of the Resistance movement by submarine this evening and we only have a maximum of thirty-six hours to interview them, and to find out exactly what they have got to say and where everything is, before they are missed. We cannot waste any time. There is a submarine waiting to take you now and we have to catch the evening tide. You will be able to debrief them on the *Conqueror* and when you get them back here. They must not be given any information or indeed, any inclination, about our invasion plans. The four of you will travel with me in my car; it will be a bit crowded I know, but I'll continue to brief you on the way to Southampton, where the *Conqueror* is currently berthed.

We were quickly whisked away in the General's car and within a couple of hours we were on board HMS *Conqueror* on our way to somewhere between St-Valery-en-Caux and Fécamp, a quiet stretch of the Northern coastline. We laid off submerged about a mile from the shore and waited until dark, slowly surfacing until the conning tower was just visible, which enabled the Captain and three others to act as lookouts for any signs of activity on land. There was total silence on the boat as any noise of any description could attract attention to us. The Captain's worse fears happened as the cloud level began clearing and the moon picked out our boat like the last pea on the plate.

It was now getting close to the rendezvous time and the Captain whispered his order: 'Boat three feet and dinghy detail forward,' and with that the submarine surfaced sufficiently to allow the deck to be just clear of the water.

The forward hatch opened with a clang, terrifying most of the crew, myself included. The dinghies were pulled out and the two men allocated to each dinghy stepped in and within seconds they were on the way to the shore; the hatch was closed and the boat submerged a few feet, leaving the Captain and his men on observation duty.

It was a precise operation and once again, within a few minutes the dinghies were returning with several men. Suddenly, there was a smell of urgency about the boat. The Captain whispered loudly, 'Dinghy detail forward!' The hatch was reopened; the dinghies and the men taken aboard and the submarine submerged. But there was one Frenchman missing, which caused consternation to everyone, including ourselves.

Immediately the boat was underway, the men were searched as a precaution; following which we began to question each in turn as to the whereabouts of the fourth man. One of them thought his group from the Pas-de-Calais region had been infiltrated, or that some of his people had been captured by the Gestapo.

'I know he had hidden several sets of plans in the safe house but so far it has not been raided by the Gestapo,' one of the leaders explained in French, which I duly translated.

'How do you know that?' I asked.

'It's being watched round the clock and I know it's safe,' he said confidently.

The three remaining men had similar stories and from that moment, Winco and myself were satisfied that the men were who they said they were, but it had taken well over two hours to get to that position. It was evident from the briefings that if, which was now likely, some of the Pas-de-Calais group had fallen into the hands of the Germans, it would only be a short time before they had forced the information from them, which would possibly lead to them knowing where the plans were hidden. It was therefore a matter of great urgency to mount some sort of operation to recover them ourselves.

Once their identity had been established and confirmed with the mainland, we began to discuss the paperwork and maps they had brought with them. Duckie, Sam and I translated all the documents and discussed the meaning of all aspects of the drawings which had been made on some of the maps. Some of them, I would hasten to add, were very primitive and obviously drawn when the architect was on operations, but even they established exactly where the fortifications were along a large stretch of coastline. In the meantime, Winco tried to investigate what had happened to the fourth member.

It took over twelve hours to make contact with the Pas-de-Calais group and, yes, they had been betrayed and decimated by the Gestapo. The second-in-command, Jacques Lafitte, had escaped and confirmed they hadn't found the radio or, worse, any of the plans. Still, none of the group could go back to Calais as it was too hot for them at the moment, but they were happy to assist others if something could be done.

We landed back in Blighty where the Frenchmen were quickly taken to HQ and shown the model of the area and for a few hours, helped out with any errors or ideas they had. Afterwards, they were able to relax and meet several other members of the Free French forces, who were all feeling frustrated by their idleness while they waited to be used against the Bosh. We were not involved with the return journey and spent the rest of the time helping to ensure the German fortifications were correctly positioned.

Meanwhile, General Grisman and Winco were extremely worried about the information the captured Resistance leader had in his possession and it had also been established that most of it was hidden in a house just off the rue Royale, one of the main routes through Calais, between rue du Soleil and rue de la Mer, not far from the station and the port. They knew it would be dangerous if the Germans got hold of this information as it could put back a landing attempt for several months, if not years.

We were called into a meeting with the General and several members of the Office of Strategic Services, known as the OSS – I suppose today you would call it the American Secret Service, or Special Forces – together with officers responsible for the organising of the French Resistance. It was an acrimonious meeting, with the Americans almost accusing the Resistance of incompetence and the Free French trying to explain the difficulties they were having: there were just too many leaks to the Germans and too many operatives being captured and shot and that we should look at our own organisations for leaks. The discussion centred around whether it would be better to bomb the area in the hope of destroying the house and the plans, or to send other members of the Resistance into the area to try to get them back. The problem was that it would take several days to organise an operation like this and that several other Resistance units would have to be involved: the more people involved, the more dangerous it would become for the operatives, and higher the probability that the Germans would cotton on.

It was decided to send in a small special team to do the job. They would be dropped by boat and make their way to Calais by whatever means possible. The local Resistance leader would be asked to meet them on the shore at an appropriate time. This would be coordinated with two heavy bombing raids on Calais and Boulogne, to act as both cover and diversion.

'Do you know Calais, Squadron Officer,' the General asked.

'Yes, very well sir. But of course you know that, sir, you have read my file,' I said with a smile, trying to be humorous.

'A straight yes or no will do, young lady,' the General remarked caustically.

'Yes sir. Sorry, sir, but I am an officer, General,' I replied, angry at his 'young lady' remark. Winco looked at me, warning me with his eyes.

The General looked at me, half angry, half amused. 'We're going to have to do something quickly, by which I mean within the next two days. So, Charles, if you and your officers would like to make yourself at home for the next hour or so, I'll call you and tell you what we plan to do and we will take it from there.'

With that, the General called the meeting to an end and we were unceremoniously shunted out of the office.

'It's because he's new,' I said sarcastically, hoping he would hear. 'He hasn't learned what manners are yet.'

'Come on, don't be as bad as he is,' Winco commented as we made our way downstairs and went to the canteen for something to eat.

There were no food shortages here and it seemed they lived a normal existence. Quite frankly, I wondered whether they really realised a war was going on. Apart from our little exercise there was no urgency about the place whatsoever and, as I had found at the gate, there was no security to speak of.

The choice of menu was superb and was I actually enjoying my meal until Winco chipped in. 'Alexandra, I think he wants you to go on this mission.'

'Don't be silly! How on earth could I be of use?' I replied and then it dawned on me. It would simply be to use my local knowledge. 'I'm not trained for this sort of thing and, quite frankly, I wouldn't want to do it.'

I didn't even want to entertain the idea. I left the canteen and walked around the grounds on my own. The place was beautiful despite the enormous piles of sand bags around the entrances and windows and the machine-gun posts round every corner. I sat on one of the garden benches, which seemed to have been left to remind everyone of more peaceful times, and drifted into thoughts about my William and what he was doing at that precise moment. I suppose I had drifted off into oblivion when I was disturbed by an American corporal.

'Squadron Officer Fraser?' he asked.

'Yes, that's me,' I replied.

'General Grisman would like to see you, ma'am.'

'I don't want to see him, Corporal. If he wants to come and see me, you know where I am.'

'I can't do that, ma'am.'

'Yes you can, Corporal.'

'Please, ma'am.' He was becoming quite distressed.

'OK, take me to him,' I said impatiently. 'Much against my better judgement I would add.

'Come on,' I continued, to the very much relieved Corporal, as I left my lovely garden seat and the brief moment of pleasure it had afforded me.

We entered the General's office and I was invited to sit down with my colleagues, who had been waiting for me, along with various other officers.

'Thank you for joining us, Squadron Officer,' he said with a hint of irony. 'I'll come straight to the point. We want to send a six-man team to Calais to try and recover the plans. The operation will be supported by the local Resistance and, because of your local knowledge, Squadron Officer we would like you to assist the team.'

'No, I'm sorry, I can't, sir. I've not been trained for such work and–' I began.

I was interrupted by Winco.

'The Squadron Officer has already done more than most in this war and I think it is totally unreasonable that you should even think about it,' he said angrily.

'I also have many staff that have done their bit, as you English say, and I'm asking several of them to go, too,' the General shot back haughtily.

'General,' Winco said, showing his great annoyance. 'Are you familiar with the British decorations for bravery because before you say any more and offend all of us, I would suggest you look at the one she wears on her jacket. It's the King's medal for bravery, the George Cross. It's the equivalent of the Victoria Cross. Every rank salutes it, including generals, so don't tell me, General, that all your staff have done what she has done. I would suggest you look up the citation . . .'

There was a deathly silence and everyone in the room readied themselves for an explosion.

'I'm sorry. I've made a complete ass of myself,' the General replied to everyone's astonishment. 'I had no idea and I'm sorry for the insensitivity.'

You didn't expect that sort of comment from a general and quite frankly Winco should have been told off for his insubordination. There was another strained silence.

'Now where was I?' the General remarked as if nothing had happened. 'Ah yes. We believe David LeClerc, the leader of the Resistance movement in the Pas-de-Calais has been taken by the Gestapo and is being held in the basement, with one or two of his lieutenants in the Hôtel de Ville in Calais, which is their headquarters.

'We don't know the exact details yet, but it will only be a matter of time before they are broken. It's possible they won't realise that the Resistance have been gathering intelligence on Nazi fortifications and won't take their questioning in that direction. However, we can't take a chance, so we must do something within the next forty-eight hours . . . Now, if the rest of you gentlemen wouldn't mind waiting, I would like the Wing Commander and Squadron Officer to join me outside of the meeting.'

We both knew what the General was going to say to us as we left the room and followed him into the garden. We were correct. He spent the entire time telling us how vital it was for us to go to Calais; my local knowledge would make the whole operation easier for everyone. He finished by assuring us that, although it was a very dangerous mission, no one would be pre-warned we were going, except just one Resistance leader.

'And of course, Squadron Officer,' he finished by saying, 'you would be protected by a captain and six men from the Special Forces.'

Both Winco and I laughed.

'But the entire bloody German Army is over there, sir!' Winco commented.

The General was silent for a few minutes and then resumed his sales pitch from another angle. 'This really is an important thing for your country, for the whole free world, and many innocent lives will be saved if we can rid the area of the Germans, once and for all.' His voice was soft and gently persuasive. I almost imagined he was trying to see me in a pair of nylons, like some pin-up, the way he was behaving.

I suddenly felt a gear shift inside me. It wasn't so much love of England, but a love of France, of those wonderful holidays spent on the beach at Le Touquet.

'Your words, General, will never persuade me, but I want to see a free France. That is very important to me. I'll go, but I would like to speak to my husband before I do.'

'No, I'm sorry, that won't be possible. We will, however, permit you to write a letter . . . We must go back to the others. We have a lot to do,' the General went on, totally businesslike again, now that I had agreed.

We returned to the office where he quickly announced I had agreed to go and also the names of those going with me. Suddenly, Sam commented: 'I want to go, too. My

German is better than anyone's round here and I think I would like to help Alexandra.'

The General had no objection and the two of us were whisked away, with hardly a minute to say our goodbyes and for Winco to wish us the best of luck. I think the worst moment was when we were asked to put our affairs in order and for me to write the letter to William.

This is the letter, Mr White. I'll read it to you. It's very short but it was the most difficult thing I have ever had to write. What it cost me in tears I can never tell.

Darling,

I wanted to see you, but I wasn't allowed to; I wanted to hold you, but I'm not allowed to; I wanted to talk to you, but I wasn't allowed to; so all I have left are my dreams of the moment when our eyes met for that first time, when we kissed for the first time and when we made love for the first time.

If it ends now, I want you to know my life has been fulfilled and that I have loved you since those moments and I'll love you forever.

Alexandra

We were quickly taken to what I presumed were the HQ of the OSS and briefed on what was to take place. We were each given typical French clothing, several hundred French francs, given a short lesson in how to handle a firearm and how to behave if caught. I was even handed, Mr White, a cyanide pill as an alternative to being tortured or worse. The mere fact we would be in civilian clothes would mean that, if we were caught, we would be shot as spies. Sam and I were both given pistols with silencers together with German and French identification papers.

Within twelve hours, we were once more on the *Conqueror* heading towards the French coast. We knew exactly what we had to do: it was simply a matter of going to the rear of 5 rue de la Mer, retrieving the papers and returning as quickly as possible.

We met the rest of the team the moment we arrived on board; they were all members of the American Special Forces and would not be wearing civvies. Security was left to Captain Len Mayerling, but the actual responsibility for obtaining the papers rested jointly with Sam and me, although I was actually senior to him. We would say what we wanted to do and the Captain and his team would suggest the most practicable and military way of making it possible.

Mr White, once more this was like going out to bat. Once you were at the crease and off the mark, your nerves went and you were no longer worried. Here I was at the crease, facing the first ball and there was no time at all to become nervous.

We felt the submarine begin to slowly surface and once again the Captain told the dinghy detail to go forward. We could sense the air of expectancy amongst the crew.

'Good luck, miss!' one of the ratings said to me as I made my way to the foot of the conning tower.

'Thank you. That's nice of you,' I said with a smile.

The boat stopped surfacing for several minutes as the lookouts checked and double-checked before the Captain quietly ordered the boat to surface and the dinghy detail to launch the dinghies. We climbed up the conning tower and onto the casing, making our way towards the dinghies. It had been agreed by the Captain that the *Conqueror* would lie off the rendezvous point between 10 and 11 p.m. each and every day for the next six days.

We were ordered into the three dinghies: Sam and me with the Captain in one and the others in the two remaining. It wasn't very pleasant as there was quite a swell and we had four or five hundred yards to paddle before we reached the shore. I turned round to see the *Conqueror* disappearing beneath the surface and for the first time I felt afraid as I realised we were now on our own.

We all continued to paddle like mad and I was wondering how on earth we were going to be able to land with the swell as it was. The Captain of the *Conqueror* had made contact with the Resistance on land and I was thankful to see him when we actually hit the shore. I was soaking wet and already fed up.

The men had been well briefed, as, the moment we landed at a deserted point near a village called Hardelot, he led us into the nearby woods and then through the fields towards Calais. The dinghies had been well hidden and we had all been issued with weapons, ammunition and equipment. Within about ten minutes we were well on our way. We parted company with our guide after about an hour and then were well and truly on our own. I already began to recognise many of the landmarks and it was now left to me to guide the party to their destination.

It was decided to travel at night and rest up in the daylight. We were approximately fifty miles from Calais and, unless we were unlucky, we had two days to get there and the same to return, leaving two days to find the paperwork.

We walked in total silence with Sam and I frequently exchanging nervous smiles; the Americans were alert to every movement, every sound, ensuring we were alone. We walked at the side of the road, never on it, keeping to the hedgerows in the darkness.

The occasional German truck or car passed with its complement of officers or soldiers en route to some late duty, causing us all to fall to the ground like nine pins hit on a strike. We waited two or three minutes after each vehicle had passed, still in total silence, to ensure the sound of any vehicle didn't mask another coming in either direction. It was longwinded, but the safest thing to do.

A little past midnight we heard another lorry approaching and we all fell to the ground again. Sam broke the silence. 'I've got a plan,' he said to the Captain. And before we could stop him, he ran into the road and began waving. The driver of the lorry braked hard, stopping some ten yards in front of him. The passenger in the lorry got out cautiously, pointing his rifle at Sam.

'I'm Major Franz Metz,' Sam shouted in perfect German. 'I

need to get to Calais urgently. I have some important information. Here are my identity papers. Hurry please; I do not want to be seen on the road.'

The passenger walked closer, still pointing his gun.

'What have you got on the back?' Sam asked.

'A gun crew, sir,' he replied, adding, 'They have just finished their duty and are going to Boulogne.'

'How many are you? Sam asked.

'Six.'

'Six what?' Sam yelled.

'Six men, sir,' the passenger said, pointing the gun away.

'I have another officer with me, Captain Shultz. Come,' Sam said, directing me to stand up. I was shocked as I stood up and walked to the lorry.

He then turned his attention to the passenger. 'Don't ask questions but we need to get to HQ as soon as possible. You get in the back with the others and we'll sit with the driver. Schnell!' he roared.

The passenger scurried to the back, followed by Sam; however, when the covers were pulled back it revealed six other men and two women.

The latter appeared to be French women who were obviously collaborating with the Germans. The soldiers were shocked at being caught with the women in the back.

Sam took his opportunity. '*Raus*!' he shouted. 'All of you get out!' The soldiers got out of the lorry very sheepishly, leaving their weapons inside.

'What is this?' he yelled at them and then shouted to me to bring the driver.

I got the driver back out of the cab and took him to join the others. The moment he had them all out, Sam drew his pistol and aimed it at the driver. 'Now!' he shouted to the rest of our team.

A look of absolute surprise appeared on the faces of the men as the Special Forces officers came out of the bushes. Two of the Germans turned and ran and were shot; the others immediately put their hands up.

The Captain turned to Sam. 'Yep, you have got us transport, but now we've to kill these six people, dispose of the bodies and then get rid of the lorry. Do you appreciate the problems you have caused me? No you bloody don't!' he said quietly.

One of the soldiers could speak some English and knew what his position was and began to plead. He wouldn't tell anybody; he wouldn't do anything. Please let him go.

For me it was terrible. I had been in that position before and I knew what was going through their minds. Two more soldiers made a run for it and were also shot and then the girls started to scream.

'Shoot them!' the Captain ordered. 'Shoot them all!'

'You can't do that! They're unarmed,' I protested.

' Are you bloody stupid? There's a war on. It's kill or be killed,' he said as his men finished them off.

All the bodies were put back into the lorry; the women with their pretty dresses were thrown in last, on top of the men, exposing their legs as they fell. The blood from their wounds was running down their legs like open veins. What had they done to deserve this? They were only collaborating to survive. What else had they got to give the Germans, I was thinking as I got in the lorry and sat there sick to my stomach at what had happened and sitting among the results of what we had done.

We drove on to the outskirts of Calais, with Sam, the Captain and one of his men acting as the driver and the rest of us in the back. I couldn't say a word and every time I looked down and saw the women I wanted to cry. What had they done to deserve it, I kept thinking again and again.

The Captain had seen an area of woodland where it looked safe for us all to hide up for the night. There appeared to be some rundown sheds at the edge of the wood and he ordered the driver off the road and sent two scouts to check out the area. Within a few minutes, it was as expected: the area was clear and we were told to collect our stuff together and make our way as quickly as possible with the two men. Two others were detailed to take the lorry miles away and destroy it. We would wait for them to rejoin us. The orders were if they became separated they should either return to the rendezvous point and wait for us, or find some alternative way back.

The lorry drove away and was soon out of sight as we quickly went into one of the old huts, but as we entered, some of the roof fell in, making a hell of a din. I was worried it would wake up the entire area. The Captain sent one of the men to the outskirts of the wood to reconnoitre the area and also to mount guard as it was on slightly higher ground and therefore had a better view of the surroundings. It was obvious that the area had not been used or even visited for years so at least we all felt pretty safe. Even so we were only allowed to talk in a low voice as sounds carry a long way during the night.

'Look, Sam,' the Captain began, 'in future, before you do anything, we have to discuss it first. I know we're nearer to where we need to be and a day early, but the lorry could have been full of crack troops and the mission would have failed before it got off the ground. As it is, we have nine dead people on our consciences and the possibility that, if they're missed, someone will suspect something's afoot. They may not suspect it's a special operation, but they will think it's the Resistance and there will be reprisals. More dead people! What's more, two of my men are going to have to traipse for miles without any sleep. You need to think and then share your thoughts. This isn't a game!'

Sam nodded. 'Sorry!' he said quietly.

'You weren't to know,' the Captain commented, a little more kindly. 'Now everyone, get some rest. We've a lot to do tomorrow.'

Sleep for the moment was out of the question. I kept worrying and trying to rationalise what we had done and to what degree I was culpable by the mere fact of being there. I could not get the women's faces out of my mind. At least it was quick, I continued thinking; they wouldn't have suffered. But

I knew that of course they would have. I had seen it in their eyes. Even if it was only for a few seconds they would have suffered the most unimaginable terror. My troubled mind was overtired and I eventually drifted off to sleep as rain began to fall. I was woken up in the early hours of the morning by the unexpected return of the two men who had disposed of the lorry.

They reported back to the Captain that they had crashed the lorry into an oncoming personnel carrier killing the driver and had quickly set fire to them both. They were disturbed by a German outrider on a motorbike who stopped to investigate the crash. The moment he got off the bike they shot him too and put his body on the fire. They took the bike and hid it in some shrubs some distance away. The Captain changed the lookout and we drifted back to sleep, feeling a little more relaxed.

Apart from the lookout, we had all managed to keep out of the rain and have some rest, but now it was time to make the appropriate plan of attack. It was decided that we, Sam and myself, would walk into Calais, a journey of at least three miles, and make our way to the rear of rue de la Mer. Hopefully, we would make it there unhindered before the curfew clicked in, which was just before dark. The Americans would, as far as possible be keeping an eye on us.

We set off, allowing ourselves two hours to do the journey, arriving just off the place du Théâtre about thirty minutes before curfew. You couldn't help feeling that everyone had their eyes on you and you couldn't help thinking you were drawing attention to yourself. Was I walking and talking naturally? Did I even look French?

My thoughts were suddenly interrupted by a shrill command: *'Halte! Ihre Papieren, bitte! Schnell!'*

My heart skipped a beat as I turned to see a French police officer and a German soldier. *'Moi, monsieur?'* I replied in French.

'Yes, you!' the German shouted. 'And you!' he snapped

at Sam.

We had been stopped by the police for a routine identification check. Both Sam and I slowly took out our papers and gave them to the German with the French policeman looking us up and down. He began to question us.

'What is our business in Calais?' 'Where do you live?' I nearly died, but after some minor questioning they seemed to be satisfied and we were allowed to go. We made our way to the railway station, where we thought it would be easy to get a cup of coffee at the little café there. As we sat there, the same policeman and German walked in and again asked for our papers.

'But you just checked them!' Sam protested.

'Ihre Papieren, bitte!'

'I'm Major Franz Metz,' Sam whispered to the soldier as he gave him his papers. 'Take me outside now and don't do anything silly or I'll cause you some real problems.'

The soldier nodded. 'You stay there!' he ordered me.

Sam went outside and pretended to be in trouble showing his French papers and his SS Major's I/D which was inside them. He tore into the German for almost blowing his cover.

'Next time you ask me for my papers, I'll have you shot, soldier. Don't salute me.

Now go on back in and check everyone else's papers.'

'Jawohl!' came the sharp reply.

'Idiot!' Sam said as they parted company and returned to me.

We quickly drank our coffee and then scurried along to the rue de la Mer via a maze of little streets and terraces. We had a few minutes to get there to avoid breaking the curfew. Eventually, we found number 5 and with the aid of Sam's knife we let ourselves in. There was no time to waste and we began the search straight away, to catch the last of the fading light. We didn't dare light the lamps as it was impossible to tell when the house was last used and obviously we didn't want to draw attention to ourselves. Soon the light vanished and we gave up our search. We decided to sleep until dawn and lay down on a bed fully clothed.

An hour or two later, we were disturbed by noises downstairs. I nudged Sam as he was sleeping next to me.

'Ssssh!' I said with my hand over his mouth. 'There's someone or something downstairs!' I whispered the moment he woke up.

We both took out our pistols, fitted the silencers and made our way to the top of the stairs, well away from each other in case our weight made the floors creak. I looked over the stairs and in the darkness I could just make out a figure starting to climb the stairs. I quickly retreated into a one of the bedrooms, while Sam stayed put. I could hear my heart beating as I held my breath, not wanting to risk the slightest sound. The intruder was now at the top of the stairs.

'Don't move a muscle!' I heard Sam say in French as he held his gun to the back of the man's head.

Then within split seconds, I heard Sam grimace as he was disarmed and his mouth covered to prevent him screaming. I heard another man begin climbing the stairs and moving quickly. I was terrified and pointed my gun at the area I thought they were in. I was shaking with fear and if the gun had gone off I doubt whether it would have hit anyone.

'It's all clear, Captain.'

It was the Americans!

I groped my way back to the head of the stairs. Suddenly, the clouds uncovered the moon and I saw the Captain and two of his men. The Captain was grinning. Sam looked sheepish.

'Have you found the plans yet?' the Captain asked. 'We got worried.'

'No, it was too dark. We were going to search at first light,' I explained.

'Right, we'll all get some shut eye. By the way Sam, you don't wait till you see an assailant. You shoot and ask questions afterwards. Never mind, you'll learn.'

We woke up at the crack of dawn and straight after eating some of our emergency rations, we began searching the house.

We looked everywhere, but to no avail. Perhaps the enemy had already found them, or they were just too well hidden. Suddenly, we were disturbed by the arrival of a fifth American officer, in fact, the radio operator.

'We've just heard that the two Resistance leaders and A.N. Other, have been taken to the Hôtel Princesse at Boulogne. It's an old hotel which has been taken over by the Military and the Gestapo,' the officer said immediately he entered.

Captain Mayerling thought for a moment. 'If we don't find these papers soon, we will have to think of ways to talk to LeClerc. That, of course, would mean springing him out of jail! Where the hell is the Hôtel Princesse in Boulogne anyway?' the Captain added despairingly, 'and where do we start?'

'It's right on the seafront,' I replied. 'It was very glamorous before the war started. As to where we start, I think we should go there and take a look at what's feasible. That is, if we can't find these papers now.'

'There you are, Sam,' the Captain pointed out in a sardonic tone, 'we've had a discussion and now we'll be setting off to Boulogne immediately. I'm pretty sure we're not going to find these papers unaided. It's probably our only chance to complete the mission.'

The Captain sent his radio operator back to join the others and gave him some coordinates for them to meet us as soon as possible, but in any event before 10 p.m. Sam actually suggested that he and I would be better travelling alone, as we were dressed in civvies and could catch a train as our papers had been good enough so far. The Americans would make their way by whatever means possible.

'OK, we will make contact with you at the station before curfew and if we're not there, you'll have to make your own way back to the rendezvous point,' the Captain concluded. An hour later, Sam and I were at the station booking office.

'*Deux billets pour Boulogne, s'il vous plaît, monsieur. Troisième classe,*' I asked and the thick card-like tickets were handed over.

We had very little time to wait as the Calais to Paris via

Boulogne arrived within minutes. It was actually a wonderful service and we were walking out of Boulogne Station within twenty-five minutes.

'It was the right decision, Sam,' I said in French as we began walking to the seafront, via the town centre, in order to get our bearings.

I knew Boulogne well, as it was the largest town near to Le Touquet and we had often gone on excursions there as well as it being our port of entry. We eventually arrived at the seafront to find that the Hôtel Princesse had been almost fenced off. The beach was hardly a beach at all anymore, owing to the large number of defensive obstacles that had been erected there and no civilian was allowed to use it. However, just in front of the Hôtel Princesse was an area of beach which was still used for its original purpose and only Germans with their wives or their French mistresses were allowed to use it. It was midday when we arrived. There was a gentle breeze blowing and it happened to be the beginning of a three-week spring heat wave, allowing men and women to rush into the sea like lemmings; their giggles and laughter could be heard a hundred yards away.

The Hôtel Princesse seemed impenetrable. We wandered around as inconspicuously as we could, trying to spot a weak spot, but eventually, somewhat disconcerted, it was time for us to go to the station to meet the Captain. We entered the station café chatting in French and sat at a little table pretending to be a couple of newly-weds, all the while thinking how on earth we were to get into the hotel and find out where they were holding the three prisoners. Suddenly, we were interrupted by a German officer.

'Major Metz, I believe,' the officer announced.

We looked up in absolute astonishment as we saw Captain Len Mayerling take his hat off and join us at our table. He could speak fluent German! We didn't like to tell him that he had inadvertently blown our cover to the French people around us, who must have now considered us to be some kind of German agents.

However, soon afterwards the Captain took us to a small hotel, one where we could get an evening meal and as we walked into the reception we were greeted by a little smiling Frenchman, but the moment he saw who he thought he was dealing with, he became very businesslike and the smiles vanished.

'I want you to give my colleagues your best rooms and your best attention and I'll be back in the morning. This is Major Metz and this is Captain Schultz. They have no luggage with them, but they are under my jurisdiction. Do you understand?'

'*Bien sur, monsieur*!' the little man replied.

We had a peaceful night. I detected that the Frenchman was definitely anti-German, and it was here I made my biggest mistake; a mistake which could have put everything in jeopardy.

Captain Mayerling came to collect us as arranged at approximately 10 a.m. and as we paid the account and were about to depart, I could not resist giving the Frenchman a knowing wink. He looked at me curiously for a moment and then smiled.

'*Bonne journée, madame, messieurs,*' he said in a much friendlier tone.

The moment I had winked I realised how dangerous that could have been. I really didn't know where his allegiances lay.

We walked around the Hôtel Princesse trying to find a route in, but still believed it was impossible. Then we all walked to the sea front and spent a few minutes watching the pretty young girls and their officers, some swimming, some paddling and others playing on the beach. It was almost reminiscent of my times at Le Touquet: there were the striped umbrellas and changing tents and even a man selling ice-creams. We were watching all the fun and excitement when our attention was drawn to a somewhat portly German officer who came out of his tent accompanied by his good-time girl. They both ran down the beach, with her screaming and skipping with delight as they jumped into the sea and began to swim out. There was a fair swell and, as the young woman stopped swimming and stood up to her waist in the sea, she was almost covered by the waves each time they came in. The German was showing off and swam right out, only stopping to encourage her to follow him. He continued swimming out and once again stopped and paddled for a while, waving his arm towards his *petite amie*.

'I know a way I can get in!' I said excitedly. 'Next time he waves, I'll pretend his life is in danger. Play it by ear, Sam,' I said hurriedly.

The German swam a little further out and repeated his pleas for his friend to follow him, but she refused and I could see that some of the onlookers were concerned.

'I'm going. Hold my stuff!'

I raced to the entrance to the beach, taking my clothes off as I did so, and the moment I arrived at the security point, I was already down to my knickers and had a simple vest on.

'He's in danger!' I yelled in French. I was followed by Sam in his perfect German who explained to the shocked guard what the situation was as I ran down the beach and dived into the sea, passing the young lady who was on her way back to the beach. The German officer was at least two hundred and fifty yards out, which was stupid if you were not a good swimmer, but in fairness he was competent. I really made a spectacle as everyone was standing up, watching my attempts to 'save' him. I must have looked good as I am a strong swimmer and front-crawled my way to the German, who was a little surprised when he saw me arrive.

'Are you all right, sir,' I asked in German.

'Of course!' he answered pompously. 'Why?'

'I'm so sorry, sir. I saw your arms waving and I thought you were in difficulty. I'm so sorry. I didn't mean to embarrass you,' I said, putting all my newly acquired feminine wiles into play.

He burst out laughing as he gently doggy-paddled.

'Well, *Fräulein*, that was a very courageous gesture and I

appreciate it,' he said, bursting into laughter again.

'What's your name?' he asked as we began to swim gently back to shore.

French, German. French, German? What should it be? I plumped for French. 'Yvette Tessier,' I replied.

'Where did you learn to speak German like that, mademoiselle?' he asked.

'At the Sorbonne, sir,' I replied modestly.

'Well, Miss Tessier, it isn't every day an intelligent and an attractive woman tries to save my life. I want to buy you lunch back at the hotel.'

'That would be very nice, but I'm wearing what I had on and I don't think they will allow a poor soaking-wet French girl into such an establishment,' I said, still trying out my girlish charm.

'Don't worry, mademoiselle, I'll see to that,' he added as we reached the shore.

He got to his feet and suddenly announced, laughing at the top of his voice, in a way only portly German officers could do, 'This little girl tried to save my life!' As I got out of the water, he held my hand up and laughed again as my sea-soaked knickers, and French wartime vest clung to my figure like cellophane. A gallant young officer came rushing to my aid and gave me a large towel to cover myself.

'*Merci, monsieur. C'est gentil*!' I said in my perfect French.

Mr White, I should have been used to it by now, but I actually received a round of applause from the people on the beach. It really made me feel uncomfortable and I once again apologised to the officer. 'I'm really sorry if I have embarrassed you,' I said and turned to go and get my clothes back from Sam, who had gathered them up and now stood waiting for me rather awkwardly.

'Where are you going?' the officer shouted.

'To collect my clothes and get these dry,' I replied.

'No, come with me. I'll organise that for you,' he roared. 'It isn't every day you are saved by an angel.'

'Can my boss bring my clothes please, sir?' I asked.

'Of course he can, my dear,' he replied, signalling the guard to allow Sam through the checkpoint at which Captain Mayerling took the opportunity to slip through as well.

'Wait there!' the officer said, raising his eyebrows and cocking his head. 'And who are you?' Sam twigged instantly.

'Major Metz, sir!' he snapped and clicked his heels, which threw the officer a little.

'Come, *ma belle française*,' the officer said, taking me by the hand and almost pulling me into his tent. There he invited me to take my clothes off, gave me another towel and promised to give me a robe to put on.

'Turn away, please, sir. This isn't fair. You're taking advantage of me!' I said as girlishly as I could. He turned away, but as I was busy drying, he kept taking a peep.

'You're looking,' I said, laughing and he would turn away for a few seconds and we would repeat the exercise. 'I've no dry underwear. I can't get dressed like this.'

'Don't worry! You can come up to my room and I'll get you some new clothes.'

'No, you can't do that. I'll just dry these out and will be on my way. I have a lot of work to do, you know.'

'I'll not hear any more of this nonsense. You will come to my room. I have to repay you somehow. Not many people round here would do that for me.'

'Sir . . .' I paused for a second. 'I don't even know who you are.'

'General von Rettenburg,' he replied, standing up straight, clearly proud of both his rank and pedigree.

'*Enchanté, monsieur*!' I said in French, holding out my hand to shake his. He took it immediately and pulled me towards him. He tried to kiss me but I slipped his grasp. 'Come now, General, you hardly know me and it wouldn't be fair to take advantage of me, would it?' I asked.

The General smiled, showing his teeth. 'Of course not, Miss Tessier. You must put this on!' And with that he gave me his bathing robe.

'Help me on with it, please, sir,' I asked.

He held it out and I slipped it on.

It was far too big for me but at least I must have looked pretty, as it stirred his cockles even more.

He was still wet from the sea and I saw another opportunity to play the coquette.

'General, you're sopping wet. Let me help you,' I said, taking up a fresh towel. I started at his feet and slowly began to rub in between each toe, then the ankle, the calf and the thigh . . .

He was putty in my hands, literally weak at the knees. He got dressed and told me to follow him. As he opened the flap of the beach tent, memories of Alice and me exiting our beach hut in our new costumes came flooding back. I thought I would be mischievous and the moment I made my exit I exclaimed: 'Ta-da', making all present chuckle.

'Follow me, Miss Tessier!' the General said as we left the beach.

On the way we passed the little French girl who had been in the sea with the General; she was a lovely little thing with dark hair and a Mediterranean tan to match, which was covered by a very attractive red-and-black swimsuit. I did feel sorry for her as she did have a living to make, but there again I had a job to do and what is the cost of losing a bit of money against the possibility of saving thousands from tyranny?

'General, will you please give my boss, Major Metz, and his colleague permission to come in and wait for me,' I asked, almost pleading.

'Of course. Werner, give Major Metz and his colleague the appropriate passes and one for Miss Tessier here,' the General ordered.

'Yes, sir!' the Lieutenant replied and proceeded to take Sam and the Captain into the hotel.

I followed the General through the revolving doors, much to the astonishment of all the guests.

'This young lady saved my life!' the General bawled as we

entered, causing all present to clap, including my two colleagues who were now waiting for their passes. The General led the way up the stairs with me trailing behind, barefoot and beautiful in my giant bathrobe.

He led me to his quarters and as he opened the door, I was dumbfounded.

'*Comme c'est belle*!' I exclaimed when I saw the elegance of the rooms. It was sheer opulence.

I ran across the room and jumped onto his bed, lying spread-eagled. The General just stood, staring at me, 'drinking me in' as they say.

'Stop it, General, you're embarrassing me!' I said coyly.

'There's something about you I just can't put my finger on,' the General said a little strangely. My heart skipped a beat, thinking he was worried about my motives.

'What do you mean?' I asked, taking the bull by the horns.

'You have such a mischievous boyish quality and you are very, very beautiful. It's strange. I have only known you a few minutes and already I want you, and what is even stranger, it's not just for sex. I just seem to want you near me.'

'General, we shouldn't be talking like this. You're naughty. You're trying to lead an innocent young lady like me astray,' I said, trying not to let him get too serious.

'I'm not, I'm not!' he said, raising his voice, almost pleading his innocence.

'General . . .' I began but was soon interrupted

'My name is Friedrich . . . Please call me Friedrich.'

'That's a lovely name, Friedrich . . . Now, what about allowing me to get dressed?' I asked, smiling, beginning to tempt him again as I walked over to him, still wrapped up in his robe and slowly gliding over the floor to peck him quickly on the cheek.

He tried to grab me but I was too agile and slipped under his arm.

'General, you have only just met me and we still don't know one another. I can't just sleep with you. What would you think of me and what would my mother say?' I added, making him laugh again.

He asked me my dress size and phoned the reception. He spoke to Werner and within a few minutes we were interrupted by a *couturière,* who brought in a selection of dresses and underwear to try on. The General allowed me to choose one and he chose the other. I must be honest, the German officers seemed to like their women dressed as whores and the dress he chose was just that – whorish – but it was for the cause. It was bright red and trimmed with black, with a long slit up the left leg – very similar colours to that worn by the little girl on the beach. Thank God, William couldn't see me. The other one, which was my choice, was much more tasteful. Friedrich chose all the underwear and silk stockings and when the lady had gone he took great pleasure in dressing me, in the red dress of course.

'Where are your shoes?' he asked gently. I shrugged. The General picked up the phone. 'Werner, order me twenty pairs of shoes suitable for this lady.' Within less than a minute, the hotel porter came up to the room and measured my feet and within fifteen minutes, another lady arrived with a large number of pairs of shoes for me to try. Even William doesn't spoil me like this, I thought, which brought a smile to my face.

'You look beautiful when you smile,' Friedrich said, still unable to take his eyes off me. He bought me three pairs of shoes. It was almost like that day when William had chosen everything for me, though I hated myself for even thinking of the comparison. The woman left us alone and I couldn't just leave things at that, war or no war; he had bought me all these things, so I simply went over to him and kissed him. I knew that would satisfy him and it did. I must admit I felt a little like a French whore, when I saw myself in the long Louis Quinze mirror as I passed it on the landing on my way to a very late lunch with a general; but he liked it and that's all that mattered.

Chapter 19

The General was a gentle man, a bit obsessive in his sexual desires but nonetheless considered a gentleman. He was certainly well mannered and knew how to please a lady. It was obvious he wasn't one of the new generation German officers who were arrogant and rude and thought of nothing but the Third Reich.

During our conversations, it was obvious that he didn't want the war and wished Hitler had sued for peace and left things as they were after they had taken the Sudetenland. He knew he would be shot if he dared say that outside the present company.

We arrived at our table in the dining room, by now the only guests. Like any gentleman, he made sure it was he who pulled the chair out for me, leaving the maître d' with the simple job of handing out the menus.

'No thank you,' I said to him as he handed me one. 'The General will choose for me. I'm sure his choice will be wonderful,' I continued, seeing that I had touched the right spot. This, of course, was one of Madge's tips.

'Now,' the General began, 'I know very little about you. What are you doing with those officers?'

'Really, General! Please don't let us spoil this lovely occasion. Can we talk about it after this lovely meal?'

'Yes of course, my dear,' he replied as he put his hand on mine across the table.

'Are you married?' I asked.

'Not now. My wife was killed in a motor accident just before the English declared war. I felt at that time I had lost everything and I didn't care what happened to me.'

'Usually an officer tells me his wife is dead or divorced because he wants to get into my knickers. Do you want to get into my knickers, General?'

He roared with laughter. 'That's what I like about you! There's an impishness about you. You don't care about authority. You say exactly what you feel. I like you, Miss Tessier,' he said, squeezing my hand.

'General, may I leave the table for a second or two? My boss wants a quick word with me and I am supposed to be working,' I said. I had spotted the Captain signalling me to go to him.

'Of course, my dear!' he said and then loudly called to the maître d' to order another drink while I left the table.

I quickly left and joined the Captain and Sam, who had both subtlety moved out of the General's view.

'Wow, this is what you get up to, is it?' the Captain whispered with a supercilious American drawl.

'I haven't really had time for anything, except get my clothes wet, have I? And *parlez francais ou allemand* unless you want us all to be shot, you bloody idiot. Now hurry, what do you want?' I said angrily.

Sam explained what the situation was. They were holding the three Resistance fighters in the basement but they were going to be moved within the next forty-eight hours to Château d'Aumont, where they would effectively be out of reach. It was therefore essential to do something quickly. They were going to obtain the appropriate transport and release the men from downstairs, but their hotel passes would be running out and they needed them extended.

'Can you help us there?' the Captain asked.

'By that you mean will I use my wiles to get the General to extend them, don't you? Well, I don't really want to do that. I'm not sure I can hold him off much longer . . .'

We were interrupted by the General.

'Now, gentlemen, how long are you going to keep my guest

away from me?' he asked abruptly.

'Not a second more. I've already explained who is the most important and I'm not the one who's going to upset a general!'

He roared with laughter. 'That's what I like about her: she's so straightforward. Like a book. You've got two minutes,' he said as he walked away.

'I'll do my best,' I promised Sam and the Captain. 'I'll keep the General happy. You get on with your rescue!'

I quickly returned to the table to see my date pouring another large glass of wine.

'You shouldn't drink too much. It's not good for you,' I scolded as I rejoined him at the table.

'You sound like my wife!' he remarked, as he once again held my hand over the table, squeezing it gently, and then simply stared at me without another word being spoken for several minutes.

'You know I do like you, Miss Tessier!'

'I know they're lovely but you're not getting into them,' I said, beginning to laugh.

'What?' he asked.

'My new knickers,' I replied, now laughing uncontrollably and he too couldn't stop laughing.

Eventually, we left the table and returned to his suite. We walked slowly up the stairs and as we did so I linked my arm in his, which made him feel even better.

'Thank you for a wonderful meal. It was very kind of you, but I suppose I really must go. Can I keep the clothes? It's so hard to find clothes these days, let alone pay for them!' I said sadly as though I really wanted him to ask me to stay.

'Would you at least have dinner with me tonight then?' he asked as we reached the door to his room.

'How could I refuse another wonderful meal like that?' I replied.

'No, I want you to come because it's me, not the meal.'

'Of course I'll come. I would love to and it will be for you and not the food. But it's nearly that time already. Wouldn't you like to go for a walk?' I asked. 'Along the front?'

'My dear, it's not the place it was. But yes I would love to,' the General replied.

'Will you order me to stay? I know my boss is scared of you so at least I'd then have the excuse not to work.'

'Now, young lady, you can tell me what you do,' he asked as we stepped into his room.

'My parents were arrested because my brother was fighting with the Resistance. They're being kept alive on the promise that I help capture enemies of your country. I'm not very good at the job,' I said, looking at him somewhat defenceless.

'Don't say any more. We're all in the same boat.' He changed the subject immediately 'We will have this walk and then dinner tonight. That's settled.'

'Wonderful!' I replied as I got onto the bed, lay down and sighed. 'Wouldn't it be nice if this was all a dream and we could sunbathe on the beach, enjoying ourselves instead of bombing our neighbours over there?'

Friedrich lay down on the bed next to me. I leaned over and rested my head on his fat stomach and said, 'If you were married to me, I wouldn't let you have that!' I prodded him.

He sniggered and said quietly, 'I wish I was!'

Mr White, I don't want you to think I led every man I met up the garden path. I didn't. The men I met and became quite fond of, I know they fell in love with me and it was the case with Friedrich. I really didn't want to hurt him and maybe in another life I could have felt something for him, but now I hated having to do my job and I vowed if I could do things without hurting him I would.

I changed into my new non-whorish dress, again with the able assistance of the General and then once again stepped down the stairs, arm in arm. I was beginning to see the look some of the soldiers were giving me. I could almost hear them saying: 'Oh she's just another of the French whores out for what she can get!' But I knew the reality of the situation and that was good enough for me.

'Just one moment, my dear,' he said as he left me in the foyer and went into a nearby room. I waited for a few minutes and, pretending to become inpatient, went to the room and knocked.

'Is the General here?' I asked.

'No, mademoiselle,' the officer replied. 'Shall I get him for you?'

'Oh, there's no need. I'm sure he won't be long,' I replied, but in those few seconds I had seen enough. It was the entire defence structure along the Channel coast to almost the port of Dieppe. I wished I had that little Leika camera with me then!

It was another fifteen minutes or so before Friedrich rejoined me, full of apologies for his rudeness, and took me out onto the front.

'Where are you from originally?' Friedrich asked as we began our stroll.

'I've lived all over the north of France, but mainly in Le Touquet. I knew this town before the war started and I haven't been near it since, until I met you,' I replied.

'I too used to visit Le Touquet. It was very fashionable in the twenties,' Friedrich remarked.

'But it's all so horrid now! Let's not go any further,' I implored, as I invited him to sit down on a wooden bench. We sat down just out of view and I began to feel quite sorry that I was betraying him. I turned round and lay with my head across his lap and almost dosed off as he caressed my hair.

We must have sat in total silence for at least half an hour before the peace was shattered by an air-raid siren blasting out, followed immediately by a sortie of attacking Spitfires. The Germans returned their fire. In one awful moment, I wondered whether my dear husband could be up there among them, though of course it was impossible. But there were men just like him, of course. Thank God none of them were hit, I thought.

Friedrich said we had to get back for reports on the damage.

'That was a lovely interlude. Thank you, Friedrich,' I said genuinely.

'I wish we could do it again.' He leaned over and kissed me. I held back, which made him stop and look at me, as if to ask, 'Don't you like me then?'

'Come here!' I said, grabbing him around the neck and pulling him into me. We kissed for a good five minutes and as a result he had to rush back to survey the damage.

'I'll see you for dinner. Be here at seven o'clock.'

'How can I get back in?' I asked.

'Sort it out with Werner. He'll organise things!' he shouted back to me and within a second or two he was away.

I went back into the hotel and sat in the foyer watching a succession of German officers go in and out until I saw Werner and was able to get three more passes for the next three days. I confessed to Werner that I really liked the General, but I would have to leave soon as I would be in trouble.' He smiled at me. 'He's a good man, Miss Tessier. I wish we had more like him. We wouldn't be in this mess,' he said quietly.

'Werner, don't say that! It could get you into trouble and I would hate that,' I whispered.

'Thank you, Miss Tessier,' he said, handing me the passes.

I thanked him, left the hotel and went in search of my colleagues. I was wearing my new green dress and shoes and felt like a million dollars until I saw the looks I was getting from the indigenous population. They knew how and where I had got them, or thought they knew. I walked into the station in the hope of seeing Sam and the Captain there and was stopped on a routine papers check.

'I'm General Rettenburg's friend,' I replied in French, handing him my pass.

'Until the next one!' the officer retorted and guffawed.

'How dare you talk to me like that? Do you want to tell him that, Officer? I'm sure he won't like it and I know who would be off to the Russian front then. What's your number?' I was genuinely annoyed at this lack of respect for the General.

'I'm very sorry. It will not happen again,' the soldier replied.

'I know it won't,' I said, almost shouting as I went storming out of the station.

I spent at least two hours looking for Sam and it was almost time to go back when I saw the two of them making their way back to the Princess.

'Alex, you look lovely!' Sam remarked as we stopped to talk.

'Thank you, darling,' I said humorously. 'But you should see the looks I've been getting from the locals. They all know who I've been working for!'

'Well, it won't be for long,' he remarked as we talked for several minutes while they outlined their plan of action for the following day.

It was well known that everywhere the General went, his entourage went with him and, in consequence, the Captain gave me strict instructions to keep him occupied and to make sure he wasn't in the foyer or the basement area of the hotel between eleven and twelve o'clock tomorrow morning. It was an ingenious and audacious plan. Sam was to go with the Captain, who would be accompanied by five 'SS officers', and arrest the officer in charge of the basement for treason. At the same time they would release the three Resistance fighters and advise the officers of the watch they were being taken to Château d'Aumont, together with the officer in charge, where he would get the same treatment. It was hoped that this wouldn't cause too many suspicions, as they were due to be sent there in any event.

Château D'Aumont, incidentally, Mr White, had become a prison for all the enemies of the Reich. Prisoners were often tortured to death, or simply executed, and those that were allowed to survive were sent to one of the death camps.

We continued our way to the hotel and I gave them their passes, which made matters much easier. I told them about the room with the plans and model in it. 'I may be able to get a look at it,' I said.

'Alex, be careful! You're in the viper's nest there, you know,' Sam remarked. 'If things go wrong tomorrow make your own way back to the rendezvous point and I'll hope to see you in

Blighty.'

We parted company and I returned to the hotel. Friedrich hadn't arrived back and I was told to remain in the foyer until he did so. I sat waiting for a while and had the chance to really look at the place.

The hotel itself was divided into various sections: the ground floor was the kitchens and dining areas; the basement was under the control of the Gestapo; and the first and second floors were the accommodation areas for the very senior officers. All the upper floors were administration. The decoration still retained the glamour of the hotel's halcyon days, but was now badly in need of a coat of paint to freshen it up.

'Why didn't you go up, my lovely?' Friedrich asked the moment he arrived.

'Your security wouldn't let me into your room on my own. It's the right thing to do. We do not want you getting into trouble, do we?' I said jokingly and looked obviously pleased to see him.

'Let her have the key in future!' he said, addressing the clerk.

'Yes, sir!'

We went up to the room and he flopped in a chair, almost exhausted, 'Come here,' he ordered. I went across to him and sat on his lap. 'You know, you're not like the other . . .'

'Sssssh!' I said, putting my finger across his lips to stop him talking. 'It can't last so let us make the most of what is a lovely thing, which I didn't think could happen.'

'Will you stay with me tonight?' he asked, almost pleading.

'Yes I will, but I won't make love to you,' I answered. 'I don't really think you would want that anyway.'

'I don't care. I just want you with me tonight.'

'What do you want me to wear, the red one again?'

'No!' he replied as he handed me a box with the most glorious blue gown I had ever seen. 'I want you to wear this tonight. It's yours for being just you.'

I couldn't believe it; it was beautiful. I felt like a spoiled child and for the next few minutes I must have behaved like one. I had seldom had such kindness from anyone, especially someone who did not want something in return.

'I'm taking you to an officers' ball, at what was the Hôtel de Ville. They are having a special meal to celebrate the third year of the Occupation.'

'I can't really do that, can I?' I asked.

'No, but you can enjoy the dinner and the dance. Can you dance?' he asked.

'A little but not very well,' I replied modestly.

'Well, we'll see,' he replied as we began to get ready.

A little later I had poured myself into the beautiful blue gown.

'Do me up, please,' I called out.

He came over to fasten the back of my dress, kissing my neck at the same time, sending tingles down my back. In a way, Mr White, I had fallen a little in love with my portly General. He was protective and kind, like a father.

The General was the most senior officer at the ball and when we arrived you would have thought he was royalty, such was the fuss and fanfare. I was without doubt the centre of attention and looked good to boot. It was a wonderful meal and again I felt really guilty, as my compatriots over the Channel were going short. I felt sick at heart as speaker after speaker condemned my country and its leadership, portraying Churchill as a drunkard and a lunatic, but again I sensed that some of the older officers didn't want to get involved with all that; some, I believed, actually respected Churchill – after all, he had been a soldier and a brave one at that. Suddenly, the strangeness of the whole situation struck me. Here I was, a young Englishwoman at the centre of this wonderful dinner celebration! I doubted whether they had a German spy at Churchill's table.

At last the meal and speeches ended and the General was invited to start the music and dancing.

'Don't worry! You'll be all right,' he said, gripping my hands and leading me onto the dance floor.

He quickly showed his astonishment. 'Where did you learn

to dance?' he asked.

'The Sorbonne, General,' I replied.

'And I suppose you learned to swim there too!'

'Yes, General,' I replied.

No one else dared join us on the floor; they were too much in awe of the General and his partner, and then, without warning, he suddenly stopped dancing and raised his hand to stop the music.

'*Meine Damen und Herren* . . .' He paused for a moment. 'This morning, this young lady dived into the sea, thinking I was in trouble. She swam out two hundred metres to rescue me. I find that extraordinary and that is why she is my guest tonight.'

The hall erupted into applause and cheers and I nodded my thanks and appreciation. The official photographer took a series of pictures of me and Friedrich, after which I was allowed to dance with other officers.

We eventually returned to his suite about 2 a.m. and quickly went to bed. Friedrich was embarrassed and stayed in the bathroom for a long time. He came out to find me sitting up in his bed.

'Come on, get in, it's late,' I said, persuading him to get into bed, which he did reluctantly. He climbed in and lay on his side and I snuggled into his back. 'Thank you for a wonderful day. I'll never forget it. Thank you!'

We were both shattered and were soon asleep.

The following morning we were still in the same position when Friedrich was woken by a knock on the door.

'*Ein Minuten, bitte*!' he shouted and rushed out to stop his aide-de-camp from entering. He had come to give him early-morning damage reports as there had been another massive bombing raid on Dunkirk and he was required to go there quickly.

'I'm sorry, my dear, I'll have to go. I'll see you when I get back.'

He was dressed and away within twenty minutes. He kissed me goodbye and whispered in my ear. 'I'm sorry, *Fräulein*, but

I'm in love with you!'

I too got dressed quickly, packed all my new clothes into a bag, dressed in my now dry old clothes and went down to breakfast.

Sam was waiting in the foyer for me and joined me.

I kept my voice low in order not to create suspicion and told Sam that the General had been rushed to Dunkirk to inspect the bombing damage. Well done, William, I thought, laughing.

'I don't know when he will be coming back. It could be some time from what he was intimating. You must tell the Captain. It should work in our favour.'

'I'll do that,' Sam replied.

We finished our breakfast and I charged it to the General's room. I must admit, I didn't like all the different sausages but the eggs and bacon and particularly the fresh baguettes were wonderful. It had been years since I had smelled a freshly baked baguette and just to break it into two brought back all those lovely memories.

Sam continued, informing me what he wanted me to do. 'It's going to happen this morning at eleven thirty precisely. Hopefully, your General won't be back, but I want you to get to Calais station and into the café there no later than four. There may be hell to play and it will be safer if you are away from Boulogne. If we're not there by four fifteen you must make your way to the rendezvous point on your own.'

I couldn't leave the hotel knowing that Sam would be in danger so I hung around in the foyer reading whatever I was able to get my hands on, which included the battle reports on how well the Germans were doing and how badly we were doing. If you had believed it, it would have been very depressing. At eleven thirty prompt, Sam, together with the Captain and his five 'SS officers', marched into the hotel and told the reception what they were doing and then hurried down to the basement. I couldn't believe Sam. He was wonderful, full of such power and command. Even I was terrified at his presence. There was a deathly silence in the place as they all listened intently to what Sam was commanding and then he shouted, as only a senior SS or Gestapo would do, for *everyone to mind their own business and carry on as normal,* at which they all did.

I know for one split second he disapproved of my presence, as I saw it in his eyes when they all had to troop past me on their way down to the basement. At that moment, I decided that I would cover their backs and keep watch and in that respect it was a good job I did as they had only been gone four or five minutes when I saw one of the other Gestapo duty officers arriving at the door of the hotel. I knew I couldn't intercept him as it might cause suspicion, so I allowed him to pass and when I thought the way was clear and no one was watching, I followed him at a discreet distance. I could hear some sort of commotion as I got nearer and nearer and I heard Sam shouting at him to mind his own business, but the officer didn't seem convinced.

'I want to see the authorisation from d'Aumont and your papers before I allow you to take them. And where is Liebsch?' he demanded.

'He's an enemy of the state and is also being taken to d'Aumont,' Sam replied. Even I wasn't convinced by the way Sam had dealt with it.

'I want your papers!' the officer shouted.

I had to do something and continued slowly down the stairs. I could hear Sam telling the Captain to go and get the papers, but the officer wouldn't allow him to leave, so I presumed he had a gun pointing at them. The carpet on the stairs ended. I deposited my shoes and stepped onto the marble, proceeding barefoot to prevent the clatter from my shoes giving me away.

I quickened my pace as I made my way towards the noise and heard the officer telling them not to move until he had phoned d'Aumont to get confirmation. The noise got louder and I was sure they were in the end room. My heart was pumping as I was almost there. I could hear the officer pick up the phone and bang down the bar several times to urge the operator to answer quickly. I could now see him. He was pointing a gun straight at Sam and I had nothing to attack him with. Distraction was the only thing I had in my armoury as I had given my pistol to Sam the previous day to prevent it being found on me in the hotel.

'Herr Liebsch!' I called out as I approached. 'Herr Liebsch!' I called again as I was almost at the door. I walked in.

The Gestapo officer turned for a split second, but that was enough; he was shot through the head by one of the men. Sam picked up the phone and told the operator to forget it as he would call later.

'Well done, Alex,' he whispered. 'Now get out of here as fast as you can and get to the station, or anywhere away from here. See you as agreed.'

'Bye!' I whispered back as I quickly left the basement, collecting my shoes on the way and returning upstairs to where I had left my bag with my pass and newly acquired clothes. I walked over to my seat, but I had been seen returning from the basement by the reception officer. Attack is the best form of defence, so I immediately went over to the reception officer and said, 'There are terrible screams coming from the basement. I think you should go and do something. Someone may be in trouble.'

I could see the relief on his face as he said, 'Don't worry, mademoiselle, that is nothing to do with you or me. It's best if we just ignore it.'

'Are you sure?' I asked with an element of concern in my voice.

'Yes I am. You go back to what you were doing and everything will be fine,' the officer replied and carried on with his work as though nothing had happened.

I thought it was safer for me to go and I decided to leave the hotel. Apparently, Sam and the others had no further hitches as they calmly walked out of the hotel with the Resistance leaders, handcuffed together, almost unable to walk. Liebsch, the Gestapo officer, was simply dragged out by his feet. 'This is what happens when you become an enemy of the Third Reich,' Sam shouted as he went through the lobby – a rather theatrical note, I thought. They put their 'prisoners' into the truck, which I noticed on leaving the place was being guarded by one of the American team in full SS uniform.

In fact, Mr White, I never did find out where they got all the uniforms from and at the time there was so much going on that I didn't think to ask.

I made my way slowly to the station via the shops and the odd café. The pass Werner gave me was worth its weight in gold, as I had been stopped several times, for routine checks, particularly as I was a woman on her own. But when I said I was a friend of General Rettenburg, staying at the Princesse, I was left alone.

I took the train to Calais and again spent several hours wandering around what was left of the town before returning to the station café. I tried to look casual, just looking around at everything and everyone, but after an hour of this my worry must have shown itself on my face. I was just convincing myself it would be better to make my own way to the rendezvous point when in walked Sam over an hour late and I could tell he was furious.

'What's the matter?' I asked hurriedly.

'Come on, I'll tell you outside,' he replied.

We left the café and he immediately blurted out the problem. 'The stupid bloody Yanks have kidnapped a German officer, shot his driver and stolen his car and now all hell has been let loose and they're closing everything off. Talk about me doing idiotic things! We've got to go quickly, so hurry! Two of the Yanks are with me. We're meeting the Captain and the rest at four in the morning,' he said as he took me by the arm. 'Look, take this back,' he said, giving me back my gun which I put inside my sweater.

'Look, there's the car!' he said suddenly, pointing down a

quiet side street.

I got into the back with Sam next to one of the Americans. I couldn't believe my eyes.

'What's this? For God's sake!'

At the front of the car was Friedrich. He was bleeding badly and his face was bruised terribly.

'Oh my God, what have you done, you bastards?'

'We're at war,' one of the Yanks said as we drove off to the rendezvous point.

They had held up the General's car, shot his driver and stolen the car, with the General still in it. They had beaten him up until he was almost unrecognisable; they had sat him in the front seat next to the driver and supported him upright by tying chicken wire around his neck, which was being held by the American in the back seat. His hands were also tied up behind him. He tried to turn to look at me but the wire and the American prevented him moving.

Sam could see I was becoming angry and was trying to calm me down. The car sped off into the country, trying to avoid any possible routes where there could be road blocks, with me becoming more and more angry and disgusted at what was happening. I wasn't going to take any chances with Friedrich's life and suddenly I drew my gun and put it to the head of the driver.

'Stop the car!' I ordered, 'or I'll blow your head off.'

'Are you fuckin' daft,' the Yank replied. I clicked the gun and repeated my order.

'Stop the bloody car!'

He refused, so I fired one right through the side window. 'The next one is through your head,' I repeated.

He stopped the car. Then turning to the other American I ordered, 'Let go of that wire or I'll kill him and then you,' I said, putting another bullet almost in the other man's ear. 'Now get out! Sam, put your gun to that man's head and if he moves, kill him and that's an order.'

I got out of the car with the Yank, making sure he could feel the gun, while Sam held the gun at the driver's head.

'Now, you bastard, give me your gun!' And to make sure he did, I shot one round within a centimetre of his toe. He handed me his weapon. 'Now help the General out and put him on the back seat.' He struggled, as the General was no lightweight, but managed eventually. 'Now you get in the front and sit away from the driver. Sam, take the driver's weapon off him. It's your bloody fault that we're in this mess. You had to be bloody clever and steal a General's car and bring the entire German Army down on us.

'You've got no bloody brains. Now you drive on and dump the car and I hope for your sakes that we're not attacked by the Germans.'

I paused for a few minutes while we continued in total silence and I just looked at poor Friedrich and his injuries. 'Sam, do not take your eyes off them and I'll try to tend to the General.'

Friedrich was in a bad way and I really tried to help him with what limited means I had, even tearing a strip off the red dress to help dress the wounds, which I thought made him smile.

I couldn't untie his hands for obvious reasons, but I did try to make him feel comfortable.

'I'll kill you for this, you fucking little bitch,' the Yank snarled at me.

'Don't be a silly little boy,' I replied in a patronising manner, which made him even more annoyed.

It was no use: there were road blocks everywhere; it was as though there was a blanket over the whole region and we were now forced to abandon the car. Our only chance as far as I could see was to head for the coast and travel along the shoreline past Cap Gris Nez and then past the village of Wimereux, turning immediately inland through the forest areas.

We stopped the car and I ordered the Yank to take it away and destroy it, following which I would meet him around the shore area of Cap Gris Nez in three hours. If we were not there he must make his own way back. We would only wait until eleven p.m. and it was already eight now and getting dark.

I had set myself an impossible task: one, the Yank wouldn't help Friedrich and wanted to kill him; two, we had to cover some very open terrain with an injured man and, three, time could easily run out. While the journey was only a few miles, the area was swarming with the enemy and we wouldn't be able to travel during the daylight hours.

I felt like a traitor when I whispered to Friedrich, 'Don't worry, I'll see you are all right.'

I wasn't going to allow cruelty of any description, whoever was on the other end of it.

Mr White, I hope you understand; I had been the underdog for years, I had been treated cruelly for no other reason than I was different and now I had grown up and I seemed to have made it my business to ensure no one else was treated that way. I know Friedrich was the enemy, but he deserved proper treatment and behaviour. It wasn't that I wanted to help the enemy; I just wanted us to be fair. It all probably sounds a little naïve, doesn't it?

I waited about an hour before we set off to the beach, with Sam and I supporting Friedrich and the Yank almost enjoying the difficulty we were in, especially when the General stumbled, bringing us both down with him. We had managed about a mile when we stumbled again, causing the Yank once more to laugh and then to tell us he was leaving as he wasn't going to put his life on the line for a 'bloody Kraut'. He made to go.

'Look, you bastard. Get one thing straight. If you leave us, that's desertion, for which you would be shot. I'll tell you what I want you to do. I want you to help support the General and we will take him to England with us. If you don't, I'll shoot you! I swear.' I took my gun out with the silencer already fastened onto it and once again fired at his feet, just missing. 'Next time, I'll aim at a bigger target, your arse, and I won't miss that.'

The Yank thought for a moment. 'Gag him and I'll support him.'

'OK. Do it but hurry up. We need to go!' I said, watching the sadistic bastard enjoying hurting his captive.

'Would you like the Germans to treat the Americans like this?'

No of course not, but they're the enemy. We're the good guys,' he replied in his irritating drawl.

'Well, think about it. Don't do it to them. Good guys don't do things like that,' I added, knowing I was wasting my time even talking to him.

We were in luck: it became very dark and heavy rain began to fall as we set off for the beach. It had taken us about two hours to cover the half mile, taking cover at the slightest movement or noise.

Chapter 20

On arriving at the shore, we took cover under the cliffs with the intention of resting for a few minutes. However, our driver was already there and waiting further along.

'Do you want to tell the whole fuckin' world you're here?' he asked, whispering sarcastically. 'I heard you coming a mile off. I'll tell you something, Missy,' he continued, trying to put me down in front of the others and then proceeding to tell us what he had seen on his way there. 'I have just seen the biggest set of guns imaginable. They would blow ships out of the water at Pompey let alone Dover. It's a fuckin' huge battery and a mass of concrete. It'll withstand any thing we've got.'

This, Mr White, we found out later was a new battery and part of Hitler's Atlantic Wall. It was named after its designer and called Battery Todt and was certainly effective as it could hit Dover and other nearby coastal towns and often did. The most important aspect of these batteries was that they could blow even the biggest of our ships out of the water, but I'll come to that later.

I was fed up with the attitude of the Americans. 'We haven't got time to talk; let's crack on. We can't take any chances, can we? Just make a mental note when and where and what you saw,' I remarked as we picked up our stuff and began to set off for Wimereux. 'You help him with the General and we'll make better time,' I added.

We did make good time and, in spite of the obstacles, reached the outskirts of Wimereux by 2 a.m. taking a thirty-minute rest before turning inland and into the woods to meet our colleagues at the agreed map reference. We had no food but plenty of water and even now the Yank refused to share any of his with Friedrich.

However, both Sam and I made sure he was all right. I know Friedrich would have alerted his troops if given the chance – he was that sort of soldier – and the American was right to gag him, especially as we were in the midst of an enormous defensive garrison and as we went along, we were all noting the cliff batteries with their big guns and all the ground positions.

To our horror we found the woods were also crawling with German mobile patrols, so it was a nightmare keeping to the schedule.

After dodging various patrols we at last arrived at the meeting point. The rest of the team and the Resistance fighters had successfully returned to Calais, collected the information and made their way to the rendezvous via Eperlecques, having seen the extent of the V1 and V2 experimental missile base. They had also discovered the fact that much of the building work was being done at night. It was now absolutely essential we got back to report. We reported on our sorry affair, and, although the Captain seemed as angry as I was about the soldiers' actions, he requested me to give them back their guns.

We had only two hours of darkness left before it would be impossible to travel further and now we had the injured Resistance fighters to contend with. We managed to get near to the Forêt de Boulogne before dawn and then had to bed down for at least twelve hours before making any further moves. I hadn't noticed the rain until I stopped moving when the cold and wet began to sink into my skin. I was frozen, but I couldn't let Friedrich suffer and took his gag off to give him a drink of water.

'Mademoiselle, I'll never forget you, as long as I live. Thank you!' he whispered as I gave him a drink of water and some chocolate.

'What's the Kraut saying?' my favourite American asked.

'He's just thanking me. Even he has more manners than you,' I said, regretting the "even he" as though Friedrich was some third-class citizen.

The Yank crawled over and replaced the gag in Friedrich mouth, adding: 'We can't have you two lovebirds fraternising now, can we?' before returning to his position.

We each took our turn on watch, two at a time in two-hour stints, while the rest of us tried to get some sleep. I must admit I found it difficult as I was sure in my mind the Yank would slit Friedrich's throat and I was determined not to let it happen. He did make gestures with his knife and then simply laughed; it was unnerving but nothing happened. Almost the entire day was spent in silence. I spent it thinking of better times, when I was in France almost on the same spot for my holidays and my days on the cricket field; at least it passed the time until the Captain shared out all the ammunition and gave the order to move out.

We had successfully crossed through the Forêt de Boulogne, making our way towards Hardelot and our pick-up point. En route we had to cross a large tidal inlet and of course the tide was in, so it was necessary to backtrack and cross via a bridge on a narrow road which led to Desvres, a small village about five miles away. It was a high-risk strategy, but one which had no alternative. We made our way due east, with two of us in turn helping the General and the Resistance fighters to move as quickly as possible. It was a nightmare of a journey as the injured seemed to become heavier and heavier, with me volunteering to carry Friedrich, when there was any dissent amongst us. I felt worn out when we eventually hit the road and began to make our way towards Desvres and the crossing point.

Three of us, me, Sam and an American, had successfully crossed the bridge, together with the General, and were waiting for the others. The bridge itself was positioned just after a sharp bend in the road, the other end of which was concealed by the forest. Foolishly, perhaps, we hadn't posted lookouts to check on traffic movements. The fourth man was beginning to cross when we all heard vehicles approaching. It was a terrifying noise as the engines of the personnel carriers had a distinct high-pitched whining sound, which could normally be heard a long way away, but the trees had masked the noise. We could also hear the sound of other vehicles approaching, but had no idea how far away they were.

The American immediately turned back and caught his pack in the balustrade of the bridge. The more he pulled at it, the more it became stuck.

'Come on!' The Captain yelled at him, but it was no good he was stuck. 'Take it off and leave it and get out of sight!' he ordered.

The American slipped off his pack and dived back under cover, just in time, as two German vehicles arrived around the corner. There were just two of them, an armoured car as expected and a covered lorry. They passed us, but it was obvious they had seen the pack on the bridge, as the front vehicle slowed down and both eventually stopped a few yards on. An officer got out of the car and walked over to the bridge to inspect the pack and, although we were out of the way, I could sense what the others were going through. We all lay absolutely motionless as we watched the officer walk towards the Americans' position.

He stopped and shouted some orders, which I didn't catch as my heart was beating so loudly. The result of that order was that six soldiers got out of the truck, while two remained inside, pulling back the covers to reveal a heavy machine gun. My heart sank.

I knew if the machine gun opened up we wouldn't stand a chance and so did the Captain, who instantly gave the order to fire. The Americans unleashed a tremendous fire fight with great courage and the machine gun, too, opened up and was ripping everywhere. I asked the American next to me to give me cover as I was going to try and put the machine gun out of action.

'No!' he shouted over the noise.

'Just cover me!' I shouted as I pulled the pin out of a grenade. 'I'm going over there.' I kneeled as though I was in the starting blocks and began to talk myself into going. 'Come on! Come on! They're running for two.'

I stood up and ran across the road flat out, flinging the grenade as I went with pinpoint accuracy into the back of the lorry.

I didn't see the result as I dived for cover on the other side of the road. But I did hear the result: the explosions were enormous as several packs of ammunition, too, were set off. Success! The machine gun and its operators were out of action. It wasn't long before the Americans had finished off the rest of the Germans.

We didn't have long; the explosions would soon attract more enemy personnel. The rest of the group made their way warily across the bridge and revealed that we had sustained two serious injuries. We now had three walking wounded Resistance fighters, two seriously injured Americans and, of course, the General. The first three had sufficiently recovered to act at lookouts while the others carried the Americans and I helped Friedrich, much to the annoyance of my favourite American. We were, I can tell you, a ragbag party.

We left the area as quickly as we could, with the sole purpose of reaching Hardelot and the beach before dawn; we knew there would be a chance the submarine would be there waiting for our signal and we all knew we had to clear the forest area quickly, as this would be extensively searched at dawn when the vehicles were discovered.

I was struggling with the General and beginning to hold the group back when the Yank called out, 'Drop the fucker, or do you fancy him that much you can't let go?'

I ignored the remark and carried on, but it was beginning to be a problem and the Captain ordered the Yank to help me. I would have preferred Sam, but he was helping the others.

The Yank came over and began to take the weight of the

General and deliberately slipped, dropping him to the floor. He began kicking him and yelling, 'Get up, yer fat bastard!'

I took my gun out and pointed it again at his head. 'Touch him again and you are dead and I mean it. Captain, take him away from here or I'll kill him now.'

'I'll have you for that, you stupid bitch,' the Yank snarled, as he was told to go and change places with his colleague.

'Look, sonny, I have eaten little boys like you for breakfast,' I said, trying to act harder than I was. 'Now get on with your job. We can sort our differences when we get back to England. But let me tell you: if you touch that man again, I'll kill you. Do you understand? You vicious little bastard. Now that goes for you all. He is my prisoner of war and if any of you break the Geneva Convention, you'll face a war crimes investigation. Do you understand?' I shouted.

'Do you?' I shouted again as there was no reply.

'Yes, ma'am.'

'OK, OK, but please keep your voice down!' Captain Mayerling whispered loudly.

Friedrich was now in a worse state, but I could tell he knew I was doing my best for him and that I wasn't going to let him down. We were still obliged to have his hands tied behind his back and his mouth gagged, but at least he was a little more comfortable.

We got within a hundred yards or so of the beach when one of the seriously injured Americans took a turn for the worse and my helper had to leave me alone with the General. We were all worn out but the General could now hardly walk and was a dead weight.

'Now you've got a big mouth! You try and carry him now,' the Yank said sarcastically.

I was determined to show the pig I wasn't beaten and told Sam to carry the supplies and my pack with the paper shopping bag tied to it. 'That is very important,' I said, pointing to the paper bag. I saw Friedrich smiling. He must have realised they were the presents he had given me.

The Yanks were looking at me with some scepticism as Sam helped me to put the General over my shoulder in the fireman's lift. My legs almost gave way on several occasions but I managed to carry him the hundred yards to the beach, much to the disgust of the poisonous Yank. We all stopped about twenty to thirty yards away from the shore while the Captain, who was beginning to lose control over his men, sent two of them to scout the beach for potential problems.

We struggled on in the dark with our injured and made our way to the dinghies, which were undisturbed and ready to use. The two seriously injured Americans were placed in the dinghies, ready to be pulled and floated into the sea and the Captain and three of his men would be going with them. The third dinghy had the three Resistance fighters, the remaining American and Sam. I elected to stay behind with the General and wait for the return dinghy. The problem was there had been no sign of the *Conqueror*, despite an hour of intermittent signalling.

'Where's that damn sub?' the Captain said again and again. He was becoming more and more stressed as one of the seriously injured Americans became delirious and noisy. 'Shut the fuck up!' he whispered loudly. 'Do you want everyone to hear us? Just keep him quiet.' He was becoming very nervous and jittery. Then to his relief he received a return signal from the *Conqueror* and he became calm again.

'Get the dinghies into the sea and start paddling out to the signal; there will only be one flash at random so keep your eyes peeled and hurry. We've only got twenty minutes before dawn breaks. Alex, we'll be back as quick as we can!' he said as the others dinghies were already on the way. It was a totally dark night and, although there was a hint of rain in the air, it had so far kept off, though I suppose it didn't really matter as we were all wet and filthy from our adventure anyway. There was one worrying factor: a stiffening breeze had blown up, causing the dinghies to struggle a little, as they made their way towards the sub.

I was left on the shore with Friedrich and I could no longer see him in this state anymore so I took his gag off; I don't know why but I knew now it was just me and him; he wouldn't shout for help.

'Friedrich, I'm sorry. I wouldn't have had this happen for the world and I promise you I'll not allow anything to happen to you.' I kissed him on his forehead and as I stroked his head, he whispered, 'Don't worry. It's the war. There's no sense in any of it!'

The dinghies arrived at the *Conqueror* and began to offload the Resistance fighters and the others into it. In spite of the imminent dawn, it was several minutes before a dinghy returned to pick us up and of course it had to be that Yank.

I could now just see the dawn breaking and calculated we had less than seven minutes before we would be seen. I struggled with Friedrich to the water's edge, paddling in a few yards, waiting for the dinghy and immediately helped him in the moment it was near enough.

'I'll have you for this, you bitch,' the Yank said for the umpteenth time, still spitting out the words. I just ignored him and continued paddling. We both paddled furiously to the sub, arriving with only a few minutes to spare. We threw the rope to one of the ratings, who held it while I climbed onto the casing, followed by the Yank, who held his hands out for the General, but of course the General's hands were still tied. The Yank then took hold of the rope and threw it back into the dinghy, which was immediately taken a few feet away from the submarine by the breeze. By the time anyone had realised what was happening, the dinghy and the General were twenty feet away.

'Give me your knife, soldier,' I shouted. He just looked at me, stony-faced. 'Give it me!' I yelled, drawing my gun. He reluctantly gave the knife to me and I yelled to the Captain, 'If you have to go without me, just go!'

Sam yelled, 'No, Alex, don't go!' It was too late. I dived into the water with the knife between my teeth and began to swim out to the drifting dinghy. I really had to push hard as the tide was against me, but eventually I reached him.

'Friedrich, darling, I'm so sorry. I wouldn't have wanted this. I'll never forget you,' I said as I began to cut his hand ties. 'Will you be all right?'

'Yes, thank you. I know I'll always love you and I hope when the war is over, and if we survive, we will meet again,' Friedrich said as I reached in and gave him the paddle.

'Bye, darling!' I said in English and began an easier swim back, with the tide on my side, but even so I was at least one hundred yards from the sub. I could see it was now becoming daylight and the submarine was in full view to anyone on shore. I swam as if my life depended on it, which of course in reality it did and arrived at the boat just as a shore battery opened up. The decks had been cleared and it was just me and the rating who was detailed to help me onto the casing when I arrived. Even before I had actually climbed aboard the submarine was beginning to submerge and you could hear the shells getting closer and closer as they began to find the range.

'Thank you, Captain,' I said to the submarine commander as I got my breath back after, almost falling down the conning tower in my haste to get into the sub. The moment we were submerged and on our way, I was taken into an area to change from my wet clothes and into some poor unfortunate rating's things, which caused some of the crew to whistle. We were all totally exhausted and either fell asleep, or sat in total silence for the six-hour return voyage to Southampton Water. The injured men were given the appropriate emergency treatment and prepared for disembarkation the moment we landed.

I thanked the American Captain for his patience with me as we all left the boat and were then taken speedily back to HQ and General John Grisman for a debriefing. There Sam gave me back my paper carrier bag back, undamaged.

'Sam, you're an angel,' I said, giving him a big kiss on the cheek.

'Alex, I nearly was!' he replied, laughing as we walked into the General's office.

We stood waiting around for a few minutes for the General to make an entry, all of us still pretty exhausted. At last he walked in, looking mighty pleased with himself. 'My-o-my, what a fantastic performance. Sit down, gentlemen ... madam ... I want you to split off into groups and detail everything to the debriefing officer that you have noted or you can remember. Well done!'

Suddenly, the Yank who had caused all my troubles stood up and addressed the General: 'General, I want to state that I think it was ridiculous that we took an inexperienced woman on this trip. She put the whole of us in danger and cost us two serious injuries. All she has done is lie on her back, fucking the enemy to death.'

I stood up and slowly walked around to where he was sitting. I looked at him for a second or two and, with a straight left to his nose and a right to his chin, I knocked him clean off his chair.

I lifted his head up by his hair and thundered another right to the side of his face, repeating the exercise four more times before I was pulled off him by one or two of the others.

I turned to the General and said, 'If this man is typical of what you can provide, I think we can win the war without you.' I began to leave, but as I got to the door, the General shouted: 'Officer, come back now!'

I ignored his call and walked out.

He sent a couple of the Americans after me to persuade me to go back.

'Well done, ma'am,' one said when he reached me. 'He had it coming!'

I smiled and gracefully agreed to go back.

'Thank you, Squadron Officer, you were obviously overwrought and we will say no more about it,' the General said, rubbing salt into the wound.

'General! How dare you! My father is a very senior general here in Britain and I can assure you he wouldn't address anyone in that vein, particularly someone who's been through what I've been through. Your soldier's behaviour has been abysmal . . . No. Criminal!' I went on to give an account of our whole adventure, my own role in it and the barbaric behaviour of the Yank. I left nothing out and brooked no interruption.

'General, my colleagues here, I hope, will corroborate my account and will expect a full investigation to be made into this soldier's behaviour. One more thing: in the twenty-four hours I was with General Rettenburg, I found him to be a fine and honourable officer who in every way abhors what is done in the name of Germany!' With that I turned and left the room, taking my large paper bag with me.

'What have you got there?' the General asked curiously.

'A present, sir . . .' I paused to let the next words sink in. '. . . for sleeping with the enemy!'

I had been back in London a week, having returned to normal duties, when Winco called me into his office. 'I've got a surprise for you, Squadron Officer. You have been awarded the DSO and the Air Chief Marshall wants to see you this afternoon. I hear they wanted to award you the George Cross, but you already have one of those!'

I was pleased and surprised. After my outburst down in Dorset I thought I might have been in trouble, but Sam and several of the others including the Captain had put him in the picture and he too had put me in for an award, as it was an American operation.

I arrived at the Air Ministry with Winco and was introduced once more to the Air Chief Marshall, who naturally congratulated me on the award and told me the presentation was once more to be held at Buckingham Palace the following Wednesday. I could take a guest if I wanted to.

'Sir, I need your help,' I said to the Chief.

'What is that Squadron Officer?' he asked.

'I have been trying to get hold of my husband at Lincoln since I have been back and I have been unable to reach him.'

'Give my adjutant the details and I'll see what I can do,' he replied.

Winco, or Charles, I should now call him as were off duty, and I left the Air Ministry and went straight to the Services Club for dinner. There were the usual formalities, the only real difference being that the menu was very limited as Covent Garden had been hit and even the drinking water was cloudy because the mains had been damaged in a raid. We left shortly after 8 p.m. and made our way to Chelsea where I had promised to make Charles a very special cup of coffee with condensed milk, as I hadn't any fresh.

We had only been in a matter of ten minutes when the front door opened and in walked my William. I had never been so pleased to see him and I'm sure after that Charles felt like a spare part, especially as I must have spent fifteen minutes in a clinch. I made the introductions and William then explained what had happened.

'I had a phone call from the Chief's adjutant, who told me I was ordered to take seven days' leave to take my wife to the Palace to receive some award. And, as you know, Charles, orders must be obeyed,' William said and continued by ordering *me* to go and make some coffee.

We spent a couple of hours in Charles' company, and I told William everything about what had happened in France. I even showed off the presents, including the red dress with the strip torn off. William was proud but clearly a tad jealous that someone else had bought clothes for me. But I told him it was for King and Country and that I had my fingers crossed all the time.

Wednesday soon came around and I was spruced up and looking my best as I stepped up to the King to be presented with the DSO. He had been briefed about the mission and what I had done and said he thought I was very brave. What was also lovely was that Sam, too, was at the presentation receiving his DSO. I hadn't seen him since we returned and didn't know he was in for it as well.

Mr White, it was a wonderful day but even so I looked out to see if I could get a glimpse of my father; but it wasn't to be.

Chapter 21

By late 1943, Britain and the Allies were making headway against the Germans and the Italians in Europe and even in the Pacific the Americans had made strides against the Japanese. The bombing raids were beginning to dent the German capacity to fight, as they were running out of materials and fuel in certain sectors.

At Christmas I went to Lincoln and spent several nights with my husband and was delighted to meet Tom once again, who was stationed in South Lincolnshire and didn't see William so much. It was pleasing to know that he was still with Madge and that they were getting married sometime in the next twelve months. It was an even bigger surprise when she arrived for the mess party. It was lovely to talk about old times and their plans to get married. Tom had been reluctant to tie the knot because he was worried that he might be killed and she would lose the opportunity to find someone else. She had no intention of wanting anyone else; she just wanted him. I think I actually bullied him into setting a date – 20th July 1944 – and that's where it was left.

It was a lovely Christmas, but the war was keeping us apart. William was so busy and as the Allies became more successful, our little section also became busier.

Not long into the New Year, I was called into Winco's office where I was greeted by three others: Colonel Wilmer Hunt from an American airborne division, Lieutenant Grant Baker and a man in civvies, who turned out to be a major in the American OSS (Office of Strategic Services), which was effectively their war intelligence department.

'Cup of tea, Alex?' Winco asked, immediately picking up the phone to organise one. 'We operate more informally in my group; we're a close-knit team, hence we use Christian names,' he said as he introduced the visitors to me. I could sense there was something in the air as even Winco seemed a bit sheepish with me.

We chatted about everything in general – the weather, the war and how well we were now doing and then finally my last adventure in France. They all seemed to know a great deal about it, even about the Yank and his behaviour towards the General.

'He's not getting a medal, I can tell you,' Major Davis quipped.

'He's been shipped out to the front line to a completely different unit. You know, of course, there's been a medal recommendation, for you, I mean?' he added.

I nodded, though I hadn't been that impressed with the way the Americans had operated. I could not help myself, Mr White; I pretty much told him what I thought. I was still very angry.

The Major interrupted me in full flight:

'Hold on, hold on. Wow, I heard you had some spirit, but I didn't know you were this hot-headed.'

I laughed and much more calmly asked him to go on.

'Well, we've heard all the detail of your actions and how you've the ability to think on your feet and we're very impressed with your courage in action, especially in the way you disarmed that machine gun. This is the reason we want you to go back!'

There was total silence and they could see from my reaction that I was shocked.

'I don't want to do it,' I said in a tired tone.

Mr White, I really was just too tired of it all, tired of the whole bloody war. Excuse my language. I wasn't scared, I was just tired.

Every time I was away, I knew I wouldn't be able to see

William and, stupid as it may seem, that was the most important thing in my life. Right from that first meeting at the Lyons Corner House that was all I wanted: to be with him. It was really only because William was out almost every night doing his bit, trying to end the war that I wanted to do something too. I wanted to shorten the war, not to kill as many Germans as I could. After all, they weren't all bad, as I had discovered.

They wouldn't take no for an answer of course and they began to outline what they wanted me to do. I was to be attached to the OSS and guide another group of soldiers to the various targets in Dunkirk, Calais, Boulogne, and even as far as the Le Havre regions. It had transpired that during my last mission we had identified various large gun emplacements and that these needed to be destroyed before the big invasion took place. As I said earlier, these huge guns could easily blow our ships out of the water and hundreds if not thousands of men could be killed or injured before an Allied foot even touched French soil. Little did we realise at the time, of course, that this was another one of the Allied subterfuges to lead the enemy into thinking that the invasion was to take place in this northern region.

The Major showed us a plan the heavily defended Battery Todt with its huge guns and an aerial photograph which had been taken by one of our own reconnaissance Spitfires. 'Sadly,' the Major added, 'the RAF lost one of its Spitfires trying to get this for us.'

This at once touched my Achilles heel; I couldn't bear to hear of one of our lads being shot down, as it always made me think of William. I foolishly agreed to go.

'Alexandra,' Winco began as he moved over and sat next to me. 'Don't make any rash or quick decisions. You've done enough. You don't have to do this.' He put his hand on my shoulder. 'You really don't have to do this. No one will think less of you.'

'No I'll do it. If only for the Spitfire pilot,' I said. 'When do you want me there?' I asked the Major.

'In two days. Is that OK?'

'Yes,' I replied and then rather cheekily asked if someone could pick me up from my Chelsea flat, to which they agreed.

Winco and I got up to leave when I turned and asked, 'Out of interest who will the party consist of?'

'Twenty-four Special American Forces, with three officers and another English officer whom I think you already know.'

'Sam!' I said, almost shouting his name.

'There will be Resistance fighters, too, joining you in France, though how many I don't yet know. But what we do know is that we'll make a hell of a row and hopefully do some lasting damage,' the Major added.

I did try to contact William to let him know I had a forty-eight hour pass and that I would be away for a few days, but as usual he was not contactable, so I had to make do with Winco, who took me to dinner at the Services Club.

'I promised William I would keep my eye on you and now look what's happened!' he said, opening the conversation as we sat down to our meal.

'He never told me,' I responded.

'Why should he? It was me he asked . . .' He paused for a moment. 'They asked me if I would persuade you to go and I told them an emphatic no . . . and then you let me down. This one's no picnic.'

'The last one wasn't either, Charles.'

'No, I didn't mean that. This one will involve combat and, Alexandra, you haven't been trained for such work.'

'I'm just the guide!'

'Alexandra, you know very well you can't just stand there and let the others do the fighting, and what if you're captured? What will they do to you? You will undoubtedly be shot.'

'Oh God, Charles, make my day for goodness' sake and shut up. It's bad enough already,' I said, almost pushing the meal away.

We didn't talk anymore except about the weather and cricket

of course, as Charles could see I was nervous. We finished the meal and hurried back to the flat for a quick cup of Camp coffee, as I had none of the real stuff left.

'Give William my love,' I shouted as he went down the steps.

'I will and, don't worry, everything will be all right,' he replied, disappearing round the corner.

I spent a worried and almost sleepless night alone in the flat and, when I did get to sleep, I was woken at some ungodly hour by an American corporal, knocking on the door, telling me he had come to pick me up.

'What in God's name do you call this time in the morning?' I said as I answered the door in my dressing gown.

'400 hours, ma'am. I have orders to pick you up as soon as possible,' he replied.

'Well, you can see I'm not ready; you'll have to come in and wait. Come on, close the door and follow me,' I ordered. I took him up to the flat and asked him to make us both a cup of coffee while I got ready.

***

Within two hours I was being introduced to the other members of the team. Sam, like me arrived somewhat late, but it was a joy to see him again.

'Congratulations!' I said, rubbing the DSO ribbon on his uniform and making sure the others heard.

'And you!' he added.

'Welcome, Squadron Officer,' the Major said. 'Thank you for joining us and now I want to introduce you to other members of the team and to the task ahead of us, which I'm sure you will find interesting.

'I'm Major Bill Preedy and the two men on my right are Captain Dave Brummel and Lieutenant Akers. We're members of the Special Forces attached to the OSS for this mission; they are organising the mission along with the French Resistance.

'On my left we've Sergeant Wallis and Corporal Ben Bennett. Now, gentlemen, I want you to meet Squadron Officer Fraser of the Women's Royal Air Force and Flying Officer Reason, both of whom are experts in their own field and have already experienced covert activity in France. Both have earned their medals for this work.'

Without doubt the team were looking somewhat aghast at a woman being brought along on the mission.

'Sir!'

'Sergeant Wallis?' Major Preedy asked.

'The mission is dangerous and will involve action. Why have –'

The Major interrupted him before he asked the question. 'Sergeant, do you know your way round the northern part of France. Well, do you?'

'No, sir.'

'Well, that's why we have this woman officer on this mission; she knows the area blindfold and you sure will need her.'

Sam also chimed in. 'I can guarantee that she will not let you down; in fact, Sergeant, I would trust my life to her hands more than to yours. She's earned her place.'

'It doesn't matter what anyone thinks at this stage,' the Major intervened. 'The die is cast and we're a complete team and we're all stuck with each other. Now I want to explain the operation: we've a total of twenty-nine men who will be divided up into five teams; four with six men and one with five. I'll lead the first team of five men, assisted by Corporal Bennet, who will lead the second team of five men. Captain Brummel will lead the third team of six men assisted by Lieutenant Akers, who will lead the fourth team of five men. The fifth team of five in total will be commanded by Squadron Officer Fraser and will contain Flying Officer Reason and Sergeant Willis, who will have the operational responsibility to offer full protection to our English officers, as they are our guides, translators and explosives expert, together with two other members of the team to be selected by Sergeant Willis. Remember it's a joint operation with members of the Resistance and us. Is that clear?'

'Sir!' the group shouted in agreement, but not before I heard Sergeant Willis comment: 'I'm a bloody nursemaid!'

'Explosives!' I exclaimed to Sam quietly. I didn't know.'

'Yes, that's me!' Sam interjected. 'I was with the Royal Engineers, before transferring to the RAF. Initially, I was used wherever explosives were needed, in the construction of runways for example, but then they were asking for translators in Winco's group. I thought I had taken the easy way out!'

'You're a quiet one, aren't you?' We both smiled.

We spent the next seven days training, with me being given training in unarmed combat, use of a knife and other weapons, and Sam familiarising himself with the latest plastic explosives, following which we spent the remaining days on the actual plans of attack. We were to be met by the Resistance and divide into our five groups. We had three primary targets which had to be attacked and destroyed: first, the Battery Todt which had been causing so much trouble in Dover and the surrounding villages. Second, the massive cement works at Desvres, where Hitler was obtaining all his materials for the huge concrete fortifications along the coastline, the 'Atlantic Wall' as he called it; and thirdly, the ammunition and fuel dumps, which the Allies knew existed but were not sure exactly where they were, despite numerous reconnaissance sorties.

We had three days to complete the task and were to return to the coast and await a signal from the *Arkansas* as we did with the *Conqueror*. It all looked so simple on paper. 'It'll be just a walk in the park!' the Major quipped to a nervous laugh from the rest of us.

On the big day we left our base and joined the *Arkansas*, one of the latest American submarines, and within two hours we were on our way. As predicted, it was a very dark rainy night, ideal for a covert landing.

We all waited nervously, in spite of the Major trying to talk up our morale. The journey was made almost in total silence, which was only broken when we heard the sub Captain order: 'Up scope!' and after a few minutes, 'Lookouts to the ready . . .

Surface!' And soon after we could feel the cool air rush through the boat as the conning tower trap was opened. 'One, two and three dinghies to the ready.' the Major ordered, and within the space of a very few minutes, the first three dinghies were on their way, leaving us on board. They were almost on the shore when one of the lookouts shouted, 'Enemy activity on the shore, sir.' All the lookouts immediately turned their attention to the land as they could see the reception committee opening up. The men turned their dinghies round but they didn't stand a chance. They were either dead, injured or in the water.

Our running commentary was disturbed by one of the lookouts shouting: 'MTBs on the starboard side approaching fast.'

An MTB, Mr White, is a motor torpedo boat and very fast over the water.

'Dive, dive, dive!' the Captain shouted to the crew. 'Full ahead and secure for depth charges.'

The Captain took us as fast as we could go into deeper water. At least there we would have a better chance, but we could actually hear the roar of the engines from the MTBs as they got nearer and nearer. It was an eerie and frightening feeling and it felt like being trapped in a steel coffin with no chance of escape; we simply had to hold on and hope for the best.

'Stop engines and lay her on the bottom, Mr Wise,' the Captain ordered. 'And not a sound!'

The MTBs seemed to be almost on top of us; the sound was awful as they slowed down and you could hear the catapulting of the depth charges and the splash as they hit the water and then silence as they floated down and then 'BANG!' as the first one exploded, then 'BANG!' as the second one followed suit, and then the third, fourth and fifth, and each time the whole sound seemed to shake the boat to its rivets. It felt as if the boat would crack open!

Something inside the submarine fell from its mounting. 'Stop that thing rattling,' the Captain whispered. 'Why don't you bloody tell them where we are!'

The whole place seemed to smell of fear and when you looked around, everyone was in the same situation with sweat pouring out of them, holding onto anything which would give them support. It was obvious that the *Arkansas* had not been involved in defensive activity before and some of the ratings were naturally terrified.

Then suddenly there was silence: the boats above had stopped their engines to see if there was any sign of damage. You could hear the swish of the water as they drifted slowly around looking for us.

'They're in the wrong area!' the Captain whispered loudly. You could hear the mass exhaling of the breath we had all been holding during the attack. 'Silent running. Half ahead, boat,' the Captain said, issuing his orders. 'Let's get out of here!'

We slowly moved away, listening to the sound of more depth charges being dropped, but thankfully nowhere near us.

'Damage report, number one.'

'No damage, sir!'

'Good. Now take over. I need to talk to what's left of the team,' the Captain said as he came over to us. 'We will have to abort this mission. We have lost the two Senior Officers and most of the team may be dead or captured. The French Resistance fighters must have been slaughtered, too . . .'

Sam interrupted: 'Why? We have everything ready and all the equipment we need. We certainly don't have enough men anymore to take on the gun battery, but we could still hit the cement works and the dump if we can find it, and of course we've the element of surprise!'

I agreed with Sam. 'We could be dropped off three or four hours from now. They won't expect us to be trying again so soon and if we've got a traitor among the group, there will not be time for him–'

'Or her!' Sergeant Willis interjected.

'Yes, you're right. Or her,' I repeated, 'to warn anyone. Shall we go then?' I asked.

'I'm for it,' the Sergeant said, followed by his men and, of course, the Lieutenant.

We all knew the Germans had been tipped off and we all knew that, while the operation was still on, there was a danger of them being tipped off again, so I asked the Captain to radio that the mission had been aborted, with the loss or capture of the entire landing party. The Captain agreed with our analysis and we arranged to go back to the area about an hour before daybreak, which would give us time to move into the forest and prepare for the following night.

We lay off the French coast for over three hours before the Captain moved us close to our former position and repeated his orders: 'Periscope depth!' And now we could once again feel the boat lifting. 'Up scope!' He scoured the shoreline and asked his number one to check before giving the orders, 'Night lights, lookouts, to the casing!' Once again you could feel the rush of fresh air as the conning tower trap was opened; this time, however, it was more than welcome as we had been submerged for over four hours. There was now no sign of activity so we decided to go and within minutes we were in the dinghies, paddling ashore. Our hunch was right: there was no sign of life and we beached just west of Boulogne at Hardelot. I couldn't help wondering if Friedrich had been picked up and was safe. The Sergeant brought me back to earth with a bang.

'Come on, we haven't got all day,' he whispered loudly as he signalled for me to pull the dinghy inshore. We had no alternative but to carry the dinghies into the forest area which was some two hundred yards away, fully loaded with our equipment, in order for us to hide them properly and give us the means of escape later on.

'Take five,' the Sergeant ordered, allowing his men to rest and then, turning to me, asked, 'Ma'am, can I have a word?'

'Sergeant?' I answered as we walked away from the group, almost out of hearing.

'Ma'am,' he began in his strong Midwest accent. 'I appreciate you are the senior officer, but neither you, Lieutenant Akers nor Sam Reason has had operational or combat experience. I think it would be better if I took command. With respect, ma'am, I think, we would be safer.'

'Sergeant Willis, I agree with you,' I replied, putting him in a mild form of shock as I had been so pragmatic. 'But I still want the three officers to be included in all planning. Agreed?'

'Agreed!' he replied and saluted me.

'Come on, I'll tell the others what's happening.'

We walked back to the others and I told them that Sergeant Willis was in command and, whatever he said and to whomever he said it, his orders had be carried out. There was certainly agreement from the other ranks and Sam and Akers saw the logic to the decision. We quickly discussed our options and I explained where all the targets were and how to get to them. I then handed matters over to him.

'Right, listen up, everyone,' Willis began. 'We'll hit the easy target first – the cement works at Desvres and as we've half an hour before it's light we will go south and pick up the road to Samur and then Desvres. Come on!'

He had allocated everyone their duties and we set off as the first chinks of light were appearing. We had just hit the road when we stumbled across a machine gun pillbox.

'Sergeant,' Sam whispered, 'we can take the box easily. Come with me, I'll call them out.'

They crept up to the door; there was hardly a sound coming from inside. Sam banged on the door and in his fluent German shouted, 'Are you asleep in there? Out now!'

You could tell there was total confusion inside and with that the Sergeant and Sam just opened the door and walked in. I told the others to keep watch as I joined the two of them in the box.

'Ma'am, we've got three of them!' the Sergeant said, as I looked at the terrified bundles of flesh, each with their hands up.

'Perhaps there were survivors from the earlier launch. They may know something.'

'Ask them where they've taken the Americans,' he said to Sam. There was no response. He fixed the silencer on his pistol.

'Ask them again!' he repeated, this time putting a gun to the head one of the terrified Germans. There was once again no response and he fired.

Mr White, I couldn't believe it. I was almost physically sick at the coldness of the man, but I had put him in charge and now I couldn't argue.

Sam then asked the second man the same question, again with no result, except this time the trembling man said he didn't know. Once again the Sergeant shot him in the head. He turned to the third, who was now just a quivering mass of jelly and was pleading for his life.

'You have to answer three questions to save your life,' Sam said, knowing the Sergeant would have no compunction in shooting him. One: where have they taken the Americans?'

The Sergeant pointed his gun and cocked it.

'La Coupole near Boulogne,' the man replied nervously.

'I know it,' I announced excitedly.

'Where do you store all your ammunition?' Sam asked.

'Capure,' he replied nervously, looking around.

'And where's that?'

'Near Le Portal on the outskirts of Boulogne,' he answered; his teeth wouldn't stop chattering.

'Now the last one. Where do you store all your petrol?'

'There's a huge store near Ardres in the woods. No one is allowed to go there, but I've been there,' he answered, hoping to ingratiate himself. 'Please don't shoot me, I have a wife and family!' he pleaded, looking towards me. I stepped forward as if to comfort him.

'Don't worry, young man,' the Sergeant said in English, 'I won't shoot you.' And then with one quick movement, the German fell to the floor, his nerve ends quivering until every bit of life left his body. The Sergeant had broken his neck.

'Ma'am, we can't take prisoners, and he would have given us away. Make no mistake, if you had let him live we would all eventually be killed. Now we must make this look like the work of the Resistance. We don't want the Germans to know that we're here in case they've been told about potential targets,' and with that he scratched the wall with the Cross of Lorraine. 'Come on, let's get out of here; daylight will be here in a few minutes.'

We hurried back to the others and moved deeper into the forest to avoid detection. 'Hardwick, James,' the Sergeant called quietly to two of his men, 'take point, two hours. Lieutenant Akers, come with me. We'll take a look around. Rest of you take a rest. Williams, Jenson, relieve those two on point in two hours. Ma'am, don't send anyone to look for us if we're not back in three hours.' With that they were off and we rested.

I must admit it was useful to have someone as experienced as Willis leading the team and I certainly had confidence in him and actually fell asleep in spite of the drizzle that had been falling ever since we landed. I was only woken up when I heard the Sergeant return.

'Ma'am, the immediate area is clear. We've two choices: the first, to cross the forest north-north-east, meeting the road from Boulogne to Desvres, then swinging right on that road we will hit the north of the town in about two hours. Second, if we continue on this route from Samer to Desvres, we will reach the south of the town in about an hour, The terrain is much easier, but the risk is greater, as there appears to be a lot of enemy traffic.'

'I remember the northern road was also busy when we were here a few weeks ago,' I said. It's really the main route from Boulogne to Amiens and the Germans have a main barracks there. The cement works are to the north-east of the town and it would be easier to attack from there, as we could get cover from the forest. I know Desvres very well and it certainly would be better if we approached from that side, as there are a few small streets and rows of houses around the church where we could take cover. It's very primitive – the roads are unmade – but I would suggest we take a look.'

'You're right, ma'am. Let's move out and not a sound!' the Sergeant ordered.

He led the way through the forest with Lieutenant Akers,

sending one man well to the fore to check things out, then one man to guard the rear, following some twenty to thirty yards behind us, and with the rest of us keeping in close order to the Sergeant. Amazingly, we made good progress and kept reasonably quiet; there was only the occasional crack as someone stood on a twig or the occasional flutter of birds as we disturbed their peace and quiet in the forest.

We could now see the road.

'Get down and stay down!' the Sergeant signalled. 'Ma'am, you and I will go recce the town. Can you use one of these?' he asked, throwing me a Sten gun?

'Yes, Sergeant,' I replied, not wanting to say that I only practised on it for the first time last week. 'Lieutenant, wait here. We'll be back in less than two hours. You know what to do.'

We set off to the road, checking for every sight and sound. The road was clear and we crossed without problem and then headed towards Desvres as there was far more cover available to us on that side. Arriving at the outskirts of the town, we made our way slowly but surely to the cement works. To our delight it was totally undefended. In fact, it was so lax I actually walked to the entrance unseen. We quickly surveyed the area, making notes of where the charges were to be laid and began the journey back to the group.

We were heading towards the church on the way back when Willis heard what he thought was a German patrol.

'Into the church, quick!'

Inside we dropped down behind the pews, but we had been seen by the cleaner, who now came running over.

'*Americains, americains*!' she exclaimed with delight.

I signalled for her to be quiet. '*Je suis française, madame. Je suis en train d'aider ces soldats. Mais il faut absolumment que vous vous taisiez*!'

She grabbed hold of my hand and kissed it.

The commotion had caused the priest to come into the church and the moment he saw the American, he too became ecstatic. His joy was momentary, for almost immediately we heard the

German patrol coming along the street and we held our breath. They passed by and the priest and the cleaner were once again beside themselves with joy.

'What are you doing here?' the priest asked in broken English.

'We're helping the Resistance,' I explained, 'and mapping out potential targets. We're going to be bombing the cement works and we want to avoid civilian casualties.'

'Ma'am!' the Sergeant exclaimed, exasperated.

'I'm sorry, Sergeant, but I'm not going to have my countrymen killed or injured unnecessarily.'

The priest seemed happy. 'What can we do?'

'The Bosh needs this cement; they're building massive defensive structures on the coast and we want to stop it, or at least slow it down.'

The priest nodded and appeared to be thinking. He was clearly pleased to have found a way to hit back at the occupiers.

'Simone,' he said to the cleaning lady, 'go to Michel de Payol and bring him to the church quickly, but don't tell anyone the Americans are here. Do you understand?'

'Yes, Father,' she said as she hurried out of the church.

'I'm afraid we have to go, Father,' I began to say. 'We can't wait.'

'You don't trust me?'

'I don't trust myself,' I replied, 'but there's a war on and strange things happen in wartime.'

'I understand,' the priest said, 'but I won't let you down.'

'I'm sure, Father. Forgive me for being so cautious.'

We sneaked out of the church and found an observation point to wait for this Michel de Payol.

After a few minutes we saw Simone return with a man whom one might describe as a typical Frenchman, especially as he was wearing the traditional beret. We waited a few more minutes to check whether they had been followed and, once we were satisfied, we both re-entered the church, where Michel simply embraced Willis, kissing him on both cheeks and hugging him and thanking him for coming.

'The Bosh have taken everything,' he began. 'We work for very little money and often they do not pay us. JP is the only one making any money and he's in their pocket.'

'JP?' I queried.

'Jean-Patrice LeClerc. He's the owner of the cement works and he's not very popular in Desvres.'

Once again I explained what we wanted to do. 'The RAF has a plan to bomb the factory, but that could endanger lives in the town. Can you get us into the factory so that we can lay charges and prevent the bombing?'

'Of course I can. I'm the foreman, mademoiselle. When do you want to do it? I would give anything to see that man get what he deserves.'

'Today, as soon as possible,' I replied.

'The place is closed at noon until three. Other than JP, only I have keys, and at the moment he goes away to be with his little tart, who also fraternises with the Germans . . . and one day . . .' He sighed. 'Seeing you here gives me hope.'

'We could meet you here at midday,' Willis said, asking me to translate. 'Ma'am, you stay here with the priest and I'll fetch Sam and two others and we'll do it now. OK?' he asked.

'OK,' I replied and he was away.

I don't think I have ever known anything in wartime that went so easily as this particular operation. Willis returned with Sam and the other two and they were then taken by de Payol to the cement works; Sam laying the charges. I stayed with the priest, who told me the entire history of Desvres under the Occupation. By two o'clock, they had returned and we were on our way back to the forest. At 2.30 precisely the charges went off. There was an almighty explosion, which must have been heard in Boulogne some thirty miles away.

'Ma'am, I don't know what you said to the Frenchies, but that was brilliant. Let's hope the next operation will be as easy,' Willis remarked.

We headed north-east to Ardres and the fuel dump. The ease

with which we had blown up the cement works had put us almost a day ahead of schedule, with the result we thought we could hit the fuel dump that evening, especially if we kept at it and made good time. Furthermore, apart from the two bullets Willis had used on the sentries at the pillbox we hadn't fired a shot.

We followed the road from Desvres to Marquise, posting points well to the fore and rear. Unfortunately, there was too much activity as hundreds of troops were being despatched to Desvres as a result of the explosions, which forced us back into the woodland area for cover. We had been moving fairly quickly for the last three hours or so when Willis told one of his men, Simenz, to go with the Lieutenant and see what they could find to the north-east. 'Lieutenant, make sure he looks about him. He's a good soldier, but he doesn't think much. Do you, Private?'

'No, Sarge,' he replied.

'Make your way back on this bearing and we'll come to meet you. Is that clear?' Willis asked.

The Lieutenant dutifully agreed and they set off, while we thankfully took fifteen minutes to eat and drink. I don't know how the Lieutenant or the private for that matter could stand going on without a break. I know I couldn't. I was shattered, but they did it without question. There were a few false alarms when those on point thought they saw and heard things, but the forest was comparatively dense and all in all we had it easy.

On the dot, however, Willis ordered us all to check our equipment and in particular our weapons and ammunition and be prepared to leave in five minutes.

We had been travelling for well over the hour when we were ordered to take cover; someone or something was coming in our direction. It was the Lieutenant and the Private and they arrived to a torrent of abuse from Willis. 'You made enough noise to wake the entire German Army! Are you stupid?' he bawled in a low voice. You could have been followed and you wouldn't have heard.'

'Sorry, Sergeant,' the Lieutenant said, totally embarrassed.

'Remick, go take a look and come back quick. Right, you two, what have you got for me?'

The Lieutenant reported back: 'We found the dump. It's massive, surrounded by a double fence with loose barbed wire in between. It's very well guarded. There are constant patrols around the inside of the perimeter and there is constant traffic in and out of the depot. We're about half an hour away. The gasoline is stored in three or four dumps well inside the perimeter.'

'Well done! Take five,' Willis said, giving them five minutes' rest which was his way of being nice.

An hour and a half later as promised we arrived at the depot and it was exactly as described. The lights had now gone on as it was dark, which made matters worse. We would be picked off like flies, if we attempted any kind of direct attack. The four officers took a look around the perimeter, which proved to be at least half a mile all the way round. There was one weak point: part of the fence was at the bottom of a steep incline, which made it easier to see into the site.

We decided the only way was to attempt a diversionary attack and hope this would give the others enough time to break in. We were also going to attempt to block the entrance. Willis gave us our duties: I and three privates were to control the entrance; Willis was to attempt the wire; Sam would attempt to blow a hole in the wire and the Lieutenant would hopefully support us from the top of the bank.

'Set your watches to 19.30 and fifteen seconds . . . now. At 19.40 we go!'

'What if we have the opportunity to stop a lorry before then? It would really give us a fighting chance?' I asked.

'Do it. We'll hear the noise and we'll take it from there. If not, it's 19.40. Go!' Willis whispered loudly.

'Best of luck,' I added, giving Sam a hopeful smile. He showed me his crossed fingers and we went our way.

We were now within a hundred yards of the entrance and

saw several lorries queuing to leave the site. Like all the German forces they ran on paper and orders, and nothing would make them deviate from that practice.

'We can hit them easily with grenades,' I told my men.

'Ma'am,' one of the men, Remick, protested, 'with respect, I don't think that's wise. I think we should wait. It's only another few minutes.' The others agreed, but were not brave enough to say it themselves.

'We haven't got a few minutes,' I replied, taking my coat off. 'I want four grenades at the ready. Now!' I ordered. I put three in my pockets; the one in my hand with the pin already out. 'You three stay down and be prepared to give me cover if I'm fired at. Understand?'

'Ma'am!' they replied in unison and began looking at me as though I had gone mad or had a death wish.

'Now ready?' I asked.

'Yes, ma'am.'

I crawled to the edge of the clearing, slowly getting to my knees, grenade at the ready. I jumped to my feet, ran a few paces and threw it. The 'ball' was in the air and I hadn't been seen. I took the next one out, ran a further few paces and another one was in the air. That practice Father had given me was paying off. I had hit the first lorry with the first ball and it blew up as the grenade exploded underneath. It held aviation fuel and had the desired effect. The other one missed the second lorry as the throw was too long.

Mr White, I had been seen and all hell let loose. My three men opened up, giving me enough cover to get back to the woods. I could now also hear the others had started their attack and there was general confusion. At this moment, the entrance was hidden in a ball of fire and the second lorry blew up. The other lorry drivers had the sense to drive their vehicles out of danger, not too far from the inside perimeter.

'We can't do much here. Let's go and help the Sergeant!'

'Yes, ma'am,' Remick whispered loudly as though he was proud of what I had done. They followed me round the edge until we could see Willis and his men at the perimeter. They were almost through.

'Come on,' he signalled to his men, who now followed him through. Then we too entered the site.

'Over there, quick!'

We all ran the fifty yards or so to the nearest buildings, but we had been seen and two or three of the enemy turned on us. Two of our men fell. The others engaged the enemy while I looked at the back of the building where to my surprise, I could see one of the dumps. There were hundreds of barrels stacked. It was an absolutely appetising target. I had never thrown that distance before. I took my jacket off and threw my grenade towards the barrels. Alas, I was well short of the target and it exploded harmlessly. I rejoined the group and asked for their grenades, too. Willis took exception.

'We can't afford to waste the fuckin' things!'

'Give them to me!' I ordered, almost snarling.

I took two grenades and, as with the first, I was just a little short. Never mind, there was the next one.

Mr White, I'm not brave; I didn't make a conscious decision to put myself in danger; I just pulled out the pin and ran twenty yards and let the grenade go. It must have landed right at the foot of one of the barrels because the explosion was immense. I hadn't noticed but the Germans had turned their attention to me and bullets were whizzing round me from all directions. However, I fell to the ground and lay very still. I could see where the main firing was coming from. I had one grenade left. I turned as little as I could and shouted back to the others. 'Cover me, three o'clock!'

My comrades let go a torrent of fire which forced my assailant to duck down. I took the remaining grenade out of my pocket, pulled the pin and from an almost sitting position I dollied the ball right into the keeper's gloves. The firing stopped and I seized the opportunity to get back to my team.

'Ma'am, I don't know why I ever doubted you!' Willis said graciously. 'Now let's get out of here. Follow me,' he ordered as he pulled the dog tags from the two dead men. He picked up their weapons and ammunition and we took cover as the firing picked up again.

I looked back and saw that Sam's unit were under heavy fire but were giving as good as they got. Sam was some hundred or so yards away from the third fuel dump when I saw him make an effort to throw explosives into the middle of the store.

Moments later he went down; he had been shot. He fell to the floor and I could see no movement.

'Sergeant, give me your binoculars, quickly!'

I looked at Sam. He was alive and I could see in his hand the explosive device he had made.

'Cover me!'

I flung the Sten round my neck, took one of the last grenades and ran across to Sam. He had fallen into a trench which was being constructed around the store itself and this gave him some protection from small-arms fire. I dived into the trench like some scrum-half diving across the line to make the winning try, accompanied by a shower of bullets. Sam was only half with me and tried to signal about the explosives.

'Two minutes, that's all,' he whispered and lapsed into unconsciousness.

I could see both the Sergeant and two of Sam's men and I signalled them to cover me. It was a 'tails I lose, heads you win' situation; Sam's explosives would without doubt kill us both and if I threw them I would probably get shot. It was Hobson's choice. The men opened fire and I prayed I would hit the target. The Germans were engaging the others as I talked myself into it.

'Come on, Alexandra, they're going for two. Quick!'

I stood up and in one movement hurled the 'ball' as hard as I could to the wickets and fell to the floor. I couldn't believe I hadn't been hit. I lay in the trench, for what seemed like ages and began to think Sam had got it wrong. I looked up to see Dev Preston, one of Sam's men, looking at me and I waved with my arm for him to keep down.

The firing stopped as there seemed to be an uneasy truce and then suddenly there was an almighty explosion. The ground shook and it seemed like it was the end of the world. Everywhere you looked was covered with burning fuel or flickering debris falling out of the sky. We were more in danger of being killed by that than by the enemy. The trench had saved us, but Sam's men hadn't fared too well, though it appeared they were still alive. The enemy, too, was in shock so this was our chance to escape. I picked Sam up, threw him over my shoulder in a fireman's lift and then ran, keeping as low as I could, towards the Sergeant.

The Sergeant signalled to the others to join him and we all made our way back to the hole in the fence. The area, thank God, was clear. However, a small platoon of Germans had seen us running across the perimeter and opened fire. We hit the ground as there was very little cover and were now faced with either edging back to where we had better cover or each making a dash for it while we had covering fire. I'm afraid we chose the latter. We did have one point in our favour, though, as two of Sam's team could see the Germans and could hold them down, even if they did have only a little ammunition left. It was a case of short bursts as each of us made the run.

'You first, ma'am,' the Sergeant said. 'I'm sorry, you'll have to leave the Flying Officer. He'll slow us down.'

'No, Sergeant. I'm not going without him. He's alive, badly injured and he'll be shot if he's caught. I'll take full responsibility for him. Get the others out. I'll cover and we will come last.'

The Sergeant wasn't one to wait; he was too experienced. He had to get his men out and some inexperienced woman wasn't going to stop him.

'Right, you two,' he said, pointing to two of the men, 'on yer way and cover us when you're there. Covering fire now. Go!'

The two men dashed across the perimeter and dived for the wire, but were now at their most vulnerable and then all hell let loose. The Germans opened up and one of our men was hit.

Sam's men returned fire and forced the Germans to momentarily take cover. They made it, but as I said one was now walking wounded.

'Have we any grenades left, Sergeant?' I asked, seeing that one of the loaded trucks had been left in the inside perimeter, well within throwing distance. 'I think I can get that one, Sergeant,' I added, as I pointed the lorry out to him. 'I want two grenades!'

'Two grenades now, is it!' the Sergeant bawled with a grin and handed them to me after one of the men had thrown them to him.

'How many have we got left?' I asked. Including the ones I had been given we had just five. I had to get the lorry in one; we couldn't afford to waste any. I took my jacket off and the pin out of the grenade. 'On the count of three, Sergeant.'

'Ma'am,' he answered, signalling to the others for cover.

I began counting, 'One, two, three!'

I jumped up to a deafening noise, as my cover had opened up, and ran two or three spaces and threw. It went between the cab and the back and wedged. It couldn't have been better: the flash and explosion were spectacular.

We now saw that Lieutenant Akers and his men had at last managed to enter the compound and were on higher ground, which gave us, for a short while at least, the advantage.

'Out now!' the Sergeant shouted. He turned to me. 'You can't take him, ma'am! It's suicide!'

'He's coming with me, or I'm staying!'

I noticed Sam mouthing me to leave him. I just ignored him. All the men managed to get through unscathed, thanks to Akers, and now it was my turn. I flung the Sten over my shoulder and quickly bent down to pick Sam up. Suddenly, I felt a huge crack to my side and was knocked over. For a moment or two, I didn't know where I was; I felt I couldn't get up. I could hear the noise of gunfire, which slowly brought me to my senses and then, as though a tap had been turned on, I was back to normal. The side of my back felt as though I had been kicked by a mule, but I was unhurt. The Sten had taken the force of the bullet; it was now useless but it had saved my life. Over the noise I could hear the Sergeant shouting: 'Are you, OK, ma'am?' I raised my hand to answer. I had just one grenade left, otherwise I was unarmed.

I had to run for it or be captured; the latter was no option as even I knew our action wouldn't be considered a normal military one by the Germans and I would be shot. I shook myself as if to say 'Pull yourself together' and got to my feet again, to the sound of the men giving me cover. I had a chance and had to take it – it was now or never. By the time I had bent over Sam, taken him by the arms, and yanked him over my shoulder, the adrenaline had taken control. I felt him tense with the pain and, as I ran with him to the wire, his body went taut. I reached the wire and could hear the odd bullet zinging past; but I was on autopilot. I dropped Sam to the floor and went backwards into the hole of the fence, pulling Sam as I went. I don't know how long it took and I can only remember pulling him through the fence, picking him up again and running into the surrounding woods and then falling over.

The Sergeant was in full control and was organising the retreat from the area. He gave me a drink from his flask and, to my surprise, said, 'Well done, ma'am! Come on, we've got to get out of here!' He had already sent men into the forest to scout our way out as we all knew we would only have a few minutes before the Germans would have brought in reinforcements from another base.

The Germans would have seen that the troops were American and would probably think there was another, larger force somewhere near the coast and that we would be trying to rejoin them.

At least that was the scenario Akers, the Sergeant and I considered as we turned east and went inland.

'They won't be looking for us there,' I said somewhat forcefully. 'We're over a day ahead of schedule, so we've a chance to lay up a while. As we still have a radio, we could even lay up until the heat dies down,' I suggested. 'What do you think, Sergeant? I asked.

'It's a good idea, but I think it will be dangerous to stay too long. Let's go east,' he replied.

He began by taking us in the direction of St-Omer, with the intention of skirting the north-east side of the town to enable us to keep to the cover of woodland area. We had been travelling quickly for about an hour when the scouts came hurrying back.

About a hundred yards further on, they had run into a platoon of German soldiers who seemed to be waiting in ambush. They had set up a heavy machine-gun position with two men in control. The Sergeant was taking no chances, and as we could easily outmanoeuvre these few soldiers he allocated each man a target.

We waited until everyone was in position and was about to attack when we were disturbed by the sound of lorries approaching. He immediately signalled 'Down!' Within seconds, two lorries appeared and stopped at the edge of the area. The green canvas curtains were pulled back to reveal a very sorry-looking but defiant bunch of men.

'*Raus, raus, raus*!' the guards shouted as they jumped out of the lorry to pull their prisoners out. In the first lorry there were eleven Frenchmen and when we saw our own men in the other we knew they must be the Resistance fighters that had been captured. In the other lorry, there were ten members of the US Army including our own Major Bill Preedy. We felt a mixture of both relief and anxiety.

'Sergeant, we have to attack now. We've the element of surprise. I'll take the machine gun,' I said as I saw them getting ready to use it against the captives. The Germans were very nervous as the French knew what was going to happen and now, having seen the gun, so did the Yanks.

'Now!' I whispered.

'Fire!' the Sergeant yelled.

It was short and sweet. With one simple throw I killed the two German gunners and everyone else hit their targets. Their prisoners took the opportunity to throw themselves into the action and the few Germans that were not instantly killed threw their hands into the air, only to meet the same fate they intended for their captives. We didn't lose a single man . . . or woman.

We ran over to the lorries to help the captives. The Frenchmen were in a bad way and it was obvious they had been tortured. As Sam was too poorly, it was left to me to communicate with them.

The Major was astonished. 'My God, Sergeant, where did you spring from?'

'It's a long story, Major, and we haven't got time to tell you right now. We have to get away from here quickly as we will soon have half the German Army after us.' He turned to his men.

'Get the uniforms off those bastards and shove the bodies in the forest out of sight and hurry. Get the machine gun into the back of the lorry and see if it works. Any of you that can walk, collect their guns and ammo . . . we're going to need it. When you've finished that, put the injured in the back of the trucks and get ready to move out in five minutes!'

I chatted for a few minutes with the French deciding what course of action they wanted to take. Four wanted to take their chances with us and the other seven wanted to go back to their areas as they had unfinished business. They all knew who had betrayed the operation and they were going to make them pay.

I suggested to the Major that he left the operational matters to the Sergeant until he was up to speed, which he thought was sensible and then discussed with the Sergeant that we needed to try and drop the seven Frenchmen off at different points. I must admit the idea was very dangerous, but they were all near to Boulogne and Hardelot, where we had left the dinghies. It was a chance worth taking, as the Germans would without doubt concentrate on the forest area and wouldn't for a moment think we now had transport.

Within ten minutes we were in the lorries and away and thankfully, it was becoming dark. The drizzle that had lasted all day now turned torrential, which I suppose also helped. I had to sit in the front of the leading lorry to help with directions while the Major, Akers and the Sergeant decided what sort of action we should take.

We dropped all the Frenchmen at their destinations, following which we made our way to the beach. A mile or so away, I instructed the driver to pull off the road and we were naturally followed by the others.

'Major, I think we have to have some kind of action plan before we approach the area,' I said.

'How far away do you think we are?' he asked.

'Ten to fifteen minutes, sir. We can take the lorries onto the beach,' I said.

'Sergeant, what's the diagnosis?'

'Jackman here,' he called quietly. 'You left the dinghies in order?'

'Sergeant,' he replied, signifying he had.

'Right, I want you to go and check them out. It's all been too simple. There's no activity and even if they are all in the forest looking for us, I think they would have left a few troops to guard the area. Take six men, but only you go and check the dinghies. It would be unlikely they would try to capture just one man. It would just blow their cover. The other five I want you to keep a hundred yards apart and work round in an arc. Keep an accurate mental note of what's there. Clear?'

'Does the machine gun work?'

'Yes, Sergeant,' one of the men replied.

'What ammo have we got?'

It seemed we had sufficient to start a minor war, but we only had fifteen fit men, which included three walking wounded, and two seriously injured, which included Sam, who appeared to be a little better.

'Check the radio works but don't call.' The Sergeant had thought of everything and was satisfied. 'Right get some rest.' he said, addressing the men.

He took the first watch himself and Akers volunteered for

watch at the other end.

Everything was building up inside us. We were so near the beach and the dinghies and we knew it wouldn't be long before the Germans would find the dead soldiers and there would be no mercy for us. I even imagined swimming the Channel in a bid to escape. We were all looking nervous, wanting to talk but not being able to, and all beginning to shiver as the freezing rain poured down outside.

Jackman came back and a few minutes later the others returned one by one.

'The boats have been touched. Everything's there, paddles, the lot, but they have definitely been looked at and I knew I wasn't alone. I could sense them all around me. I thought I saw the hint of an armoured car a hundred yards away.

The others were questioned, too. The place, it seemed, was surrounded by at least forty men. There was one armoured car and a light machine gun, together with an open-topped half-track in which at least fifteen of the forty men were waiting.

The Major began to take back control of the group. 'We know where most of the danger lies. I want you to take six men armed with the grenades, with each pair taking out the three major problems. The Lieutenant can take three men with the machine gun and the ammunition and set it up as appropriate. The two injured men will drive the lorries to the beach and wait there, but get out of the vehicle and walk round as though you are waiting. Do you understand?'

'Yes, sir!' everyone answered in unison.

'What do you want me to do, Major?' I asked.

Do you know, Mr White, I thought he was going to say just stay there and look pretty or something of that kind. However, what he said was almost as bad: 'We need experience in this sort of action, Squadron Officer.'

'Major, I must protest,' the Sergeant began, but was given short shrift.

'Those are the orders, Sergeant!'

'Sergeant, give me a few of our grenades and another Sten

or something similar,' I asked. 'At least allow me to defend myself!' I did not even wait for a reply.

I picked up the grenades and my new German gun and went off with the Sergeant. The machine gun was hidden near the road to the beach and could be easily isolated. We left two men there and then went to the armoured car, as this was the nearest, leaving three men to demolish that. The Sergeant flattered me by taking me to sort out the half-track with him.

'I'm sorry about the Major, ma'am,' he began, but I put my finger to lips and nothing more was said.

We had all time-checked our watches and the attack was to begin at 7.45 p.m. Three minutes to wait.

'Sergeant, I'll put two grenades into the men and you go for the front and the tracks,' I whispered as we were now within a few feet of our target, crawling nearer and nearer, like two snakes. We knew they wouldn't hear us as the rain was too heavy, so the nearer we could get, the safer we all would be.

I counted down to myself: 'Ten, nine, eight, seven, six, five, four, three, two, one . . . GO!'

I pulled the pins and waited for a second or two before lobbing two grenades into the well of the half-track. They didn't stand a chance and were either killed or seriously wounded. The Sergeant polished off the two in the front of the half-track with a quick burst from the Sten and then called me to follow him.

The rain was bucketing down and, even though we had the light from the explosions, it was very difficult to identify our own men from the Germans. We ran, keeping very low as we heard the armoured car kick into action.

'Down!' the Sergeant shouted, almost pushing me over as he hit the deck. 'Two o'clock: seven or eight of them.'

We lay, watching them. He passed me his grenades. 'I'll cover. Now!'

The first one was on the way milliseconds before he started firing and the second followed immediately afterwards. The Sergeant stopped firing and said hurriedly, 'Wait there, ma'am.

If you see any of them run, shoot 'em.'

He scurried round the back of the half-track where they had been keeping low. I suppose he went to finish off any survivors. I didn't see him after that, until he touched my back and gave me a fright.

'You must be more careful; I could have been the enemy,' he whispered.

Suddenly a bullet whistled past my ear.

'Sniper!' he whispered loudly.

One of the bullets hit one of our men and he fell to the ground.

'He's picking us off, one by one. He's an expert,' the Sergeant said as he began to crawl across the wet ground, acting clumsy so as to attract his attention. 'Try and pick him off, ma'am,' he said as he left.

I could now see the sniper easily. He was right in my sights and I pulled the trigger.

And 'click'. I pulled again, and 'click'. I had run out of ammunition. There wasn't time to reload, I had put the Sergeant's life in danger and had no alternative but to use my knife. I jumped up screaming and charged towards the sniper. Perhaps he didn't expect to see a woman, but he behaved as if stunned to see this new Jeanne d'Arc before him. I struck at him and the knife went in. He was as shocked as I was, but I wasn't an expert and the knife merely went deep into his arm. He screamed and dropped his weapon.

I rolled away, but now he was towering above me. He pulled the knife out of his arm and smiling, held it up as he prepared to bring it down into my chest.

The smile froze on his lips as he fell to the ground. The Sergeant had finished him off.

The battle was calming down, but who had won, we couldn't tell at that moment. I reloaded my Sten and joined the Sergeant as he made his way towards the sporadic bursts of fire.

We had won! The Germans in the armoured car, we discovered, had surrendered. We had lost five men including two of the Frenchmen, but the Germans had lost all but five. The element of surprise was the chief factor in our victory, I suppose. The Sergeant sent several men to check the dead and wounded and they returned with the dog tags of the three Americans who had lost their lives.

Mr White, I cannot describe the terrible feelings I get when I talk about removing the dog tags from the dead. It's just a number, I know, but it feels as if you are ripping their souls from their bodies.

Anyway where was I? Ah yes. It was at this point that the Major joined us. 'Sergeant, what arrangements have you made to contact the submarine?'

'Major, the Germans may speak English,' the Sergeant replied, as we were all standing next to the six Germans who had surrendered. 'I think you have just cost them their lives!' He turned to see one of the officers from the armoured car grimace.

'You do speak English, don't you?'

The German nodded.

'Major, our action was quite independent of yours and the Squadron Officer was the officer in command. I think you better discuss the matter with her.'

'Sergeant, get the dinghies to the sea and make sure we take the radio,' I ordered, much to the disgust of the Major.

'Take a few weapons and ammo. We may need it and kill those prisoners,' the Sergeant yelled as everyone sprang back into action, but the Major refused to let the prisoners be killed and ordered that they be tied up and left there. We therefore had to take the chance they couldn't be freed until at least we were away.

There was now a mad dash to the beach and fortunately the dinghies were still in one piece and even the oars were still there. We began to get into the dinghies.

'What are you doing, Sergeant?' the Major asked.

'We can't wait on the shore for the submarine to arrive, sir. Not only would we put ourselves in danger, we could lose the sub, sir,' he said, again in a somewhat insubordinate fashion. 'Which, I would hasten to add, Major, we nearly lost last time. Now, drivers, get those lorries into the water as far as they will go and everyone into the dinghies.'

'I could blow them up, ma'am,' one of the men suggested.

'The explosion would be seen for miles. So we don't want to make it too easy. Do we?' I countered. 'Come on, let's go. Tie the dinghies together, we don't want to drift apart. Let's get as far away as we can before we use the radio.'

We could all sense the Major was annoyed that his nose had been put out of joint as we were paddling like mad to get away and he tried to reassert his authority, by controlling the paddling.

'All in time! Pull! Pull! Pull!' he repeated as we made progress. We were now some few hundred yards off the beach and still paddling strongly, each taking it in turn to paddle. The Major suggested calling up the sub.

'Major, with due respect, just round that headland they have two motor torpedo boats. Tonight is a clear night; we could be seen easily by anyone with the naked eye. We must get well away. They'll be listening to any radio messages and will be able to guess our bearing,' I said politely.

We had now been paddling for about four hours and we had made good progress. The Sergeant, though, was right – in the distance we could see the MTBs circling the area. They must have released the prisoners and found out what we were up to.

We now kept as low as possible while still trying to paddle, which of course was extremely difficult and we drifted further along the Channel.

The Germans circled for about an hour before finally giving up. At that point we broke radio silence and spoke to the *Arkansas,* relaying our position and hoping we wouldn't have given ourselves away. We continued to relay our position at random as the wind was freshening and our position was far from constant. We could now see a ship approaching from the north and logically thought it was from England, but, at night and at sea, one's imagination takes a hold. It was a wonderful sight when we saw our rescuers and were eventually picked up by a Royal Navy corvette from Plymouth.

We were under orders not to discuss the operation until we had been debriefed by the Americans, which came within four hours of our return as we were whisked away from Plymouth the moment we had landed.

Sam had received medical treatment the moment he was taken on board and I made sure he was all right and taken to hospital the moment we had landed. He had begun to come round and the last thing he said to me before we were separated for several weeks was: 'Alexandra, if William doesn't want you, I do. Thanks!'

I kissed him on the head and waved goodbye. His words had brought me back to earth with a bump. He mentioned William. I hadn't had the time to think about him for three or four days and I now felt dreadful. Was he all right? Had anything dreadful happened?

The moment I arrived I was hustled into an office for a debriefing and was met by Winco, Colonel Wilmer Hunt and the Major. I must admit, I chose to ignore the Americans for a few minutes, directing my conversation at Winco.

'How nice to see you, but don't ask me again as the answer is no,' I said, smiling, He could obviously see I was pleased to see him.

'William is fine and sends his love,' he said, turning my attention to the others.

'Colonel,' I said, acknowledging his presence.

'I can understand you not wanting to go again,' the Major added, 'it's no place for a woman.'

'Major, it was no place for anyone, but how would you know? You weren't there!'

We began the debrief and I was asked to explain the details of the raid on the fuel dump and here I told the story just as it had happened, very modestly, Mr White, leaving out some of the things I did, but explained the circumstances and how we had destroyed three-quarters of the reserves, but ran out of supplies.

'Squadron Officer, I understand you abdicated your responsibility to a junior officer, namely Sergeant Willis, and in fact even took the responsibility from Lieutenant Akers. Is that true?'

'Excuse me, Wing Commander,' I said, turning to address my superior, 'am I facing a court martial? Under the circumstances, I find that offensive.'

Winco took my side and told the Major to be careful after which I answered his question. 'Major, for the record, you had been captured and as far as we were concerned you were out of it for the duration. As it turned out, had we not stumbled on you in the forest, you would have undoubtedly been shot. Neither Lieutenant Akers, Flying Officer Reason, nor myself had any combat experience whatsoever, so I suggested Willis take combat command, which turned out to be the best option.'

We discussed the operation for about thirty minutes when the Colonel said, 'Thank you, Squadron Officer, that's all.'

The Major said, 'I'm going to recommend the Sergeant for the Congressional Medal of Honour.'

'Sir, don't you want to know about the cement works at Desvres, one of the primary targets we were set?'

'What about it?' he asked.

'Well, we destroyed it without a shot being fired,' I answered and then went onto describe how we did it. The Major was absolutely devastated; he had not been told about this and felt embarrassed about the matter. Of course, Winco was enjoying every moment of his discomfiture. However, this ended the brief and I was released into the care of Winco who took me back to Chelsea, where I was given a week's leave and a well-earned rest.

It was lovely to be home, but it would have been lovelier to have William at home with me if only for a day, but it wasn't to be. I remember I almost slept for two days and when I tried my uniform on it was a little too big as I had lost a few pounds during the operation.

A few days later Winco called to see me and said that Sergeant Willis was being presented with an award for bravery. He had been invited to take a guest and had requested that he be allowed to take me. I naturally agreed and we went together.

The award was to be presented by General Eisenhower at the American Embassy in London on behalf of President Roosevelt. It was without doubt a very fancy affair and several of the others were also receiving awards, so all in all, it was a lovely occasion. When I met the Sergeant I told him to call me Alexandra.

'My name's Brian, ma'am.'

'Right, Brian, let's go and enjoy ourselves.'

We walked in and renewed our acquaintance with the men with whom we had been on the mission and began to really enjoy the moment. I'm sure if there had been a dance I would have been on the floor all night, particularly as there were only three women. We were called to order as the top brass made their entrance. There was General Eisenhower, Air Chief Marshal Bomber Harris, several others and none other than my hero of the day, Winston Churchill. I couldn't believe my luck seeing him again.

Of course, my evening was a little spoiled by Major Preedy who had been assigned to the top brass to make the appropriate introductions to them and it was now our turn.

What happened next, Mr White, was pure theatre and without doubt, a one-off. The entourage arrived and the Major introduced the Sergeant. 'One of the bravest men in the American forces, Sergeant Willis, sir. You will be presenting the medal shortly, sir.'

The General then turned to me.

'And this is . . .' The Major paused. 'This young lady was the interpreter on the mission, sir.'

Bomber Harris turned to me and saluted.

'This young officer is Squadron Officer Alexandra Fraser and is one of the most highly decorated members of our forces. She is holder of the George Cross, which should be saluted by all members of the British armed forces – officers included.'

Major Preedy was devastated and even worse was to follow when Winston came up to me and introduced himself, reminding everybody how I had won my medals including the DSO. Eisenhower had seen my discomfiture and made me feel better by telling me that my contribution was an important one and must not be forgotten.

The Americans were called to the presentation, the first being the Sergeant's medal of honour.

The Major was called on to make the announcements. 'For consistent bravery beyond the call of duty and for taking command in a very dangerous situation the Congressional Medal of Honour.'

The Sergeant walked towards Eisenhower and received his award to the cheers of all present, but then in full view he took the medal off and put it round my neck and this action was followed by all of the men, who handed me their medals, as they received their awards. It was very embarrassing for all the top brass, until the Sergeant began to speak.

'Sir,' he said, addressing the General. 'When I saw we had a woman on the team I was disgusted as I thought this action would endanger the lives of all of us. Several of the men felt we would have to nursemaid her. This wasn't the case; she not only saved the entire team on three occasions, by her ability to accurately throw grenades; she single-handedly blew up the entrance to the fuel dump and rescued, under very heavy fire, Flying Officer Reason . . .' He continued for a few minutes to recount my exploits.

'General,' he concluded, 'at first, when I saw we had a woman on board, I was worried but now I can say this, as all the men will, including Lieutenant Akers: we would have her on our team anytime. No, General, I would be proud to serve *in* her team at anytime!'

There was a huge cheer from all in the room and how could

I not be in tears after what had been said. I even had to be propped up by Winco due to the weight of the medals. The General came over to apologise and promised me an award but I replied that it was a pleasure to have served with such a wonderful bunch of men and that awards weren't important. Of course, I handed them back to the men, thanking them for their kind words because they deserved them.

It was a lovely evening and everyone enjoyed themselves. At the end of it, as the men from the team left the room, they each in turn gave me a kiss on the cheek and then saluted. The Sergeant, well, I simply gave him a huge hug and a kiss on the cheek. To hell with protocol!

Chapter 22

D Day arrived and at last the Allies had a foothold in northern France as we pushed deep into Normandy. There was bitter fighting as the Germans felt it was now or never.

Our section was ordered to go over to France to assist in interrogations, as we had been taking large numbers of prisoners of all ranks, from generals to privates. It was necessary to identify those Germans who were claiming to be French and also those who had committed war crimes. The Americans had already pushed the enemy past Caen and they too had captured many men, so we were also asked to go across and assist them.

We had been told to report to Caen and were driving along the main road into the town. However, they had neglected to tell us that the Germans had recaptured the area several hours earlier.

We set off in two American open Jeeps; in the first were five American soldiers; in ours, their two male translators, our Corporal driver and myself. I was effectively the senior-ranking officer, though I had no say in what action should be taken as I was part of the non-fighting force.

We set off with the Americans leading the way as they knew the direction in which to go and we followed about thirty yards behind. The noise of battle was all around; the big guns were blasting positions in the distance and you could hear the cracks of machine-gun fire almost everywhere. Although we were surrounded by noise, the immediate vicinity seemed strangely calm and I was wondering if it was because it had been demilitarised.

We drove a further mile or so, with the Americans, without a care in the world and seemed to be totally unaware of what was around them. Suddenly, there was a loud bang as a shell exploded in front of our Jeep and we were almost blown off the road, but fortunately it rolled gently over into the ditch. I extracted myself from the vehicle, not knowing our driver had been killed by shrapnel. I had received no training for anything like this, but I knew I had to get away from the Jeep as quickly as possible. However, I quickly saw that the others were in difficulties as they had been thrown out of the Jeep. One colleague had broken his leg and the other, as a result of the blinding flash, was suffering temporary blindness.

The Americans had stopped and were turning round when they came under fire; they jumped out of the Jeep and into the ditch and began to fire back. I managed to lift my colleague and ran down the field and into a wood, which was about 50 yards away. My other colleague followed me, holding onto the injured man's leg. He fell over that many times, it was a wonder that the Germans didn't catch us. However, it was a small enemy force and the Americans were able to contain them for a time. I hid in the wood along with my colleagues and made sure they were well and truly hidden.

'Don't do anything! Don't get up or make a sound until I get back. We don't want to get captured, do we?' I whispered as I crawled out of the wood to see what was going on. The WAAF blue uniform, I admit, wasn't the best of covers to have in the countryside. I could see in the distance a German tank arriving to finish off the Americans, who soon ran out of ammunition and were forced to surrender; they were taken prisoner and marched away with their hands on their heads accompanied by several German troops. I saw the German officer check the vehicles and put a bullet into our Corporal, so I presumed he hadn't been dead after all and the officer then went off in the same direction as the others.

I waited an hour for things to calm down, at least in the immediate vicinity, but it was still the same everywhere else.

The noise of the bombardment supported by our fighter bombers was incessant.

I crept over to the Jeep to look at the Corporal and to see if there was anything of any use to us. The Corporal had been shot in the side of the head, but it did look as though he had been dead before he was shot, as there was no sign of any blood. I took his dog tag off him and put it in my pocket and couldn't help getting emotional, as this was the only thing that would be left of him for his grieving family.

The German had missed three grenades which were loose underneath the Jeep, so I took those together with a map of the area. I went back to the two men and summarised our position and we opted to try and get back to our lines. We would have to carry Alan, and James would have to hold on to Alan and use him as his guide.

I felt we should travel by night as it was the only way we stood a chance of not getting caught. It was sad really as both Alan and James felt they were a hindrance and said that I should leave them as it was the best chance I had; but we were a team and we were going to remain as a team and there was no way I was going to leave them. It was therefore essential we had something to transport Alan, so I went scouting round to find whatever I could before the light failed. I had noticed several houses to the south of our position, but it was one of those decisions to make: would they be French or would the houses be occupied by Germans? I decided not to chance it and left them alone. There were, however, the outbuildings, so just before dusk I crept round and found several posts which had been cut ready to repair a fence and took two of them. I returned to the wood to prepare to move out.

We made the seat out of the two fence posts, which we carried like a stretcher, putting two pieces of wood across. It was difficult to sit on because there was no rope to secure them and also there was a question of the difference in height between James and me, but Alan did a wonderful job of balancing on them and being James' eyes. We started off with our home-made seat but within two or three minutes we had tripped and fallen. We got up and within thirty seconds we had fallen again.

'James, you have to trust me. I won't go too quickly or go over rough ground,' I said, trying to be firm. 'Alan, you must try and keep your eyes peeled and, if you see anything, you must tell us quickly.' I knew Alan was in terrible pain and it must have been difficult for him, but he struggled on.

'I'll do my best, Alexandra,' he replied. We had long ago stopped using our ranks in conversation; it worked much better that way.

However, our main problem was that many of the field hedges, long neglected owing to the war, had become covered in brambles, which in itself had allowed the odd sapling of hazel and hawthorn to grow through. It was tough going and we made only slow and painful progress. Around us the noise was still deafening and the sky was ablaze with flares, bomb and shell explosions and the flashes of big guns. It never stopped the whole night through and I was worried that we might be seen in the sudden illuminations as we struggled along.

We reached a narrow lane, but it was too dangerous to walk along. Cross country was our only option. I checked along the lane in all directions and it seemed quite safe. The entrance to the field opposite was some fifty yards down the road, and, I can tell you, it was the longest fifty yards I had ever run in my life. I was absolutely exhausted when we reached the field and fell, bringing all three of us to our knees; Alan stifled a scream as he twisted his broken leg. We sat down in the hedge to get our breath back and to take stock. I decided it would be sensible to make for the top of a nearby hill where we could get the protection from the wood and be in a position to get our bearings.

Once again, the ground was very rough and last year's brambles, brown and stiff with age, wound their way along the floor. Fallen twigs made nature's own alarm system, as they cracked loudly whenever you trod on them, making it almost impossible to walk quietly.

'Down!' I whispered urgently as I thought I saw someone or something at the edge of the wood about one hundred and fifty yards to our right. We dropped to the floor and lay there for several minutes before I dared to get up.

'Alan, prop yourself up and look over there and, if you see something, tell me when I get back. I'm just going to take a look.'

I went on all fours towards the wood, but when I entered the thicket it was too dark to see. I returned and Alan confirmed what I had thought: he had seen what appeared to be German lookouts. They were less than fifty yards away. Our current position was dangerous, so I knew we had to get to that wood, where at least we would be safe for the rest of the night.

It took ages to get there. Every footstep had to be thought out and double-checked just in case a snapping twig or sudden fall alerted the Germans to our presence. At last we were there and in a temporary hiding place, but already the dawn was breaking. It was about eight o'clock when it became light enough for us to see anything properly and it appeared we were situated on the northern edge of the wood, which actually turned out to be extensive. Things were becoming more difficult as Alan was beginning to succumb to the pain and it was obvious he needed medical attention urgently.

I once again decided to have a look at our position and promised James and Alan that I would be back shortly. Keeping low, I managed to pinpoint the various landmarks and, using my map, I calculated that if we kept to the northern edge of the wood we would find a road which would take us back in the direction of Caen. First, though, I had to check out the woods. I had travelled about three hundred yards when I thought my eyes were deceiving me. We had stumbled onto a crack SS Division, which was backed up by Panzer tanks. Now there were other reasons to get back quickly: to tell our troops what was lurking in the woods.

I slowly made my way round the edges of the German forces. I went as close as I dared to the edge of their encampment, lying flat on my stomach. By the time I had got to the far side of the wood I had been cut to ribbons and every damned inch seemed to shove another splinter into me somewhere. I could now see vehicles hidden in the other copses, but there was no doubt in my mind that the Germans had two or three divisions hidden away, ready for a massive counterattack.

I was making my way back to the others when I spotted the American servicemen who had been with us the day before. The five men were tied up with their hands behind their backs; they were sitting on the floor, underneath a tarpaulin; they had obviously been beaten as they were in a terrible state.

Mr White, I couldn't believe what I saw next: a classic example of 'man's inhumanity to man'. This tall thickset SS officer came along and ordered his soldiers to get the men up on their feet. They pulled them out of the shelter and stood them facing in my direction. I just hoped they couldn't see me as I lay in the thicket, but I could see them. I could see the terror in the young ones' eyes and the determination and hatred in the others. They knew what was going to happen next. The officer told them to get onto their knees. Three of them did but the other two refused, so he shot them both in the legs. He laughed as they writhed in pain on the floor. He then proceeded systematically to shoot the other three in the back of the head and they fell forward. He turned to the others and as he did so one of the Americans spat as hard as he could, the saliva landing on the officer's boot. He looked down in disgust and slowly walked over to one of the dead Americans and wiped his boot on him.

'You dirty Kraut,' I heard one of the Americans say. Then the SS officer leant down and said, 'Yes, but I'm alive!' and then shot the American in the head, though not before he had received a second dose of American phlegm between his eyes. The German officer calmly took off his helmet off and wiped his face, allowing me to get a good look at him.

He shot the surviving American in a matter-of-fact sort of way and walked off, laughing and joking with his subordinates. I couldn't help thinking of Friedrich and the way he had been treated by the American and the warning I gave him about treating prisoners properly.

I went back to the others and told them what I had now seen. Our only chance was to get away in the dark. Alan, however, was becoming very ill and needed a doctor almost immediately; he wasn't yet delirious but I felt it wouldn't be long as he had already started shivering.

'Look, our best chance is for me to create a diversion. There's a small fuel dump up there. I'll throw a grenade into it as soon as it gets dark and then we'll make our move, but until then we've got to lie down and not make a sound . . . And Alan, whatever you feel, you have got to bear it for another twenty-four hours. I know it's difficult but, if you try and get some sleep, it will pass the time quicker.'

Sleep, though, was out of the question. The noise of battle was intense and, given what I had witnessed, it was obvious that a German counterattack was imminent. You could even hear the big guns and the tanks being rolled up into position and I couldn't understand why our side hadn't already seen all this activity going on and done something about it.

It was the longest fourteen hours I have ever known. We lay almost motionless all that time, sweat pouring out of Alan all the time; he was dehydrating dreadfully and then when the time finally came to do something I could hardly move, I was that stiff.

However, I put the grenades in my pocket and went back to the place where the fuel dump was but, to my horror, I found it had been moved. I had to go almost to the back of the wood before I found where it had been relocated. There were a number of fuel trailers strategically placed at the rear and I hoped that, if I could hit one, it might spread to the others. It was a big hope but the Germans weren't daft and they had protected them to some degree. The other problem was the dump had been moved deeper into the wood and there was little leeway for an accurate throw. I had only one chance: an accurate throw or failure.

I lay on the ground for a few minutes and it began to rain heavily. Some of the Germans had taken temporary cover but others were still very active preparing for an attack. It had become very dark and it was clear we were in for a storm. I took the pin out of the grenade and held the clip down and began to talk myself into action.

'They're running! Quick, throw it at the wickets. Quick, quick!'

I stood up and in one arching movement threw the grenade and fell immediately onto the floor. I began crawling away.

I had done it. The explosion was enormous and the burning fuel fell everywhere, including on me. I didn't wait to see the results of my handiwork, but ran like some monkey on all fours back to the others.

I must have ignited a small store of ammunition because there were tremendous bangs and cracks as exploding bullets whizzed in all directions. The sky was filled with trails, crackles and explosions, bright and smoky, making Bonfire Night seem like a garden tea party. We were in danger ourselves as the bullets pinged against the trees and we could hear the 'wheeeeee' as they passed nearby.

My success had its downside as now the British and American big guns opened up on us and the shells were not too particular where they fell. The noise was terrible; you couldn't hear yourself think, especially when, soon after, the German guns began to return fire. This was a diversion on the grand scale.

'Come on, let's go!' I said to the others.

We managed to cross the field away from the wood and then to the other side of the hedgerow, where we sat down to get our breath back. I knew at the end of the next fields we should, according to the map, arrive at a road, which would lead back to our lines. I signalled to the others to get ready, but Alan was now too ill to sit in our makeshift stretcher. My only option was to try and carry him.

'James, hold onto Alan's foot. I'm going to carry him. Don't let go! We'll get home, I promise!'

I lifted Alan up and almost threw him over my shoulder as we began to struggle along the edge of the field; but as we approached, I heard a burst of machine-gun fire which was returned by several volleys of small-arms fire. We got nearer and nearer and I could clearly see a machine-gun post at the corner of the field. It was controlling the road and nothing could get near.

'Down!' I whispered loudly as I fell to the floor, with Alan desperately wanting to scream with pain.

'Stay there!' I ordered. 'I'll go and see if we can get round it.'

The bombardment by both sides was intensifying and you could almost feel the shells as they fell and exploded nearby.

I set off crawling on all fours, thinking I would be able to surprise them. As I got closer I saw it was a radio coordination point with several German soldiers relaying messages; the machine gun was in a raised position, surrounded by sandbags, which obviously helped to protect their position. All the same, I decided to throw the grenade, and once again it was a one chance-only situation. I had to stand up in almost open ground to make the throw and with the machine gun active in all directions I had only seconds to do it.

I deduced that the machine gun was being attacked by our side, from two directions as it was spraying bullets in those directions. I therefore lay down and waited until it turned away from me, calculating how long I had before the machine gun would turn back in my direction. I had three or four seconds at the most and began to count myself down. I pulled the pin and held the clip tight.

The gun turned away.

One two three . . . and it turned back.

It moved away, I stood up and ran for a few feet and threw at the wickets. I fell to the ground.

'Right over the top of the stumps!' I shouted to myself as the grenade went off. It was a direct hit and there was a huge explosion as the machine gun disappeared in a ball of fire. The radio operators had seen me and began to fire as I ran off zigzagging into the woods. They were met with small-arms fire and retreated. I went back to the others and, with a new burst of energy, picked up Alan and led James to the road.

The rain was now absolutely torrential as we turned left at the field gate and started to struggle down the road; we had gone about fifty yards when I fell and must have passed out...

I woke up late the following afternoon in a British field hospital. I don't think there was an inch of my body that wasn't scratched in some way and my uniform was ripped and burned through in many places. In other beds there were soldiers who had lost limbs, and still probably didn't know it, so quite frankly I was a lucky one.

I stayed in hospital only for a day and was allowed out the following morning, after I had been given my spare uniform. I called to see James and Alan. The latter was under heavy sedation but I was told that they would both make a good recovery. James was already beginning to see a little more than shapes. Soon after I reported to Winco to ask what my next assignment would be.

'Good God, woman!' Charles shouted as I walked through the door. 'You look as though you've been pulled through a hedge backwards. What an earth have you been doing? Don't begin to tell me! I've already been told. You've been at it again, haven't you?'

'What, sir?' I asked.

'What have I told you, Alexandra, about when we're on our own?'

'Sorry, sir . . . sorry, Charles!' I replied.

'You've been at the bravery stuff again, haven't you?'

'No not really, Charles. It was a case of carrying Alan a few yards in the dark,' I replied.

'Alexandra!' He paused and just stared at me in silence.

'Charles, you're embarrassing me,' I said in a polite way.

'Alexandra, you are a remarkable young woman.'

'Thank you, Charles,' I said and he then told me to make myself scarce until ten o'clock tomorrow morning. We had to go and finish what we were about to start when we were so rudely interrupted.

'You may be required to make a report today so let us know where you are, but, if not, I'll see you tomorrow,' Charles said.

I left to relax and get some sunshine.

I had been absent for three days and, although I had spent a few hours in hospital, I was still exhausted. I was also worried that William had been told that I was missing and was desperate to talk to him. It's at times like these that you need to talk to someone you love. However, it was impossible to communicate in any way and I just had to grin and bear it.

The Wing Commander was right. I had to make a report on the incident and had to report to the general headquarters. I did not forget to tell them about the murders committed by the SS officer.

***

The Allies had been very successful in resisting the counterattack. The fighting had been intense and very bitter; it was as though the Germans were making a last-ditch attempt to keep control of France, and it was a case of win this or lose the war. It certainly was a decisive moment, but our determination was unbeatable and it resulted in the capture of thousands of officers and men. As a result, I was ordered to go over to Caen, at the end of the battle, to begin the interviewing of the POWs.

I arrived safely this time and was introduced to the various personnel involved in the interrogation of prisoners and found we were faced with the usual problems. Fearing reprisals, many officers – some of them perhaps guilty of war crimes – claimed to be Frenchmen, or suddenly demoted themselves to privates. It was part of our job to sniff out the murderers and bring them to a speedy justice. It was this that brought me into contact with my first war criminal – the officer who had murdered the corporal driver only a few days earlier.

He entered and I immediately recognised him. I tried not to show the anger that suddenly welled inside me, and to remain neutral. I led the interview as my colleagues listened and took notes.

'Name?'

'Eberhard Herold.'

'Rank?'

'Captain, but I'm not in the SS,' he replied, visibly shaking.

'Would it be a problem if you were?' I asked.

'Yes!' he quivered. 'They've been very ruthless and refused to acknowledge the Geneva Convention and I don't want to be included in that.'

I allowed him to continue as long as he wanted to, not interrupting him in any way because we had found from experience that, the more you let them talk, the more they would betray themselves or their comrades.

At last, however, I took control again and began by asking him what he had been doing during the last four days. He had been wandering around, trying to find his unit, he told me.

'So why did you shoot an unarmed British soldier in the head after his Jeep had been blown over? And then why did you assist in the illegal detention and murder of five American soldiers last Wednesday?' I asked.

'I didn't!' he protested loudly.

I could see he was absolutely shocked at what he had been asked and when I added, spuriously that we had been informed that he himself had given the order for the murders, he started to panic.

'It wasn't me! It was the SS Major, Gerhard Fischer. He made all the decisions with regard to captured prisoners and I know he was personally responsible.'

'But, Captain, if you have nothing to hide, why are you sweating profusely?'

'Someone is lying and trying to put the blame on me.'

'Captain Herold, do you think I'm a liar?'

'No, of course not. You can only go on what you have been told. I'm an officer of the German Army and I wouldn't lie to you. Whatever the consequences to myself!'

'What if I said I *saw* you murder the Corporal in the Jeep, would you say I was a liar?'

'But you didn't! You weren't there!' he replied, stuttering, realising he had made a mistake. 'I saw the Jeep. It was blown up and everyone was killed.'

'Which Jeep are we talking about? I only thought there was a Corporal in it. You're now saying everyone was killed. Tell me about this one then.'

'I'm confused!' he replied, trembling. 'You are trying to trick me.'

'Captain, I simply asked you a question about a Jeep and you replied and I quote . . .' I looked down at my colleagues' papers to check the accuracy of his statement. ' "I saw the Jeep. It was blown up and everyone was killed." ' I paused to let it sink in.

'Now, Captain, tell me which Jeep are you talking about?'

'I can't remember,' he stuttered, almost choking on his words.

'OK. Let's stop playing games, Captain. I have good evidence to suggest that you went over to a Jeep and shot the driver in the head as he lay there injured.'

'I've told you, whoever told you that is lying. I didn't do it!'

'Shall I tell you what the evidence is, Captain? I saw you and you know I wouldn't lie, because you said so yourself. What do you say now?'

'You're mistaken. I didn't do it!'

'But I *saw* you murder the Corporal driver . . . I saw you shoot him in the head because I was thrown out of the same Jeep and hid a little further away. I saw you very clearly . . .'

He was now in full panic and shouted, 'I was ordered to do it. It was Major Fischer who gave the order!' He was sweating profusely; it was almost like tears as it ran down his face.

'So now you admit you shot the Corporal in cold blood, whereas a few minutes ago you didn't know anything about it. But you do remember that it was Major Fischer who told you to do it?'

'Yes!' he replied somewhat reluctantly.

'Yes. It was Major Fischer who ordered it, or yes, you killed him in cold blood.'

'Yes, I killed him on the orders of Major Fischer,' he replied; now almost whispering.

'Now,' I said somewhat triumphantly, 'I want to ask you, what you know about the five American Serviceman whom you ordered to be tortured and shot?'

'I didn't, I didn't!' he shouted. 'It was Major Fischer. He did it. You will have to ask him.'

Where exactly is this officer, Major Fischer?' I asked.

'I don't know. He disappeared when our positions were overrun by the Americans. I think he escaped,' he replied, calming down a little.

'Then he can't corroborate your story then, can he?' I continued.

'Are there any questions you would like to ask this officer before we terminate the interview?' I asked my colleagues but neither had anything further to add or ask.

'Captain Herold, have you anything further to say or is there anything you want to ask before you are charged?'

'Charged! What do you mean charged?'

'You will be charged with murder under the Geneva Convention . . . Guards! Take him away and lock him up.'

'No, no, no! It was Fischer, not me!' he pleaded.

Finally, I lost my composure. 'At least, Captain, you will have the chance to defend yourself in a court of law, which is more than was granted to the victims whose lives were taken by your unit!'

We had been working in the area for about a week and I was walking past one of the temporary stockades where the prisoners were held. I noticed a particularly raucous group playing cards and one of them I couldn't mistake: it was the thickset SS officer who, I had seen murder the five American servicemen. He and his friends were wearing the clothes of ordinary enlisted soldiers.

'Major Fischer?' I shouted in my best German accent, hoping that his instincts would get the better of him.

He immediately looked round, then, thinking on his feet, immediately looked back at his cards.

'Bring him to the interview room in handcuffs,' I ordered some nearby guards.

I went to the interview room to wait for his arrival.

'Good afternoon, Major,' I said, greeting the prisoner. 'Please sit down . . . Leave the handcuffs on for a moment,' I said to the guard. 'We won't be a moment, Major. We're just waiting for my colleagues to arrive.'

I sat there simply staring at the man, who without doubt was beginning to feel very uncomfortable. He tried looking away but then tried to stare me out.

'Why do you keep calling me Major?' he asked.

'Oh sorry, I forgot you were demoted from the SS,' I replied sarcastically.

Just at that point my colleagues walked in and sat down; we introduced ourselves and explained the reason for the tribunal and the questioning began.

'What is your name?'

'Friedrich Bresson.

'Rank?'

'Private.'

'Now let's start again, shall we?' I asked. 'What is your real name?'

'Friedrich Bresson.'

'OK Private, what were you doing in the woods at Colline-Ste-Colombe along with the rest of your unit?' I asked.

'We were preparing to attack the American positions and I was carrying out the duties I was required to do by my superior officer.'

'What were those duties?'

'We were moving fuel to the rear of the wood and taking ammunition to the troops.'

'Good, that confirms what I had heard.'

'I have a signed statement here to say that you were on the northerly side of the wood and that you were seen with some American prisoners . . .' I paused to wait for a reaction and for a split second I detected a shudder of fear before he regained his composure.

'It goes onto say that you offered them cigarettes and a drink. Is that so?' I didn't wait for an answer. 'Do you remember how many there were?'

'Five,' he said confidently, not realising he had put himself at the scene of the crime.

'Good, so you were there and you did give them cigarettes?'

'Yes. They were prisoners. They must be treated properly,' he added, trying to ingratiate himself.

My colleague leaned over and said in English, 'Overconfident, don't you think? If you ask me, he's got something to hide.'

'Let's see then, shall we?' I replied.

'Do you know a Captain Herold?'

'Yes. He is one of our commanders.'

'Good, good. Is he a good commander?'

'Yes.'

'Good, good,' I continued. 'Would he tell you a lie?' I asked.

'I don't think so.'

'What do you mean, you don't think so? Would he tell you a lie? Would you expect him to tell you a lie?'

'No, I wouldn't expect any German officer to lie,' he replied confidently.

I went over to the guard standing by the door and asked him to step outside for a second. We both went out and I told him I was going to ask him to take the cuffs off the prisoner in the hope it would give him extra confidence, but he must keep his gun trained on him at all times and to shoot him if he tried anything.

I went back in the room and after a few more questions, I called for the guard to remove the handcuffs, which he did, much to the relief of the prisoner, who thought he was in the clear.

'I want to return to Captain Herold and the fact that you stated you wouldn't expect him to tell a lie. That's right, isn't it?'

'Yes, that's right.'

'That's good, very good, because I have a signed statement here,' I said, flashing a piece of paper in front of him, 'signed by Captain Herold which says you murdered five American POWs in cold blood.'

'He is mistaken.'

'But what if I told you that I actually saw you kill the men. That one of them spat on your boot and then in your face; that you took your helmet off and I saw your face quite as clearly as I am seeing it now. What if I told you that I saw you wearing the SS insignia and that we know your name is Fischer!'

'I'm Frederic Bresson and I'm a private in the German Army and I insist that I'm treated as a prisoner of war as defined by the Geneva Convention.'

'Major, just as you wish! You will be classed as a war criminal and will be charged with the murder of five Americans and I'll confirm that I will be giving evidence against you! . . . Lock him up,' I ordered the guards, after advising him of his rights.

I felt absolutely marvellous that we had caught the man so soon and that he would face the death penalty, but it didn't compensate the five families who had lost their loved ones. Both officers, Mr White, were executed for war crimes some six months later, just before the war ended.

My time in Normandy was not all gloomy. In fact, something I could even describe as delightful happened a week or two after the events I've just described. I remember I was sitting in the mess tent, taking a break, when one of my colleagues came in and joined me at the table.

'Alex, I think we've a little problem,' he said cautiously but then paused uncomfortably.

'Go on, what is it? 'I asked.

'I have a photograph here. It was taken from a German officer, a General no less, and he appears to be with you!'

He handed me the photograph. 'Friedrich!' I shrieked 'Where is he?'

'It is you then?'

'Of course it is. I must see him,' I said excitedly.

We walked the two hundred yards to the officers' quarters, where all the very senior officers were being held, prior to permanent billeting and questioning. There were about thirty officers dining as I walked in.

'General Rettenburg!' I shouted as I walked into the room. Suddenly, this proud, somewhat older, but much slimmer-looking man stood up and turned. He stood in silent surprise as he saw me approach.

'Tessier, my dear, how lovely to see you!' he said in German.

He held his arms open wide. I couldn't help myself; I went over to him and we hugged. The guards were too astonished to do anything.

'What are you doing here?' he asked.

'I'm helping to interview POWs. You'll be pleased to know that that American was disciplined for his conduct towards you.'

'I knew he would be; I knew you wouldn't let it go, if you got back. By the way; I knew you weren't French all along. It's a small world, Tessier. I used to have a house in Le Touquet . . .' He paused for a second. 'There was just something about you . . .' He didn't go on. For a moment I even wondered if he had seen me as a little boy playing on the beach.

'If you knew I wasn't who I claimed to be, why didn't you do something?' I asked in French, in case everyone understood what we were saying.

He leaned over and whispered, 'Because I fell in love with you!'

I gave him back the photo and said: 'We were never enemies, you and I! And aren't we handsome now that we've lost our big stomach?' I continued, laughing. We reminisced for a few minutes about the dance and the wonderful meal.

'How did you get back to the shore?' I asked.

'I was too injured to take much notice of what was happening to me. As luck would have it, I just drifted onto the shore. There had been a massive search for me and when I was eventually found I just told them I had escaped and Hitler gave me a medal.

. . . So, if you're not Mademoiselle Tessier, then who are you?'

'I'm Squadron Officer Alexandra Fraser and I'm married,' I replied, watching his mood change to one of disappointment.

'Gentlemen!' the General stood up and roared, 'I want you to raise your glasses to a very brave young woman who saved my life . . . twice!'

The assembled officers stood up and drank my health with water.

'Thank you, gentlemen,' I replied, acknowledging the toast. 'Here you have one very honourable man. I'll see you later, Friedrich.'

I kept in touch with Friedrich after the war and I'm pleased to say he flourished in the new West Germany; he even helped to form the BDR's army. Sadly he died in 1955, but not before we had had a lovely holiday with him at his home in Bavaria. He never married and always had a soft spot for me.

The war was now running in our favour on all fronts and it was only a matter of time before we would win, so there was a better spirit in the air and a feeling of confidence.

One day Charles, my Wing Commander, called me into his tent and told me I had been awarded a Bar to the DSO and I was being given leave to report once more to the Palace to be presented with the medal. Communication with home was almost impossible so I had to wait until I got back to England before I could speak to William, but when I did, by telephone in Southampton, the news was worse than one could imagine. Tom Collingham's plane had been shot down the previous night and he was missing.

His fellow airman had seen everyone bale out and that Tom had been the last. The problem was no one was sure his chute had opened and, even if it had, they thought he had left it too late. He was posted missing and after that, I hadn't the heart to tell William of my troubles, save to say I had a fourteen days' leave.

William was naturally very upset, in fact devastated, as they had been friends for a long time. Unfortunately, Madge wasn't the next of kin and therefore would possibly not be told of Tom's situation. William asked me to tell her for him.

Mr White, what a horrid job, to have to tell your best friend that the one she is in love with is missing and might be dead. I decided to go down to Pangbourne and see Madge there.

I arrived around teatime and immediately went to look for her. She was busy as the squadron was pre-occupied over France mopping up stragglers that were trying to escape back to Germany.

I walked into her department and one of her colleagues nudged her and indicated I was there. She turned and I smiled at her, but almost instantly she knew something was wrong and her smile turned to anxiety and then tears. She tried to be brave in front of her staff, but as she walked over to me, the tears were rolling down her cheeks.

'It's about Tom, isn't it?'

'Yes, my dear friend, it is,' I replied sadly.

The room of over twenty personnel fell silent as I put my arm round her shoulder and walked out with her. You could tell from the reaction of the staff, she had earned their great respect and they were now feeling some of her pain with her. We walked slowly out of the room and along to her billet, sitting together on the bed as I explained what the circumstances were and the fact that there was still a chance for Tom.

'I don't believe he is dead!' she said quietly, almost thinking the words. 'I don't feel that I've lost him. I'm sure he will be safe.'

She paused for a moment to take my hand, squeezing it, perhaps just to give her a little comfort. 'Come on, I'm not going to dwell on it. Let's go back,' she continued, trying to be brave.

'I've cleared it with the CO. We've got two hours. Let's go into the village and have a cup of tea and a chat.'

We managed to hitch a lift with one of the lorries and went to our little café that we had used over previous years.

'What's this?' Madge asked, pointing to the fact that I had been promoted to Squadron Officer.

'I've got a lovely CO who wants to keep me so he gave me this as a present,' I said, trying to make light of the matter.

The two hours went so quickly; we seemed to have only sat down when it was time to leave. We said our cheerios and I made my way back to London and to our flat. I felt miserable.

I phoned William to tell him that I had spoken to Madge and asked if he could get some time off as I was on a two weeks' leave. I didn't want to put pressure on him as I knew they were extremely active in supporting the push. But I did want to see him so badly. I wanted him especially to be with me when I met the King again. He told me he would see what he could do. I returned to the flat somewhat deflated; I was on my own for the first time in ages with nothing to do and still not knowing whether or not William could take time off.

I did some shopping for the usual supplies, using what coupons I had to get what I could and made myself as comfortable as possible. The following morning I had at last someone to talk to, in the form of Charles, who had come to tell me the date of the ceremony and to take me to lunch.

'Don't make too many plans, the push is on and it won't be too long before we need to be in Germany sorting the wheat from the chaff,' Charles commented almost as if giving an unofficial order.

We had a lovely lunch at the usual place and then took a short walk to the War Office where I was introduced once more to one or two of the senior staff and then returned to the flat alone.

I walked in and was slowly trudging up the stairs when I heard a noise; there was someone in the house and they were searching through the drawers!

I crept up the rest of the stairs and listened outside the door. I was terrified. What if there was more than one? Suddenly, there was a bang; it sounded as though a suitcase had fallen down off the wardrobe.

It was my chance; I opened the door and burst in, sounding like a Red Indian on the warpath. It absolutely scared William out of his skin as the look on his face was one of total shock.

'William! I exclaimed. 'What are you doing here?' I asked as the colour gradually came back to his face and I began to embrace him.

'I live here, you know,' he replied a little out of breath. 'I have a wife who keeps secrets from me and I wanted to know the truth.'

'What have I done? I asked somewhat despairingly as I clung to him.

'You've been out with another man!'

'I've what?' I yelled.

'You've been out with another man to lunch today.'

'You devil,' I said loudly and pulling him onto the bed. 'How did you know that?'

'Do you think that this rank,' he said, pointing to the rings on his arms, 'doesn't entitle me to find out what's happening to my brave wife? Why didn't you tell me?'

'I didn't have a chance. You had just lost Tom and I was told you were very busy, I presume planning the raids on Germany, and my little problems were small in comparison,' I replied.

'Nothing is small in comparison to what you did. Alexandra, you are an incredible woman.'

'You're biased,' I replied as I gently rolled him over onto the bed, pinning his shoulders onto the pillow. I lay on top of him and we kissed for several minutes and then began to gently undo his tunic.

Mr White, can you imagine being separated from your loved one by the ravages of war, with the thought that one of your best friends was missing? If you can, then please imagine how we spent that evening. It was one of the most wonderful evenings of my life.

William had seven days' leave and during this time our hands were never parted except when I went to collect my bar to the DSO from the King. I would like to think His Majesty remembered me, but with the amount of bravery that abounded in our country at that time and the thousands of servicemen that were more deserving than me, how could he remember just one out of all those?

The week was a mixture of sadness and happiness. It was that week that I discovered that the lady who ran the lingerie shop in the Kings Road had been killed by a direct hit in an air raid. We had meant to go and do some shopping there, but all we found was a pile of rubble. It had happened just the night before.

'She wouldn't have suffered,' the air-raid warden said when we asked him. 'At least that's one consolation.'

Mr White, that's how we saw life and death, then: 'At least she didn't suffer.' The whole of our philosophy was live for today because we may not see tomorrow and that's how William and I spent the week. We of course had to visit the Lyons Corner house, which, thank God, was still there, and of course we did our favourite walk along the Embankment back home to Chelsea.

William called in at the Air Ministry in order to contact his team while I sat waiting and being saluted by everyone. He had been away about half an hour when he came back smiling.

'Everything OK?' he asked.

'Yes, fine,' I replied. 'With you?'

'Yes. Oh, by the way Tom has been taken prisoner and is OK!' he said casually. But then we lost it and we both began whooping for joy in the corridors of the Air Ministry.

I immediately telephoned Pangbourne and told Madge. You will appreciate how important that was to her – to know that Tom was safe and that he would be effectively safe for the rest of the war, however long it lasted, and from the look of things at that time, it wouldn't be much longer.

I returned to France the following week and was duly shipped to Belgium and Holland as the Allies had advanced further towards Germany. I had been in Europe for about four weeks when I had my most startling news, I had become pregnant. I couldn't believe it as the consultant, Mr Evans, had indicated only a possibility of this happening and both William and I had been resigned to not being able to have children. I couldn't wait to tell William and then I began to realise that I knew nothing about having babies.

Mr White, you couldn't imagine how difficult this was for me; I had had no education about what to expect. I had no mother to talk to about what to do. No doctor who could tell me what to expect; no one I could turn to. As a woman I was supposed to know about these things, but I was brought up at a boys' school where this sort of thing wasn't even mentioned. I was on my own and the war was still on.

My only salvation, I saw, was Alice, who had not long since had her second child, and I couldn't wait to get back to England to talk to her. But my unit was very busy and I wondered if I would be able to get any leave. My only chance was to discuss the matter with Winco and it was then that I saw a stumbling block. If I told Winco, I would instantly become a persona non grata. I would lose my job; they would start looking for another person to replace me. There was no such thing as maternity leave, and pay in those days.

These worries now began to play on my mind: what if anything happened to William; what if I had no money; what if, because of my past condition, I had difficulties and became ill. What if William didn't want me to have it anyway? All these 'what ifs' were preying on my mind and I really needed to get back to England. I was prepared to face the most terrible ordeals on a combat zone, but I was mortally afraid of having a baby.

I dreaded going to see Winco, but I had no alternative as he had to know. We were stationed at Venlo at the time, just on the border of Holland and Germany. I walked into his office.

'Good morning, Alexandra; how nice to see you. Now what can I do for you?' he asked.

'Sir, I don't quite know how to start . . .' I began.

'Alexandra, you can start by calling me Charles.'

'Sorry, Charles.' I paused for a moment and then took the plunge. 'Charles, I believe I'm pregnant.' I shut up, waiting for some reaction.

'That's a pity! I wanted to see the war out with you,' Charles replied. 'I knew that it would happen one day, but I must be honest I was hoping it wouldn't be just yet . . . How long can you give me?'

'I hope April, May.'

'That will do me. This war will be over within six months and then you can live happily ever after,' he replied. 'Now don't worry. Let's get this job finished and we can all go home.'

I was astonished at his attitude. I was expecting him to be angry or annoyed, but it was the opposite. He really did want me to last out as long as I could, but I still needed his help, however.

'Charles, I need to ask a favour. I'm a trifle naïve about these sorts of things and I need a few days off to see my sister. Would you please let me go for a few days, just to sort matters out, and then I'm yours for the duration?'

'Five days starting tomorrow! You can leave now. Give us a kiss?' he asked and then whispered, 'Well done, you deserve it!'

I caught the first lorry back to Dunkirk and then managed to catch a boat back to Blighty. Believe it or not, I was back in seven hours. I don't think you could do that today by boat, do you, Mr White?

The moment I arrived at Dover I telephoned my sister and she promised to be in Chelsea by the evening. I then telephoned William who was unavailable and I left him a message and told him I was at Chelsea for four days and asked if he could get a twenty-four-hour pass.

I arrived early evening, as the trains were now almost back to running on time, and it was pleasant to go through London without the worries we had had over the last few years. It was lovely, too, to be in my own bed, after sleeping in a variety of places over the last four or five weeks. Alice, though, didn't turn up.

The following morning I had overslept and was woken up by a loud banging on the door. I raced downstairs to find a frustrated Alice waiting there.

'Darling!' she said exasperatingly. 'Where have you been? I've been knocking on the door for the last five minutes. I was nearly going back home.'

'You cheeky little devil. Come on in,' I said, so pleased to see her and giving her a hug. 'What happened last night?' I asked. 'I waited up till late.'

'There was an unexploded bomb by the line, just outside the station, and nothing could be moved, so I went back home,' Alice replied. 'Now, what's this trouble you're in? You wouldn't have asked the way you did if it wasn't serious. Come on, what is it?'

Sit down, you will need to,' I began.

'You're expecting!' Alice exclaimed 'Crikey that will be one in the eye for Father, won't it?'

'It's one in the eye for me too,' I replied.

'Does William know?' she asked.

'They're fully operational and I've not been able to speak to him yet. I've left a message but that's all I have been able to do.'

'Darling, you're cold. Go and get dressed and you can tell me all about it,' she said as we made our way up the stairs to the flat.

'Alice was wonderful. You've always been wonderful, haven't you, dear?' Mrs Fraser said to Alice. She smiled and leaned over to take hold of her hand.

'Do you know, Mr White, she gave me a crash course in what to expect and what I should do. All the mysteries of motherhood were laid bare and I began to think that, after all, I should have remained a boy.

At this point we were interrupted by Sybil who came to remind me it was 4.30 and that I had to leave for a meeting at the office. It was true. The sun was low in the sky and it was a little chilly. Alice had fallen asleep in her chair but now woke up in time to say goodbye.

Part 6

Motherhood

Chapter 23

I next went to Mrs Fraser's house a week later. This time we were alone and sat inside, in the sitting room once again, surrounded by her things. She was looking more tired than I had ever seen her but as soon as she took up her story, she became animated again.

Alice could never forgive my father for putting me through all this trouble and in some ways treated my pregnancy as one in the eye for him.

'Darling, I'm on the phone. Ring me if you have any difficulty at all,' she said, as she got into the taxi and was whisked away to the station.

I was now left to my own devices, and I think when anyone is alone and has any sort of problem one begins to worry about the situation and I was no exception. What was I to do when I began to put weight on? How does the damn thing come out? What would I have to do? I had heard of backstreet abortionists and wondered if I could get rid of it. I know it sounds terrible but that was the state of my mind. I was so confused.

William arrived only the day before I was due to return to Holland. He was so excited to know I was expecting and couldn't understand what I was worried about.

'Thousands of women have babies every year and they don't worry.'

But I wasn't thousands of women, Mr White, and I think William had forgotten that he was obsessed by the photo of the glamorous confident woman he kept in his pocket book.

Mr White, I think nowadays I would be considered neurotic. William began to lose patience with me; I put it down to the fact he was under stress from the war, but he really had no sympathy and whatever I said he made light of it. I began to feel I had married a man who was lacking in understanding and wouldn't support me when I needed it.

I tried to rationalise what was going on in William's mind, and basically it was similar to the thoughts I would have had as a boy. He will have been brought up as I was and it would be to him 'women's work'. He now looked on me purely and simply as a woman and nothing else, so why would I be any different?

I returned to Holland to resume my duties and out of sheer cussedness I didn't even write to William. I was so cross with his 'It's not my problem attitude' and I thought it might make him think about my dilemma. It didn't work as he was too busy to write and he was flying again, which then put the pressure back on me.

I hadn't received a letter or any word for four weeks and was beginning to panic. I had tried to bury myself in my work, which to some degree was successful as I had caught two very nasty individuals who had been responsible for the deaths of many members of the Dutch Resistance. However, after eight weeks, I was putting on the pounds and it was almost impossible to get into my uniform skirt. I managed to obtain a larger size which would keep me going a bit longer, but everyone now knew I was pregnant. The only advantage I had was that the officers were more polite and often gave up their seats in the mess when they saw me.

I was moved to Dortmund as the Allies advanced and spent Christmas in an appalling billet. The military tried their best to make Christmas special for us, but everyone was putting maximum effort into the push forward. I remember it was Christmas Day and we were all sitting at our tables in the officers' mess when Father Christmas came in. There wasn't a thing I wanted less than a jovial Father Christmas trying to cheer me up or make fun of me. It was bad enough him just being there.

He sat down and, looking at me, tapped his knee invitingly. I shook my head furiously but the other officers insisted, no, pretty much dragged me to go and sit on his lap.

'What do you want for Christmas, little lady?' he asked, as he put his hand on my knee.

I pushed his hand away in an exaggerated way, which made the officers all cheer.

'Come on, tell Father Christmas. What you would like?'

I didn't answer but just glared.

'Who do you miss most?' he persisted, putting his hand on my knee again, which I angrily I took off, almost slapping it as I did so, much to the amusement of the others.

'I miss my husband most,' I replied proudly, trying to make sure everyone realised I was married and that I loved my husband.

But all it brought was more huge cheers, clapping and laughter.

'Do you mean that?' Father Christmas asked.

Then suddenly he whipped away his beard and there before me was Group Captain William Fraser.

'Of course I do,' I said, beside myself with joy but playfully thumping him at the same time.

The mess erupted with whistles, cheers, claps and whoops as William took the costume off and picked me up and gave me a wonderful smacker on the lips.

We all had a lovely Christmas dinner and for the first time I felt I wasn't on my own to face these new problems. William took me for a walk through the bombed-out ruins of Dortmund and, in spite of the desperation I saw before me, he made me feel secure for the first time for a long time.

'Darling, I'm so sorry I treated you in the way I did. It began to dawn on me what you must be feeling and facing. I can't believe that I couldn't see your situation; I can now and I'll never let you down again.'

'William, you didn't let me down. You didn't understand and neither did I until the truth began to dawn on me. I have never had the education to cope with this,' I replied reassuringly.

'Well, I wanted to find out how my little girl, with my little boy, is getting on and this was the only way I could do it. I hitched a ride on a Dakota. It was almost like the days when I came back from Canada . . . And now I have got a few days' leave,' William continued.

'Darling, you've made me so depressed, I can't get any more leave now and anyway I promised Charles that I would work until the last moment . . . Another thing, darling, it may be a girl!'

'Darling, Charles is now a friend of mine and as such he has already granted the wife of his friend a few days' leave in Germany. So when we can find a decent hotel we can have a Christmas holiday.'

'You're lovely!' I said, grabbing hold of him and giving him a tight squeeze.

We spent the time discussing the sorts of problems I faced and how we could overcome them and by the time we had finished we were both excited at the prospect of our first child, which William was convinced was a boy. From that moment on, I became excited about the prospect of having a child.

When Christmas was over, William had to return to his base; for me, too, it was business as usual as the Allies moved ever closer to Berlin. While William's bombers were blasting Berlin into submission, I was becoming bigger and bigger; I had got through the morning sickness problems without too much difficulty but was now convinced I was having a litter. I had scrounged an even bigger skirt in the hope my appearance wouldn't be too bad.

January saw the last offensive efforts of the German Army but in February we crossed the Ruhr and surrounded several Divisions of the German forces and captured many SS Officers. Winco almost begged me to stay on as long as I dare, as he was convinced that it would all be over by May. I agreed and sure enough on the 8th May 1945, Germany surrendered and the war in Europe was over.

I left the WAAFs three weeks later, on the 29th May 1945. There was a small parade held in my honour, and Winco made a lovely speech on what a wonderful job I had done. The assembled officers gave me three cheers and I left in the arms of my husband who had arrived to take me home. We made our way back to Dunkirk but the port was blocked, so we decided to go to Calais and then onto Boulogne and try those, but it was the same story everywhere. There were simply too many home-coming troops and the Channel was chockablock with ships.

We had at least two days to wait so I suggested we had a quick look at Le Touquet, to see what had happened to our house. William had never seen it before, or in fact ever been to Le Touquet, so at least it was a chance to introduce him to my favourite place. We managed, believe it or not, to get a bus, which had just started running again, from Boulogne to Paris-Plage, Le Touquet, but I wish we hadn't gone there. The devastation was dreadful. The beach was a mass of barbed wire and concrete. There were pillboxes everywhere, and the only thing that was left of our lovely beach hut was the strip of concrete which we had used to pitch the ball. I couldn't think of anything except those lovely holidays with Alice as I stood on the pad, feeling rather sad.

The worst was yet to come. We walked slowly to our house as my condition wouldn't allow anything else. As I expected, the garden was totally wild, but what I didn't expect what was the ruin that the house had become. It was obvious it had been hit by a shell which had demolished two of the walls. The staircase, amazingly, was still upright, but it went nowhere; the rest had gone. The furnishings had obviously been stolen at the outbreak of the war.

Mr White, you can imagine what my mental state was like when faced with this. I couldn't control myself; I was in floods of tears and was almost inconsolable. Without William with me I couldn't have faced it. The one lovely thing which came out of our visit was that I met one of our former neighbours, a somewhat older Georges Le Blanc, who had returned to his house only the day before. Unfortunately for him, it was in the same condition as ours, but at least he had started to repair it and life was beginning again. I had knocked on what remained of their door and found Georges living with his wife in a makeshift part of the house under tarpaulins and tin sheets.

'*Bonjour*, Monsieur Le Blanc!' I shouted.

He looked at me curiously, not knowing who I was. Madame Le Blanc appeared.

'*Mais c'est Alice*, Georges!' she shouted to her husband.

'*Ah, bonjour, ma petite. Bonjour, bonjour*!' he said to me as he put his arms around me and squeezed me. Madame did the same.

'It's not Alice, is it?' she suddenly asked me, looking at me closely.

'No, Madame, it's–'

She interrupted me. 'Alex!' She seemed strangely unsurprised, even if Monsieur Le Blanc looked perplexed.

'Yes. It is, Madame.'

'How many have you got now?' she asked, touching my stomach.

'This is the first and this is the cause,' I said, introducing my husband William.

We chatted for a couple of hours and they told us of how it had been for them and how the Bosh had taken everything and how it had been impossible to get food and even fresh water. Mr Le Blanc had been a printer before the war, but the Germans had confiscated his printing works and used it to produce propaganda. However, he had managed to save some of his materials and produced a clandestine single-sheet newspaper for the Resistance. He had managed to start work again, albeit on a small scale.

My father, incidentally, later agreed that William could restore the house and that we could take it on as our own. It was finished in 1952, along with our little beach hut, and we took our first holiday in Le Touquet in the summer of that year, thirteen years after the start of the war. We all used the house, William's family too, and we spent many wonderful holidays there. In fact, I never wanted to go anywhere else.

I'm getting ahead of myself. That day we took the bus back to Calais, stopping off at Boulogne, just for old time's sake as I wanted to see the Hôtel Princesse. It was just the same and had miraculously survived the bombing.

'Was this the place where you met Friedrich?' William asked, with the vaguest whiff of jealousy in his voice.

'Yes, I rescued him from the sea, somewhere over there,' I replied, pointing in the rough direction. The beach huts and tents were long gone and the workmen were already trying to clear the stench of the Bosh from everywhere. As we wandered around, everything that had taken place only two or three years before seemed like some fantastic adventure.

I returned to Chelsea with William. For a while, it seemed as if he would be sent out to the Pacific, as there, of course, the war was still raging but the horror of Hiroshima brought all that to an end.

I spent the last six weeks of pregnancy mentally preparing myself for my change of circumstance: from being an active officer in the WAAFs, an academic and an athlete, to being a housewife and mother. Behind me was an adventurous, high-octane career. Ahead of me lay feeding a baby, washing nappies, cleaning a house, shopping for food and clothing and . . . It was a bit of this and that, and yet it was the 'that' which was tearing me apart. The last vestiges of my 'male' life seemed to be slipping away from me. I even tried to talk matters over with my mother-in-law, but all she could talk about was how it was my duty to look after her son and do women's work.

The time arrived when I had to go into a nursing home to have the baby. William had insisted that it was perhaps the best thing for me, as it had to be a caesarean section, which as far as I was concerned was definitely the best thing possible. I walked in with William carrying my suitcase and was welcomed by Matron.

William introduced me to her.

'So this is our little mother-to-be then, is it?' Matron said, her patronising manner putting me right off.

Who else could it be? Does anyone else look bloody pregnant, I thought to myself, gritting my teeth so that my thoughts wouldn't be heard.

'Well, Mr Fraser, we've a lovely room all ready. I'm sure she will be very comfortable,' she continued as though I wasn't there.

It was about time I said something.

'Well, William, dear,' I said sarcastically, taking my annoyance out on him. 'Aren't you going to tell me what Matron has said, as she appears to only want to talk to you?'

He looked at me, rolled his eyes to heaven and said quietly, 'Behave yourself or I'll smack your bottom.'

She showed us into my room, still talking to William as though I was absent, explaining what they were going to do and then very kindly allowed him to stay with me for a few minutes. 'As we have to get our mother-to-be ready.'

As mother-to-be, apparently, at no time were they going tell me what was going to happen and what I was to do. I was just expected to know it all.

'It won't be long now, little lady,' the doctor said as they knocked me out.

The next thing I knew was that I woke up to find the Sister carrying in a new-born baby boy wrapped in a white cotton sheet.

'You have a lovely baby boy, Mrs Fraser,' the nurse announced, smiling all over her face.

'Is he all right?' I asked, thinking back to my own birth.

'Yes, perfectly!' she replied, still beaming. 'Would you like to hold him?'

Oh God, I knew this was coming. Why did I let this happen to me, I asked myself and then felt I had to show willing. 'Oh yes please!' I replied, trying to sound enthusiastic. Sister placed the baby on the pillow next to me.

'Oh he's got your eyes. He's so beautiful,' she said, trying to be pleasant.

I turned to look at the child and thought beautiful? He's a shrivelled-up little monster. How on earth could she say he was beautiful? What am I supposed to do with it? My thoughts were broken by the entrance of Matron.

'Now then, how is our new mother today?

'I'm fine.'

'Good, we like our mothers to be fine, don't we, Sister?'

'Now, Mother, have we fed baby his breakfast yet?' Matron asked.

Oh my God, Alice didn't tell me anything about this. What on earth is she going to do? No! what on earth does she want me to do? Oh I wish I were dead. They were the only thoughts in my head.

The lovely Sister answered for me. 'No, Mother hasn't fed baby yet, Matron.'

Why doesn't she mind her own business. Why can't she give him his breakfast. Nurses are trained to do that kind of thing, aren't they?

Then the worst nightmare in my entire life began, as Matron and her entourage walked over to me. It seemed as though the entire nursing staff had dropped down a gear as everything was happening in slow motion.

'So, Mother, let's put baby to the breast,' Matron said, picking up the little monster and peeling back my pyjama jacket.

'What!' I yelled.

'Come on, Mother, don't be silly. Baby needs his dinner, doesn't he?'

You said 'breakfast' a few minutes ago, you bossy devil, I thought, as I was trying to smile at the vicious woman who was trying to interfere with my person and who had now just succeeded in flopping my left breast out of my pyjamas, despite my attempts to stop her.

'Is Mother a little shy then?' she asked me.

I'm not bloody shy; I'm just simply bloody stupid. What on earth am I doing here?

I was thinking all these things when Matron, without warning or the decency to tell me what she was doing, just pushed this thing at my chest, which suddenly sucked into my nipple, nearly pulling it from the rest of me.

I had never sworn so much in my life as I had at this point. 'Bloody hell!' I yelled. 'What the hell are you doing?'

'Don't be a silly billy, Mrs Fraser. Baby needs his dinner and you will just have to get used to it, won't you?'

Get used to what, I thought as the monster just kept sucking. The initial shock had subsided when Matron had to put her two pennyworth in.

'Now, Mrs Fraser, we can't have baby feeding from just the one, can we? It will run dry.'

'What!' I exclaimed again. What do they want me to do now? Oh God, please wake me up! I know this is a bad dream.

'You will have to get used to this, Mrs Fraser. Baby depends on his mother and Mother must learn to do things properly, mustn't she?' Matron continued.

'Yes,' I replied with a smile that would have broken ten mirrors.

'Now, Mother, you give baby about ten minutes on the left and then–'

'Pardon,' I interrupted.

'So that baby gets enough nourishment from Mother. Then you take baby off the left and put him on the right one for ten minutes . . .'

I was thinking aloud, not realising Matron and the nurse could hear as I began to murmur sarcastically, 'I knew it. Twenty minutes of paradise!'

'Mrs Fraser, you're overwrought. Now I want you to behave like a fully grown woman! It will all come naturally, I promise.' They started to walk out.

'Come back, I'm sorry. I need you to stay,' I pleaded.

'No, Mrs Fraser, you must learn to do it by yourself,' Matron said firmly and then added: 'If you want to use the toilet, ring the bell. You must not get out of bed at all.'

I'm trapped, I'm bloody trapped. I've got a blood-sucking parasite attached to me and I can't escape. This is all William's fault. He did this to me!

'Mother, ten minutes is up. Come on swap over!' Sister ordered as she popped her head back around the corner.

'I can't! It won't let go!' I said, as I tried to pull away and couldn't.

With a sigh of irritation, Matron came over to me and pulled it away with an almighty loud 'PLOP'.

'Come on, Mrs Fraser, I'm helping you this time, but you really must try to do it yourself! And remember he needs four feeds a day . . .'

Matron left me to my own devices and, as I must have been tired, I fell asleep and was woken up some twenty minutes later with the tiger fast asleep on my right breast. Sweet, some might have thought, but I was more concerned with discovering what damage the brute had done to my nipples. It was with great relief I found out it hadn't chewed them off, though they were somewhat battered and bruised.

My inept movement woke up 'Baby' and it began to cry. And oh Lord, how it cried! Despite my best efforts – which I admit weren't much – it wouldn't stop. Eventually, the nurse came running in. Baby, it seemed, had wind and the nurse began to try to get rid of it.

'You must learn to do this, Mrs Fraser,' she said, handing the baby back to me. 'You hold him like that and then pat his back until he burps.'

I did as I was told because I knew I couldn't win, and patted the baby. She was right. It burped and spewed all down my pyjamas. The stench was awful and made worse by the nurse when she said 'There that was easy, wasn't it? You'll soon get used to it.'

But Baby still didn't want to stop crying.

'He wants changing,' the nurse said proudly.

'I know he does; I'll swap it for a dog any day,' I replied quietly, hoping the nurse didn't hear.

She came over to the bed and laid a large rubber mat across it, then pulled up a trolley with some warm water in a bath at the side of the bed and said. 'Now Mrs Fraser, I want you to pay attention. We're going to change his nappy.'

What wonderful new experience was this to be, I thought.

She told me to undo the safety pin, which in itself was big enough to hold Harry Houdini on his tightrope, and yet all it was doing was holding three little corners of a nappy together. As the nappy came away, it revealed a yellow mass of stench.

'Eeeeeerrrrrrh! What the devil is this?' I yelled as the diarrhoea came rolling off the cloth nappy, causing the entire room to stink.

'He's a good little chap. He's done his first number two,' the nurse said happily.

Oh my God, I'll kill Alice! What the hell will his number three or four be if this is number two? I was now becoming desperate.

'How often will we have to do this?' I asked the nurse.

'I have a little surprise for you,' the nurse replied, getting her own back. 'Baby will let you know, but it won't be "we", I'm afraid. It will be you. Really, Mrs Fraser, you will get used to it. You will have to, as this little chap is now fully dependent on you for everything. If you fail, so will he.' She turned to leave, but just before she went, she said sternly, 'Don't let your husband hear you say "it". He's a lovely little boy and you must be very proud. I would be if I had a boy like that.'

Well, that put me in my place; I was well and truly told off.

After the extremely active half hour, the tiger returned to his sleep and I was left alone with my thoughts. The nurse's words were ringing in my ears and when I put them in the context of what I had suffered, I knew it wouldn't be fair to put this baby through anything which resembled unkindness. My father's trauma when he realised he had made a mistake and rejected me wasn't my fault and anything I did and said wasn't this baby's fault. I had been successful in most things that I had done and it would be terrible if I failed as a mother because that is what I would be judged on, at the end of the day.

The first test of this new attitude came at four o'clock when William was allowed to visit me and I had to suffer the nurse complaining to William about me

'I don't think our mother is very happy with her lot, Mr Fraser. She has been very cross and bad-tempered with us and baby. Haven't we, Mother?' she announced as she walked over to the bed with him.

You patronising bitch, I thought, gritting my teeth and trying hard not to say anything; in fact, trying to resist the desire to get up and hit her.

William, bless him, jumped to my defence, explaining how hard I'd had to work and how brave I had been. But then I dreaded his standard patter about cricket scores and the like, so I stepped in, saying how kind the nurses had been in showing me how to do this and that, and then gave another gritted smile.

My problem then was I didn't realise how important it was to make oneself presentable for your husband after childbirth, as if it all had just been a stroll in the park. As soon as William and I were left alone, his first words were:

'Oh, you look awful! Can I have a look at Thomas then?'

I picked up the sleeping child and gave him to William, who gently and tenderly took him in his arms and cradled him. He looked so proud and when he said, 'Isn't your mum a clever little girl then?' it made me feel even more dreadful.

I was now feeling so sorry for myself that I began to sob, and I couldn't tell William why. Motherhood was supposed to be instinct, and I just didn't have it. William had more maternal instincts in him than I did. The moment Thomas, for that was his name, started to cry, William picked him up and rocked him back to sleep again. I was full of admiration.

Thomas soon woke up again as it was time for his second feed.

'Give him to me. He's hungry!' I said a little more confidently and with that, I very gently offered Thomas my breast, which he took like a magnet to steel.

However, I had committed a cardinal sin. No sooner had I begun to feed Thomas than Sister came running in, almost shouting, 'Mother, you can't do that in front of Mr Fraser! Where do you think you are? It's not the sort of thing fathers want to see, you know. Come on out, Mr Fraser,' she ordered.

I was furious and naughtily replied, 'Sister, he did help to make it!'

'We don't want that sort of talk in here, do we now?' she continued, pulling me down a peg or two. 'Go and sit in the waiting room!' she ordered, 'and I'll let you come in when Mother has finished feeding Baby.'

William went out with his tail between his legs, while I continued to feed Thomas and just drifted into thoughts about the future and how William had looked so proud to be the father.

'I know you are going to make a wonderful mother,' he said later, when he was allowed back in, giving me a squeeze and stroking my untidy sweaty hair. He then proceeded to surprise me by opening the little attaché case he had brought in and took out a large camera with a flash attached to it and announced he was going to take a picture of Mother and Baby.

'Not like this you're not!' I told him, for the first time feeling the need to look better than I was at present. I gave William the baby and proceeded to make myself look respectable.

The feminine genes were coming more to the fore, Mr White! I cradled Thomas, positioning my arms and, when I saw the look of real joy in William's face, I smiled for the camera and the photo was beautiful. He had it in his office until he retired and by his bed until he died and then it went with him. It was such a lovely picture. It was one of those golden moments that are occasionally captured on film.

On my last day at the nursing home, Peter and Thelma Wilkes came to see me. It was like having my father and mother there at last. There was sadness in Thelma's eyes when she held the baby, thinking, no doubt, how wonderful it would be if it were her own.

'None of this would have happened it hadn't been for you,' I said to them as they were leaving.

Mr White, in this life you are lucky if you can count on one hand the number of real friends you have and I can say quite categorically that Peter and Thelma were two of the fingers on that hand.

There were one or two reporters waiting to photograph me as I walked out of the nursing home and I had to hold the baby in my arms with William on one side and Sister and Matron on the other side. The report appeared two days later under the headline:

'Heroine Has Baby Boy'. It was a total shock to the nursing staff, as I had not told them anything about myself. Sister looked at me in a different way after that.

The three of us returned to Chelsea to begin our lives as a family, but William had one big surprise left for me and one, in fairness, I didn't really want: he had been offered a house near Lincoln and was expected to take up residence near the base. I agreed to go, or should I say was ordered to go. So within two weeks of leaving the nursing home, we had the first move to our new house where I began my life as a serving officer's wife, albeit the Commanding Officer's wife. I did, however, retain the Chelsea flat, and at the time I remember thinking that I could always run away there if I couldn't stand it anymore.

I'll never forget that day we travelled up to Lincoln, following the removal van. It didn't occur to me that Thomas would be so inconsiderate as to wet his nappy while we were travelling, or, indeed, want feeding. Not once but twice we had to stop at the roadside for me to do the business. The baby wailed so much that William eventually lost his tether.

'Can't you damn well do something about that smell? How do you think it will look when I arrive at Lincoln?'

'For God's sake,' I snapped back, 'What do you want me to do with it: eat it? Stop the car, *now*!' I shouted. 'And I'll go and wash him in the river over there . . . No, better still, stop the car and I'll drive. You can look after your precious little rugby player.'

This was what William had consistently called Thomas since he had been born. Didn't it occur to him that he might be a cricketer like his mother?

It was a wretched four-hour journey and quite frankly I must have looked a mess. William put the tin hat on matters, as they say. We had just passed the main gate, having been saluted by the guard and allowed to pass, when William turned to me and said, with what seemed like a touch of sarcasm:

'Darling, you look frightful. Can't you do something with your hair and straighten up a little?'

Mr White, I couldn't believe my ears. Here was a man who had shown such understanding and had been so supportive and yet now he was uttering these words. I was momentarily shell-shocked. I didn't say a word, but did as I was told. I put Thomas, beside me (we were, of course, sitting in the back), took out my comb and quickly ran it through my hair and endeavoured to tidy up. But I was so angry, I was almost shaking.

We arrived at our new home; the removal van, which was now behind us, pulled up and within minutes the men had begun to unload our possessions into a 1930s detached house with four bedrooms. The house stood in a row of similar-looking houses, all of which were for the officers with families stationed at Lincoln. Pete Seager's song comes back to me: '... all made of ticky tacky and they all look just the same.'

For the first time I felt like a subordinate, there to do as I was told; no longer a wife, but a chattel. As we alighted from the car, several other officers and their wives came to see if we wanted anything. Rather nice of them, I suppose, though I believe their ulterior motive was to look me up and down.

'Mrs Fraser, I'm Lucy May. I'm your neighbour. Now as soon as you have settled in, you must come and have coffee with us. We meet most mornings for a chat and it will help you to settle in and get to know people.'

'Thank you, Mrs May,' I said, trying to hide my irritation with the whole situation.

'Oh, call me Lucy!' she replied. 'We're not formal here. We leave that to the men.'

I cringed.

Mr White, it's amazing that on the previous occasion I visited the base – it had been a year or two before – I was the centre of attention – a glamorous female who turned heads, and yet now, when I was introduced, the men seemed to look straight through me. It was an interesting change.

I picked Thomas up out of the car and, as if on cue, he decided to wake up, causing all the females, en masse, to rush over and begin cooing.

'Doesn't he look like your husband?' Lucy May said in a condescending sort of way.

He bloody does at the moment, the shrivelled-up little devil, I thought to myself before forcing a smile and politely replying, 'Do you really think so? He will be pleased.' For a moment, I fantasised that Thomas wasn't William's at all. My, that would have put the cat amongst the pigeons.

William suddenly announced: 'I think we shall have to go in now. It looks as though we're going to have to give young Thomas his lunch.'

We? *We*? I silently screamed. When was the last time you had to flop your tit out and let a young animal try to bite the end off? Forgive my language, Mr White. It was how I felt. William was still doing his bit.

'Thank you, ladies, for your kind offers of help. I'm sure Alexandra will take you up on that and I know she will look forward to your coffee mornings. Thank you, gentlemen. I'll see you all in the office in the morning.'

And with that, William walked into the house, followed by his Indian squaw and papoose. There was no romantic 'carrying over the threshold' or welcome kiss, just a grunt from a somewhat tired and grumpy husband.

The house itself was quite roomy, though a little old-fashioned. It was let fully furnished to senior officers and we had only brought things which we would need immediately – food, cutlery, pots and pans, bedding and the like – and of course they were in the removal van, waiting to be unpacked. My CO, though, wanted his cup of tea; Thomas wanted his dinner and I wanted to run away.

'Darling, is there any chance of this cup of tea? I'm sure the men are absolutely gasping for one, aren't you?' he asked.

With that, the two automatons duly nodded in unison and replied, 'Yes sir.'

'Darling,' I said, smiling through gritted teeth, 'I would only be too happy to oblige, but I've no idea where the kettle, the cups and saucers and the tea and the sugar are at the moment.'

'Oh, of course! Well, you go upstairs and feed Thomas and then when you have done that it will probably be unloaded. You don't mind waiting, do you?' he asked the automatons, who once again duly nodded in unison.

Well, I couldn't believe it. I was ushered upstairs, out of the way, loaded up with all the equipment needed to feed and change Thomas and left to my thoughts. This wasn't the William I had married – this one was an inconsiderate bully. He had not shown any affection from the moment he got into the car. I began to ask myself: Was this what he was really like all along and was this what my life was going to be like?

I began to shed a tear or two as I sat on a bed and started to feed Thomas. Was this little thing the only friend I had now? Then suddenly my self-pitying thoughts caused me to laugh out loud. William came upstairs to see what was going on.

'How long are you going to be?' he asked. 'The van's unloaded.'

'For heaven's sake, I can't stop now! It was your idea, sir. Just put the kettle on and I'll be as quick as I can,' I replied, beginning to show my annoyance.

William went back downstairs, leaving me with my thoughts again. Well, it won't work, William, old chap. I'm not the frightened little child I once was. After all, I won the George Cross and the DSO twice!

Thomas at last finished. By now I had got the burping and nappy-changing down to a fine art and was finished in less than another five minutes; only this time, as I was in a such hurry that he missed the towel on my shoulder and spewed all down my clothes, finishing with a big smile.

I put him in his pram and, stinking like a sewer, went downstairs to finish making the tea. William always stood up as I entered the room and that day was no exception, and so did the two men who were sitting with him in what was to be our lounge. Once again William humiliated me.

'Alexandra, please go and change! You have sick all down your back!' he ordered. I was near breaking point, but bit my tongue.

'Where have you put my clothes, dear?' I sweetly asked through gritted teeth.

William told me where they were and I hurried up the stairs to change. However, he had a shock to come. One thing that Madge had taught me was how to be a quick-change artist and how to put make-up on quickly: in less than ten minutes I had put my best dress on and made up. I vamped into the kitchen to put the kettle on. Disaster number two: it was an electric cooker; the one in Chelsea was gas. I didn't know how to switch it on and had to go into the lounge to ask William for help. The men's eyes nearly popped out of their sockets.

'Could one of you lovely gentlemen help me, please? I don't know how to switch the cooker on. I've always been used to gas.'

Much to William's annoyance, the removal men both jumped up and followed me into the kitchen. Within a few seconds, they had told me what to do and I really played up to it.

'You know I wish I was technical like you. We're only good for having babies, aren't we?' I said, almost pushing my boobs into one of the men's faces, as he bent up from switching the cooker on. It had temporarily done the trick; I could actually see William was annoyed.

Anyway, Mr White, I made the tea and in the process had to pop next door to scrounge a bottle of milk, which allowed Lucy May and her husband to take a good look at the 'Vamp of Savannah'.

The men left, with William giving them an extraordinary big tip, and then I knew I was in for it. He stormed into the room and began shouting at me.

'Why do you try to embarrass me like this? All I asked was that you smarten yourself up, not come down like some tart.'

That did it. I burst into tears and sobbed uncontrollably, but he didn't stop at that.

'I have a position to keep up and in the last few weeks you have been letting yourself go. I want my wife to be tidy all the time. I want a wife that'll look after me, just as I'll look after her. I know you didn't want to come here and neither did I, but I had to and we will have to make the most of it. You will join the coffee mornings. You will take part in the officers' wives activities. It's your duty as the CO's wife!'

'Darling, why are you behaving like this? What have I done to deserve it? You complain that I'm untidy but you forget I've only just come out of hospital with your child. You're forgetting that I have had no training nor experience for this part of my life . . .'

'Please, Alexandra, don't bring all that up again. I've told you that's now in the past and you are what you are and that's an end to it!'

'But William . . .' I said, almost pleading.

'I don't want to discuss it anymore!'

William stormed off to the bedroom and finished unpacking his things.

I was truly devastated and hadn't a clue what to do next. Nothing had prepared me for the domestic life that now loomed.

I was like a fish out of water all over again. When I look back, I realise I was only thinking about myself and I never gave a moment's thought to what might be causing William to behave in this way. But I'll come to that in a moment, Mr White.

We spent the evening listening to the radio, the reports on the war in the Pacific leaving me wishing I was still in uniform and away from all this. Then suddenly, William stood up and announced he was going to bed and with that just left me downstairs with my thoughts. I wondered what I had done and whether or not he wanted to sleep with me. I gave Thomas his feed, changed him and took the risk of going upstairs. I bedded Thomas down in his own room and crept into bed.

William was dead to the world, but he was sweating profusely. I knew then he was ill in some way and that perhaps this might account for his unusual behaviour, so I resigned myself to trying not to make matters worse for him. I hardly slept a wink that night what with worrying about things and listening out for Thomas, though he was as good as gold and woke only once for his nightly feed.

William got up about six o'clock. He was soaked to the skin and the bed was absolutely wringing wet. He took a shower, dressed and went downstairs for breakfast. I was still in my night attire.

'Can't you dress before you come downstairs?' he asked.

'Yes, dear. I'll do better tomorrow when I have sorted out the clothes.'

He left for his office an hour later without a word being spoken.

Things didn't change for many weeks. Every night he would return home and say patronising things like, 'Darling, couldn't you have washed these things out earlier. Perhaps if you started earlier it would be finished by the time I got home.'

Admittedly, doing the laundry was a challenge. Of course, I hadn't got the use of the Chelsea steam laundry, so even William's shirts had to be washed and ironed by me, plus, of course, our underclothes, the bedding, the towels, the tablecloths and all little Thomas' outfits, which he always got amazingly dirty, God bless him. Once again I'd had no training for all this and no one to whom I could turn for help; it was just a question of trial and error.

William's answer to the whole problem was always something like: 'If you like, I'll get Lucy May to pop in and give you some advice.' How humiliating that would be!

Lucy May did call round, though wisely she steered clear of offering me advice. Instead, she invited me round for the first of the coffee mornings. I dutifully followed her next door, with Thomas in the pram. After the formal introductions, coffee was served and the business of the day commenced.

The officers' wives chief business it seemed was organising dinner parties and dances, various events for the wives of the other ranks, and other charitable activities. Once that was done, they would then gossip and talk about their sex lives, complain about their husbands and which of the other women's husbands they fancied. They discussed everything about everything and everyone, and nothing was sacred.

'You had better watch out,' Betty Morgan commented. 'Yours is a hunk!'

'And good looking!' Phyllis Arkwright interjected.

I thought: You can have the big ugly inconsiderate bully; I don't want him. I tried to smile.

Then, of course, when they thought my guard was down they began to question me about my life. How I had met William, which I told them; what I had been doing to help the war effort. I simply told them I was in the WAAFs at Pangbourne, helping with the stores. They nodded politely and obviously thought nothing of it. I had been, in their eyes, some kind of secretary.

As the women relaxed in my company, these coffee mornings became racier and racier, till in the end some of them were actually describing how they had performed with their husband the night before. I always kept silent during these conversations and I began to think William and I were unusual as we hadn't made love ever since Thomas' birth. I put it down to the fact that he was still unwell; in spite of my pleas for him to see the doctor, he refused and my concern even seemed to make things worse.

At one of the many Squadron formal dinners we had to attend, I was asked to present a cheque to the RAF Benevolent Fund, which had been set up to help the men wounded during the war and also the families of those killed in action. The officers' wives had worked tirelessly to raise money and had achieved £203 16s 10d, which in those days was a very respectable sum of money.

The entire officer corps had been assembled in the mess for the presentation and I was seated between William, who looked like thunder all evening and hardly spoke a word to me, and the representative of the Fund, Flight Lieutenant Ross Williams, who couldn't stop talking.

William introduced Ross to the company and he gave a lovely little talk about the Fund and how it was helping so many people and so forth. Then it was my turn: I stood up and presented the cheque to Ross on behalf of the group, making sure it was known that in this case I had not assisted in any way in raising the money, as I had not been there long. I sat down to which Ross stood up and thanked us all for our efforts.

'I had no idea the cheque would be presented by such a gallant officer as Squadron Officer Alexandra Fraser, holder of the George Cross and the Distinguished Service Order and bar. I was at Pangbourne when she won the first medal for unbelievable bravery and her name will be remembered there for a long time.'

A murmur of surprise went through the room, both among the officers and their wives.

'You're a dark horse, aren't you?' Lucy said as I called her over to meet Ross after the meal had finished.

'Oh it's all in the past now and not important,' I replied.

William left the presentation shortly afterwards and returned to his office, leaving me to my own devices, which was really quite embarrassing. Although people didn't make any comment to me, I felt that they had already begun to talk about our situation. There were questions from the girls at coffee morning: 'Is everything all right between you and William?' or simply 'What's the matter with William?' I began to wonder if William had another woman, as he was spending more and more time at his office. He was even becoming stand-offish with his officers.

Eventually, I ran the house like clockwork and, realising that William wouldn't put up with a scruffy wife, I kept myself very respectable, but I'll say in my defence that I was always clean and tidy, especially after meeting William. However, I began to lose weight with the worry and decided to see the doctor. I made some excuse to William that I was going to see Alice and made my way to Upper Hayfield to see the now very old Doctor Palin.

It was strange to see him after all this time, particularly when he hadn't heard about my life. Like others, he too thought I was Alice. Anyway, eventually he understood the situation and I began to explain what was happening to William, how he was always aggressive, how every night he perspired so much the bed was wet through and he was becoming reclusive even at work. He listened carefully to everything I had said and then told me that he simply thought that William was suffering from overwork. The fact he had flown more sorties than most people during the war; the fact that he probably felt responsible for all the friends and colleagues that had been lost; the fact that he now had a family and, finally, the probability that he might be worrying about his role and status in life now the war was over, might have led to a deep psychological crisis. In short, Dr Palin told me, he was very likely depressed.

'Alex, William needs to see a doctor and needs to take a few weeks off. Don't worry, I'm sure it won't last forever and I'm sure it's not about you.'

'Thank you so much, Doctor,' I said as I was leaving and then he repeated, 'Alex, I really do believe it's not about you. There are many men suffering similar problems now the war's finished.'

I left Dr Palin's surgery and thought I would call in at my mother's to show Thomas off. I was relieved to find that she was there on her own and that she was pleased to see both me and her grandchild; she made a great fuss of him, but there was still that same reticence, that fear that my presence would somehow offend my father.

I telephoned William and let him know I was going to stay at the flat overnight and he was furious. He tore into me over the phone, shouting it was my responsibility to be there to look after him and that I should set off back straight away. For the first time I put my foot down and told him I would see him the following day and slammed the phone down, shouting: 'Expect me when you see me.'

I drove to Chelsea, parked the car and took Thomas into the flat. As I walked in and closed the door, all the lovely memories came flooding back. How I had trapped William behind the door, how we had sat on the settee by the light of the fire and watched the shadows on the wall, and how we had made love for the first time. From that moment, I knew I just wanted to rush back and see him and help him through this crisis.

'Sorry, Thomas, duty calls!' I said as I picked him up and took him straight back out to the car, locked the house and set off back to Lincoln, all the time thinking, it's not the same man. William wouldn't do these things to me if he was well, I know it.

The journey didn't take as long as the previous one from Chelsea and as my thoughts were more positive it seemed to pass all the more quickly. I was waved through the gate and made my way home, although it was late, William was still up waiting for me.

'Where the hell have you been?' he asked, almost shouting at me, but then adding, 'I've missed you!' before I could reply.

'I've missed you too and so has this damned rugby player,' I said, which made him smile for the first time for ages. 'I've been to see my old doctor as I'm losing too much weight and he tells me I've got a few problems and that we must both be suffering the same sort of thing. Dr Palin says–'

William interrupted me: 'You've been to see him! Why not go to Donald?' Donald was Squadron Leader Donald Pitcher, the base's senior medical advisor.

'I didn't want it to affect you in anyway. I told him we were both under a great deal of pressure in the war.'

'Good Lord, Alexandra; what pressure are you under? You only have the home to look after!' I had to bite my tongue once more and make allowances. 'What else did you tell the noble doctor?' he asked sarcastically – he was beginning to return to what was now his normal self.

I couldn't help it; the words simply fell out of my mouth. 'I told him every morning when you wake up the bed is wet through with perspiration and that you were losing weight.' Then something snapped in me a little as I continued loudly: 'And you haven't even noticed that my clothes no longer fit me properly as I'm losing weight because of the worry. Then I mentioned that sometimes you had very bad moods and that sometimes even your men were asking if you were all right.'

He went mad. 'You've no right to talk about me behind my back, to a doctor or anyone else, particularly to my officers. How dare you do this to me!' he shouted. 'I'm going to bed,' and with that, he stormed out of the room and charged upstairs, slamming every door in the process. I was sure the entire camp would have heard his antics. Thomas certainly did and was now adding to the commotion.

There was an uneasy calm and then there was another almighty outburst as he stormed downstairs, banged his way into the dining room, and threw the bed sheets at me. 'The sheets are fucking wet through, you stupid bloody woman. Won't you ever learn how to run a home?'

Thomas was now screaming his head off and nothing I could do could stop him, but William hadn't finished. 'If you don't learn to do things properly you can bloody well go and take him with you. I'm sick to death of your whining. You can't do this and you can't do that. You're an incapable bloody bitch!'

Once again he threw the damp sheets at me, which not only covered me, but also Thomas who was in my arms, causing him to scream yet again. Thomas's penultimate outburst came as he shouted, 'And you can shut him up!'

I didn't say a word; I simply sat down and gave Thomas his nightly ten minutes on one side and ten minutes on the other, which caused William to yell his final order.

'I've told you before. I don't want to see you doing that down here. Get upstairs!'

I calmly picked up my stuff, with Thomas refusing to let go, and quietly went into one of the spare bedrooms to finish feeding him. The poor little devil was now oblivious to all that was happening around him and within a short time he was asleep. I put clean sheets on the bed and returned downstairs to find William sitting on the settee, with his head in his hands.

'What on earth is happening to us?' he asked.

'Nothing with us, darling. You're not very well, that's all,' I replied.

He was just about to snap back at me, when I put my finger across his lips and said. 'Sssssshhhh!'

He took a deep breath and then sighed, as though he had all the troubles of the world on his shoulders.

'Come on. I've made the bed. Let's go upstairs,' I said as I helped a willing soldier to his feet and helped him into bed.

For the first time in weeks he actually allowed me to cuddle up to him. I got up at five the next morning and made sure everything was perfect and that I was clean and proper, simply to stop him losing his temper, as I knew that wasn't doing him any good.

'Alexandra, the sheets are wet again,' he remarked as he came downstairs.

'Yes I know, darling, I'm afraid you were perspiring again all through the night. It can't be helped, but I'll get them washed and dried before you come home tonight,' I said, trying everything in my power to keep him calm. William seemed a little more receptive this morning so I took my opportunity to influence his thoughts.

'Darling, I have to talk to you. I have to let you know I love you more than life itself, but I have to let you know I want our marriage to be a partnership where we can talk to one another and share each other's concerns when we have problems. I don't want a marriage like my father and mother have, where my mother is frightened to say or do anything which might upset my father. I don't want to have to keep quiet, just to keep the peace; I don't want to be frightened to tell you things, just in case you fly into a rage. I want our marriage like it was: when I could talk to you; when you would try to understand me and where you would listen to me when I thought I had something worth saying.

'I don't want to feel embarrassed in company when you admonish me publicly and I do want to feel that my life is worthwhile and I'm not just a skivvy for the CO and I do want to be held, to be kissed and told that you love me. We've got a family to raise and we don't want Thomas to live in a house where there is constant friction. We want a home where he will know he is loved and where he will know his parents love each other and he will be able to feel it.

'I'll try harder to be what you want me to be, but you have to meet me some of the way. William, you must look at yourself. You are pale and losing weight, and every morning the bed is wet. Please, I want you to think of yourself and see the doctor because you are becoming very poorly. I love you, William, just the way you were and I don't want you to change.'

I finished my little speech and, again before he could say a word, I gave him a hot sweet cup of tea and moved away to let my words sink in.

Thomas saved my bacon as, once again and right on cue, he started crying for his breakfast. I finished cooking William's breakfast: egg and bacon and toast, as some items of food were already becoming easier to get. He sat alone in total silence and the moment he had finished, he went to the office without a word being spoken.

I skipped the coffee morning meeting and concentrated all my efforts on getting the house clean and tidy and preparing a meal which I hoped he would be proud of – with the help of Fanny Craddock's latest radio recipe. However, William had a trick up his sleeve. Late in the afternoon, he sent one of his young officers round to tell me he would be bringing four or five guests round for dinner tonight and asked me to put his dress suit out.

Quite frankly, I just wanted to run away, but, regardless of the lateness of the hour, I made the effort and trebled up on the quantities of Fanny's recipe, laid the table for seven places, tidied up the lounge, fed Thomas, changed into something that nearly fitted me and waited for our guests to arrive. Six o'clock arrived and there was no sign of anyone, and by seven, I was beginning to get worried as the meal would be ready by seven thirty.

William arrived home by himself at seven fifteen. He walked in as though nothing had happened, hardly acknowledging my existence.

'Where are your guests then?' I asked.

'Oh, didn't I tell you? They're unable to come,' he replied casually.

'Oh, William, I got everything ready. Why on earth didn't you tell me? It's such a waste.'

'Oh for heaven's sake, it's not the end of the world. I'll phone Jack next door and invite them round, the Shepherds and the Morgans, too, and then it will all be used up.'

I would have preferred for us to be on our own, but he was already phoning next door.

'Jack, can you and Lucy come round for dinner? Alexandra has had a bit of a disaster and cooked too much and I would like you to come and help eat it. Come as you are. No need to dress up!'

That, Mr White, is how he invited all three couples. Why he had to tell a lie and make it out to be my fault I do not know;

but as I promised myself, I knew he was ill and I was determined to go along with it calmly. You can imagine however, how embarrassed I felt when they arrived, first for having really no option but to accept the CO's invitation and, second, to discover that I was all dressed up. But, Mr White, I showed 'em.

Lucy and Jack arrived first and I opened the door with a wonderful smile. 'Come on in. How nice of you to come and help me out,' I said as I took them into the lounge.

'William, could you please offer Jack and Lucy a drink? I'll go and let our other guests in.' The Morgans and the Shepherds arrived together and I gave them the same treatment.

It was the very first time I had given a dinner party, Mr White, albeit an impromptu one, and thanks to Fanny, the meal was a success. The beer and the wine did loosen the tongues and the conversation didn't dry up and the food was as delicious as the post-war rationing would allow. I don't know how I managed to stay awake until one in the morning, the time when our guests departed, and I didn't know how I controlled my anger when William made some comment about how I ought to do something different next time. At no time did he say, 'Well done' or 'thank you, darling.'

Matters didn't improve over the next two to three months; in fact I think things got marginally worse. William actually began to lose interest in Thomas, having already lost interest in me, despite my having got my figure back after having Thomas and looking, I think, reasonably presentable. William still wouldn't go to the doctor's to discuss his situation as he refused to recognise there was anything wrong with him.

I now felt that I was the only one who could do something to prevent our marriage from falling apart. I decided to go and meet Alice, and with William's grudging permission, I arranged to meet her in the West End, at my favourite Lyons Corner House. It was like a breath of fresh air.

I bored her to tears with my problems, but at least I had someone who listened, which I suppose was a good thing in itself, as it got things off my chest. I thought it would be better to leave the base for a short time until William had sorted himself out.

Alice, however, became serious – a rare thing. 'It's a difficult decision you have to take. He is the father of your child and it's not fair to Thomas just to walk away– '

'But he doesn't talk to him anymore,' I interrupted, 'and he hasn't talked to me civilly for weeks.'

'Nonetheless, darling, I want you to make a list. On the one side write down all the reasons for going and on the other, all the reasons for staying. If, and only if, the going list is longer should you even contemplate leaving your husband. You have to remember it's not easy for us, particularly when we have children.

'Your world has changed and, I promise you, Alex, you would find it almost impossible to get a job and you would lose everything. If the staying list is longer, then you will just have to make the best of it.'

The subject changed and we spent the rest of the day just chatting and quite frankly, having a lovely time. I was sorry to see her go as it had been a wonderful respite from all my woes.

I returned home to spend the next few days thinking seriously about my situation and, as things didn't improve, I decided I would make that list. Reasons to Leave: One: he was cruel. Two: I couldn't think of anything that didn't come under the heading of cruel. So it was Reasons to Stay. One: I couldn't live without him. From then on I just sat looking into space and realising I had to do as Alice said and make the best of it.

The following day the country was euphoric as Japan had surrendered after the two atomic bombs had put paid to their fighting spirit. The officers' wives now had the job of organising the victory celebrations on the base. There were to be parties for all ranks and, of course, William as the overall Commanding Officer and his wife were invited to all of them.

The first was a very grand affair with all commissioned and non-commissioned ranks invited. It was to be held in one of the hangars and it was amazing the effort which was put into it; one would never have guessed what the building was from the inside.

Would you believe it, there were over two thousand people at that dance? For the duration, I acquired a babysitter, who had strict instructions to contact me if things became difficult. I fed Thomas before we left and we set off in silence. I was determined to have a good time, as I was wearing that same red dress that had gone down so well in 1941, together with my medal ribbons.

Everyone was in high spirits and everyone, with the exception of William, was determined to have a good time. The Air Ministry had done well for us, as there was a fantastic buffet and for the dance music we had Ted Heath and His Orchestra, which was very famous at the time. We all lined up to be served with our food and returned to our tables, after which it wasn't long before the band started up. William and I were asked to start the dance, which we did in spite of William's reluctance. We set off with a quickstep made famous by Roy Fox and his Band, 'I'm in Love' – very apt.

Do you know, Mr White, we danced round the floor as if it was our first time, when we were fond of each other. He held me so tight as though he wanted to let the others know I was his again. Soon many others joined us on the floor and the dance got going.

I don't think I missed a dance in the first half of the evening and I felt really good. Even the good-looking Lucy May kept commenting how much I was in demand.

The wives had spent much of the first half selling raffle tickets in aid of the RAF Benevolent Fund and I was asked to pick the winning tickets from the large drum. Ted Heath called us all to order and announced: 'I want to ask the CO's wife, Squadron Officer Alexandra Fraser, George Cross, DSO and bar, to draw the raffle.'

Mr White, there was a massive cheer from everyone; it seemed to go on for minutes and was a very emotional moment.

Cheers turned to wolf whistles as they saw me cross the floor and walk up the steps onto the platform. I felt very proud to have done my bit during the war and very proud to be one of those present in that hangar. I drew ten of the winning tickets and announced that the ladies had actually made over three hundred pounds for the fund, once again to loud cheers.

'Thank you, Mrs Fraser,' Ted Heath shouted over the hubbub. 'Now then, folks, let's begin the dancing again,' and the band struck up, beginning with all the wartime favourites, which everyone including William sang along to. Then the band played the latest fad, American jive, which I just loved. I danced round and round with what seemed like everyone until William asked me to stay around for a few minutes as he wanted to introduce me to a few people. For once, he seemed somewhat proud of me, having seen the way I was respected by everyone.

We spent time visiting all the groups at their tables and William personally thanked them for all the effort and help they had given to him and the war effort. I thought that this was the most wonderful gesture any one could give to their men and at the end of it one non-commissioned officer made an impromptu speech and gave a 'three cheers' to the CO and his wife. That too was an emotional moment and it did show what the men thought of him. Mentally, I put that down on my list for reasons to stay – he must be a decent sort of bloke if they thought so well of him.

We returned home after a wonderful evening somewhat loudly, causing Thomas to wake up and start demanding his twenty minutes. Even that, however, was done without a hitch and within minutes, he was back to sleep and we were on our own. It was the first time for months that we had made love and it was the first time for a long time that he made me feel wanted, but we had the same trouble when we awoke. The bed was soaking wet and William was shivering uncontrollably. In fact, I had to call the doctor and thankfully it was Donald who was on duty.

He examined William thoroughly and told him to stay in bed for the rest of the day and then had a chat with me. I told him everything and it was as Dr Palin had suggested – stress.

William hadn't had a break of any length for several years and Donald suggested we went away for a holiday and in the meantime he would give William a tonic which would help him.

The following day William was given a month's leave and by the end of the week we were on our way to Looe in Cornwall.

We booked into a little place for bed and breakfast and almost immediately William began to get better; by the end of the second week he was almost back to his old self and I could talk to him, without him getting annoyed. By the end of the third, he had realised what a dreadful person he had been and was forever apologising, and by the end of the fourth I had got back the man I married.

Mr White, I remember walking along the promenade like some old married couple that couldn't be parted. The weather was lovely despite it being so late in the year. It was very quiet as the season, such as it was, had ended. People were beginning to start their new lives; some had been lucky enough to get hold of some paint and began to brighten up their houses after six or seven years' neglect. Everywhere people were smiling and eager to talk, all the more so when they learned that William was a senior RAF officer taking a well-earned rest.

That four-week break was the start of the rest of our lives and from that moment William never showed any antipathy towards me whatsoever. Those difficult months had changed me, too: I never went back to my old ways; I was always up early and still am; I always kept myself tidy and the house spotless, and never gave him the excuse to have a go at me. So I suppose it was a learning exercise for both of us.

Shortly after our return from Looe, there was an unexpected knock on the door. William, of course, went to see who was there. I heard the door open and then a very loud shout:

'Tom!' William yelled.

I raced to the door and yes it was Tom Collingham standing there; I had never been so pleased to see another man before, as I was to see Tom.

He had just been repatriated and hadn't even seen Madge yet. He had come simply to ask William to be best man at his wedding. Madge was still at Pangbourne, but, although the war with Japan was over, she was still waiting to be demobbed and he wanted to marry her before she was. He met her in the RAF and he wanted, for some strange reason, to marry her while she was still in the RAF.

It may be something about uniforms, Mr White. I understand that some men like a woman in a uniform and I think William was like that, because he did so like mine off.

'Oh God, you'll think I'm a wicked person, won't you, Mr White?'

Anyway William agreed and we all drove down to Pangbourne to meet Madge. I have never seen so many people pleased to see a man before. All Madge's staff who had been so supportive when he had been missing were euphoric to see her beaming face as he walked in. Tom proposed immediately to the delight of all the others and the date was set for a quick wedding. Tom wasn't going to let a chance like this slip out of his hands again, he said.

They were married at Lincoln Register Office within twenty-eight days of his return, with William as his best man and me as a witness. I was allowed to wear my uniform again and I too felt good and proud.

Life returned to normal for a few weeks, except now Thomas was teething, but what made me suffer wasn't so much the loss of sleep, but the cruelty which the little fellow dished out to his mother at feeding time. Mr White, it was bad enough when he would suck hard on the teat, just with his gums, but now he seemed almost to get sadistic pleasure from using his new sharp teeth on me, giving me a toothy mischievous smile as he did so. I tried feeding him on the bottle, but the National Dried Milk wasn't popular with this baby piranha.

Like William, Tom was offered a position in the RAF after the war and was stationed not too far away, so I had Madge close to me and we were able to resume our friendship. Within twelve months, she had a daughter and we were able to compare notes. It was a great time for squadron parties and functions, too, so we also had lots of opportunities to escape from our daily chores.

My cricket career did not entirely vanish either. That first summer there was an RAF knockout competition and William was keen that I play. I was thrilled, as I thought I would never play again. He had to cheat somewhat to get me into the team game, by putting me on the books as a temporary RAF clerk, as that was one of the conditions of entry, and initially putting down his own name. I made a practice bat out of a broom stale – the one my father gave me was at the flat in Chelsea – and began to practise against the wall of the house. My neighbours, Lucy in particular, thought I had gone absolutely mad; in fact I know it became a bit of a joke amongst the officers' wives, but I was determined not to tell them anything and spoil the shock. I got my coordination back and by the time the day came I wasn't in bad fettle.

We were a scratch team put together from players who had been keen on cricket before the war, so we were all somewhat green, but anxious not to let the Station down. The ladies were to organise the tea and I was asked to assist. I felt terrible having to tell a white lie and to say that I had to do something for my husband. The day arrived and most of the Station was there to watch, plus some of our opponents' supporters, which made it a respectable crowd. I was concerned as the pitch had been made out of the grass field at the side of the runway and the square had been cut out of that. However, I need not have worried as when I went to look at it, the ground staff had done a fantastic job.

We arrived at the ground at one thirty ready for a two o'clock start and immediately William went up to Flying Officer Peter Frost, our Captain, and apologised that he couldn't play.

'Good afternoon, sir . . . Mrs Fraser,' he replied, nodding in my direction.

'Look, Peter, I can't play and in fairness I had no intention of playing, but I have brought you someone who will do just as well.'

'Right sir, let's have him and we'll all go and change,' Peter replied.

'She's here,' William added to the utter consternation of the officer.

'But sir?' Peter started, obviously in shock.

'Don't worry; I'm sure she won't let you down,' William said, interrupting him.

One could feel Peter was very cross and embarrassed at what his CO had done to him. In fact, he was so cross that he commented:

'And I suppose you want her to open the batting as well?'

'No, number three will do!' William retorted with a wink at me. Peter was flabbergasted.

We went into the offices to change and they allowed me to go into the empty one next door, but unfortunately I could hear every word that was said about me.

'It's bloody ridiculous! The skipper has used his position to get his wife in the game. What the hell does she know about cricket?'

It was Peter speaking but most of the team seemed to agree.

'We'll be humiliated!' one said.

There, was, however one lone voice who supported me – Flight Sergeant Andrew Mellor's: 'I've heard she's played before.'

'Yes, Flight Sergeant, but cricket played by girls is hardly enough experience to play against a team of men, is it? What's she going to do when their fast bowlers come on – ask them to bowl underarm?' This caused a guffaw around the room.

I decided it was time to go round to meet the team. Peter

Crabtree introduced me to the rest of the lads. 'What shall we call you, Mrs Fraser?' he added.

'Alexandra will do,' I replied. I could see the disdain in the men's eyes, although they dare not say anything.

We walked across the field to sit with our respective players or partners and, of course, I went to sit next to William, who was taking charge of Thomas. Madge and Tom had turned up to watch the match, too.

'What are the lads saying?' William asked.

'They're furious,' I replied, 'particularly Peter, but it's understandable.'

Peter joined us.

'We've just lost the toss, sir, and we've been put into bat. Would you pad up, Mrs Fraser? Alexandra . . . sorry. You're number three,' he added, glancing at William.

'Yes sure,' I replied excitedly. For some reason, I had no nerves; I just wanted to get out there and bat. I didn't have to wait long as our opener was out on the last ball of the over and I walked out.

'Best of luck, darling!' William said, which made my day.

'Go get 'em, Alex!' Madge shouted.

'He's very fast,' the batsman warned me as he passed me.

The other opener faced his first ball and it went off the edge of the bat for four, to the grimaces of the bowler, the wicketkeeper and slips, but that didn't matter. He was caught next ball, so our score was just four for two. Then we had the mighty Peter, who gave me a pep talk on what I had do if he called me for a run. But he, too, was out for a duck the second ball. So far I'd done nothing.

We were four runs for three wickets when the Flight Sergeant walked in.

'One run!' he shouted as he pushed the ball out.

At last, I was to face my first ball since the start of the war.

'Calm down, take your time!' I told myself almost out loud. I needn't have bothered; it was a full toss, which I square-cut for four and I was off the mark, much to the delight of William and the servicemen.

I had scored 105 when I stupidly lost concentration and was bowled. The Flight Sergeant was 35 not out and our score was a presentable 150 for four. He walked out a little way with me and said, 'Well done, lass! I knew you could play!'

'Sorry, I doubted you,' Peter said as I came out. 'But where on earth did you learn to play like that?'

'I played first-class cricket for the Combined Universities, until they discovered I was a woman,' I replied proudly.

William put his arm round me and gave me a big fat sloppy kiss. My critics were silenced.

'Their loss!' Peter commented.

The match was won. We finished with a respectable 190 and they were all out for 75 and we were through to the next round.

William didn't have to get me picked for future matches. From then on I was picked on merit and in the next four matches, I scored 15, 93, 73 and 47. We reached the group final, which was to be played on Cambridge University's ground – a cracker of a pitch compared with what we had been used to and I really looked forward to playing on it. There was the usual fuss about my eligibility, but given my service record, it was decided that it would be best to let me play. Refusing to allow me to play might have given the RAF bad publicity, not that it could do much wrong in the eyes of the public.

It was a lovely day and Peter, our Captain, won the toss and elected to bat. We had improved from the early days and the openers scored 33 before we lost our first wicket. I walked in to cheers from William and Madge and to the rapturous applause of our whole Station. I faced the first ball.

It was a batsman's paradise. I raced to a hundred and was out just before tea for 185, my highest score to date – since the war, that is. It was fantastic. I have never felt so good, but in fairness any good batsman would have scored those runs as the bowling was mediocre and the wicket was true. We finished up with a massive 293 for six wickets and the opposition scored just 120.

See that tankard on the piano, Mr White? That's what we each received for winning the match.

On the whole, however, the RAF was embarrassed by the affair and decided that as from the next year only full-time employees would be eligible and that only men would be allowed to play, although they didn't press that point too much. There was a lot of discrimination against women in those days, so no matter what I did or said, I couldn't win. I went back into retirement and continued to raise my family. I did miss the cricket, but I had to accept the verdict of the times – it certainly wasn't a world for women.

A few months after the war in Europe ended, I received an invitation to dinner at the French Embassy in London. The invitation was also for William; we naturally accepted and it stipulated medals should be worn. I felt very proud of both of us as we as a family were highly decorated. To our delight, when we arrived both Winston Churchill and the great General de Gaulle were there, but perhaps even better was the presence of both Sam and Winco. I remember it was a lovely meal and, after de Gaulle stood up and made a short speech in French, I was called up along with Sam to receive the Croix de Guerre for what we had achieved in France on those missions. De Gaulle told the assembled company what Sam and I had done and I was once again very proud.

Sam told us he had been demobbed and was now at the German Embassy in Frankfurt, working as a junior diplomat; not as interesting as his former life, perhaps, but at least it was safe.

When he asked me what I was doing now, I simply said. 'I'm a mother.'

William and I continued to live happily in the house, making the best of everything. I became involved with many charities and helped many of the local lads to learn to play cricket. Life, although pleasant, had become routine: for example on Mondays I took Thomas to the baths for swimming lessons; on Tuesdays we, the officers' wives, worked for the various charities, and so on. I suppose you would call it humdrum, but we were happy enough.

The winter of 1947 was the worst I can remember; the snow was on the ground for months and it was almost impossible to do the normal things in life. But when the winter lifted we had a glorious summer. I followed the fortunes of my favourite team, Middlesex, and particularly those of their star batsman, Dennis Compton, who actually hit eighteen centuries during the season. It was a fantastic performance and I believe the record still stands.

There must have been something in the air that summer as I found myself pregnant again; the problem was I could still remember the torture caused by my last pregnancy and I wondered what on earth I had done to deserve it, especially when William had booked me into the same nursing home, or Stalag 1 as I preferred to call it. Mr White, I had the same Commanding Officer and the same chief torturers and I was actually given the same cell. This time, however, at least I knew what to expect. I knew I would wake up to find another shrivelled-up little monster that would endeavour to devour me from the moment it breathed life.

I woke up, having had another caesarean and was drifting in and out of consciousness when I remember the nurse coming in with a large bundle of blankets. She walked over to the bed and for some reason I turned to her and said, 'She's called Alice.'

'Yes, she's a little girl, a lovely little girl,' the nurse replied, as I drifted back to sleep.

There was the same routine – Mother must do this, Mother must do that – and I couldn't believe they didn't recognise an expert when they saw one. They must have known I could tell them a thing or two about having babies and what terrible monsters they grew into. What did surprise me, however, was that, from the start, I actually felt somewhat maternal to Alice and to a larger extent, enjoyed having her.

It was a little harder to manage looking after two youngsters, but I was determined to do so and the fact that we were not badly off financially. William could afford to buy many of the then luxuries in life; a refrigerator, a Hoover cleaner, a radiogram and a new electric cooker. The latter item was bought for me in the hope my cooking standards would improve, but I didn't think I was doing too bad, even with the old one.

Chapter 24

Britain was in the middle of a political minefield and William had to work day and night, as all the bomber stations had been put on alert due the start of the Korean War. There was even a distinct possibility of his entire unit being shipped to Seoul in South Korea to support the troops, but in the end, thank heavens, his station was stood down. The downside was that his outfit was one of the few responsible for carrying the atomic bomb.

Then, in 1951, the Russians started to blockade Berlin and were in fact trying to starve the West Berliners into submission. William was involved in the Berlin Airlift, taking food and supplies round the clock to the stricken population. His squadrons and pilots were on duty permanently until the crisis was over, and even then they remained on a permanent state of alert as the Cold War deepened. Peace, Mr White, really hadn't lasted that long.

That year, 1951, also saw the birth of our third child, James. It really was an amusing pregnancy as I had to attend an antenatal clinic, which was something new back them and enormously popular. I remember one particular demonstration a nurse gave using a grapefruit.

'Now, ladies,' she said, 'I want you to imagine that this is your baby. It will pass down the uterus and you will then be told to push and it will pop its head out . . . and Bob's your uncle!'

'Nurse, are you trying to be funny?' one of the ladies said. 'That bloody grapefruit isn't even as big as my last baby's head, let alone its body. I can tell you it's not as easy as Bob's yer bloody uncle!'

Despite such dire warnings, this time I was determined to have a natural birth. It was the beginning of the new fashion for everything natural and the nursing home told me that it would help me to relate better to my child. Mr White, I wouldn't recommend any male trying to do this; when you've got a six–inch object trying to come down a two-inch hole and everything has to stretch to allow it to, I'm sure you can imagine the difficulty. I can only say it's the worst form of torture that has ever been thought of. My labour lasted about three hours and all ended when the nurse began shouting at me: 'Come on, Mrs Fraser. Push!' and I began to swear at her, yelling in pain.

The nurse even had the gall to say, 'And I thought you were brave, Mrs Fraser!'

'So did I, but you're not a bloody Nazi, are you?'

'Now come on, don't talk like that now; it's not nice. Come on. Push!' she shouted and then it was all over.

Make me relate to my child! I could have drowned him then and there for what he had put me through.

Being the CO's wife and raising three children was extremely hard work. The washing alone seemed a Herculean task, though I absolutely refused to accept William's offer that we get in help. I wasn't going to admit defeat, and so I became easy prey to the Hoover direct-selling salesman, who knocked on my door and introduced me to the new Hoovermatic Twin Tub washing machine. It seemed like a life-saver and I was in love with it at first sight. Unfortunately, William had no belief in such gadgets.

'What have you wasted my money on this for?' he said when he saw the machine.

'Darling,' I answered sarcastically, 'if you would like to spend four hours a day washing yours and your lovely mucky little children's clothes and your son's nappies, you're very welcome. This, I'm told will cut the work in half.' I turned to walk away adding, 'And another thing: I thought this was a partnership and it was our money.'

I was interrupted by James who had woken up and was now hungry. 'Are you going to feed him then?' I snapped. 'No, of course you're not!' I continued as I picked up James and pushed him towards my breast.

William just started laughing. 'I can't take you seriously, when you shout at me with him on your left tit!'

'I don't believe it. How on earth did we win the bloody war, when you don't even know your left from your right'.

'What do you mean?' William asked quizzically.

'He's on my bloody right one,' I replied, putting an end to any conversation as we couldn't stop laughing.

It was amazing how quickly the time had passed. This year Thomas was to start school and, despite my own problems there, I wanted him to go to Bankworth, particularly to the Junior School, as I felt the school had given me tremendous courage to do and try things and helped me gain leadership skills.

Mr White, I know you will find it strange, I wanted to send all my children to Bankworth, after all the heartache I suffered, but times had changed. Perhaps I wanted to lay a few ghosts to rest; perhaps I wanted my children to do that for me; there was moreover no mix-up about any of our children's gender. I don't know in my heart what the true reason was; but what I do know is that the education the school was giving at the time was very good and we wanted to give the children a good chance. Furthermore they had begun to take day students, but unfortunately we lived too far away and I certainly didn't want Thomas to board. So his first preparatory school was at the RAF camp and like his father, he developed a passion for rugby. I was jealous that he had no interest in cricket, but then he was his father all over. I suppose it was my childhood all over again.

The next three of four years were much the same and saw the birth of my fourth child, Charlotte, on whom I doted. I had developed into the boring matriarch of the family, nursing everyone through all their illnesses because no one else would;

preparing all the meals because no one else would, and doing all the household chores for that same reason. I didn't wholly dislike my life and it was good to see our handiwork develop into what were undoubtedly reasonable children. I had given everyone stability and the children knew they could come to me with anything.

I had kept in touch with all my friends and of course Alice, with whom I still had that special friendship, but I suppose my favourite non-relatives were Peter and Thelma, whom the children now called Uncle Peter and Aunt Thelma and it was wonderful to see the bond of love that formed between our children and them. I made sure I saw them at least once a fortnight. Of course, my biggest regret was that my father still didn't want to have anything to do with me.

In the summer of 1951 everything changed as William was posted to the Air Ministry in London to assist with the planning and supply of materials to Berlin and Malaya. We moved to a small village called Whitton, not far from London. The good thing as far as the family was concerned was that William's new position was almost a nine-to-five job and he found more time, too, to indulge his passion for rugby, becoming involved with the coaching of the County rugby team. Furthermore Thomas could now at last go to Bankworth as a day student, though sadly he had now missed out on the Junior School. He had grown into a fairly big, confident lad and I felt he would be able to hold his own. Alice, of course, could go to the Junior Girls' School. William had bought me a little car, one of the first Ford Populars and it was my job to take Thomas and Alice to Bankworth every day.

Before they started there however, we had taken Thomas and Alice to an open day school to show them what it was going to be like. William was very keen when he saw the facilities they now had for sports.

There were numerous pictures around the school of past achievements, and one in the Senior Boys' which drew Alice's eye was a picture of me as Alice in the play.

'Is that you, Mum?' she asked.

'Yes of course,' I replied, feeling proud that she recognised me.

Thomas started to ask, 'How could you play . . . ?'

William put an end to the conversation. 'Your mother was very special, that's all.'

'And beautiful,' Alice said proudly

'And beautiful,' William repeated with a smile.

I was thankful, in some ways that Thomas wasn't interested in cricket, as he didn't take much notice of the numerous team photographs about the place and one or two individual ones of me, not to mention the fact we never used the Chillington-Henry name.

We walked all over the school, past the new swimming pool and the new tennis courts and back through the boiler house yard, when the memories came storming back. I tightly gripped Alice's hand, which made her ask, 'Mummy, are you all right?'

'Yes, of course, dear. Just a bit light-headed. Nothing to worry about,' I replied reassuringly, but William had seen the change in me and put his arm round me.

'Is this the place?' he whispered so the children couldn't hear.

'Yes, darling, it is. It brings back terrible feelings and sends shivers all over me. I know I should be over it by now, but I just can't seem to forget it.'

'Don't try! Just stay with me and you will never have to be afraid again,' William said, squeezing my shoulders.

Mr White, you can now see why I fell in love with him and why I married him and why I wanted to spend the rest of my life with him. Can't you?

On Thomas' first day, William and I dropped him off in my new car. I deigned to kiss him goodbye and wish him the best of luck, and you would have thought I had committed a very serious crime.

'Mum, don't do that! You know I don't like kissing anyway. Do you want the other boys to think I'm a sissy?'

William and I looked at each other in stark amazement and simply shrugged our shoulders.

'No! Of course not, sorry,' I replied, fully put in my place.

'We'll pick you up at six tonight then?'

'Yes, all right. Try not to be late. Dad's taking me for practice. Aren't you, Dad?'

I just stood there open-mouthed, wondering what I had reared. 'I blame you for this, William Fraser. He takes after you. You always were a bossy boots.'

William smiled and we drove home. I worried the entire day whether he would be all right. Had I let him go to Bankworth to allay my old ghosts? Was I trying to prove a point? I couldn't wait until six o'clock, I was that nervous.

'Why did you worry?' William asked, as Thomas came out of the school with a huge smile on his face.

'I played my first practice game today, Dad. And what do you think? I scored a try!'

All the way home he chatted excitedly how he had done this and how he had done that and all the time it was to his dad that he addressed himself. It was lovely that Thomas had this relationship with his father, just as I had had with mine, but I could now see myself doing exactly what my mother had done: standing back and taking second fiddle. But I was so different from my mother: I was active, a good sportsman, sorry, – woman, and had a useful brain. I didn't think I could just sit back and stagnate. I had four children and a husband to look after and, although it was at the time a full-time job, I could see it was becoming easier and I wanted to prepare for the freedom that would come.

Thomas, of course, flourished at Bankworth; he fitted right in as if he had been born to go there. A little difficulty arose when he was selected for his house cross-country team. Suddenly, alive to the prestige of competing in this event, he spotted a photograph of me, as Alex Henry, collecting the winner's cup.

'Mum . . .' He paused for a moment. '. . . I saw your photo in the school hall . . .' He paused again, and I could almost see the cogs turning as he asked, 'How on earth could you compete in the boys' cross-country when you're a girl?'

Once again William was on the ball. 'Thomas, your mother was very special and could beat any of the youngsters until she was about fifteen. Then they grew stronger and could beat her.'

'I haven't dared to tell the others that that was my mother,' Thomas said. They would never believe me anyway. It is true, isn't it?'

'Of course it is and don't worry about it. Mr Wilkes will tell you if it's true or not, but I would leave it at that. It will save you the embarrassment of having Tarzan as a mother. Just show them the ones where she was in the plays; they will believe that,' William concluded.

Things had changed since my day at school and the war had accelerated the change: we had more freedom and people's opinions were more diverse, more tolerant . . . That was, unless you were a young eleven-year-old who suddenly finds out that his mother has put her name down to play for the parents cricket team against the First XI in the annual Prize Day Match.

I had warned Peter Wilkes who was now the Deputy Head and I could see his smile as I heard him chuckle down the phone.

'Don't tell anyone,' I said. 'I want this to be a surprise.'

'It will certainly be that. Alexandra. But you can rely on me: I won't say a thing,' he promised.

William, too, had decided to keep it a secret that I would be playing so when Thomas saw my special cricket bat being put into the car on Prize Day he assumed it was his dad that would be playing. As soon as he realised it was me, however, he 'threw a wobbly'. I'll never forget his little face; he looked so desperate.

'Mum, you can't do this to me. What will everyone think? I'll be the laughing stock of all the school. Please, please don't do this to me, I beg you!' he said, almost in tears.

We took no notice until he finally said, 'I'll kill myself, I will.'

He was then castigated by William for being so stupid. Then at the cricket ground, William picked up my kit and carried it into the pavilion and was immediately directed into the changing room with the rest of the players. 'It's my wife that's playing not me,' he said, to the utter consternation of the young man showing him the way.

'Excuse me, sir?'

William repeated what he had just said. The lad gulped, not knowing what to do.

'Don't worry, young man,' I added kindly, 'I'll change in the gents. You guard the door and stop any prying eyes and we'll be fine.'

I came out of the gents having changed into my new cricket wear, which included my new divided skirt, which was all the rage for sportswoman at that time. There was a deathly silence as I walked into the changing room and put my bag with my bat and pads on the bench and then hung my clothes on the peg. The playing fathers just stood and stared.

'Come on, lads, haven't you seen a woman before?'

'Are you playing for us?' one of them asked.

'Of course I am. Do you think I would be in here with you if weren't?'

'Good God! A woman playing with us!'

I stood up in front of them and looked at myself up and down. 'Good God, you're right. I am a woman. Well, we'll just have to make the best of it, won't we?'

Our Captain lost the toss and the School XI won and elected to bat. We walked out on the field, to numerous whistles and cheers especially when I took the field. Poor Tom was hiding behind his dad, hoping not to be seen, and I was sent out to my usual position on the boundary, out of harm's way.

We put up a pitiful performance in the field and allowed them to score 202 for four wickets. I was never given the chance to bowl even though Mr Wilkes advised our Captain to give me a chance. When it was our turn to bat, I noticed I was being dropped down the intended batting order. Again, Mr Wilkes intervened on my behalf and persuaded them to let me stay at number three. His parting shot to the Captain was: 'What have you got to lose?' The Captain nodded resignedly.

Our openers put on twenty runs before the first man was bowled with the last ball of the over and it was my turn to walk out onto my favourite ground. I loved it as I strode out to the crease. I didn't care about the cat calls and the shouts and the wolf whistles, I felt wonderful. Especially when I saw William standing up cheering with poor old Tom still cowering with shame because of what his mother was doing to him. I saw the smile on Peter Wilkes' face as I stood next to him, waiting for the next ball to be bowled.

'Thanks, Peter. I needed this!' I said to him quietly.

'Best of luck, Alex,' he whispered, 'and take your time.'

'Thanks.'

The ball was bowled and the batsman called me for a run and now I was facing my first ball on my favourite ground for almost eighteen years. Watch your guard. Watch the ball on the leg side. Take your time. All the phrases that Peter Wilkes used to say to me were running through my mind.

I hit the first ball for a gentle two and was off the mark. The next I hit for a single; I was feeling better. The following ball, the other opener was also bowled: we were 23 for two. The next batsman to come out was the one who had expressed shock at a woman being picked. He managed to survive the over and I thought I would be cheeky and rub salt in the wound.

'I do hope this woman can hold the team together, don't you?' He went red as a beetroot.

Peter Wilkes whispered to me, 'Don't get over confident!'

'No you're right.'

I began to bat and scored freely, deliberately taking singles at the end of the over. I had scored 20 to his one, with William cheering every run. Then I noticed Tom had actually started looking at me bat. I hit nine off the next over and Tom actually stood up next to his father, while William still cheered. Another

11 off the next and I was at 40. I then hit a beautiful six off the next which made Tom shout: 'Well done, Mum!' The other young man was suffering the indignity of a maiden at the other end. It was once again my turn to face the bowling. I could sense the apprehension in the crowd, particularly Tom who now had his hands in the air every time the ball was bowled. My fifty came up after three successive twos, much to the delight of my family. William and Tom held hands and jumped round and round.

I reached my hundred in the next nine overs and to my absolute delight, the man at the other end had only scored seven when he was out, caught behind. I scored a further 51 when I signalled to the Captain I thought I'd had enough. He called me in, to the rapturous delight of Tom, who ran on the pitch and put his arms around me. He walked down to the pavilion with me as though he had actually scored the runs.

He was so proud of me I almost cried with joy and then I heard him say to another lad. 'That's my mum!' I couldn't help myself then.

William came across, put his arm round my shoulder and proudly said, 'I'm proud of you, too, darling.'

I walked into the dressing room and was reluctantly congratulated by the pompous individual who had so decried me before the match.

'Sorry, but I felt I couldn't leave it to you; you were just too slow,' I said mercilessly 'and never judge a book by its cover!'

The Captain came in and asked all the other players to leave so that I could change and very nicely told me that Mr Wilkes had told him that he wouldn't be disappointed in me but that he hadn't believed him. He then said he had been playing cricket for twenty-five years and had never seen an innings like that.

'Where did you learn to play like that?' he asked.

'At home with my father, and here. Mr Wilkes taught me,' I replied, at which he was just stumped for words.

'You were a pupil here?' he asked.

'Of course, there was a girls' side as well, you know,' I replied.

'Ah yes, of course!' He left me to get changed, still looking confused.

I walked out of the pavilion with my kit packed, with a very proud husband and a no longer embarrassed son. We sat down and watched the rest of the match, which we won easily. We took Tom home after all the excitement of the day and naturally, he had to be in the front of the car, with me in the back, a place which seemed to be reserved for ladies back then. Suddenly, out of the blue and without any prompting from his dad, he said something that is usually only reserved for grownups.

'I'm sorry, Mum.'

'What for?' I asked.

'For doubting you!' he replied.

The newspapers had a field day and my innings were reported even in the national editions. Of course, they did some research and discovered that I had represented the universities; they felt I should be playing for the English Ladies' team and following all the publicity, I was asked if I would like to play for the Kent Ladies' side, which I gladly accepted, though I played only four matches for them, in the end averaging 55 for that season.

I had become the local reporter for the *Whitton Gazette* and my amateur job was to collect all the local news – the births, deaths and marriages, the local sports and business, as well as all the social events in the village. I loved this job as I could pry into everyone's affairs and listen to all the gossip. This little job, however was to give me one more opportunity of taking revenge on another of those rapists that had attacked me all those years ago and it was another financial disaster which gave me that opportunity.

The Suez Crisis was one of the most awful periods in the post-war history of our country and on the 29th October 1956, twenty-seven years to the day of the Wall Street Crash, we created another economic crisis when we made the mistake along with France of attacking Egypt to prevent President Nasser from nationalising the Suez Canal. The world's stock exchanges tumbled with both Britain and France losing a lot of international friends because of their actions. There was much diplomatic activity between all the nations involved and many diplomats were busy at what we today would call damage limitation.

Bankworth was one of those public schools that had a reputation for producing the top flight in the Diplomatic Service and I was astonished to see the name of Edwin Jagger appearing in the media, as the spokesman for the Government. I wondered if he was the Edwin Jagger whom I had known at school and asked the Editor of the *Whitton Gazette* if he would allow me to cover the briefings. He agreed but I would have to wangle my own pass. 'How can I stop you?' he added. 'You're my only unpaid reporter,' he replied, laughing.

I pulled lots of strings, one of which was via the Editor of the *Daily Mail*, your paper, Mr White. He had done several stories on me over the years and I called in a few favours. I told the Editor I wanted the Gazette to run the story first and he could have it afterwards. But when he heard which paper I was talking about, he just laughed. We had a circulation of 2,600 and that the paper was even owned by the *Mail* group, which I hadn't realised. 'I'll do it for you, Alexandra,' the Editor, Tom Small, confirmed.

I discussed everything with William and told him what I wanted to do and he became very worried. 'You're hitting at the Establishment now and you'll never win, darling. Please be careful!'

'I will, but I can't let these people get away with it. Remember, sweetheart, they didn't just rape me; they actually considered murdering me and burning my body to get rid of the evidence,' I said defiantly. 'Would they have put me into the furnace alive?'

'I'm always with you, darling, whatever you do. I just want you to be careful, that's all,' William replied with a worried expression on his face.

I went to London and stayed alone at the Chelsea flat, making plans as to what I would say if I got the opportunity to ask a question. The following day I went to the *Mail*'s office and introduced myself to the Diplomatic Editor, John Stafford-Harries, and told him I was hoping to speak to Edwin Jagger.

'That will be difficult, Mrs Fraser. You'll be one of many and they generally just allow the reporters from the BBC and the bigger newspapers to put their questions. It's always the people they know. But what's this all about then?'

'Please, just you wait and see,' I replied, trying to be a little secretive in the hope it would whet his appetite.

'What I suggest is that you come to the briefing and be as glamorous as possible, as it will help you to get noticed. I should warn you, though. These diplomats are very clever at sensing trouble and at the first hint of something being awry, they'll just clam up and the briefing will end.'

I did exactly what Stafford-Harries told me to do. I dolled myself up and I looked pretty good, although I say it myself. We were all waiting in the Ministry briefing room for the representative to appear; it was like some club as there were many conversations taking place as the various reporters acknowledged one another. My problem was I wasn't one of its members.

I had butterflies in my stomach and I felt like I was going into bat as the hubbub suddenly died and the spokesman walked in. 'Was this really him?' I asked myself. He looked so old, so grey. He stood at a lectern and began to brief the press. Even his voice didn't sound the same. I have to take a closer look, I thought to myself, and I stood up and slowly walked towards the front, as there was a vacant chair. Stafford-Harries was right: an attractive woman can stop the traffic.

One hundred pairs of eyes followed me as I walked from the back to the front and even the speaker stopped momentarily. I smiled as he continued and noticed how he kept glancing in my direction. Could it really be him?

He finished his briefing and called for questions and turned in my direction and smiled. That was his big mistake – I recognised his smile. That same smile he had given me as he had watched Norman pushing something inside of me on that terrible day.

I'm going to have you, you bastard! I said to myself.

'Any more questions?' the rapist asked and I put my hand up to attract his attention. 'I'll take your question next, my dear,' he said, acknowledging my request.

Patronising bastard! I thought to myself. What on earth was I going to say?

'Now, Mrs . . .'

'Alexandra Fraser of the *Whitton Gazette*.'

'Mrs Fraser, how can I help you?'

'Do you enjoy your job, Mr Jagger? I asked, smiling sweetly.

'Yes of course I do!' he replied, a little taken aback by my line of questioning.

'Do you think you are a suitable person to be doing this very important job?' I asked, allowing a little bitterness to creep into my tone.

'Yes of course I do. I wouldn't be doing it if I didn't.'

There were a few disgruntled comments from the floor that I was wasting everybody's time.

'Now next question, please,' he asked.

'No, Mr Jagger, I want you to answer the question properly,' I shouted over the demands for me to sit down. 'So you think you are a proper person? May I remind you of a little incident with some boys in a school boiler house in the 1930s?'

The room went silent as everyone saw the ashen look on Jagger's face. It was as if he wished a hole could appear and he could fall in it. You could now hear a pin drop and then the hundred pairs of eyes returned to me.

'Well, do you remember it Mr Jagger, and are you still so sure you are a fit and proper person?'

Jagger didn't answer. He stood there mesmerised, unable to move and was eventually helped out of the room by one of the aides. I was besieged by reporters wanting to know the story, but Stafford-Harries hurriedly ushered me out of the room.

'You'll have to speak to my Editor!' I said, rushing out. The Suez Crisis had taken a back seat for the moment.

The following morning my Editor rang to say that he was under siege. There were dozens of reporters at his offices. They were actually waiting for me to arrive at work; they little realised that this non-paid gossip writer worked from home.

I had heard from Stafford-Harries that Mr Jagger had been taken very ill and I couldn't do anymore to him. If he had recovered he would have a difficult enough time explaining everything. However, he didn't recover and was pensioned off from the Foreign Office on the grounds of ill health. My Editor gave the story to Stafford-Harries and the *Daily Mail,* but it was never published. I think perhaps they felt he had already had his just desserts. Had it been ten or more years later, the press would perhaps have had a field day.

Chapter 25

During the following summers I had very successful seasons with the cricket bat, playing for Whitton First XI, where I had become a regular player and very well accepted, so much so I was considered one of the lads. In those days it was unusual for men to swear in front of a lady, but on the field, I heard all the curses under the sun. On the field I was Alex and off the field, Mrs Fraser. One of my chief pleasures was that I began coaching the youngsters, including my own children. It took a bit of time for the young players, and for that matter their parents, to take me seriously, but when they heard about my achievements they too accepted me. I even tried all my father's techniques and so I developed several decent batsmen. Alice wasn't a bad player until she became too much of a lady and felt the game wasn't for her.

On the whole, though, it was rugby that became the main focus of our family, especially after Thomas had been picked for Surrey Juniors County side. I spent hours taking him to training sessions and watching and waiting for him, while his father was busy with his work. William was now employed part-time by the RAF and part-time by the Surrey Rugby Club, where he worked as a training manager. This, of course, left me to do all the running about. Thomas was turning into a keen all-round sportsmen and I had high hopes for him. He was constantly finding new things to excel at and had his opportunity when Bankworth School was gifted a large piece of land down by the Thames and they decided to add rowing to their list of activities, which Thomas took up and dare I say, soon proved himself a fine oarsman, too.

In time, Bankworth became affiliated with one of the rowing organisations and as such the members and their families were invited to Henley Rowing Regatta. It was a splendid day; there wasn't a cloud in the sky and the champagne and strawberries made it special. The boys went to play football in the surrounding fields while the two girls preferred to stay with William and myself.

We had been sitting down just enjoying watching the world go by when we were suddenly accosted by a tall, athletic-looking man. He introduced himself as Don McRitchie, a sports correspondent for the *Daily Telegraph*. He had recognised me and had just come over for a chat. Both he and William were both fanatical rugby supporters, and within the space of a few minutes, I became second fiddle. Nonetheless, after he left us, it seems that Don McRitchie went along to several of the organisers and suggested that I should present the winners' trophy for the two junior races. I was honoured to accept, even though it meant we had to stay until the last race, as the presentations would not be made until the end of the day.

In preparation for the little speech I would have to give, I decided to look round and do some research. I was wandering round, casually listening to the chat, visiting the various stalls, the tea tents and the like, when suddenly I heard a loud voice hailing me.

'Ah, Alexander Henry! What are you doing here? Are you a boy or a girl this time?' he guffawed.

I turned round in shock, but quickly composed myself. It was my old teammate, Willoughby, from Oxford.

'Willoughby! Fancy seeing you. Are you keeping the prostitutes busy or are you still a eunuch?'

It was as though I had 'castrated' him all over again. The look of shock on his face and that of his companions was unbelievable.

I walked away feeling cock-a-hoop that I had got one over on the pompous idiot and continued my little tour. I was looking at the crews getting in and out of the boats at the river's edge when I felt someone grab hold of my arm and pull me round to face him. It was Willoughby.

'How dare you say that in front of my wife and friends. I want an apology at once!' he said, almost shouting.

'What for?' I asked rhetorically. 'Everything I said was true, wasn't it. Or don't you remember that night at your father's club.'

I stared at his hand on my arm as if to say, 'Take it off me,' but he took no notice and was once again trying to bully me. 'If you ever dare to say anything like that to me again, I'll finish you.'

'And how exactly will you do that?' I retorted. I had grown up a little since my Oxford days.

He didn't have time to answer. William and the children had been looking for me, and had seen Willoughby behaving badly towards me. William and Thomas came running over.

'Take your hands off my wife, you imbecile!'

Willoughby stood there in amazement, still holding my arm.

'I said take your bloody hand off her!' William shouted, but didn't give the poor man the chance to respond. He simply picked him up and shouted: 'Cool off in there then!' as he threw him into the Thames.

'Well done, Dad!' Thomas shouted. He was so impressed with what his father had done that he added, 'Next time you touch my mother, you'll have to answer to me as well!'

I felt so proud that I had William and 'Son of William' as my great defenders.

A large number of people saw William's actions but I simply told them that Willoughby had been making an indecent proposal, and so all sympathy for him evaporated.

A little later I was called to the presentation tent and made my way with William and the rest of the family following on. To my amazement, I again saw Willoughby, who had changed his clothes and now wore a smart rowing cap. He clearly hadn't twigged that I was the Alexandra Fraser who had been called to the tent. Once again he repeated the threat:

'I'm warning you! I'm not without influence,' Willoughby said nastily.

'Willoughby, dear, you're a nonentity and a silly little one at that,' I replied and made my way into the tent.

Inside, I was greeted warmly by the President, who made me most welcome, fussing around and then explaining what they would like me to do. He then made an apology for the difficulties I'd had with one of the spectators.

'Oh it was nothing! Just a silly little man who wanted to have sex with me,' I replied, knowing full well I had absolutely shocked the poor man. 'But don't worry, my husband soon put a stop to his perverted antics. He tried it before, when I was at Oxford, you know,' I said, putting "the boot in" as they say today, knowing that Willoughby was a club member.

The presentations started and the juniors were to receive their trophy first. The President stood up in front of the packed marquee and began to make his formal speech, finally introducing me:

'I have asked my first guest to present the prize because she is one of the finest examples of what the British spirit really is. She won the George Cross during the war, together with The Distinguished Service Order and bar and was presented with the Croix de Guerre for her bravery in France by none other than General de Gaulle himself. Her heroism and bravery is the stuff of legend.

'She became a Squadron Officer and was responsible for the capture of many of the Nazi war criminals. She is, as everyone knows, also a successful cricketer. I take great pleasure in introducing none other than Alexandra Fraser!'

I walked almost from the back of the hall to the stage at the front, to enthusiastic applause. I walked up the steps, to be greeted by the President, and handed the card with the winners' names on it. I was supposed to just announce the names and present the cups, but I could see Willoughby sitting at the front, open-mouthed as he saw me walk onto the stage, so I thought I better say something more appropriate.

'Thank you, ladies and gentlemen for the warm welcome, and for the honour you have given me by asking me to present the trophy. But it wasn't everyone's wish I should do so. Mr Willoughby here made it quite clear he didn't want me to do it and made quite a fuss. But I don't blame him . . .' I paused as a few people were murmuring 'Shame, shame!'

I continued: 'No, I don't blame him. He was brought up in a world where certain beliefs were paramount – that it wasn't the place of a woman to do anything but cook and raise children. Today, we're seeing a new generation of young people growing up who will sweep away Mr Willoughby's world and encourage everyone, no matter what their sex, no matter what their background, to take a full and active public part . . . and yes, on the sports field, too! Many of the women here in this room did their bit during the war and fought hard for our country and now we're at peace, they deserve their chance to fulfil their every potential.

'I lost my opportunity to play first-class cricket because they found out I was pretending to be a man, as that was the only way I could get a game, but the views, beliefs and standards of Mr Willoughby's world put a stop to it. I hope you don't let these views put a stop to today's youngsters from competing on an equal basis, rowing included. Fitness, team spirit and friendship and most of all, a superb competitive spirit are things we all have the right to enjoy.

'But now we come to the real purpose: to present this wonderful trophy to John Davies, the young man who rowed a fantastic race and deserves every bit of your applause.' The whole place erupted into cheers, as the young John Davies walked up to collect his trophy.

I walked down the steps of the stage, glancing at Willoughby as I did so, but only his wife had the courage to look at me. He looked like a ghost and must have wished for that proverbial hole.

The President began to introduce the next guest, but felt he had to say how my words had hit home and how we all needed to change, if we were to become more competitive in all sports. He then asked me to return to the stage to present the very first trophy to the winning ladies' team, which I enjoyed doing.

At the end of the presentations, I saw Willoughby coming out of the tent; he was once again with his wife, who was looking at me with daggered eyes.

'Willoughby, old chap,' I said sarcastically. I leaned over and whispered to him, 'Don't ever threaten anyone by telling them you have a lot of influence before you check what influence they may have. I'll tell you what I'll do for you tomorrow: I'll tell the press about that evening in your gentlemen's club. I hope you've told your wife, because I've told my husband. Please don't threaten me again. Good evening, Mr Willoughby,' I finally said out loud.

Of course, I didn't go to the press with the story, but it must have made him uneasy for a while. The one good thing that came out of the event was William's chance meeting with the *Daily Telegraph*'s sports correspondent Don McRitchie.

Unbeknown to me they had arranged a lunch meeting to discuss the possibility of William becoming a Board member at Twickenham. It would appear that one of the senior members was retiring and there was a vacancy. The meeting went very well and within six months, William was on the Board and had left the RAF with his pension.

Although it was a full-time position, he still retained his coaching interest in Surrey, as this was one of his real passions. From my own point of view, I no longer had to worry he might be called to a war zone.

My success with the Kent Ladies cricket team got me chosen for the English Ladies cricket XI and for several years, I became a regular. However, I will never forget the 26th June 1958, when I received a telephone call from Emily Trenchard, the England Ladies Cricket Captain, informing me I had been selected to play for England, against the Australian Ladies Team in the first test of a two-match series starting at Edgbaston two weeks later.

I arrived at Edgbaston ground for the first of the test series. The weather had been very wet prior to the start so Emily decided to bat, thinking the pitch wouldn't do a lot for the bowlers in the first instance. Our opener, Jennifer Smith, didn't do well and was out for ten and I came out onto the field with my usual fan club shouting from the pavilion: 'Come on, Mum!' I batted quite well but stupidly lost concentration and was out for 44 just before lunch. I sat in front of the pavilion with my family to watch the match, when I saw a gentleman in his late forties walking towards me, holding the hands of two young girls. He came directly up to me and for a moment I was lost. Then suddenly it twigged.

'David?' I asked. It was the boy on the beach at Le Touquet all those years ago.

'Yes!' he replied. 'I needn't ask your name. My daughters already know it.'

'Are you on your own?' I asked.

'No, I have my wife over there. We're here for the day to watch you play.'

'Oh, that's nice of you. Thank you. Come on, where is your wife?

'She's just over there,' David said and waved to the woman sitting some distance away.

I also waved to her and signalled for her to come and join us.

William, Tom and Alice were confused at this sudden appearance of a stranger, but I quickly put them out of their misery.

'William, this is David. We met when we were on holiday in Le Touquet. I had a crush on him when I was fourteen. You're very lucky,' I said to his wife. 'I would have run away with him, but he told me I was too young.'

His wife, Valerie, was a little timid, but his daughters were developing real personalities, with minds of their own. I know this sounds big-headed but I believe he only came to the match in the hope of seeing me. David still had that puppy-dog look when we talked.

'Would you like to have lunch with us?' I asked.

David accepted but Valerie said, 'We've brought sandwiches.'

'Oh come on, you can have those for your tea,' I said, trying to persuade her. Valerie gave in and I treated them to lunch in the 'posh tent'. It was a very pleasant couple of hours.

'How is Alice?' David asked

'She's fine and has got two children now and is still as lovely as ever,' I replied.

David turned to William. 'We played cricket with Alexandra and her sister on the beach and, believe it or not, she knocked us all over the place. We couldn't get her out and it really annoyed Phil, my friend, as he fancied himself as a bowler.'

I could see Valerie was feeling out of it so I quickly changed the subject and invited them to Worcester for the next test match. I told them I would leave tickets for the three days on the gate for them, should they so wish, though I think Valerie had had enough of our company and wanted to go. We were saved by the bell as we had lost another three wickets, so I had to go back to the pavilion in case there was a collapse and we had to go out to field. We said our goodbyes and I felt in a mischievous mood; perhaps it was that little bit of Alice that was in me. I kissed David on the cheek goodbye and whispered, 'You naughty boy! You gave me my first kiss.'

At least he went away with a smile on his face. They didn't turn up at Worcester and in fact we never saw them again, but it was nice to have 'a blast from the past' as they say today.

The match hadn't gone very well for us, especially as we had been lucky with the toss and had favourable batting conditions, which I squandered, and we were all out for 279. Deborah had batted well for 52 and Emily for 66, but it wasn't enough and the Australians had thrashed us about in the field and had actually scored 450 before declaring some 171 runs ahead.

We had to survive the third and final day to save the match. The openers survived the final ten minutes of the day without loss and resumed for the final day with ten runs on the board. Deborah and Jennifer put on 58 for the first wicket, which was a good solid start, and more important, they had batted until just after lunch. Deborah was the first out for 22 and as I walked to the crease, Emily the Captain shouted, 'Stay there, Alexandra. Just stay there! Her words were almost drowned out by the cheers of encouragement from my family.

Well, Mr White, I had got my orders. I had to stay there and this, for a free-flowing batsman, wasn't my game. I really tried that day and at the close, Jennifer had scored her maiden hundred and I was 89 not out. I would have loved this to have been a five-day match, as I think, after that, we would have beaten them. They would never have got us out in that match, which ended up a draw, with Jennifer taking the honours for England, which I was very pleased about.

Around this period, Mr White – I think perhaps you were too young to remember – Macmillan was Prime Minister; the economy was good, we were recovering from the war, and, to quote Mr Macmillan: 'We had never had it so good.'

At one point he made some changes to his Cabinet and he had brought in a new youngish MP to be Foreign Secretary. The papers had a field day with his past: how he had been a star pupil at Bankworth Public School; how he had gone to Cambridge and taken a degree in French, and how he was a future Prime Minister in the making. He was pictured with his wife and two children on the front of every newspaper under headlines: 'There's More to Come from Morton'. You could tell from his face he was full of himself. And, of course, Mr White, you will remember he was one of the animal rapists; in fact had held my body as they tried to push me into the furnace.

When I read these headlines over the breakfast table with William, I nearly choked; I didn't even realise that Morton had gone into politics.

'That man . . . Foreign Secretary! I almost screamed. 'No! I won't allow it!'

'Don't do this to yourself. Don't make it an obsession. It will destroy you,' interjected William.

'That animal would have burned me in a furnace, William, if Hazard had not had a change of heart. I can't, I *can't* let him get away with it,' I said, raising my voice and becoming upset.

'All right, all right, don't worry, calm down. Please don't get yourself in a state,' William added.

I had made up my mind. Somehow I was going to get an interview with him and confront him. Reluctantly, William agreed to help me and in fact almost planned the entire operation.

'You can get into anything you want with your credentials!' he said. 'It will be difficult to get an appointment with him, but you'll just have to persevere. Tell him it's a personal matter and that it will be to his advantage to meet you. You'll find that no politician will be able to resist that sort of approach. Pretend that you're writing some story on him,' William said.

Well, I tried for a week, sounding more desperate by the day; I told his secretary that I would be breaking the story within the next few days but that I really needed to speak to him first. I wouldn't keep him more than ten minutes.

It worked! The secretary relented and made me an appointment for Wednesday morning at 10.30 a.m. On the day I turned up as glamorous as any forty-year-old woman could look.

'Good morning, I'm Alexandra Fraser. I have an appointment with the Foreign Secretary at ten thirty,' I said confidently.

'Yes you have,' she replied superciliously. 'You're very lucky. Normally, the Minister doesn't see members of the public.'

'I understand that,' I replied, 'and I'm very grateful. I'm sure it will be to his advantage. He's done very well, hasn't he?' I continued, simply to make pleasant conversation.

'Yes he has,' she replied coolly. 'I understand you were a Bankworth girl?'

'Yes that's right,' I replied.

'The Minister too is from Bankworth; from the boys' side of course.'

'Is he really? How lovely. I think we will have many things in common,' I continued also with a hint of irony in my voice.

'I hardly think so,' she replied haughtily. 'Do you?'

'No perhaps not,' I said, smiling my most sour-sweet smile.

The intercom rang and the secretary left her desk and bounced into the Minister's office, on her four-inch stilettos, tossing her hair as she went, as if to let me know how important she was to him. Five minutes later, the young lady came out.

'The Minister will see you now, Mrs Fraser.'

I stood up gently, slowly replaced the magazine I had been reading, and glided into the office. It was one of the little things Alice and my father used to say: 'Stand up straight and walk in as if you owned the place. I did just that and when I entered I wished I did own it. What a beautiful office! I really was taken aback by its splendour; it took your breath away.

'Yes it's rather beautiful, isn't it?' Morton said, breaking the ice.

'Breathtaking!' I replied.

'Well, Mrs Fraser, what can I do for you?' he asked, gesturing for me and his secretary to sit down. 'I understand you are a Bankworth girl?'

'Yes.'

'When were you there?'

'I'm not telling you that. You'll guess my age.' It was a stupid thing to say but it was the first thing that came into my head.

'I understand you won the George Cross.'

'I was lucky!' I interrupted.

'And you are currently playing cricket for the England ladies' team.'

'Yes,' I replied, thinking he would recognise me if he asked any more questions. I tried to divert his attention to the business in hand. Minister, is it possible to speak to you on your own?'

'I'm afraid not, Mrs Fraser. It's simply not done. I have no secrets from Phoebe, I mean Miss Carstairs, here. Do I?' he asked, as her supercilious little face lit up.

'That's fine,' I replied, and then began speaking to him in fluent French. 'I only wanted to talk to you about eight boys and a man named Norman Guest, and how they raped a little girl in a boiler house at Bankworth School.'

His face turned ashen, as I turned round to the secretary and asked. 'Do you speak French, Phoebe darling?' I asked, returning to English. 'I do hope so and then you can take things down word for word.'

'Oh no . . . no I don't!' she replied, somewhat confused.

'Then I'll explain as well as I can in English. Shall I, Minister?' I asked.

'Err . . . err . . .' Morton stumbled to find the right words.

'Well there were these eight . . .' I started to say.

'No, Mrs Fraser, please . . . I'll see to this Phoebe. You can leave us now.'

'Perhaps you're not as important as you thought, dear,' I added condescendingly as she got up to go.

Morton had lost all his composure and was stumbling for words and even stumbling behind his desk as he tried to walk round to me. Phoebe, poor little love had lost all composure too and was so confused when she left the room. 'Shall I leave it open, sir? she asked.

'No shut it and get out!' he suddenly exploded.

'Now come on, don't take it out on your poor little Phoebe. You don't have any secrets from her after all. You've told her, of course, that you raped a fourteen-year-old girl and then attempted to murder her by pushing her into a furnace while she was still alive. You have told her that, haven't you, Minister?'

'Who are you?' he spluttered. 'You're here to blackmail me, aren't you? You think just because I have been made Foreign Secretary, you think you can gain some advantage, don't you?'

'You don't deny it then? I asked, keeping the pressure on him.

'What?' he demanded.

'That you are a murdering, buggering rapist!' I replied.

'Of course I deny it. I don't know what you're talking about.'

'Then, Mr Former Foreign Secretary, why are you getting so flustered?'

The intercom rang. It was Phoebe.

'Are you all right, sir?' Phoebe asked. 'Your ten forty-five appointment is here.'

'Oh go away. Damn it!' he stammered and then turned back to me. 'Well, what do you want?'

'Nothing, Former Foreign Minister, except your immediate resignation.'

He stumbled back into his chair in a daze and we sat in total silence for several minutes, during which he tried to regain some self-control.

Suddenly he said, 'I could tell the police that you're trying to blackmail me, and who would they believe? A blackmailer or a minister?'

'That's funny, former Foreign Minister, I can remember you saying something very similar all those years ago – about the authorities not believing a bitch who chose to whore herself around.' Again I paused to let things sink in. 'No, former Foreign Secretary, I'm the holder of the George Cross, the Distinguished Service Order and bar, the Croix de Guerre and I play cricket for my country. I wonder who they would believe now. Me,' I said, raising my voice 'or a sleazy rapist who attempted to murder a child, a terrified fourteen-year-old girl?'

'But how do you know all this? Who are you?' he asked, somewhat despairingly

'I'm the former Alexander Henry,' I replied slowly so that he could take it all in.

'Henry!' He paused and then repeated in a whisper, 'Henry. It was you with Jagger. Wasn't it? But Henry was a boy!'

'No, darling, Henry was a girl! Now, former Foreign Secretary, I would advise you to resign before – well, can I put it nicely – before you are pushed! Now I must go; I have taken far too much of your time already. Thank you for seeing me, former Foreign Secretary, I'm sure we won't meet again.'

I got up to leave and he came speedily round to me and put his hands on my shoulders.

'What can I do to stop you doing this?' he begged.

'Oh it's that you want, is it?' I said coolly as I pulled the zip down on his trousers and put my hand inside his pants. He stared at me horrified, as once again the tigress embedded her claws into her prey, causing the bright-red blood to pour from his torn testicles. He screamed and fell to the floor, but of course, the former Foreign Secretary's office was soundproofed. I walked into his private little cloakroom, washed my hands, smartened myself up and walked out of his office.

'Goodbye, Phoebe dear,' I said, as superciliously as I could. 'We did have loads of things in common, but do you know what? I don't think he has got the balls for the job anymore.'

Morton resigned the same day, saying that he had made a mistake accepting his new position and that he wanted to spend more time with his family. I really don't know how he explained his torn testicles to his wife, or to his secretary or to the hospital, but I know he would have dreaded, for the rest of his life, the possibility of me giving my story to the papers.

Well, Mr White, I had revenged myself on all of those boy rapists except one – Joseph Smith. I cannot say I was in any way enjoying my 'spree'; to the contrary, I was reliving every moment of my ordeal when I saw these men. But I needed to know that there was justice in the world and only then could I be finally free of my demons. I phoned Peter Wilkes and asked him to help me track Smith down and he agreed to give me the information, though his voice told me he did so with a heavy heart.

'I'll give you his address if you hold on a bit,' Peter said.

I waited for a few minutes and he returned. 'Last known address; The Presbytery, Thornbury Road, Frenchay, Bristol.'

'Thank you, Peter. I appreciate what you've done for me,' I said and put the phone down.

I talked everything out with William, who as ever was supportive and agreed that I had to go and see this man, if only to put an end to all the torment.

'Be careful, darling,' William said, as I caught the train from Whitton the following day.

The journey reminded me of our trip during the war, when we went to Torquay via Bristol Temple Mead and had to stay in Bristol because of the bombing. This time I was hoping to drop a bomb from another direction.

It was about four o'clock in the afternoon when I arrived, too late to go to the presbytery, so I spent the time booking into a hotel and doing some shopping.

I didn't have a very good time as I missed William and had the task in hand on my mind. I felt like a naughty woman as I sat at the bar alone before dinner and fended off the numerous reps and sales managers who had stopped at the Trust House Forte Hotel. The chat-up lines they used hadn't changed much but it was nice to be told by strangers that you were still lovely.

The following day I went to the church next door to the presbytery and sat in a pew until I saw someone whom I could ask if Joseph was still here. A little old lady came in and walked to the side of the church so I scurried over to ask, following her into a room at the side. She was, it turned out, the cleaner and she told me that 'dear Father Joseph' would be coming shortly; so I returned to my pew and waited.

I didn't have to take a close look at the animal, but I knew from the moment he walked into the church it was him – the Doctor Mengele of the boiler house. I hoped desperately he wouldn't recognise me before I had chance to put my plan into operation, but I took my chance as I walked into the confessional.

He entered the box and slid the little cover off the window. 'My child?' he began.

'Father, I have sinned. I have committed a grave, unforgiving crime against several people who raped me as a child. I have taken revenge and ruined their lives and I'm in terrible pain.'

'God will always ease your pain,' Joseph Smith replied. 'How did this happen, my child?'

'I was taken by eight boys down to a boiler house, where they raped and buggered me. The eighth boy then suggested that they try to get rid of me, to murder me. I can remember one of them shouting: "Kill her! Kill her!" But I thank God that one of them was moved to pity me and prevented the worst. I have already taken revenge on seven of them and I have now found the eighth and I do not know what to do.'

I paused to let what I had said sink in. 'Father what would you do if you found out that the last one was a priest! I am in agony, Father. This priest put my feet into a furnace and wanted to push me in! Is such evil imaginable? What shall I do, Father? Would God forgive me if I exposed this man?'

I stopped as I heard him take a deep breath.

'My child,' he said quietly at length, 'this was a long time ago and that man must have suffered terrible torment for what he did. The most Christian thing that could be done would be to forgive, as this priest has tried to make amends for the suffering he has caused.'

'But how can I risk this priest being allowed to continue his terrible trade?' I countered, emphasising the words 'murdering' and 'rapist'. 'I have a little child the same age. Can I allow my child to be touched, given the Blessed Sacrament, by a priest who has done these things, who might do them again? Father, would you take that chance? Because I do not believe I can. I do not know what to do. But I know I have to do something.'

I stood up and walked out of the confessional, knowing he wouldn't say anything. Knowing he wouldn't follow me, but knowing he would be tormented just as I had been.

I returned to my hotel and phoned William and told him all that I had said and done and that still I didn't know what to do.

'Come home, darling, we miss you. It's all behind us now. He knows how you feel and the hurt he has caused you. Let that be the end of it!'

Wise old William, I thought as I rushed to the station and caught the first train back to London and then Whitton.

I didn't hear anything else about Joseph Smith until a few years later, when I was told that the priest had hanged himself, leaving a simple note pinned to his cassock saying, 'Father, I have sinned.'

Chapter 26

I told you I had been selected to play for England in the second and final test to be played at Worcester. It's a beautiful little ground and to me it almost compares with Canterbury and the Old Gloucester pitch at Stroud, full of old-world charm. It was to be a three-day test; they couldn't risk allowing us to have a four or five days because 'us ladies' would never last that long. However, that's another story.

While I loved the cricket, it was really my family I loved and I was beginning to feel it was impinging on my time with them, so after having many heart-searching discussions with William, I decided that this would be my last 'professional' match. I must be honest, William didn't want me to stop playing, and in fact he was very sad I had made up my mind to retire. Still, we decided I would still play for Whitton as long as I felt capable. Anyway, William booked three days' holiday; we took the children from school and we all went to Worcester.

The weather was glorious. I don't think we could have picked better weather if we could have ordered it specially and the Worcester ground was bathed in sunshine for the whole three days. I was, however, forty-one and really didn't want to be running round the boundary in that heat. I was thankful when the Australians won the toss and elected to bat first and Emily, our Captain, put me to field in the slips. We had a good crowd for a ladies' match of at least 2,600 of which 75 per cent were screaming young girls, but it was nice when you heard clapping when you did something well.

William, Tom, Alice and James were my honoured guests in

the pavilion and they were there when we walked out onto the field. They stood up and cheered, but I knew it was just for me. I think it was the 'Come on, Mum!' that Tom shouted, which the entire ground must have heard, that confirmed it for me.

Our bowlers toiled against the Australians on a perfect batting wicket and by lunch on the first day they had scored 125 for two. By tea they had moved into the two hundreds and by the close they had put us into bat, having scored 315 for seven declared and we were 14 for none. The next day our openers had scored 39 when Deborah Hollingsworth was out LBW. It's easy to complain about the umpiring, but she was very unfortunate to be out. However, it was now my turn to go out to bat. The little wicket gate was opened for me, to the cheers of my family and the lovely English supporters. I crossed with Deborah as I walked to the crease. I looked around and took guard.

'Middle and leg!' I shouted to the umpire.

'That's it!' the umpire replied and I was ready to face the first ball. I don't know what it was – perhaps it was the fact I had decided not to play again or perhaps it was I had played too long already, or I was overconfident, I don't know, but for the first time in my playing life I didn't feel nervous.

I faced the bowler and as usual was talking to myself. Take your time. No hurry! The Australian bowler ran up and released the ball. I was off the mark with one run, much to the delight of Tom and Alice.

It was certainly my day as I finished on 80 not out, but as far as the other girls were concerned, we didn't do too well. We only just avoided the follow-on and the Australians had an hour before tea and all after tea to pile on the runs. At close of play, I was interviewed by various members of the media and the following days' papers were full of glowing tributes to my career.

It did have the effect of swelling the crowd on the final day to over 4,000, though the ground still looked empty.

The Australians batted for the first hour and then declared

leaving us 290 to score to win – an almost impossible task. We made a positive start with Jennifer Smith and Deborah, each scoring freely when Deborah nicked one and was caught behind with the score at 41. I went out to bat in an emotional state but even more so when I spotted Peter and Thelma Wilkes out in the crowd, with a busload of girls and one or two boys from Bankworth.

William ran down the steps to open the little gate for me. 'Best of luck, darling. I'll love you whatever you do!'

The crowd actually stood up and clapped as I walked out to the crease. Even the Australians stood still and paid tribute to me by joining in.

I had to pull myself together and do my best for the team. Now take your time. Look round. Don't take chances.

I took guard and faced the bowler . . . The first ball was short on the off, which I cracked for four. My fifty came up after lunch and Jennifer and I had put on 60 runs. At tea, I was 111 not out and we had a distinct chance of victory as Jennifer was on 30. I had scored 173 not out when Jennifer hit the winning run.

I cannot tell you, Mr White, what a wonderful feeling that was. Jennifer and I hugged each other in the middle of the wicket as the umpires handed us each a set of bails from the wickets. We walked back to the pavilion and every player stood back to allow me to lead the players off.

I was sobbing my heart out as I looked up and saw a tall blurred figure standing by the gate. He didn't move and I still couldn't see him through the tears. I wiped my eyes on my sleeve and stood still. It was my father! I couldn't move for a second or two and neither could he; but then he held his arms wide open and I just dropped my bat and ran to him as I did along the platform all those years ago.

For a second we were silent and then he said, 'Alex, darling, I'm so, so sorry. I couldn't face losing my son, but I now realise that I gained a wonderful daughter whom I have always loved. I'm very proud of you!'

'Father, I did all this for you,' I said, sobbing my heart out.

Jennifer brought my bat and gloves in for me and I walked with my father's arm around me up the steps and into the pavilion.

William, bless him, was waiting inside, with Peter and Thelma and our children. I walked in with my father, who went straight up to William, put his arms around him, with the tears rolling down his face, and simply said, 'Thank you, for what you have done for me, for looking after her all these years . . .' Then the tears took over and he was incapable of anything for a few minutes.

We had a fabulous time catching up on all everyone's news. But it was my father whom I most wanted to be with, although as we talked he would keep saying, 'You must see to your other friends. We can catch up later.'

Mr White, he told me how terrible he felt when he saw my face on the day he walked out and how that image had lived with him ever since. He told me how he had wanted to come and talk to me when he came to see me play for the Combined Universities. He had watched every ball of my innings of 52 against Bradman and my match at the Oval against Surrey and all my matches for the England Ladies side.

He told me how proud he was when I went to receive the George Cross and the Distinguished Service Order and how he wanted to put his arms around me and tell me how sorry he was.

Do you know, Mr White, I knew my father had been there every time. I knew I had seen him and sometimes, I felt he was near me, with his hand helping to guide me. I was just sorry we had wasted all those lovely years!

William, it seemed, had planned the whole thing and now who should walk in, but my lovely sister Alice and her family. Lucy was there too together with her new husband, and my poor, dear mother. William's parents were there, but his mother still couldn't take it in that I played cricket. 'It's a boy's game, dear!' she said at one point, taking me aside. 'You should try and be a little more feminine.'

'The problem is, Mrs Fraser, the boys just aren't good enough!'

She shook her head and sighed. 'You really should have been a boy, Alexandra. You should have been Alexander!'

William and I looked at each other and smiled and then he had another lovely surprise for me as Harry Whelan and his wife, Doreen came into the pavilion.

No wonder we had a bigger crowd today – they were all my friends.

I know one cannot replace lost time; those moments were gone forever, but it was resumption from where we left off with my father. He never missed a match at Whitton and was always making the effort to see our family and his grandchildren, whom he adored and this too applied to my mother. "What a pity we wasted such wonderful years," he would often say to me.

Perhaps I should end my little story there, Mr White, but I have just one more event to relate to you; one that also connects with my strange, unhappy boyhood.

I was shopping in Whitton High Street with little Charlotte and was waiting to cross the road at the new pedestrian traffic lights. They changed to 'Go' and like any good parent, I was teaching my youngest daughter the rights and wrongs of crossing the road. I stepped off the pavement, holding Charlotte in one hand and a shopping bag in the other. To our absolute amazement, the moment my foot touched the road a car came screeching towards us, just missing my legs as it tore past. Instinct made me pull Charlotte back and we tumbled backwards. Many people came to our aid as we collected ourselves together, but it was a shock to us all and a very near miss.

Many people had seen the cream-coloured Wolseley do its worst, but no one had noticed the driver or taken a note of the number plate. The police were called, but naturally enough, they put it down to an impatient motorist and, to be honest, I thought nothing more of it.

It had been at least three months since the incident when once again I was crossing a side road just off the High street when the same cream Wolseley sped round the corner at speed, its horn blaring, and once again, Charlotte and I were almost knocked over.

'You were lucky there, dear,' some old gentleman said. 'You must look where you're going! It's not the best way to teach youngsters to cross the road.'

I had to bite my tongue in order not to shout back at him. Once again, I phoned the police, but once again they told me it was probably just a case of careless driving. I wasn't so sure, particularly as it only seemed to happen when I was with Charlotte.

Absurd thoughts came into my brain. What if the driver was trying to kill Charlotte? What if, more likely, he was after me? What if . . . ? What if . . . ? It was a very worrying time.

It was shortly after that incident that we moved here into Glengarry. My father and mother thought the house was too big for them and decided that it would make the perfect home for our large family. They bought a smaller house in the town, only a few streets away, and we moved in. I could not have been happier or busier, Mr White, and I really did forget about the whole Wolseley business.

It was the middle of the cricket season a year later when I had become suspicious of a green and cream A40 Austin parked outside Glengarry. I had noticed it on the odd occasion before but had not thought much about it. Then a day or two later, I saw it again outside Charlotte's school. I mentioned it to William who immediately phoned the police and they sent a patrol car around on a regular basis for a couple of weeks. It was at this time, too, that I started getting a few silent phone calls, always when I was at home alone, making me think I was being watched.

On one occasion I asked, 'What do you want?' There was a long pause when he whispered: 'You, Alexandra, just you!' But that was it. I reported all this to the police, but there was very little they could do. There was much worse to come. It was the first of July and a gloriously hot day. It was a Friday and the roads were chockabloc with day trippers. As usual, I set off to collect Charlotte from her school, but because of the traffic I arrived a little late. I raced in to collect her and was met in the corridor by the teacher.

'Hello, Mrs Fraser, you're too late. Your neighbour has just picked her up. He's taking her home for you.'

I panicked. 'What neighbour? Where is she, for God's sake?' I yelled.

There was no one at home, so I rang Sybil, now our housekeeper, who lived just down the road and asked her to visit the house and see if Charlotte was there. It was one of the worst ten minutes of my life and when she returned to the phone and said Charlotte hadn't arrived, I almost passed out with shock. A normally controlled Alexandra Fraser was an uncontrollable jelly.

The Headmistress, who had arrived on the scene, tried to soothe me.

'Just phone the police for me, would you?' I begged. 'You really shouldn't have let her go with someone she didn't know . . . I've got to phone my husband.'

The Headmistress began to realise that the school had dropped a clanger. 'Don't worry, I'm sure everything will be all right. Would you like a cup of tea?'

'No thank you. I just want to see Charlotte!' I said, trying really hard to be brave.

The police arrived with all bells sounding, screeching to a halt outside the school. No fewer than six officers came rushing in and so too did a Chief Inspector. I clearly had some influence left, Mr White.

'I'm Chief Inspector Fellows, Mrs Fraser. Please be assured, we'll do everything we can to find your daughter. From what I've heard so far, I'm afraid to say it sounds as if she has been snatched. Have you any idea who may be responsible for this?'

'Yes I have!' I replied as William walked through the door. I jumped up and fell into his arms. 'William, it's all my fault! The traffic was so bad. I couldn't help it, really I couldn't!'

'Of course it's not your fault! I just can't believe, Headmistress, that you allowed this to happen,' William said, directing his attention to her. 'What person in their right mind would allow another person they didn't know to walk in and pick up a child? It's bloody disgraceful!'

'Now, Mr Fraser,' the Chief Inspector intervened, trying to keep things on track, 'I need a statement from your wife so that we can start looking. We don't know yet what it's all about.'

I told him all about the incidents with the cars and the anonymous phone calls. I told him also, somewhat impatiently, that we had already reported all of this to the police, not that they had done a great deal about it.

'I'll stop you there, madam, do you have the registration number of Austin? the Inspector asked.

'No I don't, but the last letters are UK,' I replied. 'I'm certain of that.'

'Excuse me for a moment. I'll pass this information on. At least we can be looking out for the car. I'm sure we'll have Charlotte back safe and sound very soon, Mrs Fraser.'

But we didn't, despite reports in the press and on television. A week later, nothing had been seen or heard of either the captive or the kidnapper. On the eighth day, however, the police had a breakthrough, or I should say a piece of luck. There was a block of flats in Whetstowe, a town about twenty miles from Upper Hayfield, and a neighbour had reported hearing a little girl crying in a flat belonging to an old man who lived on his own.

'He's a bit of a loner apparently,' one of the officers told us. It took a further twelve hours for the police to confirm that there was a little girl in the flat and about another two to confirm that the man inside was armed with a shotgun, having demonstrated the fact by firing it into the air from the balcony. The police thought it was a good idea for us to be there and rushed us over to the scene. The flats were newly built, typical of those built in the sixties, and he was on the thirteenth floor. Everywhere had been sealed off and even the neighbouring flats had been emptied.

A huddle of reporters had arrived and soon after a TV camera crew. We had well and truly entered the media age, Mr White.

The negotiations had already started as they had an officer at the top of the stairs trying to talk to the man through the door.

But all the man kept saying was: 'Go away and leave us alone!' The officer then asked if he could go in and talk to him, but that just made the man agitated. Once again he discharged the firearm on the balcony and we all heard the little girl scream high above us. This was followed by pleas of 'Mummy! Mummy!

'It does sound like Charlotte,' I screamed, wondering whether it was just wishful thinking on my part.

'It's quite likely,' the officer replied.

The Inspector arrived to speak to us. 'We have a direct phone line into his flat so we can communicate with him easily.'

'I could willingly kill him,' William said fiercely.

I felt all my wartime courage welling up. I had faced the Nazis, for heaven's sake. What did I have to fear from a lonely old pathetic man? I told the Chief Inspector I was going to go the flat and started to walk across towards the tower block entrance.

William and the police tried to dissuade me, but William at least knew it was no use.

I arrived at the lift and found they had cut the electricity off to it, which meant walking up thirteen storeys. The staircase was on the outside of the building and was open at every floor. I looked down as I reached each of these points to wave at William to get some moral support. I could see the TV cameras following my every move. It made me feel sick to see how our grief and torment had become a media sensation.

I finally arrived at the thirteenth floor and walked slowly and carefully to the front door, passing several policemen all waiting for instructions. I knocked on the door and waited, but there was no sound, so I knocked again much louder. I heard the man shout, 'Shut up!' as Charlotte began to scream.

'Charlotte!' I yelled. 'It's Mummy. Don't worry, darling, I'm here.'

I heard the man shuffling around and he was obviously trying to drag Charlotte around as well as come to the door.

'Are you on your own?' the man shouted through the door. 'If you're not, I'll shoot her.'

'I am, I promise. There's no one with me!' I replied in sheer panic. 'Please let me in and let her go. I promise there'll be no tricks. I'm on my own.'

There was silence once more, but they were obviously close to the door as I could hear Charlotte being silenced. It was as though he had his hand across her mouth.

'I'm going to open the door . . . I warn you, there's a gun to her head. If there are any police there, she'll be shot!'

That voice. I could swear I knew it.

'Please, please don't do this. I'm on my own. I wouldn't risk the life of my daughter. Please open the door,' I begged, leaning my head on the door to hear her muffled cries.

There was another silence for a minute or two and then a bolt was drawn back, followed by the key in the lock being turned. The door only opened a few inches as it was prevented by a security chain. He pushed Charlotte forward. I could now see her little frightened face as the man held the shotgun to the back of her head.

'Please don't do this! Can't you see she's terrified? She's only a little girl. Let her go. I'll take her place.'

He pushed the door to and I heard him removing the chain and then he opened the door wider. The shotgun was immediately put against my head as he pushed Charlotte out of the door.

I grabbed her and hugged my terrified little girl as she broke down in tears. 'Mummy, Mummy, he's horrid! He said he would kill me if I didn't behave!'

'Well you did, darling–'

He interrupted me. 'Bloody put her down now or you'll lose your head and she won't have a mother, if that's what you are.'

I put Charlotte down and gave strict instructions on what she was to do. 'Now you go down the stairs there. It's quite a long way, but Daddy is waiting at the bottom and I know this gentleman will let Mummy go in a few minutes, so you tell Daddy I won't be long. Can you do that for me, darling?'

'Yes, Mummy!' Charlotte replied, sobbing her heart out. I watched her go to the stairs. She turned round, the tears flowing down her face, and waved. 'Bye-bye Mummy!' she sobbed.

'Go on, darling, you'll be all right. Go on!' I said again, as I could see the reluctance in her face. 'Go on! Be a good girl for Mummy. Go on.'

Charlotte started down the stairs as I was roughly pulled into apartment and thrown onto a settee with the shotgun still pointing at my head. The man relocked the door and put the bolt and chain back on, always with the shotgun pointing at me.

'I'll shoot you if you try any funny stuff,' he continued. 'I really have nothing to lose.'

'Why are you doing this and why did you pick on that little girl?' I asked.

For the first time I was able to look at my aggressor. He was somewhat scruffy, with several days' growth on his beard. He looked as though he had had a hard life and was about sixty, and yet his voice seemed to be that of a younger man. He had held Charlotte captive for eight days and yet she didn't seem hungry. The apartment, too, was reasonably tidy and clean. I became upset when I saw the rope he had used to tie Charlotte up to prevent her from moving too far. The rope was looped and tied to a specially installed steel hook in the wall and on the other end was a set of handcuffs. He now placed one of these on my right wrist.

'What do you want from us?' I asked, almost pleading.

'I want you, Alex,' he said to my absolute shock. 'I've wanted you since I was sixteen and at least at the end of my life I've got you.'

I looked at this man as he sat opposite me and just stared. For a moment I couldn't think of anyone whom I had known that long who would fit the description of this man. Then suddenly as though the clock had been put back twenty-five years, I saw him looking at me.

'*Hazard*!' I screamed. 'It's you, isn't it? Oh my God no!'

I remained in shocked silence for several minutes, while he just stared at me saying nothing. Eventually, I broke the silence.

'What are you going to do now? Please, don't do that again. Please!' I begged, suddenly filled with the same fear, the same weakness, I had felt all those years ago.

'I'm not going to harm you, Alex. I just want to be with you for a few hours. Just you and me, something I have wanted all this time. Just to say sorry. I have never wanted any harm to come to you and I have always wanted to say how much I'm in love with you and that I always have been and I always will be.'

'Then if you love me, *why this*?' I began shouting. 'Why did you do that to my little girl? Don't you realise that she will be scarred for life? Don't you think every time she closes her eyes to go to sleep she'll think of this and cry out for her dad, just like I have done for all these years?'

'I've told you,' Hazard said, 'I'm not going to harm you. Taking your little girl was the only way I knew to get you to come to me.'

'But you've nearly killed us on several occasions!' I continued, once more raising my voice. 'Why did you do that? Are you mad?'

'I suppose I am, but it's you that's made me this way, Alex.'

'Don't talk such bloody drivel! You made yourself this way. You were the cruel one. You were the bully; *you* and *you* led the others into doing what you did. Your bloody henchmen – the Barratt brothers, Smith, Morton, Wales, Jagger and Shepherd. I remember them all, and none of them succeeded in the end.'

'I didn't want to!' he shouted. 'I didn't. It was me that

stopped them. I couldn't bear to see what they were doing to you. I didn't want to take part.'

'Then why did you for Christ's sake?' I snapped. 'Why did you let them, especially that dirty, filthy bastard Guest?' I said, spitting the words out.

'I couldn't help it. I was frightened of what they might do or say. I didn't want to be ridiculed.'

'You know, Hazard, you're just like the Nazis. When the war was over they would look at me straight in the face and they made the same, lame excuses. It wasn't me. I was told to do it. I saw one Nazi shoot five American soldiers in cold blood, torturing and laughing at them as he did it, and yet when he was caught, he pretended he was a victim, just like you. And yet when he went to the gallows, this big bully of a man screamed like a baby. He struggled, Hazard, like a little girl being put into a furnace, begging for her life. Do you remember a little girl begging for her life, Mr Hazard?'

'Everything got out of hand,' Hazard continued.

'Yes!' I interrupted. 'Just like Nazism got out of hand.'

He banged the butt of the gun down on his table in anger and confused sorrow, losing his patience with me. I could sense he wanted to leave me for a few minutes to calm down, but then suddenly he asked: 'Do you want a cup of tea?'

'No. I don't want anything from you, thank you,' I replied, somewhat haughtily.

Hazard left me tied up on this long rope with the handcuffs attached to my wrist. He had cleverly made sure that everything that could have helped me was out of my reach. Once again, he was in some way tormenting me.

A few minutes later he returned with two mugs of tea.

'It's no good. You won't be able to escape and I won't let you go until I've finished. So you might as well sit down and have this cup of tea, as I have got something I want you to see.'

I was beginning to feel a little more secure when the phone rang.

'Answer it. It's the police. They'll want to know if you are all right. Tell them, though, I'll kill you if they try to break in. But Alexandra – may I call you Alexandra, I know you prefer it – if you tell them who I am I'll kill you. Please promise me you won't. I'm known to my neighbours as Mr Treadwell and I've lived here for about a year, ever since I found out where you lived. Promise!' he repeated.

'I promise,' I replied.

It was the police.

'Is that Mrs Fraser?' the voice on the other end asked.

'Yes,' I replied.

'I'm Detective Chief Superintendent Wilson. I'm coordinating our actions in this matter. Are you all right?' he asked.

'How's Charlotte?' I asked almost in desperation.

'She's fine. She's with her daddy and she's fine. Are you all right?' he asked again.

'Yes, I'm OK. I'm handcuffed and I know he will kill me if you try to break in, but at the moment we're talking and everything is calm.'

Hazard approached and snatched the phone, shouting, 'Just fucking stay away!' He slammed the phone down.

'I'm going to show you something that I have been saving for years,' he said, suddenly calm again.

He opened the door of the sideboard and took out a large scrapbook and brought it over to the settee and sat next to me. I moved away just to keep him out of reach.

'For God's sake, I'm not going to do anything. If I had wanted to I could have done it the moment you came in. You can make this easy or hard. It's up to you. Come on, move closer. I promise I won't touch you.'

I reluctantly moved closer and he opened the first page of his scrapbook. It was a picture of me as Wendy in *Peter Pan* and then others of me in the other shows. My whole life was set out there: copies of newspaper articles, pictures of me cut out from the photographs; little scribbled notes about what I had done.

'Why have you done this? You couldn't have liked me that much, or you wouldn't have bullied me so.'

I told you, I have loved you ever since I was sixteen and when I first began to notice you in the dining room. I remember I would be staring at you and you would occasionally catch me looking and I would turn away sharply. I couldn't help myself. I just had to look. Some of the other boys started to make comments that I fancied you and began calling me homosexual. I couldn't stand that, so I had to pretend I didn't, by doing unkind things to you. Nothing terrible. Just hiding some of your clothes or joining in the teasing. But the strange thing was, the more I did it, the nearer I felt to you.

'It was obvious to everyone that you were a girl and none of us could understand why you were left in the boys' school for such a long time. I thought it was cruel, but at least you were near me. When you appeared as Alice, half the school fell in love with you and the other half just wanted you. You were always very pretty, but this part made you look fantastic and, believe it or not, I became jealous of all the attention you were getting and had to put a stop to it. I wanted you so much that I began to be cruel and pretend that I was doing things just to be in control of you. Instead I did it because, even then I wanted to make love to you.'

I moved away a little.

'Oh don't worry! I can't do anything on that score; you saw to that. Mind you, it was my own fault when I look back. I deserved everything you dished out and more. It caused the break-up of two marriages, which, I must be honest, were little more than wartime affairs and wouldn't have lasted.'

'What did you do during the war?' I asked, trying to change the subject.

'Nothing as glamorous as what you did, Alex. I served as a private in the infantry. I didn't care if I lived or died, so I took ridiculous chances and became a minor hero myself. I was offered promotion, but refused. I wanted to die in the trenches so to speak. When the war was over, I sent the medals to my father and disappeared. In fact, I started searching for you. But you had moved around and the trail went cold, until one day I saw an article about you in the newspapers and from then on it was easy.' He laughed as if delighted by his own cunning, but then suddenly he became serious.

'Alexandra, I'm going to kill myself today and you'll be free of me.'

I looked at him totally shocked.

'I want to die with your picture beside me. This one!' he said, tearing the picture of Alice out of his book. 'It's my favourite.'

'You can't do this; you can't just simply throw your life away,' I said, shaking myself out of my stunned silence. 'They can give you help these days.'

'I'm not mad. I don't need a doctor,' he replied impatiently. 'I have decided what I want to do, and why I want to do it. There is nothing left in my life worth living for. I have tidied up my affairs. My father believes I have had a breakdown and gone missing. I don't want him to think otherwise. I want you to once again promise that you won't tell the police about my real identity. When I have finished I'll be unrecognisable so it's important to me, you keep your word. I know no one will miss me when I'm gone; I only hoped . . .' He paused as tears began to fall from his eyes onto his cheeks and drip onto his trousers.

'Well, it doesn't matter. Nothing matters as I have caused you too much pain and misery and now all I want is to make my peace. The keys for the handcuffs are in the drawer there. As soon as I've gone, pick up the telephone. The police will answer it and they'll come and free you.

'Alexandra, please forgive me for all the wicked things I did to You. Please forgive me for causing little Charlotte that misery. I promise you I didn't touch her. I made her as comfortable as possible. I didn't tell her anything about me or you. I just used her to see you once more. The last thing I want you to know is that I love you and only wish I had been a decent human being.' He paused for a second or two. 'Please give me your hand.'

I held my hand out and he took it in his. He leaned over and kissed it on the back. He put the picture of me under his shirt, took his shotgun, and walked out onto the little balcony. I watched through the window as he climbed onto the balustrade, and shouted, 'I love you, Alexandra!' He then shot himself under his chin, effectively blowing his face away and fell the thirteen storeys to the ground.

I sat motionless. I didn't have to phone the police; they arrived within seconds of Hazard's death.

I left the flat in William's arms. I was in tears, but these were tears of relief that, after all these years, it was all over. I had forgiven all the rapists, but I could never forget them . . .

***

There is just one other thing, Mr White. Do you remember the strange affair in Oxford – the German spying ring? On the 1st January 1998, the secret papers about the incident were released to the public. It was reported that I, as Alex Chillington-Henry, had helped the Secret Service to foil the ring. One or two of the clever journalists managed to put two and two together and connected it with me. There were one or two headlines and they even tried to get a story out of me, but I refused.

I'll pass over the many years that followed, Mr White. They were ones of contentment; of watching the children grow up and raise their own families, of enjoying the company of our friends and dividing our lives between Upper Hayfield, Chelsea and Le Touquet. We had been through a lot but we were very lucky, I know. Above all, I was blessed with the best and most generous husband and we loved each other deeply and truly. But all good things must come to an end.

William, though long since retired, had been working too hard and the doctor had told him to ease off. He loved the garden here and he would spend hours in it, tending to the plants and generally pottering around. It was his paradise and I, elderly as I am, was his Eve. Then, one day, I woke up and went into the bathroom. Normally, he would get up and start to get himself ready, just as we had done for sixty years, but when I came out of the bathroom he was still sitting up in bed.

'I'm a bit tired, darling, I'll just have a few more minutes,' he said softly.

'Yes, you stay there, darling. I'll give you a treat. You can have breakfast in bed,' I replied.

I went downstairs, prepared a boiled egg, toast and marmalade and a pot of tea with two cups. I took it upstairs and there he was still propped up with his two pillows, waiting for this rare treat.

His eyes were closed and he had a beautiful smile on his face. I didn't really want to disturb him but I couldn't resist him. I put the tray down and walked over to him, gently put my arm around his shoulder and kissed him and then whispered softly in his ear:

'Come on, you lazy monkey. I have got the most wonderful breakfast for you. It has taken all of my culinary skills to prepare it.'

'Just leave it there. I want to say something to you.'

I knew something was wrong and I tried to hide it from him.

'Come on, I don't want any of this sentimental mush. I want my husband to eat his breakfast.'

'You know, sweetheart, you have made my life complete. I have loved you from that first moment I saw you. It has been truly wonderful!'

'Come on. I told you, none of this sentimental mush. We've got things to do, darling,' I replied smiling, but trying to hold back my tears at the same time.

'Darling, I can't. I'm going,' he said quietly.

For a moment I was lost for words and for the first time since I had met him, I felt totally vulnerable. 'Don't be silly, come on.'

'Darling, hold me, please. Hold me tight!' William gently whispered.

I put my arms further round his shoulders and clasped my hands together. He looked at me and smiled, then whispered, 'I love you.'

His eyes closed, his head fell gently back onto my arm and he had gone. My rock, my staff, and my life, as I knew it, had ended. He had taken me from hell to happiness and had never asked anything from me except to give him all my love, which I did.

I stayed with him for over an hour, holding him where he had rested and then gently laid his head on the pillow and kissed him.

I couldn't think of anything else but to phone my sister, Alice.

As she picked up the phone I said softly, 'Alice, William has gone.' She knew exactly what I meant and within the hour she was with me. She walked in, took me in her arms and almost cried her words.

'Darling, I'm so sorry . . .' She paused for a moment and then asked, 'Where is he?' I told her where I had left William and she asked, 'Can I see him?'

'Of course,' I replied as I took her upstairs.

William looked so peaceful as he lay there, as if in total contentment. Alice went to him, leaned over and kissed him, with tears rolling down her cheeks.

'Thank you, William, for what you did for my lovely sister.'

I too kissed him again and we walked out of the room in each other's arms. We were the last of our generation and we simply sat on the top step of the stairs holding each other, letting the happy memories drift over us as we sat staring in total silence.

The silence was only broken when Alice said, 'Do you remember David and Phil in Le Touquet and I said let's go and have some fun.'

'Yes I do!' I replied, smiling, 'and you conned them into paying for the ice-creams!'

'Yes, but we did have fun, didn't we, and, darling, haven't we lived!'

Epilogue

Mrs Fraser fell silent as she remembered those moments; tears were rolling down her cheeks. It was several minutes before she was capable of any conversation. She was stirred from her thoughts when Sybil brought in what was to be my last tea and scones, but even then the emotion was creeping through her strong façade.

'Well, Mr White, you have heard it, warts and all, as they say. The good and the bad, but I wouldn't have changed a bit. Even the bad bits helped shape what I became and helped me to experience the real love a person can give – which is what my William gave to me.

'We've few real friends in our lives, Mr White; in fact I have found you can count on one hand those who would support you through thick and thin. I was lucky: I had William, Alice, Peter and Thelma Wilkes, Harry Webster and David Rice at school and now I have Sybil too. There was Madge as well but I never really knew what happened to her. But that was all; that was all the people I could count on through thick and thin, but that was enough and that is enough for anyone.

'I know I have done things that are, as they say, the stuff of legend, but I never actively went looking for fame or celebrity. I know that, had things been different, I might have done even better, but I know I would have missed the true happiness I was given in the end.

'What lessons have I learned from my life? Well, I know I couldn't be unkind to a living soul. Look at the torment that Joseph Smith and Hazard went though, how they paid for the torment they inflicted on others. It's not worth the risk. Kindness is a better route. We need to offer encouragement and love to all those around us. They are the lessons I have learned.

'If you do decide to publish the story, Mr White, I must make it

absolutely clear, while I do not want any payment. I would like some of the profits to go to the RAF Benevolent Fund. We owe such a lot to the RAF and the other Services for our general security and many have given up their lives . . .'

She paused and sat thoughtfully for a minute or so, which gave me the opportunity to interrupt her.

'Mrs Fraser, it will be an honour to publish your story. Quite frankly, though, I shall miss coming to your lovely home and listening to your strange and wonderful tale. I shall miss Sybil's scones! You know how I enthralled I've been, but I've also been very moved and inspired.'

We sat for several minutes in silence. Outside the sun was setting and the shadows lengthened across a room that was filled with so many memories – the photographs, the trophies and, there in one corner, the old seasoned cricket bat.

'Do you think you will make your last hundred, Mrs Fraser?' I said at last.

'Mr White, my sister Alice is ninety-four and I'm eighty-nine not out. It's a batsman's . . . sorry, batswoman's wicket. What do you think?'